ETRUSCANS

BY MORGAN LLYWELYN
FROM TOM DOHERTY ASSOCIATES

FICTION

Bard
Brian Boru
The Elementals
Finn Mac Cool
Lion of Ireland
Pride of Lions
Strongbow
1916

NONFICTION

The Essential Library for Irish Americans

ETRUSCANS

BELOVED OF THE GODS

MORGAN LLYWELYN

AND

MICHAEL SCOTT

TOR®

A TOM DOHERTY ASSOCIATES BOOK
NEW YORK

ETRUSCANS

Copyright © 2000 by Morgan Llywelyn and Michael Scott

Edited by David G. Hartwell.

A Tor Book
Published by Tom Doherty Associates, LLC
175 Fifth Avenue
New York, NY 10010

www.tor.com

Tor® is a registered trademark of Tom Doherty Associates, LLC.

Design by Lisa Pifher

ISBN 0-312-86627-5

First Edition: March 2000

Printed in the United States of America

0 9 8 7 6 5 4 3 2 1

Earthworld
Otherworld
Netherworld

These are the realms of our existence
These are the worlds that bind us
Flesh is tied to Earthworld
Spirit to Otherworld
Death to Netherworld
Between the three, only the Ais *travel*
    without restriction.

Etruscan proverb, Second Century, B.C.

ETRUSCANS

PROLOGUS

Extracted from LIBRI FATALES,
The Hidden Will of the Gods,
as found in the ETRUSCA DISCIPLINIA

A NEW TRANSLATION BY LLYWELYN & SCOTT

We have always been.

We, the Ais, existed even before the beginning. But it was humankind who named us gods, assigning us form and attributing omnipotence to us as well. Then they bowed before us and we were pleased by the taste of worship.

When humans learned to fear the gods we reached the zenith of our power.

Although we are what man aspires to become, in many ways we resemble humankind. We are fickle. The Ais can love and hate, destroy life and create it anew. We amuse ourselves by elevating our favorites and tormenting those we do not like, and occasionally, just to vary the entertainment, we reverse their positions.

Ostensibly humans are the slaves and we the masters; yet in truth the relationship is far more complex. Some of the Ais say we would be better off without humans because their incessant demands are a nuisance and a distraction. Others, however, point out the ways in which we depend upon humankind and insist we dare not destroy them. The argument between the two points of view has raged for eons.

Humans will always require gods.

We give their lives a meaning: often we are the meaning. Our existence is taken as their command to exist. We provide them with someone to blame other than themselves. We satisfy their inborn need of ritual. We give them reasons to celebrate.

But we, the Ais, also need humankind. Without them we have no definition. Human imagination imbues us with form and face, shape and substance.

Interaction with the Earthworld has become an imperative for us, involved as we are in such a symbiotic relationship. Over the millennia we have grown dangerously dependent. We stimulate awe, and resultant faith through demonstrations of power such as storms and plagues and celestial marvels. We must, because if humankind stops believing in us the Ais may cease to be gods.

Man born of dust is incorrigibly cunning. Like the rat, he sniffs out the smallest advantage. He constantly strives to overcome his limitations and enlarge his sphere of influence by manipulating the gods through his priests. Usually we ignore the pious mouthings of the priesthood, which have little to do with our own intentions and desires. On the occasions when the two do coincide, however, and we appear to be answering some human prayer, man invariably claims he has influenced the gods. This makes him more arrogant than ever.

Nor is man above trying to create gods who are more amenable to his wishes than we are. For this purpose even his dead ancestors are employed. Unfortunately, the same belief with which man shapes us can transform one of his own into a deity . . . of sorts.

Such man-made gods have abilities exceeding those of mere mortals and in addition embody all the vices of humankind. They inevitably hate the Ais, whom they see as rivals and superiors.

We call them siu, *the evil ones.*

Demons.

ONE

Silent, deadly, and immense, they came whispering out of the bright sky with talons extended. By their unnatural size and behavior he recognized the great white owls for what they were: minions of the dark goddess.

Their golden eyes burned with ferocity. Their silver claws sank into his scalp and the shoulders of his naked body, ripping his flesh. He bit down hard on the inside of his cheek until he tasted blood to keep himself from crying out. If she was watching from the Otherworld, he refused to grant her that satisfaction.

At some distance beyond the trees, he detected a faint but unmistakable glow that could only mean one thing: he must be approaching an area of Sacred Space.

He stumbled as the ground beneath his feet turned to a gelatinous morass, sucking him down, then solidified almost instantly to trap his feet and ankles. With the palm of his hand he struck the earth, spending a valuable portion of his remaining energy to break the surface tension and release himself.

As he pulled his legs free, he felt the draught of wings brush his face. He promptly threw himself back down and cradled his head with his arms. The trio of hunters swept in low above him, the susurration of their wings all the more menacing for its softness.

At the last instant he surged to his feet. With flailing fists he struck one of the birds in the chest, bringing it down in an explosion of feathers. Before it could hit the ground he snatched up the creature and held it to his face. The distinctive, musty odor flooded his mouth and throat as he sank his teeth into the owl's neck. Trying not to gag on the cloud of plumage, he clamped down hard and inhaled deeply.

The owl screeched and writhed.

He took another, even deeper breath, forcibly drawing into his lungs a thin vapor torn from the very core of his victim. He was ravenous for the creature's *hia*, the living spirit it contained.

As he inhaled its essence, the energy that animated the owl began to replenish his waning strength. But one breath was not enough, he must have more. The pursuit had been so long; he was so weary. . . .

Sensing his intent, the owl redoubled its struggles. Its legs extended abnormally until they could reach around his torso and tear the flesh from his back in order to lay bare the spine, to seize and crush the vertebrae with its mighty talons. But he did not give it the chance. Opening his jaws, he twisted the bird's head to one side and snapped its neck with his bare hands.

Swiftly he sucked the last of the *hia* from the dying body, even as the creature shriveled and decomposed in his hands. Then with a cry of disgust he flung the liquefying object from him.

Drawing on his new strength he ran on, pushing his way through closely spaced ranks of sentinel trees. He had escaped the Otherworld, tearing through the fabric that separated it from the Earthworld only to find the earth itself conspiring against him. Could the dark goddess extend her reach so far?

As if in answer, branches twisted into skeletal limbs that clutched at him, holding him back. A coiling root emerged from the soil, catching his foot and sending him crashing to the ground. As he fell he was already wrapping his arms around his body and beginning to roll. If he gave up now the forest would claim him as its victim before his pursuers could.

At least he would have the small satisfaction of cheating her minions.

Lurching to his feet, he risked a glance backward. Thus he stood clearly revealed to his pursuers; a slender, swarthy man of somewhat less than average height, with a hooked nose and sensual lips. His eyes were almond shaped, his flesh fine-grained. But that flesh looked old, worn, almost as if it had long ago turned to parchment. And his eyes, rimmed around with scars, were very tired.

The remaining owls ghosted toward him on silent wings, banking sharply to clear the trees. Their pale plumage glimmered as they passed through patches of shade. To a casual observer they might have seemed beautiful.

But no normal owl would hunt during the day.

Fighting back fear—but not regret; no, never regret—he staggered on.

Sacred Space lay ahead. Once there he would be safe from their attack because no matter what form they took, these creatures were animated by *hia*. A *hia* might be the ghost of someone who had died, or the life force waiting to occupy a person as yet unborn. It could belong to an animal or a tree or a flower, for no life was possible without spirit. Nor were *hia* exclusive to the Earthworld; quite the contrary. In the Otherworld there were many spirits who would never manifest themselves in tangible bodies. But all *hia* had one limitation. Without invitation or very special powers they could not enter space consecrated to the gods.

No such restriction applied to the *Ais*, of course. If the goddess who was now his enemy chose, she could come after him herself, even into Sacred Space. He had no doubt that she was angry enough.

Why had she sent the owls instead?

He must recover and decide what to do next. He had to find sanctuary, if only for a little while.

As he burst from the forest, his thoughts were so firmly fixed on this goal that he reached the riverbank before he knew it. The muddy verge was treacherous. At his first step it slid away beneath his feet and plunged him headfirst into the Tiber. The icy shock drove the breath from his lungs and stole the warmth of *hia* energy from his body, leaving him weak again.

A powerful current battered him, dragging him away from the bank. Small round mouths lined with vicious teeth gaped just beneath the surface as ribbonlike eels fixed on his flesh. Pain seared up his legs. Frantically he fought to keep his balance while he pulled off the sucking eels. If he went under he would never resurface.

A whisper on the air warned him just in time. Turning from one battle to another, he struck the owl in midair and sent it spiraling down to the water. As it fell, the creature made a desperate effort to recapture its long-lost human shape. Swirling, melting, it presented a blurred image of a woman with the talons and snowy plumage of an owl and panicky golden eyes set in a human face. Embodied in this hybrid form the *hia* had neither the advantages of the owl nor the human.

With a terrific splash it fell into the river, the unforgiving waters swallowing its scream.

The eels were distracted from their original prey by the floundering of this new victim. Flowing away from him, they attacked the owl-thing before it could recover. They circled the dazed form, entwined themselves around its limbs, and dragged the hapless creature beneath the surface, where larger, darker creatures lurked.

Splashing wearily out of the river, he dragged himself up the bank on the far side. His breath was coming in sobs. The flesh of his legs was red from the cold and redder still from the blood pouring from scores of ragged wounds. The owls had torn his body and the eels had shredded his lower limbs. As he staggered on, drops of blood spattered the soil.

Deep in the earth something shifted, as his blood excited ancient memories. The banks of the sentient rivers throbbed with somnolent life, which normally required great amounts of blood and passion to rouse it to full consciousness. But this blood was different; vibrant with spiritual energy and fragrant with the scent of the Otherworld.

A shudder ran through the ground like the first tremor of a quake.

When he had dragged himself to the top of the rise he saw Sacred Space just ahead. He narrowed his eyes to call upon the weary remnants of his Otherworld sight for a better look. The sanctuary's glow was blurred, its holy radiance not fully developed. Consecration of the *templum* was not complete then. But that did not matter. He would be safe enough there for as long as he needed.

He had only moments left. He could feel the ground beneath his feet moving and shifting, rippling in long, slow waves. The air began to tremble as before a storm. Who knew what ancient madness lurked in the earth in this place?

Caution dictated that he advance warily; there were undoubtedly traps in the lush landscape ahead of him. But there was no time for caution. Summoning the last of his energy, he broke into a shambling run toward the *templum* while behind him the earth began to rise in a great, curling wave. A few steps, just a few more . . .

He had almost reached safety when the last of the owls struck him. It swooped out of the sky to sink triumphant talons deep into his flesh.

His cry of pain was swallowed as he pitched forward and fell headlong to the ground.

TWO

Beyond the bend of the river, Vesi strolled in the sunshine. She loved being out under the bright blue sky. Let others shelter themselves in houses, in cities. Above all things she enjoyed unfettered freedom.

Suddenly she detected a change in the atmosphere. An unexpected chill, though the day was warm; a brief bitterness on the wind, overriding the perfume of ripening grapes. Vesi shivered in spite of herself, then laughed off the sensation. She would not let anything spoil her mood on this radiant late summer day.

Tossing back hair the color of a moonless midnight, the girl closed her eyes. Wide-set eyes, dark and bright as onyx. Her sheer *peplos* was dyed with saffron, complementing her olive complexion. A crimson scarf was draped across her shoulders. Strings of tiny silver bells were laced around her throat and wrists, making music with her slightest movement.

The bells tinkled as she breathed deeply, savoring the sweetness of the air. Without visual distraction her other senses came to the fore.

She measured the weight of the wind on her shoulders, as light as a lover's caress, and turned her face to welcome its breath. Warm again. The momentary cold had been just an aberration. Thankfully, the girl abandoned herself to the delights of the season.

With a delicate sniff she identified the smells of summer one by one. Dew-drenched grass, sun-warmed earth, flowers in the meadow, droppings of sheep and scat of fox, the odor of a young bullock grazing not far away, and an old wolf bitch tardily coming into season. Underlying these was the verdant scent of trees at the edge of the forest and the fecund mud of the nearby river.

A hundred fragrances assailed Vesi's nostrils, each telling their story of life.

There was just one smell she did not recognize.

A faint but acrid tang still lay like a stain on the air. She curled her lip in distaste. How monstrous that something ugly should mar the otherwise perfect day! She would ignore it and surely it would go away.

Tilting her head, the young woman redirected her concentration to the natural music surrounding her. She could recognize sixty species of bird by their song, differentiating between those that were native to Etruria and those that merely visited the lush meadows on their way to the northern Darklands or south to the realm of Aegypt, the fabled Black Land.

One by one, Vesi sorted through various sounds until she found one she could not identify . . . a distant, labored gasping, occasionally punctuated with a groan.

An injured wild boar perhaps. But no, this was no animal. Vesi knew all the animal voices. Perhaps she was hearing a member of one of the primitive tribes her people had dispossessed in claiming this land long ago.

Her forebears styled themselves the Rasne, the Silver People, although others referred to them simply as the Etruscans. In a time recalled only by storytellers they had moved into the territory between the rivers Magra and Rubicon. Eventually their control was total in an area bordered by the Arno on the north and the Apennines and Tiber to the east and south, extending as far as Latium. Force of arms and superior intellect made the land theirs. None had been able to stand against them, neither the indigenous inhabitants nor the subhuman beasts who infested the mountain wildernesses.

Not all the vanquished had left the land. Those who remained, in the high mountains and primeval forests, were in the process of creating legends. Tales of the Silver People.

Opening her eyes, Vesi blinked against the bright sunlight, then shaded her face with both hands and gazed toward the south.

The bitter smell and gasping breath both seemed to emanate from the site of the incomplete *spura*, the Rasne city being built beyond the bend of the river. But the place was uninhabited at the moment. Although the ground had been cleared and the *purtani*, the priests, had blessed the boundaries, the final sacrifices had yet to be made. Vesi knew that none of the Rasne would break the taboo and enter unhallowed Sacred Space without being accompanied by a *purtan*.

Yet someone was there.

As she stood, puzzled, the wind changed, carrying to her the unmistakable odor of fresh blood.

Drawing her long-bladed knife from its tooled leather sheath, Vesi glided silently forward. Since earliest childhood she had loved to play at hunting, like a boy—to the despair of her mother, who wanted her daughter to be feminine and delicate. Rasne women were works of art.

But Vesi had no desire to be a work of art. Such a static image bored her. Life was to be *lived*. She thrilled to the prospect of adventures. Now her callused bare feet slid through the long grass, testing every step before trusting her weight. One could never be too cautious. A patch of quicksand might be anywhere. *Spurae* were sometimes sited to take advantage of such natural defenses.

She drew another questing breath. The blood-smell was stronger now, identifiably human but disgustingly tainted with something foul.

Another groan sounded. There was no mistaking the voice of a man in pain. Abandoning caution, the girl started forward just as a rising wind whipped her hair into her eyes. It might have been an omen; the Rasne believed the gods spoke to them in such signs and portents. The girl paused long enough to take a gleaming silver fillet from the leather purse she wore at her waist. She settled the band firmly on her brow to hold her hair in place.

Then she began to run.

Since none of her people would have ventured on their own into the unfinished *spura*, she assumed the groaning man must belong to one of the native tribes. Or, more dangerously, be a hawk-faced Roman from Latium, an advance scout for an army hoping to extend Rome's territory. Such raiders had become a constant threat. Once the Etruscans had feared no one, dominating not only Etruria but much of Latium. With increasing prosperity their aggressive impulses had diminished however. The Rasne had become tired of war, tired of the casual butchery, the stink of the dead and the dying. They had taken their martial arts and turned them inward, using them to create rather than destroy, to build rather than pull down.

And now the jackals were gathering.

Vesi hefted the knife in her hand, her thumb caressing the hilt with its encrusted carnelians. But she did not hesitate. At the back of her mind was some romantic, childish notion of taking an injured Roman warrior prisoner at knife point and leading him home in triumph. No Rasne woman had ever done such a thing before.

She sprinted up a hill, then dropped flat at the crest so she would not be silhouetted against the sky. From this vantage point she could look down upon the *spura* spread out below like some child's toy.

The area had been cleared, foundations dug, drains installed, streets laid out. Each house, shop, and public building was already allocated a site that would contribute to the symmetry of the whole. Squares and rectangles were pegged with fluttering strips of pale cloth. Stone footings would be placed to support walls of sunbaked brick covered with tinted plaster. Courtyards and roofs would be tiled; murals would be painted on every available surface. Terra-cotta piping was stacked to one side, waiting to serve the fountains that would sparkle throughout the city.

The choicest site of all was reserved for the great *templum* at the center of the *spura*. Plinths would be placed at intervals along the approaching avenue; statues of the *Ais* would stand there, gazing down with blind eyes upon their people. But before this could happen, the entire area must be consecrated with blood and flesh and smoke. Then a city wall would be raised to protect Sacred Space and construction could begin in earnest.

The result would be the finest *spura* ever built, even more elegant than Veii, which was celebrated as the most beautiful city in Etruria. And as everyone knew, Etruria was the most beautiful land in the world. Its inhabitants were the special favorites of the *Ais*.

"Great are the gods and precious their love," Vesi murmured automatically.

She shaded her eyes with one hand so she could make out details of the scene below.

There!

In the center of the site designated for the *templum* lay a huddled body. Desecration! When Vesi leaped to her feet with a yelp of outrage she accidentally dropped her dagger. It struck the soft earth point first and stood there quivering.

She was quivering herself, with indignation. Injured or not, the man had gone beyond all bounds of decency! The most Sacred Space of all had been defiled. The priests would not use it now; the lengthy process of selecting another site for the city would have to be undertaken. It might be many seasons before an equally propitious location was determined.

To add to Vesi's dismay, she glanced down to discover that her knife was stabbing the earth. With a soft moan the girl stooped and withdrew the blade. She removed the clinging soil with reverent fingertips, then tenderly pressed the tiny particles back into the ground as she murmured a prayer to the goddess Ops. "May the earth spirits forgive my carelessness; I meant them no harm."

Straightening, she drew a deep breath.

The blood-smell was stronger than ever. The figure lying in the center of the *templum* space was not moving.

Keeping a firm hold on her knife, Vesi trotted down the hill toward the *spura*. When she reached the edge of the first marked foundation she stopped, reluctant to cross the invisible line that bordered the most dangerous of Sacred Space: unhallowed ground, designated but not protected from the more inimical inhabitants of the Otherworld.

Pacing along the line, she stared at the man lying on what should have become the floor of the *templum*. From a distance she had thought he wore a tattered cloak; now she saw it was the flesh of his naked back, torn in bizarre strips. Vesi wondered what animal could have inflicted such wounds. Neither bear nor boar nor aurochs, whose marks she recognized. Could it be one of the legendary monsters said to inhabit the mountains of Latium? Would such a creature have come this far into Etruria in search of prey? Surely not.

Yet obviously some predator had been at work. The injured man must have been caught and mauled and then dragged here, suffering terribly.

Vesi caught her lower lip between her teeth as she pondered a new mystery.

Where was the trail of blood?

Crimson had seeped from the man's body to puddle beneath him, yet there was no gory pathway across flattened grass to the place where he now lay. An animal dragging him would have left one. Instead there were only spattered droplets, indicating he had walked there by himself. Furthermore he looked wet, as if he had recently emerged from the nearby Tiber. Swimming? So wounded?

Suddenly the fallen man gave an appalling shriek and convulsed like a fish on a hook. Fresh blood began oozing from his wounds.

His anguish was so acute Vesi could almost feel it herself. She could go for help, but by the time she returned he would surely be dead. Fortunately she was not afraid of blood. Had she not watched

21

from hiding as the *purtani* set the silver plate into her father's crushed skull after the hunting accident that eventually claimed his life? She could help this man if he was not too far gone, if he had not lost too much blood.

Vesi looked over her shoulder. The rolling hills were tapestried with flowers, many of them possessing healing properties. She could cleanse the wounds and apply a poultice to staunch the bleeding. The *purtani* would criticize her for usurping their healing functions and probably punish her for entering unhallowed Sacred Space. But if she were to allow a man to die needlessly when she might have saved him . . . was that not the greater crime?

Vesi pressed her forefinger and middle finger to her lips, kissed them, and bowed her head in reverence. "Culsan, the god of destiny; Tuflas, goddess of healing, guide me. What I do now, I do through you."

Then she stepped over the line.

Walking through the unmade city was terrifying. In unhallowed Sacred Space the fabric between the worlds was very thin. Vesi was certain she could hear *hia* and *siu* whispering in the Otherworld.

She could even catch the faintest scent of the Netherworld where Satres ruled and Veno protected the dead. As long as she was alive its mysteries were denied her. But the perfumes that wafted from that dark kingdom were spiced with myrrh and cinnamon and subtler, more alluring fragrances that promised and beguiled. She felt their temptation, potent as a stirring in the loins.

Death, the Aegyptians claimed, was a jewel of incomparable brilliance.

On every side shadows twisted and dissolved, hinting at wonders, each one attempting to draw her into the darkness from which she knew she would never return.

Fragments of songs, ghosts of winds, the distant trilling of unknown birds called to her, and behind them the faintest whispers that might have been prayers, incantations, secrets. . . .

With an effort Vesi forced herself to concentrate on the injured man. To allow her spirit to be distracted would leave her vulnerable to vengeful spirits lurking in wait for the unwary. The young woman was trembling with tension as finally she stepped into the rectangle of the *templum.*

It was as if she had walked into a maelstrom.

Dark hair tore free of her silver fillet; saffron *peplos* molded itself to her body. The air within the area was so thick she had to force herself through invisible density. The beings lurking beyond human sight in the Otherworld were frenzied as she had never known them to be . . . but then she had never walked through unhallowed Sacred Space before. They clustered and gibbered at the very edges of her vision, vanishing when she turned to look at them, reappearing as writhing shadows when she looked away.

The absence of a bloody trail was more puzzling now, but only because there was so much blood around the man's body. Vesi forced herself to kneel beside him, drawing her linen skirt up onto her thighs to keep from staining it any more than necessary. She gently examined the wounds on his back—deep punctures and long, raking claw marks that flayed the flesh. Then, sliding her hands under the man's body, she turned him over.

She was startled to find the broken body of a huge white owl underneath him, downy feathers plastered to his bloody chest. Then when she looked upon his face, she realized this was no ordinary man.

Vesi was about to scream when he opened his eyes.

THREE

Though he was half a mile from the river, Artile caught a whiff of the tainted breeze. Instinctively he dropped to the ground and rolled a short distance down the terraced slope. Yet even as he rolled, the stench followed him.

Twice before he had encountered a similar putrid chill. The first time had been when a Babylonian magus loosed a minor *utukki*, an *ummu* demon, on a caravan Artile was leading across the Great Sand Waste. The *utukki*'s presence had been heralded by a foul, icy breeze. Artile had smelled the odor again many seasons later on the day he came upon the remains of a human sacrifice high in the Black Mountains. Although the day had been warm, the telltale chill had lingered around the butchered corpses.

The *purtani* said the foul wind slipped through whenever the fabric between the worlds was torn.

Lying flat on the ground, Artile raised his head cautiously and sniffed. The air around him smelt only of loamy earth and healthy grapevines. The noxious odor had vanished.

And yet . . .

Artile fumbled for his pruning knife and got to his feet with the inadequate weapon clutched in his hand. He crouched like a man ready to run; there was no shame in running. In his youth he had been a mariner, a guide, and a mercenary warrior, surviving all three dangerous occupations because he had learned to trust his instincts . . . and run when the occasion warranted.

His instincts were telling him now that something was wrong, terribly wrong.

Shading his eyes with one hand, he turned full circle. His vineyard spread out before him, vines laden with grapes just beginning to ripen. In the distance he could see some of the workers moving slowly along the rows and filling their baskets. None of them appeared uneasy.

Beyond his land a fold of hills sloped to meet the forest and the river. Nothing disturbed the scene. No spiral of smoke warned of fire among the trees. The Tiber was as placid as a snake basking in the sun.

Artile looked up. The birds that circled in the sky above, always hopeful of snatching some fruit, seemed equally untroubled.

Perhaps he was imagining things; were his aging senses at last beginning to betray him?

Tightening his lips, Artile gave a firm shake of his head. He could not accept the possibility; he had not imagined that odor. His nose was still sensitive enough to detect the first hint of rot upon the vine or the telltale sliminess of diseased soil. His other senses might fail, but that of smell would be reliable until the end.

Limping slightly, he walked the width of the vineyard terrace and climbed the hill beyond. His left thigh muscle had been torn by a Nubian spear eight seasons past. The *purtani* had healed the injury, but the residual awkwardness finally convinced him he was getting too old to be a mercenary. So using the small fortune he had secreted away over the years, he purchased a vineyard with a modest but comfortable villa. There he had settled down to spend the rest of his life getting acquainted with peace.

The gods, Artile told everyone, had been good to him.

But the *Ais* were fickle; they could rescind their kindness at any time, as he knew.

At the top of the hill he paused to catch his breath. Automatically he glanced northward, in the direction where the new *spura* soon would rise almost on the boundary of his vineyards. Another gift of the gods, the opportunity to sell his wines so close to home. He would . . .

The man grunted in surprise. There was a moving splash of color—gold and green and red—against the cleared earth. He rubbed his eyes, then looked again.

Someone was crossing unhallowed Sacred Space.

Keeping his eyes fixed on the distant *spura*, Artile hurried forward as swiftly as his game leg would allow. Those colors indicated a woman; the female costumes of the Rasne were famous for their exuberant hues.

Surely none of the Silver People would knowingly enter unhallowed Sacred Space!

Yet he was seeing a woman there, of that Artile was certain. His mobility was impaired, but the keen sight that had stood him in good stead for so many years was undiminished. Once it had been his proud boast that he could tell if the eyes of an eagle flying overhead were yellow or gray.

The woman seemed to be moving toward a dark form in the very center of the *spura*. The old man frowned, trying to make sense of the vaguely human shadow. Artile saw the woman pause, bend over . . . then the path dipped and the scene was hidden from him by the next hill. Cursing under his breath, he hastened forward.

Before he reached the summit of the hill he heard her scream. The sound was high-pitched, terrified . . . and abruptly cut off.

Without hesitation, Artile tried to run.

When he could see the *spura* again, only the figure in bright clothing lay on the cleared earth. The dark form she had been examining had vanished.

Artile's heart was pounding fearfully in his chest by the time he reached the margins of the *spura*. He hesitated, unwilling to enter until he realized that Sacred Space had already been compromised. No city would be built here now, he thought with a pang of disappointment. No market on his doorstep. Then he berated himself for his petty and selfish thoughts. Limping, he hurried across the foundations toward the area designated for the *templum*.

The still figure within was lying on her stomach with her head twisted to one side. What he could see of her face was puffed and bruised; dark hair was matted to her skull by blood. Torn from her body and strewn on the ground beside her were the tatters of her bright clothing.

Artile's fist closed with the index and little fingers extended. He brought his hand to his mouth and breathed an ancient prayer into the fingers, warding off evil.

Kneeling beside the woman, he gently turned her over. The breath caught in his throat. He knew her. She was Vesi, a maiden, a daring girl who played games and ran races like a boy, a girl filled with spirit and courage. Of all the children of the Rasne, Vesi was among the brightest. Watching her had made him long for a daughter of his own, though Fate and old war wounds had decreed he had none. Now to see her like this . . . !

Artile had traveled far and fought in many battles, and more than once had observed what men inflamed by blood lust could do to a woman. Yet never had he seen a woman so peculiarly mutilated.

Deep parallel gouges ran the length of the girl's body, slicing open her breasts and cutting deeply into the soft flesh of her belly. On closer inspection, they looked as if they had begun low on her abdomen and ripped *upward*. He measured them with his broad hands. There were four cuts spaced wider than the span of human fingers. More blood stained her thighs.

Making sympathetic noises deep in his throat, Artile removed his cloak. She was a strong girl and well-nourished; with his bad leg he would not be able to carry her all the way back to his villa. He must go for help. But he could not leave her naked amid the gaudy ruins of her dress.

As he was tucking his cloak around her, the crushed remains of a bird fluttered from her hands. From the feathers Artile identified the corpse as that of an owl.

The old man picked up a feather and turned it in his gnarled fingers. A white owl, in a land without white owls.

FOUR

L ong before consciousness returned, Vesi could hear voices. Dream voices circled and spun around her, some murmuring almost inaudibly in a misty distance, others loud and immediate. A few she recognized. Her mother's was suffused with anger. The *purtan* was soft-spoken in counterpoint, conciliatory.

There was another whose words were like the crack of a whip, Pepan, Lord of the Rasne.

Vesi grew dimly aware of the hiss of candle flame somewhere nearby, of water tinkling from a fountain a little farther away, of the particular ambient sound of space embraced by stuccoed walls. From beyond those walls came a low buzz, as of a distant crowd.

Through ears that never slept, such details informed that level of Vesi's mind that also never slept. The sounds created a pattern she recognized. She knew this place by heart, was familiar with each crack in the plaster and every tile on the floor.

As with most Etruscan houses, the structure was a hollow square with stone foundations and walls of unfired brick, built around a roofless courtyard that provided both light and air to the interior. The rooms that comprised three sides of the house gave onto this space. At the rear a solid wall formed the fourth side of the square. A fountain in the courtyard kept the house filled with the delicate tinkle of water music, and the air was perfumed by flowering plants growing in terra-cotta tubs. Beyond the entrance door at the front of the dwelling lay the *spura* of Vesi's birth. She was in the main room of the house she had lived in for all of her fourteen years. She was . . . home.

Safe.

Following that first conscious thought, her other senses began to awaken one by one. She caught a whiff of the herbs and spices used in Etruscan cooking, then the lush fragrance of the flowers blooming in the courtyard. Gradually, feeling began to return to her nerve endings. At first she was but dimly aware that she lay on a couch piled high with cushions, but then . . .

. . . with the restoration of total tactile sensation came *pain*, an explosion of agony that enfolded her body like a sheet of flame!

Vesi screamed.

"I tell you no man could have done this," Repana was saying angrily to Caile, the *purtan*. A big-boned, middle-aged woman in a sky blue gown of elaborately pleated linen, Repana prided herself on being considered still handsome. Surely someday Pepan would notice.

But her own appearance had become irrelevant. She fixed her eyes on the *purtan*'s face rather than look any longer at the damage that had been done to her daughter's body.

The paunchy priest was an easterner, not a full-blooded Etruscan, and excessively fond of the pleasures of the vine and the table. His thick lips were still glistening with grease from his most recent meal as he replied, "The man who found your daughter is a former mercenary, and we all know what they're like. I feel quite certain he was the one who . . ."

Pepan dropped his hand onto the *purtan*'s shoulder as lightly as if the touch might soil his fingers. A slender man with long-lidded eyes and a thrusting, aquiline nose, the Lord of the Rasne moved with the deceptive languor common to his race. He could be identified as a prince of Etruria by the way he wore his beard. All facial hair was plucked from his cheeks and upper lip, but from his chin hung a precisely coiled pair of dark brown curls. His clothing consisted of a narrow, short-sleeved white robe with a red border over which he wore a triangle of darker red, finely woven wool, drawn to one side and fastened high on the shoulder with a silver brooch set with lapis and carnelians.

"The man who found Vesi is Artile the winemaker," Pepan told the priest in crisp tones, "and is well known to me. A man of impeccable honor. I trust him implicitly, and on his behalf I resent your slander."

Caile widened his eyes. "I meant no harm, my lord! Certainly not! It was just a suggestion . . . one looks first at the most obvious . . ."

Pepan locked his hands on either side of Caile's head before the other man had time to flinch. He forced him to bend over the young woman lying on the bed. "Then look at the obvious!" Pepan commanded.

Roughly he thrust the *purtan* down, holding his face just above the girl's torn breasts. When the priest squeezed his eyes shut, pressure from Pepan's thumbs made him open them again. "Look, you coward," snarled the Lord of the Rasne. "Does this damage resemble the work of any human weapon . . . or human hand?"

The *purtan* focused his eyes to find himself a mere finger's length from mutilated flesh. He wrinkled his nose at the scent of blood and a smell as foul as excrement. His stomach heaved.

"Repana is right, no man did this," Pepan asserted, satisfied to have made his point. "We must seek elsewhere for Vesi's attacker." He released the *purtan* and stepped back, deliberately wiping his fingers on the red wool as if the touch of the priest's flesh had insulted him. "I need some fresh air." Folding his arms across his chest, he stalked into the courtyard and stared up at the twilight sky.

The evening was sweet with summer, the first stars a handful of jewels flung against a peacock blue dome. Normally such beauty enthralled Etruscans. They composed countless poems to celebrate the first star, the warm night wind, the constantly changing hues of the heavens.

But this evening Pepan's outraged senses took no pleasure from beauty.

A widower, he had long admired the widowed Repana. At the most unexpected moments he found himself thinking of her warm smile, her long-fingered hands. His sons and daughters were grown, and his house and his heart were lonely. He could not simply take Repana as wife however. Under the law, first the spirits of his own dead mate and Repana's would have to be located in the Netherworld and propitiated, and these arrangements took time. The Lord of the Rasne had many responsibilities and put his responsibility to himself at the bottom of the list, something he would get around to . . . in the future.

So he had done nothing as yet about his feelings for Repana. But he had developed a paternal affection for her daughter; if—when—he wed Repana, Vesi would become his child. He could taste, as bitter as bile on his tongue, fury at the wanton damage that had been inflicted upon the lovely young woman.

"If no man is responsible, then the girl must have been mauled by a beast," Caile was saying in an effort to regain his dignity. "That stench, that wild smell, could come from a bear or . . ."

Repana uttered such an exclamation of disgust that the *purtan* backed away from her, fearing she might strike him. "Look around, what do you see?" she demanded to know, making a graceful gesture that included the entire house. "The fur rugs underfoot, the tusks of boar and horns of aurochs that hang on the walls . . . every one of those trophies was taken by my husband. He prided himself on his skill with the spear; it was an art form, he said.

"Usually he killed his prey and made a sacrifice of propitiation to its spirit. But sometimes the beasts left their mark on him. I have tended and stitched many such wounds, including the one that ultimately proved fatal when a bear ripped off the top of his skull. I also saw the damage done by the pack of wild boar that killed my sons when they tried to follow in his footsteps as a matter of family pride. You might say I am an expert on hunting injuries," she added, with a bitter twist of her mouth.

Pointing toward the four terrible raking wounds on her daughter's body, she concluded, "I tell you, priest, there is no wild animal in Etruria that leaves marks like these."

"If it was neither man nor animal, it must have been some monster that strayed into our territory," Caile suggested. "Perhaps a creature from the Darklands, one of those things with the head of a boar and the body of a lion and great leathery wings. We know such monsters live there."

"*We* know?" Pepan called scornfully from the courtyard, not even deigning to look over his shoulder at the *purtan*. "Who is this 'we,' priest? You never venture outside the *tular spural*, the city boundaries. I have scouted the forests and mountains and found them inhabited by debased tribes one could scarcely call human, yet they fear us more than we fear them. In all my travels I have seen no such monster as you describe. Nor have I seen anything like what has been done to this girl."

"But if you eliminate man and beast and monster," the *purtan* argued, throwing up his hands, "what does that leave? What else is there?"

"*Hia*," breathed Repana. Suddenly her courage failed her. "*Hia!*"

To the terror of all, occasionally some corrupted *hia* would break through from the Otherworld or, more terribly, from the Netherworld. Ravening and uncontrollable, the thing might fasten upon a living person. Once it had selected a victim, it would use its malign influence to drive the unfortunate to commit the most appalling acts, even self-mutilation. But Vesi could not possibly have done this to herself . . . and Artile had seen another . . . if the old man had not disturbed her attacker, Vesi might have endured a fate beyond imagining. The thought sickened Repana.

But as she shuddered with horror, a cracked whisper said, "No, this is not the deed of a mere *hia.*"

Repana whirled around as Caile dropped to his knees and pressed his forehead to the floor. In the courtyard, Pepan did the same. A slight, bent figure stood in the doorway of the house, ignoring the men who prostrated themselves in reverence.

"Not *hia?*" Repana asked hoarsely.

"No. Something worse, I suspect. Much worse." The shape at the door moved and an old woman hobbled into the room. She was almost hairless with age, her skin taut across the bones of her face, giving the impression of a skull.

"Uni Ati," Repana murmured. She attempted to kneel, but the old woman placed a restraining hand on her arm.

"Stand with me, daughter. Lend me your support while I examine the child."

In silence the two women gazed down upon the suffering girl. After her one scream Vesi had made no further sound. Tears seeped from beneath her closed eyelids however.

"Leave us," the old woman ordered the men. "We have no need of you now. I can do whatever needs to be done for this girl."

Without protest, the *purtan* and the Lord of the Rasne scrambled to their feet and left the house to join the crowd gathered outside. Not only the Rasne, but even the humblest of their slaves had been drawn by news of Vesi's injury—and the more astonishing and unprecedented visit of the Uni Ati to a private residence.

The Uni Ati, whose title meant First Mother, was the oldest of all the Silver People. She had been the senior elder of the Council for as long as anyone could remember. The most serious disputes of the Rasne were referred to her; her judgment was final and irrevocable. In addition, she was a skillful healer, and many who had been given up as hopeless by the *purtani* were taken to her and subsequently cured.

It was claimed that she never changed the rags she wore nor left the hillside cave that was her only home. Yet she had come to Repana's house this evening.

"No *hia* caused this," the old woman repeated. Extending her left hand palm downward, she rotated it in a sunwise circle above Vesi's torn body. Her knuckles and joints were so knotted with age as to resemble the mangled claws of birds. But when she moved her fingers through the air, the bones glowed through her skin with an eerie green light.

Vesi convulsed.

Repana tried to gather her daughter in her arms but the old woman blocked her with her own body. "No!" she cried, continuing to make gestures above the girl's torso. "These are not fatal injuries," she remarked after a time, "only very painful ones. But . . ." She drew a deep breath and moved her hand in a different pattern, allowing it to rest for a moment above Vesi's torn belly. Once she darted a glance at Repana and swiftly looked away. Moments later, she grunted as if confirming some suspicion.

With a sigh, the Uni Ati folded her hands and withdrew them into the sleeves of her tattered robe. "Your daughter was attacked and violated by a *siu*," she told Repana. "That is demon's stink on her flesh." One hand reemerged from the sleeve of her robe holding a ceremonial knife with a curved bronze blade. "She would be better off dead."

"No!" Repana gasped. "No, First Mother, she is everything to me! I gave birth to four children: three boys and this girl. Over the years I have attended the dying not only of my husband but also my beloved sons. I am not ready to put my last child into her tomb. Can you understand? I want to enjoy her living. Please! Why do you want to do this?"

Still holding the knife aloft, the old woman replied, "I tell you your daughter has been impregnated by a *siu*. Even now the demon's seed swells within her; she will give birth to an abomination. Is that what you want for her? Do you wish her to be feared and loathed by the rest of the Rasne? Do you think they will even allow the two of you to remain in this *spura*?"

Pressing the knife into Repana's numb hand, the Uni Ati closed the woman's fingers around the handle. "It is up to you to sacrifice your daughter," she said. "You must offer her to Veno and request that your ancestors be allowed to come for her. Assure her of a proper dying, and implore the *Ais* to destroy the *siu* spawn."

Repana was very pale. "What if I refuse?"

"Then someone else will do the deed, for it must be done. But remember—only Vesi's nearest kin can summon the *hia* of her ancestors to conduct her spirit to sanctuary in the Netherworld. Without such guides, she is not likely to find her way there alone. She could be lost to wander frightened and confused through the Otherworld instead, a helpless ghost. There she would easily fall prey to evil spirits."

From the hollows of her sunken eyes, the Uni Ati gave Repana a searing look. "You have no choice," she said. Then she hobbled from the house.

As Repana stood beside her daughter, clutching the knife in fingers turned to ice, she could hear the old woman's cracked tones beyond the door. "Caile, we will require your services after all. Dress yourself in your ceremonial robes and summon the townspeople. There is to be a Dying."

"A Dying? But why?" Pepan demanded to know. "Appalling as they are, Vesi's injuries need not be fatal. You can heal them, First Mother. Your skills are . . ."

"Be silent and do not interrupt me! Repana has chosen to give the girl to Veno because she is carrying the spawn of a *siu*," the old woman snapped. "Were Vesi to live, her child would bring disaster to the race of the Rasne."

FIVE

From its source on the northwestern slope of the Apennines the water flowed relentlessly downward. At first an inconsequential rivulet that sang to itself in the sun, the stream gathered force as it descended. In time a mighty river swept seaward to a raw young city sprawling across seven hills.

Long before the birth of Rome, the Etruscans had named the river Tiber, meaning notched. Of all the watercourses that flowed through their land, this was the most important: Father Tiber.

Like fertile Sister Nile and dark Brother Styx, the Tiber was both a barrier and a conduit. Unpolluted and pristine, the living waters of the great rivers straddled the divide between the worlds of flesh and spirit. Strange beings inhabited the three realms—Earthworld, Otherworld, Netherworld—traversed by these rivers.

Only rarely did the occupants of one realm venture into another.

The great river gave life and took life. On its journey to the sea it drained meadowland and fed marsh; incubated dragonflies, dissolved the flesh of carrion, and scrubbed the bones clean. Some worshipped it, some feared it, and only the fool ignored it.

The river was unforgiving.

Denizens of the Otherworld clustered most thickly around the Tiber's banks, and Earthworld hunters found the richest bounty there.

Wulv pressed the tip of his bronze dagger into the pile of dung in the center of the path. The outer crust cracked open to reveal a moist and steaming interior. The man smiled to himself, but the expression was distorted by the scars that covered the left side of his face, pulling his lips away from his teeth in a permanent leer. Unkempt hair straggled to his shoulders; eyebrows as tangled as briar thickets overhung his deep-set brown eyes. Even among his own tribespeople, the Teumetes, Wulv was considered ugly.

But he knew how to track animals.

The boar had passed this way recently and was keeping to the trail, a well-worn animal trail winding through the forest west of the Tiber. If the beast followed the usual pattern, it was heading for a familiar lair.

Of course, there was always the possibility that it would break with the pattern. Throughout his life Wulv had hunted bear, wolf, and wildcat, but of all creatures, boar were the most unpredictable. Bears were not much better, however. The bear that had torn open his face should have been hibernating when a much younger Wulv stumbled across its den. The bear had taken his face—but he had taken its hide. Made into a mantle, the trophy still hung across his broad shoulders.

Wulv had been tracking this particular boar for three days, patiently, biding his time. Any other hunter would have abandoned the pursuit and returned to the comfort of friends and family, but Wulv had neither to distract him. All he had was single-minded determination.

The boar he was following had rampaged through the fields bordering the Teumetes village on the fringe of the Great Forest. What the animal had not eaten, it had trampled in wanton destruction. A hunting party composed of the young men of the village had gone out and eventually killed a boar—a young, wiry-bristled female they'd trapped in a patch of marshland. They had hurled as many spears into the animal as the fingers on two hands, slung the dead boar from a pole, and carried the carcass back in triumph to their village.

One look at the beast convinced Wulv it was the wrong animal. The slain boar had a broken hoof that would have left a distinctive track and was not nearly as heavy as the animal that had ravaged the crops. But when Wulv called attention to these facts, he was shouted down by the triumphant hunters. Their beardless leader even threatened him. Only the patience Wulv had learned while waiting for his bear injuries to heal had prevented him from removing the youth's liver with his knife.

Instead he had gone home to wait. He did not live in the village, but some distance away on an islet in the middle of a marshy lake at the very edge of the Great Forest. Wulv preferred to spend his days where no man would laugh at his ugliness and no woman would shrink from his touch.

Four days later the village elders paid him an unprecedented visit. They implored him to forgive the rash behavior of the young men and begged him to go in search of the original boar. The beast had returned, doing even more damage than before. In addition, it had killed a tiny boy child whose mother was working in the fields. The sight of her half-eaten toddler had, the elders related, driven the woman to madness.

Wulv listened without comment, his arms folded and his eyes staring into some misty distance. He let his visitors work up a sweat as they strove to persuade him and accepted, with apparent reluctance, the bribes they pressed upon him. Then at last he gathered his weapons and a few supplies and set off—as he had meant to do all along.

The boar was a challenge.

As if the beast knew it was now being hunted by an expert, it abandoned the area, moving deeper and deeper into the forest. Wulv had no difficulty picking up its trail. Perhaps, he speculated, the boar was deliberately leading him somewhere for reasons of its own. The creature was intelligent and cunning, and obviously learned from experience.

He must be doubly wary.

Determined to maintain a precise distance, a margin of safety, between himself and his quarry, Wulv ate as he traveled, satisfying his hunger with strips of dried meat he had brought with him and berries snatched from bushes he passed.

In the middle of the third day of his hunt, the man halted and took a half step off the trail. In his bearskin mantle and untanned leather tunic he blended into the forest background. Turning his face up, he peered through the branches of the giant trees above him until he was able to locate the Great Sky Father. Past High Day it was. Great Sky Father had begun his journey down to the horizon.

Wulv came to a decision: If he had not tracked the boar to its lair by nightfall, he would turn back. Three days was long enough to be wandering through the forest without feeling sun on his head. He was growing bored.

As the afternoon wore on, the temperature fell and what little light penetrated to the forest floor soon vanished. Wulv caught the scent of rain on the air. The hard rain typical of the region could obliterate all traces of the boar, dissolving fresh spoor and washing away its characteristic odor. A less experienced hunter might have tried to close up the space between himself and his quarry so as not to lose the trail, but Wulv had learned caution the hard way.

Unconsciously, he rubbed at the scars on his face.

Borne on a howling wind, the rain swept in from the north. Icy drops as vicious as stones slashed through the canopy of the leaves, driving earthward at an angle. Wulv paused long enough to unsling the leather pack on his back and remove a piece of oiled deerhide, which he carefully wrapped around the head of his spear.

Some of the mountain tribes still used blades of flint or obsidian, but the Teumetes were proud of their metal weapons and intensely protective of them, knowing their worth to be greater than jewels.

With the rain now at his back, the hunter moved even more cautiously. The wind was blowing his scent up the trail; surely the boar had already picked it up. Wulv had heard of a boar turning aside from a track and waiting until its hunter passed by, then lunging out to kill the man with its savage tusks.

One foot set precisely in front of the other, Wulv continued to advance. His wary eyes peered out from beneath his tangled brows; his spear was balanced in his hand, ready for action.

Lightning flashed, illuminating the forest in stark black and white. The God Who Roars boomed an angry response. Wulv halted abruptly and made the Sign of Horns, index and little finger pointing straight out to ward off evil. It was not good to be in the way when the God Who Burns and the God Who Roars stalked the land, warring between themselves. Capricious and deadly, they trampled man underfoot as carelessly as a man trod on ants.

Lightning cracked again. In that instant, Wulv saw the boar. The beast was standing immobile in the track ahead of him, with its body at an angle, its great head bowed, razor tusks gleaming. He saw the boar start to turn . . . and at that moment the lightning exploded again and the world vanished in white brilliance as the boar began its charge.

The hunter's eyes were seared by the light. Momentarily blinded, he hurled his spear.

SIX

Some distance to the south, a lone figure was sitting on his haunches in a small cave. He appeared to be human: a slender man somewhat less than middle height, with almond-shaped eyes and swarthy skin as worn and crumpled as old parchment.

Drawing upon inhuman abilities lingering from his Otherworld existence, the *siu* had reformed the walls of the cave to glassy smoothness. This vitreous substance rendered him invisible from any prying eyes that could see beyond the physical.

Secure within this stronghold, he sat.

In the sky above the cave clouds gathered; thunder rumbled.

On reflection, his earlier actions now dismayed him. But they were not his fault; nothing was ever his fault. The minions of the *Ais* had hunted him relentlessly until he became so desperate and exhausted he could not think. By the time he escaped from the Otherworld into the Earthworld he was acting on sheer instinct. Encountering the human girl had been . . . his mouth twisted in an ironic grimace . . . like a gift from the gods.

An incomplete gift, unfortunately. Eating the still-living heart of a virgin should have been sufficient to restore him to full strength. But a moment's intense excitement, a loss of control . . . when he had a warm human female in his hands once more after so long a time, he had been unable to resist the temptation to rape her. The mistake would have been rectified by devouring her heart afterward and thus killing her. But as he was about to tear out the organ, the limping man had come hurrying toward them. Knowing he still lacked the strength for a confrontation, the *siu* had been forced to abandon the girl and flee.

Leaving a part of himself in her living body.

Mistake, mistake!

In spite of the distance between them, he was physically aware of the child that had been conceived. The call of its unborn spirit drew him like a beacon.

In another age the demon might have allowed his seed to mature to birthing. He would either have been indifferent to the child or taken malicious pleasure in teaching it evil.

But the era when humans and inhabitants of the Otherworld could freely mingle with one another was over. As a result of manipulation by the *Ais*, the different planes inhabited by sentient beings had boundaries now. A demon could exert influence in the Earthworld, but he, or she, could no longer take a tangible form there. Thus had the gods ruled.

This particular *siu* had willfully ignored their ruling and made himself part of the Earthworld with a tangible body. The Earthworld he had once walked as a human man himself. The Earthworld for which he still lusted.

Here he could act with impunity, knowing that little could harm him . . . except the flesh of his own flesh. As a carnate element of the *siu*, his spawn made the demon vulnerable.

The unborn infant and the woman who carried it must be found and destroyed. As long as the child existed it posed a very real threat, one he could not tolerate.

Closing his eyes, the scarred flesh wrinkling and twisting, the being in the cave concentrated on the faint but distinctive song of the unborn life, tracing it to its source. Occasionally he paused to scratch himself, tiny slivers of skin peeling off beneath his nails. Too many centuries had passed since he was truly a man; now he was vaguely uncomfortable in skin. To the casual glance his looked like human flesh, but with a decidedly greenish cast he could not eradicate. And it was very dry, which annoyed him. Any small failing on his part made him angry.

There! The telltale song of life, a wondrous threnody that never failed to infuriate him.

Lightning flashed across the sky.

He began a low, monotone humming as he expanded his inner sight to encompass territory far beyond the cave. He knew where they were now; it only remained to find a form in which to attack and destroy them.

Lightning flashed again. The final flash blinded not only Wulv but the boar as it charged. In that instant it was slain. By sheerest accident the hunter's spear entered its left eye and pierced its brain.

Before it could even feel the pain of the fatal blow, the great beast crashed to the ground. Heart stilled, lungs frozen. A gush of bright blood poured from its nostrils. For a few moments there was no sound but the gurgle of organs dying within the carcass.

Slowly Wulv regained his sight, searing monochrome fading to familiar colors. He approached the body one wary step at a time, intending to reclaim his spear and collect his trophies. Sometimes an animal could play dead until the hunter was right on top of it. But not this one. A once-in-a-lifetime throw and the beast had run right onto the spear, driving it deeper. The boar was slain. Wulv was silently exulting as he reached for his spear.

With a shudder, the dead boar staggered to its feet.

Wulv flung himself backward, scrabbling for his knife.

The first tottering steps the boar took were as uncertain as those of a newborn. It lurched, almost fell, gathered itself, and lurched on. The beast's mouth opened but no breath emerged. Its right eye continued to glaze; no lashes batted across the fixed stare. The thing paid no attention to Wulv however.

There was one brief moment when the shadows around the creature suggested a crouching man. Then the image vanished as if absorbed into the beast's body. Sullen red coals began to glow deep within its undamaged eye. Giving a toss of its mighty head, it slammed its skull against a tree trunk and dislodged the encumbering spear.

Then the slain boar trotted into the forest and disappeared.

For a time Wulv could only stare after the beast. Cold sweat was running down his spine and his legs were trembling. He should turn and walk away, forget what he had seen. But he was no coward . . . and he was curious. Curiosity had always been a weakness of his.

At last he clenched his jaw, reclaimed his spear, wiped its bloodied head on the leaves, and set off on the boar's trail.

Repana caught her daughter's hand and squeezed it as hard as she could, but the girl was unresponsive. Vesi seemed half asleep, unaware of the branches that scratched her skin or the brambles that tore her bare legs. She had already been so injured that she did not feel the lesser wounds. All her concentration was required to put one foot after the other as her mother demanded.

Looking up, Repana tried to judge time through the dense canopy of oak and elm leaves high above the forest floor. The pursuit might already be underway.

The woman narrowed her eyes in thought, considering her situation. The Uni Ati had intended to preside over Vesi's Dying, cocelebrating the event with the *purtan*. Normally any of the Rasne would have welcomed such an honor. Nothing in the lives of the Silver People was as important as the end of life itself, a highly formalized ritual circumscribed by rites and observances. Families went to the greatest lengths to ensure that a departing member was committed to the care of the ancestors and welcomed by Veno in the Netherworld. The Netherworld was fraught with hazards. Only the powerful Protectress of the Dead could keep a spirit safe there.

But Repana was not willing to surrender her last surviving child to Veno. Not yet.

While pretending to accede to the Uni Ati's demand, she had secretly given Vesi a draught of oil of poppy, then put clothes on the girl as the narcotic was taking effect. Working swiftly and silently, Repana had gathered a small bundle of food and herbs and the few essentials they would need to make good their escape. When all was in readiness, she had gone to the door of the house and requested a sacrificial knife. She spoke with pride, as befitted a mother preparing to give her child a great gift.

The Uni Ati had replied, "You have my knife already," in a querulous voice that scratched the air like a sliver of glass.

Repana had bowed her head respectfully. "I return your knife to you, First Mother, and ask that I may have another to use. One which I may keep for myself afterward, as a holy relic of my daughter."

Such a request could not be refused. Head wobbling atop her thin neck, Uni Ati nodded agreement. "When we bring a child into the world," she said, "we grant it the gift of life borne of blood. Now you, Repana, have a final gift of blood to give your daughter. Those whose deaths we make beautiful will reward us when our own time comes; they will be waiting with loving arms outstretched to guide us safely to Veno in the Netherworld.

"Give your daughter her Dying as you choose. We support you and commend you. When she has departed, we will sing songs and hold funeral games in her honor. Great will be our joy at imagining the existence awaiting her with Veno in a nightless land of fruit and music."

The assembled people murmured among themselves. Most of the Rasne and not a few of their slaves had children; all wondered if they would have the courage now being required of Repana.

Without a word, Pepan stepped forward and handed Vesi's mother a large ebony-handled knife with a curved blade. As her eyes met his he gave a slight but deliberate nod, then silently mouthed the words "glade of stones."

With an effort, Repana kept her face impassive. Any reaction on her part could arouse suspicion and she did not wish to have Pepan implicated. She was grateful however. The Lord of the Rasne seemed to be the only one who cared what she was feeling and who was willing to take her side.

Carrying his knife, she went back inside the house and closed the door, the only door. She and her child were alone together within the windowless walls. It was to be expected that she would want privacy until the mortal wound was delivered. Then she would summon the others and they would form a triumphal procession to carry Vesi to the *templum*.

There was no limit on the time allowed for a ritual of Dying. It could take a matter of moments, it could occupy an entire day. There were a hundred ways to make a Dying, from the swift and painless, which was favored for the very old or the very young, to the most ancient rite in which the victim was allowed to bleed to death over a long period of time. This was the way favored by traditionalists, who insisted that only blood could be certain of attracting the favor of Veno.

Repana never intended to find out.

Even if Pepan had not called her attention to the sacred glade deep in the forest, which was famed as a sanctuary, she had already chosen that as her destination. Hers and Vesi's. But first they must escape the *spura*.

The rear of Repana's house was actually the high wall that encircled the Rasne city. The house consisted of three small wings surrounding the courtyard, but its size was a blessing for a widow with only one child. There was another advantage, however, which Repana now appreciated for the first time.

She stood quietly for a moment, looking down at Vesi. From outside came the voices of the crowd raised in supplication to the gods as

Caile led them in a wailing singsong that grated on Repana's nerves. Bending, she wrapped her semiconscious daughter in a cloak, then somehow got the girl to her feet. "It hurts," Vesi whimpered, but only once. Whimpering was not part of her nature.

Through a combination of cajoling and brute force Repana succeeded in hoisting Vesi through a narrow vertical opening let into the city wall. Intended as a loophole to allow javelin throwers to defend the Rasne *spura*, the shaft was not meant to accommodate a human body. When Repana followed she found it a very tight squeeze. For a moment she panicked. What if she got stuck and they broke into the house and found her?

Then with one final, desperate wriggle, she was through, emerging in an angle of the wall screened from casual view by a clump of shrubbery. There she found Vesi slumped on the ground, her figure no more than a dark huddle in the darker night. Her mother caught her by the shoulders and dug in her fingernails, hoping to rouse the girl with pain. When Vesi murmured an inarticulate protest, Repana whispered urgently, "Stand up, child. I can't carry you; you will have to walk . . . or die. Walk, I tell you. Now! Walk!"

Without a backward look, Repana had led her daughter away from the only home they had ever known, across the fields and into the black maw of the forest. From behind them came the sound of chanting slowly rising toward an inevitable crescendo: the Song of a Dying.

As she made her way into the forest, Repana could not remember the last time anyone had defied a Uni Ati. Such a deed would merit the most dire punishment. Nor could she recall any Etruscan ever exiling themselves from one of their *spurae*. Immersed in beauty and comfort, they were the god-chosen, the god-blessed, the god-loved. In living memory none of her race had turned their back on such a heritage.

But sometimes slaves attempted to escape. Or thieves. Then the great hunting dogs came into their own. No one escaped the massive hounds with their sensitive noses and long, silken ears. And sharp fangs.

Repana could feel a prickling of the skin on her back as if the hounds were already right behind her. She tried to get Vesi to hurry, but the girl could barely walk. In addition, the footing was treacherous, the forest so dark that each step had to be felt out with a tentative foot. When they had gone far enough that they could no longer hear the chanting, Repana allowed her daughter to stop. While the girl leaned panting against the bole of a huge tree, her mother scooped out a shallow bed for them between the roots. There they hid until dawn, concealed beneath dead branches.

When the first daylight filtered into their sanctuary they were up again. Vesi's injuries forced them to travel very slowly; they seemed to be inching through the forest rather than running away. More than once Repana ground her teeth with impatience. When a storm overtook them, thunder and lightning signaling the fury of the gods, she did not dare stop to propitiate the elements. She and Vesi must keep going. Their defection would not be forgiven by the Rasne, whose threat seemed the more immediate.

When the storm abated the two women hardly noticed. But in the silence following the thunder, Repana heard sounds in the distance that convinced her the hounds were on their trail. Holding Pepan's knife in one sweating hand, she gripped her daughter's arm with the other and dragged Vesi on. If only they could reach the glade, they might be safe from the hounds.

And if they did not . . . well, there was no shame in being taken down by the famous hunting dogs of the Rasne. Death would be swift and sure; the animals were well trained. And it would mean Repana did not have to kill her own daughter.

At least, she told herself, they would die together. Without a formal Dying their spirits would wander aimlessly. But they would have each other . . . and hope. It was common knowledge that those who died together in such circumstances were often rebirthed together, returning to the Earthworld if they found no home in the Netherworld.

The pursuing beasts were getting closer; she could hear them crashing through the undergrowth.

Repana frowned. The hounds of the Rasne were not usually so clumsy.

. . .

As something came rushing toward them, Repana whirled around, pushing Vesi behind her. The girl stumbled and fell with a loud cry.

Repana had been expecting dogs, but instead found herself facing an enormous, battle-scarred wild boar. Cruel yellow tusks protruded from its gaping mouth. She screamed . . . and in that final, terrible moment, noticed that something was wrong with its eyes. One was blasted open and suppurating. The other was opaque and glazed, like that of something dead.

Holding Pepan's knife in both hands, Repana called aloud upon Veno and prepared to die.

SEVEN

Six hooded figures stood wordlessly staring into the pool that dominated the long oval hall. A solid beam of intense white light shafted down from a circular opening in the ceiling, turning the water milky.

Sacred water, touching both Earthworld and Otherworld.

In the distance a wild dog howled. Shadows flickered across the beam of light as bats winged their way through the warm night air.

A single bubble rose to the surface of the water, gathered, then burst, sending concentric ripples flowing outward. The silent figures turned their backs on the pool and bent their heads.

Another bubble burst on the surface and then another. Soon the pool was heaving and boiling as if with a life of its own.

Abruptly, opalescent water cascaded off polished obsidian.

A smooth head emerged from the center of the pool. A flat forehead. Blind, slanted eyes. A long, narrow jaw, a slash of a mouth. White water flowed down the black surface of what appeared to be a statue as the image was more fully revealed. The slender column of a neck, sloping shoulders, and then, like a cluster of monstrous fruit, a ribcage covered by swollen black breasts tipped by enormous ruby nipples . . . with one exception. A single breast was flat and withered, the nipple desiccated.

The statue spoke.

Her voice was sibilant but slurred, as if every word was an effort. "I have work for you."

The six figures kept their heads bent to avoid sight of the presence in the pool. "We hear, O Great Pythia," one, older than the others, murmured.

The dark goddess spoke again. "A particularly vicious and cunning *siu* has committed a crime against me. This demon is known to you by his original name of Bur-Sin. Until recently he was an acolyte of mine, the one I held in special favor. Then he robbed me. He took advantage of my trust to get close enough to me to fasten his mouth on my breast."

The listeners shuddered in a mixture of religious ecstasy and terror.

"Each of my breasts has its own attributes, as you know," the voice went on. "The one he drained has given him powers to which he was not entitled."

The six waited, but she did not elaborate.

"I sent Otherworld minions in pursuit," said the carven image, "but the *siu* escaped them in the Earthworld. During the chase they did succeed in injuring his bodily form however. To restore his strength he intended to tear out and eat the living heart of a human virgin. He was disturbed by the approach of another human before he had done more than open her flesh. He abandoned her and fled, but even now his child quickens within her body."

A crescent of darkness edged the milky pool as the moon made its way through the sky, altering the angle of the shaft of light. The obsidian image, which had never risen above waist height, began to slip back into the water. Her dark form glimmered dimly through the translucent liquid.

The words were coming quicker as the level of the water began to rise. "I charge you to seek out this *siu* in the Earthworld. Take him captive to hold for my punishment. Locate his spawn first—you will find the impregnated woman among the Rasne—then use the child as a lure to trap the father. He dare not allow it to live and thrive. Once you have the demon, destroy his child and summon me to complete his punishment. Go now . . . and fail at your peril!" she added harshly.

"We will not fail, O Great Pythia," one of the six whispered.

White water closed over a blind black head. The ripples died away, leaving the surface of the pool as smooth as polished glass.

The shaft of moonlight narrowed, disappeared.

Six hooded figures left the chamber without a backward glance, moving through pitch-black corridors without the benefit of torches. Their kind had no need of light.

EIGHT

Lowering its head, the boar charged.

Repana crouched reflexively as she struggled to recall anything useful her husband might have said about the habits of wild boar. Had he once remarked that a wild boar usually veered to the left, hooking upward with its tusks to disembowel its victim? Frantically she ransacked her memory for an echo of his words, some guidance from the Netherworld where he surely watched and waited.

She would have one chance. She must turn her body sideways to make the smallest possible target and in the same move step to the right, plunging the dagger she carried into the base of the boar's skull as it charged past.

If she failed . . .

The boar thundered across the glade; she could feel the ground shake beneath its hooves. But its behavior was most unnatural. The animal's one-eyed stare was fixed and blind, no foam flecked its lips, no breath hissed from its nostrils. When it was five paces from her, she could smell the unmistakable odor of putrefaction. The boar was dead and rotting . . . yet still moving.

"May the *Ais* protect us!" Repana gasped. The dagger shifted in sweat-slick hands. "Ancestors guide us . . ."

There was a blur of movement from her left.

Pepan's bronze-headed hunting spear buried itself to the haft in the beasts heavily muscled shoulder.

The boar should have squealed and turned toward its attacker or dropped to the ground and rolled to dislodge the weapon. It did neither. Instead it kept advancing with terrible intent, head lowered, dead eyes fixed on Vesi.

The Lord of the Rasne hurled himself forward, recklessly throwing his body onto the boar's back, using his weight in a desperate attempt to force it to the ground. He meant to dig his heels into the earth and try to get enough leverage to snap the animal's neck.

The boar jolted to a halt so abruptly that Pepan was thrown off in an unintentional somersault. Scrambling to his feet, he reached for his dagger, only to realize belatedly that he had given it to Repana the previous day. It was in her hand now. He could not reach it before the boar got him.

His hunting spear was lying in the long grass a little to one side. Closer than Repana and his knife . . . but still too far.

The boar shuddered and lifted its head, flinging it angrily from side to side. Pepan blinked at the wash of foul air the beast exuded. Patches of the boar's flesh sloughed off with its violent movements. The Lord of the Rasne discovered that the film of grease and hair on his hands was composed of decomposing flesh. As he watched in horror, a flap of skin on the boar's jaw dissolved into stringy pulp, clinging to the bone by a viscous thread. Teeth gleamed yellow in the gap.

"Walk away," Pepan said over his shoulder. He kept his eyes fixed on the beast, not daring to turn and look at the women.

"We can't," gasped Repana. "Vesi can go no farther."

"Then drag her! Wrap her hair around your hands and drag her to the lake. Wade out into the water; the boar will not follow you there. Even if it does," he added grimly, "I think the rest of its flesh would fall away at the touch of clean water."

Still Repana hesitated. "Did the Uni Ati send this thing after us, Pepan?"

"Even the Uni Ati cannot work such magic. This creature is possessed. Now go!" He heard Vesi moan and risked a quick glance over his shoulder. Repana was trying to maneuver her daughter onto her feet, but the girl resisted.

In that moment the boar gathered itself and charged again.

A terrific blow to the belly forced the air from Pepan's body, doubling him over, sending him sliding on the damp earth. He staggered to his feet with his hands pressed to his stomach. Repana was screaming behind him and there was a deeper, inner roaring as blood surged in his ears. When he tried to straighten up the pain was excruciating.

The boar was directly in front of him. Its grotesque head swayed from side to side as more gobbets of flesh fell away. The skull beneath was stark in the fading light. There was blood on the grass and blood on the creature's muzzle. For an instant Pepan thought he had injured the monster . . . until he realized the blood was his own.

The boar's tusks had torn a ragged hole through his tunic and the skin beneath. Probing with his fingertips, he felt rib bones grate together. When he lifted his hand to his face, his palms were dark with gore.

He knew all too well the signs of fatal injury. So he would die. He was not afraid. Even if his ancestors were not summoned for him, even if he were not guided to safety in the Netherworld, he had faith in his own ability to cope. His *hia* would survive.

The boar took a shaky step forward. Pepan distinctly heard a bone snap in its body and it lurched sideways. Its left hind leg was now dragging.

The Lord of the Rasne felt a surge of hope. If only he could keep the beast at bay for a few more moments, accelerated putrefaction would render the creature harmless. All he had to do was to keep it away from the women until it collapsed.

The boar staggered forward, enveloping Pepan in its nauseating miasma. Its jaws gaped, baring the cruel tusks.

At that moment a hand fell on his shoulder. He looked around to find Repana standing beside him, holding his hunting spear. "Go now," he urged her. He was shocked to find his voice so weak; shocked too at the black wall of pain that was slowly enveloping him. "Run before it charges again."

"I will not leave you." The big woman planted the spear solidly on the ground before Pepan with its triangular head facing the boar.

"You must. My wound is fatal."

"We will stand together," Repana vowed grimly.

The crippled boar lunged . . . straight onto the spearhead, which entered the animal's throat and erupted between the shoulder blades. The crossbar set onto the shaft should have prevented the boar from charging up the shaft to attack the hunter, but the beast's disintegrating flesh simply flowed around the obstacle.

In less than a heartbeat it was upon them.

Releasing Repana's hand, Pepan threw himself into the boar's gaping maw.

NINE

Because he had not stopped for food or rest, Wulv was growing very tired, but he no longer had any thought of giving up. The chase was too interesting. The thing he was tracking followed no normal pattern, meandering instead in a disoriented way as if it did not have total control of its faculties. Which, he thought, was not surprising. But whatever the boar was, living or dead, natural or unnatural, Wulv had marked it as his quarry. His tenacity was a source of pride. He would destroy the monster no matter what and celebrate victory afterward.

The beast had become progressively easier to track as it disintegrated. By the time he finally caught up with it, he was afraid there would be little left to . . . kill? But he would claim a trophy anyway; the tusks, perhaps. Properly cleaned, at least they would not stink.

He was actually imagining the arm-ring he would make of them when he heard a male cry of pain just ahead.

Wulv ran forward with his spear balanced in his hand, ready for the throw. As he burst through the screening undergrowth he tried to see everything at once so as not to be taken by surprise, but it was hard not to be surprised by the sight that greeted him.

A tall old man had flung himself straight at the moving boar in a desperate attempt to stop it. He was obviously trying to protect a woman in a sodden blue gown. Off to one side a younger woman half-slumped against a tree, with one hand pressed over her mouth and her eyes wide with terror.

"Duck!" screamed Wulv. For the second time he hurled his spear at the boar; for the second time the weapon found its target. The beast's rotten flesh no longer had enough tensile strength to offer any resistance to the spear. With a shriek like a deflating bladder, it collapsed as the force that had animated the body fled.

For a brief moment the shadows around the creature suggested a crouching man.

Then only a pile of rotten flesh remained.

Wulv drew a shaky breath. After his last experience he was reluctant to approach the boar again. Instead he turned toward its intended victims. By the richness of their clothing and the craftsmanship of their jewelry he knew them as Etruscans. "Are you all right?" he asked abruptly.

"I am," replied the woman in blue. "But my daughter . . . come here, Vesi, come here to me. It's over now." She opened her arms and the younger woman stumbled into them.

"There, there," Repana murmured, stroking the girl's sweat-matted hair. Giving her daughter a hug, she turned toward Pepan and what she saw wrung a soft cry from her. She flung herself on the ground beside the man and tenderly cradled his head in her lap. "My lord, my lord Pepan!"

The man struggled to open his eyes. His chest felt like broken pottery. "At last . . . ," he whispered.

"What?" She bent closer. "At last, what?"

"I am in your arms," he said almost inaudibly.

"You sacrificed your life to save ours!"

Pepan summoned another tiny surge of strength, enough to ask, "Was I . . . successful?"

Repana's eyes filled with tears. "You were," she told him. She did not mention the hunter with the spear.

But Pepan's pain-dimmed eyes moved past her and, with an effort, focused on Wulv. "You," he said.

"I, lord?" Wulv sounded nervous. He was not accustomed to having Etruscan nobility speak to him. The tribes of Etruria regarded the Teumetes as little better than beasts of the field and forest.

"You were the one who saved them. I am . . . grateful."

Wulv hardly knew where to look. The woman in blue was also staring at him, but he dared not meet her eyes. She must be a queen. Surely his damaged face and crude clothing disgusted her.

"You helped save us," she said in a low voice. "I too am grateful."

For the first time he could remember, Wulv felt a blush heat his face.

Pepan attempted to sit up. "Help me," he urged Repana. He slid a massive ring from one of his fingers and held it toward Wulv. "Take this," said the Lord of the Rasne, "as a token of my gratitude. And as payment for a further service you may do me."

Wulv echoed numbly, "A further service?"

"These women—Repana and her daughter, Vesi—are dear to me, and they are in danger. I must entrust them to your keeping. I bid you take them deeper into the forest, all the way to the glade of stones. You know the place? Hide them there; protect them from those who pursue them."

"I, lord?"

A little of Pepan's old command returned to his voice. "You are of the Teumetes, are you not? Therefore you know your way around the forest, and you are good with spear and knife."

Abashed, Wulv nodded.

"I cannot command you to do this. I ask you as one man to another. You have proved you are a man of honor; a lesser man would have run away. Will you do as I ask?"

The hunter nodded again. The ring was heavy in his hand.

"I will not ask you for your word," said the dying Rasne. "I will not bind you thus."

"My word is given. I will protect them."

Repana was weeping now. "But what of you, my lord?" she asked Pepan.

He tried to sound strong as he answered, "I go in a different direction to throw them off your trail. When it is safe, I will return to the *spura* and say you have escaped. I will insist that no further effort be made to pursue and punish you."

"But the Uni Ati . . ."

"Even if she does not believe me, she will not dare call me a liar in public. Go now, the pair of you. Go with . . . what is your name?"

"Wulv." Even as he spoke he recognized how harsh, how barbaric his name sounded.

But Pepan did not seem to hold it against him. "Go with our friend Wulv and be safe," he told Repana.

"I would not leave you before. What makes you think I will leave you now?" Her eyes flashed; she was ready to fight.

For the first and last time he told her, "Because I love you, and this is what I ask of you."

Repana caught Pepan's bloody hand and brought it to her lips. "Let me stay," she breathed, her breath moist against his flesh.

"If you stay, then all of this will have been in vain. And Vesi will still be slain."

Slowly Repana got to her feet. She backed away from the wounded Etruscan lord and gathered her daughter into her arms. "Will we meet again?" she asked Pepan.

"We will," he promised. "I swear it. I will always be with you. Now go. Go!"

As Wulv shepherded his new charges deeper among the trees, Repana looked back. She saw Pepan on his feet, standing erect and proud, leaning on his spear.

.   .   .

In the cave with glassy walls the *siu* lay stretched on the earth, recovering. The expenditure of energy required for possession was not normally so exhausting. But finding himself in a suddenly dead body had been a shock. His hold on the flesh had been tenuous, and his struggles to maintain it had only succeeded in speeding up the processes of decay. The hunter's second spear cast had been more than he could counteract, forcing him to flee in order to recoup.

In all his long experience, nothing quite like that had happened before. It did not weaken his resolve to find and kill his spawn however. If anything, his anger at being thwarted was an added stimulus.

Meanwhile six hooded figures made their way through the forest pursuing their own hunt. They did not speak, having no need to confer for they acted with one will. The command had been given; they had no choice but to obey.

TEN

Had Pepan not been Lord of the Rasne, he would have died where the boar first struck him. His wounds were mortal; he knew he was bleeding internally. But he must live up to his nobility and therefore was obliged to attempt the impossible. Besides, he was one of the Silver People who believed that one's Dying was the most important aspect of one's Living and must be accomplished in a particular way. He had to reach his own *spura*.

His extremities were cold and numb and he was only able to walk by a supreme effort of will, clasping his locked fingers together across his abdomen and breathing between the stabs of pain. Something gurgled deep in his lungs with each breath he drew.

The injured Vesi had recently covered the same distance. So he could do it. He must.

He went on. When he could no longer stand, he crawled.

·   ·   ·

Through the roaring in his ears he began to hear the sibilant snickering of malevolent spirits watching from the Otherworld, hopeful of seizing and feasting upon his *hia* if it left his body without protection.

Pepan was on his hands and knees when the hounds found him. The posture bewildered them. By his scent they knew he was not their quarry but the Two-Legs whom the other Two-Legs considered dominant. The hounds dare not be other than submissive in his presence. Yet how did it happen that he was walking like one of them?

Whining with uncertainty they capered around him, wagging their tails to demonstrate their friendship and licking at his bloodied face and hands. This was the scene that greeted their handlers when they arrived. They could only stare, as baffled as their dogs.

The Lord of the Rasne managed to groan, "Pursue the women no more. Just carry me to . . . Sacred Space," before his final collapse.

Caile prepared for the Dying of the Lord of the Rasne with exceptional care. *Purtani* came into their own at a Dying, the focal point of their profession. But when the Dying was for a noble lord, a priest must excel himself. In a crimson robe of heaviest silk rewoven with silver thread, and wearing a headpiece of silver set with lapis lazuli, Caile was more vividly attired than any woman. This Dying demanded an explosion of joy.

Even before he left his chamber and made his way toward the *templum*, he began to sing. He called first on Pepan's nearest living kin, his sons and daughters, to summon them formally. They fell into step behind him. They too were clothed in their best as befitted the occasion. Silver glinted on throats and sparkled on fingers and dangled from earlobes, gemstones glowed in arm-rings, hair was pomaded and curled and coiled into a dozen elaborate shapes.

They were people on their way to a celebration.

As they passed through the streets of the city, every door was thrown open. The Rasne—male and female, old and young—came flocking out of their houses to join the parade, taking up the glad song.

The Etruscan *templum* was large enough to accommodate the population of the city. A structure of flawless symmetry, it was built of the finest materials and followed a design handed down for untold generations. A deep, colonnaded portico ran the width of the building, allowing the maximum number of people to stand beneath the roof of the *templum*. Within the sacred precincts themselves, a long flight of steps approached a high podium upon which the final rites of Dying were celebrated. The atmosphere was at once solemn and joyous, as befitted a place where people celebrated kinship with the immortals.

If a city outgrew its Sacred Space, a new *spura* had to be built and a new and larger *templum* constructed according to the same plan, for it was unthinkable that even one person be denied access to the rituals. The throng that gathered for Pepan's Dying could barely crowd under the roof, straining forward so as not to miss a thrilling moment.

Only the Uni Ati was not present. Her absence was interpreted as censure. As he lay dying Pepan had sent for her and demanded she forgive Repana, but the ancient crone had merely listened in silence then returned to her lonely cave.

There she now did her own praying to the *Ais*.

Meanwhile Caile led the Rasne in Songs of Summoning to the dead kin of the dying man. Their *hia* must make the journey from the Netherworld and be near when Pepan's spirit left his body, to accompany it safely back to Veno. Sacrifices were offered to lure them; incense was burned to guide them.

Tingling with anticipation, the Silver People prepared to celebrate the advancement of their lord to a higher, richer state of existence. Children vied with adults for the best places in the *templum* in order to be the first to feel the rush of invisible forces gliding past. The exact moment Pepan's *hia* sprang free of his ruined body would signal a great outpouring of joy.

Oblivious, the Lord of the Rasne lay stretched on an elaborately carved cedarwood altar in the *templum*, beneath a purple canopy embroidered with sacred symbols of sky and river and sea. A wisp of life remained to him. Like a curl of smoke it extended from his body into a hazy distance, already halfway to the Netherworld. He had only to let go and be drawn along that nebulous pathway.

But he was not ready to let go. His kin had not arrived; he could not sense their *hia*. So he waited, caught between life and death.

In the cave with the glassy walls, the being who lay there became aware of a vortex of forces gathering in the distance. Someone was initiating a Dying. He forced himself to focus, gathering the last of his depleted energy, allowing his consciousness to expand, to take in the surrounding forests and mountains, the rivers and valleys. Tiny spots of vibrating light shimmered and danced, pulsing with life and living.

Where . . . ah, yes . . . there! The city beyond the river was beginning to vibrate with a ritual summoning of the Rasne's dead ancestors.

The prospect was tempting. If he timed it right, he could arrive before the ancestors, invade the Dying ceremonies, and snatch the departing spirit from the very grasp of its kinfolk. Such a trophy was the envy of every other demon.

The *siu* had a more immediate need however, to destroy the life he had inadvertently planted in the human female. The child's fleshly link with him was too dangerous. And he had not the energy to do battle with the enraged ancestors of the dead.

There would be other Dyings, other chances for pleasurable predation. The Etruscans were preoccupied with death and all its trappings. He could remain here and feed off their dead, growing ever stronger and more powerful. Before he could take advantage of them, however, he must seek out the young woman he had violated. Her and her unborn child.

As his thoughts lingered on the woman, he became aware that she was the object of other thoughts. He was not alone in seeking her.

A surprising number of others seemed to be looking for her as well!

·   ·   ·

Wulv did not know just who was pursuing Repana and her daughter. Neither they nor Pepan had told him. Perhaps it was not even necessary that he know. Protection was protection, and he would defend them against all dangers. He had given his word and that was enough.

For the first time in his life the scarred Teumetian felt important. The Lord of the Rasne had entrusted him with an important mission . . . but more importantly, he had looked beyond the ruined face, the unkempt hair, and the crude clothing to see the man beneath. And had trusted him.

But as he led the way through the lightless depths of the Great Forest, Wulv could not quench his curiosity. Later, when they had stopped to rest the wearied young woman, whose name he gathered was Vesi, he asked the older woman, "What are you running from? Thieves? Romax invaders? A jealous husband? It would help if I knew what pursued us."

Repana hesitated before replying. "My daughter and I defied the traditions of our people."

Wulv waited, but she told him no more. He understood the power of traditions however. They were more important than laws, since they were enforced with emotions rather than regulations. One could disregard a law; one could not flout a tradition. Repana and Vesi were being pursued by their own people, then, who would probably hound them to their dying day.

Wulv nodded bitterly; one's own tribe could be the cruelest of all.

When Vesi finally collapsed with exhaustion, he made camp for the three of them and stood guard. Repana fed herself from the supplies she carried and urged a few bites on her daughter, feeding her by hand, but Wulv rejected the food she offered him. Rasne food was sweetened and spiced, as if its natural flavor was not good enough. To eat such things would make a strong man weak. Instead he speared a rabbit for himself and roasted it over a small fire, devouring it when it was still half raw. He refused even to season the meat with some of Repana's salt, though he appreciated the generous gesture. The possession of a commodity as valuable as salt confirmed what he already knew: his charges were nobility.

After Vesi fell asleep, Wulv tried to talk with her mother. They had little common ground. Repana was plainly uncomfortable with anyone so crude, though she tried to conceal her distaste. But when she unthinkingly drew aside the hem of her stained and torn gown rather than let it be contaminated by his foot, Wulv felt the gesture like a knife to the heart. Once such an occurrence would have aroused him to a terrible anger, but now . . . now it merely saddened him. Perhaps he was getting old.

At length Repana asked, "How long will it take us to reach the glade of stones?"

Sucking on one of his broken teeth, Wulv calculated distances. "Traveling as slow as your daughter does, we can't be there much before tomorrow sunset."

"She is injured; she can go no faster," Repana said. "And besides . . ." She broke off abruptly, realizing that in her weariness she was about to say too much.

But Wulv would not let it be. His hunter's instincts were alerted. "Besides what? Is there anything else I need to know that might be important if I am to protect you?"

She turned and looked squarely at him in the somber glow of the dying campfire. He truly was an ugly creature, with that scarred face and twisted smile, and the dancing firelight lent his features a macabre cast. She came of a race devoted to beauty, mistrusting and abhorring ugliness as an abomination before the *Ais*. But these were hunting scars—bears' claws, she thought—and thus honorably earned. Her own late husband had been scarred . . . and Pepan had trusted . . .

Repana could not bear to think of Pepan. "My daughter is with child," she said in a voice so low Wulv could hardly hear her. "A most undesirable child. Our people want to kill her with the infant in her womb."

Wulv thought he understood. Some inferior, a slave perhaps, had defiled Vesi, and now both she and the unborn infant were outcasts.

His heart went out to them. He was to some degree an outcast himself. "While I live your daughter and her baby will come to no harm," he vowed. "I am strong and I know the ways of the forest. I can protect you from the wild animals and from outlaws; I can find food for you and show you where there is pure water to drink. You can trust Wulv; he will never let you down."

His voice rang with such unsuspected fervor that Repana was taken aback. Tentatively, she laid one hand on the arm of their new ally. "I thank you, Wulv."

Touching him was not as unpleasant as she expected. His face was hideous but his skin was warm; he felt like any other man.

ELEVEN

lthough they were Rasne and the hunter had always been a little contemptuous of the effete Silver People, Wulv had to admit he was impressed by Vesi's courage. When time came to be on the move again, she got to her feet without complaining in spite of her pain. He watched as her mother tended her wounds, so he saw how terrible they were.

But when he asked Repana what beast had caused them, she merely pressed her lips together and shook her head. "No animal did this," she said shortly.

"No beast either," replied Wulv.

"An . . . enemy," Repana reluctantly admitted.

"You do have dangerous enemies," Wulv conceded. "But you'll be safe from them at the glade of stones."

Or so he hoped. He was beginning to get an itchy feeling at the base of his skull, an old hunter's wordless warning. As they forced their way through the dense thickets of the Great Forest, he kept his spear at the ready. His movements were stealthy, cautious; his gaze ceaselessly examined the dense undergrowth. Nothing attacked them, yet he felt the weight of watching eyes.

They reached the glade of stones, as he had predicted, late in the day. Gesturing to the women to stay in the shelter of the trees, Wulv went forward to reconnoiter the time-honored sanctuary before he would allow them to join him.

He walked into an eerie stillness.

This place always chilled him, so in the past he had avoided it whenever possible. A blood-red sun was setting, casting a lurid hue over the scene. The glade contained a circle of standing stones each as high as Wulv's head, so roughly hewn that it was impossible to tell whether their shape was natural or carved. In the crimson twilight, with the shadows writhing down the ancient stones, they resembled a circle of gnarled and twisted old men. Local lore named these stones the Twelve Whisperers. At certain times of night and certain times of year, or so folk claimed, a question whispered into the ear of the tallest stone would result in a whispered response.

Wulv only half-believed that it was the wind.

But he knew that nothing living occupied the glade.

Relieved, Wulv beckoned to the women.

They set up camp between the stone circle and the trees. Wulv used fallen branches to build a wattle shelter and made a surprisingly comfortable bed for Vesi and her mother out of boughs and leaves.

"You are very skilled. And you are being very kind to us," Repana said, as she observed the little touches he added: the crushed flowers and herbs among the boughs to scent them, the mud chinked into the walls of the shelter to keep out the wind.

The Teumetian mumbled something in embarrassment and looked away. But he was pleased she'd noticed.

"We will stay here," he told the woman, "until . . ."

"Until what?"

"We receive word from your friend that it is . . . safe."

A twinge of pain tightened the skin around Repana's eyes. She doubted that they would ever receive word of any sort from Pepan. She knew also, from the look in the hunter's eyes, that he too believed that Pepan was dead.

I will never see him alive again, she mourned silently. Oh, my love! My lost and never-to-be love. Why did I not speak to you as I should? Why did you not speak to me?

Guided by the sound of chanting, six hooded figures made their way toward the Rasne city. They moved slowly, with a peculiar gliding motion, but they never stopped. When they saw the walls ahead of them, glowing with the pale golden hue of delicately tinted brick, they lowered their hoods and exchanged congratulatory glances. Gathering closer to one another, they offered silent prayers to Pythia. Then they raised their hoods once more and approached the city.

The single guard remaining on duty at the gates of the *spura* was feeling sorry for himself. He resented being excluded from the Dying. There had been no Dying for several moons. He had felt cheated when the Repana woman ran off with her daughter rather than providing such a ceremony.

When he saw the six approach, he reacted more aggressively than he normally would have. "Halt!" he cried, striding toward them and dramatically flourishing his spear. Pilgrims, farmers, brigands—they could be anyone; they had no business in the *spura* when a Dying was in progress. As he drew nearer to them, however, the quality of the cloth in the heavy robes they wore put him in mind of the last Roman trade delegation to visit the city. Best to address them carefully. "Halt and state your business," he called in measured tones.

The six continued to advance. He could not see their faces, overshadowed as they were by the large hoods, but a hollow voice replied, "We are looking for someone."

The guard leveled his spear at the speaker. "Who?"

Again the answer came: "We are looking for someone."

"I have to have a name," insisted the guard, taking one prudent step backward but continuing to point his spear. The voice set his teeth on edge and caused a peculiar unease in the pit of his stomach, as if he had eaten spoiled meat. "I cannot let just any stranger off the road come in here."

"We are not just any strangers; we mean to enter," replied the hollow voice.

As they continued toward him, the guard grew nervous. There were six of them to one of him, and though they did not appear to be armed, their attitude implied menace.

He reached for the horn hanging at the side of the gate to warn of intruders.

A nauseating odor swept over him. Suddenly his head seemed full of swirling mist. He drew a breath to cry out but that only sucked the foul air deeper into his lungs. As he choked, the lead figure had almost casually brushed aside his leveled spear. The other five followed.

Within the *templum* Caile and his fellow *purtani* were chanting incantations over braziers clustered at one end of a high podium to form a five-pointed star. At the other end was an altar on which a motionless Pepan lay. When the Dying was successfully completed, the emptied husk would be placed in an elaborately painted and decorated tomb, there to spend all eternity surrounded by beauty.

In a precise order the priests alternately trickled powders and water into the flames of the braziers. Scented smoke billowed; colored flames plumed. The sons and daughters of Pepan promptly used consecrated scarves to wave the smoke toward the doorways, while they repeated their own chants of summoning.

Supine on the altar, Pepan lay beneath his purple canopy and felt no sense of time passing. He was suspended between worlds. The weight of his flesh seemed an increasingly slight impediment. Soon he would break his last bonds with his physical body and go. And he would be pleased to go. He had no fear of Death. His only regret was that he had been unable to help Repana when she most needed him. It gave him some consolation to know the hunter would look after them however. Obviously this path was ordained by the gods.

Though he had often doubted them during his lifetime, here and now Pepan found it easy to believe in the *Ais*.

Suddenly rising voices interrupted the ceremony. They buzzed like insects around Pepan. He just wanted to drift . . . away . . . away . . .

"Who are those strangers?" someone was asking.

Another replied, "I felt dizzy the moment they passed under the portico."

"Where did they come from?"

"They have a dreadful smell about them, did you notice?"

"How silently they move. Have they no feet?"

"How dare they enter Sacred Space uninvited!"

"Are they . . . gods?"

Reluctantly Pepan became aware of six dark shadows looming like vultures around the altar. He could feel cold thoughts probing his dying brain, unnatural ideas and bizarre images flickering behind his fading eyes. Panic rose in him. These must be *siu*, come to claim him. . . .

Though the *hia* of his dead kin had not arrived to protect him from the encroaching Otherworld and guide him safely to Veno in the Netherworld, he could wait no longer.

With a great burst of energy Pepan leaped free of his body and fled along the nebulous, misty pathway that opened up before him. In the distance he could see dim shapes; he prayed they were the *hia* of his ancestors approaching.

Behind him, clustered around the empty shell of his flesh like carrion crows, the shadows gathered.

The six surrounding the altar turned as one, filed down the steps, and left the *templum*. An unspoken thought was shared between them: We have failed; the one we seek is not in this place. Pythia will be displeased.

Silently they returned through the city, making their way toward the gates. People from the *templum* started to run after them; some fell back as their minds were gripped by an inexplicable awe, leaving them weeping and shaken on the streets.

"The moment the strangers gathered around him, Lord Pepan died," one person whispered to another. "They must indeed be gods."

Several bowed down and touched their foreheads to the ground, pressing their flesh into the soil recently walked upon by the gods.

Embarrassed by his earlier fear and terrified anew by the reappearance of the six, the guard at the gate made no effort to stop the six from going out the gateway. But when the Rasne came staggering up, he gathered the remnants of his courage, strode boldly into the road, and hurled his spear after the last figure.

With a solid thud the weapon sank into the cloaked back, impaling him; arms flung wide, crucified on the air, he fell silently. Without breaking stride, his companions caught his body beneath the arms and dragged him away with them.

A heavily armed company from the *spura* soon set out after them but came to a dead end. The peculiarly imprecise footprints of the six simply vanished off the dusty track. The Rasne searched for a while, then had to admit defeat. They returned to their city with a sense of persistent unease.

With the resilience of the young, Vesi began to recover as soon as she had some rest and food. Wulv worked to make their shelter a secure hut without defiling the sacred nature of the place. With additional leaves and branches he camouflaged the hut so skillfully that it looked like nothing more than a windblow of forest debris. Inside it was dry and snug, with enough headroom and even a smokehole so they could build a tiny fire, the opening canted at an angle to allow the smoke to drift away horizontally, rather than straight up into the heavens.

That evening, following their supper of rabbit, berries, and a nourishing broth of roots, they sat around the tiny thread of a fire and talked. Their voices were whispers in the gloom, only their eyes visible in the shadows.

"I have known about this place all my life," said Wulv, "but I never entered the circle of stones before."

"Are your people, the Teumetes, afraid of the stones?"

"Not afraid, exactly; we revere them. This is a place of sanctuary. We shed no blood within the circle, and any animal that flees a hunter is safe as long as it shelters here. To my people, this is sacred space."

"Do you know why the glade is sacred, Wulv?" Vesi wanted to know. Her voice was thready and weak, but at least she was beginning to show interest.

"My people have their legends, as I'm sure the Rasne have."

Repana smiled. She needed to keep Vesi awake and interested in her surroundings; anything to prevent her dwelling on the horror that had occurred. The older woman leaned toward Wulv. "Time spent waiting is long indeed. Shorten it for us. Tell us the stories of your tribe."

Wulv was flattered. To the best of his knowledge, no member of the Silver People had ever shown the slightest interest in the history or customs of the Teumetes.

He gently stirred the fire with a stick, careful not to raise any sparks that might ignite the thatch. Then he cleared his throat several times and, rather self-consciously, began. "When I was a child I used to listen to the elders of my tribe talk. That was before my scars made me so ugly my people scorned me."

Repana made a small sound of sympathy in her throat. It was, Wulv thought, the first such sound he had heard from a woman in many years.

"The ancestors of the Teumetes lived in forests even darker and denser than this one. We were the Children of the Bear. That was our name because we were not men and women, you see. We walked upright but our bodies contained the spirits of bears."

"*Hia,*" Vesi murmured. Her mother gave her a sharp look.

Wulv nodded. "Our bear-spirits were fierce and brave, *hia* a man would be proud to welcome into his body. But then a new people came up from the south, following the seacoast in boats made of timber and reeds. They also walked upright but their spirits were those of the river serpent. Members of a subtle, cunning race, they invaded our homeland in search of certain herbs and stones, metals and crystals to use in their rituals.

"The Serpent People could not outfight the Children of the Bear but they were far more clever. In the fighting that followed, my ancestors were defeated. They fled their home forests and at last reached this region, only to find it was already inhabited by an ancient and venerable tribe who practiced a form of magic involving the spirits of the stones. They tolerated us as long as we respected their customs and did not desecrate their sacred sites.

"We were weary of running, so we stayed. A few of the Serpent People pursued us almost this far, but they would not go near the sacred sites of the stone-magicians. Eventually they went back across the mountains to the land they had stolen from us. In the seasons that followed we waged constant war with the serpent folk, harrying them along the rivers that bordered the two lands. As time went by, they changed: they were no longer as cunning, no longer as fast or as deadly . . . but we had changed too; we were no longer powerful and virile. So there came a time when the descendants of the serpent folk simply disappeared from our lands. But by then there was no going back for us; we had become men and women. Our bear-spirits simply . . . faded away." The hunter touched his scarred flesh. "Though bears are with us still," he added somewhat ruefully.

Repana understood more of Wulv's simple tale than he knew. The Silver People had legends of their own origin that were not totally dissimilar, stories of an era when existence had been in a state of flux, with flesh and spirit interchangeable. The ancestors of the Etruscans had, of course, been nothing so crude as bears or serpents. In ancient times the *Ais* had invaded their bodies and minds, impregnating them with the divine. Thus the Etruscans became the embodiment of all that was fine and noble, avatars of love and war and wisdom transcending mortal limitations. They could interpenetrate the various planes of existence at will, wearing their flesh into the Otherworld or reclaiming their *hia* from the Netherworld.

Slowly, choosing her words with care, Repana tried to explain this to Wulv, so he would understand the natural superiority of herself and Vesi. But he had the sort of blunt and basic mind that kept asking irritating questions.

"Why can't you still do that?" he wanted to know. "If the Etruscans are almost gods, why can't you move instantly from place to place without needing either protection or a guide?"

"The *Ais* are easily bored," Repana replied, speaking as patiently as to a child, "so all things change after a time. For their own reasons the gods chose to alter the relationship between flesh and spirit. Some of our ancestral *hia* were permanently lodged in mortal form, becoming the tribes of Etruria. The best of them, of course, became the Rasne, my own people. Other *hia* retained an independent existence. They never put on flesh; they never accepted mortal limitations.

"The men and women of Etruria revered their ancestors, as they should. These were beings who had been almost gods. But this competing homage made the *Ais* jealous. By way of retaliation they caused some ancestral *hia* to embody all the vices of humankind but none of the virtues. Thus were the *siu* created, to keep us torn between good and evil."

Repana glanced sidelong at her daughter. "And the *siu*, like the *Ais*, are with us always. Each cruelty, every crime, has, at its heart, a *siu.*"

At this the girl entered the conversation. "The people your ancestors found when they first came here—were they Etruscan?" she asked Wulv.

The Teumetian shook his head. "I don't think so. The Etruscans began somewhere to the east, or so the stories of my people claim. They settled here later. They are a very different race from the stone-magicians."

"Then what happened to the stone-magicians?"

"I don't know. Some of our elders believe they simply melted into their stones," Wulv concluded in a hushed voice. He glanced out into the night, fingers touching the bone amulets stitched into his clothing.

Silence filled the hut, a silence permeated with invisible beings who must be taken into account and ancient events that continued to affect the present. Only the little fire dared to hiss.

TWELVE

The five cloaked beings were not accustomed to running, but now they ran, seeking a place where they could learn the extent of their comrade's injuries in safety. There was always the chance that the Rasne might send armed warriors after them. The awe they had sought to exude through sheer mental power obviously did not work equally on all the Silver People, as the guard's action had shown.

If they fell, they would have failed Pythia. Then even death might not protect them from her anger.

They set out toward the nearest river, the Tiber, to seek aid. Water was sacred to Pythia. Certain rivers had special powers, not the least of which was the ability to cure followers of the dark goddess. Or so her acolytes believed. The time had come to put that belief to the test.

The one they dragged made no sound. He might already be dead, but was at least beyond feeling pain. They stopped long enough to shoulder him like a sack of meal, then hurried on. The last in line kept turning back to watch for the pursuit that never came.

. . .

As he recovered from the shock he had endured, the being in the cave grew increasingly hungry. He was now afraid to return to the Otherworld; she was surely waiting there to exact her punishment. But if he remained in the Earthworld, the flesh he had acquired at such cost must be nourished.

He began to lust for food.

He allowed his consciousness to roam into the forest beyond the cave, seeking a developed life-form. He could subsist off the flesh and spirits of birds and beasts, but they provided insufficient energy. He needed richer fare.

Gradually he became aware of the existence of the six. Though still some distance away they were headed in his direction and one was seriously wounded. Its life force was bleeding away.

Gathering himself, the *siu* left the cave. Sustenance must not be wasted.

By the time the five reached the river, all semblance of life had left their comrade. Without hesitation they plunged down the bank anyway, intending to immerse the body in the water and beseech holy Tiber to restore him. But the task that awaited them was not an easy one. Yesterday's storm had swollen the Tiber to flood strength and now it rushed headlong between its banks, hissing like an angry serpent. The five struggled to keep their footing on the muddy bank while lowering their companion into the river.

Abruptly, his robe ballooned as water flowed beneath the fabric. Within moments he was torn from their grasp. The rampaging river whirled the body away, tossing it like a log in the current, sending it spinning down the river course to disappear around the nearest bend.

Only a short distance below the bend, the being from the cave trotted along the riverbank, anxious eyes searching.

He stopped abruptly and scanned the river.

81

The Tiber was carrying an appalling mass of tree branches and uprooted bushes toward him. The *siu* ignored the debris, his attention arrested by someone caught in the flood. As he watched, the river tossed the body of its helpless victim to and fro. The flailing limbs provided a spurious life that excited the *siu* almost beyond bearing. He began to run along the bank in hot pursuit. Food! *Energy!*

The river course narrowed, the water boiling white through a defile. The body tumbled in the rapids and then paused, snagged on an outcropping of stone. To the *siu* watching anxiously from the riverbank, it appeared as if the figure in the water had caught hold of the rocks to save itself.

The *siu* eagerly waded into the river to claim his prize.

The pure water of the Tiber shrank from his glaucous flesh. But he managed to catch one end of the sodden robe and drag the body onto shore, hauling it through mud and briars with apparent ease. Grinning, the *siu* crouched to examine his catch.

The corpse's hood had become dislodged. A thin patina of serpentine scales covered his flattened, almost triangular skull.

The *siu* spat in disgust. He knew these creatures of old and considered them abominations. He should cast this one back into the river. But he hungered, hungered desperately for the life he thought the body still contained.

Losing control of his greed, he tore off gobbets of flesh and thrust them into his mouth while he dug for the heart. It was not the meat he craved, but the living essence. He chewed perfunctorily, then gulped, swallowing hard . . . and gagged violently as a shudder ran through him.

There was no essence of life.

The only essence was death.

He had ingested dead flesh!

Abandoning his prey, he staggered away from the river. Twice in a short period of time the *siu* had joined himself not with life but with death. First with the boar, now with this creature. Slow black waves rolled through his body, battering at his consciousness, leaching away his personality, his memories.

He was . . .

He was . . .

He . . .

As the madness claimed him, the violence of his derangement sent a shrill discord jangling through the Otherworld. Those who heard and understood the sound laughed at his pain.

Thoughts flowed around Pepan; he swam through them as through water. He had a sense of millions of swarming intellects, some sparkling like fireflies, others as dull and muddy as frog spawn. This was a plane separate from, yet impinging upon, the reality he knew. The consciousness of Earthworld trees and plants cast constantly changing reflections here, and the movement of every Earthworld animal caused a parallel vibration in the invisible realm.

Looking down at himself, Pepan discovered that an image of his body continued to cling to his spirit like the afterimage of the sun on one's eyeballs. He also became aware that his *hia* was sending out an auditory signal as distinctive as birdsong, a deep, musical ululation that echoed through the Otherworld. This was the song of his soul.

Pepan's call was soon answered. A dense cloud materialized in the distance, pulsing with a rhythmic beat as familiar as his own heartbeat had been. Without even thinking about it, he recognized the sound and knew its source, listened as his own sound melded and became part of the greater symphony. His ancestors were coming for him . . .

Abruptly Pepan's attention was distracted by a faint and very different signal coming from the opposite direction.

A mere thread of music, lyrical and heartbreakingly sweet, it evoked a powerful response in Pepan.

Three strains in delicate harmony, soaring together. They were not his family, yet he recognized them with a loving heart.

Repana.

Vesi.

And the child!

The child already quickened within her then. So soon . . .

Separated from them by death, Pepan felt more concerned about them than ever. In the Otherworld everything touched upon everything else, so perhaps he could continue to have influence on their lives. Perhaps he could finish what he had set out to do: protect Repana and Vesi . . . and the baby.

With this thought uppermost he hurried to intercept his escort, eager to explain what he required of them.

THIRTEEN

T he child is growing far too fast," Wulv told Repana. "I have had little experience in such matters, but I know a woman should not swell like that. Not so soon, so quickly."

Repana cast a critical eye toward her daughter. The Teumetian was right; he had confirmed what she had only suspected. After only a few days Vesi's belly was already large enough to contain a seven months' child. Had it been the siring of a human father such development would have been frighteningly abnormal.

The father was not human.

But she did not want to admit this to Wulv. How could she admit to this primitive woodsman that her daughter was carrying a demon's child? Such an admission to one's inferior would be extremely embarrassing. And who knew how he might react? Those like him were superstitious brutes. He might slay them out of hand; she dare not take the chance. "My daughter has probably been pregnant for longer than anyone thought," she said. "It is easy to misjudge such events."

Wulv was saying, "Only yesterday her belly was almost flat."

"Sometimes that happens," Repana replied with a calm she did not feel. "Infants grow in spurts, you know."

He looked dubious. "I've watched the breeding of animals. The unborn inside them grow slow and steady."

"My daughter is not some beast!" Repana snapped. "I ask you to remember that she is Rasne." The woman turned away before Wulv could ask any more awkward questions.

Vesi was aware of the child's extraordinary swelling within her. She knew she should feel terror at the very thought, but onrushing motherhood produced a calming effect. Whatever the baby's sire, the unborn was also part of her and she could not fear part of her own self. Sometimes she just sat beside the fire with her fingers laced across her rounded stomach and crooned to the child inside, promising to love it no matter what its nature might be.

Watching her, Repana wanted to cry, remembering the times she had sat before a fire, cradling her own stomach, murmuring to the infant Vesi within. She had wanted so much for her only daughter, had promised her so much. Now those dreams and promises would come to naught because of another child . . . the demon's child.

At night she lay on the bed of boughs and held her daughter in her arms. "There are ways," she whispered, "of getting rid of the child if you want to. Herbal preparations I can concoct for you or a diffusion of hazel bark with . . ."

Vesi stiffened. "No. It is my child."

"But . . ."

"No!"

"It might be a monster. You know that."

"If I had been deformed in your womb—and you knew it—would you have gotten rid of me?"

By way of answer Repana simply clutched Vesi harder, unwilling to answer. The Rasne worshipped beauty. No mother ever wanted to be forced to use her sacrificial knife.

·   ·   ·

Traveling, Pepan discovered, was not the same in the Otherworld. Time and distance were measured differently. But that did not mean his *hia* enjoyed unhampered freedom of movement. As he tried to reach his ancestors, a peculiar viscosity wrapped itself around him, forming a barrier that he thrust against until it gave like a weakened membrane. He slipped through to find himself in what appeared to be a long tunnel. Translucent walls surrounded him, yet when he reached out to try to touch one he felt nothing.

Just ahead he could see the cloud that contained his kinsmen, but reaching them required a complex set of trial-and-error maneuvers. It was like learning to walk all over again, and he was elated at each small success.

Nearing the cloud, he tried to get some idea of its size. But its opaque mass constantly expanded and contracted. At the end of one of these contractions a form emerged.

My son, said a voice without words.

The form flickered and . . . Pepan found himself gazing upon the face of his father, Zivas, former Lord of the Silver People. A gifted linguist, Zivas had studied and mastered the languages of a dozen other tribes, even those in Latium, for no reason other than the joy of learning. He displayed the characteristic long-lidded eyes and aquiline nose that marked their family, but his visage was slightly faded, like mosaic tiles that had been too long in the sun.

Is it really you? Pepan wanted to know, reaching out. Then he peered eagerly over his father's shoulder. *Is Mother with you?*

Zivas gestured toward the cloud behind him. *Only one from each generation of the bloodline responds to a Dying. Your mother is safe with Veno in the Kingdom of the Dead. Come now; she is eager to welcome you.*

Pepan strove to understand the details of this new existence. *If one from each generation is with you, does that mean your sire, and your grandsire, and . . .*

By way of answer his father moved backward and the cloud swallowed him, expanded, contracted, and a new figure emerged. These features also bore the familial stamp, only more faded still.

I am your grandfather's grandfather. Within our bloodlines is carried the history of the Rasne. My immortal spirit is that of the warrior I once was when under my command Etrurians stood shoulder to shoulder with allies from the Attic nations and beat the Carthaginians to their knees. I returned home in triumph only to discover an invasion force from Latium had attacked our city in my absence. After I had driven them away, we held a festival of celebration and sacrificed to the Ais. Then we rebuilt our spura on undefiled ground according to the plans long ago set forth by my revered ancestor. . . .

The cloud convulsed, another figure replaced his and went on, the words blending into a lyrical paean.

I am the Planner. From the talents the gods gave me sprang the great cities of Etruria, during the glory days when we spread out across this land. Whenever our warriors claimed new territory, I oversaw preparation of the most auspicious site the priests could identify, then laid out streets and drainage systems, designed buildings, and selected construction materials. In the blink of an eye I could envision an elaborate plan and know just how to bring it to fruition. So it was that the mark of the Silver People was carved into the very stones of this country, as long ago foreseen by . . .

Almost instantly he was replaced by yet another form, one so faint Pepan could scarcely see it at all. In the tones of a woman this new image told him, *I am the Prophet. In my day the Ais spoke directly to us. We were not so proud then as we later became,* the voice added regretfully. *We were willing to listen.*

In the reign of Atys, Son of Ghosts, the place in which we lived suffered a great famine. But by following the direction of the gods we were led out of starvation to this much more fertile region, where we grew and prospered. Life became more pleasant; we no longer had to struggle just to survive.

Then the Ais encouraged us to develop a sense of beauty so we could appreciate them more fully. Under their tutelage we developed our arts until eventually we became known as the Silver People.

Another voice interjected, *Generations of craftsmen such as myself have captured stunning images of the Ais in sculpture—some no larger than a thumb. We have designed jewelry beyond compare for our beautiful women; we have decorated our tombs with images of the dear dead so lifelike they*

88

almost breathe. Far beyond our borders the Rasne are famed for luxury and elegance. But all that we achieve is simply a gift from the gods, who love us.

The gods who love us, echoed the Prophet.

Marveling, Pepan realized he was in the presence of the most able of his race. Just when he needed them.

Using his new-found ability to speak without words, he struggled to communicate his problem. *There are two exiled women, Repana and her daughter, Vesi, who are very dear to me and are in great trouble. I want to help them, but I am new to this state of being, I do not know what abilities I may possess here. I ask you, my ancestors, to teach me. Help me to help my friends.*

Why should we involve ourselves? The women you name are not your wife and daughter, his warrior ancestor pointed out. *They are not our bloodline. They have their own ancestors.*

But they are Rasne, Pepan argued, *so we must share common ancestors.*

A multitude of voices debated among themselves. Then, sounding faintly amused, the female voice of the Prophet spoke from within the cloud. *Some of us had many children. All rivers are born from the same rain.*

Pepan said eagerly, *You will do as I ask then?*

Because you ask it, his father's voice replied, *and I could never refuse my sons anything.*

The voice of the Planner countered, *If we do this, will you come with us afterward?*

Instinct told him he could not lie to the dead. *I cannot say. I only know I cannot go to the Netherworld leaving things as they are.*

The Prophet intoned, *You would not be the first who remained behind to conclude unfinished business.*

But will he come afterwards? someone demanded to know.

Possibly. He is guided by love. The ability to love even after death is common to all hia *and is the one emotion no* siu *can feel. Pepan invokes the love we bear him and asks us to extend it to those he loves. I say we shall.*

The cloud roiled and from its depths came the sounds of not three or four but hundreds of voices, some little more than animalistic grunts. Pepan could tell some mighty argument was taking place. He waited, unable to measure the passage of time in a world where time was not, until at last the Prophet spoke to him again. *All things happen as they should*, she said. *Lead us.*

It was easier to move now that he had had some practice. He still had no sense of direction however, and when the Prophet bade him to lead them he was momentarily uncertain. Then he heard once more that lovely, distant music and followed it eagerly.

As he approached the glade, he discovered that the circle of stones continually emitted a humming sound. At close range the hum distorted the music that guided him and set up a disturbing vibration in the Otherworld. That vibration could repel many entities. Pepan forced himself to go on.

At his back pulsed the opaque cloud.

Wulv lay on the ground just outside the shelter he had built for the women. Clothed in leather and bearskin, he looked like a wild animal himself. Pepan hovered over him long enough to ascertain that he was sleeping peacefully, then entered the hut.

Walls were no longer a barrier. The *hia* of the dead Rasne passed effortlessly through interlaced branches and chinked mud. Inside he found Repana and Vesi lying in each other's arms. Each was contributing a note to the Otherworld music that had guided him this far. Repana's identifying sound was rich and melodious; Vesi had a higher, clearer note, achingly pure in spite of all that had happened to her.

But it was their physical voices that caught Pepan's attention. He arrived just in time to overhear the conversation between mother and daughter about the possibility of aborting the infant. To his surprise, he felt their pain as sharply as if it were his own. Since he had no flesh to serve as a buffer, their emotion came into him naked and raw.

Vesi obviously cherished the unborn infant, but Repana secretly regarded it with resentment amounting to loathing. The child would begin life with every possible disadvantage. Like its mother it would be an exile with no property, no status—and the added curse of a demon father. Only the *Ais* knew what face it would wear in the world or what deformities of body or spirit it might carry. Pepan could understand

Repana's reservations, but life was sacred, even this life. He must do what he could to ease the way.

Silently he called out to the unseen cloud that had taken up a position in the center of the circle of stones. *This is the woman I should have wed. This girl should have become my daughter. I did not give them enough of myself in life, but I would rectify that now. Help me. Help us.*

It has never been done . . .

Never been done . . .

Never. . . .

When the argument raged into silence, the Prophet said simply, *Put your hand on her belly.*

Pepan protested, *I have no hands now.*

His grandfather replied, *The memory of your earthly body is still strong and we will add all our force to yours. It will be enough.*

Pepan did as he was instructed and approached Vesi. His fingers were as transparent as glass when he held them up to his face; through them he could dimly see Vesi's body, as if she were made of slightly thicker mist. When he laid his palm—delicately, tentatively—on her mounded flesh he had no sensation of solidity. There seemed nothing to keep him from reaching farther, from reaching inside her and actually putting his hand on the womb. As he stared at her belly, its flesh became translucent and he could see the shape of the baby within.

Yes, said the voice of the Prophet, *that is what you must do. Reach inside, feel the child.*

Pepan obeyed. Neither of the two women on the bed seemed aware of the invasion, but the infant floating in its small, warm universe responded to his touch by opening its eyes.

Beyond the shelter, the stone circle began to hum.

The unborn child heard. Its eyes opened wider, looking upon scarlet and crimson tides as its tiny hands clutched at the mist of Pepan's fingers.

Do not move now, Pepan, commanded the Prophet.

The cloud within the circle began to glow with a lambent green flame, while sparkling white fire shivered across the stones.

In his dreams, Wulv stirred and mumbled but did not awake.

The cloud contracted violently then expanded to cover the hut. Tiny emerald fires flickered over the carefully arranged branches. The air smelled of storm. A rushing wind howled through the primeval forest, whipping the trees until they groaned in protest, sending the forest creatures scurrying for shelter.

Pepan felt a great weight descend upon him, as if he had been floating in the river for a long time and just come out on land again. The weight pressed down unbearably, threatening to crush him though he had no body. Desperately he fought to remain upright and stay still—until the weight flowed through him and his *bia* caught fire.

This he could feel. He writhed like the storm-tossed trees in an agony beyond description. His spirit was burning hotter than the forge, hotter than the sun, consuming him.

The essence of a people was raging through him.

And from him, into the woman and her unborn child.

Chieftain and warrior, craftsman and Planner and Prophet and all the generations before them poured along the conduit Pepan provided, emptying their knowledge into Vesi's womb.

The baby convulsed. Vesi sprang up with a shriek, clutching at her belly. "It's being born!" she cried. "It's being born now!"

FOURTEEN

A s with a Dying, there were certain rituals that must attend a Birthing. The newborn *hia* required protection as it entered the Earthworld from a very different plane. It would take awhile before he or she learned the rules governing this new type of existence. But the more immediate problem was the danger imposed by malign inhabitants of the Otherworld.

Siu, as well as corrupted *hia* who had never made their way safely to the Netherworld, were very aware of a newborn's vulnerability. While a mother was still in labor they crowded close, hoping to subsume the baby's spirit and thus acquire a being of flesh and blood who would obey their dictates.

If Vesi had given birth at home, midwives and *purtani* would have been with her constantly, caring for flesh and spirit. Protective symbols would be painted on her belly and on the special birthing stool handed down from mother to daughter. Priests would chant and burn incense whose sweet smoke dulled the pain. Silver bells would ring to ward off evil spirits, while elsewhere in the *spura* young goats were sacrificed to lure them to other prey.

Instead she was alone in a crude hut in the forest with only her mother and a primitive Teumetian—and the combined wisdom of a hundred generations of Rasne.

As Pepan watched, Repana worked over her daughter. Wulv had been awakened by the girl's shrieks but was forbidden to enter the hut. "You would just get in my way!" Repana shouted at him.

Hurt, the woodsman sat on the ground outside and sulked. From time to time he flexed his callused hands with their dirt-rimmed fingernails and stared at them, unable to comprehend their uselessness in the current situation.

Pepan understood the impotence Wulv felt. All he could do now was defend the little family against the Otherworld predators already swarming toward the site.

The atmosphere had grown thick with demonic shapes. *Siu* hissed and growled, writhing obscenely as they advanced. Instead of bodies, in the Otherworld they displayed grotesque manifestations of their favorite vices. Some appeared as gaping mouths with slimy tongues and endlessly working jaws. Others were little more than oversized genital organs, throbbing with lusts that could never be eased.

Hia were different. Many had never been embodied but existed as pure, crackling energy. *Hia* who had been corrupted by *siu* gave off a distinct smell of decay. They tended to stay close to their corrupters, basking in the sulfurous glow of concentrated evil.

As this hideous assemblage gathered, Pepan braced himself. He still did not know enough about the Otherworld to know how to fight them but was trusting to instinct. And the ancestors. But they seemed to be drawing back, pulling away.

From within the hovering cloud came the voice of the Prophet. *The child is not without resources of its own*, she said. *Watch . . . and learn.*

When labor began, the infant had ceased to emit its characteristic tonal signal. For a time it was silent, all its energies focused on the convulsive struggle to escape the womb. The birthing was swift, but no sooner had the child emerged from Vesi's body than it sent out a new signal, a layered, complex chord of ineffable sweetness that rose and fell with its lusty cries.

The sound rang like a chime through the Otherworld.

The rapacious horde halted abruptly. A few—the older, more experienced—even turned back. The others milled around in confusion, snarling and snapping at one another but advancing no farther.

Pepan asked, *What happened? I do not understand.*

A small part of each of us is now in that child, replied the voice of the Prophet, *making him more powerful than any single member of our race has ever been. Demons and those they influence are destructive rather than creative. A lack of creativity means a lack of imagination. Without imagination they cannot encompass a new idea—and this child represents a new idea. He frightens them.*

Abruptly, the sound the child was making changed, becoming a deep growl that provided a startling counterpoint to the original sweetness of tone. The effect was disturbing; one by one the gathered *hia* and *siu* turned and melted back into the Otherworld.

What's wrong? Pepan asked the ancestors.

Demon-song, his father replied. *You did not tell us the infant was siu-spawn.* Although there was no inflection in his voice, Pepan could sense his anger. *We have gifted the offspring of a demon. My son, do you know what you have done?*

Will you take back your gifts because of it? Pepan countered.

The cloud roiled again. At last the Prophet spoke. *All things happen as they should. What we have given, we do not reclaim. But although we return to the Netherworld, you are commanded to stay close to this child. The gifts that burn within him must have every possible good influence to counterbalance the evil. He will have further need of you . . . and so will our people.*

Pepan turned away to hide his delight. *If it is my destiny . . . then so be it.*

The voice of the Prophet darkened. *The threads of destiny grow very knotted, Pepan.*

Beware.

FIFTEEN

As soon as she was able, Vesi reached for her baby. Wordlessly Repana put the infant into her arms. The two women stared down at the head nuzzling Vesi's breast. Aside from a downy cap of lustrous dark hair, the infant looked like any other newborn, red faced and wrinkled. Vesi gave a great sigh of relief. "I was afraid . . ."

"I know. So was I. But he is no monster," Repana added to reassure her daughter in spite of the lurking doubts she herself still harbored. "You have given birth to a healthy boy who looks as normal as any other." She didn't add that she had checked the babe for additional fingers or toes and its spine for a tail.

As if to prove her words, the infant opened his mouth and gave a lusty bellow. Both women laughed. "Little man," Vesi murmured fondly. "My little man."

"Men need names. What will you call him?"

"I do not know, Mother. There are no *purtani* to take the auguries, so how am I to know what sort of name he needs?"

"You must give him a name of your own choosing then."

Vesi blinked. "That is too great a responsibility. Names have so much power over those who bear them. What if I choose wrong and do him damage?"

Unseen, Pepan bent over them. The girl feared the responsibility but he did not; he knew what name the child should have. With all his strength he tried to shout it loud enough so she could hear. *Hora Trim!*

But his strength was not enough. Though the shout resonated throughout the Otherworld, Vesi barely heard a whisper. She turned her head quickly, eyes wide. "Was that the wind?" she asked her mother.

"I heard nothing. There was a storm earlier but it is over now."

Hora Trim!

Vesi shivered. "There is a draught here."

HORA TRIM!

Abruptly Vesi smiled, lips moving as she formed words. "Hora . . . trim." She looked up at her mother. "I will call my son Horatrim."

Repana raised a quizzical eyebrow. "Meaning spirit of heroes?"

"Is that not a perfect name for a little boy?"

As she gazed down at the child, Repana was not so sure. His Rasne forebears were undoubtedly heroic, but the infant's sire was very different. Yet perhaps Horatrim was a good choice. "Such a noble name just might help counteract the influence of the *siu*," she told Vesi.

At the mention of the *siu* the young woman stiffened; her eyes became distant and glazed. "No demon had anything to do with my son. Nothing, I tell you!" Her voice rose shrilly, startling the baby, who began to cry. Vesi's eyes were wide and wild. She was as brittle as glass, threatening to shatter at the slightest blow. Her mother feared she might lose her mind.

"Of course, my child," Repana hastily agreed. "I am simply weary and made a foolish slip of the tongue. I meant to say the name would protect your son against any demons he might encounter when he is older. It is a good name, a fine name. Rest now. You have done well." She stroked Vesi's forehead and murmured soothingly until both mother and infant grew calmer.

But long after Vesi fell asleep, Repana was still trembling.

The physical attack must have been terrible indeed, she thought, *but to relive it unbearable. I have to be careful with Vesi. We must find a safe place to raise the child where no one will mention its origins and bring the memories flooding back.* Repana realized they could not return to their *spura.* Even if Pepan had succeeded in getting the others to forgive them, there was always the danger someone would say something.

When Repana announced to Wulv that the baby was alive and well, he was eager to see the infant at once. But Repana discouraged him; she was uncomfortable with the idea of allowing the woodsman too near a new baby. "They're both sleeping," she said. "There is something you can do, however. We will need moss for diapering, can you find some?"

Wulv looked almost insulted. "Some? How much do you want?"

"As much as you can carry," Repana said with a hint of a smile.

Delighted to be of use, he set off at once and soon brought back not only moss but a freshly snared rabbit for Vesi's dinner. "Meat makes milk," he assured Repana as he showed her his prize at the entrance to the hut.

"I suppose you have a great experience of nursing infants?" she remarked sarcastically.

He took no offense. "Hunters have to be observant. I have seen what the women in my tribe do. I have watched the beasts of the field feed their young."

Repana bit back an angry retort. "My daughter is Rasne, which of course means she has delicate sensibilities," she said firmly. "Vesi prefers fish. White fish."

"This deep in the forest she had better eat what she can get. We're not on the banks of the Tiber now. When you go home you can—"

"We will not be going back to our *spura.* Even . . . even if the Lord of the Rasne sends for us himself."

Wulv stared at Repana. "But I thought . . ."

"Our lives there are over."

"Then where will you go? You can't stay here forever. The forest is full of dangerous beasts who won't respect the sanctuary of the stones. And I can't protect you night and day; I have to sleep sometime."

"Are you saying you would abandon us?"

"I am not. I gave my word to the Rasne lord. I may not have much, but I have my honor."

Repana nodded. "We will rely upon it then. Pepan recognized your quality and I trust his judgment. But tell me, Wulv—you have a home elsewhere, do you not? Someplace safer, where we could go?"

"I can't take you there."

"Why not?"

"It's . . . well, it isn't much of a place, nothing like I'm sure you're used to. There's a hut like this one only bigger and made to stand winter weather. It's part of a compound with a shed for storing hides and a smokehouse for fish, all on an island I built up in the middle of some swampy ground that floods a lot. In fact, my home is usually surrounded by a lake. People leave me alone there, which is the way I like it."

Repana clapped her hands together. "It sounds perfect!"

Wulv was disconcerted. But before he could think of a way to discourage them, he heard a voice. Not a human voice, it sounded more like the soughing of the wind through the leaves, yet it spoke in clearly distinct human syllables.

Take them.

Wulv grabbed his knife and glanced wildly around. He saw only Repana, the hut, the circle of stones, and the forest beyond. Yet with a hunter's infallible instinct, he was aware of another presence. He touched the bear's claw amulet on his belt. This was indeed a cursed place.

Take them, the voice repeated. *Whatever Repana wants, you must do. Your future lies with them.*

Wulv had to fight back an almost overwhelming desire to throw himself on the ground and do worship. Surely one of the gods was speaking directly to him. In the memory of his tribe, such a thing had never happened to one of the Teumetes before. He was simultaneously terrified and elated.

"What is wrong with you?" asked Repana. "The color has left your face."

You must take them with you, insisted the implacable voice.

"I will. Oh, I will!"

Repana was perplexed. "You will what?"

"Take you to my home as soon as your daughter can travel. That's what you wanted, isn't it?"

She gave him a hard look. But just then Vesi called to her, and forgetting everything else, Repana ducked inside the hut.

Once more Wulv swept his eyes around the glade. There was nothing noteworthy, only the sentinel stones standing their eternal vigil. A bird's cry drew Wulv's attention upward. Although the sky was a delicate eggshell blue, a gathering of clouds portended rain. One in particular puzzled him. Its shape changed so swiftly. One moment it looked like soft billows of foam, the next it resembled rugged mountain peaks. As Wulv watched, the mountains became an army marching away into the distance.

From the Otherworld things looked different.

Wulv, the hut, even the circle of stones were to Pepan no more than misty and somewhat indistinct shapes. The cloud, however, was very solid.

Pepan, intoned the voice of the Prophet, *we must go now.*

What will happen to me if I stay here?

You are vulnerable in the Otherworld, Pepan. A siu *could contaminate your* hia, *making you one like them. It would be a great pity to see such a noble spirit corrupted. Your ancestors would grieve; our happiness in the Netherworld would be marred.*

But I cannot die?

No, his father's familiar tones replied, *you cannot die. Only flesh can die, and you are done with that.*

Then I will watch over the women and the infant all their lives. I am strong, stronger than any demon.

The hovering cloud darkened. *You are also overconfident,* proclaimed yet another voice in accents he could hardly understand. *I was like you once, a thousand years ago. But you will learn, Pepan. We all learn.*

With a mighty roar the cloud turned an inky purple and began to twist into a giant knot. The roar increased. The cloud convulsed, folding in upon itself. Abruptly came a sound like the boom of a monstrous drum and the knot unwound into a long, thin rope the color of spring violets, stretching all the way from the circle of stones to the horizon.

The sky shimmered with rainbows.

The air smelled of the distant sea.

A hush fell upon the Otherworld.

As Pepan watched, the violet rope grew thinner and thinner until only one filament remained. Then that too was gone and he was alone.

Alone in a way he had never been before.

Within the hut, the baby began to cry.

SIXTEEN

T hroughout his life, Wulv had lived intimately with nature. Later he told Repana, "I've seen every weather there is and every sort of cloud too. But never one like that one. It was unnatural."

"How can a cloud be unnatural? The Rasne believe that clouds are nothing more than heated water, rising as steam."

Wulv looked shocked. "The Teumetes know that clouds are the exhalations of our gods." His voice trailed away as he gazed, awestruck, into the heavens once more. "The gods spoke to me from the clouds. I swear it. And that one cloud in particular sailed away in the direction of my home. I am to take you both there as soon as possible. Do you think your daughter will be strong enough to leave here tomorrow?"

Repana of the Silver People was not about to argue with one who had a message from the gods, his or anyone else's. "We will see how she feels in the morning, Wulv."

As it happened they had to wait a few more days until Vesi was able for the journey. Childbirth combined with her injuries had weakened her more than she would admit, but her mother's keen eye would not be fooled as to her condition. "When my daughter is strong," she argued with Wulv, "she will be able to travel faster. As it is, we would have to stop too often to let her rest, we would hardly make any progress. So go and bring us some fresh meat. I will make her a nourishing broth. You will eat some too; you look as if you need it."

On the morning before they set out for Wulv's home, the Teumetian carefully demolished the little hut in the glade, smoothing away every trace of its existence.

"This is a sacred place," Wulv pointed out. "We must leave it as we found it."

Repana nodded. The Rasne understood all too well the importance of keeping any sacred space undefiled . . . unlike the brutal and warlike Romans, who were said to burn other people's temples and throw down their gods.

Carrying her baby close to her breast, crooning constantly to it, Vesi followed Wulv with her mother at her back as they made their way along the narrow forest trails. Even at High Day it was very dark beneath the primordial oaks. Repana kept glancing over her shoulder, convinced she could hear something behind her. But there was nothing she could see, only a few thin shafts of light slanting down through the canopy of the leaves overhead. Yet each time she looked back she felt certain there was more undergrowth than she remembered and the forest had a more pungent, fecund odor.

As he followed the little party, the *hia* energy that Pepan radiated left its mark on the forest. Branches dipped greedily to absorb some of it; leaves burgeoned and grew glossy with their share. In Pepan's wake, roots clawed through the soil, clutching after the last tendrils of the nourishing force. The *hia* of the dead fed the living, who in turn would die, decay, and feed new life-forms in a never-ending cycle. The integrity of the whole depended upon the death and rebirth of its parts.

The only constant was change.

Pepan's strength was continually dissipated and then restored by the surging emerald energy of the living forest.

Just when it was most needed, Wulv called a halt. "I'll find some drinking water for Vesi," he said. "You sit here with your back against this big tree and close your eyes and rest. I'll be only a shout away." Not for the first time, Repana was impressed by Wulv's consideration.

When weariness began to take its toll on Vesi, he volunteered to carry little Horatrim. She demurred. "What can he know about babies?" she hissed to her mother, her whisper loud enough for Wulv to hear. "You carry him," she said, thrusting the child into Repana's arms.

But Repana was weary as well. When she stumbled and almost dropped the infant, Wulv caught her and steadied her, then gently eased the babe from her arms. "I won't hurt him," he insisted. "I like babies."

Repana raised an eyebrow. "Have you ever held one before?"

The Teumetian thrust forward his lower jaw in a way she was coming to recognize. "I like babies," he repeated stubbornly.

"But have you ever . . ."

"I've held bear cubs and fox kits, day-old wolves and orphaned fawns. I know what to do," he said, wrapping the baby in his bearskin mantle.

Too tired to argue, the women gave in. For the rest of the journey their guide carried Horatrim as carefully as any mother could wish. From time to time he even murmured to the baby and was rewarded by a gurgle that pleased him inordinately. "I think he likes me," Wulv confided shyly.

Shortly before sunset the forest gave way to a marshy expanse fed by a tributary of the Tiber. Wulv stopped and pointed. At the marsh's lowest point a lake glinted; a tiny islet was barely discernible in its midst. "My home," he announced with shy pride. "I built it myself. Piled up earth and rocks until I had a raised place that was always dry.

Made that causeway leading to it too, so I can get home even in time of flood."

Repana was too tired to be interested in the details of the place. It looked appallingly primitive, but at least it was a sanctuary. "How much farther?" she wanted to know.

"We'll be there before dark. Take care to follow in my footsteps. If you step off the path you could find yourself neck deep in water."

Now Repana was doubly glad that Wulv was carrying the baby.

The path twisted and turned, dipped and doubled back on itself in an ever more intricate pattern meant to confuse invaders. Beyond the forest marsh grass took over, slender, supple leaves that gradually grew higher and higher, until they were walking through a verdant tunnel. The ground underfoot was boggy in places, making every step an effort. The Teumetian moved with confidence, barely glancing at the route he followed. He was concentrating on the baby in his arms. Finally, he stopped and allowed the women to catch up. "Welcome," he said simply, stepping aside at the neck of the narrow causeway that ran out to the artificial island in the center of the lake. Several thatched huts stood on the island. "All this is mine," the Teumetian added, indicating the little compound with a wave of his hand.

Gratefully, Repana and Vesi stumbled along the causeway and collapsed together on the bed inside the largest hut. As Repana's eyelids drifted closed, the last thing she saw was Wulv carefully handing Horatrim to his mother.

In the morning, while Vesi was nursing Horatrim, Repana allowed Wulv to show her around his little domain. Although it was very crude, Repana was forced to admit to herself that Wulv had achieved a surprising level of domesticity.

"The spit over the firepit rotates—look, I'll show you; it works with this foot treadle I made—so meat roasts evenly," he explained proudly. "And in this shed here, where I smoke fish, I've arranged flaps in the roof so I can control the amount of smoke."

"Is there only one way onto this island of yours?"

"Only one. And I can barricade the causeway if wolves or bears get too close."

"What about two-legged predators?" wondered Repana. "What is to stop them from swimming across?"

"Nothing—except for the pointed stakes I sunk into the mud around the margins of the lake. And the water here is full of eels. I feed them on blood and scraps of meat. If any attacker were to jump into the lake and injure themselves, the eels would be drawn by the blood and do a bit of attacking of their own."

"Eels cannot kill a man," protested Repana.

"No, but it would take an extraordinarily brave man to attempt to swim through a swarm of biting eels," Wulv told her with a grin.

Repana subsequently commented to Vesi, "He is a resourceful man and more intelligent than he looks. In fact, if I did not know Wulv was a Teumetian I would not take him for a savage."

"Perhaps the Teumetes are not savages," Vesi suggested.

Repana's eyebrows flew toward her hairline. "Of course they are! You heard what Wulv said about being descended from bears." But privately she was beginning to have doubts as to just what constituted a savage.

In the days and moons and seasons that followed, Repana's good opinion of Wulv continued to grow. She and Vesi found him unfailingly courteous according to his own standard and gifted with a sense of humor that made their exile more bearable. When winter closed in, he brightened the long nights by telling rambling jokes that had no point but were somehow very funny and singing bawdy, equally funny songs in a husky voice.

Repana tried to pretend she did not understand their meaning, but sometimes she blushed.

Wulv found her blushes beguiling. At night he lay sleepless thinking about them, and when spring came he brought her armloads of wildflowers. "There are more flowers around the lake than I ever saw before," he commented.

"What am I to do with these?" asked Repana, bending her head to sniff their fragrance.

"I don't know. I just thought you would enjoy . . . something beautiful, after looking at my scarred old face all winter."

"I stopped looking at your face a long time ago," Repana said quietly. "My people worship beauty in all of its forms, but you have taught me that there is a deeper beauty, a beauty of spirit. I think our people lack that, and we are the poorer for it."

Wulv bowed, his cheeks flushed. He did not entirely understand what Repana was saying, but he understood the emotion behind the words.

"You like him very much," Vesi remarked.

The older woman shrugged and concentrated on gathering the flowers together. "He is good to us."

Pepan also was aware of a burgeoning affection between Wulv and Repana. In the Otherworld the emotional attraction was expressed as a lyrical strand of melody whenever their eyes met. The former Lord of the Rasne was astonished that Repana could so react to a primitive woodsman. He was not exactly jealous; the longer he was in the Otherworld, the more such emotions seemed irrelevant. Rather he felt a fading, wistful envy. Life was going on without him. How strange.

Yet he remained involved, watching with something akin to paternal pride as the infant Horatrim crawled, then stood, then took his first precocious steps. There was no doubt the boy was developing with astonishing rapidity. One could almost see him grow.

Meanwhile Vesi's youthful face took on more matronly plumpness, and a sheen of silver frosted Repana's hair.

Because in the Otherworld Pepan had no sense of time, each

change took him by surprise. The swiftness of the changes surprised him even more. During his life in the Earthworld, had things altered so quickly? Had time passed with such extraordinary rapidity? Perhaps it had . . . and perhaps he had been too busy to notice the changes.

Eventually he realized he was having his own effect on the Earthworld. The energy of his *hia*, remaining in one place as it now did, was causing an explosion of growth most clearly demonstrated by the vegetation surrounding Wulv's lake. Ancient marsh willows that had been on the verge of dying reclothed themselves with new leaves. Spindly seedlings developed into luxuriant shrubbery in less than a season. Vivid, fleshy orchids of gold and azure blossomed along stems the length of a spear shaft, while from early spring until late autumn the air was perfumed by masses of white roses.

And day after day, Wulv brought Repana flowers. When she took them from him, their hands touched and lingered. In the morning there would be more blossoms for the Teumetian to bring to Repana.

Horatrim continued to grow with astonishing rapidity. The first words he spoke were, "Give me!" as he reached for his grandmother's flowers, displaying early the Rasne passion for beauty.

The three adults laughed with delight.

In the Otherworld Pepan laughed too, a rich warm sound.

Laughter was not irrelevant, for while it lasted the sound of joy acted as a shield that kept dark forces at bay. The musical chord of Horatrim's spirit had the same effect, Pepan observed. In the immediate vicinity of the child no *siu* lurked; no corrupted *hia* sniggered. But he knew they were not far away, circling, stalking. Rapacious.

There were other watchers as well. He was aware of them as vast shapes on the horizon emitting a sound like the ringing of silver bells, a barely perceptible tintinnabulation that underlay all other sounds: this was the song of the *Ais*, the music of the gods. Their looming presence made Pepan uneasy. He was willing to challenge a *siu* but he had no illusions about his strength compared to one of the *Ais*. They could crush him without a thought if they chose, if his actions displeased them. So far they had not interfered, but he had no way of knowing what they might do in the future.

He wondered why they were also taking an interest in the demon-sired child.

SEVENTEEN

T he half-human child of a siu has always been considered an abomination, a creature who belongs in neither world.

Yet would we be justified in destroying such a child?

He is innocent of his father's crime. Because of her own sense of outrage, Pythia wants the boy Horatrim killed. But if we do so, we will be no better than the siu, matching one destruction with another.

There is also the matter of the child's exceptional heritage.

A powerful spirit, newly entered into the Otherworld, gave the unborn infant an assortment of gifts donated by older, even more powerful spirits from the Netherworld. Thus the child is special to Veno, Protectress of the Dead. Veno argues for the boy's survival as forcibly as Pythia argues against it.

We, the Ais, shape all three worlds according to our own designs, which humankind can never understand. Humans have their own effect on the Earthworld, of course . . . and on us, who conform in some degree to the images they give us. So one influences the other.

The outcome is not certain.

Wild forces and inexplicable energies are gathering about the boy called Horatrim. We feel their power but are uncertain how to proceed. Although we *pretend to omnipotence, we have to admit among ourselves that even we do not know everything.*

Therefore we agree that it would be a mistake to move against these forces until we understand them better. Such an action might not only destroy Horatrim, but also destroy the delicate balance he represents between the three worlds. The risk is too great.

We shall content ourselves with watching, and waiting . . . for a while.

EIGHTEEN

R omax!"

Even before Wulv reached his native village, he heard the first shouts. Those living in outlying areas were swiftly passing the word.

"Romax," they warned, using the Teumetian name for the most powerful tribe in Latium. "Romax warriors are headed this way!"

It was high summer and Wulv was making a rare journey to his birth village to trade pelts from the forest for wool and linens with which Repana could make new clothes. Three years had passed since she and Vesi had fled the Rasne *spura*, and the gowns they were wearing had long since worn out. They were, as they frequently told Wulv, tired of improvising with scraps.

Little Horatrim was happy enough to wear furs and leather like his hero Wulv, but women required something more.

As time passed Wulv was learning quite a bit about women—and small boys. They had become his family, the only family he would ever know. Whatever any of them wanted, he felt obliged to provide. But for their own protection he had never told anyone about them and allowed no one from outside to approach the island.

For once, when he entered the village no one called out, "Here comes Scarface. Hide the women so he doesn't frighten them into fits." It was an old joke and not a funny one. But this time the Teumetians had something more urgent on their minds.

"Five or six raiding parties have been seen in our territory," Wulv was told by the headman, a grizzled veteran of many battles. "As usual they're looting and burning, then trying to claim the land for their own. But they won't succeed here!" The headman brandished his favorite battle-ax by way of emphasis. Several strips of dried and blackened skin were knotted together just below the ax head, trophies taken from the backs of old enemies.

The Romax were the most hated enemy of all, the mere sight of one arousing the Teumetes to blood-fury.

"Stay here and stand with us," the elders implored Wulv. "There will be plenty of good fighting."

"I can't. I have to go back."

"Go back to what? That swamp you live in? You stupid maggot. If you stay here and fight with us, you can have your pick of the Romax weapons we capture. Forged metal!"

But Wulv was stubborn. "I don't need metal. I have this great lump of precious metal right here to use for trade." He held out the ring Pepan had given him. "I want to exchange this for wool and linen to make clothes."

The headman sneered, although he took the ring readily enough, holding it to the light before pressing it between the nubs of his worn teeth. "Wool and linen? Why? What happened to that filthy bearskin mantle you usually wear? Getting soft in your old age, eh?"

"The weather is too hot now. Besides, I need something better than that for my women."

"Your what?" The elders gaped at him, but the headman burst into laughter. "Wulv, with women! I don't believe it. Who would have anything to do with you? Your scars aren't even wounds of victory; you got them in some battle you lost."

"A fight with a bear," Wulv corrected, "which I didn't lose. I made his pelt into that mantle you mentioned, and he's kept me warm every winter since. But Rasne women are used to finer fabrics so I need—"

"You don't have any Rasne women. You're lying."

Wulv growled and locked his fingers around the other man's throat, but at that moment a cry from the sentry at the gate rang through the village. "Smoke! There's a fire in the distance. The Romax must be heading this way."

Dropping his hand, pushing the headman away from him, Wulv whirled around to look. A column of black smoke was rising toward the sunny sky—from the direction of his lake and island. Without a word, he turned and fled.

Horatrim had been disappointed that morning when Wulv refused to take him to the village. "I've never met any other people," he had complained. "I've only heard you talk about them. I want to know what they look like. I want to see how they live."

But his grandmother was adamant that he be kept hidden away. With the passing of the seasons Repana had grown accustomed to their isolation and increasingly fearful of any exposure. Meanwhile Vesi's bright, adventurous spirit had been subdued by her misfortunes, leaving her content to bow to her mother's authority. She rarely spoke and was content with sitting quietly by herself, humming tunelessly. At night, her dreams were often troubled.

"You're better off here," Repana told Horatrim, "where you are safe."

"Wulv can keep me safe," Horatrim had insisted. "Wulv can do anything. Tell them," he appealed to the Teumetian.

"Your grandmother's right," Wulv affirmed.

But in the end Wulv went off without him, leaving the little boy to amuse himself. His mother and Repana were busy grinding emmer wheat in a stone quern that they had set out in the sunshine, so for want of anything better to do, he ambled over to watch them. The ground wheat would make dumplings for the main meal of the day, but that, Horatrim thought regretfully, was a long time away.

His small round belly rumbled. "Dumplings taste better with meat," he remarked to his mother.

There was no response and although Vesi's hands were busy, her eyes were distant and lost, seeing another time and another place where her dream lover took her to his couch of silken sheets.

Horatrim appealed to higher authority. "Grandmama? I can get us meat."

"You're too little," Repana said automatically.

He thrust out his lower lip. "Am not."

The pouting little face was so comical Repana bit the inside of her cheek to keep from laughing. He had the appearance of a boy of seven or eight, though only three years had passed since his birth. The three adults were with him all the time so hardly noticed how exceptional his growth was. But once in a while his grandmother took a long, serious look at him and marveled. Life was, indeed, full of mysteries, including the mystery of the way her own feelings toward the child had changed.

It was impossible to continue to resent such an engaging little fellow. Sometimes Repana just wanted to grab him in her arms and hug him. She did not always resist the impulse, but today she was trying to be serious. "You're just a child, Horatrim. Providing meat is man's work."

"I am a man!" he flung at her, standing with his legs wide apart and his pudgy fists braced on his hips. "Almost."

Repana shook her head. When the boy was in a stubborn mood, there was no dissuading him. "All right then, bring us a bit of meat if you can. But don't wander far away and be careful in the forest. If you see any strangers, hide, or I will never let you go off on your own again."

Horatrim ran to collect the slingshot and miniature fishing spear Wulv had made for him before she could change her mind.

He was still a child. When he he stood on tiptoe the top of his head came only to his mother's breast. Yet under the tutelage of the Teumetian he had learned to kill hares and spear fish in the streams that fed into the marsh. He was not big enough to hunt for the venison and wild boar that Wulv brought down, but he could pretend they were his quarry.

The day was blindingly hot. Almost every afternoon in summer a spectacular storm would erupt somewhere in the area, sending great white spiders stalking across the land on their long legs. The touch of one of those legs was known to be fatal. Each morning Vesi and Repana offered a sacrifice of burned feathers to Tinia, the deity of lightning, to spare their home, and whenever he left the island they warned young Horatrim to avoid the trees if a storm broke.

But he was a boy who tended to forget the warnings of women.

Now, carrying his spear lightly balanced in his hand, the boy trotted along the bank of his favorite fishing stream. The stream was not swift running but quite deep and snaked its way in and out of the edge of the forest. Where it ran close to the trees, fat fish lurked in caverns beneath thirsty roots reaching down into the water.

Today Horatrim had decided to trace the water all the way to its source. He had never seen the birthplace of a stream before and the prospect excited him. He had a remarkable ability to find adventure where no one else thought to look.

A sturdy little boy with dark hair and eyes and the olive complexion of the Rasne, Horatrim himself did not appear remarkable—except to the watcher from the Otherworld.

Pepan could see the *hia* encased in the boy's body and there was nothing childish about that spirit. Enriched by the talents and abilities of a pantheon of gifted ancestors, Horatrim's *hia* was already more powerful than Pepan's. A hundred forms of genius fed its flame.

You do not yet know what you are, Pepan thought. *When you do, that body will be too small to hold you.*

He watched in fascination as the child painstakingly traced the stream. At one point Horatrim picked up a large piece of bark and, using a sharp stone, began drawing a map of the watercourse with all the detail and accuracy of an adult planning a drainage system for a city. As he worked he hummed to himself in a childish treble. But the tune he was creating was one of the ancient love songs of the Silver People, a song the boy had never heard before.

Pepan was aware of the Roman scouting party long before Horatrim was. A brazen clanging rang through the Otherworld, destroying harmonies.

Beware! he called silently to the boy.

Horatrim tensed.

Throughout his short life he had been aware of certain intuitions he could not explain, of half-glimpsed images, barely heard sounds, snatches of conversation, the intentions of animals. Now, suddenly intuition was warning him to hide, so without hesitation he abandoned the open ground beside the stream and ran toward the nearby forest. Panting, he dived into the first thicket.

No sooner had the child burrowed into the undergrowth than the leaves swelled and expanded, hiding him.

He heard the invaders coming long before he saw them.

Tramping feet, marching to a rhythm. They too were following the open ground beside the streambed but approaching from the opposite direction.

Cautiously, the little boy parted the leaves and peered out.

A company of men was passing no more than a spear's throw from Horatrim's hiding place. Could they be the Romax Wulv spoke of with such loathing? They wore molded tunics of boiled leather and metal helms with flaps that protected the backs of their necks. They walked two abreast, each carrying a round shield on his back and wearing a short sword in a scabbard at his hip. In front of them their captain marched alone, with sword drawn.

"Are we near Etruria yet?" a man in the third row called up to the first. His clipped, abrupt speech was unfamiliar, yet to his surprise Horatrim could understand the language. "I want to see one of those rich Etruscan cities."

"Forget about the cities; I want to get my hands on one of those perfumed Etruscan women," remarked another man. "They have skin like thick cream, or so I've heard. Can you imagine nuzzling into . . ."

"You think their fathers and husbands will just hand them over to us?"

"I don't mind fighting for a woman; I've done it often enough before."

The captain said over his shoulder, "You won't have to fight for women. I know the Etruscans; their men have become as idle and pleasure loving as any female. There was a time when they joined with the Hellenes to extend their influence from the Darklands to the Sunlands. But success went to their heads. They stopped trying so hard and devoted themselves to wine cups and banquet tables and dancing. Now it takes intervention by the gods to force any of them to fight. The Etruscans are said to be the most religious people on earth," he remarked as an afterthought, "for whatever that's worth."

There was coarse laughter from the rear. "They'll be praying to their gods right enough when we get through with them!"

"We won't see them for a while," retorted the captain. "We're in a pocket of Teumetian territory now and those square-headed bastards love to fight, so keep your weapons at the ready."

Hidden by the sheltering leaves, the little boy watched the company pass by. He found them very strange. They made no effort to muffle their footfalls. Twigs snapped loudly beneath their tramping feet. Their leather creaked, their metal clanged. Since earliest childhood Horatrim had been taught by Wulv to move as silently as any forest creature, and he found the actions of these strangers disturbing, a desecration of the peaceful countryside. One even took a swing with his shortsword at a little willow sapling, cutting the young tree in half for no reason. He brayed with laughter.

Horatrim was horrified. He felt the willow's pain and heard its anguished cry.

The wind shifted, carrying a wave of pungent body odors to the boy. The Romax stink, he observed. His nose twitched with disgust at the smells of garlic and sweat and long-unwashed clothing.

Mama and Grandmama insisted Horatrim bathe every day, and fresh clothing always awaited him. "You are Rasne," Grandmama frequently reminded him. She had even encouraged Wulv to begin bathing.

He was not too sure what "being Rasne" meant. But he felt confident it was something very different from the nature of the invaders crashing through the countryside. He would be glad when they were gone. He had wanted to see others like himself, but these men were not like him at all. And he had no desire to be like them.

When the last sounds of their passing died away, he crept from his hiding place and resumed tracing the watercourse. The sky was darkening with a summer storm and he knew he should head for home, but he was stubborn. What he began, he would finish.

Yet his mind kept skittering back to the strangers. What sort of place did they come from? He would ask Wulv about them when he returned. Wulv would know. Wulv knew everything.

NINETEEN

Wulv ran as hard as he could, while with every step his foreboding increased. Dark clouds gathering overhead added to his sense of impending doom. He regretted having built his sanctuary so far from the village. At a walking pace it had always seemed a satisfying distance, assuring him privacy and freedom from the pitying stares of others. But he was running at top speed now.

Even at that he was too late however. He burst from the forest at the edge of the marsh to discover that his home was ablaze. The island was swarming with Romax warriors. Several were silhouetted against the flames of his burning house as they busied themselves with the two women.

Vesi lay unconscious beneath her ravager, but Repana was fighting back.

"Monsters!" Wulv screamed at the top of his lungs. "Monsters!" He hurled himself forward with no sense of personal danger, only a vast, reddening rage.

Within that rage a great shadow took form. As Wulv, roaring with fury, pounded across the causeway, the nearest Romax turned around in time to see a human running toward him embedded in what appeared to be the transparent image of a giant bear.

"Ho . . . !" cried the startled warrior. But he made no further sound. Wulv struck him such a mighty blow across the throat that his vocal cords were paralyzed. A second blow snapped his spine, sending him spinning into the lake, which immediately boiled with wriggling eels.

The nearby warriors were so taken aback that they hesitated, and in that slim space of time Wulv killed two more. Then they closed on him, swords thrusting, spears jabbing. Screams and grunts tore through the air as a company of highly trained warriors attacked, and were attacked by, something that might have been a huge and savage bear—or one desperate man.

"Repana!" Wulv called with all his might from the heart of the fray. He thought a faint voice answered.

The Teumetian was hopelessly outnumbered, yet somehow he stayed on his feet. A blade sliced through the big muscle in his upper left arm but the pain never reached his brain. Anger blocked all sense of agony; he felt only a desperate desire to get to his women.

Repana had heard him call out to her and it gave her renewed strength. From the moment the warriors had emerged from the forest she had anticipated her fate, but she was determined not to give up her life without a struggle. Life, to her surprise, had become very sweet again, even though Pepan was lost to her forever.

Besides, she had her daughter to protect.

"Kick and bite," she had instructed Vesi when the warriors first approached the causeway. "Vomit on them if they try to rape you; that puts men off. Get your hands on a weapon, any weapon, and take as many into the Netherworld with you as you can."

"And you, Mother," gritted the younger woman as she rummaged through the household's meager supply of implements in search of weapons. She equipped herself with a fish scaler and gave her mother a hand ax. Shoulder to shoulder they stood waiting in the sunshine for the enemy.

They had not long to wait.

With howls of delight the war party had pounded across the causeway and attacked the compound. The women fought back with a ferocity that gave the lie to the Roman belief that Etruscans were weak and soft, but soon they were overcome by superior numbers.

"Now you'll lick my feet, you scrawny bitch!" a warrior had demanded as he ripped the fish scaler from Vesi's fingers and flung her backward onto the ground. He hurled himself on top of her, neither noticing nor caring that she had struck her head on the stone quern as she fell. Panting, he tore at her helpless and unmoving body.

Meanwhile others had pillaged the compound. When they found nothing of value they set fire to the buildings and amused themselves by taking turns with the women. Vesi remained lifeless and unrewarding, so was spared the worst of it. Repana proved a more worthy trophy, fighting like a tigress. Each new man had to subdue her in turn, and she left the mark of her teeth and nails on every one. But she was growing tired, terribly tired. It was only a matter of time before pain and shock released her to unconsciousness, perhaps to death.

When at last Wulv's cry reached her ears, she struggled to free herself from her latest rapist and get to the Teumetian somehow. She meant to shout his name . . . but instead she heard herself scream, "Pepan!"

TWENTY

He never left Horatrim, yet part of him was always with Repana. His *hia* became aware of her pain. Then he heard her call his name, a cry of distress winging to him through the Otherworld. He had no flesh with which to go to her aid, but he had another resource.

Horatrim! Pepan shouted voicelessly. *Horatrim, listen to me!*

The child stopped in his tracks.

You must go home. Now!

The little boy cocked his head to one side, listening. But all his ears heard was the singing of the stream, the sighing of the wind.

Go home!

Now!

Dropping his fishing spear, Horatrim whirled around and began to run.

As he sped back the way he had come, the sound of the wind turned into the malicious hiss and snicker of a thousand evil voices.

The boy's heart began to pound in his breast. His feet thudded a frantic rhythm on the stream bank. The sky continued to darken as a massive summer storm advanced, but it was not fear of the storm that propelled him.

Hurry, urged the silent intuition that drove him on. *Faster, faster!*

He had not realized how far he had come; the journey back seemed to take forever. But at last he saw the lush marshland spread before him, with the small lake, shallow in the heat of summer, at its center. Relieved, he raced toward the glint of water. And stopped in horror.

Wulv's compound was ablaze. Invaders swarmed over the little island like ants, and in their midst some sort of struggle was taking place. With sweat pouring into his eyes Horatrim could not tell just what was happening until he wiped his forearm across his face. Then he saw all too clearly.

Outlined against the purple storm clouds a creature like a huge bear stood on its hind legs, surrounded by warriors. Roaring in fury, it flung itself from one side to the other while they slashed and jabbed at it with their weapons. A woman was staggering toward the creature, holding out her arms imploringly. Her clothing was bloody and torn to ribbons, exposing her bare breast. Long strands of gray hair streamed wildly over her shoulders. As the child watched she fell to her knees with her arms still outstretched, and her wail of despair drifted across the lake.

"Grandmother!" screamed Horatrim.

He must get to her, but there were warriors on the causeway so he flung himself into the lake instead. Thrashing wildly through water up to his chest, he waded toward the island. The eels surged toward him, then writhed in agony when they touched his flesh. Horatrim was unaware of them. Too late he remembered his abandoned fishing spear. What could one unarmed little boy do against a company of warriors? Remembering the stakes Wulv had driven into the mud, he reached down and wrenched one free with surprising strength.

The boy pushed through the water. But the viscous mud at the bottom of the lake sucked greedily at his feet, holding him back. He gave a violent lunge to free himself.

From nowhere a shrill, mirthless laugh sounded in his ears. Something was watching; something was enjoying.

The sound distracted him. At that moment he lost his balance and tumbled face forward, inadvertently swallowing a mouthful of brackish liquid.

Choking, strangling, fighting panic, Horatrim struggled to get his feet under him. When his head at last broke the surface he desperately gulped air into his lungs. It burned like fire but it was better than drowning. The dark water terrified him; it seemed determined to claim him as a victim before he could reach Repana. And his mother . . .

"*Ais*, help me!" gasped the little boy.

His mother and grandmother believed in the gods implicitly and made sacrifices to them for every occasion. Aside from standing obediently silent throughout the rituals, he had never taken part in their devotions, which seemed very adult and mystifying. But if ever there was a time to seek supernatural aid, this was it.

"Help me," he repeated urgently. "I'm frightened!"

You must not be afraid, replied a voice. He could not tell where it came from; it was simply there. In him, around him . . . almost a part of him.

Fear can cripple you, the voice warned.

Before Horatrim could recover from his astonishment a different voice spoke up, enunciating as if with great effort, *Fear is something you can step out of as a beetle leaves its shell. Walk away from your fear. Leave it behind you and never look back.*

"I can't!"

You can. I did. And, having mastered the technique myself, I have given you that ability, it was my gift to you.

"But . . ."

Stop resisting! You make this too difficult. Just listen. Listen!

Never before had Horatrim conversed with *Ais*, but he was certain the gods were talking to him now. In their divine wisdom they were assuring him he could walk away from fear.

Your fear is like a shadow that is always with you. Look around. See the darkness that hovers close by? That is your fear.

The boy did as he was told. A faint, smoky cloud hung like a stain on the air beside him.

Now that you have seen it, recognize it for what it is, the voice instructed. *Then walk away. Leave your fear behind you.*

. . . and so he did.

Gritting his teeth, Horatrim floundered out of the shallow lake and onto the rocky but solid earth of the islet. Behind in the mud he left his capacity for fear, never to be reclaimed.

What he saw next would indeed have crippled him if terror still had any power over him. A sudden blast of lightning against the storm dark sky illuminated the scene with painful clarity.

The thing that Horatrim had mistaken for a bear was only Wulv— valiant Wulv—locked in a fight to the death with a score of men who were systematically hacking him to bits.

Thunder boomed.

Repana, obviously dying, was trying to crawl forward to meet her fate with the Teumetian. Beyond them Horatrim glimpsed the figure of Vesi lying on the earth like a broken branch while one of the warriors kicked her.

The lightning struck again, very close. Horatrim felt the hair lift on his scalp and forearms, then a great shudder ran through him.

Wulv's fading cries were nothing compared to the roar that now burst from Horatrim's throat. It was not the shriek of a child but the full-blooded howl of an enraged man. His vocal cords swelled to accommodate the sound; his neck thickened, his shoulders broadened accordingly.

Faster than he had ever thought before, his racing brain analyzed the situation and made a decision. Wulv and Repana were almost beyond help, but Vesi's condition was uncertain. She might be saved. Horatrim raced toward her, the pointed stake clutched in one white-knuckled hand.

But they were not the hands of a little boy. The Romax who was kicking Vesi, more out of frustration than cruelty, stared in disbelief as a figure came toward him. With every step the child grew larger, older. The warrior's foot paused in midswing. The boy—the youth—the young man hurled himself forward in a great leap calculated to disable.

As Horatrim left the ground he heard yet another voice instructing, *Swing your arms for balance.*

He landed easily before the Romax.

Twist, then kick.

His left foot shot out, slamming hard into the Romax's unprotected kneecap. The sound of breaking bone was clearly audible, and the warrior pitched forward.

Now use your weapon, drive it up beneath the chin.

Horatrim rammed the stake into the Romax's throat, pushing it up through the roof of the mouth and into the brain. The man was dead before he hit the ground.

Horatrim bent over Vesi. She was still breathing, though both her eyes were swollen shut and a thin trickle of blood ran from the corner of her mouth.

Put your fingers to her throat and feel how the blood pulses, said another of his voices. *Ah, she is strong. She will recover in time if no further harm comes to her. Go to the others now.*

Leaving his mother, Horatrim ran toward Repana and Wulv. With a coldness that surprised himself his brain was planning strategy to free them from their tormentors. One piercing cry caught the attention of the warriors surrounding Wulv and they turned toward the newcomer.

On their faces Horatrim saw blank surprise. He would never know what they saw, for as he approached they began scrambling backward. When he was within a couple of paces of them, he pretended to lunge to the right, then darted to the left instead and scooped Repana into his arms. The child Horatrim would never have thought of lifting his grandmother; the young man he had become did so easily.

"Who are you?" she managed to gasp through bloody lips.

"Vengeance," replied a voice—a voice she recognized even in her extremity, for it was Pepan's. Yet the face looking down at her belonged to the child Horatrim. But the features had matured inexplicably however, as if years had passed since the morning. Now he was both man and boy, familiar and a stranger.

Moaning, Repana closed her eyes.

Horatrim's actions caught the warriors off balance. One of them took a wild swing at him with his sword, but he easily ducked beneath the blow and in the same movement laid Repana at Wulv's feet. The mortally wounded Teumetian slumped down beside her and cradled her against his chest with a little sigh that might have been contentment.

The Roman warriors were tough and experienced; they swiftly regrouped. In a unit they rushed at him, then separated to flow around him like a river around a rock in order to trap him within their circle.

A child would have been overwhelmed by the strategy. The person Horatrim had become found himself drawing on the experiences of men who had been dead five hundred years. He fell to the ground, hugging his knees and rolling between pairs of running legs, then as soon as he was in the clear he was on his feet and turning to fight.

He had no weapons but his spirit and all it now contained: the accumulated wisdom of generations of people who had lived intimately with the gods.

Balancing a spear, a cursing warrior took aim at the man-boy who had appeared so unexpectedly. Horatrim met the man's eyes, then glanced up almost casually. "Tinia," he murmured as if calling to an old friend.

A bolt of blinding light seared out of the boiling clouds to detonate at the feet of the Roman and engulf him in a ball of fire. In the resulting dazzle Horatrim envisioned a flame-haired figure with no face, no indication of gender, and yet a terrible beauty. In one hand the figure held a whip. When the whip was cracked, lightning crackled and snapped.

Cowering, the Romans shrank back as the smell of their comrade's crisping flesh tainted the air.

"Tinia," Horatrim murmured again in acknowledgment and gratitude. Then from deep within himself came other names. "Sethlan, god of metals, give me fists of iron. Tuflas, goddess of healing, let me not

feel my wounds. Culsan, god of destiny, grant me victory. Sancus, god
of cities; Satres, ruler of the Netherworld; Ani, guardian of the gates;
Veno, Protectress of the Dead; all you who are sacred to my people, be
with me. I honor you now and fight in your name!"

His mother and grandmother had spoken those names within the
hearing of the child Horatrim. Now he identified them with the multitude he felt inside himself. He had long been aware of the crowd of
presences flooding his mind and his muscles, filling him with strength
and cleverness and courage. He had never known their origins, but
now he made the assumption that they were gods.

Surely the *Ais* were with him.

How could a mere band of mortal warriors hope to stand against
one whom the gods loved?

He attacked in fury, and in terror the Romans attempted to flee
from him. They saw what he did not.

Behind the infuriated youth, bearing down upon them, strode a
whole army. Led by the image of an aging figure dressed in the gar-
ments of a nobleman of Etruria, a shadowy host of men and women
marched implacably forward. Through their spectral flesh could be
seen the dying fires of the compound behind them. Spears hurled at
them passed through them as if through thin air.

The youth from the lake commanded an army of ghosts.

"*Manes!*" shrieked the Roman captain. His eyes rolled in his head.
"*Manes!*"

Without effort, Horatrim understood what the word *manes* meant.
But why did the man claim he was seeing ghosts? Was it supposed to be
a trick? "Fool," Horatrim muttered contemptuously. Locking his fists
together, he slammed them against the Roman captain's temple and
grinned with satisfaction as the man slumped to the ground.

Being a warrior is fun, thought what was left of the little boy inside
Horatrim. He looked for the next man to hit.

Storm clouds had swallowed the sun, and smoke from the burning
compound further obscured the scene. In such a premature twilight it
was hard to tell what was happening. Horatrim knew only that he

fought and fought, knocking down one man after the other. With every blow he landed he seemed to grow stronger.

He never thought to look behind him.

In his wake, specters strode among the fallen Romans, extracting a terrible vengeance and taking more than lives. Souls were torn from the stunned bodies Horatrim left behind him souls bound and ensnared by magic that was ancient when the world was young. The *hia* of the Roman warriors belonged to the shades of long-dead Etruscans now, forced forever to do their bidding. But their captors did not content themselves with taking slaves. Lovers of beauty, they must create beauty where none had existed before. The *hia* of the Rasne had spent many centuries in the Netherworld perfecting their talents. Moments of terminal terror were extracted from dying minds by the most skilled physicians, twisted and shaped into intricate, bloody beads by the greatest artisans, strung onto wire spun by the finest craftsmen from filaments of pain.

When the Etruscan spirits were finished, only the man-boy and the mortally injured bodies of Wulv and Repana and the unconscious Vesi remained. No Roman flesh, no spilled blood spattered the earth where moments before a company of trained warriors had been slaughtered.

Horatrim stood rocking slightly on his heels, rubbing his knuckles and looking around with a dazed expression. "Where did everyone go?" he asked in bewilderment.

There was no answer.

A faint groan caught his attention. He dropped to his knees beside Repana and Wulv, who looked up at him with glazing eyes. "Don't touch her," snarled the Teumetian.

"Wulv . . . it's me, Horatrim."

"Horatrim?" The Teumetian scowled. "You're not Horatrim."

"I am, but something happened to me," the boy replied. "And I came too late," he added miserably. Suddenly he was a child again, eyes brimming with tears. He reached for Repana.

Wulv twisted sideways, interposing his body between them. "Leave her! She's mine now."

"I only want to help; she's my grandmother."

Wulv responded by clutching Repana still more tightly to his chest and baring his teeth like a wild animal. It was obvious he no longer recognized the child he had helped raise.

Repana turned her head and tried to look into Horatrim's face, but the effort was too much for her. She uttered one soft moan, then slumped lifeless.

Wulv's scarred features blurred with a grief too great to survive. He struggled into a sitting position and shook the still body. "No! You have to live, you have to live for me! With me! I'll do better. I'll get you soft cloth. I'll catch such lovely fish for your meal. Please. Oh, please. My . . ."

The Teumetian drew a long, anguished breath. In his throat Horatrim could hear the death rattle. Wulv made a final effort. "My dear one," he murmured, the words of tenderness crossing his lips for the first and last time. Then he too was gone.

At the moment of Repana's dying, Horatrim had felt a pain as if something had torn loose inside him. The sensation was not repeated when Wulv died, but his sorrow was just as intense. Fighting back tears, he turned away—so he did not see two shadowy figures slowly materialize to bend over the woman who lay on the earth. One was tall and elegant, the other stocky and coarsely formed. Each held out a hand to her.

Repana's *hia* hesitated, then accepted them both. Like a scarf of sheerest silk it floated upward from her corpse and, together with her two companions, faded into the Otherworld.

Meanwhile Horatrim, wiping furiously at his eyes, was stumbling back to his mother. Vesi was still unconscious but at least she was alive. He was determined to keep her that way.

TWENTY-ONE

The Roman garrison occupied a hill fort overlooking the river. Built many years before by a now vanquished tribe, the fort had been modified and reinforced by the victorious Romans to take full advantage of its position. A high timber palisade surmounted walls of rammed earth and rubble. New timber gates had been installed and secured by massive bars. Pyramids of stones warned of ballistae mounted atop the walls.

From a level summit the hill fell sharply away, with clumps of parched cedar clinging to its steep flanks. Treacherous scree made any approach to the top difficult. Bronze-helmeted guards were stationed at the gates at all times, each equipped with a two-edged sword in a scabbard, a dagger, and a pair of throwing spears. Over linen undervests and woolen tunics they wore corselets of hammered bronze plates fastened together with rings to allow for mobility, while scarves around their necks served to keep the armor from cutting into their skin. The entire outfit was meltingly hot in the summer sun, bitterly cold in winter.

Because the garrison was situated north of Rome on a tribal frontier, the guards were under orders to be constantly vigilant. They were human; occasionally their attention wavered.

"This isn't a frontier, it's a backwater," Paulus complained to Sextus as they stood on either side of the main gate. "There's no fighting, no action. No opportunity for loot," he added petulantly. "There're rich pickings on all the other borders—I've heard of men making fortunes in Thrace, where even the slaves are bedecked in gold. But here . . ." He shook his head and spat into the dust. "The Samnites haven't come down from their mountains recently because they're too scared of us, the Vestini are subdued, and as for the Etruscans, they've gone as soft as melting wax. The king says we'll be overrunning them soon."

"You can be burned by melting wax," Sextus reminded him. He had stood this watch with Paulus every day for a month and was weary of the younger man's constant complaining. Paulus wanted most desperately to be in the midst of battle; he longed for the clash of weapons and the stink of blood and the promise of loot. Since joining the military his only assignment had been guard duty, and he was frustrated.

Sextus, on the other hand, had fought in many campaigns and had his belly full of battle and bloodshed. Paulus did not appreciate how lucky they were to be simply standing here, doing nothing. He now tried to transmit this to his companion. "I fought the Etruscans . . ." he began.

Paulus groaned audibly. He had heard the tales of Sextus's exploits a hundred times.

"I know the Etruscans well," Sextus continued undeterred. "If they should decide to declare war on Rome before our king marches on Veii, we had better be ready."

"I'll wager anything you care to name that it never happens." Yawning, Paulus scratched himself in the armpit. A trickle of sweat ran down under his body armor and he dug with one forefinger in an unsuccessful attempt to reach his upper ribs. "The Etruscans have no interest in Rome. I've heard descriptions of the cities in Etruria. They have brick cities with public buildings as fine as temples and private houses fit for princes. What would they want with an overgrown village of mud-and-timber shacks on seven rocky hills? You worry unnecessarily, Sextus. In the meantime I'm mightily bored and that sun is too damned hot. There's no one in sight. Why not step into the shade of the wall and have a quick game of dice? We can see just as well from there, and I'd welcome the chance to win that cloak I lost to you in the barracks last night."

A sharp voice cut through the stifling air. "If either of you desert your post for an instant, I'll personally skewer your guts."

Paulus and Sextus froze as their captain, Antoninus, strode through the gateway with a grim expression on his sunburned, hawk-nosed face. "You're supposed to be standing guard, attentive and watchful. All I can hear is your chatter. And you underestimate the Etruscans," he told Paulus. "They may seem peaceful now, but I wouldn't trust one of them if we had exchanged a blood oath and I was married to his sister. Guile is as natural to them as fighting is to us. They are an ancient, decadent race; they make the Egyptians look honest. Their current nonaggression could be just a clever ploy to make us relax our vigilance. While you two are dicing your pay away, a whole army could be sneaking past us under cover of those willows along the river down there, determined to sack and loot Rome."

"That's hardly likely; we're not the only guards," Paulus replied, smiling easily. His cousin was married to the captain's son, and he imagined it allowed him a certain familiarity.

Antoninus's backhanded blow drove him to the ground. "When you stand at this gate you stand as if you are the only guards between the barbarians and the gates of Rome. So keep a sharp lookout. And let me hear nothing further about playing dice!" Antoninus added as he walked away. "You ignorant whelps may not realize it, but the Etruscans you sneer at *invented* dice!"

Below the garrison, the Tiber undulated lazily through a land baked ochre by the relentless sun. Only the sway of willow branches against the wind betrayed any activity, but by the time Sextus and

Paulus resumed their silent surveillance of the terrain, the trees were immobile. The bird song, which was the eternal heartbeat of the region, had been stilled.

The dark-haired young man leading the woman along the river's edge was careful to keep the trees between himself and the fort on the hill. Seeking cover in unfamiliar territory was as natural to him as breathing.

Vesi had been badly damaged in the raid. Her distraught son had held her in his arms and tended her wounds as best he could, using mud and leaves and scraps of half-remembered lore, lore that he should not know, had never been taught. Yet it came to him in his need and he accepted gratefully.

Horatrim had poured his love into his mother and was finally rewarded when she opened her eyes with a weary sigh. But when he looked into her eyes they were blank. No matter how much he pleaded with her to come back to him, there was no spark there, no sign of recognition. Yet she was alive; he comforted himself with that much. She was at least alive.

When Vesi had regained enough physical strength, Horatrim had taken her away from the island and its unbearable memories. He had set off through the forbidding, endless expanse of the Great Forest with no real destination in mind.

Then at night Horatrim began having vivid dreams of a wide river running through a fertile valley of rich black earth. In this unfamiliar land, exotically robed, dark-skinned healers worked in high-ceilinged temples. As he watched, they cured the sick and repaired the injured with incredible skill.

Where such dreams came from he did not know. But he awoke convinced the healers existed. Somewhere. In the Black Land, wherever that was. If he could only find them, perhaps they could help his damaged mother.

In the meantime, however, he decided to take Vesi to her own people. They might be able to heal her themselves, or they could at least look after her while he went in search of the Black Land and the wondrous healers of his dreams.

He did not discuss his plans with Vesi. Conversation was no longer possible with his mother. She could only be gently guided, told to sit here, lie there, eat this, drink that. He fed her by hand, pressed soft food into her mouth, then waited while she chewed slowly and swallowed, then fed her some more. When she soiled herself he cleaned and bathed her, unaware how recently she had been doing the same for him. Obedient as a child, Vesi followed his instructions. Sometimes she made small, erratic gestures or gaped dumbly with her mouth hanging ajar. But she did not speak; she had not spoken since that terrible day when Wulv and Repana died.

Slowly, limited by Vesi's ability to travel, they had made their way through the forest. Thanks to the hunting and foraging skills Wulv had taught him, Horatrim was able to keep them both fed. He asked for nothing but directions from the occasional Teumetians they encountered.

During endless, sleepless nights, he tormented himself with memories of his grandmother and Wulv and the life they had led together before the coming of the Romax. The little family on the island had bothered no one, done no damage. In retrospect he realized they had been happy.

Yet the Romax had destroyed all that for the sheer pleasure of destruction. His stubborn mind re-created the images of that last terrible day again and again, refusing to accept them, refusing to forget.

He was taller than his mother, taller than most of the hunters or trappers or even the occasional Romax scout they encountered. He had burst from his clothes and been forced to make new ones from hides and pelts he trapped along the way, stitching the pelt with tiny neat stitches although he had never sewn before. Almost overnight his body had turned into that of a powerful young man. Yet deep inside a small boy still lived, peering out at the world through wondering, baffled eyes, and with the universal question of the child: Why?

Why had the Romax come?

Why had his grandmother and Wulv been slain?

Most important of all, where had his mother gone?

They had been traveling for the best part of a ten-day journey when they had stumbled—almost accidentally—upon a Teumetian village deep in the heart of the forest. While Vesi sat on a log, Horatrim chopped wood, using an ax with fluid ease, in return for some cheese and bread and sour wine.

Later that day, as he was being paid, the Teumetian headman had looked at him appraisingly, admiring the breadth of the young man's shoulders, the rippling muscles in his bare arms, the brawny length of his legs.

"Stay with us and join our warrior band," the headman urged Horatrim. "We could use a big powerful fellow like you to stand with us. And in return you would enjoy the safety of our village. Wandering the forest is no longer safe; every year there seem to be more raiders from Latium. These are dangerous times."

"I cannot," Horatrim replied. "We are going to find my mother's people."

"And who are they?"

"The Rasne. They have some sort of . . . of city, I believe my grandmother once said. On the other side of the Great Forest. We will be safe there."

"I wouldn't expect to find safety among the Silver People," advised the bandy-legged village chieftain. "The Etruscans produced great warriors—once. But not anymore. Now they lack the will to resist any determined effort at conquest. And conquest is what the Romax intend. They won't always be satisfied with raiding. Why settle for some loot when you can have all of it? The Teumetes will prove too tough for them, but remember my words, we'll see the day when they swarm over the Etruscan cities and make them their own. The Romax may be maggots, but at least they're lively maggots. The Silver People have become slugs."

"That may be. But I have to take my mother to her own people. You see how she is; I cannot care for her by myself."

"You won't get any help from the Etruscans. Just look at her, dressed in rags and as mad as a mouse under the full moon. The Silver People want everything to be perfect; they'll never accept her as one of their own. They'll either turn her away or sacrifice her to one of their gods."

The headman rubbed his hands together, skin rasping. "But you're right," he went on, "a young man like you should not be looking after a grown woman. I'm sure you have better things to do. Tell you what; I'm a generous man. Although I've already got two wives, I'll take her off your hands." He grinned toothlessly. "Wouldn't mind having a woman who can't talk."

The man's eyes glinted lasciviously; a thread of saliva drooling from his lips. Horatrim, repelled, took a step backward, pulling Vesi with him. The chieftain had followed. In one hand he brandished a knife; with the other he reached for the woman. "Even a madwoman has her uses."

But just as his grimy hand clutched the front of her gown, Horatrim's fingers closed around the man's hand. He squeezed so tightly he could hear the bones grinding together. "I think not," he said softly.

For a single heartbeat the chieftain had contemplated driving the knife in his free hand into the youngster's chest, but the look in Horatrim's eyes stopped him. He knew without the slightest doubt that the boy could and would kill him first. He spun around and scuttled back to his village, leaving the young man and his mother standing alone.

That night as he had made camp for the pair of them in a forest glade, Horatrim thought over what the chieftain had said. What if Vesi's people would not accept her? Absentmindedly he scratched the stubble that had recently bloomed on his jaws. His body was becoming a man's, and men were supposed to know what to do. Wulv would have known.

In the dark, in the night, alone with the massive responsibility of his helpless mother, Horatrim felt like a very small boy indeed. Tears prickled at the back of his eyes, but he brushed them away with the back of his hand. He had used that same angry movement almost from the moment he learned to walk, whenever tears threatened. He had never seen Wulv cry.

"I'm worried, Mother," he reluctantly admitted as he fed small sticks to the fire. "I fear nothing for myself, but I am concerned about you. The world is a dangerous place. Until the Rasne take us in, we have no one but ourselves."

Vesi had sat cross-legged beside him, fingers idly pleating the threadbare fabric of her gown, staring eyes fixed on the flames. She did not think, did not feel, did not care. From the moment her head struck the stone quern in Wulv's compound she had been little more than an empty vessel, a woman's body with no functioning intelligence inside. The bright, brave girl was gone. But on some level deeper than thought the mother had responded to the son's anxiety. A prayer was formulated in her blood and bones. And into her emptiness, something came, using her . . .

Her disused throat worked convulsively.

Forget about the Rasne, said a voice.

Horatrim jumped. The voice was not Vesi's, was hardly even human. He dropped the sticks to crouch before his mother, taking her cold hands in his. "What did you say? Mother, did you speak?"

She sat unresponsive. He was beginning to think he'd imagined it when he saw the flesh of her throat working.

Forget about finding the Rasne. You have a different future. In Latium. Among the Romans.

Horatrim had seized his mother's hands. They were icy cold. Her eyes did not meet his; she seemed as stupefied as ever. Yet though her lips barely moved, she was undeniably speaking. The voice was thin, strained, without gender or emotion. Yet curiously it reminded him of the voices that had spoken to him the day Wulv's island was raided, the same voices he sometimes thought he heard whispering to him at the very edges of his consciousness.

Desperately trying to establish some conscious contact, Horatrim had squeezed her hands hard enough to cause pain. She never flinched. "Are you talking about the Romax, the ones who hurt you?"

In Latium they are known as Romans.

"You want vengeance, is that it?"

Listen.

Speaking directly is difficult, though we find it easier through this woman because she does not resist us. You must go to Rome. Your future is there.

"Mine? How can that be? And what about you, Mother, what am I to do with you? I do not understand what you want."

A silence had followed while Horatrim waited patiently, eyes fixed on his mother's throat and lips, waiting for them to move.

You must. For the first time there was emotion in the voice, an imperative command.

And take me with you.

There was no further sound but the crackle of the fire, the calls of the night birds, the distant yapping of a fox.

Horatrim did not hear them. He sat with his elbows propped on his knees and stared at his mother.

She did not speak again.

The next morning they resumed their travels. Eventually they emerged from the Great Forest to find themselves on a deeply rutted dirt road that bore signs of frequent cart travel. Horatrim had looked both ways, up and down, but saw no one, no indication of habitation in either direction. Yet this was a road; it must lead somewhere. But in which direction? Stooping, he examined the ground, sensitive fingers tracing the cracked lines in the earth.

Knowledge came unbidden: cart wheels generally turned outward, so they were deeper on that side, and laden carts would usually be heading toward a town. With a boyish grin, Horatrim caught his mother by the hand and set off down the road. After the first time Vesi stepped in a rut and almost turned her ankle, he was careful to keep her to the center of the track, which provided a relatively level surface.

Before long they had begun encountering other travelers, as many as three or four in a day. Instead of asking for the city of the Rasne,

Horatrim had sought directions to a place called Rome. To his own astonishment, he found himself speaking to each traveler in that person's own language. The courtesy earned him a friendly response and occasionally a cart ride or a meal as well.

"Rome! You don't want to go to Rome. The Romans are the most aggressive of all the Italic tribes," he was informed by a Picene merchant making his way west with a train of oxcarts driven by whip-scarred slaves. "They've subdued most of their neighbors already. They claim to be descended from twins who were suckled by a wolf, if you can believe it. One of the twins was known as Romulus so they call their stronghold Rome after him. Their current king is Tarquin the Superb."

"Superbius," corrected a Campanian merchant heading east the following day. "He styles himself Lucius Tarquinius Superbius, a name meant to impress the *plebeians*, the commoners. He boasts of having royal Etruscan blood but he's really just the latest in a long line of opportunists. Kings come and go. Romans are difficult to govern; the place is always a nettlepatch of intrigue. Look for a better destination, young man, unless you're interested in trade. Rome loves doing business." He had glanced sidelong at the silent Vesi. "Maybe you want to sell this woman in the slave market. If you do, Rome is where you'll get the best price."

Horatrim had listened to this advice without comment, but after they left the merchant he said to Vesi, "Are you certain you want to go to Rome?"

She did not answer. Her mouth hung ajar like the door to an abandoned house.

"We can turn back," her son suggested, wiping a trail of spittle from her chin.

In response the woman had shuddered as if a cold wind blew through her. She straightened until she stood perceptibly taller. Her chin came up, her shoulders went back. From somewhere deep inside had issued one of the voices he was coming to know.

We never turn back.

He did not question the voice. Command was implicit in every syllable.

"We never turn back," he had repeated. On his lips the words became a vow.

Thirty days after leaving Wulv's ruined fort, Horatrim and Vesi were skirting a garrisoned hill; a garrison on the frontier of Rome. The man-boy paused to listen to the voices of the guards carrying on the still air. Peering through the screening willows, he watched the captain appear and wondered yet again at the wisdom of traveling into the city.

Then he glanced down at his mother. Vesi was sitting contentedly on the earth beside him, picking at the countless tiny flowers that had sprung up around his sandaled feet.

He crouched beside the woman and lifted her chin to look into her empty eyes.

"Rome lies ahead. Are you still sure?" he asked.

Vesi ignored him and concentrated on weaving the flowers into an intricate garland.

Horatrim looked back over his shoulder. But that way lay the past, with its bitter memories of pain and death. Rome was waiting. Whatever it contained could not be worse than what they had already experienced.

"We never turn back," he whispered, lifting Vesi gently to her feet. As his head was bent, she slipped the garland of flowers around his neck. For an instant he thought he saw a ghost of a smile on her lips.

TWENTY-TWO

I n the beginning Pepan's *hia* had been content merely to follow them. As long as there was no actual danger to the woman or her son he remained a passive observer. But when the Teumetian chieftain openly lusted after Vesi, Pepan had responded.

With an effort of will, he had concentrated all his thought on a summoning. A sound like a trumpet rang through the Otherworld. From the mist shapes had appeared, dim shapes that had no faces, but faces were not needed. Form was important, and these had the form of an army.

As Horatrim spoke with the Teumetian an invisible army of ghosts had materialized at Vesi's back. Gray, wraithlike shapes had raised their arms in silent menace and a cold wind had blown out of nowhere, lifting the hair on their heads so it writhed like snakes.

The startled chieftain forgot all about Vesi's round hips.

When Horatrim led his mother safely away, a peal of laughter had reverberated through the Otherworld. *I am still involved with life!* Pepan had crowed with delight.

The nearer Horatrim drew to the borders of Latium, the more closely his invisible watcher followed. He wondered if Horatrim was thinking of revenge. If he were still a living man, Pepan would have desired revenge himself.

Repana—his Repana—had lost her life to the Romans, and though her spirit continued to exist, the path of her destiny was forever altered. Wulv was part of her future now. Having died together, they were linked in a way Pepan and Repana were not. He knew that once they got used to the changed condition of being dead, they would have gone off together to the next stage of being. Wistfully, Pepan wondered if he would ever have that luxury. But he had chosen his own path. Now he must follow it wherever it might lead.

We never turn back.

That had been his credo in life—the credo of the Rasne—and he had carried it with him into death. Now Horatrim had taken the oath as his own.

Life, Pepan mused, *is strange, and afterlife is stranger still. Death is the true meaning of life.*

In addition to Pepan, other beings were following Horatrim. After the death of one of their number, the surviving minions of Pythia had retired from the pursuit of the *siu*'s child—for a time—to recover themselves. One of their own had been slain. The loss was almost incomprehensible.

Returning to the long oval hall with the moon pool, they performed the summoning ritual and awaited their goddess. When the surface of the water stirred they prudently turned their backs.

From the depths of the milky pool an obsidian image rose. Droplets of opalescent water clung to the ruby nipples of her multiple breasts like obscene milk. Her mouth was an angry slash from which a voice hissed in anger.

"So you have not succeeded?"

"We were thwarted, O Great Pythia, by—"

The dark goddess interrupted, "Out of cowardice you abandoned your mission, that is all there is to say. You were to find the *siu* and kill its spawn and you have not done so."

"We did find the *siu*, O Noble Queen," began the leader of the five. "But he . . ."

The statue's voice had dropped to a liquid purr more frightening than its former sibilance. "Perhaps you should die instead," murmured Pythia. "I could take my pleasure from your torment."

"That will not be necessary, Divine Goddess! We will resume our quest at once!" Flinging themselves to their knees, they had groveled in the dirt, being careful to keep their backs turned at all times toward the fearsome figure in the pool. To gaze upon her was to court destruction.

"I am merciful—foolish with my mercy perhaps—it has always been my greatest failing. I will allow you to return to your quest because I know you will not fail me again." The goddess paused. "Now that you know how vulnerable you are, you will be more careful. Remember, everything that walks the Earthworld can be slain in the Earthworld. Including you."

As the goddess began to sink back into the pool, she added, "Usually creatures in the Earthworld die only once. But fail me again, and I will take pleasure in killing you a thousand times. I can promise you an eternity of the most exquisite agony."

With these chilling words ringing in their ears, the five set out again upon their quest. The trail had grown cold, however, and they dared not call upon the goddess for help.

There followed a frustrating time of trial and error, questions asked and bribes paid. The seasons raced by. The five were painfully aware of the goddess watching. But the quarry they sought seemed to have disappeared from the earth.

Then at last, on the far edge of the Great Forest, they picked up the trail again. In that remote region they learned of Wulv's compound and succeeding in tracing the fugitive Vesi to the islet in the marsh. But they arrived too late. The ashes had been cold for a long time.

They fell upon the nearest Teumetian village instead and

destroyed it in a blind rage, torturing the inhabitants for the slightest scrap of information. In an effort to save his own life, the last survivor told the five of a muscular youth and a mute, mindless woman who had fled the territory after the Romax raid. The woman was reputedly Rasne, he said, and they were last seen heading south.

In payment for this information the Teumetian was ritually slaughtered as a sacrifice to the dark goddess. The five then feasted upon his liver.

"We have them!" the leader of the five exulted. "That is surely the youngster we seek, for he has grown more quickly than any human offspring could. When we find him we can be certain his sire will not be far behind. Demons follow their own."

Eyes glinting with a fanatic light, the five then made their way south. Toward Latium and Rome.

Horatrim and Vesi were still within sight of the Roman garrison on the hilltop when she gave a hollow groan. At once he put his arm around her. "What is it, Mother?"

Danger, said one of the voices he believed to be gods. *You are being pursued.*

"Pursued by who?"

Five.

"I can fight five," he confidently declared.

These are not ordinary warriors. You could not hope to stop them all.

"Then what am I to do?" It did not occur to Horatrim that it was foolish to ask advice from a madwoman. By now he understood he was not talking to Vesi, but to something else.

Five cannot stand against two score, came the cryptic reply.

"What are you saying?"

Leave me here and double back. Go up the side of yonder hill, but do not follow one of the obvious approaches. Drag your feet, scuffle dirt. Then halfway up, stop leaving a trail and return to me.

Obediently, Horatrim worked his way up the southeast face of the hill toward a blank garrison wall, dislodging stones and crushing small clumps of cedar with deliberate clumsiness. Before he reached the top he veered off sharply and made his way down again as light footed as a deer, using the techniques Wulv had taught him. He ran silently to the willows where he had secreted Vesi. Finding her mute and unresponsive once more, he took her hand and led her away.

It was almost twilight before the five cloaked figures came within sight of the Roman garrison. They searched the surrounding area until the one with sharpest eyes discovered Horatrim's trail going up the hill to the fort. "This way, we have him now."

Paulus and Sextus were still on guard at the gates, though the day was almost over. The enervating heat lingered however. The ground seethed; the horizon shimmered. Sticky inside their clothes and with pounding headaches, both men were in bad humor. Twice more Antoninus had emerged from the fort to bawl orders at them, finding fault with everything they did, from the way they stood to the angle of their spears.

Once the sun extinguished itself in a sea of flame beyond the western hills, the guard would change. Already the two men were anticipating their daily ration of beer and meat. "I could drink goat piss, I'm that thirsty," Paulus remarked.

"The beer they give us is goat piss, do you think frontier guards rate barley brew? I tell you, it wouldn't take much to induce me to throw down my weapons and go back to . . . Ho! What's that?"

"I don't see anything, Sextus."

"Some fool's trying to sneak up on us. Off there to the side, down below that outcropping. Look where I'm pointing, will you?"

Taking a step forward, Paulus peered down to discover several cloaked figures crawling up the hillside on hands and knees and bellies. Delighted with something to do, something to relieve the boredom, he promptly whipped his sword from its scabbard, hammered it against his shield, shouting, "Attack! Attack!"

Gate guards were chosen for their carrying voices. A moment later his cry was taken up inside, followed by a clashing of weapons and a thunder of feet as the entire garrison came pouring through the gates. There were only forty of them, but they were tough, aggressive veterans bored with inactivity. The intention to kill was stamped on every sunburned face. They could successfully have fought a number half again as large as their own.

At the first sight of them, the five cloaked figures halfway up the hill realized they stood no chance. With a wail of "Pythia protect us!" their leader jumped up and turned to run. His companions followed. But their talents did not include fleetness of foot. The first Roman caught up with the last of them and delivered a savage sword-blow through the cloak to the flesh beneath. A scream rang across the hillside.

The angle had been calculated to chop off his leg at the knee, yet the wounded figure continued to run although something flopped on the ground behind him. When the Roman paused in midstride to pick up the severed limb, he gave a gasp of revulsion and flung it from him.

What he had amputated was no leg, but a muscular, scaly tail as long as his arm.

By that time Horatrim was a considerable distance away, but the sound of the scream was borne to him on a rising wind. He stopped and turned to his mother. "Did you hear that?"

She did not answer. She stood beside him with head bowed and hands hanging.

"There's fighting back there," he told her as he listened intently. "Whoever was chasing us must have met the Romans instead. Like running into a nest of hornets, I would say from the sound of it." He smiled, thinly. "That was a clever plan, Mother."

He knew the plan was not Vesi's, but how else was he to address her? And where, he found himself wondering, did she go when someone else was speaking through her?

Suddenly the little boy inside him wanted to weep. Vesi might still walk and breathe, but his mother was irrevocably lost to him.

·   ·   ·

Stumbling and slithering, the mutilated creature fled down the hill with his four companions. Behind him he left a trail of thick, brownish ichor smeared across the sunbaked earth.

The Romans pursued halfheartedly. The horror of the severed tail demoralized even such hard-bitten warriors; no one really wanted to catch up with the cloaked figures. They shouted threats and beat their swords against their shields, but when the order came to turn back they responded with enthusiasm. They had been raised on stories of the creatures of myth that inhabited the dark northern forests.

"What in the name of Great Mars was that thing, do you suppose?" Paulus asked Sextus as they trudged back up the hill.

Wiping his sword blade again and again on every stunted cedar they passed, Sextus replied, "I don't know and I don't want to know. I never saw anything so awful in my life." Lifting his sword, he examined the blade ruefully. The metal was pitted as if it had been dipped in acid.

Antoninus, who was hardly less shaken than his men, said in an unsteady voice, "It was a demon. They were all demons, that's why I gave the order to turn back. You can't kill demons."

Paulus gazed down at an ugly smear on the ground before him, the viscous, stinking ooze from the wounded creature. "Perhaps they were demons and perhaps not. Look there, Sextus."

His friend kept his eyes fixed on the garrison ahead of them. "I don't want to."

"You certainly did the thing great damage; you should be proud."

"I'm scared, that's what I am. What if it comes after me seeking revenge?"

Paulus's own courage was seeping back. He managed a lopsided grin as he punched his friend on the arm. "At least you can't say you've been bored today."

Sextus glared at him. "I don't think that's funny."

Emboldened, Paulus teased, "Where did you throw that tail? We should keep it as a trophy."

"Leave it alone, will you!"

"A demon's tail? I think not. I want it if you don't. We can hang it on the wall of the barracks along with the captured trophies." Paulus made a great show of searching among the rocks and bushes while some of the other Romans sniggered at Sextus's discomfort. But just as Paulus found what he sought half-concealed in a clump of cedar, Antoninus barked, "Get on, you lot, I want us all back inside the walls before the dark catches us. Those things might come back . . . with reinforcements," he added for emphasis.

Paulus reached for the severed tail. On closer inspection it did not appear to be a tail, but more nearly resembled the nether part of some huge serpent. He did not want to touch the repellent object but he could not back down now; he had carried the joke too far.

His fingers had barely grazed the scaly surface when the thing whipped around his wrist and crushed every bone.

TWENTY-THREE

I t was important to take care of the family.

Whenever Young Ones wandered away from the mouth of the cave, He would growl and wiggle his eyebrows, and She would run after their errant offspring, chittering anxiously. She was responsible for herding Young Ones back to safety. He did not tend Young Ones. He provided meat and mounted She whenever She invited him.

He remembered an Old One like himself who had brought meat to the cave when He was little. And an old She with drooping dugs who chased himself and other Young Ones. There had been more like them living in other caves throughout the hills. But not now.

Where had they gone?

When He tried to think about them his head hurt. It was not easy to construct a thought. Hunting was easier and required no thought. He liked hunting. Whenever He returned with meat, He would devour his fill, then let She take her turn. Afterward they would sit in the sun outside the cave and watch Young Ones rend and tear what remained of the bloody flesh. Sun was good. A full belly was good.

Mounting She was good; locking his fingers in the shaggy yellow hair that grew along her shoulders and sides, thrusting deep into her, feeling the bursting feeling. Afterward He liked to sleep. She liked to sleep then, too, but Young Ones would take advantage and run outside and She would have to go after them.

Young Ones were a lot of trouble. They made a lot of noise racing and romping in the cave.

The cave smelled good. It smelled of rotten meat and dried blood, reminding He that his belly was empty. But no matter how He searched, there were no shreds of meat to be found. Not even a cracked marrowbone. All gone. Young Ones had eaten the last of the food.

One of them came too close and He growled and cuffed it with the back of his hand, but not too hard. Young One ran and hid behind She, peering out with bright, beady eyes. He growled again. Young One blinked.

She growled back at He, warning him not to threaten her baby. In response He showed her his teeth but She only growled again. Usually She would back down, but not where Young Ones were concerned.

He sighed and began picking through the thick mat of russet hair on his torso in search of fleas. She came over to him then and made a whimpering noise. When She pressed insistently against him He began grooming her, catching her fleas between thumb and forefinger and popping them into his mouth. But they were too small. They did not fill the belly. He must go in search of more meat now or sleep hungry.

When He pushed her away and stood up on his two bowed legs, She gave a grunt of protest that He ignored. From a pile of debris at the mouth of the cave, He took a gnarled branch He often used as a club. If He hit meat on the head, meat would fall down and die. He swung the branch onto his shoulder and strode away without looking back.

She stood in the cave entrance and watched him go down the hill in the twilight with his peculiar, rolling gait. Soon He disappeared into a stand of cedar trees.

Licking her lips in anticipation, She sat down to wait. She knew what it meant when He took the club.

They would eat soon.

TWENTY-FOUR

The Roman matron called Delphia was stout and handsome, with oiled hair arranged in sculptured curls across her brow in a style copied from an Etruscan wall-hanging. Silver Etruscan beads hung in graduated strands around her neck. Like her husband Propertius, she exuded an air of prosperity. As she reclined at her ease in the cart, she was chattering merrily and examining her hennaed fingernails.

The couple was returning from a trip to view their latest acquisition, an estate near the border of Roman territory. Propertius sat facing his wife, going over accounts in his head and wondering whether their hired driver would try to extort more money from them before they got home. He was annoyed to realize they would not reach the gates of Rome until well after dark, and beginning to worry. He hated traveling at night. In spite of the warriors the city assigned to patrol the approaches to Rome, the roads were not safe. The most trusted drivers had been known to betray their passengers to outlaws for a share of the profits.

As a member of the Roman Senate and the owner of a far-flung trading business, Propertius Cocles sometimes engaged in a bit of spying. Following his recent report on current Etruscan military strength, he had been rewarded by King Tarquinius with an estate in the country. The understanding was that in return, Propertius would put his property at the service of Tarquinius whenever required. Roman kings occasionally found themselves in need of a secret hideaway.

In truth the estate was little more than a sprawling farm bisected by a tributary of the Tiber, but the soil was fertile and with enough slaves, a man could produce an excellent profit. And there were always enough slaves, more than ever now that Rome was beginning to expand.

As they jolted along in the high-wheeled wooden cart behind a bristle-maned Thracian horse, Delphia was enthusing, "Now that I've seen the land I have so many ideas, Propertius. We must build a villa for ourselves overlooking the river, so we can get away from the heat of Rome in the summer. It never seems to bother you, of course, but myself and the children suffer dreadfully. I want an enclosed garden where the younger children can play, and separate slave quarters, and perhaps a . . ."

Propertius was used to Delphia's chatter. The bulk of her conversation consisted of demands to which he responded with unfailing agreement—although he never really listened. He would build what he wanted and his wife would have to . . .

"What is that? Gods defend us!"

Propertius's musings were cut short by Delphia's shriek of horror. At the same time their driver began furiously plying the whip, but the Thracian horse was fat and sleepy. It broke into a trot instead of the gallop the situation demanded.

The monstrosity that came hurtling toward them down the cedar-covered slope was enough to chill the spine. Though man-shaped, it was not a man but a massive shaggy horror. The curious rolling gait of the thing was deceptively swift; in spite of the driver's frantic efforts, in a few moments it had reached the road and was bounding toward the cart in prodigious leaps.

Only then did Propertius's numbed brain realize that one of the monster's disproportionately long forelimbs was carrying a club.

Springing to his feet, the Roman shouted, "Help! Someone help us!" as loud as he could. But there were no patrols within range of his voice. The hilly, wooded countryside through which they were passing was empty except for occasional scattered farmsteads. There was no one nearby to save them—and their hired driver was useless. He could only gape in horror as their attacker leaped for the horse.

Too late the animal realized its danger and plunged forward. Simultaneously the shaggy creature hit it between the eyes with a mighty blow. The sickening smash of the skull was clearly audible, even above Propertius's calls for help. The horse fell dead in the traces, bringing the cart to a shuddering halt.

Lifting the club to its mouth, the monster licked at the blood and brain matter clinging to the wood and grunted with pleasure. It might have been satisfied with its equine prey had not the driver panicked and leaped out of the cart at that moment, slashing at the creature with his knife. With a roar, the thing took a swipe at the man that knocked his head from his shoulders.

Delphia's screams drew the creature's attention to the white-faced passengers. Curious, it started toward the cart, nostrils flaring, trying to decide if these hairless ones were its own kind or simply meat. The brute was making appalling noises, a combination of growls and grunts that so unnerved Propertius that his knees gave way. He slumped back onto the seat, moaning in terror and clutching his chest.

Seeing her husband on the verge of fainting had quite the opposite effect on Delphia. Her terrified shrieks were transformed into an ear-splitting yowl of anger as she snatched up the whip the driver had dropped and lashed it across the face of the monster. The brute paused for the briefest moment, staring at her in obvious surprise. An overlong pink tongue traced the bloody cut on its hairy cheek.

Then, with a grunt, it scrambled over the side of the cart.

Seen up close, the creature was even more horrific than Delphia had realized. Its skull was grotesquely large, back-slanting, with a shelflike brow extending over sunken eyes. The broad, flat nose had cavernous nostrils, the slobbering mouth stretched in a disgusting grin. Except for its face, the monster was covered with filthy reddish hair, and the breath that washed over Delphia was so foul she thought she would vomit.

Worst of all, however, were the eyes. Staring at her with an expression of murderous hunger, they were obviously intelligent and very close to being human. At this realization, Delphia came close to fainting herself.

The monster's grin stretched even further to display cruel yellow fangs. Leaning back to give itself room in the cramped confines of the cart, it raised the club for the killing blow—just as the first stone hit it in the back of the head.

He gave a grunt of surprise. Turning, He saw another hairless one running toward him. With incredible agility the human was scooping up rocks from the road as he ran and hurling them one after another.

The next hard-flung stone struck He squarely on the nose. His roar of pain echoed across the countryside. When the sound reached the cave on the distant hillside and his waiting She, the female responded.

Her mate was in danger!

Frantically, She called to him again and again, raising her voice in an eerie, ululating cry that rebounded from hill to hill; a cry born of the swiftly descending night and an even more ancient darkness.

It was the loneliest sound in the world.

When the stranger leaped into the cart to grapple with the pain-dazed monster, Delphia seized the opportunity to scramble out. Then she reached over the side and tugged desperately at her husband. "Come, Propertius, hurry! While they're fighting we can get away."

The Roman almost fell as he stepped to the ground; only his wife's outstretched arms saved him.

Meanwhile the stranger had succeeded in wrenching the club away from the monster. The thing possessed extraordinary strength, but its reactions were slow. When he pried the club from its grip and threw it as far from the cart as possible, the brute turned to watch it rather than concentrating on fighting its opponent.

In that moment Horatrim wrapped his hands around the creature's neck.

TWENTY-FIVE

From the moment he heard the first screams for help, he had been aware of a singing in his blood. "Stay here and stay out of sight, Mother," he had told Vesi, seating her on a large stone behind a screen of cedars. Then he began to run in the direction of the screams.

Pepan's *hia* followed.

The singing had intensified as Horatrim ran. It became the sound of a thousand bees—or a thousand voices—humming confidently through his veins, giving specific directions to his limbs and muscles. By the time he came in sight of the cart on the roadway, his body had known exactly what to do.

The stones Horatrim threw distracted and then briefly disabled the monster, allowing him to enter the cart and close with it. His hands were hardly large enough to encompass the massive, muscular throat, but his fingers knew just where the nerves and veins were located beneath the skin. He pinched the windpipe shut, then compressed the thick artery that brought blood to the brain.

The creature slumped immediately, not unconscious but shocked by the pain and confused by the shadows that had gathered so quickly, the numbness that threatened its limbs.

Step by step Horatrim forced it backward, out of the cart. They staggered together to the ground. Once it felt solid earth under its feet, the creature erupted in a frenzy. It broke free of Horatrim and ran off into the darkness, leaving him holding a handful of russet hair and a patch of flesh torn from its hide. As it ran the monster emitted another chilling, inhuman cry. In the distance, something answered.

Horatrim threw down the hair and torn flesh in disgust and turned to the couple from the cart. They were both trembling but unhurt. Gently, he led them away from the road and helped them sit down. They wrapped their arms around each other and sat watching him like two terrified children as he went back to the cart to examine first the driver, then the horse. Nothing could be done for either.

Horatrim returned to the pair he had rescued. "You cannot stay out here in the open tonight," he said to the man, a short, stocky individual with a fringe of graying hair around a head rapidly going bald. The man merely stared at him. Horatrim tried again, finding a different language on his tongue. "Where were you going when you were attacked?" he asked.

Propertius shook himself as if awakening from a bad dream. A sense of relief washed over him. Their rescuer was not only a man like himself, but also spoke Latin, albeit with a strange accent, a man of some learning. "My wife and I were returning to Rome," he replied in a voice that still quavered slightly. "I am called Propertius Cocles, and I am in your debt for saving our lives."

"The . . . the gods were with me. They sent me to you. You owe me nothing. But come, we should move away from here; the bodies will bring scavengers." He urged the couple down the road toward the hiding place where he had left Vesi.

"I am in your debt," Propertius insisted on repeating as they walked. "I am a man of no small importance, and my honor is precious to me. I always pay what I owe. You can ask anything of me and it is yours. Just tell me your name and family, that I may do you—and them—proper honor."

"I am called Horatrim. As for my family . . ." The young man hesitated, then went on, still guided by the strange music surging through him, "My mother is my only family. We are Rasne. Travelers on our way to Rome."

The woman brightened. "Etruscan? How wonderful! I do admire the Etruscans, they are so very elegant." Delphia, a person of warm affections and instant enthusiasms, was ready to welcome this new hero unreservedly.

Her husband was more cautious. Horatrim's background gave him pause. For generations there had been sporadic conflict between Etruria and the tribes of Latium, although never enough to put an end to trade. Frequent intermarriage had done little to lessen the tension. The Etruscans resented the rise of a more vigorous culture, the people of Latium were jealous of past Etrurian achievements.

In spite of this stormy relationship, in Roman society an ancient Etruscan bloodline was highly desirable. To be considered *patrician*, a member of the nobility, it was almost essential to have at least one Etruscan antecedent. The present king was a perfect example. Lucius Tarquinius Superbius frequently called attention to the pedigree of his Etruscan father and tended to overlook his mother's Latin family.

Years of experience trading with the tribes of Etruria had made Propertius wary however. The Etruscans believed that every aspect of their lives was influenced by gods and demons, by the shades of their ancestors and the malice of disembodied spirits. The result was a complicated culture where countless invisible entities had to be placated before the smallest action could be taken. It often got in the way of business.

Propertius mistrusted mysticism; he put little faith in things he could not see and count. In this he differed from most of his contemporaries. Burgeoning Rome was seeking an enhanced spiritual identity. Simple pastoral gods of field and forest were being superseded by more esoteric deities, each with its own priests and rituals shrouded in mystery, though as a businessman, Propertius could appreciate that there was money in religion.

In the privacy of his own home Propertius scoffed at the proliferating religions. He was particularly contemptuous of the Cult of Magna Dea to which many of the women, including his wife, were devoted. "It's nothing more than the attempt of idle women to usurp power for themselves," he said. "The only god Romans need is Mars. War is good for business."

Still, one must admit Etruria had attained a level of prosperity that was the envy of Latium. For generations wealth had poured into their cities from copper, lead, and iron mines, from farms and vineyards, from Eastern trade and Western piracy. The Etruscans insisted they owed their entire success to the benevolence of their gods.

Now this young man had appeared just in time to save the Roman and his wife from a monster. He had accomplished the feat with extraordinary skill and agility and was not even breathing hard afterward. "The gods were with me," was all he offered by way of explanation.

Propertius was prepared only to believe in what he could see and touch. Tonight, perhaps, he had seen a miracle: the gods working directly with and through a human. An Etruscan. A young, handsome Etruscan, obviously educated and therefore from a good family.

Propertius had a daughter of marriageable age.

Arranging his face in his best trust-me-I'm-an-honest-trader smile, he said, "Since you're going to Rome anyway, Horatrim, we would be grateful if you would accompany us. I fear we shall have to travel on foot the rest of the way, but it's not far now. You will stay the night with us of course; in fact, I insist you stay for as long as it pleases you. I want to hear more about these gods of yours." He eyed his rescuer's filthy clothing of uncured hides. "And surely we can find you something better to wear. I have a son almost your size."

"I would be happy to see you safely home, but I'm not alone. I have my mother with me. I left her at a safe distance when I heard the screaming."

"Bring her too!" Propertius insisted. "Any woman who gave birth to such a hero is welcome under my roof. We'll treat her with every courtesy, I assure you. Where is she? I want to congratulate her on her son."

Horatrim hesitated. Here was an offer of shelter and protection for Vesi, but it was coming from one of the Romans. Yet was he not being led into the very heart of the Roman world anyway? The knowledge that mysteriously had been imparted to his muscles was of no help in this situation. He needed to confer with Vesi—or rather, with the gods who spoke through Vesi. But he dare not leave the Roman couple alone, not with the monster's voice still reverberating across the hills.

"Come with me," Horatrim said to Propertius and his wife. "I'll take you to my mother."

Night had fallen by this time; a humid, overcast night, an obsidian night in which unseen entities whispered and rustled. He was accustomed to a presence at his back that he assumed was that of the gods, the *Ais*. But there were other invisibles too, less benign ones. He could feel them, watching, waiting.

Horatrim was anxious to get back to Vesi.

When Horatrim had run off in the direction of the screams, Vesi had waited patiently where he left her. Waiting did not bother her. Nothing bothered her. The boulder on which she sat radiated residual warmth from the sun.

When the hooded figures slunk out of the night, she paid them no attention.

They had been trying to find a safe place where their injured comrade could be left to recover, if possible. They stumbled upon Vesi quite by accident. It was one of the tenets of their religion that nothing ever happened by accident however. Finding the woman was surely part of the goddess' plan. So while Vesi looked on mute and uncomprehending, the hooded beings addressed their deity and asked for guidance.

An answer came, very soon.

They were delighted to discover that Pythia was no longer displeased with them; in fact, she congratulated them for having done well indeed.

Then she took control of the situation.

Horatrim found Vesi just as he had left her, sitting on a boulder in the darkness with her fingers laced around her knees. Hurrying to her side, he put his fingers under her chin and turned her face up toward him. She did not speak but he liked to believe that she recognized him. He needed to believe.

"This is Vesi of the Silver People," he told the two Romans.

The woman on the rock said nothing.

Propertius leaned forward to peer at her in the gloom. "Is she ill?"

"No, just . . . quiet. We were . . . attacked by brigands, and she was badly injured some time ago. As a result she stopped speaking."

"Ah, that's a pity. Have you had a physician look at her? We have several in Rome who might be able to help. I will arrange for the best of them for you."

"Truly we have been led to you by the gods," replied Horatrim.

He put his hand under Vesi's elbow and lifted, and she came obediently to her feet. "We are going now, Mother. These kind people have offered us aid and shelter."

"I am Propertius, dear lady," the beaming Roman introduced himself. "And this is my wife, Delphia. I hope you will consider us your friends."

"We are indebted to your son for our lives," the woman added. "What he did was so wonderful; you should have seen him!"

Vesi said nothing.

Delphia turned to Horatius. "Does she never speak?"

"Rarely."

"And you have been looking after her for how long?"

"Most of my adult life," Horatrim replied with truth.

"You are indeed a hero," declared Delphia. Her voice choked. "A son any mother should be proud of."

TWENTY-SIX

Horatrim kept his arm around his mother, Propertius had his around Delphia. The road was deeply rutted with cart and chariot tracks and difficult to walk upon, and occasionally the Roman or one of the women stumbled. But Horatrim never stumbled.

The warm night air smelled of cedar and cypress.

At last Propertius exclaimed thankfully, "See there, ahead? The gates of Rome!"

By comparison with the *spurae* of Etruria, Rome was very crude. To anyone who had seen stately, symmetrical Veii, Rome was a confused jumble of ramshackle huts and half-built halls, its lack of planning all too obvious. But Horatrim had seen no Etruscan cities. He walked along open-mouthed, swiveling his head from side to side in astonishment at the size of the place, the crowds, the noise. . . .

At night the narrow streets were alight with flaring torches and bustling with people. "This is the city that never sleeps," Propertius announced proudly.

Many of the buildings were constructed of timber and sods plastered with river mud, giving them the look of something thrown up in a hurry. Houses and shops and flat-roofed warehouses crowded together, clinging to the hillsides and to one another as if fearful they would slide down. Rome smelled of cooked food and rotting fruit and olive oil and animal dung and raw timber, of new construction and old midden heaps.

Hawkers thronged the streets in spite of the lateness of the hour, trying to persuade people to buy jellied eels and cheap trinkets. Garishly painted women stood outside the numerous *tavernae*, beckoning in a way Horatrim did not understand. A burst of profanity erupted from the open door of one *taverna*; a woman's laugh gurgled merrily from another direction. Elsewhere someone was playing a pipe with a shrill, brassy tone that grated on the eardrum.

Suddenly Vesi's feet slid out from under her and she almost fell. Horatrim caught her before she could hit the ground. Gathering her into his arms, he stroked her hair and murmured soothingly. Then, indicating the torrent of raw sewage flowing down the street and turning its mud into slime, he asked Propertius, "Why don't they pave these streets and install gutters?" He did not know where the concept came from; it simply appeared in his mind.

Propertius paused in midstep. "Pavement? Here? Impossible, the streets are too steep and too crooked."

As if he were listening to someone else, Horatrim heard himself say with explanatory gestures, "You could begin with a series of temporary timber supports laid at angles . . . like this . . . then dig out above them and set permanent stone slabs across like this. . . ."

The Roman was looking at him thoughtfully. "You are the most astonishing young man. I want my brother to meet you. Like myself, Severus is a member of the Senate, but he's also the king's chief builder. Tarquinius is constantly demanding new schemes to improve Rome— for his own greater glory, of course—and it's Severus's responsibility to find them. I think he will be very interested in what you have to say. But that is all for the morrow. First, however, we all need a bath and a good night's rest."

Propertius led the way up first one narrow street and then another, eventually reaching a hilltop overlooking the city. The summit was crowned with houses. He halted before a door let into a plastered wall and beat a tattoo with his fist. After a time, the door creaked open. A slave holding an oil lamp stood in the doorway, blinking uncertainly. "Master? Master!"

"Of course it's me. Let us in, you fool. We're exhausted and we want to go to bed."

Guiding his mother by the elbow, Horatrim followed the Romans inside.

Pepan had never dreamed his *hia* would someday enter Rome. But where Horatrim and Vesi went, he followed. The nearer he got to the city, the more he disliked the sound that characterized Rome and Romans in the Otherworld, a brazen, strident staccato of muscle and might.

Viewed from the Otherworld, the house of Propertius was a mere translucent shell. Pepan easily penetrated the walls. Finding himself in the large, square room that formed the bulk of the dwelling, he surveyed his surroundings with distaste. No murals were painted on the walls, no tiled mosaics set in the floors. There were no flowers, no fountains, and only one statue, a crude clay representation of Mars in a small niche off to one side. Where was the household art? How could people survive without a clutter of beautiful things around them?

These people are pitifully unpolished, he thought with contempt. *The few pleasing things they possess, like the jewelry the woman wears, are merely copies of Etruscan styles. Do Romans create nothing worthwhile of their own? Or do they steal it all?*

As he mused, Pepan became aware of a swirling viscosity slowly filling the room. Like himself, other intangible beings had penetrated the walls. They were never far away, the denizens of the Otherworld. Lacking palpable bodies, they could have no physical effect on humankind. But that did not prevent their having influence.

Since joining their number, Pepan had witnessed demonstrations of their power. Disembodied spirits could fill a living human with elation or dread, could make the imagination soar or turn dreams into unrelenting nightmares. More to be feared than sword or spear, *siu* and corrupted *hia* could induce an insanity from which there was no returning.

And they were always vigilant, awaiting their chance. The bright lights of the physical world drew them like moths to a flame. So Pepan must be vigilant too. Never for a moment could he cease watching over Horatrim and Vesi, protecting them from all the things they could not see. He regretted that he was unable to protect them from physical dangers as well, but the gifts of the ancestors that surged through Horatrim's body were doing a good enough job of that.

The invisible beings that invaded the Roman house in Horatrim's wake had followed him from the northern verdant forests. Latium was not their natural home; the sunbaked hills were foreign to creatures of mist and mystery. But they were here now, prancing and gibbering and beckoning, flinging their snares, competing furiously with one another over the extraordinarily endowed spirit of Vesi's son.

Someone else thought young Horatrim well endowed.

In spite of the lateness of the hour when Propertius and Delphia returned home, their older children thronged around them. When Propertius told them of the attack and rescue, all eyes turned toward Horatrim.

One pair of eyes belonged to a girl Propertius identified as his eldest daughter, Livia. Aside from a few coarse-featured girls hiding behind their glowering and suspicious mothers in a Teumetian village, Horatrim had never seen a young woman before. At sixteen years of age, with a well-developed figure and a generous mouth, Livia already had considerable experience of young men. But she had seen no one like Horatrim; no one whom her father glowingly described as a hero.

She sidled close to him and gazed up from under her dark lashes. "Did you really save my parents from a monster?" Her voice was soft and sweet, with a delicious little trill at the end. She spoke in such a soft whisper that Horatrim had to lean forward to hear her—a trick she had learned from her maid.

Horatrim was quite unprepared for the effect she had upon him. He had reached physical maturity in an astonishingly short time; his emotions had lagged behind. Now they were beginning to catch up. His throat closed; his mouth went dry. He was certain she could hear his heart pounding.

"I . . . uh . . . that is . . ." Where were those voices in his head when he needed them? Why had they no guidance to offer now? He cast a beseeching glance toward his mother, but Vesi was equally noncommittal. She stood where he had left her, just inside the door. Her blank gaze took in the entire room and saw nothing.

Delphia was at no loss for words however. She already had decided that a brave young Etruscan would be a fine catch for one of her daughters and bring a touch of ancient elegance to the family. Her friends would be so jealous; they were already envious of the Etruscan baubles Propertius brought back to her from his travels. "Horatrim not only saved us both," she told Livia, "but has agreed to accept our hospitality so we can repay him properly. He—and his dear mother, of course—will be staying here with us for a while. We want you to make them feel welcome."

The girl smiled at Horatrim and dipped her head so that she could look at him through overlong lashes. "There is nothing I would like more," she said for his ears alone.

The bedazzled Horatrim grinned back.

Pepan, watching, was filled with misgivings. He did not want Vesi and her son to be in this city or this house. Rome was too raw and too new, the Romans too hungry for conquest. His *hia* was made uncomfortable by the strident martial music that identified them in the Otherworld, drowning out all other sounds. Why, he wondered, had the ancestors been so determined to bring Horatrim here? What had Rome ever meant for anyone—but trouble? What Rome could not assimilate, it destroyed.

TWENTY-SEVEN

L ivia liked to sleep late. Yet this morning she rose early, bathed carefully, and paid particular attention to her cosmetics, squinting at her reflection in the polished silver mirror. Having learned from one of the house slaves that Horatrim was in the garden, she managed "accidentally" to find him there. He was sitting on a bench in the sun at the side of the house tenderly feeding Vesi.

She observed him critically in the early morning light. His jaws were freshly shaven. A slave had attempted to perform the service for him, but Horatrim had refused. "I can do it myself; I know how to use knives." He did not want any stranger close to his bare throat with a naked blade in his hand; Wulv would never have approved. Now his cheeks were bare of stubble although a plethora of cuts and nicks showed he still had to master the technique.

For clothing he wore a toga borrowed from Livia's brother Quintus, a plump and petulant youth. A slave had folded the garment around Horatrim's body in the precise pleats of current Roman

fashion, which he thought a bit silly. What use were pleats, he wondered? He only tolerated the fashion because it was part of learning
about Rome.

His heavily callused feet were strapped into leather sandals. He had
never worn shoes before and disliked them intensely. From time to
time he stopped feeding Vesi long enough to scratch his calves, which
were irritated by the snug sandal thongs.

"Can't your mother feed herself?" Livia asked as she watched him.

Horatrim shook his head. "She has no interest in food. If I don't
put it into her mouth, she doesn't eat." Using a round-bowled olive-
wood spoon he tipped some lentil porridge into Vesi's mouth, then
offered her a sun-ripened fig. She would not bite into the fruit; he
had to tear off a tiny bit and place it on her tongue, but then she
chewed and swallowed. Vesi was wearing one of Delphia's old
gowns. Neither of them knew that it was cut in the Etruscan fashion.

Watching him attend his mother, Livia raised her eyebrows. She
found his attentions touching. "How very curious! I believe my father
said that she doesn't speak, either?"

"No, not really."

The Roman girl's eyes danced. "Well, I wager I can make her say
something. Just watch me." She spoke with the assurance of a pam-
pered and petted child who had never been refused anything.

Throwing herself down at Vesi's feet, Livia caught the woman's
hands between her own and gazed earnestly up into the impassive face.
"How lovely you are," she said. "At least you would be if you were
tidied up a bit and had your hair curled. I have pots and pots of cosmetics, some from as far away as Crete and Aegypt. My father is a
trader, you know; he imports all sorts of things. Would you like me to
paint your face for you?"

Vesi's vacant eyes stared through her.

Nonplused, Livia tried again. "Why were you wearing rags last
night? I thought Etruscan women were always exquisitely dressed. I see

Mother has loaned you one of her gowns, but mine are much nicer. You will have your choice of my best. Which would you prefer, my pleated yellow linen or my Aegyptian cotton with red embroidery around the hem?"

Something flickered at the back of Vesi's eyes.

"Aha—I told you," said Livia triumphantly.

Horatrim knelt in the dust beside Livia and took his mother's free hand. Maybe this was what she needed; female company.

Vesi's jaw sagged open and her features began softening like wax in the sun. An altered bone structure appeared beneath the flesh, subtly changing the shape of the face.

Livia dropped Vesi's hand as if it were hot.

Vesi's skin darkened and coarsened. Her throat muscles began to work, but the voice when it came was not Vesi's. Nor was it any of the voices Horatrim had heard before. Slurred, sibilant, it rose and fell in an eerie cadence that raised the hackles on his neck.

In her tomb among the Campanians, your mother's mother sleeps in a peplos *of fine wool, with amber at her breast.*

Livia gave a gasp. "What was that? Who spoke?"

Horatrim said honestly, "I don't know. But it was not my mother."

He would have been relieved that someone else heard the voices speaking to him through Vesi—had it not been for the fact that this was such a frightening voice.

He had walked away from fear once, but now it closed around his heart like an icy hand. Fear not for himself but for Vesi. Yet he could not have said just what he feared.

He said, "I've never heard my mother speak like that before."

"But I made her talk," Livia insisted shakily. "Didn't I?"

"Yes. Yes, I suppose you did."

Delighted with herself, Livia left Horatrim with his mother and rushed into the house to boast of her achievement.

But when she related the incident—and Vesi's puzzling words—to Delphia, the Roman matron gave a shriek. Followed by her baffled daughter, she ran outside.

Delphia bent over Vesi. "How did you know?" she demanded, grabbing the other woman by the shoulders. "How did you learn my grandmother was entombed at Campania? I never told anyone she was not Roman. And what gave you the idea that her funeral dress was a woolen *peplos?* Or that she wore an amber brooch? Nobody knew that, not even my husband."

Vesi stared up at Delphia.

"You're frightening my mother," warned Horatrim. He stepped between them, gently but firmly pushing Delphia aside. But Vesi did not look frightened. Nor were her features misshapen; the distortion had faded, as had the peculiar dark hue. She looked like herself again, except . . .

Except that once or twice, he thought he saw something move in her eyes. Something peered out of them. Something terrible.

Until that moment Pepan had been unaware of any change in Vesi. When Horatrim ran to answer the Romans's cry for help, Pepan had gone with him, fearing he was in danger. Then once Horatrim joined the Romans, their Otherworld signal, a strident blare of horns, had blotted out any other music. So Pepan had not detected the loss of the solitary pure note that identified Repana's daughter. Now he realized it was gone. Instead she emitted a faint but ceaseless sibilance.

Pepan was horrified. He had failed in his self-appointed duty; he had not protected his beloved Repana's daughter against invasion by a malign force.

When he sought to discover what had possessed her empty shell, his efforts were rebuffed by a solid core of blackness within Vesi. The voices of the ancestors, who had found it easier to speak through her unresisting mouth, were silenced, driven out.

Though Pepan had thought himself beyond human emotion, he was stricken with guilt and the terrible feeling of helplessness.

He had failed Repana and Vesi once, and now he had failed Vesi again. This time the cost would be much higher.

.　　.　　.

When Delphia told her husband about the incident, Propertius said, "The woman must be what the Etruscans call a seer. Such people are holy, beloved of the gods."

"I thought you had no religion. 'Sacrificing livestock to stone statues is a waste of saleable meat,' you said. 'I'm too practical to be taken in by hysterical priests and clouds of incense,' you said."

"I am practical. Practical enough to recognize an opportunity when it is beneath my very roof. This Etruscan pair is exceptional. It only remains to decide how best to exploit their assets to our advantage."

"What assets? I suspect they are fugitives; we've seen such people before. Perhaps Vesi made an unpopular pronouncement and fell out of favor with her tribe. I'm sure Horatrim will tell us the story when he feels he can trust us enough. In the meantime they have come away from Etruria with nothing more than the clothes on their backs."

Propertius gave his wife a pitying look. "Those rags are the least of their fortune," he told her. "I think we are going to hold a banquet, Delphia. A feast in honor of our rescue and our rescuers—and to introduce our pet Etruscans to a few select members of Roman society."

"Banquets are costly. Not that I'm objecting," she added quickly. "We don't entertain as much as any of the other Senate families. Do you plan to invite the king?"

"Of course."

Delphia stared at her husband. "Then the banquet will be twice as costly. There must be something in it for you aside from the expense?"

"Oh, yes," Propertius assured his wife. "Yes, indeed there is." He was positively glowing with anticipation.

The household was thrown into a frenzy of preparation. Horatrim found himself very much in the way; everyone seemed to have something to do but him. Within the walls there was no place where a boy used to the silences of the forest could find peace and quiet.

174

The front door of the Roman house opened directly into one large, rectangular room where most daytime activities took place, including meetings with Propertius's business clients. Off this were several cramped cubicles that served as bedchambers for family and guests. Slaves had to be satisfied with sleeping on the floor in the kitchen or in one of the overcrowded storerooms at the rear.

The house was stuffy and poorly ventilated, with only small windows high up under the eaves to keep passersby from peering in. In spite of the lamps that were kept burning throughout the day and polluting the atmosphere with malodorous smoke, the interior remained dark and gloomy.

As he walked around the rooms, Horatrim could not help but imagine the alterations he would make if the house were his.

Like all meals, the banquet was to be served in the main room. Couches were arranged around a large table so guests could recline as they ate. Horatrim was not sure he approved of eating while lying propped on one elbow. His mother and grandmother had done so, but Wulv had always insisted on squatting on his haunches while he ate, claiming it made the food easier to digest.

"I miss Wulv," he was saying to Vesi when the slaves Delphia had assigned arrived. It was their duty to bathe her and dress her and make her presentable for the king of Rome.

Horatrim wondered what a king would look like.

A dozen other guests arrived before the man known as Tarquinius Superbius was expected to appear. Several of them were members of the Senate, identifiable by the broad purple stripe on their elaborately folded and draped togas.

"Only kings and senators wear purple," Propertius had explained to Horatrim beforehand. "The color is very rare and precious because ten thousand murex shells must be crushed to produce a usable quantity of dye. Whenever you meet a Roman wearing purple you must show the utmost respect."

"What is so special about senators?"

Propertius was surprised that anyone could be so naive, but replied patiently, "Every senator is the head, the *paterfamilias*, of a leading Roman family. Upon the death or discredit of the king, it is the function of the Senate to nominate a new king from among our own class, the *patricians*. The nominee is then voted upon by an assembly of the people, but in my time Rome has never failed to accept the choice of the Senate. Although the king has supreme power, the senators serve as his advisors. Our influence therefore is considerable."

Horatrim, who understood only a little of this, had contrived to look impressed. "So you are really the power behind the king?" he asked.

"But of course," Propertius lied.

As his guests arrived, Propertius introduced the Etruscans as if they were at least as important as senators. "These are our valued friends," he would say, while Delphia chirped, "They are of the Rasne, you know, the Silver People. The oldest and most noble line in Etruria."

Horatrim smiled politely and tried to remember names, but Vesi responded as usual, with no response. She merely stood, powdered and perfumed and silent.

When Propertius's brother Severus arrived, he proved to be as tall and lean as the trader was short and stout. He was accompanied by a fine-boned man with a dark complexion and a closed, enigmatic face. "This is Khebet, an Aegyptian, a trusted and honored associate, who is visiting me for a time on a matter of business," Severus announced to the other guests, "so I brought him along."

Propertius already seemed to know Khebet; the two exchanged brief nods. The Romans took the Aegyptian's appearance for granted, but Horatrim could not help staring at him like any small boy confronted with marvels. Khebet wore a narrow gown of striped, lustrous fabric fitted very close to his lean body and cinched at the waist with a broad swath of supple leather. Folds of white cloth formed an elaborate headdress, completely covering his bald head. But his clothing was not the most remarkable thing about him, Horatrim decided. Never before had he seen a man whose eyes were outlined with kohl, nor whose lips were touched with some red cosmetic. The young man briefly wondered if Khebet could be a woman.

Introductions concluded, Severus caught Propertius by the elbow and led him off to one side. "Are you mad, brother? Whatever made you bring such a pair into your home?" he asked, nodding toward Horatrim and Vesi. "People you know nothing about—did it never occur to you they could be spies?"

"Would you know a spy if you saw one?"

"I am sure I would."

"And would the Etruscans send a mute woman and a mere youth to do their spying?"

"Perhaps not," Severus reluctantly conceded. "But they look hungry to me, particularly the woman. They look like the sort of beggars who will rob you blind."

"You always were a good judge of character," Propertius replied sarcastically.

"And here you are displaying your foolishness to the rest of the Senate and in front of the king."

"As it happens, Severus, that young man over there saved my life. That's all the recommendation he needs. In addition, however, he has some very interesting talents. You'll be sitting next to him at table tonight; I suggest you ask him what he thinks of Rome's streets." The trader gave his brother a cryptic smile.

When at last a yellow-haired slave announced "Tarquinius Superbius, King of Rome!" Horatrim turned eagerly toward the door. The person who entered was a profound disappointment. Although he wore a robe of royal purple and was flanked by a towering pair of Numidian slaves, Tarquin the Superb was a skinny little man with a nose like a vulture and the eyes of a ferret.

"So that is what kings look like," Horatrim whispered to Propertius.

The Roman chuckled. "That's what *this* king looks like, but he's hardly typical. Anyone with the right bloodlines can become king if he's determined enough or crafty enough or wealthy enough."

"Which is Tarquinius Superbius?" Horatrim wondered. "Determined, crafty, or wealthy?"

"All three," Propertius replied. "In addition, his father was once king of Rome himself. He was the late lamented Tarquinius Priscus of the tribe of the Tarquins."

As soon as the king had been greeted effusively, all females with the exception of the hostess were ushered from the room. This, Horatrim understood, was the Roman custom, although Livia threw a wistful parting glance over her shoulder as she left and made sure Horatrim saw her flutter her eyelashes at him.

One other female did remain however. When a slave tried to lead Vesi away, her eyes came alive.

I stay, said that peculiar, sibilant voice.

The slave threw a questioning look toward Propertius.

That one has no power over me, the voice announced.

A silence fell over the room.

When the moon hangs by its horns, a trader will pass through the gate and a king will dance with the black goat.

Now all heads were turned toward Vesi. The voice did not seem to come from her mouth in the normal way, for her lips did not move. Rather, it issued from some cavern deep within her, echoing eerily as if it had traveled a great distance through subterranean passageways.

Khebet the Aegyptian sat bolt upright on his couch.

"What did she say?" Tarquinius demanded to know, blinking shortsightedly at the woman. "Is there something wrong with her?"

Delphia immediately shoved the slave aside and put her own arm around the Etruscan woman. "Vesi," she told the king, "is a seer of visions. She described my grandmother in her tomb with details she could not possibly have known."

Propertius added, "This is a very holy woman, Lord Tarquinius.

One of the reasons for tonight's banquet was so you could meet her. I had planned to have her join us again after the meal, you see, and . . ."

Tarquinius was not listening. With his bodyguards hovering close on either side, he approached Vesi.

For a moment her eyes glittered like black stones seen through a thin layer of ice.

"Do you know who I am?" the king demanded.

Although her gaze turned in his direction, he had the disquieting feeling that she was not seeing him.

"I am Lucius Tarquinius Superbius, King of Rome."

The gleam began to fade from Vesi's eyes, and her head drooped.

"Explain to me what you meant by what you just said about a king dancing with a goat?" Catching hold of Vesi's chin, he raised her head. But the eyes into which Tarquinius glared were dull and lifeless, all intelligence extinguished.

Tarquinius turned toward Propertius. "What's the matter with this woman? Is she a fool? How dare she refuse to respond to me!"

"She was badly injured some time ago, lord," Propertius hastened to explain. "But she is a holy woman, I assure you. A prophetess, as you have seen. It's just that her gift . . . ah . . . comes and goes. I fear it is not under anyone's command, even a king's. While we await its return, perhaps you would care to sample the feast we have prepared for you?"

Giving Propertius a threatening look that indicated Vesi's "gift" had better reappear before the evening was over, Tarquinius allowed himself to be shown to the table. But he insisted the Etruscan woman remain in the room. "Stand her over there where I can see her," he ordered.

Pepan was dismayed. The arrival of the king of Rome had thrown the Otherworld entities into a frenzy. *Hia* who had never been incarnated in the flesh were able to see past and future as one and therefore were aware of Tarquinius's destiny. Something about his future excited them unbearably.

Will he die soon? Pepan wondered. *Are they hoping to capture his* hia?
The atmosphere darkened, portent of a struggle.

Pepan hovered close to Vesi and Horatrim in order to protect them
from whatever was to come. But he knew he could really offer little protection. Horatrim's gifts were formidable and he was learning more
about them all the time. Soon he would need no help from anyone. As
for Vesi . . .

She stood where the slaves had stationed her, half a dozen paces
away from the table. Her blank gaze stared off into space. But she was
no longer empty. Pepan was all too aware of the darkness within her,
the seething blackness that roiled and hissed.

The banquet Propertius had prepared was the finest the house could
offer. As the guests reclined on couches around the table, slaves served
the first course, which consisted of bowls of black and green olives and
platters of dormice seasoned with poppy seeds and honey. This was followed by hens in pastry, horsemeat boiled with juniper berries, and an
enormous roast pig.

When the pork was presented, Propertius scowled in monumental
displeasure and shouted at the slaves carrying the platter, "This pig has
not been properly gutted! Send for the cook."

The cook was a handsome yellow-haired slave from Thessaly who
appeared at a trot. Propertius repeated the charge. Bowing low, the
man replied, "Oh, but it has been gutted, my lord. I would never
embarrass my master with improperly prepared food."

"If you lie I will have you flogged. Slash open the belly and prove
your words if you can."

Producing a large knife with a dramatic flourish, the cook slashed
open the belly. Out tumbled a vast quantity of spicy blood puddings and
steaming sausages, overflowing the platter and spilling onto the table.
Propertius and the cook burst into laughter at the guests' amazement.

Even Tarquinius smiled. "Well done, Propertius. I trust you will
breed more pigs like that and have them delivered to my kitchens?"

"As soon as they can fly," the trader assured him. Laughter rippled around the table. Horatrim's childish whoop was the loudest of all.

Flagons of wine and beer were kept refilled as course after course subsequently appeared, offering everything from globe artichokes to bulls' testicles. By watching the other guests, Horatrim discovered how to eat both delicacies. He was quite enjoying himself, though he was uncomfortably aware of his mother standing like a statue in the background.

He had been placed between Severus and Delphia. Between courses, Propertius's brother turned to Horatrim. "For some reason known only to himself, my brother suggests I ask you about Roman streets?"

New concepts leaped into Horatrim's mind. He began describing drainage and paving techniques, sketching ideas on the edge of his toga with a finger wetted in red wine, while a rapt Severus listened and watched. "You could use the same method on the approaches to the city," the young man elaborated. "Paved roads leading to Rome would surely improve trade."

Overhearing, Tarquinius leaned forward. "Does he know what he's talking about, Severus?"

"I think so, my lord. I've never seen that type of paving myself, but I believe it is common in Etruria, where the streets have stood the test of centuries."

"Maybe I should order them built, eh?"

At that moment an eerie, sibilant voice rang through the room.

He who builds that which endures, becomes immortal.

Tarquinius sat bolt upright as everyone turned to look at Vesi. "That prophecy was meant for me! Did you hear what she said; she said I could become immortal. I must have that woman!"

TWENTY-EIGHT

A demon follows its child.

Though the *siu* could not feel love, it was bound to Horatrim by invisible bonds that could not be severed while the child lived. And while the child lived, it remained a danger to its sire.

Of all the creatures that were stalking Horatrim, the *siu* was the most deadly. It was in no hurry to close with its quarry however. Once the *siu* picked up the trail, it was confident Horatrim could not escape. Vesi was a handicap the youth could not overcome. The capture could be made in its own time; the kill in its own way. The *siu* followed the young man patiently, savoring the luxury of anticipation. Enjoying, too, the opportunity to observe the changes that had taken place in the world since it last walked upon the earth with human feet.

Its human life had always been characterized by intellectual curiosity.

. . .

The walls of Rome did not impress the *siu*.

He recalled a much grander city, a citadel of unrivaled splendor where once his name had been almost as respected as that of the Great King, the Lawgiver. He had walked its streets in those long-lost days when he wore flesh, holding his proud head high while people excitedly pointed him out to one another.

"There he is! Bur-Sin, with the light of genius in his face. See the wealth of the jewels on his breast, the gold and glass and lapis lazuli. They are gifts from the Great King, small payment in return for the fabulous creation he is erecting."

A small return indeed, Bur-Sin had thought. As the days passed and work progressed, he had been increasingly aware of how unique, how spectacular his achievement would be when it was finished. Nothing remotely like it existed in the Kingdom of the Two Rivers or even beyond.

As chief designer and architect, Bur-Sin had labored for years over the plans before building began. On countless mud tablets he had drawn elaborate construction details. When his plans were finally approved by the Great King, he had become responsible for training and overseeing the laborers who did the actual building. At the same time he had personally searched the land for the rarest, most beautiful plants, jewels to be placed in the setting of the Hanging Gardens of Babylon.

Tier upon tier the gardens rose. They did not actually hang in the air, but were roof gardens built within the walls of the royal palace. Laid out in a series of ziggurats, or pyramidal towers, they were irrigated by pumps of the architect's own design, drawing water from the Euphrates River.

Almost every day the Great King came to see them. At intervals he would bestow another gift upon the architect, more jewels or a supple dancing girl with honeyed hips. The Great King knew his architect had an insatiable passion for women.

Then Bur-Sin began to notice that in conversation, the Great King invariably referred to the gardens as "my gardens." The name of the man who was creating them was never mentioned.

A thousand slaves labored, a thousand times the sun rose and sank, and still the Hanging Gardens were not completed. The Great King grew impatient. "How soon can I dedicate my gardens?" he demanded to know.

Bur-Sin lost his temper. "On the day when they bear my name, the gardens will be finished!"

The Great King had responded with a burst of temper of his own. "Arrogant servant, how dare you usurp the royal prerogative!"

"I am entitled to recognition for my work. It is not too much to ask. The people of Babylon already know who is responsible for the gardens. They will remember and revere me long after I am dead. I merely request that when foreign dignitaries come to view the gardens, as they will, they too should honor the builder's name."

"I am the builder!" thundered the Great King.

Bur-Sin had felt his rage turn to ice. "Then complete the Hanging Gardens yourself. As for me, I will offer my services elsewhere. Perhaps the Aegyptians will appreciate me. I can erect an equally splendid construction for them."

The Great King's rage knew no bounds. "I will never allow you to build a rival for my gardens! Seize him!"

Guards had tried to grab Bur-Sin, but he ran. He fled through the halls of the royal palace until at last he came to the Inner Temple, the private precincts where the Great King offered sacrifices to the god Marduk. In an alcove curtained with crimson silk the image of Marduk stood, an upright crocodile sheathed in gold.

Bur-Sin had prostrated himself before the statue. "Great Marduk, deliver me!" he pleaded.

They had found him there, cowering at the feet of the gilded saurian. Breaking the laws of sanctuary, the guards had dragged him away and taken him before the Great King. Then did Hammurabi the Lawgiver, the Just and Wise, pass the most unjust decision of his life.

"Put out his eyes," he said.

.   .   .

That was long ago. Now the *siu* who was once Bur-Sin walked again, not the ancient avenues of Babylon, but the muddy streets of Rome, stalking its prey.

TWENTY-NINE

The woman was red-eyed and weary. Since sundown she had been in and out of *tavernae* soliciting business, but the loins of the Romans were not responsive to her decayed charms. She hated the prospect of going home. Home was a tumbledown hut at the foot of the Palatine Hill. Built into the hillside above were a number of tombs, bleak reminders of mortality. On the summit stood some of the finest houses in Rome. Their sewage combined with noxious liquors seeping from the tombs to rot the footings of her walls. She had grown so used to the smell that she no longer noticed it.

Her shack was dark and lonely, and without a client for the night, Justine could not even buy oil for her lamp. There was nothing to eat either, but that scarcely mattered anymore. Her teeth were so rotten she could hardly chew and had to stifle her hunger pangs with soggy bread and overripe fruit when she could get them. There was little pleasure in such a diet. At last she admitted defeat and set out for the Palatine.

The night seemed darker than any she could remember. "I am too old for this," she said, talking to herself for company. "When I was young and beautiful they all wanted me; oh yes, I could command any price then. Now they laugh at me."

Almost every statement she made was prefaced by, "When I was young and beautiful," until the phrase had become a joke. "When you were young and beautiful that old she-wolf was still suckling Romulus and Remus!" her listeners would jeer.

People could be so cruel. Justine's eyes brimmed with self-pity. Once she had laughed at older harlots who were glad to settle for marriage to some rough farmer from the country and the security of food on the table every night. In her youth she had believed such women were foolishly sacrificing freedom for the drudgery of slavery. Now she would have accepted an offer of marriage from even the most impoverished goatherd or lime digger and been grateful, but the offers had dried up with the last of her beauty.

"This winter I'll be forced to get a bowl and beg," she muttered to herself. Then a remnant of almost-forgotten pride surfaced. "No, I won't beg. I'll kill myself first. I will. I'd rather be dead."

In the enveloping darkness, something snickered.

The woman froze. "Who's there?"

Silence. But the silence was not total; she could swear she heard breathing close by. She reached into the neck of her gown and fumbled between her scrawny, sagging breasts and produced a sliver of metal. "Who's there, I say. I warn you, I have a dagger here and I know how to use it."

This time there was no mistaking the low chuckle. The sound came from off to her right, in the direction of the marshy waste ground that comprised much of the valley between the Capitoline and Palatine Hills. The path she usually took home lay across that space, but she felt a curious disinclination to follow it. "Perhaps if I go back to that last tavern my luck will turn," she murmured to herself.

Facing around, she began to retrace her steps. The breathing followed her.

Other sounds accompanied it now, whispers and murmurs and obscene smacking noises. She felt a sudden relief. She was being followed by young boys then, males still embarrassed by their burgeoning sexuality and resorting to childish games. But she knew how to deal with them.

Halting abruptly, she threw wide her arms. "That's all right. You needn't be afraid. Step up and show me what you're made of. I'll be good to you; I'll break you in right. Come now," she wheedled, "come to me."

Out of the darkness, something came.

Justine had thought nothing could shock her anymore, but she was wrong.

From the shadows swarmed amorphous apparitions that hissed and growled and sniggered, writhing obscenely as they advanced. Some appeared as gaping mouths with slimy tongues or slobbering lips that mimicked sucking. Others were oversized genital organs, a phalanx of throbbing phalluses advancing on the horrified woman. Still others were mere sparks of sulfurous light that gave off the stench of carrion.

Central among them was a figure who appeared human yet moved in rhythm with the disgusting phantasmagoria. He chuckled again.

"You called me?" asked the *siu*.

Justine tried to run. He caught her before she had gone more than a few steps and threw her to the ground. Gibbering, the other horrid forms closed around them in anticipation.

"You must forgive my admirers," the demon growled. "From time to time they follow me like shadows, and they are just about as useful. Let us dispense with them, shall we?" He whirled on his companions with such a ghastly roar that they faded into the night, leaving him alone with his prey.

Justine fought with all her strength and the experience of too many years spent on the streets. She knew how to hurt a man. She kicked and clawed until he pinned her wrists with one hand, squeezing them tightly enough to block circulation. He stopped her from kicking him by the simple expedient of throwing his full weight on top of her.

To her surprise, he was not nearly as heavy as he looked. But he stank abominably.

She tried to scream then. He covered her mouth with his own and swallowed the scream, then drew back enough to say, "I suppose it is too much to hope you might be a virgin?"

Before she could reply he chuckled again. The sound was mirthless and cruel. "No, I suppose not. A pity."

"Do whatever you want; just don't kill me!"

"Kill you? I assure you, the mere thought of a corpse disgusts me." Justine felt a shudder run through the body pressed against her own.

"I'll do anything . . ."

"Good, very good. I appreciate compliance in a woman. Tell me, what do you want most in all the world?"

"To get away from you!" she snapped.

"Oh, we can't allow that. Try again. Consider your situation. You are a harlot, I suspect, and thus in the business of selling yourself. If in exchange you could ask for anything you liked, no matter how impossible, what would you ask for?"

Her frantic mind skittered sideways and she said the first thing that popped into her head. "I'd ask for my youth back."

"Better, much better. I think that could be arranged."

"Don't be ridiculous. I'm old; I'm thirty," Justine confessed in a whisper. She turned her head to one side, trying to avoid his fetid breath.

As if he read her mind, he said, "Do you dislike my odor? Someday you will smell even worse, unless you find a way to stop time. That is what I can offer you. In exchange for something I require, I can make you half your age and keep you young forever."

"You're mad."

"The gift I describe is in my power to give, I assure you."

"Only a demon could do such a thing!"

He stroked her sunken cheek. "And what do you think I am? I can make this flesh bloom again and do more besides, much, much more. In return, however, I have special needs that must be satisfied."

Justine could not imagine what "special needs" this repulsive being might have. She was convinced he was mad and dangerous as well. In her years walking the streets of Rome she had met any number of madmen and learned it was best to placate them whenever possible.

"Just let me get up," she urged, "and we can talk. I'm not used to doing business like this."

He chuckled again. "On the contrary, I should say this is the very position in which you are most accustomed to doing business. But you may get up. If we are going to be partners, you deserve that courtesy."

Partners. The idea repelled her. But if she could stall for time, perhaps she could find a way to escape. A few minutes ago she had been ready to consider dying; now she wanted most desperately to live.

"Do you indeed?" he asked abruptly, reading her thoughts, which were a clarion call in the Otherworld. In one lithe movement he was on his feet and reaching down to offer her a hand up.

Although she tried not to, Justine shrank from his touch. His hand was icy cold and very dry, the skin rough and flaking. His sharp nails bit into her palm like tiny fangs. "Take me home with you," he said. "We can talk there."

The last thing she wanted was to lead this lunatic to her home, but she had no choice. With fast-beating heart she made her way across the fetid waste ground at the foot of the hills. He followed close behind her. She did not have to look back to know he was there. She could smell him. Just knowing he was there made the flesh burn on the back of her neck. In fact, her skin felt peculiar all over, as if she had been in the sun too long. A hot flush radiated from the top of her head to the soles of her feet. She toyed with the idea of claiming disease—a trick a Scythian whore had taught her in her youth— then remembered that he could read her mind.

In the end she simply kept walking. For so many years she had done as men asked; the habit was deeply ingrained.

At last she came to the pitiful shack that was her home and tugged open the splintery door. There was no lock; she had nothing to protect, so she could not slam the door in his face and lock him out. But he was too close behind her anyway. She felt him brush past her into the darkness. Then she heard the scratch of fingernails on pottery.

"I have no oil for that lamp," she started to say just as her one small lamp flared into light. He stood holding it in front of him while its flame threw eerie shadows on his face.

The sight made her nauseous.

"Do you not find me handsome?" he asked sardonically.

She could not bear to look at him. In the wavering light, his face was the color of putrid meat. "You must be diseased. Your skin is flaking off."

"Unfortunately that is correct, but not because of disease."

She could not resist asking, "Does it hurt?"

"You dear child. So tenderhearted."

"I'm not a child and I'm not tenderhearted either."

"But you would help me if you could?" he persisted.

"Of course, but I don't see how I . . ."

"In return for your youth, you will do anything?"

"Anything."

" 'Tis done, then. Now it is your turn." Reaching for her with one hand, he caught her by the wrist and drew her closer to the light. "Look down," he commanded. "Dear child."

Justine looked down.

The arm he was holding had been sunburnt and scrawny, scored with old scars; but even as she watched it began to change. The contours grew as plump and prettily rounded as in her youth. Her gnarled fingers became white and supple once more; then the broken fingernails were whole again, forming perfect arcs.

He slowly moved the lamplight along her arm, then across the front of her body. "Observe yourself, Justine."

She did not ask how he knew her name. Her attention was focused on the full, firm breasts plainly visible in the low neck of her gown.

He released his hold on her. Her discolored metal mirror appeared in his hand and he held it before her face. "What do you see, Justine?"

"Is that me?" she asked tremulously, lifting a wondering hand to her cheek.

The girl in the mirror copied her gesture exactly. The girl was barely fifteen, with eyes like sloes and a ripe, red mouth. Not a line marred her perfect complexion; she was vibrant with life.

Staring into the mirror, Justine said, "I used to look like that."

"You look like that now. And you will forever, unless I withdraw my gift. Or . . . if we should fail to conclude our business arrangement. . . ." He twisted the mirror away, then held it back. This time Justine found herself gazing upon the old familiar face that greeted her each morning, haggard and wrinkled, with pouches under the eyes and an apathetic expression.

She caught his hand. "Ah no, bring her back!"

"Are you certain?"

"Yes. Yes! I will do anything. Anything."

His lips quirked into a smile. "Somehow I thought you would," the demon said.

THIRTY

Horatrim was dismayed to hear Tarquinius demand possession of Vesi. But before he could leap to his feet in
protest, Delphia caught hold of his arm, squeezing firmly.
"Don't be rash. The king's bestowing a great honor on
her. Your mother will live in the royal palace and be treated like a
queen."

"I won't let my mother be any man's harlot!" Horatrim had never
heard the word before, yet it suddenly burned through his mind.

Tarquinius overheard the outburst and blandly replied, "You misunderstand my intention, Horatrim. I don't need her for my bed; I
have plenty of willing women. I want to install her as my personal
soothsayer."

Slowly Vesi turned her head and met her son's eyes. For a single
instant he thought he saw his mother's true expression: terrified, lost.
Then it faded and was gone.

.   .   .

It was close to noon the following morning when a sedan chair arrived at the house of Propertius Cocles and obsequious slaves offered their bowed backs for Vesi to step upon so she could climb in. She seemed quite content to go.

Severus had been too drunk to go home after the banquet, so he and Khebet had been given beds for the night. They now joined the party gathered at the door to wish Vesi farewell. Severus had a cloth soaked with vinegar wrapped around his head, but the Aegyptian showed no sign of a hangover. He was bathed, shaved, and neatly dressed, every hair in place. Even his fingernails were buffed and shining, and he exuded a throat-catching aroma of pungent herbs and exotic spices.

"I charge you to take good care of my friend," Delphia told the king's servants.

"And remind him that it was I who found her for him," added Propertius. Turning to Horatrim as the sedan chair disappeared down the street, he said, "You could not possibly have made better arrangements for your mother's welfare. Relax and be happy for her."

"But she speaks so rarely," Horatrim protested, "and when she does much of it is so obscure."

Severus interjected, "No matter how obscure her pronouncements, they will be taken as messages from the gods. Propertius doesn't set great store by the gods, but I assure you Tarquinius does. As does my friend Khebet," he added, indicating the Aegyptian.

Severus continued, "Unfortunately the rest of us have to work a bit harder at pleasing the king. I want to hear more about these paving ideas of yours, Horatrim. Propertius, do you mind if we take your guest on a little tour of the city? Perhaps the air will help clear my head."

"Go right ahead," said the trader with an indulgent wave of his hand. "I thought you would find Horatrim interesting. Just remember who introduced you to him."

"He will probably try and charge me an introduction fee," Severus grumbled as they strolled out into the street.

Rome by daylight was sprawling and squalid but still seethed with energy. The earliest settlers had been farmers who built their huts on the hills overlooking the Tiber in order to leave the fertile river valley free for grazing and cultivating. With the passage of time the pastoral settlement had gone through several transformations, becoming a market town for local produce, then a regional market involved in both export and import, then finally the headquarters of a fledgling bureaucracy devoted to managing the wealth of Rome. Now ambassadors and trade delegations from friend and foe alike made frequent visits to the city on the seven hills.

Horatrim noticed other kohl-eyed Aegyptians. Khebet even bowed politely to one, acknowledging recognition though nothing was said between them.

Khebet, it appeared, was a man of few words. He and Severus exchanged an occasional remark, but for the most part he was content to pace sedately beside the others. The only obvious interest he showed was in the new Temple of Jupiter, Juno, and Minerva that crowned the stony Capitoline Hill.

"I built that," Severus said proudly. "Completed it within the time allowed and under budget. Observe the Etruscan-style portico. That was to please Tarquinius, of course."

Rome was a city of wonders to Horatrim. He had never seen so many people in his life, and he was becoming increasingly aware that each person emitted a distinctive musical sound, a barely audible chime or lilt or even percussive beat. Some were pleasant, others discordant. Because he knew no different, Horatrim assumed that everyone else could hear this music, too.

"Listen!" he exclaimed.

Severus and Khebet stopped and looked at him quizzically.

"Do you hear that?"

"Hear what?" asked Severus. The Aegyptian said nothing, merely raised one eyebrow.

"That!" Horatrim insisted, turning his head from side to side. He was trying to identify the direction of the martial music he was hearing, a sound as of trumpets in the air. His gaze fell on a side street just as an unusually tall, strikingly handsome man came striding out into the sunlight. The man, who appeared not much older than himself, walked as if the earth was hardly good enough for him. He was followed by a company of ceremonial bodyguards wearing plumed helmets and carrying highly polished spears at a uniform angle. They too moved with arrogance and grace.

The tall man's eyes met Horatrim's. They were a clear green with no gentleness in them. Theirs was the look of an eagle. They examined the young man, then flickered across Severus and the Aegyptian . . . and dismissed them.

He strode past and was gone.

"Who was that, Severus?" Horatrim wanted to know. The force of the tall man's personality had jolted him across the space between them. "And wasn't he . . . splendid!"

"Him? He's Lars Porsena, a prince of Clusium."

"Clusium?"

"Hill country in Etruria, which makes him one of your own in a manner of speaking. He's visiting the king as head of a trade delegation. My brother knows him; Propertius knows everybody."

"A prince," murmured Horatrim, "from Etruria." He turned to watch the bodyguard march away up the street. They were tautly muscled, clean-shaven, well-drilled. He thought them more impressive than the Romax . . . Romans. "Were you ever a warrior?" he asked Severus.

"Me? I'm not such a fool as to be willing to lay down my life for someone else."

"But surely to be a warrior is a noble calling."

"I'm a senator. We do battle in a different way. When it comes to physical combat I prefer to be a spectator. I go to the arena whenever there's a performance scheduled and wager on my favorite fighter—or the bear—but I have no interest in risking my personal hide."

Eyes fixed on the fast-disappearing Lars Porsena and his men, Horatrim said, "I think I would like to be a warrior."

"You're a bit late. The Etruscans have lost their enthusiasm for warfare."

The young man smiled almost dreamily. "We might find it again."

"Better not let the king hear you say that. Our Tarquinius boasts of his noble Etruscan forebears, but he's really a Roman at heart. He truly believes the accident of having been born here makes him superior to anyone else, be they Hellenes or Carthaginians or even Etruscans. The welcome he gives trade delegations is all on the surface, good business for the city. If Lars Porsena or his warriors so much as waved a spear out of turn they would never see Etruria again.

"And speaking of Tarquinius . . . since we've come to a particularly steep street, why don't you show us what you mean about laying paving, so I can discuss it with the king?"

They spent the early afternoon wandering around Rome. The Aegyptian, Horatrim eventually learned, held an exalted position in his own country. "I am a priest of Anubis, the Jackal God," Khebet elaborated, briefly breaking his silence.

Severus took up the conversation. "Aegyptian priests are experts in mathematics, the science of numbers. They build quite remarkable temples by relying upon complex calculations no one here understands. Propertius knows Khebet through his trade connections in Aegypt, so he arranged for him to come and work with me for a time, instructing my men."

Khebet gave a faint smile, the merest tightening of his lips over his teeth. "In return you pledged sacrifices to Anubis, remember."

"Yes, yes, of course!" Severus hastily assured him. "Bounteous sacrifices, just as we agreed."

As they continued their stroll Severus called Horatrim's attention to the situation of various streets and asked for comment. In responding, the young man displayed a knowledge of construction that led the Roman to remark, "You certainly learned a lot in the cities of Etruria."

"I've never seen the cities of Etruria."

Severus's jaw dropped. Then he grinned. "Surely you jest with me."

"It's no jest. I was born and raised in the Great Forest. Rome is the only city I've ever seen."

197

"But that's simply not possible! How could you concoct such ideas out of nothing?"

"They don't come out of nothing. I . . . it's difficult to explain this, Severus. But I simply know these things. And sometimes I hear voices."

Khebet turned and gave him a penetrating look.

"Doesn't everyone hear voices?" Horatrim asked, surprised by the expression on the Aegyptian's face. "They tell me what to do. Sometimes," he added ruefully, thinking of the girl Livia.

Severus hardly knew how to react. On rare occasions, perhaps once in a generation, someone produced a totally new idea. He had heard of such god-gifted geniuses, though he had never met one himself. Yet if Horatrim spoke the truth he was one of that number. "If your knowledge originates in your own head," he told Horatrim, only half-joking, "we must be careful to see that no one chops it off."

Late afternoon found them approaching an expanse of damp, rat-infested waste ground in the valley between the Palatine and Capitoline Hills. Here was dumped every sort of rubbish from oyster shells and dead dogs to aborted infants. Around the perimeter stood an assortment of makeshift shacks, some little more than rotten planks leaning against each for support like drunkards leaving a tavern.

Horatrim remarked, "If this were drained you could build decent houses here. Or a market square or even some fine public building."

"How would you suggest draining it?"

The young man squatted on his haunches, picked up a stick from the ground, and began drawing diagrams in the mud. Severus and Khebet leaned over his shoulder, watching. From time to time the Aegyptian gave a murmur of approval.

His first diagram concluded, Horatius went on, "As for the river, I am surprised you have no substantial bridge across it. Surely it would be to the city's advantage to unite both banks by something wider and more stable than that flimsy wooden structure you have now. Look here. You could span the Tiber like this, starting at this point, using arches for support . . ."

Lost in his work, he drew furiously as the two men watched him in silent amazement.

At last Severus found the voice to say, "I want you to work for me, Horatrim. In fact, I insist upon it."

"Work for you? Why?"

"I'm the king's personal builder, his architect. When Tarquinius wants something constructed he commissions me to draw up the plans and contract materials and labor. There's always a nice profit to be made; he never questions the costs I quote him. No business head at all," Severus added with a wink. "While you, my young friend, have a quite remarkable head. If you're willing to come up with ideas exclusively for my firm, I will reward you handsomely. Very handsomely." He winked again.

"You want to buy my ideas?" Horatrim asked incredulously.

"Something like that, yes. An arrangement rather than a purchase however; one that would benefit us both. You would be apprenticed to me to learn the building trade, and in time you might even have a share of the business. A very small share, of course. What do you think?"

A short time ago Horatrim had been a primitive child living in the Great Forest. Now he was being accepted as a man and offered work of importance in the city of Rome.

For one wild moment he almost laughed, but he was afraid they would misunderstand. With an effort he kept his face serious. "My mother foresaw this, Severus. She said my future was here, though neither of us had ever been here and we did not even know any Romans. But she insisted we come. You know the rest."

The older man gave a low whistle. "She is obviously a great seer. But for great seers to survive, they must temper their pronouncements with discretion. I wonder what she'll foresee for our Tarquinius."

As the day wore on the three men were too preoccupied to think of food. Only when a bank of dark clouds swept in over the river did

Severus realize how late it was. "We had better go back to my brother's now, Horatrim. If I don't deliver you in time for dinner he'll suspect I've kidnapped his guest or begin charging me for your time."

When they reached the house, the first person Horatrim saw was Livia. The Roman girl was sitting casually by the door as if she had just paused there for a moment. In truth, she had spent an impatient day awaiting the young man's return. At sight of her, all of Horatrim's plans and designs went out of his head. Once more his inner voices failed to guide him, but he was beginning to feel more confident.

I can do this myself, he thought.

But when he attempted to strike up a conversation with the girl over dinner, the presence of so many other people in the room was a serious distraction. Severus was talking to Propertius; Khebet was wandering around the room, thoughtfully stroking his chin and ignoring everyone else; Delphia was instructing the steward; other slaves were preparing the table and couches for the evening meal; Livia's younger brothers and sisters were scampering back and forth or hovering close, giggling whenever Horatrim paused to talk to the girl, laughing aloud when she tried to open the conversation. There was no such thing as privacy.

"Is there somewhere else where we can talk, Livia?" he finally asked with an air of desperation.

"We could always go outside, but it's getting dark and the air smells of rain. Rain will ruin my hair." She patted her carefully arranged curls and smiled disingenuously. "You wouldn't want to see these dis-arranged, would you?"

"Ah, no. Of course not. They are . . . beautiful. But . . . is there no place else? Inside?"

"Only the sleeping chambers, and I share mine with my two sisters. If we go there they will come after us immediately out of curiosity."

"This is no way to construct a house."

Livia's laughter was gently mocking. "I suppose you know a better one?"

Now they came to him unbidden, singing through his blood.

"A house should be built around an unroofed courtyard so it forms a hollow square," said Horatrim, echoing his inner voices, hands moving to shape the design. "The exterior wall is blank, but every room opens onto the courtyard which lets light and air into the interior."

He could see it so clearly; as clear as a personal memory. "The house is two houses, really. The front portion is the public one, with a large reception area rather like your main room now, only much more elegant and comfortable. To provide additional light to this space there is an opening in the center of the ceiling. The tiled roof above slopes down on all four sides, throwing rainwater through spouts into a marble pool set in the center of the floor. This gives a sense of coolness and peace, while the reflection of the sky in the water provides an ever-changing work of art."

The girl was looking at him wide-eyed. The young man's voice had deepened, become stronger, more commanding, with the faintest hint of an accent.

"Off the principal reception area are chambers for dining or playing games and dice, whatever entertainments the host wants to provide for his guests. Or in fine weather he may take them into the courtyard, which has a columned portico down either side. Behind this portico are the servants' quarters, readily accessible to either part of the building. The rear half of the house comprises the private residence, with ample apartments and bathing facilities. Here the women of the family can enjoy themselves while the men conduct business and entertain clients at the front. The entire structure is light, airy, spacious, and affords total privacy within, no matter how busy the streets beyond its walls," Horatrim concluded.

He was so rapt in his vision he was unaware of Delphia, who had abandoned her task and come to stand slightly behind Livia. She listened to him with fascination. When he stopped speaking she turned and called, "Propertius, come over here at once! This young man has just described the perfect house. Every matron in Rome is going to want one like this. I know I do. You must build it for us, Severus."

After that Horatrim had no opportunity for a private conversation with Livia. The evening was spent with Severus and Khebet extracting every bit of construction information they could from him, while Propertius insisted on talking about how best to market the design and how much money could be made building the houses.

When everyone was exhausted and a yawning Severus finally announced he was going home, Propertius said abruptly, "We will expect a sixty percent share of the profits of this venture, of course."

Severus was suddenly wide awake. "What do you mean, we? Horatrim's going to be working for me. I'm the builder."

A bland smile spread across Propertius's face. "So you are. But while you were wandering around the city today, I paid a little visit to the royal palace. The king is delighted with Vesi. He believes having his own personal oracle will enhance his stature enormously; and when I pointed out that I had found her for him, he was in a humor to grant me any reasonable request."

"And you made a reasonable request?"

"I asked to be allowed to adopt Vesi's son."

Horatrim turned to look at Propertius.

"Horatrim is henceforth to be known as Horatius Cocles, and this family is entitled to share in whatever he earns. As *paterfamilias*, I demand you pay him sixty percent."

"Fifty."

"Fifty-five."

"Done!" cried Propertius. With a grin, he turned to Horatius. "Welcome to my family!"

THIRTY-ONE

The hour was late; the rain had long since blown over.

Horatrim was sharing a stifling cubicle off the main room with Propertius's sons. Three were much younger boys. The fourth, Quintus, was a sullen fellow of his own age who resented having so suddenly acquired a new brother.

They slept on pallets on the floor in order to be cooled by any stray draught of air, but no air was stirring. Only Horatrim's thoughts were churningly active. Horatius Cocles, he kept saying to himself. I have become a Roman!

For a while that evening he had feared Propertius and Severus would come to blows, but eventually they had struck upon a mutually acceptable arrangement. Horatrim was certain each man privately thought he had the better deal. No one asked the new Horatius what he wanted.

So much had happened to him so fast, the old patterns were breaking down. Childhood was sloughing away like dead skin. He could not sleep, there was no point in trying. He wanted . . . he needed . . . when he ran his hand down the length of his body there was an immediate stirring in his groin.

He arose from the pallet, wearing only the tunic in which he had slept, and went out into the main room of the house. The front door stood invitingly ajar. He stepped outside. And found Livia. As he knew he would.

She was there, leaning her back against the wall beside the door as she gazed up into a star-spangled sky. She was aware of him but did not look around, allowing him the pleasure of looking at her.

She wore a shift of sheer Aegyptian cotton, exposing her arms to the shoulder and her legs almost to her groin. He could smell quince-seed pomade on her hair. He was achingly aware of her, an unsettling experience for one who had so recently been a child.

"You came to us a stranger, yet now you are my brother," Livia remarked. "You will live here with us. Your fortune is assured, and with that fortune your place in the Senate. Using your ideas, father and uncle plan to bring new glory to Rome. Furthermore, work will soon begin on a new house for us with a private apartment of my own where I can entertain you." She spiced this last remark with a mischievous grin.

"How? I mean, entertain me how?"

She gave her trilling laugh. "Not with games or dice. Surely we can find something much more pleasurable." Turning toward him, she ran one speculative fingertip along his arm. A thread of invisible flame sprang up in the wake of her touch. With languid grace she tilted forward to lean on Horatrim instead of the wall. For a moment he staggered, more from surprise than the weight of her body. He could feel the heat of her flesh through the fabric of her shift. Then his arms closed around her and he held her close. When she lifted her face to his, her breath smelled of wine and honey.

Horatrim had never exchanged a kiss with a woman. He only knew how to plant a childish pucker on his mother's cheek. But Livia allowed him no time to be awkward. She pulled her arms free of his embrace, cupped the back of his head with her hands, and pressed her open mouth to his.

"I know what you are; you're a demon," Justine accused. Pointing to the immense phallus, erect and throbbing, between them, she said, "*That* gives you away. I've seen enough of the other kind to know it isn't human."

The *siu* glanced down. "Oh, I assure you it is—or was. During my human lifetime my member was a great source of pride. An abundant sex does not make one a demon, dear child. In my time this was not considered unusual, though nowadays I believe that males are less generously endowed. Even the gods have gender, although it may have been attributed to them originally by humankind, an example of man making gods in his own image. But now deities take as much pleasure in their sexuality as any human—more. Appreciating that sex is the quintessence of creation, the ultimate magic, they celebrate passion with a splendor you cannot even imagine. Even such a one as Marduk, the Crocodile God, is famous for . . ."

He paused.

They were lying together on a heap of rags and straw that passed for a bed in her miserable hovel. Justine had just taken part in a sexual act outside of anything in her prior repertoire, a comingling of pleasure and pain that exploded her senses with ecstasy while filling her mind with revulsion. She did not ever want to repeat the experience.

And yet she knew she would again . . . and again . . . and again. . . . It was the price she must pay.

Meanwhile she hung on his words with professional interest. How many harlots had ever heard a demon describing the sexual lives of the gods?

"Yes?" she urged. "What about Marduk?"

His voice was dark with anger. "There was a time when I prayed to Marduk to save my life. Seeking protection from the Crocodile . . . I was a fool to ask! I lived, but he let them put out my eyes with a hot poker. The pain was indescribable, yet that was not the worst. I who had been an architect, the designer of great palaces and magnificent gardens, was nothing without my eyes. Less than nothing—a beggar with a bowl. I who had been so proud!

"In fear and fury I turned against Marduk then. If one god fails you, I reasoned, try another. There are a multitude of gods; the trick is to find one who suits. I redirected my prayers to the goddess Pythia, a deity from the land of the Nile, because I had always been fond of females. Restore my sight, I promised her, and I will be your slave forever.

"Pythia did indeed restore my sight. When I awoke the next morning and gingerly touched my cauterized eye sockets, they were swelling with new orbs. A miracle! Within a few days the first dim glimmers of light appeared to me. I was so grateful I never thought to ask the cost. No gift, even one freely given, is without its price. This would be a salutary lesson for you, dear child, were it not too late.

"The price Pythia demanded proved to be more than I wanted to pay. The dark goddess restored my sight—and allowed me one night and a day to enjoy it. I went to bed one night strong and healthy and with a beautiful woman beside me.

"But the morning never came. While I slept the dark goddess extracted my spirit from my body as neatly as you would pull a tooth. I found myself stranded in the Otherworld, a disembodied being still tormented by an insatiable appetite for life. It was even worse than being blind.

"It should have been the end of me. But it was not.

"In the Earthworld, people who had admired me while I lived continued to revere me. They passed on my legend to the generations who followed them, telling the story of the builder of the famous Hanging Gardens and adding their own flourishes as the years went by. Eventually the Babylonians began to make statues of me and offer sacrifices.

"But because a human spirit cannot be so idolized without incurring the wrath and jealousy of the gods, deities I had once worshipped transformed me into a demon. Unfairly," he added bitterly. "I deserved to be worshipped myself; I had been an extraordinary man!"

Justine bit her lip and said nothing, desperately concentrating on the sagging ceiling, unwilling to allow the *siu* to read her mind.

"Pythia should have protected me," he went on in an aggrieved tone, "or at the very least argued with the other gods on my behalf. But she allowed them to abuse me. Finally, when it was too late and I had become the demon you see, she took pity on me and adopted me as her personal servant. But perhaps pity is not the right word. I think she took pleasure in my abasement. When I realized this I vowed to be revenged upon the dark goddess. I bided my time, always pretending to be devoted to her, while centuries passed in the Earthworld."

Justine smiled in the darkness. Men—either from modern Rome or ancient Babylon—never changed. They always wanted to talk about their favorite topic: themselves. "Did she never suspect you?" she asked.

He replied with his bitter chuckle. "Gods are not as omnipotent as they want us to believe. I was able to deceive Pythia because in her arrogance she thought herself above deception. And at last I found a way to even the score with her.

"From the dark goddess I stole enough power to clothe my spirit in flesh, enabling me to live once more in the Earthworld. Such transformation is within the gift of the gods, although they hoard it jealously. But I wanted my life back. I had a right to it!

"The power I took from Pythia was sufficient to form a tangible body through sheer force of will, so I undertook to re-create my own self. Alas, however, I am not a god. I did not perform a perfect act of creation. The body I attempted to restore proved to be a rather blurred copy of my original form. I became what you see now.

"I experimented with other forms, sending my spirit into the body of a beast—a beast that was soon slain, unfortunately. I tried to use the body anyway, and the result was disastrous. For a time my spirit went mad. When I recovered, I returned to this body resolving not to make the same mistake again. My next mistake was almost deadly; I consumed dead flesh . . . and the madness that overtook me once more almost engulfed me.

"Maintaining my hold on the Earthworld is difficult. In spite of all I can do, I feel my body fading. Every day it becomes less substantial; and as you have remarked yourself, the skin is flaking off. I look leprous. I do not blame you for being repelled by me, Justine.

"Nourishment is vital to me, nourishment of a very particular sort. But very soon I am going to require another body to inhabit. Something young and strong and original, not a copy of one long in the tomb."

He smiled. She found his smile more sinister than his chuckle.

"I have been seeking a perfect body for a long time, and now, at last, I have found one. Tell me, dear child—are you familiar with the royal palace?"

THIRTY-TWO

T he royal palace of Rome stood some distance from the Tiber in order to avoid the smell of the river. As the city expanded, its river was becoming an open sewer. The intense heat of summer caused the water level to fall alarmingly, exposing mud flats that added their own stench to the effluvium. But the city could not grow without Father Tiber, which provided access to the sea and thus to foreign markets.

Like every Roman household, the palace served a number of functions. In addition to being the residence of the king, it provided guest apartments for visiting dignitaries such as the prince, Lars Porsena.

This evening's entertainment included an appearance by Tarquinius's latest discovery. "From now on, the king of Rome will have his own personal holy woman to interpret messages from the gods," he had informed his chief steward. "I want to present her after the banquet and under the best possible circumstances. Arrange a high seat for her in a private chamber. Surround her with all the trappings appropriate to one of her calling."

Guests in the palace on this particular occasion included not only the young prince from Clusium but also a wealthy Sardinian shipowner, the leaders of a trade delegation from Smyrna, and a major Aegyptian dealer in slaves and exotic beasts. After dinner they were shown into the windowless chamber where Vesi waited. While Tarquinius watched with a proprietary air, they gathered around a tripod supporting a huge bronze bowl. Within this peculiar perch sat a woman.

She was dressed in a gown of bleached linen, cross-banded beneath her breasts. Her arms were bare, her head crowned with a laurel wreath to signify honors. On either side of the tripod were bronzed laurel branches, and at the feet of the stool was a brazier filling the room with clouds of white smoke and the fragrance of bitter herbs. The effect was every bit as impressive as Tarquinius desired.

"Speak to us, O Prophetess!" he intoned.

Silence.

Vesi sat immobile in her bronze bowl and stared over his head.

"Speak, I command you!"

Something came alive behind her eyes. Something terrible.

No mortal commands Pythia, said a voice that seemed to come from very far away.

Vesi's lips did not move.

When he heard the name of the dark goddess, the Aegyptian slave dealer blanched beneath his olive skin. Pythia was not a major deity in the pantheon of his people, but she was an horrific one, her name invoked rarely and always with trepidation.

Tarquinius bowed low before the woman on the tripod. "Forgive us our presumption. We merely seek wisdom."

Wisdom is a tree with ten million roots that feed on blood while the branches die.

Tarquinius cleared his throat. "Ah . . . indeed." He had never heard the number ten million before.

The Aegyptian, however, was impressed. Turning to the king, he said, "What you have here is something remarkable. I commend you. Where did you find such a valuable commodity?"

The king of Rome knew enough to refrain from divulging gratu-
itous information to trading partners. Airily waving one hand, he said,
"She is from Etruria, of course. Who else has such an affinity with
magic and mystery? Who else converses regularly with the gods? And
she's not for sale, if that's what you're hinting. She's like one of my own
family."

The Sardinian shipowner was skeptical. "I never heard the name
Pythia mentioned in connection with any Etruscan tribe." He glanced
accusingly at the Aegyptian. "Pythia's one of yours, isn't she?"

"We have a goddess by that name, I believe," the man replied warily. No one could see his fingers clutching the amulet sewn into his
robes in an attempt to ward off evil.

"Well, I've never heard of her," Tarquinius said with a shrug. "But
I dare say the name will become famous in time. This woman merely
needs a larger audience, which I will provide. Have any of you questions you wish put to her?"

Uncertainly at first, then with growing fascination, the party
addressed the woman seated on the tripod. Sometimes she did not
answer. Then for no apparent reason she would fall into incoherent
raving. Seizing the bronze laurel branches, she shook them wildly as
she chanted. Out of the chaos an occasional phrase would make stunning sense to one or another of the men in the room.

Her most cryptic comment was reserved for the handsome prince
of Clusium, Lars Porsena. When he stepped close to the tripod to get a
better look at the woman through the smoke, she fixed her eyes on his
face and solemnly declaimed, *Beware the empty nest. That which hatches
from the eagle's egg will rain fire on the wolf's cubs.*

When the evening was over Tarquinius was euphoric. The Etruscan
woman had far exceeded his expectations. "Having her entertain my
guests was a brilliant idea, positively brilliant," he confided to his
favorite body slave as he took his evening bath. Beaming with self-
congratulation, the king absentmindedly fondled his genitals in the

warm water. Recognizing the signals, his slave ran through a mental list of the concubines, trying to guess which one Tarquinius would want tonight.

But his master's mind was still on the Etruscan woman. Though her pronouncements had been few, they had been relevant. It would be but a short step from the genuine prophecies of the seer to those he would have her make for political reasons. In a month, perhaps less, he would announce that she had proclaimed him the son of a god and that his line would rule for a thousand years. Then she would really earn her keep.

"Do you wish a woman sent to you tonight?" his slave inquired as Tarquinius emerged from his bath. "Perhaps the yellow-haired one you bought last spring?"

But Tarquinius was too overstimulated for anything so ordinary. "No, I'm not in the mood. Bring me the seer instead, so I can talk with her privately. Perhaps she will have some prophecy for my ears alone."

The slave bowed low so the king would not see the smile on his face. He could imagine the type of conversation Tarquinius had in mind.

They brought her to him in the anteroom that led to his bedchamber. The ruler of Rome was casually attired in a robe of orange silk dyed in Syria. Vesi wore a sheer, pleated gown of the sort favored by the palace courtesans, and scented pomade had been used to dress her hair. In the soft light of the oil lamps, which rendered the gown virtually transparent, she appeared surprisingly youthful . . . and innocent. Tarquinius liked his women young. Suddenly he was interested in something more tangible than her oracular abilities.

Rising from his bench, he led her through the doorway into the next room. She followed without resistance. A massive bed waited half-hidden behind swathes of sheer fabric that could be drawn to keep out biting insects. Tarquinius drew the curtains back and, still holding Vesi by one wrist, stretched himself upon the bed. She continued to stand at the edge of the bed until he tugged imperiously at her arm, then she lay down beside him and closed her eyes. When he released her wrist she folded her hands across her breasts.

Seen thus, she looked like a corpse.

The image was troubling. "Open your eyes," he requested.

She did not move.

"Open your eyes, I said!"

She raised her lids to reveal huge dark eyes that held not the slightest hint of intelligence. Tarquinius was excited by her docility. She was his; he owned her.

"I appreciate your cooperation tonight," he said. "You will be amply rewarded, as are all my favorites. But you must reserve the true prophecies for me. You understand that, don't you? Anything of real importance that the gods tell you, you are to divulge only to me. And in a little while I will need you to make certain prophecies for me."

She lay unresponsive. Seen from this close she was even younger than he had thought. How could that great hulking Horatrim be her son? The king's eyes strayed to her hips. They were full and rounded, with swelling pubes clearly visible beneath the soft fabric.

"Do the gods really speak through you?"

Tarquinius had never possessed a holy woman before. What divine visions might present themselves to her when the king of Rome entered her body? He was thrilled at the idea of being so close to the gods, entering a vessel they had so recently vacated. Perhaps a vestige of their godhood would have remained, a scrap he might claim for himself. Gently, with respect, he attempted to arouse her.

But she was as indifferent as a statue. He began to feel insulted. He was Tarquin the Superb; what right had she to ignore him? His anger and his lust grew together. When he could control them no longer, he caught the neck of her gown and ripped it open.

In one of the guest apartments, Lars Porsena was still wide awake. He was young and virile, but he had deliberately refused the king's offer of a woman for the night, just as he had been careful not to drink too much wine. In the morning there would be complicated negotiations with the king present. It was best to keep one's senses sharp when dealing with Romans.

In the meantime he was mentally preparing himself by going over the moves and countermoves to come. One must be prepared to be firm, yet flexible. He lay on his couch with his fingers laced behind his head, gazing at the ceiling and calculating just how much grain he was prepared to give in exchange for the goods his people wanted. The flickering light cast by the lamp beside his bed cast weird shadows on the walls around him.

Then he heard the scream.

Since even a *hia* could not be in two places at the same time, Pepan had chosen to stay with Vesi rather than with Horatrim. She was all but lost; whatever had possessed her was too old, too powerful for him to combat. All he could do was stay close to her and hope for an opportunity to help her.

The Rasne lord found the palace of the king of Rome as disappointing as the houses of his subjects. Pepan thought the royal residence resembled a glorified rabbit warren, with countless chambers and passageways tacked onto one another as need dictated. There was no coherence to the plan, merely a cancerous growth sprawling unchecked. *Perhaps Horatrim will improve the place*, he thought. There was a delicious irony in having a Rasne design the capital of the Romans.

While Vesi entertained the king's guests, Pepan watched. He was perfectly aware her mysterious mouthings did not originate with the girl he had known. She was being well-treated, however, which was his immediate concern. He could only hope that sooner or later he would find some way to free her from the black miasma enveloping her spirit. If the spirit of the girl Vesi still existed at all.

When Tarquinius Superbius took her body into his bed, Pepan was

distressingly aware of his inability to prevent rape. And it would be
rape; Vesi was incompetent to give her consent. Yet something in her
recognized the impending violation—and screamed.

A scream carries on the night wind, and the senses of an embodied *siu*
are far more sensitive than those of an ordinary human. Any cry of pain
can draw a demon. To their kind, pain is food and drink.

"Hurry!" he ordered Justine. "We may be just in time!"

Lars Porsena was on his feet before the woman's scream stopped
echoing through the halls of the palace. He raced in the direction of
the scream. As he came around a corner he surprised a pair of guards
who tried to intercept him, but he seized the spear from one and
slammed its shaft against the temple of the other, knocking him
unconscious. The first man hesitated, reluctant to fight the tall Etruscan nobleman alone. That moment's pause cost him dearly, for
Lars Porsena hit him a blow on the jaw that laid him on the floor
beside his companion. The Etruscan leaped over them and entered
the king's private chamber.

Tarquinius looked up, enraged by the intrusion. "How dare you
burst in here! Where are my guards?" Lurching to his feet, he started
toward the door to summon them.

Lars Porsena moved to block his way, towering over the much
smaller Tarquinius. "I heard a scream."

"Nothing to do with you," Tarquinius snarled.

Lars Porsena looked over the smaller man's head. The Etruscan
seer lay stretched on the bed unmoving, her gown shredded around
her.

"What are you doing to that woman?" he demanded to know.

"I already told you it has nothing to do with you. Now get out of
here or Clusium can forget about ever doing any business with Rome."

Hot blood flamed the Etruscan's cheeks. "You can't threaten me!"

"I just did. Now get out."

On the bed, Vesi moaned.

Forgetting the king, Lars Porsena whirled around and went to her. "Are you all right?" he asked solicitously. "Has he hurt you? I'll make him pay for insulting one of . . ."

Tarquinius hit him over the back of the head with a bronze lamp.

Lars Porsena collapsed without a murmur.

Panting, Tarquinius stooped over the woman on the bed. The incident had shaken him. He was not accustomed to being thwarted, certainly not in his private chamber. Now he was determined that nothing should stop him. Taking hold of Vesi once more he roughly thrust her legs apart. He was not looking at her face. But then something in the way her body felt to his hands alerted him and he raised his head.

The expression in her eyes was the last thing Tarquinius saw before she tore him apart.

In the early years of her harlotry, Justine had been beautiful enough to command high prices and count some of Rome's most powerful names among her clients. On a number of occasions she had visited the royal palace, and even after so many years, its rooms and passageways remained clear in her mind.

At the gates she presented herself as a whore answering a royal summons. "And this," she said, indicating a figure swathed in robes, face hidden, "is my protector and bodyguard."

"With that body, you'll need one," leered the guard.

Her restored beauty was sufficient. Justine and Bur-Sin were swiftly passed through.

Once inside, she led the way to the king's apartments. Each time a guard challenged them she flashed a dazzling smile. "Tarquinius Superbius sent for me," she would say. The king's tastes in young women were well known, so no one questioned her.

When they reached the royal chamber she was astonished to find two guards lying unconscious outside the door. "Be careful," she started to warn Bur-Sin. Then she laughed. How foolish to warn a demon! With him close behind her, she entered the chamber.

The room was like an abattoir.

A tall man lay unconscious in the middle of the floor. On the bed a woman in a torn gown crouched in a pool of blood. Her hands were hooked into talons clutching gobbets of flesh. The light of madness burned in her eyes.

There was blood everywhere, spurted in long streaks up the walls, dappled across the ceiling, pooled on the tiles. Half on the bed and half on the floor sprawled a mutilated body, so badly disfigured that it took Justine several moments to recognize the king of Rome. She gave a moan of horror.

The *siu* hardly glanced at the corpse—or the woman. All his attention was fixed on the unconscious Etruscan. He bent over him and stroked his face with a lover's touch. "See how strong he is, how healthy! Dear child, this is a gift," Bur-Sin chuckled, "from the gods."

Pepan could feel the whirlpool of energies swiftly gathering around the embodied *siu*. He knew him now, knew his name and his history. This was Bur-Sin, architect in life, lover of the goddess Pythia in death. He was now somehow trapped in rotting human flesh, his very presence in the Earthworld an abomination. His current state of existence disturbed the delicate web of energies that linked the worlds, creating pools and vortices of discord.

All of Pepan's strength was necessary to keep from being sucked into one of the vortices. A low humming sound filled the room. The air grew cold, colder, freezing.

Justine hugged herself. Her lips were turning blue. "Let me out of here," she pleaded.

The woman on the bed whimpered. Then with an effort she got to her feet and began to stagger toward the door.

The demon rolled his eyes in her direction. His features were livid; with every movement of muscle, more skin pulled loose. Completing the transfer would require his total concentration, but even so he was briefly distracted by something he saw on the woman's face. Something familiar.

He had no time to think about it now. "Yes, go, Justine," he managed to say in a voice distorted by the collapse of his vocal cords. "Go to that shack of yours and take the woman with you. I will come for both of you soon. Soon."

"Where will you be?" asked Justine.

"I'll come to you presently. I have some work to do here first. Go!"

Justine caught Vesi by the wrist and fled.

THIRTY-THREE

The slaves who came to prepare their master for bed were alarmed to find the guards unconscious on the floor outside. They hurried into Tarquinius's chamber. What they saw sent them gibbering in terror.

Flavius, captain of the royal guard, arrived at the run, sword in hand and a company of men at his back. One look inside the chamber was enough to tell him the king had no further use for his services. His body had been torn apart. Flavius shrugged. He had always known that one day he would find Tarquinius slain.

His constant prayer had been not for the king's safety but that he himself would not be in the way when the assassination attempt was made. Obviously, the gods had answered that prayer. He must go to the temple when he had the opportunity and offer a sacrifice of thanksgiving.

At the foot of the bed was a small heap of decomposed meat, as if someone had thrown a meal on the floor and left it there to rot. Flavius stepped over it, idly wondering what it was doing in the king's bedchamber.

Then he crouched down beside the nobleman from Clusium.

From the general condition of the chamber, he expected to find Lars Porsena dead. But the Etruscan was still alive, although he appeared dazed and groggy. Flavius helped him to his feet. "What happened here?" he demanded.

Lars Porsena slowly opened his eyes. "We were talking. Someone burst in . . ." His pupils rolled back in his head, showing only the whites before his eyelids drifted down again and he fell silent.

Flavius's men had by this time restored the guards in the hall outside to consciousness and marched them into the room. They looked at the dead king and then at Lars Porsena with expressions of shock and horror; but before either could speak, the Etruscan said, "The king was attacked by a band of assassins who must have sneaked into the palace. The two guards stationed at the doorway fought valiantly but were unable to overcome them. They should be commended; I have never seen anything so brave. If they were mine, I would make them both officers."

His eyes were still closed.

The guards kept their mouths similarly closed. The word of an Etruscan nobleman would be believed before the testimony of two lowly plebeian guards. Better to be lauded as heroes than condemned for failing to save the king.

"What of you, Lord Porsena?" asked Flavius. "How did you manage to survive?"

"I defended your king to the best of my ability," the other replied. Then he opened his eyes and looked down at his right arm. He extended it for Flavius's inspection. The arm was badly lacerated and a purple bruise was appearing from his temple to his jaw. "I am afraid my best was not good enough, although I would gladly have given my life for Tarquinius. He was one of us, you know, a man of Etrurian blood," Lars Porsena added with convincing sincerity.

Flavius was examining his wounds. The longer the captain looked at them, the more horrific they became. "Your defense of Tarquinius does you credit," he said. "Do you know what became of the assassins?"

Lars Porsena shook his head. "Sadly, I do not. I was struck a blow on the side of the head and everything went black. The next thing I knew you were helping me to my feet. Will you allow me to assist in searching for them? If I get my hands on them, I will do to them what they did to . . . to . . ." He indicated the mangled body of Tarquinius with a nod, obviously too emotional to speak further.

Pepan was aghast at the turn of events. Watching helplessly from the Otherworld, he had observed the serpentine shadow wrapped around Vesi's spirit. He had seen the ancient evil peering through the empty eyes of Repana's daughter and knew it for what it was.

He wanted to warn Horatrim, but his first duty under the circumstances was to Vesi. Abandoning the gore-spattered chamber, he followed the fleeing women. He was aware that the strength to do the deed had not come from Vesi herself. The girl he had known would never have been capable of such horror.

She was different now. Possessed. But not totally lost. Not yet. Faintly, very faintly, wind-blown and weakened yet persistent in its grip on life, came the thread of sound that identified Vesi's *hia*.

In the Otherworld Pepan also could hear the tonal discord surrounding the beautiful young woman called Justine. She was not possessed but she had been warped in some way; her song was distorted and off-key. Having Vesi in her custody was worrying. Pepan didn't sense any malice in the woman, however . . . only greed and a deep sadness.

Pepan hovered close to them as they made their way through the warren of corridors. Justine knew the palace well; she managed to avoid each point at which guards were stationed and in time led her charge safely through a side entrance and out into the night.

No one in the palace was paying much attention to women anyway. The guards were concentrating on finding a band of assassins. Foremost among the searchers was the wounded Lars Porsena, who valiantly ignored his injuries as he ran up one corridor and down another, indifferent to danger, inspiring the men who followed him.

Streaks of angry red light appeared in the eastern sky before Flavius reluctantly conceded the murderers had escaped them. "We should summon the Senate immediately," he said.

"What will happen now?" asked Lars Porsena. The prince from Clusium looked very tired, with dark circles under his eyes. Yet those same eyes were fever bright.

The captain shrugged. "It will be up to them to decide what to do next. It's not the first time we've had an assassination, nor I fear will it be the last. Being king of Rome is a lifetime occupation, but sometimes that means having a rather short life." He stopped, and looked intently at the wounded prince. "Of course, certain kings—those who inspire the respect of the military—tend to live a little longer."

By the time Justine and Vesi reached the harlot's shack, the Etruscan woman's energy was exhausted. In spite of the fact that the slain man's blood was drying to a stiff paste on her hands and clothing, Vesi tumbled onto the rags piled in the corner and was asleep at once.

Justine stood looking down at her for a time, wondering what Bur-Sin wanted with her. She was not attractive by Roman standards; just mute and god-touched. Justine's own brother, in their distant childhood, had been god-touched. He howled at the moon every month with white froth bubbling on his lips. One morning she had awakened to learn that their father—or the man they assumed to be their father—had given him to the Tiber.

Justine blew out the lamp and stretched herself beside Vesi. Strange, she mused, she had not thought of her brother in a long time. Just then a sudden, sickening chill washed over her. The ancients believed the sensation presaged death. In the gloom, her teeth flashed in a grim smile. She was not going to die. Not now. Not for a long time. She had a demon on her side.

Pepan waited nearby until Justine feel into a troubled sleep; then he turned and fled back toward the palace.

·   ·   ·

222

Horatrim awoke with a start. At first he did not know where he was. Then he was not sure who he was. Slowly, memory came dribbling back. He was in Rome. And he was no longer Horatrim. He was Horatius Cocles. Propertius's adopted son.

And he was a man. Last night Livia had kissed him. The memory was sudden and vivid. The man in him knew there had been the promise of more . . . the boy in him was unsure what the promise entailed.

The pale lemon light of an early Roman morning was beaming through the one small window. The other "sons" with whom he shared the room were already up and gone. Yawning, Horatius rose from his pallet. He stood tall, stretched, yawned again. Where was everyone?

He jangled the string of silver bells that hung by the door, but no slave came running to dress him. After waiting for a time, Horatius began to laugh at himself. The sound was strangely hollow in the quiet room. "I've dressed myself all my life," he remarked aloud. "I can do it now."

He fumbled awkwardly with the folds of the toga, trying to achieve a fashionable effect, then gave up and simply twisted the cloth around his tunic as best he could. He gave the sandals a long look, then decided to leave them for later. After a life spent barefoot it would take a while to get used to having his feet encased in leather.

Next he splashed his face with water from a pottery bowl on a nearby stand. Lifting the bronze razor Propertius had given him as a gift, the young man looked at his reflection in the mirror beside the bowl and decided that he really should practice scraping the hair from his face. Roman men did not have facial hair, unlike the Teumetians, who prized it as a sign of virility.

"Horatius," he said, practicing the name as he scraped the blade across his cheekbone.

Horatrim.

His old name echoed in his head.

"Horatius."

Horatrim.

The sound was louder, clearer.

He squinted into the mirror. His image was curiously blurred. Bending his arm, he scrubbed the polished silver with the sleeve of his toga. "That's better." He raised the razor again and looked into the mirror.

A face gazed back at him—but not his face.

Horatrim, your mother needs you.

The razor slipped and cut a deep gash in his cheek. He brushed at the wound, then ran his bloody fingertips over the silver, leaving a crimson streak.

The face in the mirror solidified.

Your mother needs you.

"But my mother is safe in the royal palace!"

She is no longer there, and she is far from safe.

"Where is she then? And who are you?"

Vesi was taken from the palace during the night. She is in grave danger.

"Who are you?" Horatius repeated, his voice rising. "Are you one of the gods?"

Alas, I am no god. Nor do I have a physical body with which to save hers. That is why I need you to . . .

"But I can see your face!"

You see my memory of my face. I am—I was Pepan—and now I am what you would call a ghost, I suppose. A spirit without flesh. Throughout your life I have watched over you out of love for your grandmother.

Suddenly Horatius became aware of noise outside; people were shouting to one another in the street beyond the window, and there were distant horns blowing.

"My grandmother? Repana? You knew her?"

I knew them both. Listen to me, Horatrim. You must go to your mother and make her safe.

The razor dropped forgotten from Horatius's fingers. As soon as he turned his back on the mirror Pepan could no longer appear to him. He hovered at the young man's right shoulder; invisible, calling but unheard.

Horatius ran from the room as the noise outside grew louder.

In the Otherworld Pepan was almost overwhelmed by the brazen blare of Rome's voice.

Propertius's house, Horatius quickly discovered, was empty. Even the servants were gone. He opened the front door to find the street crowded with people milling about and calling questions to one another.

"Something terrible has happened; I just know it," a woman was saying anxiously. "I heard an alarm just now."

Horatius caught hold of her shoulder and turned her to face him. "What alarm?"

"Horns blowing at the palace."

Horatius began to run. The face in the mirror had told him that Vesi was in danger . . . and now an alarm was sounding from the palace. The two events could not be unconnected.

Where was Propertius? He must find the Roman. Propertius would know what to do. Elbowing people aside, Horatius pounded off down the hill, intent on reaching the palace, unsure what he would do when he got there.

Then he turned a corner and ran headlong into someone he knew.

Khebet the Aegyptian staggered under the impact.

Horatius caught the man before he could fall. "Have you seen Propertius?"

"I have not," Khebet replied, rubbing his bruised chest. "I was looking for Severus myself. He was summoned from his house abruptly; I thought he might have come up here to his brother."

"There's no one in Propertius's house, but people are saying there's some sort of trouble at the palace. I'm going there now. My mother is . . . but she may not be . . . I must find her!" Horatius cried, increasingly frantic.

Khebet was practiced at remaining calm when others were emotional. Observing that a slash across Horatius's cheek was oozing blood, he touched the wound with his long, slender fingers.

When Khebet, priest of Anubis, made contact with Horatius's blood, his third eye opened.

The Jackal God always responded to blood.

Never before, however, had mystical vision come as vividly. Khebet found himself staring at a veritable horde of beings, male and female, old and young, clustered so tightly around the young man that their forms overlapped into an ever-changing, fluid shadow. They had no bodies, merely the memory of flesh.

Khebet knew he was looking at the naked *ka*, the soul. Scores of souls, hundreds of souls, generations of souls, every one of them interlocked with the spirit of Horatius. Beside the young man, standing by his right hand, was a powerful *hia* who wore the flickering form of a Rasne lord.

For once even the imperturbable Aegyptian was astonished.

But his long years of training in the temples along the Nile stood him in good stead. He appreciated the wonder of what he was seeing and understood that he was in the presence of a very special human being.

Recovering his poise, he put a hand on Horatius's shoulder. "Thou art blessed," he said in the secret and formal language of the temple, an archaic tongue long-forgotten by ordinary Aegyptians. "Doubly blessed," he added, looking at the lordly shadow beside Horatrim.

His astonishment returned, Horatius replied in the same language, "I do not feel blessed, Khebet. I am so worried about my mother and . . ." he broke off abruptly. Moving past the Aegyptian, his eyes had fixed on a large metal ewer standing on the counter of a streetside shop. Reflected in the polished metal of the ewer, Horatius saw the face that had stared at him out of the mirror. When the Aegyptian turned to follow his gaze, three faces were momentarily reflected in the metal.

"Do you see that?" Horatius whispered.

"I do."

"Then it is real?"

"Very real."

Horatrim pointed toward the third face. "Just a little while ago he told me my mother was in danger, and that I should go to her."

Khebet nodded. "Believe him."

"Will you help me, Khebet?"

With grave courtesy, the Aegyptian bowed. "I would consider it a great honor," he replied.

THIRTY-FOUR

As members of the Senate, Propertius and Severus were among the first to be informed of the king's murder. They were wakened in the dawn by messengers who spoke in hushed whispers. Hastily throwing on their clothes, the two men came at the run from their separate houses and arrived almost simultaneously at the palace.

"Stop blowing those cursed horns!" Propertius shouted to the guards on the palace wall.

Unless the horns were silenced, all Rome would soon converge on the palace, he knew. Once news of Tarquinius's assassination was public knowledge, vast crowds would besiege the gates, either to declare their undying loyalty to the dead king or to learn who was going to replace him, more often the latter. Every foreigner in Rome would be trying to arrange for passage home at a time of social upheaval. Army officers would come pouring into the city, hopeful of improving their individual power bases. In the midst of all this, enterprising vendors would be hawking sausages and dates and leavened bread baked in the shapes of dogs, and taking wagers as to the name of the next king.

Pandemonium. There might well be riots—and riots were bad for business.

Any sensible, reasoned plan of action would be rendered impossible.

"Stop those horns, I said!" Propertius screamed at the guards.

The strident horns fell silent, but the air was still torn. Tarquinius's wife and concubines were in full mourning; their shrieks and wails echoed from the palace. Meanwhile companies of grim-faced warriors continued to search the grounds, although no one really believed the assassins were still inside.

"A dark day," Propertius panted to his brother by way of greeting.

"It is for a fact." Severus wiped sweat from his brow. "Have you ever noticed that just when you think you have everything going right, it all goes wrong?"

The trader nodded. "Hubris."

"Eh?"

"The Hellenes have a word for everything, you know. *Hubris* means never count your accomplishments or you tempt the gods."

"I thought you didn't believe in the gods."

"Things change," retorted Propertius. "Do you recall what the seer said at my banquet the other night?"

"Aaah . . . not precisely, no."

"She said, 'When the moon hangs by its horns, a trader will pass through the gate and a king will dance with the black goat.' Last night there was a crescent moon. I'm a trader, and I'm about to pass through the palace gate. And in Etruria a black goat is a symbol of death. I believe the gods spoke through that woman, Severus. Her prophecy is already . . . Ho, Antoninus!" he broke off to call to a passing warrior. "You certainly got here fast!"

The Roman captain strode briskly toward Propertius. "I was coming to the city anyway to make a report to the king. Something quite bizarre happened at the northern frontier a few days ago, and we thought he should know about it. But I won't be telling him anything now."

"Not unless you care to follow him across the Styx. Have you been inside yet? Do you know what's happening?"

"The captain of the guard is questioning Lars Porsena right now."

Propertius raised his eyebrows. "The prince from Clusium? Why, is he a suspect?"

"Far from it. He tried to fight off the assassins and was badly injured in the attempt, so he's quite the hero now. Flavius is hoping he can identify the murderers."

Severus spoke up. "They must be taken alive. It will be up to the new king to execute them once they are captured."

Propertius was thinking fast. "The new king indeed. The Senate will want to choose a nominee before news of the murder is made public, so we must ensure that not a word of what has actually happened gets out, at least for the present. A panic is the last thing we need. We will have to warn the servants and swear the guards to secrecy. Quiet those caterwauling women inside. Keep out everyone who does not have legitimate business in the palace. We can't afford to deny all entry though; that would look suspicious. Antoninus, will you pass us through the gates?"

"I'll take you in myself; but I warn you, the place is in chaos."

"I'm a trader; I'm used to chaos. Come, Severus. There is much to do."

Antoninus conducted the brothers into the palace. However he seemed less interested in talking about the assassination than in describing some peculiar incident on the frontier. ". . . and hacked off what he thought was a leg," he was saying, "but it proved to be a snake. Or part of a snake. It actually crushed the wrist of one of my men and . . ."

They passed a small antechamber just as Flavius, captain of the palace guard, came out. Over his shoulder they could see Lars Porsena inside. At the door Flavius turned and bowed low to the prince of Clusium. Very low indeed, Propertius noted.

Taking Antoninus by the elbow, he said in an undertone, "Would you mind arranging it so that we have a few moments alone with Lars Porsena? Just to discuss a bit of trading business. I will, ah, make it worth your while the next time I cross the northern frontier."

Antoninus promptly engaged Flavius in animated conversation and steered him off down the corridor. As soon as they were gone, Propertius beckoned to Severus to follow him then entered the chamber. "I understand you're the hero of the day," he greeted the Etruscan.

Lars Porsena looked at him blankly.

"I'm your old friend, Propertius! We've done business together. I bought a quantity of fine silver jewelry from your craftsmen just last summer. Paid above the going rate for it, in fact. Under the table, of course."

Something shifted behind Lars Porsena's eyes. "You must forgive me; I took a blow to the head last night. Now I remember you, Propertius. A man of my own stripe."

The Roman took this as a compliment. The prince was, he thought, looking unwell, with sunken eyes and a faintly greenish cast to his skin. "If Flavius has finished questioning you, Lars Porsena, have you time for a word or two with us?"

"I already told Flavius what I know."

Propertius gave an impatient wave of his hand. "I'm sure you did, and they will or will not catch the assassins and we'll have a grand trial and a splendid execution and that's the end of that. It really doesn't matter. What is important is the future."

"Forgive me again, but I do not understand what you mean."

"It is the responsibility of the Senate to nominate a new king as soon as we can agree on one. But that may take time. In the manner of all politicians, we're more inclined to disagree. Furthermore, there are very few at the moment whom we would consider suitable candidates. But you, as a hero, a man who like Tarquinius can claim the most ancient noble blood . . . you are well-qualified to be king, Lars Porsena."

Severus looked at his brother with awe as he realized what was coming next. The plan was extraordinarily audacious, a plan worthy of Propertius in his youth, when his boldness and cunning had made his fortune.

"I don't think we could nominate you right now because you're not well enough known."

"You are suggesting making me king! But I was not born in Rome," Lars Porsena protested.

Propertius shrugged. "A minor handicap. Such inconveniences can always be overcome if one is determined. If we can stall the deliberations for long enough, Severus and I may be able to bring the other senators around to our way of thinking in time. I trust you would not be averse to rewarding us for acting on your behalf?"

In the eyes of Lars Porsena laughter sparkled, as if at some dark and secret joke. "Perhaps I have a better idea," he said. "We can discuss the repayment of obligations later."

By the time Horatius and Khebet reached the palace, there was a crowd at the gates being held back by noncommittal guards. No one knew what disaster had occasioned the sound of the brazen horns, but every imaginable rumor was being floated. Some said the king was ill; others claimed there had been a military revolt. As the people grew increasingly frustrated in their efforts to gain information, they were turning sullen.

The Aegyptian sensed danger in the air. Though his face remained impassive he tensed inwardly, wanting to turn back. "If your mother may no longer be in the palace," he remarked to Horatius, "why did you want to come here?"

"Because this is the last place she was." His eye fell on a familiar face in the crowd. "There's Quintus!" Horatius pushed his way through the throng to his new brother. "Is Propertius here?"

Quintus turned a sullen face in his direction. "You mean *my* father? He's inside with Uncle Severus. Why?"

"I need his help."

Quintus said smugly, "They'll never let you go in to him. No one's being allowed inside but senators and a few foreign officials. Important people," he added. "And in spite of my father's recent action, you are simply not important."

Horatius drew himself up to his full height. "Is that a fact?"

.   .   .

232

Within a matter of minutes he and Khebet were inside the palace.

The Aegyptian remarked, "I have never been introduced to palace guards as an ambassador before. And as for calling yourself the son of a member of the Senate . . . !"

"I am. Now."

"That may be, but it only worked because the courtiers are so distracted. Something is seriously wrong here. What do you want to do first, look for Propertius?"

"First, I want to find out where my mother was kept. Perhaps I can pick up her trail."

"This is no forest; there are no tracks to follow."

Horatius replied incomprehensibly, "Wulv taught me how to read all sorts of spoor."

"Wulv?"

The young man did not answer but set off down the nearest corridor, sniffing the air. Khebet hurried along in his wake. When they were challenged by a guard, Horatius cried, "Make way for the Aegyptian ambassador!"

The guard bowed as the imposing Aegyptian swept past in a cloud of almond perfume.

"Do you know where we're going?" Khebet asked in a low voice.

"No, but I have noticed that all of these Roman houses and palaces are built to a similar design. I'm hoping that the king's chambers will be down . . ." Suddenly he skidded to a halt. "In there; she was in there!" Darting through a doorway, he entered a spacious chamber. This opened into one still larger, where a bed stood on a dais enshrouded with badly torn draperies. Khebet followed, slipping one hand up the sleeve of his other arm. In a moment more there was a knife in his hand.

The bedchamber reeked of blood. The cloying stench hung heavy on the air, a sweetish-rotten odor that made Horatius gag. But after one shocked inhalation, he relaxed. "That isn't my mother's blood," he said. "Her scent is still here though. And something else, an awful stink . . ."

233

The Aegyptian's nostrils dilated. "The smell of a demon," Khebet said hoarsely. One step at a time, fearful of what he might see, he approached the ruined bed and drew the curtains aside. The linen sheets were soaked with clotted gore. On the floor beside the bed was a veritable lake of blood.

For a long moment Khebet stared down without speaking. Then he crouched beside the pool and used the tip of his knife to crack the hardening surface of the blood. His lips began to shape an incantation. "Accept this gift, great Anubis. Not spilled in your name, but freely given to you. In return, I ask for the revelation of the blood."

The surface of the blood, already darkened by coagulation, turned black as jet.

Khebet leaned closer as a vision began to form. Shaping itself from the essence of lost life, an image appeared of a woman on the bed with a man bending over her. Then another man rushed into the room and a scuffle ensued. Fascinated, the Aegyptian watched the recurrence of deeds whose sinister vibrations still resonated within the chamber. Once he gave a gasp of alarm.

"What is it?" asked Horatius, peering over his shoulder. "What are you looking at?"

But the blood revealed its secrets only to the priest of Anubis. Horatius saw nothing more than a tar-colored puddle. Khebet, however, made a choking sound and waved his hands as if warding off some invisible horror. The smell that he had identified as the stink of a demon grew stronger in the room. The surface of the blood began to bubble. "Oh, wretched being," Khebet moaned, "thou art evil, evil!"

Suddenly Horatius had a sense of immense vistas just beyond his gaze. A singing thundered through his bones. Unconsciously using the Aegyptian tongue, he said, "What are you seeing, Khebet? You have to tell me; I command you!" No longer was he a child asking questions. Power resonated through him, the imperious force of a hundred chieftains.

Even a priest of Anubis could not resist. Bowing his head, Khebet murmured a different incantation and swept his hands in circles over the boiling pool. Its black surface quieted slowly. Then, just as slowly, gleamed silver.

"Look," said the Aegyptian as he moved aside to make room for Horatius. "This is the blood lore, the tale of life carried in the red liquid of life. See the past through the generosity of Anubis."

THIRTY-FIVE

The king's death would have far-reaching ramifications for Rome's trading partners and her military alliances. The most immediate effect, however, would be upon the Romans themselves. Although politically conservative, they were emotionally volatile. Without someone strong in charge, they could stampede like cattle in a thunderstorm. The assassination of Tarquinius was tantamount to a major thunderstorm.

The members of the Senate who gathered on the morning following the king's death were aware of the precariousness of the situation. There was always the possibility that the assassination had been carried out by some ambitious *patrician* outside their own circle, who would then attempt to capture the allegiance of the Roman military. It had happened before. If successful, he could be declared king by popular acclamation. And if he was not one of their own, he might abolish the Senate altogether. That too had been threatened before. The ultimate power rested with the king.

As soon as all the senators had arrived at the palace, an urgent meeting was convened. Propertius and Severus were last to enter the large chamber—walking on either side of Lars Porsena. His presence excited a buzz of conversation. They went to the head of the room and stood facing their colleagues. While they waited for conversation to die down, Lars Porsena said to the brothers in a low voice, "Remember our deal. You help me, then I help you."

"Agreed," Propertius murmured.

"Absolutely," echoed Severus. "We have your word on this?"

"You have my word. And you know how much I value it." Lars Porsena smiled.

The room fell silent.

Lifting his arms, Propertius announced, "Today we stand at a crossroads. We can undertake to nominate a new king immediately, knowing that suitable men of sufficiently noble blood are in short supply at present. The best are too old, too young, or simply unwilling to take on the responsibilities and hazards of the office.

"Or we can consider something else."

His fellow senators stared at him dumbfounded. "But Rome must have a king," someone said.

Severus pointed out, "The Hellenes have no king."

"Oh, well, the Hellenes," came the dismissive reply. Roman contempt for the Greeks was well known.

"I am not suggesting we adopt a democracy," Propertius went on, his mouth shaping the word with disgust. "However kingship offers many opportunities for abuses. I, as much as any of you, prospered under the reign of Tarquinius Superbius, but ultimately he behaved in a way that could only bring discredit to Rome."

Turning to Lars Porsena, he said, "Please tell us what happened last night. What really happened."

The prince from Clusium cleared his throat. "I did not wish to make this public out of respect for the kingship itself," he said, "but my friend Propertius has persuaded me to do so. The statement I originally made concerning the king's death was not accurate."

A low murmur ran around the chamber, like surf beating on a distant shore.

"I am Etruscan, as was Tarquinius. As indeed was the prophetess he recently brought into the palace. Last night, while relaxing in my chamber, I heard a woman scream. I ran to the king's chambers only to find him raping the seer. Brutally raping a holy woman!

"I lost my head and attacked him. I have no excuse other than my revulsion at what he was doing. I attacked my fellow Etruscan to prevent him completing an act that would have brought undying shame upon his name, his race, and the kingship of Rome. But even as I was dragging him off her helpless body, the gods of Etruria intervened.

"You have been shown the body, and many of you remarked that nothing human could have wrought such terrible damage upon it. You were right, wise Senators.

"It was the *Ais* who tore Tarquinius to pieces. I was helpless to stop them, though I tried and was wounded in the attempt. Who can prevent the gods doing anything? Thereafter I could only watch in horror as they delivered their terrible punishment.

"When it was over, I did what I could to make it look like an outside assassination. Not out of fear for myself, but to keep from having to reveal the king's wickedness. I did not want the proud line of the Tarquins to suffer humiliation."

Lars Porsena's speech was met with a stunned silence. After a suitable time, Propertius said humbly, "We are very much in your debt, Lars Porsena. If the king's depraved attack upon a holy woman became public knowledge, it would severely undermine governmental authority."

"Governmental authority is already undermined," Lars Porsena replied. "The king of Rome has insulted the gods. The gods know even if the people don't. And now that the gods have turned their eyes to Rome . . . we must be very careful. . . ."

Severus was nodding agreement. "Following such an event, whoever replaces Tarquinius must be absolutely above reproach," he told the other senators. "It could take months, even years to find such a man. To allow us adequate time, the prince of Clusium has offered an alternate suggestion that we feel has great merit."

"For the immediate future, Rome might be better off with a division of power," explained Lars Porsena. "While waiting for the right king to manifest himself, appoint two men from your own ranks as joint interim governors. Surely no one is better equipped to rule Rome than its senators."

The *patricians* in the chamber responded with flattered smiles. But one toward the rear called out, "What about Tarquinius? He's dead, no matter how it happened. We have to deal with that issue first."

Propertius said, "Under the circumstances, the less that becomes known about this shameful affair the better. Publicizing the king's death would serve no constructive purpose. I suggest we announce that, as a result of unspecified abuses of power, Tarquinius has been expelled from Rome by a unanimous vote of the Senate. The people will see that we have acted in their best interests and their trust in us will be enhanced."

The prince of Clusium nodded and bowed his head. An almost palpable tension radiated from him, but those who noticed put it down to simple nervousness, the discomfort of a warrior mired in a puddle of politicians.

Severus clapped a hand on the prince's shoulder to lend him support. A spark leaped from Lars Porsena's skin, nipping the builder's fingers sharply enough to draw blood. At the same time the prince shot a sidelong glance at Severus, who blinked in surprise.

The light in the chamber briefly reflected in his eyes, turning them a vivid green. Lars Porsena smiled; the color faded.

The prince bowed his head and folded his arms across his chest, holding his body tightly. An invisible wave emanated from him, a tide that rippled across the room in concentric waves. Its greatest influence was felt by those closest to him at the front of the room, the oldest and most respected members of the Senate.

"What we have heard makes sense," a venerable, silver-haired *patrician* said thoughtfully. "You know that I have always advocated such a path." The other senators looked at him in astonishment. They had never heard him say any such thing. "Perhaps it is time the Senate took control of Rome. I move we appoint two consuls to serve as joint governors."

Another suggested, "Why not elect consuls annually until we find a new king? That way they won't have a lifetime lock on power."

"And if we give them the right to veto each other's actions," said the man to his left, "their decisions will have to be taken in concert."

But one lone senator at the farthest edge of the room remained dubious. "We would have to be certain the two we chose could work together. We must not rush into anything, my friends. Calm deliberation is required here. Reasoned debate. Perhaps we should name a committee to look into the matter further and draw up a list of possible candidates."

A suddenly impatient expression flickered across the face of Lars Porsena. Lifting his head, he fixed his coldly burning eyes on the silver-haired senator who had spoken first. After a moment the man exclaimed, "There is no time for committees and lists. But you are right, we need two men who can work well together; I nominate Propertius Cocles and his brother, Severus, to be consuls of Rome. And we'll vote on them here and now!"

THIRTY-SIX

Horatius was badly shaken. The scene Khebet showed him in the pool of blood was horrific beyond his imaginings. As the two men stared at the shocking vision, Khebet said in a surprised voice, "I recognize that man, Horatius. You saw him in the street, remember? Severus identified him as an Etruscan prince called Lars Porsena."

"I think I remember him," Horatius said vaguely, "but he is nothing to me. We just saw my mother dragged away, perhaps to some awful fate. That's all that matters. Come on, we have to find her!" He bolted for the door.

With the greatest reluctance, Khebet followed him. The priest's horoscope for this moon had promised revelations and excitement and the prospect had tempted him. Now he was beginning to wish he had stayed in Aegypt, where he knew how to avoid danger to his person.

Throughout his career Khebet had stood apart from every murderous court intrigue and repeatedly shifted allegiances within the jealous ranks of the priesthood to be certain he was on the safe side. Let others suffer the assassin's dagger or the poisoned cup.

Fear of death was not something an Aegyptian priest could admit. His people considered death the brilliant climax of life, the blazing sun following life's pallid moon, and spent fortunes to prepare for the Afterlife. Yet the idea of dying terrified Khebet. His real reason for joining the priesthood of Anubis had been hope that the god of death might relent for one of his own priests.

He had promised to help Horatius and so he would. For the moment, pride was as strong in him as fear.

Horatius ran straight for the palace gates. Khebet pounded along at his heels. When a guard challenged them with a leveled spear, Khebet summoned enough priestly authority into his voice to shout, "Urgent business! Aegyptian ambassador!"

The disconcerted guard stepped back and the two men ran out into the chaotic streets of Rome.

They did not go alone. Pepan, the invisible companion, hovered close to Horatius as he had done since early that morning. The Lord of the Rasne was even more desperate than Vesi's son. He had a better idea of what was at stake. *Hurry!* he kept urging, although Horatius could not hear him. *Hurry!*

Whenever they passed some reflective surface there would be a brief glimpse of an aristocratic face with an aquiline nose and a beard composed of two long, corkscrew curls, a face whose anxious gaze was fixed on Horatius. The young man was too distracted to notice. But the observant Aegyptian saw the image clearly, just as he had seen the shades that were joined with Horatius's spirit.

The skills Wulv had taught the boy Horatrim proved invaluable. Horatius was not far from the palace before he caught a whiff of her scent, that particular combination of skin and hair that would always mean Vesi to him. For a time he was able to follow the trail through the narrow, crowded streets, but then he lost it again. The smells of Rome coming awake on what promised to be a hot morning overwhelmed the scent of one woman. Horatius cast back and forth like a hunting dog, desperate to pick it up once more.

Fate seemed to be conspiring against him. A cartful of fish blocked an exceptionally narrow street; a crowd of children playing a ball game ran into Horatius and Khebet full tilt, then swirled around them, shouting and laughing, hindering their progress.

As he accompanied them, Pepan could hear the sibilant hiss that had replaced Vesi's identifying music. Sometimes it seemed to be getting closer, then again it faded when Horatius took a wrong turn. Pepan knew exactly where Vesi was, but the knowledge did him no good. Try as he might he could not transmit it to Horatius.

Then he became aware of another being hurrying toward Vesi. Mortals on the streets of Rome that morning noticed only a tall Etruscan prince emerging from the palace and setting out across the city. They gave way before him out of respect for his size . . . and the air of purpose and menace he exuded.

But seen from the Otherworld, there was no mistaking the *siu* that now occupied the prince's body. Bur-Sin reveled in the strong, virile flesh. This body, he promised himself, he would keep and enjoy for a long time.

Just as Horatius found Vesi's trail again, his nostrils were assailed by an appalling stench. He recoiled in disgust. Khebet cried, "I smell a demon!" But in the crowded, narrow streets they caught no glimpse of Lars Porsena.

The smell evaporated or was drowned in a hundred other odors.

Horatius resumed the search, instinct and the unseen urging of his invisible companion drawing him on until they eventually came to the edge of the fetid waste ground below the Capitoline Hill. Suddenly Horatius stiffened and threw up his head. With a broad grin he broke into a run. "Thank the *Ais*, I've found her, Khebet!" he called over his shoulder. He was sprinting toward a shack at the foot of the Palatine Hill on the far side of the waste ground.

Before he had covered half the distance he was attacked.

They came out of the heaps of refuse, and they came in their hundreds. An army of huge black rats swarmed toward Horatius as if guided by a single mind. The first few to reach him hurled themselves at his bare feet and ankles and began to gnaw furiously.

Horatius gave a violent kick but only succeeded in casting off two or three while still more ran up his other leg. Razor-sharp teeth bit deep into his upper thigh. A questing head rummaged beneath his toga, seeking his genitals.

Horatius screamed in defiance. Springing high into the air and simultaneously pummeling them with his fists, he at last dislodged his attackers and leaped clear of them—but only temporarily. Within a heartbeat they were on him again.

Meanwhile Khebet, badly frightened, ran back to the edge of the waste ground. The rats paid no attention to him. Their fury was concentrated on Horatius.

The young man fought with extraordinary agility, moving, moving, always in constant motion, knowing that if he stood still he would die. He used two broken lengths of wood to strike at the rats that came too close. Horatius leaped across a fetid pool. The rats in his wake poured into it, those behind landing atop those already in the water, pushing them down, until the pool was thick with bodies. Still the vermin came.

Horatius was tiring.

Khebet found it hard to believe that any human could battle so many rats at one time and stay on his feet. Summoning all the courage he could muster—and furious with himself for being in this situation in the first place—the Aegyptian looked around for a weapon. There was nothing but broken planks and bits of stone. He seized the nearest piece of timber and tried to make himself go to Horatius's aid . . .

. . . as a second army appeared on the scene.

This one was composed of thousands of warriors in armor, black, jointed armor. Individually each was the length of a man's forearm; together they formed a dark sea of chitinous terror. They waved audibly clashing pincers while their curving tails dripped poison.

"Scorpions!" Khebet froze where he stood. Although normally scorpions were solitary individuals, these were acting in concert. What malign force controlled them the Aegyptian could not say, but it was obvious they had a single, deadly purpose.

When the rats saw the scorpions they ceased their attack on Horatius. They gathered around him in a semicircle—and waited. The scorpions hurried toward them. Rat and scorpion bracketed the young man between them. Inexorably, they began to close on him.

Khebet shouted an unnecessary warning; Horatius was fully aware of the danger. He dodged to one side toward a perceived opening, but the rats were even faster than he. They filled the hole with their bodies and kept coming.

Horatius turned in the other direction, but the scorpions wheeled and blocked the opening. Then, when they were almost close enough to touch him, they inexplicably halted.

He took a tentative step. They reared up and menaced him with clashing pincers and he stopped.

The rats swiftly moved in behind him.

He was completely encircled with vermin now. Their ranks had grown so deep that even the most spectacular leap on his part could not clear them. He turned all the way around, slowly, looking for the tiniest avenue of escape.

There was none.

The rats watched, eyes fixed and unblinking. He noticed that their

245

eyes were green—but did rats not usually have red eyes? When he turned to look at the black carpet of scorpions, he saw that they too were sheened with a greenish hue.

Now that they had him trapped, Horatius expected them to attack from every direction. But they did not move.

He cast a frantic look toward Khebet. "Help me! I have to get to my mother, don't you understand?"

"Yes, yes, of course. I understand *now*," the Aegyptian added. He did not know the reason, but he recognized the magic. There was only one way to fight magic.

Throwing back his head and lifting his arms toward the sky, the priest of Anubis began to chant.

"Great Anubis, Jackal Lord, god of the dead, hunter of souls, devourer of *kas*! Hear me!"

Moments ago the sun was high in a cloudless sky, but suddenly black clouds came boiling out of the south. Across the waste ground a warm wind began to blow sharp particles of sand that stung Horatius's skin like a million tiny insects. But there was no desert close to the city.

The wind blew harder, hotter. Howled out of a black sky.

The earth rumbled beneath Horatius's feet. A quiver ran through the hills of Rome, a shaking of the earth that grew steadily stronger. Carried but faintly on the howling wind came the terrifying ululation of a hunting dog.

A jackal.

Within the tombs on the Palatine hillside, something stirred.

Something awoke.

One by one, the heavy stone doors of the tombs were pushed open from the inside. Out into the day shambled a parade of decaying forms, bodies phosphorescent with decomposition. Bodies long since vacated by their spirits, but obedient to the command of the god of the dead. Many were so rotted they had no discernible gender. Some were child-size; others still bore remnants of white hair clinging to their emerging skulls.

Step by awful step they came down the slope.

THIRTY-SEVEN

The rats were the first to notice. They lifted their heads and sniffed the air curiously, then began an excited chattering among themselves. A moment later the scorpions responded, turning in unnatural unison to see what was happening.

Following their movement, Horatius looked in the same direction. At first his mind could not comprehend what his eyes were reporting. Scores of dead and rotting bodies were making their way down the hillside toward him. They could not be described as walking, for many no longer had feet to walk upon. Yet they were capable of a form of locomotion. Staggering, sliding, dragging themselves as best they could, they set out across the waste ground toward Khebet. The smell of death went with them, wafted on a hot wind.

The Aegyptian never stopped chanting. "Great is Anubis, god of the dead! Eater of souls. Heart-render. Bone-cleaner. Skull-crusher. Flesh-shredder. Great is Anubis."

As the rotting bodies drew closer, the army of rats found the charnel odor too tempting to resist. Abandoning Horatius, they scurried in pursuit of the corpses. After a moment's hesitation the giant scorpions scuttled after them. The young man promptly seized the opportunity to run in the opposite direction, toward the shack.

As soon as Horatius was free, Khebet ceased his chant. The dead bodies promptly collapsed where they stood; the vermin swarmed over them.

The Aegyptian hurried to join Horatius, hands pressed to his ears to drown out the disgusting sounds of feeding.

Above it all, the jackal howled with delight.

The tall man filled the doorway, blocking the light.

When his shadow fell across Justine, she instinctively recoiled.

Lars Porsena laughed. "You are not glad to see me, dear child? Do you not recognize me? I have transformed myself for your pleasure. Think what delights we can experience together with your renewed youth and this fine strong body."

The lovely girl sitting on the pile of rags said nothing. The woman lying beside her moaned, however, deep in her throat.

Crossing the room in two long strides, Lars Porsena bent over Vesi. He took up Justine's lamp and studied her face. "Yes, she is who I thought she was," he said with satisfaction. "Excellent! This is excellent. He is searching frantically for her—and I have her. If he wants her, he must come to me. How very convenient."

"What are you talking about? Who is she? And who's searching for her?"

"I never knew her name, but I knew her body—briefly. Some time ago. Now her son is searching for her. She is the bait he cannot resist, but I must not let him find her. Not yet and not here. First I need to separate him from any possible ally so I can destroy him without interference."

"Why do you want to destroy him?"

He ignored the question. "We must go now, and quickly, before he catches up with us. I have put barriers in his way but they may not hold him for very long. On your feet, Justine, and the woman with you. I must admit there is a certain inconvenience to having a body; it has to be physically moved from place to place and that takes time and effort. But in my opinion the pleasure of solid flesh far outweighs its disadvantages. Come on!" He gave her arm a cruel tug.

Horatius found the door ajar. Stepping inside, he discovered one small room furnished with bits of rubbish scavenged from the waste ground. A cracked *amphora* contained the dregs of sour wine, but there was no sign of food. The place was much poorer than Wulv's old hut. The thought of his mother in such squalid surroundings sickened him. Vesi, who had already been through so much. His throat burned with grief for her sake.

He was almost relieved to find her gone.

A faint trace of her scent remained, however, lingering in spite of the pervasive odor of burnt cloth. A pile of rags in the corner was smoldering where a lamp had been hastily overturned.

"Is she here?" asked a voice from the doorway.

"I'm afraid not, Khebet. See for yourself."

The fastidious Aegyptian had no intention of entering the shack. Pressing his perfumed sleeve to his nose and mouth, he swept his eyes around the interior but remained resolutely outside. "Was she ever here?"

"Yes, and quite recently too."

"You were deliberately prevented from getting to her in time," said Khebet. "But I wonder why they did not overwhelm you when they had a chance."

"You mean the rats and scorpions? Who could make vermin obey them?"

The Aegyptian allowed himself a modest smile. "With the aid of Anubis I was able to make the bodies of the dead obey my will. Magic is all around you, Horatius. You yourself have more than one shadow."

"What are you talking about?"

before Khebet could reply, another being finally succeeded in
himself heard.

rom the smoke of the smoldering rags that had once been Jus-
's bed, Pepan formed a body. It was not much of a body, hardly substantial enough to exist for more than a few moments, but by using all
his strength he was able to give it a voice. *Vesi*, he said, forcing a simu-
lation of sound through a simulated throat.

Horatius whirled around to confront a shadowy figure vaguely
resembling a man, a man with a face he remembered. Had it been only
that morning? In the mirror?

Vesi, said Pepan again.

"I tried to find my mother and make her safe, as you said. I fought to
get here only to find her gone. She should have known I would come,"
Horatius complained to the creature of smoke. "She should have waited!"

Khebet thought Horatius sounded surprisingly like a small boy
who has just discovered that the world is not fair and one's best effort is
not always rewarded. He liked the young man better for it. But the
image in the smoke said, *Do not be unreasonable; she could not wait for you.
They have taken her to the caves.*

"What caves?"

*The Caverns of Spasio, east of Rome. If you follow her, there is grave dan-
ger to yourself. You must be on your guard every moment. Use the protections
I have given you. It is not Vesi he wants, but you.*

"Who? Who is doing this?"

Before Pepan could reply, the tiny fire that fueled the smoke finally
died.

Horatius turned to Khebet. "Was that what you meant about my
having other shadows?"

"He is but one of many, not all of them benign."

"Why are they following me?"

"I can only speculate. Some may have something to share with you;
others may want something of you. As a priest, I find your situation
most intriguing."

Horatius felt his temper fraying like old rope. "My situation isn't important; it's my mother I'm worried about! Those caves he mentioned—have you ever heard of them by any chance?"

"As a priest," Khebet repeated with emphasis, "I know a lot about the Caverns of Spasio. They are believed to be one of the entrances to the Netherworld. I had not been long in Rome before I made a point of seeing them—from the outside only, of course."

"Take me there, Khebet. Please!"

The Aegyptian shook his head. "I knew you were going to say that. Revelation and excitement," he added cryptically.

Later, four inhuman hunters crowded together at the doorway of the shack, peering in. The atmosphere inside still trembled with vibrations but he had gone. Yet at last they were closing in on him. The long hunt would soon be over.

Pythia would be pleased.

THIRTY-EIGHT

T
he country was rocky and rough, the trackway all but invisible. They were walking single file along the path, with herself in the lead and Vesi in the middle. From the rear his voice guided, "Left here. Now up through that defile, then off to your right. Move faster. I want to reach our destination while there is still enough light for him to follow."

"Where are we going?"

He responded with the familiar, demonic chuckle that had nothing of Lars Porsena in it. "My plan is simplicity itself, dear child. We are taking the mother to a place where the son can only follow by dying."

Suddenly Justine knew. Her stomach contracted with terror. "The Caverns of Spasio!"

"And through them to the Netherworld," he replied.

"You can't take me with you; I wouldn't . . ."

"Survive? Not under normal circumstances, no. But with sufficient power I can keep both you and this woman alive in the Netherworld for a time, just as I can maintain this body. I merely need a little nourishment. We spoke before about my nourishment, remember? That is why I need to keep you with me—even there.”

Half-fainting with fear, Justine felt her knees give way beneath her. Then to her astonishment the mindless woman behind her reached out and caught her. *“Courage,”* she whispered in a voice only Justine could hear.

“What can he possibly intend to do with my mother, Khebet?” Horatius asked over his shoulder as he trotted along the road the Aegyptian had indicated.

Khebet was struggling to keep up. He was a lean, fit man, as Aegyptian priests were inclined to be, but Horatius’s speed and stamina excelled his. “I cannot say, but he is evil, Horatius, evil. Whatever he means to do can only harm her.”

“Yet the face in the smoke said it was me he wants.”

“What better way to lure you into a trap than this?”

“I don’t care if it’s a trap,” Horatius said stubbornly. “I have to go to her; I don’t have any choice. No one else can help her.”

His fiercely possessive attitude toward his mother once again reminded the Aegyptian of a small boy. When boys became men and found women of their own that emotion was tempered. But although Horatius had a man’s body, the spirit within was still immature.

“Look sharp,” Khebet said aloud. “Somewhere up ahead there is a turnoff. Watch for a narrow path partially obscured by hemlock and cedar.”

No mortal was needed to guide the four. That fragment of Pythia which possessed Vesi provided a sufficient beacon. They were hampered by a lack of physical speed, but they were relentless. They would eventually catch up with their quarry.

Four cloaked and hooded figures glided along a Roman road,

speaking to no one. When they encountered a man on a horse the animal shied so violently it threw its rider, who sat cursing in the dirt and shaking his fist at them. They never stopped, never even looked around.

The dark goddess was waiting.

In the late afternoon sunlight Justine looked deep into Vesi's eyes, just for a moment. Then Lars Porsena gave them an impatient shove from behind. "Go on, go on! We are almost there."

"I thought I was going to faint."

"Gather your courage, dear child. I expect better of you than fainting. What is about to befall you is a simple transaction, nothing more. You need only think of something else and it will soon be over. Surely in your former line of work you were accustomed to thinking of something else during business transactions?"

Justine shuddered. His insinuating voice tore the scabs off old wounds.

The Caverns of Spasio were a series of interlinked caves extending into the bowels of the earth. Initially very large, they became smaller as they went deeper. Unlike other caves, a constant flow of air moved through them, claimed by the Romans to be the breath of the Netherworld. Through the caverns wound a river of black water. In its lightless depths no fish swam. The Romans believed that it was a tributary of the Styx.

Everyone knew the caverns had been fashioned by the gods at the dawn of the world. No human had ever explored the caves fully; no sane human wanted to. The few who did—brave or foolhardy, drunk or mad—had never returned. One cave led to another, then to another, all the way to the Kingdom of the Dead. If one went too far, one could never get back.

The entrance to the foremost cave was screened by scrub cedar and a tangle of white-flowered hemlock. Lars Porsena caught the hemlock and drew its blossoms to his face, inhaling the fragrance. "Wonderful," he breathed. Then he pushed the shrubbery aside to reveal a great dark cavern like a gaping mouth waiting to devour Justine.

"I can't." She screwed her eyes shut and clutched Vesi's arm. "I can't. I'm too afraid!"

"You can," insisted the demon's implacable voice. "Step inside, Justine. I grow impatient for my meal."

Pepan stayed close to Horatius and Khebet. He found no further way to communicate; so many restrictions applied to a disembodied *hia* in the Earthworld. Yet he remained within an arm's length of Vesi's son at all times, hoping Horatius would somehow sense him there and draw strength from his presence.

As they drew nearer the caves, his anxiety increased. First he heard a ripping noise and then a shrill screech, the unmistakable sound of pain transmitted through the Otherworld. Shortly thereafter, Vesi's identifying sound began to grow faint; fainter . . .

Hurry, Pepan urged Horatius, *hurry, before it is too late!*

But he feared it might already be too late. Death was only the least of what might happen to Vesi.

By the time Horatius and Khebet reached the caverns the daylight was beginning to fade. Peering through the opening into the first cave, they saw only darkness until their eyes adjusted. Even then the interior of the cave was grimly shadowed.

Horatius drew a deep breath. "I smell my mother's scent; she was here recently. Now her trail leads deeper into the caverns. She's going away from me all the time, Khebet; what shall I do?" he asked in the voice of a desperate child who expects adults to have all the answers.

"She has led you to a very dangerous place, Horatius. I most urgently suggest we turn back."

But no sooner did the Aegyptian speak than Horatius felt the familiar singing in his blood, filling him with knowledge and certainty.

We never turn back, he replied.

It was not his voice.

Khebet closed his eyes in a moment's silent prayer. *Great Anubis*, he thought, *do not desert me. I am in the presence of wonders*. "Horatius, please listen to me. We cannot pursue her through these caves. They lead to the Netherworld. Do you understand what I'm saying?"

"I do understand. But if that's where they've taken my mother, that's where I must go. Now you can come with me or stay here. It's all the same to me. You have a choice. I do not." The young man shoved his way through the shrubbery and disappeared into the cavern.

"Nor do I," Khebet murmured. Perhaps this was a punishment, though he could not recall any deed of his so heinous. Some unpropitiated crime in a previous life perhaps? "The only way I know to enter the Netherworld is through death," he argued as he reluctantly followed. "The *ka* must leave its body in order to cross the Styx. If your mother has been taken that far she is already dead, so there is no point in your . . ."

Horatius turned to face him. In the dimly lighted cave he stood with his hands on his hips and his feet wide apart. "I won't let her be dead," he said stubbornly.

"You have no choice!" the Aegyptian cried in exasperation.

"I do. I'm going to go get her and bring her back."

Khebet rolled his eyes skyward. "Anubis help me!"

"*You* help me, Khebet. You can work great magic. You brought the dead back to life."

"No, I did not. You saw dead bodies move, which is not the same thing. They were briefly animated through the power of Anubis, whose priest I am."

"Then when I bring my mother back from the Netherworld, you can do the same for her."

"You do not want an empty shell!"

"There is little more than that of her now," Horatius remarked ruefully. "I'm going after her, Khebet. Help me or not as you will."

The Aegyptian drew a deep breath. "Very well, I will do what I can. But if you have faith in my magic, you must obey me completely. Agreed?"

Horatius hesitated. Wulv was the only man he had obeyed. At last he said in a low voice, "Agreed."

The Aegyptian began to pace back and forth, talking as much to himself as to Horatius. "We cannot let you attempt the journey in your physical body; it will have to remain here, so you have something to come back to. I will release your *ka* to travel to the Netherworld. First I will need hemlock from those bushes outside to make a potion and some of the niter from the walls of this cave. Then . . ."

"Will you go with me?"

Khebet shook his head. "I cannot. I must remain behind to stand guard over your untenanted body. There are many malign spirits who would possess it otherwise."

"When my spirit leaves my body, will I be dead?"

"Not if the ritual works." The Aegyptian hesitated. "But I must be honest with you, Horatius. I have never performed this ritual before. It was old when the world was young, and only the greatest of priests would ever dare attempt it. Alas, I am not the greatest of priests," he added ruefully. "If I cannot reunite your *ka* with your body once you return from the Netherworld, you will be dead. Worse than dead, because while your *ka* wanders lost in the Otherworld, your body may be possessed by some foul spirit. There are many such who are always eager to seize uninhabited flesh. The gods alone know what crimes may be committed by something wearing your face and form."

Horatius shrugged. "I have no fear of death." That much was true. The other horrors Khebet described however . . .

He swallowed. Hard. "I trust you to bring me back," he told the Aegyptian. "But if you cannot, then you must destroy my body so nothing can use it. Promise me this."

"I promise."

THIRTY-NINE

At first the way through the caverns was all but lightless, yet Lars Porsena never faltered. With one hand locked on Vesi's wrist and the other on Justine's he plunged ahead, down and down and down, dragging the women with him.

Beside them ran the river. Merely an inconsequential trickle along the floor of the first cave, it broadened with each cavern. Try as she might, Justine could not discover any tributaries feeding the river, yet it continued to gather strength as it descended until the caverns echoed with a mighty roar. The sound beat against her skull. The water gave off a foul, disgusting odor like rotten eggs.

Once when Justine whimpered with pain, Lars Porsena pulled her to its very brink. "You can have a drink if you like," he said.

She turned her face away.

He laughed. "Come then, we have a distance yet to go."

They went on; her pain did not lessen. He had hurt her very badly and she marveled that she was still able to walk. As if he read her mind, he remarked, "You can stand an extraordinary amount of pain, you know. You are young. And I chose you because you are strong. You had to be, to survive the life you led." He chuckled. "If you think you suffer now, just wait until we cross to the other side of the river."

"I can't cross that river; it's the Styx."

"Have you so little faith in me? I told you—you will survive. You both will survive for as long as I need you to. Come now, dear child, do not scowl at me. I have restored your beauty. Why ruin it?"

"What are you going to do to me after we . . . after we cross the river?"

"I have not yet decided. The Netherworld offers many opportunities for pleasure; what I call pleasure, that is. You may not agree. But you will be able to explore at first hand aspects of your sensual nature whose existence you have hidden even from yourself. Does the prospect not intrigue you?" he asked archly.

"Of course not!" she shot back. Yet she was lying and he knew it.

The dishonesty of her reply pleased him. As a reward he lessened the severity of his grip on her wrist. "All mortals lie," he said. "Only the hopelessly mad, like our friend here," he jerked his head in Vesi's direction, "are innocent. Hers is the purity of mindlessness."

But Justine had looked deep into Vesi's eyes. There was a mind behind them, a cold, calculating mind that watched everything—and understood.

As they went deeper the caverns did not become darker. Instead a pale gray light, barely discernible at first, grew stronger as they progressed. By this light Justine was able to recognize a change in the life-forms within the caverns. At first there had been numerous common spiders scrabbling over the damp stone. Past a certain depth the spiders disappeared to be replaced by creatures that never saw the light of day. Translucent land crabs scuttled sideways at their approach, and albino bats hanging in packs from the ceilings mewled at them like cats or chewed the finger-thick white slugs that lurked in stony crevices.

Deeper still, the shadows partially concealed beings of such frightful, distorted shape that Justine could not bear to look at them, but averted her eyes and hurried past. Bulbous forms leaped from the dark river and fell back with a squelch rather than a splash. Once or twice long, sinuous tentacles broke the surface and waved hungrily, questing in the air for a moment before retiring to the depths again. Once one brushed against Lars Porsena and recoiled with a hiss.

"What sort of creatures live down here?" Justine asked him in a ragged whisper.

"Live? You can hardly say anything *lives* this close to the Netherworld, dear child. Beings do occupy this region, but their existence is very different from yours."

Something huge and hairy came bounding forward to press itself against Justine like an affectionate dog, but within the hair it had no bones, merely a jellylike form that molded itself disgustingly to her leg. She gave a gasp of horror and pulled away, almost breaking free of Lars Porsena's grasp.

His fingers swiftly tightened again on her wrist. "You do not want to do that," he cautioned her. "If you break contact with me I cannot keep your body alive, not down here. Look ahead and you will see light. We have almost reached our destination, dear child. Blessed art thou among women, for you are about to experience wonders."

FORTY

Khebet sat beside the body of Horatius, trying not to look down at the emptied face.

I should have gone with him, thought the Aegyptian. Or I should go back to Rome. In fact, I should never have come to Rome.

Regrets were futile. He could not leave the comatose body. He could only sit and wait.

Daylight beyond the mouth of the cave, already partially blocked by shrubbery, gradually disappeared. The creatures of the night began to make their presence known. Owls hooted, predators emerged from their burrows and began to take prey. A tiny voice shrieked in pain.

Khebet sat cross-legged on the floor of the cave in the dark and waited. Thirst began to torment him. He found himself dreaming of golden barley beer with beads of moisture running down the side of the cup or crystal flagons of melon and pomegranate juice or a great pitcher of cool water from the well in the temple courtyard. And rain. Slanting silver rain replenishing the Nile, making all things green.

When he ran an exploratory tongue over his lips they were cracked and dry.

When this was over, he was going to return to his own land and immerse himself in the Great Mother of Rivers until her water soaked into every pore of his skin.

He had used water from the tiny stream that ran through the cave to make the potion he had given to Horatius, preparing the mixture in a naturally hollowed-out stone the size of an infant's head. The water had seemed pure enough, though foul-smelling, but he was strangely unwilling to drink any of it himself. A priest of Anubis could surely overlook such a small inconvenience as a dry mouth.

The body he guarded was indifferent to discomfort. It merely waited.

Periodically Khebet put his fingertips against the broad, strong throat. The faintest sluggish pulse beat there, like a candle guttering just before it goes out. So far the ritual had worked, but Khebet knew full well the hardest part lay ahead, if Horatius returned at all.

He heard someone approaching. Rustling bushes betrayed the presence of several large bodies.

"Who is out there?" called Khebet. "I warn you, I am armed!" His hand dropped to the hilt of the small ceremonial knife he always carried tucked in his sash.

The rustling of the shrubbery ceased. Something was breathing out there, a stertorous breathing that did not sound quite human to the alarmed Aegyptian.

Khebet bent and fumbled on the floor of the cave, searching for the hollowed-out stone that had contained Horatius's potion. Then he slipped his knife from his sash and held the blade between his teeth. Untying the sash, he knotted one end of it around the stone.

Now he had two weapons. Yet he had never been so afraid.

·　　·　　·

The four outside the cave conferred silently with one another. Those whom they sought had gone within; there was no doubt of it. They must follow. But there was an obstacle.

Their leader thrust his body through the shrubbery until he stood in the entrance to the caverns. At that moment there was a silken, whirring sound; then a missile struck him a painful blow on the side of the head.

He staggered backward out of the cave.

"Got one!" Khebet gasped around the knife he still held in his teeth. He could hear them milling around and was not comforted by the fact that they did not speak aloud. The sounds they did make were sufficiently alarming. To Khebet's anxious ears it seemed as if something very heavy was being dragged through the undergrowth. And there was a curious dry sibilation like that of scaled bodies rubbing against one another.

Khebet was reminded of a nest of newly hatched snakes he had disturbed on the banks of the Nile in his boyhood, long before he learned serpents were sacred . . .

. . . and the glee he had taken in throwing brush down upon them and setting fire to the nest, watching the little snakes twist and writhe in agony.

No sooner had the image flashed through his mind than there was a concerted rush at the mouth of the cave. Flinging up his arms, Khebet spat out his knife so he could cry with all his might, "Great Anubis, empower me!"

A jackal howled.

Fire.

And the Little Ones burning.

The four had responded in fury to the picture in Khebet's mind. Sacrilege! The dark goddess would never forgive them if they did not punish the perpetrator of such an obscene act. Gathering around their leader, they attacked the cave with every intention of slaughtering the person inside. Pythia was always pleased by sacrifice.

As they filled the entrance a wall of fire blossomed just in front of them.

So intense was the heat that Khebet staggered back, but he did not lower his arms. He had called the flame from the living rock through the power of Anubis. This was the most potent of magics. He had secretly believed himself incapable of such great work. Thankfully, he was wrong.

When he felt Horatius's body against the back of his ankles, he shuffled his feet to push his friend farther from the flames. But Horatius was powerfully built, not easily pushed. Khebet would have to take hold of him with his hands and drag him, and that he dare not do. If he lowered his arms, the flames would die.

And so would he and Horatius.

The obedient flame roared upward to the ceiling of the cave and licked along it greedily, seeking out and feeding upon the tiny lichens that clung there. The fire-voice roared.

"Great Anubis, Jackal Lord, all praise to you from this your servant!" shouted Khebet to be heard above the fire.

Maintaining the wall of flame required a vast expenditure of physical energy. The Aegyptian could actually feel the heat being drawn from his body, even while it radiated back to scorch his face. He did not know how long he could continue to provide the barrier. His fingers were growing numb, pins and needles radiating down his arms, locking his wrists and elbows into knots of pain.

Then through a momentary break in the flames he caught a glimpse of the four hooded strangers. They lurked just inside the cave mouth, waiting, waiting. Only the fire could drive them away.

Khebet tried to summon courage. When he acted it was not bravery, however, but terror that impelled him. He would die unless he made himself move. He stepped forward toward the four, driving the wall of flame ahead of him into their faces.

There came a hiss of pain and the stink of scorched cloth.

When the fire bellied out to meet them they tried to hold their ground, but nothing living could resist flame. Tiny blue lights danced on their oiled skins and they retreated beyond the mouth of the cave and stood huddled together there, trying to decide what to do next.

Within the cave the Aegyptian desperately held up his tiring arms and wondered what to do. It was getting hard to breathe. The fire was using up the oxygen in the cave and drawing in replacement air from the lower caverns. Air that smelled of sulfur; noxious air that lay heavy in the lungs.

Khebet was wracked by such a fit of coughing he momentarily lowered his arms.

The flames dipped; the four beyond the cave mouth glided forward.

"Back!" screamed Khebet, recovering. His arms stretched high once more; the flames leaped higher.

The four stopped.

The man within the cave shivered violently in spite of the fire. "I do not want to die here, Lord Anubis," Khebet said in a hoarse whisper. "Not here, so far from the valley of the Nile. This is not my place, and the cause in which I fight is not my cause. Have mercy on this your servant!"

FORTY-ONE

He was dead.

Yet not dead.

The boy within him knew he should be terrified. But since that dreadful day when he'd left personal fear behind, only insatiable curiosity remained, untempered by caution or experience.

He could still feel fear for others however.

Vesi had been the hub of his life. Although his body was entering manhood, the child inside was still far too young to imagine life without her. To restore her to himself he would undertake anything, even the ritual that made him dead and notdead. For a fearless child the prospect was a great adventure.

There had been a brief, unsettling moment after he emerged from his fleshly shell when he found himself staring down at his own body. Khebet was crouching over him with long fingers pressed to his throat. In his other hand the priest still held the drinking vessel he had fashioned of huge leaves, containing the dregs of narcotic poison.

The Aegyptian twisted around to look up with his third eye at

Horatius's *ka*. Khebet's lips did not move, but the young man clearly heard the ancient language of the Black Land. "May the gods speed you on your mission."

Horatius had then begun the journey from which no one ever returned.

The way to the Netherworld was far from straightforward. The caverns comprised a passageway disorientingly located between different planes of existence. To complicate matters, being a disembodied spirit did not allow Horatius the ease of movement he had expected. In order to make any progress he had to force his *hia* forward through sheer concentration. Although he had no physical body this required a tremendous amount of effort.

Water was both a conduit and a barrier between the worlds of the living and the dead. He followed the course of the river because Khebet had told him it was the surest guide to his destination, but whenever he drew too close he sensed he could not cross.

Down he went, and down, ever farther from light and sun.

Horatius was still aware of physical surroundings: the walls of the caverns, the increasing volume of the river, the sulfurous stench that wafted upward from the depths. But behind stone and earth and water he saw, as if in a clouded mirror, another world.

Otherworld.

And the deeper he went, the farther away from light and life, the clearer it became.

This was a place of spirits and shades, of the ephemeral and the immortal. The Otherworld was a realm of dreams and nightmares, yet in its own way more real than the world he had just left behind.

Here myriad intangible figures swirled and danced in complex patterns much older than man. With a sense of mounting amazement, Horatius realized that earthly life as he knew it was nothing more than the skin on the surface of a sea of incalculable depth. Within that sea were glowing multicolored constellations inhabited by multitudes of spirits. Some were gorgeous; some were shocking. All were occupied with pursuits far removed from the interests of humankind. Their existence underlaid and even collided with his, yet until that moment he had known nothing about them.

Horatius was swept by an almost irresistible desire to join their seductive dance. Without the burden of a human body he could spend an eternity exploring the wonders of the Otherworld. The adventurous small boy inside him was sorely tempted. It would be so easy to leave the river and wander off. But instinctively he knew that if he did so, he would never return to the body that awaited him or rescue his mother.

Abandon her now and she will be forever lost, said a familiar voice.

A face swam toward him out of the darkness. A narrow, aristocratic face with long-lidded eyes and a distinctive beard on its chin.

Horatius's mouth worked, but no sound came out.

You have no need of a physical voice in this place. Think your words, imagine your phrases. This is the place of words made flesh.

"Who are you?" Horatius asked in his head.

"In human life I was Pepan, Lord of the Rasne. As I told you before, I was a friend of your grandmother and of your mother."

"And you are with me now?" This business of talking in one's head was intriguing.

"I have always been with you. No one walks alone. You have been reinforced more than most, however, and you will need still more help if you are to succeed in your mission. Come, we have not far to go."

"Are we near the Netherworld, Pepan? I hope to catch up with my mother before they—whoever they are—take her across the Styx."

"You cannot. You are at too much of a disadvantage here, neither totally alive nor truly dead. Be patient. Once you enter the Netherworld we will be able to give you appropriate armor and weapons. Then you can fight for your mother with some hope of winning."

Horatius said stubbornly, "I don't want to wait; I want to save her now!"

Pepan sighed. "You do not realize what you challenge. Right now Vesi is little more than an empty shell used by one of the *Ais,* a goddess who sometimes speaks through her defenseless mouth. She is also the captive of a *siu*, a demon of formidable powers. Few mortals have ever been more at the mercy of the Otherworld."

"A goddess? A demon?" Horatius struggled to understand. "Why have they chosen my mother?"

"Who can explain the motives of such beings? They play elaborate games according to their own rules. No human can understand them. But we are not without powers of our own, that is what I am trying to tell you. Once you are across the Styx . . . see ahead, where the river narrows and then rushes downward through an opening like a gullet? At that point we make our crossing."

"Will I be truly dead then?" It was a small boy's question.

"Truly dead."

"And dead forever?"

"Nothing is dead forever."

Horatius could sense the increased momentum of forces rushing toward the narrow opening. The mouth of the tunnel was formed like a skull with jaws agape. Stalactites and stalagmites resembled jagged teeth. Turbulent rapids were created as black water boiled with the effort of trying to force too great a volume through the open jaws. Back through the tunnel came the deafening roar of a mighty waterfall beyond, a wailing as of a million souls in torment.

In spite of himself Horatius hesitated. "Do you mean we have to go through there?"

"That is the only way. Are you afraid?"

"I haven't been afraid since Wulv and my grandmother were killed," Horatius boasted. "I was told to walk away from my fear and I did. But . . . this is different."

"Yes, this is different. Until you make your decision, the only help I can offer is to assure you that you are not alone."

"My decision . . . are you suggesting . . . I could turn around and go back?"

"There is still time," Pepan replied, "if that is what you want."

"More than anything else—except to save my mother."

269

"Your decision is already made then."

Suddenly Horatius felt as if a great burden was lifted from him. How liberating it was to fix on one star and let all else follow! "Yes, my decision is made. I choose not to be afraid. And I never go back."

"Good," Pepan approved. "Now we have to get you across the Styx. Look closely. Just before the river plunges downward you will see a tiny pier and a boat. The boatman is called Charun. Once you pay your fare his boat will carry you through the rapids, into that tunnel, down the waterfall that lies beyond, and deposit you safely on the opposite shore."

"Where will I be then?"

"In the Netherworld. And I will be there to help you."

"How am I to pay Charun? I have nothing."

Pepan laughed. "Usually a coin is placed in the mouth of a person at the time of their Dying in order to pay the boatman. Since you had no proper Dying, I will provide you with a coin. I am Lord of the Silver People after all. Otherwise you would have to tell Charun a secret; sometimes he will accept that as a fare."

As they drew near the pier and the boat, Horatius saw Charun waiting for them, tapping his foot impatiently. The boatman had the appearance of a very old man with a morose visage, cavernous eye sockets, and overly developed arms and shoulders. In his right hand he held a heavy hammer. As they approached he raised his left arm, hand outstretched.

A shadowy arm reached past Horatius and dropped something shiny into the boatman's open palm. Charun hefted the coin, judging its weight, then closed one eye and squinted at the silver through the other. At last he spat through a gap in his teeth and nodded. "This will do," he said grudgingly. "Passage for one. Who stays?"

Neither. A second coin fell into his hand.

"Passage for two to the Netherworld." Charun's nostrils flared and he inclined his head toward Horatius. "Are you sure this one is dead? There is the stink of life about him."

"He is ready for the Netherworld," Pepan replied, not answering the question.

"Are you being met? If you set off on your own through the Netherworld, you'll regret it. Satres rules there as god, but the only sure safety is with Veno, Protectress of the Dead. And you'll need someone to guide you to her, you know."

Pepan hesitated. "Our situation is different from most."

Charun shrugged. "Not being met. The more fool you then. But come ahead; it's nothing to me."

For such a turbulent voyage the boat seemed very small and flimsy. Horatius and Pepan had no physical bodies to entrust to its care, but their spirits could not make the crossing unaided.

"Water is too powerful for a *hia*," Pepan explained. "Water has life of its own and is holy. Our spirits must be carried across."

They did not step into Charun's boat; rather, it folded around them. Its sides were curiously spongy, giving Horatius the impression of a huge stomach. "We can't see!" he protested.

"Believe me," Charun assured him, "you don't want to look down into the waters of the Styx." He stood at the rear of the boat, hidden from Pepan and Horatius by its upcurving sides, and began to pole them through the water.

The small boat bucked like a fractious horse. Horatius had not thought the river wide, but they seemed to travel for an age, tossed violently about in the rapids. After the first few moments Horatius became accustomed to the motion and even began to enjoy it. He listened with fascination to the sounds coming from the water: horns blowing, pipes playing, wild laughter, somber weeping, voices of seductive beauty calling. More than once he wanted to peer over the sides, but Pepan warned him, "Charun is right; do not look into the Styx. What waits there could capture your spirit forever."

As the boat leaped and spun on the current they could hear Charun mutter to himself like any disagreeable old man. When he let loose with a particularly colorful expletive, Horatius could not help laughing. At once Charun snarled, "Are you not afraid of me?"

"Should I be?"

"I am Death!"

Horatius laughed again. "Why should I fear Death"?

The tunnel was a shock. The boat suddenly upended and dropped prow first with frightening speed. Nothing could be heard above the roar of the cascading water but the sound of endless screaming, as if multitudes were forever falling. Horatius wondered what it would be like to spend an eternity falling . . . falling . . . falling.

As they plunged downward he was thankful he had no solid body. Even so the sensation was sickening.

I am not afraid, he told himself firmly. I am not afraid!

Abruptly they hit bottom. The boat struck the surface of the river below the falls with a juddering impact, seemed about to overturn, then righted itself. A few moments later they felt it grate on the shore. The sides unfurled, falling away like drooping petals. From being a devouring belly, Charun's boat had been transformed by the journey into something resembling a giant lily.

Horatius scrambled from the boat. From the riverbank he turned and called to Charun, "When I return, will you take me back across the Styx?"

The boatman gave a derisive snort. "Return, you say? No one ever returns."

"I shall return," Horatius promised.

The young man found himself on a pebbled bank that gave way to rolling hills. A well-worn path meandered away from the river. Before setting out upon it, Horatius paused to look back.

To his surprise there was no sign of Charun or the boat, only the black waterfall roaring down into the black river.

He resolutely faced forward and set out along the path. "Are you still with me, Pepan?" he called over his shoulder.

"Of course. I told you, I am here to help you find your mother. You will not be able to track her in the Netherworld as you did on earth, but I can. I promise to stay with you as long as you need me."

"And then . . . ?"

Pepan did not answer.

Horatius followed the path to a promontory overlooking a small, tranquil lake of opalescent water. Around the lake grew a variety of trees resembling giant ferns, with graceful, drooping branches. From the trees unseen birds called in piercing voices. When Horatius looked up he saw no sky. Instead there was an arching ceiling far overhead, like the top of an immense cavern, lit with a reddish glow. Across this background occasional streaks of gold blazed and died abruptly, briefly illuminating what looked like cursive lines of script. The boy in him wanted to know who had written those gigantic words on the distant ceiling.

"Here we are at last," said a voice close behind him.

Turning, Horatius saw an elegant, middle-aged man in a close-fitting white robe with a dark red mantle over one shoulder. His face and curling beard looked familiar.

"Pepan?"

"I am." The man smiled and held out his arm. Horatius hesitated before reaching for it.

"But you're flesh and blood!"

"In the Netherworld all spirits are materialized. Those who have lived Earthworld lives take on the memory of the last form they possessed."

Horatius reached out to touch Pepan's bicep. "This is only a memory? It feels so solid!"

"I am as substantial," replied Pepan, "as everything around us. Only the Otherworld is insubstantial. Yet it has the greatest power of all," he added mysteriously. "Welcome." He wrapped his hand around the younger man's right forearm, and Horatius repeated the gesture.

"I have waited so long to meet you," Pepan said with genuine warmth. "So long to do just this."

Realizing he was feeling what seemed to be living flesh, Horatius looked down to discover his own familiar form. He was dressed in the badly folded toga he had put on this morning—so very long ago! Or was it?

He had lost all sense of time.

Extending his arms, he turned his hands palm up and studied the lines. "This is me all right, Pepan. But I don't understand. What about my other body, the one back in the cavern with Khebet?"

"Your Earthworld flesh remains intact where you left it. As long as it is not destroyed, there is the possibility of your *hia* returning to it. But make no mistake, the Netherworld form your *hia* now inhabits is vulnerable and must be protected. Here there are countless varieties of vicious beings with no desire but destruction. You will require weapons from your armorers."

"What armorers? I see no one but ourselves."

"No one?" Pepan echoed. Reaching out, he pressed the palm of his hand against Horatius's breast. "Although you now bear a Roman name, you are destined to become the greatest of all the Etruscans. Everything we are or were is carried forward in you. As I told you before, you have never been alone."

FORTY-TWO

At first the pearly waters of the little lake were warm against Horatius's skin. Concentric ripples spread across its translucent surface as the young man waded out from the shore.

"How far do I need to go, Pepan?" he called over his shoulder.

"To the heart of the lake. There, that's it. Now . . ."

"Now?"

"Crouch down."

"Is that all? Just crouch down?"

"Stop asking questions, Horatius, and do as you are told. Crouch down until the waters close over your head. Then you may stand again."

Closing his eyes tightly, he took a deep breath although he was not sure if he would need it. Was breath necessary in the Netherworld? So many unanswered questions. . . .

"Do as I say!" called Pepan.

Horatius bent his knees until he was submerged. The lake at its center was much warmer than elsewhere, and swirled in sluggish tides about his body, thick and cloying, more like honey than water. It insinuated itself into every orifice; almost at once his belly knotted with cramp. He hugged himself against the pain and stood up again . . . to discover that he was not alone in the water.

Another man emerged with him, a man who bore a discernible resemblance to Pepan. He wore military dress, including a breastplate of highly polished bronze that reproduced every muscle of his torso.

He responded to Horatius's look of astonishment with an amused smile.

"Fear me not, lad. I—and those who follow—are your ancestors; we are your past. I am called Zemerak and was your grandfather's grandfather. Under my leadership Etrurians stood shoulder to shoulder with Athenians and Corinthians, and beat the warriors of Carthage to their knees. As a trophy of victory I returned home with the splendid breastplate I wear, which I personally removed from the commander of the Carthaginians." He began unfastening the armor. "No weapon was ever able to penetrate its surface. I now bequeath it to you."

As he handed over the breastplate, Zemerak gazed deeply into the young man's eyes. Across his noble features a momentary regret flickered, for the life that had once been his. Then he smiled. "Hail and farewell, Horatius." Between one breath and the next he was gone.

"Give yourself to the water again," instructed Pepan from the shore.

Once more Horatius bent down, felt the lake close over his head, felt the cramping under his heart. This time when he stood up he was facing a stocky man with long-lidded, drowsy eyes. After a moment, however, Horatius realized their expression was deceptive. They watched him with a keenness he could feel in his bones.

"I am called Emnis, and I too was a warrior," said the stocky man. "In my time the tribes of Etruria were establishing themselves in many lands. From each of these we took the best and adapted it to our own use. The shield I carry is my favorite example." He held up a long, slightly curved rectangle of highly polished blue metal with a grooved bronze rim. "When the edges of several of these are fitted together they form a covering like the shell of a turtle, and several men can shelter beneath.

"Take this to protect you from your enemies, Horatius. Equally important, be generous in sharing it with your allies." The man smiled. "Enjoy your life, Horatius. Live every moment fully. Hail and farewell."

After his next submersion in the lake Horatius was joined by a lantern-jawed man with laugh wrinkles and a merry mouth. He clapped the young man on both shoulders. "So this is what my line has become! I am not displeased. My name is Tarxies. Long before Emnis was born I was a famous horse-warrior. I led raids as far away as the land of the Lydians, and took many captives . . . mostly women," he added with a wink. "A man astride a horse needs to protect his exposed legs from the knives and spears of his enemies, so I developed these greaves."

Tarxies reached down and fumbled beneath the surface of the lake, then came up with a pair of dripping shin guards. "These are molded of boiled leather so they cover the entire front of the leg from kneecap to foot, yet do not hamper mobility. You will find they fit you perfectly. While your wear them your legs at least will be invincible," he broke into a grin, "whether you have a horse between them or not. Hail and farewell, Horatius."

Horatius had barely raised his head when his next ancestor appeared in a fountain of bubbling water. "Mastarna," the man said simply, and the young man did not know whether it was a greeting or a name. Water dripped in pearly globules from the highly polished edges of the great two-headed ax he carried.

Horatius took a step backward in spite of himself. The man with the ax smiled grimly.

"They called me Mastarna of the Minoans," he said, "because I conducted a profitable trade with the sea kings of Crete. When I saw this double-bladed ax in the palace of Knossos I coveted it for myself. One head faces to the right as you can see, the other to the left. Both blades are looking for blood." He tapped the blade with a fingernail. It sang high and pure. "The metal is bronze sheathed in gold; the haft is ebony. A ceremonial weapon consecrated to the gods, it ultimately cost half my fortune and almost my life as well. But it was worth it. Now it belongs to you, Horatius of Rome." With a curiously mocking bow, he held out the ax.

When Horatius closed his hands around the haft he gasped at its weight. Turning away from Mastarna, he tried an exploratory swing. The gleaming weapon was perfectly balanced, and sang effortlessly through the air like the very voice of death.

"Well done," commented Mastarna. "I am relieved to see my prize is in strong hands. Use it well and often. Hale and farewell, Horatius."

The next donor was not a man, but a woman. Horatius could only gape at the sinewy female who rose from the lake beside him. A wealth of brown hair was twisted atop her head and held in place with a skewer of ivory that might have been animal bone. Her broad cheekbones momentarily reminded Horatius of Repana, but this woman's eyes were as wild as those of any animal in the forest. When she bared her teeth, they were very white against her deeply tanned skin.

"Bendis," she introduced herself succinctly. "The Huntress. I understand weapons. I give you my favorite." She handed Horatius a long strip of woven cloth, wide in the middle but narrowing at the ends and reinforced throughout its length with strings of supple rawhide. "You know how to use the sling," she said. "I watched you." Next she gave him a small doeskin bag and instructed, "Fill the bag with stones from the shore of this lake. Use them only when you must, but be assured you will never miss. Hale and farewell."

"Again," Pepan called from the shore, "bend down again."

The figure that emerged from the water this time bore little resemblance to the others. He was a stooped, emaciated man with only one tuft of white hair remaining at the back of his skull, sticking upright like the crest of some exotic bird. His skin was yellow with age, his nose thin and beaky, his lips so narrow he seemed to have no mouth. Across his arm he carried a folded hide.

Nodding gravely to Horatius, he said, "Among the Etrurians I was known as Waylag the Traveler, but over a long lifetime I answered to many names in many lands. Some of these names are now legend, not only to my people, but to others you may never encounter. In the reign of Atys, Son of Ghosts, I ventured to explore the First Kingdom of the Kush. There I learned forbidden secrets.

"In those days the animal kingdom was composed of our brothers, and shared its wisdom with us. One of my greatest teachers was Pardus the Cunning. When he died he left me his skin, the book in which his wisdom may be read. Clothe yourself with it; learn both patience and guile from your long-dead brother."

Reaching out, Waylag draped a magnificent leopardskin around Horatius's shoulders. "You travel in a new direction," he said. "Your feet will create paths no one has walked before. I envy you, Horatius. Never stop traveling. Never stop looking, and learning, and seeking. The answers do not matter, remember that. But the questions are all-important. And now—hale and farewell."

The young man stroked the silken pelt. It was as supple and glossy as if it had just been removed from the leopard and instantly warmed his chilled flesh. But once more Pepan gestured to him to immerse himself.

This time he had to wait until he felt as though his lungs would burst before the familiar cramp wracked him. Gratefully he surged to the surface and drew a deep breath.

The figure who emerged from the water beside him was barely half his height. Wild, coarse hair grew over most of its visible body. In appearance it reminded him, with a jolt, of the thing that had attacked Propertius on the road to Rome.

Automatically he lifted the ax. But Pepan cried out, "No, Horatius! He is the first of us!"

Without taking his eyes off the shaggy man, Horatius called, "What do you mean?"

"From that primitive creature's loins sprang the seed that one day became the Etruscans. The gift he brings you is perhaps the most potent of all."

The shaggy man did not speak; perhaps he had no words Horatius could recognize as language. But there was intelligence in his deep-set eyes beneath their shelflike brow. With great dignity, he drew something from the leather strip tied around his waist and held it on both outstretched palms.

Wedged into an antler-prong handle was a blade made of flint. When Horatius reached for the primitive dagger his fingers grazed the edge of the blade. He drew back with an exclamation. The weapon was incredibly sharp.

"Nothing cuts like flint," Pepan observed from the shore. "With tools like those our distant ancestors carved out a civilization."

Horatius cautiously reached for the dagger a second time. When he held it up to examine in detail, he was struck by the craftsmanship of the weapon. The flint blade had been painstakingly chipped into a perfect cutting edge. The antler handle was incised with a complex pattern carved into the bone. Using only the raw materials of nature, its maker had created both beauty and utility.

He looked at the shaggy man with new respect. The other gazed back across untold centuries. As their eyes locked Horatius felt a change taking place within himself. *The Silver People began with this man*, he thought, *and all the men and women who followed him. I have just met some of them. Each has given me the gift they value the most.*

For the first time in his life Horatius felt the humility that marks the beginning of true maturity. He bowed his head.

The shaggy man grunted in response.

Slowly, with a sense of ceremony, Horatius raised the flint dagger and pressed it first to his forehead, then to his lips.

Its maker understood. Light leaped in his deep-set eyes. Reaching toward Horatius, for the briefest of moments he rested his palm on the exact center of the young man's chest.

Then he too was gone.

Horatius stood alone in the water.

"Come out now," Pepan called to him. "You have everything you need to be a man of the Silver People."

FORTY-THREE

I knew he would follow her!" Lars Porsena crowed in triumph. "I knew the fool would never desert his mother. Let this be a lesson to you, Justine. Love is the greatest weakness of the human race."

"I should have thought," she replied, "love was one of our greatest strengths." She was beginning to know his mind. He liked to give lectures and expound upon his philosophies. Justine had known men like him before; men who paid for her time simply to talk. Lonely men. She found herself wondering if the demon was lonely.

The trio were crossing an arid plain beneath a crimson sky. The ground beneath their feet seemed firm enough, yet toward the horizon it wavered as if unstable, like the shimmering of a mirage.

Vesi walked between Justine and Lars Porsena with one of them holding each of her arms. When they first entered the Netherworld she had whimpered a time or two but now she was silent, docile.

They were accompanied by an ever-changing assortment of muttering, snarling entities, beings that lurked at the corner of the eye but were too frightening for Justine to turn and face. Some, she recognized. They were similar to the creatures who had inhabited her worst nightmares. Lars Porsena seemed unconcerned about them however. From time to time he even asked them questions and apparently received answers, though in a language Justine could not understand.

"There is no strength in loving," the demon was now saying to her with conviction. "Caring for anyone is always a mistake. That fool boy just proved it by walking into my trap. Love makes humankind vulnerable."

"Did you never love?"

"Only myself. I was the only person I ever found worthy."

The faintest tremor passed through the arm Justine held, as if some violent internal struggle were taking place far below Vesi's placid surface. Justine cast a swift glance at Lars Porsena but apparently he had not noticed, being preoccupied with his own discourse.

He went on describing the ways in which love invariably failed humans, but Justine was no longer paying attention, though from time to time she murmured a syllable of approval. Her mind wandered back over people she had loved—or thought she'd loved—times when the world seemed joyful. There had been many dark days in her existence and only a few bright moments. Those were the ones she wanted to remember. *What a shame*, she thought, *there were not more of them.*

"Love is the ultimate trap," Lars Porsena announced conclusively. "For the sake of love men march willingly to horrible fates, as that boy behind us will discover."

Justine awoke from her reverie. "Are you going to attack him soon?"

"Not yet. First I have some business to conduct in order to facilitate my actions here. Then I want to lead him far away from any possible help before I confront him. The Netherworld is a vast realm, most of it violent and unstable. You are already aware of some of its natives. There are others far worse.

"Satres, god of the Netherworld, makes no effort to control its inhabitants. He enjoys and even encourages their worst behavior to amuse himself. But Veno, Protectress of the Dead, provides a sanctuary of delight for those who manage to reach her. I have no intention of allowing that boy's spirit to find safe haven.

"If he gets close enough to Veno's realm, he will be able to call upon whatever kin he has there for aid. But if I catch him out in the open, I can call on allies of my own. All the advantage will be mine. I will tear his immortal essence to shreds."

"You never told me why you want to destroy his spirit," said Justine. "I can understand killing a living human for revenge, but to destroy the *spirit* . . ."

"Not easily done," the demon interrupted. "But possible. And in this case, necessary. Suffice it to say that while his spirit survives it poses a threat to me. I had long been looking for him. When I discovered his mother in the palace, I realized the weapon for his destruction had fallen into my hands."

"How did you know she was his mother?"

"I did not . . . at first. But I have an infallible memory, Justine, and soon recalled her face. I forget nothing. You would be wise to remember that yourself."

There was a chilling undertone in his voice. Justine was suddenly anxious to change the subject. "Have we far to go?"

"A distance yet. The Netherworld is much larger than the Earthworld."

Justine glanced over her shoulder. "What if he catches up with us before you conduct this business of yours?"

Lars Porsena turned to look at her over Vesi's head. In the lurid crimson light, his handsome features were strangely distorted, his wild, uncombed hair suggesting horns. "You are a clever girl. A woman with a mind—what a peculiar idea. We need something to slow him down of course. An impediment . . . ah, I know!" Releasing Vesi's arm, he raised his face to the blood-lit sky and clapped his hands together twice.

"Children of Rak-Sar-Shu! Attend me!" he called in a ringing voice.

Singly, then in small clusters, then in a blazing cloud, they formed out of the scarlet sky, the crimson light. Brilliant yellow-white sparks swirled and darted toward Lars Porsena like so many fireflies. But these insects made a sinister hissing sound as they approached. The cloud of malign spirits that had accompanied Lars Porsena fled in terror.

"What are those things?" whispered Justine.

"Fire fiends," Lars Porsena replied casually. "Infernal servitors of a Babylonian fire god now long forgotten. Only his minions remain."

When the burning sparks reached him and the others, they began circling the trio with ever-increasing speed. As they flew they grew larger until each was the size of a man's fist. The sound they made became a muted roar, the roar of a fire on the verge of exploding. The air smelled of molten metal.

Justine shrank back against Lars Porsena. "Will they hurt us?"

"Not as long as they are under my command," he assured her.

"Are they like you?"

He chuckled. "No one is like me, dear child. These fiends are very minor imps that have never been human. They possess almost no mind. Like fire they are obedient to anyone who can control them. Such beings have their uses however. Because they have little intelligence and are incapable of emotion, they are perfect tools for my purpose."

Addressing the moving balls of fire, he commanded, "Return along the way I just came until you find a young man trailing me. Surround him, harry him, do whatever is necessary to slow his progress without causing him to stop altogether."

He paused as if listening to the fiends, then chuckled his cruel chuckle. "I doubt if you have enough power to kill him," he said, "and I forbid you to try. Hurt him all you like but do him no fatal injury. He is mine. I will not rest until I have torn his spirit apart personally."

FORTY-FOUR

Waiting in the cavern with Horatius's body, Khebet listened anxiously to the sounds of the four regrouping outside. He was keeping Anubis's fire alight, but just enough to be a warning. In time his energies would fail and the fire would go out. What might happen then he could not imagine.

From time to time he looked at Horatius. The young man lay supine on the floor of the cave with his hands folded on his breast and his calm face upward. In the light from the magical fire he looked asleep. Beneath his closed lids the eyeballs moved constantly however, as if scanning the landscape of dreams.

Then, as Khebet watched in the flickering firelight, a change took place.

The landscape of the Netherworld was not a constant. As Horatius and Pepan advanced, the scenery changed dramatically. No sooner did they leave the lake than they entered into a parched, arid country. Stunted trees clawed the reddish atmosphere as if desperate for air, and the ground was baked to a hard crust. As Pepan had said, Earthworld tracking techniques were not possible here. Yet with the Lord of the Rasne at his side Horatius always knew which direction to take. From time to time Pepan would cock his head as if listening, then point. "We go this way," he would say with certainty.

"What do you hear?" Horatius asked.

"The music of her soul," was Pepan's cryptic explanation.

Horatius wanted to question him as to what he meant, but there were so many other new things to see, experience, learn. . . . There would be time later, he thought. Once Vesi was safe. Then he would sit down with Pepan and have a wonderful conversation. He would learn all about his mother and his grandmother and the land from which they came.

As he strode forward Horatius made a striking figure: a lean, muscular young man wearing a warrior's breastplate and the pelt of a leopard over his damp toga. The shield was strapped to his arm, the greaves covered his legs to the knee, and he had used the cloth sling to fashion a pouch holding the bag of stones from the Styx and his flint knife. The pouch hung round his neck within easy reach. Most impressive of all was the glittering two-headed ax he carried nonchalantly on his shoulder.

Horatius's clean-shaven face was calm, his eyes were clear and confident. Purpose was implicit in every line of his body. The bursts of childishness that had, understandably, still been part of his character seemed to have been left behind in the warm waters of the lake. Horatius Cocles was indeed a man.

I wish he were my son, Pepan told himself.

No sooner had the thought crossed his mind than he saw Horatius tense and flex his knees, dropping into a defensive crouch.

"What is it?"

"Look there, coming toward us over that hill." Shifting his grip on the haft of the ax, Horatius pointed with his free hand. A cluster of bright specks like blazing embers had appeared in the distance. They

286

rapidly drew nearer. As they approached, the two men could hear a low, sinister hum coming from the fiery swarm.

That sound told Pepan all he needed to know. "Beware, they are dangerous. By their very nature most natives of the Netherworld are inimical to life."

"I am armed."

"You are," agreed Pepan, "but your arsenal is not proof against fire."

The specks had become spinning, blazing balls that hurtled through the air at tremendous speed, trailing streamers of black smoke in their wake. Horatius stood his ground. "They may pass us by, Pepan. There is no point in worrying until . . ."

Suddenly one of the balls swerved toward Horatius. A second and third followed, then halted in midair to hover in front of him, blocking his path. When he took a step sideways the globes of fire moved with him. The others gathered until there were twenty or thirty forming a burning barrier. They would not let Horatius pass, yet neither did they force him backward.

"See if you can get around them, Pepan."

But when the Rasne lord attempted to move to one side the fiery spheres took up an orbit around himself and Horatius, effectively penning them in. As they circled the pair they continued to spin at great speed individually, throwing off more sparks. A few caught and flared briefly in the dry grass. There was an immediate smell of carbon, acrid on the tongue.

Horatius narrowed his eyes in thought. "He did this before, Pepan."

"What are you talking about? Who did this before?"

"The man who stole my mother. He sent rats and scorpions that threatened me but apparently did not intend to kill me. Well, I'm not waiting to see what these things will do!" Clenching his jaw, Horatius took a step forward.

Pepan started to say, "Be very caref——" then stopped. The burning globes in front of Horatius had given a tiny amount of ground. They allowed him to move forward one small step at a time, no faster.

Horatius looked over his shoulder. "It's all right, Pepan. Apparently we are allowed to advance as long as we go slowly. But why should we go slowly?"

As if in reply something sang through his blood, the wisdom of a wise old warrior recognizing an enemy strategy. "We are being delayed because those we pursue need more time!" exclaimed Horatius. "Time to give themselves an advantage . . . right! Let's go, Pepan. Run!" He raced forward.

Instantly the low hum became a furious roar. The globes of fire launched a concerted attack on Horatius, coming at him from every direction. He plunged ahead, through the fire, through the smoke, grimly holding on to the haft of the useless ax, possessing no adequate weapon against the flames but his own courage.

The spinning balls narrowed their orbit until they were close enough to singe hair, but Horatius never hesitated. He ran as fast as he could, with Pepan hurrying after him. In an effort to slow him, the balls of fire began mindlessly hurling themselves at Horatius's body. The first struck his breastplate a glancing blow and went spinning away. The next one hit harder, only to explode in a gout of flame and a shower of sparks. A tiny, insanely raging entity fled unnoticed from the holocaust. Undeterred, the other fiends pressed the attack. Another ball hit the breastplate and burst, the flames spinning off at an angle to graze the exposed underside of Horatius's arm. The flesh turned an angry red as a long blister erupted from wrist to elbow.

Ignoring the pain, Horatius ran on.

As Khebet watched over his body in the cave, one of Horatius's arms turned crimson. The Aegyptian lowered his own arms long enough to lift the limb and examine it, finding a huge, watery blister rising on its underside. Almost at once a second blister appeared on the upper arm. The hair on the arm crisped and smelled scorched.

There was only one conclusion: Horatius was being injured in the Netherworld.

And if he was injured, he could be slain. Khebet lifted his arms and cried to Anubis, "Great Jackal Lord, protect this man who now roams the dark realms! Let him survive this ordeal, allow him to return safely and I will offer you sacrifices of a splendor to rival that of the pharaohs!"

He made the promise wildly, rashly, with no idea how he would keep it but knowing he must find a way somehow. The gods always demanded that promised sacrifices be delivered.

But he had a more immediate worry. During his brief lapse of concentration the fire across the entrance had died down enough to allow the four to get into the cave.

FORTY-FIVE

The moon pool in the long, oval hall began to bubble. There were no mortal eyes present to see the figure that partially emerged. The multibreasted Pythia rose briefly through the white water, looked around, found herself unattended, and submerged again. But she did not leave the pool, need not leave it in order to travel from her Earthworld temple to her Netherworld palace. Water was a conduit.

Among the many palaces belonging to gods in the Netherworld, Pythia's was neither the largest nor the most spectacular. Each palace was a reflection of the nature of its builder. Some employed Cyclopean architecture on a scale beyond Earthworld comprehension, with massive walls and immense towers that bespoke granitic power. Others were as tiny and exquisite as jewels, refracting rainbow prisms from crystalline pinnacles where silken banners fluttered gaily.

Pythia's stronghold in a shadowy valley between two brooding mountains possessed a sinister quality all its own. Even among the gods, who could scarcely afford to condemn any of their own for misbehavior, Pythia's name was enough to provoke a shudder of distaste.

At the dawn of Humankind she had interfered with Man and Woman in the Birth Garden, tempting them to an intellectual independence that altered the entire relationship between *Ais* and human. For this she was ostracized.

In response she had made defiance her coda. Her palace reflected her truculent attitude. A vast circular structure surfaced with overlapping scales of metallic black, the mansion rose level upon level, coil upon coil, to dominate the valley. Any who wished to traverse the region between the two peaks found their way blocked. Should they be so foolhardy as to venture into Pythia's realm, they could expect to find agony.

As a result the coiled black palace had very few visitors. Sumptuously furnished in onyx and obsidian, the building echoed hollowly whenever the goddess was not in residence. At its heart was another pool whose waters were as thick as curdled cream and as black as tar.

Here Pythia resurfaced.

A flat forehead, a long narrow jaw, a slash of a mouth. In the Netherworld, however, Pythia was not blind. Her keen eyes were like buttons of polished jet. Turning her head slowly on its long, slender neck, she surveyed the hall surrounding the pool. Her tongue briefly flickered through half-parted lips. "Attend me!" she cried.

Servants hurried forward. Like her Earthworld acolytes, these had serpentine forms. In their case, however, the shape was natural rather than an imposition of the goddess. Pythia was fond of capturing humans and warping them to suit her fancy, but those who served her in the Netherworld were snakes at heart and had never been anything else.

"You command, we obey, Great Goddess," they replied with superficial deference as they approached the tarry pool. They did not share the fear of the Earthworld acolytes that prevented them from looking at their deity. They looked at her openly, almost insolently, as if measuring her usefulness and wondering if they might find a god more worthy.

"Have you any news of the traitor Bur-Sin?" the goddess demanded.

They writhed in indecision, urging one another to go forward. Finally one was shoved to the front. "Even now," the reluctant messenger related, "he is approaching your palace, Great Pythia."

"What! He is coming here? Deliberately?"

"So it seems. With him he brings two females from the Earthworld. Two living females. He maintains their fleshly bodies by using the power he stole from you, an act of appalling audacity. Possibly he thinks to use them to do you harm."

"Harm me? What wretched demon could possibly harm me?" With a great upward surge, Pythia began to emerge from the pool. Beads of moisture clung to her polished skin. She rarely left the water completely because her form was repellent even to herself. Once she had been as beautiful as the loveliest human woman. But in punishment for her misdeed the other gods had put a mark upon her forehead and cursed her to crawl forever in the dust.

She found it easier to hide her shame within the shelter of opaque water. For some acts, however, she must commit to dry land.

Up she came, and up. The slender column of her neck gave way to sloping shoulders, then a grotesque cluster of swollen breasts with their ruby nipples—and one withered breast, empty and useless. The elongated torso that followed was muscular and sinewy, without waist or hips. As more of Pythia emerged from the water her resemblance to anything human disappeared. Her undulating body was broad and thin, like that of a monstrous eel, and of astonishing length.

With a final convulsive heave she cleared the water and lay stretched upon the floor of the hall, half-filling the room, her many bosoms heaving. Gathering herself, she swiftly coiled into a huge and deadly spiral.

Her servants recognized their danger then and tried to slither backward. Before they could escape she reared up until the forepart of her body towered high above them. A broad hood of mottled black flesh unfolded from either side of her neck just below the jaws. Then she dipped her head and played her flickering tongue over the one who had spoken.

Pythia's jaws opened; fangs shot out, dripping a paralytic poison onto the hapless servant. Her victim could only watch with eyes bulging in horror as her jaws unhinged enough to clamp around his entire head . . . and rip it from his body.

The others fled. Alone in the central hall of her palace, the giant figure of Pythia swayed back and forth. Softly she hissed to herself, "Why? Why has he burdened himself with women?"

FORTY-SIX

The fire fiends continued to hover close, but Horatius would not be deterred. The burning globes did not attack him again however. "They seem more inclined to hinder you than to harm you," Pepan remarked.

"Perhaps I can't be harmed in the Netherworld."

"Make no mistake; you can. Only in the Kingdom of the Dead is there total safety, and you're not dead."

"What about you?"

Pepan replied, "As long as I remain outside the kingdom I too am vulnerable."

"Yet you choose to remain with me?"

"I do."

Horatius paused for a moment and turned to look the other man squarely in the eyes. "I owe you a debt," he said.

"You do not. I am atoning for failing your mother and grandmother a long time ago. I made them a promise I could not keep. Now, through you, I have a second chance. If anything, it is I who am in your debt."

They struggled on. In time they found themselves skirting a broad plain that stretched almost to the horizon. The ground was littered with immense slabs of limestone like a giant's paving stones. Leafless, spiny plants thrived in the gaps between them.

When Horatius tried to go over for a better look, the fire fiends closed around him, attempting to prevent him. Stubbornly he forced his way forward. When he reached the first of the stones the burning globes drew back. "It looks as if they can't follow us here. We can escape them now, Pepan! Come on!" He ran onto the limestone plain and began leaping from one stone square to another. Pepan hurried after him.

The fire fiends hung in the air at the edge of the rocky expanse like a swarm of frustrated hornets. The tiny plants growing between the stones crisped and flamed, only to immediately reappear, then burn again.

The rough-surfaced stones were split and fissured, frequently unstable, shifting underfoot. Running proved impossible and Horatius and Pepan were forced to slow to a walk. The young man felt an uneasy prickling at the back of his neck. Beneath the lurid red sky that was not a sky, the plain had an eerie, haunted quality. "What is this place, Pepan, do you know?"

"I cannot say I do, much of the Netherworld is unexplored, but . . . look over there, Horatius."

Pepan was pointing toward a massive framework emerging from between two slabs of stone. Like the ruin of an ancient building, a set of curved vertical timbers clawed at the sky. Horatius went to take a look. Moments later he called over his shoulder, "These are bones, Pepan!"

The Lord of the Rasne hastened to join him. Together the two gazed down at the ribcage of a giant skeleton, crushed and broken, slowly being freed by natural forces as the stones shifted and the soil wore away. Once a creature of monstrous size had been buried there. Now all that remained was its decaying frame.

"What was it, Pepan?"

The older man studied the bizarre shape, running his hand over the hard surface. "No creature you or I have ever seen. Nor are these actually bones, not as we know them. They are made from some other substance entirely. Not stone, but not bone either."

"Can you say what the creature looked like when it was alive?"

"I cannot even say if it ever was alive. This is the Netherworld, remember. Earthworld life is alien here. I . . . where are you going?"

"There's another one over there!" Careless of his footing, Horatius trotted off at a tangent across the stony expanse.

Pepan caught up with him as he bent over another recumbent form. This one was much smaller and of a different shape. It included a skull of vaguely human proportions but with curving tusks and a bony crest across the top. From the shoulder blades spread a fan of bones that might once have supported wings. The entire skeleton reminded Pepan of something only glimpsed in dreams.

They found another, a human skeleton, with the skull of a bull and curving horns. Beside it lay a creature that had the body of a horse, but the foreparts of a man. A few paces farther on was a huge skull that possessed three sets of eye sockets, three gaping mouths.

Pepan crouched to rub his hand over the three-faced skull. "May the *Ais* forgive us," he whispered. "I believe we have stumbled into a graveyard of the gods."

"But the gods are immortal, surely." Horatius was staring down at the perfectly preserved skeleton of a man—but a man four times taller than a normal human. He tried to imagine a limit to immortality and failed.

The two continued on their quest. Horatius was troubled by what they had seen. From time to time they found other relics, each hinting at some mystery, some legend. He paused by each one, struggling anew to understand the mystery.

Gods die.

And if gods can die, what hope for man?

He was turning to put the question to Pepan when he heard a low groan. The sound was soft and musical, so sweet that at first Horatius thought he was hearing a song or a melody played by the wind moaning through the bones of dead gods.

When it came again, he followed the sound to its source.

At the foot of a towering vertical stone that pointed to the crimson sky was a pit littered with bones. A huddled figure lay in the bottom of the pit. "Pepan! Look here!"

The Lord of the Rasne hurried over to put a cautionary hand on his arm. "It might be a trap."

"Or it could be someone in pain," argued Horatius. As if to confirm his words, another moan sounded from the pit. He shook off Pepan's hand and jumped down. His companion could only follow, shaking his head.

When Horatius and Pepan tossed aside the piled debris of ancient bones and knelt beside him, the being opened his eyes. Orange eyes. Star-shaped eyes set in a pale but perfect oval face, surrounded by a mane of curling, golden hair like the petals of a flower. He was very beautiful but he was not human.

When he saw them he groaned again and closed his eyes.

"Who are you?" Horatius asked gently. "Can we help you?"

The voice that answered was very weak. "You cannot help me. I am dying."

"Are you wounded?"

"No, merely starved."

"We have no food."

"I need no food."

"Who are you?"

"Why do you care? But if you do—I am what you call a god. A once-god."

Pepan tensed. "Be careful, Horatius."

"You need not fear me." The orange-eyed being attempted to sit up. "I am the one who should be afraid of you. My enemies have sent you to mock me in my weakness. I take satisfaction from knowing that their time will come. One day they too will lie here and wait for oblivion."

Horatius crouched beside the god. With tender care he gathered the being into his arms and stroked the pallid brow, brushing strands of golden hair away from the extraordinary eyes. "We have no intention of mocking you; we are not cruel. But if you are a god, why are you not immortal?"

"I am immortal; I have always existed and always will. But not with this face and form. Their substance was created by the imaginations of humans who long ago conferred godhood upon my spirit. They encased me in this image. Now humans no longer worship at my shrines. My temples have fallen; no power of faith sustains me. My beauty is dying and I grieve for its loss."

"Of course!" exclaimed Pepan. "Horatius, long before there were Etruscans other people walked the earth, people who worshipped very different gods from ours. When those folk died out, their vision of the gods must have died with them. Here we see an example of someone's god dying because the belief has died. Don't you see? The *Ais* need us as much as we need them!"

Horatius was deeply moved by the beautiful, fading creature. "Is there no way I can help you?"

The orange eyes gazed up into his. "Believe in the reality of me. As long as I am real to you, the form you see will survive. In return I will give you my help in your hour of greatest need."

"You have my pledge," promised Horatius. "May I know your name?"

"Some have called me . . . Eosphorus."

"Eosphorus," Horatius repeated, his mouth full of the word. "Eosphorus." Even as he said the name, the creature in his arms began to change. A glow appeared beneath the clear skin, then grew in power until Eosphorus was radiant. His beauty became so great Horatius had to turn his face away. "I cannot look at you; you dazzle me."

"I was once known as the Shining One," the god in his arms said.

FORTY-SEVEN

When he saw the two mountain peaks rising ahead of him Lars Porsena smiled. "We are nearing Pythia's palace," he told Justine.

"Is that where we're going? But you told me she hates you and wants to harm you."

"She does. I am tired of fleeing however. I want to put an end to the quarrel between us and rid myself of fear. Cowardice ill becomes me, dear child."

"So you are going into her den to confront her?" In spite of herself, Justine could not keep a throb of admiration from her voice. Hiding from trouble, or running from it, or not admitting its existence—these were her ways of coping. They had failed her miserably, as her life proved. Yet the one time she had taken her courage in both hands and faced a tormentor, it had proved to be this demon at her side.

Lars Porsena uttered his demonic chuckle. " 'Den' is hardly the word I would use for Pythia's palace. She is lazy and likes her comfort, as you will soon see. Her taste is a bit bizarre, perhaps, but reflects her true self. There, just ahead. Those gates in that high wall are hers. Beyond them is a long road that leads to her, ah, den."

The gates were made of metal bars cunningly contorted to resemble a tangle of briars. Large, needle-sharp thorns protruded in every direction. Anyone who attempted to force the gates open, or climb over them, would be badly lacerated. But there was a handle; a single smooth handle shaped into a serpentine curve.

"Try it," Lars Porsena suggested.

Brushing past Justine, Vesi reached forward and took hold of the handle.

From somewhere among the thorns came a dry, menacing rattle.

Vesi, unintimidated, twisted the handle until both gates swung open. Lars Porsena's eyebrows shot upward in surprise, but he recovered to reward her with a sweeping bow. "After you," he said.

Once the three had passed through the gates they heard them slam shut. Justine glanced back. No visible agency had closed the gates, and there was no handle on the inside.

Ahead lay a road that wound down a dark valley between two somber peaks. No light reached that road; it lay in eternal shadow.

"This place frightens me," Justine whispered.

"So it should," Lars Porsena laughed. "This is the Valley of the Shadow."

They had gone some distance before Lars Porsena stumbled. Then, visibly faltering, he stumbled again and came to a halt. "I am growing weaker," he complained to Justine.

"Surely not here, not so soon."

"Yes, dear child, right here. Right now! I dare not approach Pythia unless I am at my full strength. And for that I need you. It is your reason for being. Come to me now," he said in a seductive voice. "Come to me."

The demon opened his arms.

Afterward Justine walked in a daze for a time. When at last she took notice of her surroundings she discovered they were approaching a round, oily-looking black building that rose layer upon horrid layer, each successive coil smaller than the one below. There was no peak at the top of the structure, no tower, no turret. Merely an awful emptiness.

"Pythia's palace," announced Lars Porsena, striding forward.

Scale-cloaked and hooded figures guarded the double doors that led into the palace. Although their faces were concealed by the enveloping hoods, Justine sensed they were apprehensive at the arrival of the visitors.

Lars Porsena said brazenly, "Tell the dark goddess her favorite acolyte has returned. Announce the arrival of Bur-Sin of Babylon."

The guards drew back; the doors swung wide.

A second set of figures wrapped in iridescent, scaled cloaks appeared from within the palace to usher Lars Porsena and the two women into a large audience chamber. The room was devoid of furniture aside from benches of obsidian and onyx lining the black walls. Sullen yellow flames flickered in bronze braziers. Pythia's servants indicated silently that the new arrivals were to seat themselves. Then they all but ran from the hall.

The central feature of the audience chamber was a circular pool brimming with black liquid. From time to time a lazy bubble surfaced, glistened, broke. Justine found herself gazing at the pool as if hypnotized. Her mouth was dry, her tongue thick with an ancient and irrational fear of the unknown.

A disturbance destroyed the apparent tranquillity of the pool, a slow roiling that gradually intensified, a sense of some mighty body moving below the surface.

When Pythia's head emerged from the pool Justine gasped and opened her mouth to scream, but Lars Porsena's fingers tightened in a savage grip over her jaw. She choked on her fear in silence.

Vesi sat unmoving, looking straight ahead.

The goddess rose from the water just far enough to reveal the upper curve of her breasts and fixed unblinking eyes on Lars Porsena. "You."

301

"Yes."

"You never fail to surprise me, Bur-Sin; I suppose that is why I tolerated your insolence and your insubordination for so long," said Pythia in a terrifyingly soft and sibilant voice. "But this time you go too far. Or have you returned to submit to the punishment you so richly deserve?"

"No, Pythia, I have a different resolution of our conflict in mind."

"What could you possibly suggest that would give me more pleasure than reducing you to blubbering madness?"

"A sacrifice."

Justine's stomach contracted with fear. But instead, Lars Porsena gestured toward Vesi. "I have brought you this woman as an offering. Visit upon her whatever punishment you had in mind for me."

Justine observed that Pythia had yet to look at Vesi. "Why should I accede to your request, Bur-Sin?" the goddess inquired. "What makes you think she would be a sufficient substitute for you?"

"Because she is not just any woman, Great Goddess. She is quite remarkable: an oracle, a seer. I personally witnessed her prophesying for the king of Rome. We both know that oracles are favored by the gods. Therefore she is a very valuable sacrifice and one that should more than repay my, ah, misdeed."

At last Pythia transferred her gaze to Vesi. "An oracle, you say," she continued in the same conversational tone. "Unless my eyes deceive me, she is also an Etruscan. She certainly has Etrurian features; the race beloved of the gods, or so they claim."

"Therefore she is twice valuable, Pythia. And in addition—just so you will know how much I am willing to pay for your forgiveness—she is the mother of my child," Lars Porsena finished triumphantly.

"Indeed! You would do that, surrender the mother of your child to me? An impressive sacrifice, Bur-Sin. But"—the tongue of the goddess flickered fretfully between parted lips—"is one woman enough to atone for your crime against me? Even if she is all you claim."

"Oh, she is, Great Pythia! I can prove it." Lars Porsena caught Vesi by both shoulders and clamped his fingers painfully deep into her flesh.

"Say something," he growled at her. "Look into the future and tell us what you see."

Vesi did not move, did not blink.

"You are trying to deceive me, Bur-Sin," drawled Pythia. "I expected as much."

"This is no deception! She is a seer, I tell you! If you once hear her speak, you'll be convinced."

"Oh, I have heard her speak," replied Pythia in that unmistakable voice. But the words did not come from the goddess in the pool.

They came from the lips of Vesi.

Lars Porsena snatched his hands away from her shoulders as if burned by her flesh. "I have not only heard her speak," the voice went on, "but I have spoken through her. I even used her as a tool to tear apart a human for my amusement. Bur-Sin, you fool, you have brought me my own plaything as a sacrifice. The mother of your child, indeed! How ironic, since my minions have exhausted them- selves searching for your son. Once they found him, he was to be used as a lure to draw you: and I then thought I might kill him in front of you as part of your punishment. But now that I have you in my coils, I do not really need him. I can punish you quite sufficiently in a thou- sand other ways. Ah, Bur-Sin, for you I will create undreamed of tor- tures! You will die each night, awaken reborn in the morning, suffer and die again. Remember, I warned you."

As Vesi fell silent, Pythia emerged farther from the pool, revealing a second and then a third row of breasts. Justine fought an insane desire to giggle. *A whore in Rome could make a fortune with those,* she thought. Then she noticed that one breast was desiccated, as flat and flaccid as an empty purse.

Pythia noted the direction of her glance. "*He* did this to me," she hissed. "Bur-Sin, whom I trusted, whom I even loved. He crept close to me as if he found my form beautiful, and when he was nestled on my bosom, moaning with what I thought was pleasure, he . . . did . . . this!" The voice of the goddess shrilled to a screech.

Rising still higher, she turned toward the demon. The great mantle on either side of her neck flared wide. "You stole enough of my power to make a body for yourself! Several bodies, apparently. That is a fine one you wear now, Bur-Sin. Tell me, is it virile? Is it a worthy lover for a goddess?"

Her sarcasm was like the lash of a whip. Lars Porsena clung to the tatters of his courage. "Accept the sacrifice I have brought you, Great Pythia," he pleaded, "and I will demonstrate the prowess of this splendid body in whatever way pleases you."

Her cold laughter was even more unpleasant than a demon's chuckle. "Until you return what you stole from me, nothing you do could possibly please me."

"You want me to return the power of embodiment? I beg you, Pythia—reconsider. Without it, I would lose the body I now wear."

"Having a human body again seems more important to you than anything else, Bur-Sin. How very curious. I would find one rather stiff and limiting, myself. But surely you need more than the power you stole from me to support your current situation. The Netherworld was never meant for human bodies, yet here are all three of you wearing Earthworld flesh. How ever did you manage to arrange it?" Pythia's voice was soft again, silky, deliberately misleading in a way another woman could recognize.

Justine tensed.

The demon could not resist a chance to show off his cleverness. Placing one hand on Justine's shoulder, he said, "I have provided myself with an additional source of energy to draw upon, Great Goddess. One I can take with me anywhere, even here. Whenever I feel my strength failing"—in one swift move he ripped the Roman's gown open from neck to knees—"I feed!"

In the fitful yellow light of the torches the body of an exquisitely beautiful young woman stood revealed; revealed in all its dreadful despoliation. Strips of flesh had been torn away from Justine's ribcage, evidence of teeth and claw marks still visible on the edges of the wounds. A gaping wound showed where the belly had been laid open so the soft fat underneath the skin could be devoured. The breasts had been badly chewed. No injury was enough to kill her, but each was excruciatingly painful.

Dark fires flickered in the eyes of the goddess. "You are indeed a demon, Bur-Sin." Her head rotated on its slender neck until she was looking at Justine. "And what was the prize for which you paid so much?"

"My youth, Goddess," Justine whispered.

"Humans! I always knew they were fools. What value is youth? Something no one can hope to keep!" Pythia looked back toward the demon. "You bought her very cheaply."

"I did what I had to in order to survive," Bur-Sin protested.

"Your survival was assured anyway. Few spirits lose their immortality. As a demon in the Otherworld you enjoyed unfettered freedom. Had you preferred to be in the Netherworld you could have materialized here in any form you chose. But unfortunately, your insatiable appetites prompted you to steal a second Earthworld existence for yourself. A great mistake, Bur-Sin; the gods disapprove of demons incarnating on earth. They invariably try to claim our prerogatives there.

"You say you came here to offer me the woman as a sacrifice, so I accept her—but my acceptance does not imply forgiveness. Far from it. There is no atonement for what you did to me, Bur-Sin. I merely take her for my own amusement, and I will keep the young one as well. To survive what you have done to her she must have an exceptionally strong spirit. I am sure I can find an interesting use for such a spirit. Entering my service will mean the irrevocable destruction of their Earthworld bodies, of course, but no matter.

"As for you, Bur-Sin . . ." Pythia hesitated in order to prolong his agony. "As for you, obviously you will have no use for either of them any longer. You have sacrificed much for that body you prance around in, but your days of enjoying human flesh in all its forms are over. I mean to give you *exactly* what you deserve."

Surging upward, she began to leave the pool.

With a great shout Lars Porsena shoved the two women toward the goddess and ran.

FORTY-EIGHT

Again the landscape of the Netherworld changed. Guided by Pepan, Horatius entered a billowing desert striated by different colors of sand, ranging from ochre to yellow to a strange, burning white. A hot wind blew continually, stirring up clouds of sand.

At first a few pinnacles of eroded stone were the only landmarks, but these eventually merged into a wall of low, rugged cliffs pierced by occasional dark defiles. Pepan found the sullen atmosphere of the region disturbing, the scenery of nightmare.

Horatius felt differently. "I must admit, I miss green," he remarked to Pepan. "My eyes are hungry for green and blue and clear, cool colors. But this is a remarkable place all the same. The Netherworld contains more wonders than I ever imagined on earth."

"I doubt if you're aware of a fraction of the wonders that exist on earth," Pepan replied. "Only when you enter the Otherworld and leave human limitations behind do you fully appreciate the beauty of the Earthworld. To hear the music of a living spirit . . ."

"Of course, you spoke of this before. The music of her soul, you said. But I don't understand what you mean."

"How do you think I am following Vesi? Every *hia* sings a song unique to itself that cannot be heard in the Earthworld, but is clearly audible once you leave."

"You can actually hear my mother? Can I?"

"Perhaps. Listen for the particular song of her human spirit, a single pure note, tempered by experience and age, altered by pain, heightened by love. Open your heart and listen."

The young man shrugged the ax off his shoulder in order to concentrate more fully. "I think I hear . . ." Sudden alarm leaped in his eyes.

Accompanied by a curious, gobbling noise, a dozen or more grotesque beings came into view making their way among the sand dunes. Standing smaller than an average man, each possessed one head, two arms, and two legs but there any resemblance to humankind ended. Their skin was the color of rust and composed of innumerable small bubbles. They traveled with an awkward, loping gait, and as they moved the bubbles lost cohesion and burst so that bits of their surface continually sloughed away, leaving a sluglike trail in their wake.

"What are those things?" asked Horatius with disgust.

Pepan shook his head. "I have no idea and no desire for a closer look. Let's head for the cliffs, there at least we have a chance of getting away from them. Out here on the desert we're too exposed."

Trying not to call attention to themselves, the two set out for the cliffs at a brisk walk. The creatures immediately changed direction and followed them. At this ominous sign Horatius and Pepan broke into a run, but by the time they reached the cliffs the pack was closing fast. Their smell preceded them on the hot wind. They stank like the bowels of someone in the last stages of disease. A momentary wave of nausea doubled Horatius over, retching.

The pack swiftly caught up with him then. The leaders flung themselves upon him, clinging to his torso and arms like lichen on a tree. The rest encircled him to keep him from running away. They had no faces other than thick-lipped mouths in the center of their heads from which poured a foul-smelling, yellowish drool. Their slobbering mouths held curving fangs, their two-fingered hands ended in long talons that they could use either as claws or as crablike pincers. The bubbling skin was too slimy to grasp; Horatius could get no hold on them to tear them off. Against so many the shield was merely an impediment on his arm. Neither were his weapons of any use, for with the creatures crawling over him he could not swing the ax nor even get to the knife in his neck pouch.

When they discovered they could not tear through Horatius's breastplate they turned their attention to his head. They attempted to gnaw his ears from his skull, their talons slashing for his eyes. He tried as best he could to fend them off but there were too many of them.

Pepan was dismayed. To come so far and risk so much, and then fall victim to this loathsome horde . . . "No!" cried the Lord of the Rasne. Unarmed, he threw himself on Horatius's attackers and dragged the young man free. Pulling him by the straps of his breastplate, he hauled him into the mouth of a narrow defile. Then tossing Horatius behind him into the shadow, he stood squarely in the mouth of the defile and faced the creatures.

His fists sank from sight in slimy bubbles, he could find nothing solid to hit. But he screamed and kicked and flailed his arms, driving them back with the sheer fury of his attack. The creatures hesitated momentarily to regroup. "This is your chance, Horatius! Run for it, go through the defile to whatever is on the other side. I'll hold them here until you can get away. And listen for your mother's music!"

"I can't leave you alone!"

"I told you they are dangerous to life, but you forget—I'm not alive," Pepan argued. "Run, I tell you. Run!"

The young man staggered to his feet. "I cannot desert you."

"And I will never desert you," Pepan lied. "Now go!"

Horatius ran.

Sooner or later, Pepan thought as the young man disappeared into the cleft in the rock, *he will remember my telling him that I am vulnerable here too. But by that time he will be safely away.*

I do this for you, Repana. So that he can save your daughter.

The creatures attacked. Their curving talons cut through the air with an unnerving, scythelike motion, or closed into pincers attempting to rip his flesh from his bones. As if they knew how unmanning their breath was, they deliberately belched great waves of gaseous stench in his face.

There were too many to attack him all at once. Half their number were clinging to his body while the rest capered around him, gobbling hungrily, mouths opening and closing, the jaws and chests wet with noxious saliva. Pepan had no illusion about their plans for his flesh.

If only he had a weapon.

He ruefully recalled lending his favorite ebony-handled knife to Repana, so long ago. There must be some weapon he could use now; anything! But as he looked frantically around he saw nothing but sand.

Stooping, Pepan snatched up a handful of sharp grains and hurled them deep into the nearest open mouth.

The creature choked, clawed at its throat, fell writhing to the ground. To Pepan's disgust the others promptly turned upon their companion and devoured it alive, shoving chunks of bubbling flesh into their mouths even as they resumed the attack on the Rasne lord.

Since his death Pepan had learned much about the laws that controlled the three disparate planes of existence. But he did not know how much damage a Netherworld body could suffer and still host a living spirit. If his body was destroyed his *hia* would be set adrift alone and unprotected in this dreadful place. He would surely fall victim to the predators of the Netherworld long before he could find his way to sanctuary with Veno. Only the gods themselves knew what he would become.

Pepan fought to control his fear, but he was tiring. One of the creatures behind him took a terrific swipe at his back. A pain like a bolt of lightning drove him to his knees.

Repana, he thought again as he struggled to his feet.

He did not know if he spoke aloud.

His attackers were tumbling over one another in their eagerness to destroy. The pain rose to a dazzling crescendo.

So this is how it will end. What sort of destiny is this for a prince of Etruria?

Claws slashed his chest, pincers ripped flesh from his shoulders and thighs. The creatures were grunting with excitement at the prospect of a kill. In another moment they would overwhelm him with sheer numbers, but he was determined to go down fighting.

Then at an invisible signal the entire pack flung itself upon him at once. Pepan fought back with fists and elbows but the outcome was inevitable. Under their massed weight he staggered and fell sideways. He managed to get to one knee only to be knocked down again, sent sprawling by a crashing blow to the back of the head.

He could not get up again. Curling into a ball, he attempted to shield his head with his arms for as long as possible.

As he lay huddled on the ground memories flickered through his mind like a brilliantly colored ribbon. Images of his childhood, his gentle and affectionate mother, his aloof and lordly father. He recalled his youth, his first love, the taste of her lips. His initiation ceremony into manhood, his leadership of the Rasne. Wife, children.

Repana.

Above all others, Repana.

So many people, so many faces. Many of them now safe in the Kingdom of the Dead, whereas he . . .

So many images, so many lives and loves, so few regrets . . .

Repana.

When the other faces had vanished into the pain, Repana's remained. He struggled to hold onto that memory to carry with him into the darkness. Perhaps if he could take her image with him into the night, it might sustain him.

Then through the gobbling and grunting of the creatures tearing at him he heard a single sound: a rich and melodious note that went straight to his heart. Twisting around, he managed to peer through the legs of the creatures in time to see two figures appear out of the shimmering heat.

One was a woman dressed in an Etruscan gown.

Behind her, hulking huge, loomed the shadowy form of a massive bear.

The woman . . .

Pepan tried to focus on her face but he was swiftly losing consciousness. Gray mist swirled through his head. He squinted, struggling to see for just one heartbeat longer . . .

. . . as the great bear launched itself upon the creatures, roaring in righteous fury as it savaged them.

"My lord, can you hear me?" She bent closer until her face was almost touching his. "Open your eyes and speak to me."

Pepan made himself ignore the excruciating pain in his back long enough to lift his eyelids.

A face appeared. A beloved face. Younger than he remembered it, bright with youth and alive with love.

"Repana?" His voice was very faint.

"Yes, yes, my dear one."

"But I thought . . . you were safe with . . ."

"With Wulv? I was. Together he and I made our way to Veno. We faced many hazards on the way but he overcame them all for my sake. At last the Protectress opened her arms to us and we were safe in a realm of delight. But then we heard your call. And here we are."

"You left the security of Veno's realm for my sake?" Pepan asked incredulously.

"Just as you eschewed it for my sake, and Vesi's. I know what you did for us. Even in death, you remained with us, watching over us. But don't waste strength talking now. We must get you away from here before any more harm can come to you." Raising her voice, she called, "Wulv! Is it over?"

"Almost," came the reply.

The immense bear shambled into view, holding a torn body in his paws. From the body streams of tiny bubbles ran onto the ground, forming a puddle that emitted a nauseating odor.

"Get rid of that," commanded Repana, "and help me carry Pepan."

"Carry me!" the wounded man retorted indignantly. "Where?"

She smiled down at him. "To Veno, of course, where you will be forever safe with us."

Pepan tried to sit up. "But your grandson needs me."

With a firm hand, Repana pushed his shoulders back onto her lap. "You have done all one could possibly do to help him."

"How do you know?"

"Veno allowed us to watch from our sanctuary."

"You took a great risk by coming to save me."

Repana laughed, the warm, low laugh he remembered from long ago. "Ah, when one is with the redoubtable Wulv, one is in little danger."

At the sound of his name Wulv, in human form, came trotting up. There was yellowish ichor on his hands and soaking into the tunic of skins he wore, but his eyes were very bright. Pepan noted that his face was no longer ridged with scars. He was almost handsome.

"Best battle I've had in ages," the Teumetian commented happily. He bent down and helped Pepan to his feet.

"You do not have to carry me," said the Rasne lord with a hint of his old authority. "I can walk."

"Of course you can," Repana replied. "You always were a strong man. We will each take one of your arms, though, just to steady you." She smiled into his eyes. "Come, my love. It is time to go home."

FORTY-NINE

T he fire of Anubis had subsided to a row of flickering
tongues of flame just inside the entrance to the caverns.
Twice the hooded figures had gained access; twice Khebet
had fought them back. One now lay unmoving within the
mouth of the cave, its body partially consumed in the flames. There
was no fight left in the Aegyptian, nor magic either. The next time they
attacked they would leap the low flames and kill him.

Khebet felt hollow inside, numb as with some appalling cold.

According to the tenets of his religion, a luxurious Afterlife awaited
him. Gold and silver and attentive slaves, sweet wine and silken
couches and beautiful women.

His teeth began to chatter uncontrollably.

He could hear the remaining hooded horrors moving around outside. Why did they not talk to one another? Their silence was as sinister as their intent. The agony of anticipation was unbearable.

Khebet thought of the sacrifices he had to offered to Anubis over
the years, the trussed-up calves and lambs and kids with garlands of
flowers around their necks that he had placed upon the god's altar. The

animals had gazed at him with such innocent, despairing eyes as they awaited their fate, but their emotions had been of no consequence to him—then.

Now he wondered if they had been as terrified as he was tonight.

"If I survive this," he murmured to give himself the comfort of a human voice, "I vow I will never again offer a blood sacrifice to the Jackal."

Not only his teeth were chattering. His whole body had begun to tremble.

He had not succeeded in placating the gods after all. His life had been misspent, his priesthood a fraud. With death imminent, Khebet was shocked to discover he did not even believe in the Afterlife.

The realization should have increased his fear, but instead a sort of desperate peace came over him.

His trembling abated.

"Die bravely, Aegyptian," Khebet whispered to himself in the echoing cave. "If all else is lost, give yourself that much. Die as a hero, like Horatius."

FIFTY

The defile in the cliffs widened into a canyon, then eventually opened onto a broad plain. The surface of this tableland resembled black marble polished to a high gloss. Pausing at the mouth of the canyon, Horatius gazed out across the desolate landscape and tried to decide which way to go. There was nothing here that could serve as a trail, no way he could track Vesi. He needed Pepan and the musical sound the other man had followed.

Pepan . . .

Pepan should be behind him . . . and then he inhaled sharply. "But he told me he was vulnerable in the Netherworld too!"

Suddenly he understood. Pepan had offered himself as a sacrifice. Horatius turned and ran back through the defile, ax in hand. This time he would be ready for them. He would hold his breath and not breathe their poison.

But the sandy plain was deserted. There was no sign of the creatures, though the ground was encrusted with slime. There was no sign of Pepan either, only a puddle of blood.

Crouching, Horatius studied the scene. The congealing blood told him nothing. But then the pervasive, lurid light changed slightly and he made out an unusual indentation on the ground a few paces away. He got swiftly to his feet and went to look.

Moving in a straight line across the sand toward the horizon were blurred marks more nearly resembling the tracks of a bear than those of a man. They were accompanied by the footprints of naked human feet, high-arched like a woman's. Between them were the unmistakable prints of Pepan's Etruscan sandals.

Horatius raised his ax in silent salute to the man he had known so briefly—the man who had been with him all his life.

Then he retraced his own footsteps back through the defile, in the direction Pepan had sent him. His journey was not yet over.

No sooner had he set foot on the gleaming black plain than he became aware of something moving beneath him. When he glanced down he discovered his own reflection, as if he walked on a mirrored surface. At first the effect was unsettling. He kept looking down to see his face looking back at him.

Raising his eyes, he tried to estimate the distance to the horizon. But perspective was unreliable here. At one moment it seemed quite close, then when he looked again he was gazing across an endless blackness beneath a lurid red dome. The infrequent streaks of gold that blazed across the faraway roof of the Netherworld were also reflected in the black marble. Like fireflies, they provided nervous flashes of light that were gone before he could focus on them.

Nothing else moved on the dark plain.

Perhaps because he was alone now, Horatius felt increasingly apprehensive. And yet the ax was on his shoulder, the knife and sling-shot close to hand. None of these had been of any use against the creatures with the bubbling skin but they were a comforting reminder of Pepan's words: *You have never been alone.*

He walked on for a time.

An interminable time.

The landscape, and himself as the solitary figure in it, was unutterably depressing. What he had seen of the Netherworld was no place for a human spirit, he thought. What would the Kingdom of the Dead be like? Surely it was better than this. But he had no idea in which direction it lay, any more than he knew where to find his mother. He could only keep going forward, ever hopeful of discovering something—anything.

Perhaps that is what faith means, Horatius told himself.

Then in the distance he glimpsed a single figure that flickered in and out of his vision, now discernible, now seeming no more than a trick of the light. As he watched, he realized the figure was coming in his direction. Soon he could tell that it was bobbing back and forth as if running in an erratic pattern, then crouching and half-turning to look back.

These were the actions of prey fleeing a predator.

Hefting the ax, he scanned the horizon but saw nothing else moving.

As it came closer, the figure gradually resolved itself into that of a man. Every movement he made indicated terror. Horatius set off toward him, impelled by the instinct to help a fellow being in distress. Then he paused. There was something disturbing about that figure. Although manlike in every proportion, he was running too fast for any human.

Horatius took the ax from his shoulder and balanced it warily in his two hands.

Now the other noticed him, turned toward him. The unnatural speed slowed to a normal pace.

Horatius called out, "Are you in trouble?"

The man threw up one arm and waved. "Stay where you are," he called, "I will come to you." He trotted toward Horatius.

As he approached Horatius was astonished to see a face he knew: the clear green eyes, the piercing gaze of an eagle.

Lars Porsena.

The Prince of Clusium—here!

Then at once he realized that although the creature wore the handsome visage of the prince, this was no human.

At the same time Lars Porsena reacted to him. He stopped, shocked. His handsome face hardened into a look of implacable hatred. "I know you," he said through clenched teeth as he approached. "Oh, but this is good . . . good. Surely the *Ais* are playing with me. This is some jest. I know you," he repeated almost with disbelief. "You have your mother's sound."

Horatius was caught off guard. "How do you know about my mother's sound?"

Lars Porsena bared his teeth in what might have been a smile. "I know all about your mother; at least, all I need to know."

"Have you seen her?"

"Seen her? I just left her—back there." With a jerk of his head he indicated the direction from which he had come. Then unaccountably he chuckled.

"I have to go to her," Horatius began, but before he could take a step Lars Porsena blocked his way.

"You are going nowhere," said the demon in a voice vibrating with menace. "You pitiful puling pup, the gods have delivered you into my hands after all. I can snatch victory from the very fangs of defeat. When I finish with you there will be one less thing for me to worry about. When I have done with you, I may even go back and confront Pythia."

Faster than thought, the Etruscan body melted into a different form altogether. Instead of a human being Horatius was confronted with a man-size ball of metallic-looking spikes. The ball rolled toward him, pulsing rhythmically, while from its midsection two green fires burned like eyes. A spiky tentacle shot out to take a savage swing at Horatius.

He dodged sideways, barely avoiding the tentacle, feeling it brush against his hair. "What do you want?" he cried with a sense of outrage. "I've done nothing to you!"

From within the ball the voice of Lars Porsena replied, "You exist. That is your crime against me and the punishment is death."

"That makes no sense!"

The demon chuckled. "You expect logic? The rules of existence are different once you leave the Earthworld. You are totally in my power here."

Not totally, thought Horatius. *Hit me; strike my breastplate.*

With an act of purest faith, the young man stood firm. When the demon reached for him he met the blow with his chin up and his head high. The spiky tentacle snapped out, catching him full in the chest. It rebounded harmlessly off his armor.

But it suffered dreadful damage in return. A ripple of blue fire ran up the appendage from the surface of Horatius's breastplate. There was a blinding flash of light and a great crash like the voice of Tinia the lightning god. With a howl of pain, the spiky ball disappeared.

In its place stood a beautiful woman, nursing a bruised arm.

The transformation was so abrupt, the contrast so total, Horatius could only stare. She was the most compelling creature he had ever seen. A mane of honey-colored hair cascaded down her shoulders, framing naked breasts. The curve of her unclothed hips was an invitation; the golden nest at the base of her rounded belly was a lure. Meltingly green eyes smiled languorously at Horatius. "I want you," she whispered.

The young man's body responded with a surge of mindless desire.

Opening her arms, the woman urged, "Come to me. Be my lover and you will know the heights of passion."

Unconsciously, Horatius stepped forward and the woman moved to meet him.

"I will teach you wonders," she promised in a voice throbbing with invitation. But as she spoke the hair on her head began to move, to writhe and twist with a horrid life of its own. The light in her green eyes became an insane glare that held nothing of human warmth.

Fighting the lust still scorching through him, Horatius held his shield at an angle so he could catch the woman's reflection in the metal surface. What he saw was no woman at all. Instead his enemy was revealed as a figure of putrescent horror, holding out arms that dripped with the rot of the grave.

Shuddering, Horatius swung the shield in front of him to cut off the vision.

A silence fell then. He might have been alone in all creation. The loudest sounds were the roaring of his blood in his ears; the thudding of his heart. He waited, trying to prepare for the unguessable, but nothing further happened.

When he could stand it no longer he peered over the top of the shield and saw only the black plain, the red sky. Then he heard something moving and looked down.

On the ground before him crouched a monstrous lizard longer than a man. The body was the color of flame, the head saffron yellow surmounted by a serrated crest of orange cartilage. From the shoulders sprouted leathery black tendrils that waved like weed beneath the sea.

The saurian's eyes were clearest green.

Fixing a cold gaze on Horatius, the lizard vented a roar that reverberated across the plain. Its open mouth revealed a double row of pointed teeth, each one as long as a man's thumb, set in muscular jaws. The creature continued to roar as it lashed its tail from side to side, building momentum for the attack.

Horatius held his shield to one side, arms spread as if inviting destruction.

The lizard lunged forward.

Fearsome teeth clamped on the young man's shin. The beast bit down; the teeth shattered like glass against the greaves.

The lizard's roar became a squeal of pain as splintered shards tore its mouth and tongue. Black blood spurted. The monster writhed at Horatius's feet and . . .

. . . was transformed into an immense bull.

The roar of the lizard was as nothing compared to the bellow of the bull, a creature half again as large as any Earthworld beast. The hide was dead white with large patches of red, like splotches of blood, on the back and belly. A pair of sharp black horns curved out from the forehead—but it was not a bull's forehead. The beast's massive shoulders were surmounted with an outsize human head. The face was a distortion of Lars Porsena's.

Pawing the ground and snorting in rage, this grotesque brute fixed baleful green eyes on Horatius. It was powerful enough to charge through his shield. Even his breastplate could not turn so huge an adversary.

Had not one of his ancestors mentioned bulls?

Horatius spread his feet to give himself a more secure stance and hefted the gold-plated ax just as the bull charged.

Horatius neatly sidestepped the charge and put his full weight behind the swing. The ax sang with a voice of its own, a somber whir of death. The glittering blade sliced into the muscular neck of the bull just below the human jawbone. There was a momentary resistance of tough flesh, but nothing could deflect the sacrificial ax.

At the moment it sliced through the brute's jugular, Lars Porsena changed again.

In place of a bull with a man's head an even more improbable hybrid appeared. Crouching on four clawed legs was a creature with the body of a great, tawny lion—and with wings. This time the head was that of an eagle, a green-eyed eagle. The pitiless, predatory eyes burned into those of Horatius.

He swiftly took half a step backward and lifted the ax for another blow. Before he could strike, the creature unfolded its broad wings and sprang into the sky.

The ax sang harmlessly through empty air.

Tilting back his head, Horatius saw the thing hovering above him out of range of the ax. When it screamed its voice was like nothing he had ever heard before. Then it extended its clawed feet and dived toward him.

The mighty wings beat the air so hard they almost knocked Horatius down. One of the feet caught the ax, tore it from his grasp, and carried it high into the crimson heavens. Screaming triumphantly, the monster climbed into the sky again and prepared for another dive.

With gaping beak and downbeating wings, the brute could plummet to the ground with enough force to break Horatius in half.

Horatius whipped the pouch from around his neck. Tucking the flint knife into his belt, he twisted the cloth into a sling that he armed with a stone from the Styx.

The monster dived.

Horatius fired.

The stone struck between the savage green eyes. The brute, stunned, lost control and fell spinning out of the red sky.

When it hit the ground it vanished. In its place a human figure lay crumpled at Horatius's feet. The figure moaned and struggled to rise, then turned a bloody face toward the young man. "Help me," implored Pepan, reaching out. "Help me get up."

Horatius automatically extended a hand. Pepan got to his feet with an effort, wincing in pain. "What have you done to me?"

"I don't . . . but . . . I don't understand . . ." stammered Horatius. "You . . . I mean he . . . I thought you were a monster."

"I am and always have been your friend," Pepan replied reprovingly.

Embarrassed, Horatius dropped his eyes . . . and noticed two reflections on the gleaming black surface where they stood. His own was familiar, but the image beneath Pepan did not resemble the Rasne lord. It belonged to a very different man in a very menacing posture.

Horatius swiftly dropped to one knee and snatched the flint knife from his belt. Raising his arm, he struck a mighty downward blow. The weapon fashioned by the earliest Etruscan sank to the hilt in what appeared to be solid stone—and pinned the demon's reflection to the ground.

Pepan's form dissolved into that of a furious Lars Porsena. He tried to lift first one foot and then the other from the ground, but they were held securely in place. Even demonic strength could not free them from their reflection.

He was trapped.

His green eyes gave Horatius a look of such concentrated hatred that the young man took a step sideways, out of Lars Porsena's reach.

322

The demon bent to draw the knife from the stone himself, but when his fingers touched the handle a shudder ran through him. He convulsed with pain. White smoke coiled from seared flesh.

"My mother!" Horatius cried. "Where is she?"

Through clenched teeth the demon snarled, "I'll tear you to bits!"

"I think not. We just proved I am more than a match for you. But I might be prepared to release you in exchange for information about my mother."

With a visible effort Lars Porsena arranged his features in a slightly more amiable expression. "What do you want to know?"

"How can I be sure you're telling me the truth?"

"I have no reason to lie to you."

"You have no reason to kill me either."

"Ah, but I do. Did. If you release me I will consider matters settled between us however."

"First you'll have to tell me about my mother and where to find her. Did you have anything to do with her kidnapping?"

"I?" Lars Porsena sounded genuinely offended. He splayed the fingers of his right hand across his chest in a gesture of sincerity. "I dearly love women, I would cause no harm to any of them. Trust me."

"Trust you? I had as soon trust a viper. I don't know just what you are, but . . ."

As Horatius said the word *viper*, Lars Porsena went pale. His green eyes were no longer fixed on the young man's face; they were staring over his shoulder with a look of total terror.

At first Horatius suspected a trick, but it was obvious that Lars Porsena's fear was genuine as he redoubled his efforts to free himself. He was almost sobbing with terror.

Horatius turned to follow the direction of his gaze. Coming over the horizon was a huge, dark figure that appeared to glide forward, halt long enough to gather itself like a coiled spring, then glide forward again.

"No," Lars Porsena gasped. "No no no no no!"

"What is that?" asked Horatius.

"Pythia."

The name meant nothing to Horatius, but the way the creature was moving was unnerving. It advanced with astonishing rapidity. By the time it had halved the distance between them, he could make out details.

He stared in disbelief at the largest serpent he had ever seen.

The upper part of her body was female, though not human. In her coils she carried two human women. She was so huge that their bodies did not impede her progress in the slightest.

"Don't let her get me!" begged Lars Porsena.

Horatius started to ask, "What does she want with you?" but the words dried on his tongue as he recognized one of the women caught fast in the serpent's coils.

"Mother!"

At the sound of his voice Vesi opened her eyes.

"Horatrim," she called softly.

She was looking down at her son from a height, for the huge serpent was holding the two women far above a man's reach. Both women were alive and conscious. The muscular coils of the creature possessed unimaginable power, but also great delicacy. Pythia could have crushed Vesi and Justine if she chose. Instead she held them almost tenderly.

"Bur-Sin," she hissed.

The being Horatius knew as Lars Porsena crouched on the earth in abject terror.

"Did you think to escape me?" Pythia inquired of him. "You demons are so arrogant." Her glance flickered toward Horatius. Her eyes were as cold as the spaces between the stars. "I am the goddess Pythia. Release this cringing thing to me at once."

The young man calculated swiftly. Although the being before him was awesome, obviously she had some limitations or she would not have asked him to release Lars Porsena. She would have done so herself.

"I will release him to you on one condition," he replied. "Give those women to me. Then he is yours."

"No!" screamed Lars Porsena. Neither Pythia nor Horatius paid any attention to him. He had become a mere object for barter.

Lowering her head on her sinuous neck, Pythia brought it close to Horatius. Her forked tongue flickered over his face in a curious, questing gesture. He shrank inwardly from her touch but stood his ground.

"Ah," she said at last. "So that is who you are. What extraordinary gifts you possess! Bur-Sin underestimated you, I suspect. He always underestimates others: his opinion of himself is so great he assumes everyone else must be inferior. In truth there is nothing superior about him. He is a thief, a bully, and a coward and deserves whatever punishment I choose to give him. Let me think . . ."

Her voice sank to a hiss more awful than her anger. "Bur-Sin is so proud of the form he now wears. I will make it human again, mortal again, with his *hia* still inside—and kept totally under my control this time. Then I will send him back to Rome to serve as my minion there. He will have no free will, of course, but . . ."

Lars Porsena clasped his hands together in an attitude of prayer. "Great is your mercy, Goddess!"

"Your gratitude is ill-founded, Bur-Sin. Your body will be vulnerable to the pains and tortures you have inflicted upon others, and when it dies I will simply put your *hia* into a new one to suffer again. And again. You will have a most interesting future. I will make you the scourge of Rome . . . and Rome in turn will scourge you."

Lars Porsena's eyes widened with horror.

Pythia addressed herself to Horatius. "By what name are you known?"

"Horatius Cocles."

"Very well, Horatius Cocles. Give me this pitiful wretch and you can have one of the women in exchange."

For the first time Horatius took a good look at the second woman in Pythia's clutches. She was beautiful; even Livia would have seemed plain by comparison. And she was gazing at him with enough pleading in her eyes to melt iron.

But so was Vesi.

"Choose," demanded Pythia.

"I will take them both."

"Oh no, I am not inclined to be that generous. You must choose one and relinquish the other to me, together with your captive."

Horatius folded his arms across his chest. "Both, I say. If you do not agree, free him yourself." He stepped back, gambling that the serpent had no more power over the flint knife than did the demon.

If he was wrong. . . .

For a long moment she stared at him, her tongue flickering lazily between her lips. Then, with agonizing slowness, Pythia began to lower the two women to the ground. As their feet neared the gleaming black surface the serpent loosened her coils.

Horatius darted forward to catch Vesi before she could fall. "Mother!"

The face she turned up to his was haggard and exhausted. "My son," she whispered. She raised one trembling hand to touch his cheek. "Make her release me *completely*."

Though he did not understand, he called to Pythia, "You must release her completely!"

"Very well," was the grudging reply. "You drive a hard bargain."

Horatius felt his mother shudder in his arms. Then she drew a deep breath of relief and nestled her head gratefully against his shoulder.

The beautiful girl stumbled toward them, moaning with every step she took. Horatius reached out in pity and drew her into his embrace as well. "We must get away from here before she changes her mind," he told the two women.

Pythia drawled, "Oh, I will not change my mind. Unlike demons, the gods usually keep their word. I do not need you anyway. My little games with Bur-Sin will keep me as entertained as a cat with a mouse. Just remove that knife, Horatius Cocles, and you are free to go wherever you like."

Over the heads of the women, he told the goddess, "We don't belong here, we must return to the Earthworld. But the way is long and difficult and these two are very weak. We need help."

Pythia replied with vast indifference, "What is that to me?"

"You are so powerful that even a demon fears you. Surely you could do this small thing."

"Flattery only works on fools. Remember that in the future, Horatius Cocles. But yes, I could transport you if I chose." She hesitated as if weighing various considerations. Then the great coils shifted with a liquid sound of scales sliding against one another. "I will help you on one condition: that you ask me for nothing else. Ever. Make even the smallest request of me in the future and I will strip you of everything you possess, do you understand?"

"I do."

"Very well then." Opening her mouth wide, Pythia vomited a large pool of alabaster liquid onto the black plain. "Here is your roadway. Release Bur-Sin to me. Then dive into the pool with your women and let the current carry you to the Earthworld. Do it immediately; I offer you only the one chance."

"Be careful," urged the girl. "It might be a trick!"

But Horatius could not be frightened. Releasing the two women, he crouched down, grasped the handle of the flint knife, and tugged.

The knife slid out of the shadow on the stone.

Lars Porsena staggered backward.

Pythia responded with a triumphant hiss. The huge coils shifted again; the black form lifted toward the red sky.

Horatius gathered the women into his arms again and strode to the brink of the pool. Before he entered the water he took one last look back.

With dreadful clarity he saw the great serpent towering high above the demon, her body bent into an S-curve. Her eyes blazed with a murderous lust beyond human comprehension. Extending her flaring hood Pythia spread its dark shadow over the figure cowering below her.

Lars Porsena's frantic green eyes met those of Horatius. "Do not abandon me to her!" he screamed just as Horatius leaped into the pool.

"I am your father!"

FIFTY-ONE

T he opaque water was as warm as milk. No sooner had it closed over their heads than a current seized Horatius and the two women and dragged them deeper, then swept them inexorably forward. When Horatius could not hold his breath any longer he was astonished to discover that he did not choke. Breathing the water was like breathing air.

The two women he tightly grasped were making the same discovery. Vesi relaxed, but the girl writhed and kicked in a futile attempt to swim under her own power.

As Horatius was carried along, faces swirled at random through his memory.

Wulv. Propertius. Pepan.

Lars Porsena.

I am your father!

Horatius shuddered.

The demon had lied to him countless times. No doubt it would have told him anything in a desperate bid to escape the vengeance of the dark goddess.

I am your father.

Nonsense.

But the seed of doubt was planted.

As the warm white flow sped them back toward the Earthworld Horatius fell into a sort of dream. He was imagining the future. He would work for Severus, become prosperous, build a house for his mother, marry someone . . . Livia . . .

Livia seemed very far away however. Held close to his side was a different and even more beautiful young woman. As she struggled he felt her full breast against his arm; her legs entwined deliciously with his own. The gods had thrown them together. What did this mean?

Before he could speculate, the current roiled wildly around them and tore Justine and Vesi from his arms.

A moment later a geyser of alabaster liquid spewed Horatius into a clump of hemlock at the entrance to the Caverns of Spasio.

His spirit was sucked from his Netherworld body like a seed being sucked from a grape. There was a sickening swoop, a jolt . . .

Horatius opened his eyes to find himself lying on his back on the floor of the first cavern. After a momentary confusion his mind cleared.

Khebet, battered and bloody, was straddling him and trying to fight off three hooded assailants. A fourth lay unmoving by the entrance. The sound of the Aegyptian's harsh breathing filled the cave. Although he did not yet feel settled in his Earthworld body, Horatius drew up his knees and swung them to one side then swiftly rolled up onto his feet. "Enough!" he cried.

The hooded figures froze.

Khebet was at the end of his strength. He managed to mutter, "Thank the gods," then let himself slump to the ground, gasping for breath.

Horatius hurled himself on the nearest figure. He smashed his fist into a shadowy face beneath a hood. His knuckles struck a snout; cartilage crumpled. There was a grunt of pain. The other two recovered from their astonishment and joined the fight.

The three creatures were formidable, yet Horatius would not have cared if there were six—or sixty. He had the advantage of surprise. He also had a young and healthy body that had benefited by a good rest. Dancing on the balls of his feet, he pummeled each opponent in turn, taking savage joy in the release of tension. With every blow he struck his confidence grew. He did not need magical weapons, he did not need the aid of the gods.

"I'm Horatius Cocles!" he shouted, whirling, leaping. "I've been to the Netherworld and come back alive!" Kicking, battering. "I cannot be beaten by cowards who hide their faces!" He landed five blows for every one he took. He seemed to be everywhere at once and growing stronger every moment. The cave was full of him, larger than life, angry and joyous and brilliant.

Pythia's minions panicked. Abandoning their fallen comrade, they fled from the cave.

Horatius tossed a lock of hair out of his eyes. He was not even breathing hard. "By the gods, it's good to be alive!" He bent to help the Aegyptian to his feet. "We did it, my friend! We did it!"

"Did you get what you went for?" Khebet asked weakly. His legs were trembling; he had to sit back down.

Just then a shadow fell across the scorched opening of the cave. Khebet tensed—until two women entered. Vesi was leaning on the shoulder of the lovely girl Horatius had rescued from Pythia.

Horatius gave a sigh of relief. "Yes, Khebet. I brought back all that I sought—and more."

Khebet was injured and the women were exhausted. There was no point in leaving the caverns until they were able to travel, so Horatius gathered enough firewood to keep the cave warm and went looking for something to eat. Nuts, berries, a bird shot out of the sky with an improvised slingshot, a rabbit taken in a snare made of vines—with these he provided for his charges. Once more Wulv's training came to his aid. Soon he had created a comfortable little camp where they could spend a number of days if need be.

"I've made a discovery," Horatius confided to Khebet when the Aegyptian began to take a little interest in something other than his aches and pains. "Our ancestors and our friends are our true riches."

"My people store up riches for the Afterlife," Khebet said, "but what if there is none? You are right, Horatius; at least we can be certain of the past and present."

Thinking of Lars Porsena, Horatius chuckled. "I can assure you there's an Afterlife as well, at least for some of us. The only thing is it may be horrible."

"I am in no hurry to find out," the other told him.

"Will you be returning to Aegypt?"

"I am in no hurry to do that either, Horatius. I used to think I knew everything and was in control of my destiny, but I was mistaken. I would like to stay with you for a while longer, if I may. I suspect you have much to teach me."

Horatius laughed. Laughter came easily to him now, bubbling up like a fountain. "I can't teach you anything. You're a priest, an educated man."

"I am not even sure about being a priest," Khebet said with a shake of his head. "But I do believe I am more of a man than I was."

The girl called Justine was also regaining her strength. She took over the chore of caring for Vesi, bathing her face with fresh water, urging her to eat, trying without success to get her to talk. As Horatius watched them he was touched by her devotion to the older woman. It was inevitable, he decided, after what they had been through together.

One evening as they finished their meal beside the fire Horatius noticed that Justine was beginning to look haggard. Perhaps she was doing too much too soon. "Are you ill?" he wanted to know.

"Why do you ask?"

"Your face, it's . . ." Horatius paused, not sure what to say next. He did not want to insult her. Perhaps it was a mere trick of the light.

Justine raised a hand to her cheek. Was there the slightest loss of firmness? "But he promised!" she cried, aggrieved.

"Who promised?"

She bowed her head but did not explain. She did not want this extraordinary young man to know what a fool she had been, believing the word of a demon.

In Rome there were plenty of wealthy old men who would buy the finest creams and lotions for her in return for her favors, and perhaps enable her to retain her recaptured beauty. But she knew she would not seek them out. Having seen Horatius, Justine could not bear to think of returning to her past life.

She willed slackening flesh to cling tight to bone and flashed him her warmest smile.

Horatius smiled back. As the firelight leaped his smile caught someone's else's attention.

"Horatrim?" Vesi said hoarsely. It was the first word she had spoken since the Netherworld.

Horatius caught her in his arms and rocked back and forth, holding her head against his shoulder as if she were the child and he the parent. "Yes it's me, Mother. It's me."

"But you are . . . so big."

"And you are so little. I never realized how small you are, Mother."

"A long time must have passed . . ."

"Do you not remember?"

She shook her head. "Only flashes. Bright bits in a darkness. They make no more sense than a shattered mosaic."

As gently as he could, Horatius recounted their recent history to his mother. Khebet and Justine filled in their parts of the puzzle, though Justine was careful to edit hers. Occasionally Vesi asked questions; hesitantly at first, then with growing comprehension. Her bright spirit, so long submerged, began to peep through her eyes like sunshine when dark clouds roll away.

"You have restored me to myself," she said at last. The recital had tired her but it was a happy weariness. "I don't know how to thank you. All of you."

The Aegyptian said, "Thank the gods, who must truly love your son."

At the mention of the gods Horatius gave a start. "Eosphorus!"

"Who?"

"Someone I met in the Netherworld, Mother. I made him a promise. Wherever we go, we are going to set up a little shrine to Eosphorus. Once each day we will remember him and call his name."

Vesi managed a faint smile. "If it pleases you. I would like to sleep now, I think." Her eyes drifted shut. Tenderly, Horatius carried her to the bed he had made for her of fallen boughs and soft mosses.

Then he returned to Khebet and Justine, who were still by the fire. Justine was playing idly with a stick that had fallen away from the flames. "What are your plans, Horatius?" she asked as he sat down beside her.

"I'm going back to Rome with my mother and Khebet. My future is there." Taking the stick from her, with its burnt end he began drawing on the floor of the cave. Squares, rectangles, cubes. Houses and buildings. He gazed thoughtfully at the images, then turned toward the girl. "Have you a family somewhere worrying about you?"

Justine bit her lip. "I have no one. No one anywhere."

"Then you'll come with us. Having gone to all the trouble to bring you back from the Netherworld I'm not about to abandon you now."

"You know nothing about me!"

"I've seen how kind you are to my mother. And you're very beautiful. That's all I need to know."

"But . . . I will grow old, I will . . ."

Horatius laughed. "I may be old before you are. I seem to be aging more rapidly than other men."

"That will not matter to me."

"Then why do you think it will matter to me?"

Fearful that someone in the city would recognize her, she started to protest further. Then she remembered how much she had changed. *If happiness is enough to keep a woman beautiful,* Justine thought to herself, *perhaps I have a chance.*

"In Rome I can make a good living," Horatius was saying, "and you can be a companion to my mother. Perhaps one day . . ." he stopped and shook his head. There would be time for that later. When he understood women better. "At any rate our worries are over," he concluded. "We can enjoy some peace from now on."

Khebet raised an eyebrow. "Peace? In Rome? I doubt that. Rome is many things—raw, new, greedy, exciting—but I cannot imagine it being peaceful."

Rome, mumbled Vesi. They had thought she was asleep. When she spoke her voice was so low, so strange, that at first they could not make out what she was saying.

"Your mother has not yet thrown off the effects of her terrible experience, Horatius," Khebet suggested. "She is still haunted by it and having nightmares."

Vesi stirred uneasily on her bed and spoke again. This time Horatius heard her clearly. She was repeating the words Pythia had said to Lars Porsena.

I will make you the scourge of Rome . . . and Rome in turn will scourge you.

EPILOGUS

We Aïs do not always have things our own way. The fate of humankind is written not on stone, but on the wind. Man himself—blind, ignorant, irrational Man—has more power over his future than we do.

We do not want him to know this. As long as he leaves his destiny in the hands of the gods we can control him.

Control is a two-edged weapon however.

Some of us are genuinely fond of humans and seek to protect them from their own worst natures. Others perversely encourage the destructive tendency in humankind.

But if Man dies, so die the gods.

We would all do well to remember this.

Developmental and Learning Disabilities

Developmental and Learning Disabilities

Evaluation, Management, and Prevention in Children

John H. Meier, Ph.D.
Director, Office of Child Development, and
Chief, Children's Bureau
Department of Health, Education, and Welfare
Washington, D.C.

University Park Press
Baltimore • London • Tokyo

UNIVERSITY PARK PRESS
International Publishers in Science and Medicine
Chamber of Commerce Building
Baltimore, Maryland 21202

Copyright © 1976 by University Park Press

Typeset by The Composing Room of Michigan, Inc.
Manufactured in the United States of America by
Universal Lithographers, Inc., and The Maple Press Co.

Library of Congress Cataloging in Publication Data
Meier, John, 1935–
  Developmental and learning disabilities.

  Includes index.
  1. Learning disabilities. I. Title.
LC4704.M44   371.9   76-7458
ISBN 0-8391-0762-5

Contents

List of Figures

List of Tables

Preface

This book is intended to bridge a yawning chasm between several handicapping conditions. Children keep falling into the depths of a ravine where they remain out of sight and out of mind until they turn up on high school and even junior high school drop-out lists, in the juvenile delinquency courts, on welfare, and/or in other personal or social predicaments. They should be spared this plunge by a caring and able society and a community of scholars and service deliverers. The artificial dichotomy separating developmental disabilities from learning disabilities, widened by self-serving pedagogical and pedantic polemics, creates and widens the euphemistic cracks into which many children fall or are pushed.

The subject matter is admittedly complex. Attempts to establish interfaces are correspondingly difficult and are made even more difficult by challenging established traditions that have historically militated against such synthesizing endeavors. It is not the intent of this book to present an exhaustive treatment of all that is known about developmental and learning disabilities since this information is available in multiple separate sources that are mentioned as references throughout and in Chapter 10 of this book for the reader's information and convenience. Nonetheless, enough of the state of the art and science regarding development and learning is presented to support the case that the two classifications of disability are not only compatible but also in simultaneous mutual interaction with each other.

Overlaps between development and learning have become increasingly clear as individual children are evaluated and followed by interdisciplinary teams. In this regard, it is appropriate to mention the author's lengthy involvement with these multi-dimensional issues in a university-affiliated child development program. These programs exist to train inter-professional personnel and to deliver comprehensive interdisciplinary evaluations and intervention/prevention plans for the most complex childhood disabilities in development and learning.

This book does not attempt to present the nuts and bolts of the interdisciplinary process nor does it present an elaborate series of illustrative cases. A companion text by Johnston and Magrab (1976) does present the evaluation process with illustrative case histories. Wherever concrete examples are deemed helpful in illustrating these issues, they are included in order to make this book a practical guide as well as a theoretical forum. The present book is a complementary analysis and synthesis of the underlying issues arising around the child caught up in a paralysis of analysis or classified in a system stricken with a hardening of the categories—all to the disadvantage of himself,[1] his family, and society in general.

It is hoped that such a distillation of the issues will be palatable and even intoxicating to the reader, who will experience a new perspective on these salient issues and perceive and behave more knowledgeably and effectively as a result. After all, learning is simply defined as a change in perception and/or behavior. This book is written to achieve the admittedly ambitious goal of causing desirable changes in the understanding and practices of persons working with developmentally and learning disabled children.

The ultimate hope, of course, is that those who read this book will as a result provide for more effective and efficient learning and development within each child with whom they work. Such impact upon individual children is a difficult goal to make since general developmental and learning potential begin at conception. Some developmental and learning disabilities (DLDs) have deep roots in a long developmental history, making it extraordinarily difficult to uproot, prune, and replant an individual's inherent and intact abilities in more productive and fertile soil. Perhaps this book can help assure that more DLD children will realize their maximum potential, and, although some become late bloomers, they will bear their fullest fruit. May your therapeutic thumb grow greener and may you have more happy gardening.

---

[1] Masculine pronouns are used throughout the book for the sake of uniformity and brevity, rather than using the more elaborate and cumbersome "himself or herself," etc., forms. This usage is merely an arbitrary following of convention for the sake of simplicity, and it is not meant to show preference for or discrimination against either sex. This represents another "handicapping condition" of concern today. Some other field may set *it*self the task of establishing better mutual pronominal interaction and the grammatical liberation of the sexes.

Acknowledgments

It is scarcely possible to acknowledge adequately the many human and material resources that contribute to the preparation of a book. There are literally hundreds of people, organizations, events, and other phenomena with which a writer is in dynamic interaction from the conception of the germinal book's prospectus to the birth of the fully developed body of a new book. One could indeed analyze the growth and development of a book from the gleam in the writer's mind, to the many bleary-eyed late evenings, to the occasional morning sickness from reviewers' critiques, to the final production of what is hopefully a robust and useful new member of the society of ideas. Writers do not ordinarily get just a little bit caught with a new idea or a little bit pregnant. There is no cure for such a pregnancy, short of therapeutic abortion, than to proceed to the full term, however excruciating and agonizing the labor, with the abiding hope that a viable product will be born. It is hoped that the processes of amniocentesis—whereby this manuscript was subjected to various readers at various stages in its gestation to be refined, modified, and nourished accordingly—will have prevented the birth of another crippled or still-born product to take its place quietly on the shelves of various caretaking library institutions, never to be heard from again.

This book was conceived on a ski lift high in the Colorado Mountains and gained its first lease on life in the form of a skeletal outline when the writer was incapacitated in a skiing accident and unable to do much other than think and write. Because of other vicissitudes and unplanned delays, the gestational period was twice as long as planned and was extended twice by an understanding and compassionate publisher.

Mr. Linton Vandiver's curiosity about the fleshed-out version of the ungainly skeleton which he encouraged to grow and develop helped the author over his prenatal depression, especially when the going got very slow and discouraging due to the many interruptions and other demands on his time and effort.

Since there was considerable concern about the viability of this potential offspring, the writer called in an expert developmental specialist who looked at the growing manuscript from various points of view and made suggestions for improving the probability of a happy delivery and viable product. I therefore wish to acknowledge the sensitive critiqueing offered by Dr. Paula Malone.

Needless to say, the prolonged labor was painful and arduous. The midwifery of Ms. Opal Every, who typed version after version of re-edited manuscript without ever becoming prematurely discouraged or cutting the cord, is greatly appreciated. She also helped in the tireless probing for elusive and obscure references which would otherwise have made the labor unbearably tedious.

With all of the attention being given to this endeavor and only so many hours in a week, other significant persons were deprived. My wife Ann and three developing children, Rebecca, Rita, and Rhonda (the three R's), on occasion expressed some sibling rivalry over this new member of the family which was demanding so much of their daddy's time. Nevertheless, they endured and shared some of the discomforts and inconveniences of attending to this DLD individual and generally supported the effort to bring this baby of unknown potential into the literary or academic world. For this I lovingly thank them.

Last, but by no means least, are the major and sustaining sources of inspiration for this endeavor. First among these are the DLD children themselves, who are the reason for conceiving the book. The confused and often desperate parents and caregivers of DLD children gave further eloquent testimony for continued efforts to get the best of what is known together in their behalf. Second, the growing numbers of students concerned with DLDs in some respects served as procreators of this text, since they relentlessly pursued each topic to its logical conclusions, frequently causing the writer to revise, reconsider, or at least clarify obscure points. Third, my esteemed colleagues, too numerous to mention individually, encouraged me by the enlightened offspring of their own to nurture this baby to term.

chapter 1

Recent Progress
and Definitions

RECENT PROGRESS

An Introductory Allegory:
Alice in Wonderland versus Marvin in Mystery Land

Once upon a time, before most of us were even born, there was a scientist named Alfred who spent much of his life studying how humans develop and learn. He studied so many children that he claimed he could tell which ones were developing just like all good boys and girls should and which ones were not. Then one day the King wanted to know which children in his empire should go to school and which young subjects were too dumb to get anything out of the empire's fine academies. The King heard about the marvelous ability of Alfred to apply his newly developed magical tests to each child and thereby separate the good subjects, who were likely to succeed in the academies, from those bad boys and girls who should be excluded from the academies because they were not growing up properly.

This new system of discriminating in advance the successful learners from the failures worked very well indeed and the academies were filled with able and ambitious young subjects. Soon the rulers and scientists from other countries in the world heard about this new and excellent system for ensuring the success of their schools. Envoys and experts from other countries came to study the mystical new system which was ensuring the production of such good subjects. Moreover, most of the other countries were experiencing a massive proliferation of boys and girls, many more than their schools could accommodate, so they too wanted to use this new miraculous system for classifying very young boys and girls into categories according to their measured ability to do well or poorly in school.

The visiting scholars observed and copied every detail of Alfred's methods and materials so that they might use them in their own countries without doing violence to the sacred rites. Some of the very clever and

1

astute visiting scientists noted that simply and literally translating the tests into their own vernacular was not always satisfactory, especially when it made their best children perform less well than Alfred's population of children. Rather than running the risk of committing some sacrilegious heresy against the advance of science, the more pragmatic yet highly respected and sophisticated disciples of Alfred's, such as Louis, adapted his methods and materials to better fit the customs and standards of their own societies. And, lo and behold, the restandardized versions of Alfred's system worked! His genius was proclaimed and his system was promulgated far and wide among the enlightened and literate societies of the Western world. And the talented youth which Louis's version of Alfred's system identified lived happily terminally.

A whole new vocabulary grew out of this new psychometric movement. Children afflicted by the plague were named lazy, underachievers, environmentally deprived, diabolical, dyslexic, strephosymbolic, hyperkinetic, unmotivated, clumsy, messy, careless, obstreperous, mentally defective, familially retarded, culturally disadvantaged, hemispherically asynchronous, neurologically immature, genetically anomalous, SOBs (Sons, usually boys, of Bad Parentage or Blood), etc. The list of pejorative expletives goes on ad nauseum, if you're not sick already.

In the early days of the movement, only the really bad and ugly children got singled out. Most of the young inhabitants of the Western world succeeded on the restandardized versions of Alfred's system well enough at least to not be condemned to the purgatory (Blatt and Kaplan, 1966) of the labeled. And since there was a simultaneous Judeo-Christian movement toward human perfection, prompted by even greater religious zeal, the more grotesque reminders of human imperfection were put out of sight and presumably out of mind in distant institutions.

The science of psychometrics became increasingly refined and sanctioned, if not sanctimonious. Who could dispute that the psyche can be measured after the empiricists proved that insofar as something exists it can be measured? Soon the faculty for thinking and learning, often called intelligence, got broken into many small parts, each of which could be measured by one or more tests, which are basically samples of various behaviors. And the size of a child's intellectual ability was expressed by points on a scale, much as height or weight. Just as children of a certain chronological age were supposed to be so tall and so heavy, they were also supposed to be so smart. And those who weren't so smart usually weren't so lucky; with a few exceptions, this only served to prove the rule.

With the refinement of Alfred's system and the rash of inevitable defectors who went into competition with him in order to capitalize on his fame and fortune, many other systems and subsystems and their promoters sprang up. Also, more and more children with multiple variations and milder forms of defect were identified. Groups of concerned and/or guilty parents sought solace by uniting and they sought explanations for their child's maldevelopment by shopping around from system to system and from cult to cult until they found one they could live with or one that met certain of their needs.

And there was always an extant or incipient system somewhere to be found which could temporarily satisfy their desperate quest for answers while separating them from their possessions and sometimes from their child. There were systems apparently devised to indict the parents themselves by suggesting that their defective child was a punishment for their own evil ways. And the witch hunting goes on as new scapegoats are sought and old ineffective potions are marketed and sold. And yet, after three-quarters of a century, newly enlightened specialists, child advocates et al., are reflecting on their own profession's past sinful ways. They are passing laws to help remove many of these children from dilapidated institutions and to remove them from inappropriate "special" programs back into the mainstream where new techniques are helping them to grow and develop according to their full potential and where they can assume more responsible roles in their society. And, for the unfortunate few who fare best in institutional settings, these are undergoing careful scrutiny and upgrading. However, this allegory does not end happily here. As another astute observer of humanity observed, it is not appropriate to rest upon present accomplishments, since so much remains to be done.

> The woods are lovely, dark, and deep,
> But I have promises to keep
> And miles to go before I sleep. . . .
> (Frost, 1955)

What a delightful and triumphant tale this would be if that were all of it. But, alas, there seem to always be at least two sides to every story. And the present book will tell the story of those boys and girls who don't do so well when Alfred's system is applied to them, or who may do well on Alfred's system but for some strange reason perform in everyday preschool and school activities in ways that are at least disappointing and sometimes completely disgusting to their parents and themselves. The present book will also reveal how some of Alfred's overzealous or self-aggrandizing exponents (persons like Louis excepted) exploited his new system and how a hardening of the categories and paralysis of analysis spread like an epidemic throughout the world, wrongly labeling and, consequently, unfairly determining the destiny of hundreds of thousands of youngsters.

DEFINITIONS

Preliminary Definitions of Human Development and Learning

Although there are at least as many definitions for human development and for human learning as there are experts and books addressing them, two rather simple definitions are offered at the outset and will be elaborated upon as this chapter and book unfold. A simple definition of *human development* is a change in a person's function or capacity in any one or combination of four interacting domains—physical, emotional, social, and intellectual. Development is distinguished from growth. Growth relates primarily to a change in size or quantity, whereas development relates more to a change in function or quality. Development occurs during the entire life span from birth to death, indeed from womb to tomb, or even, as some would argue, from the erection to the resurrection.

An equally simplistic definition of *human learning* is a change in perception and/or behavior in any one or combination of the four aforementioned developmental domains. It is possible for a human being to learn certain adaptive behaviors, such as drinking to quench thirst in the physical domain, without any intellectual rationale or even words, feelings, or social customs to explain it. However, it is more typical for human behavior to be the manifestation of a complex interaction among two or more of the domains—drinking alcoholic beverages not so much to quench thirst as to be sociable, to relieve tension, to open conversation, and perhaps ultimately to damage the physical integrity of the organism.

Interrelationships between Human Development and Learning

The inextricable intertwining of human development and human learning has fascinated biological and behavioral scientists for centuries and remains as a great interdisciplinary challenge in each new investigation of individual differences. Discussions and debates about whether development or learning is more important are analogous to and run parallel with the controversies over the relative importance of heredity versus environment or nature versus nurture. Both development and learning are a function of the opportunities and restrictions found within an individual's natural endowments and the millieu in which he can realize and enhance them.

Learning can take place in any of the developmental domains and yet no observable change in behavior may occur because of either a subtle shift in the balance of the domains or a different meaning now attributed to the same behavior. For example, a competent mother may learn new information about the learning and developmental potential of her new-born child and yet continue to behave toward the child in the same facilitating and loving way, but with a much keener sensitivity and appreciation for his needs. Moreover, the mother might not even have been interested (emotionally motivated or developmentally ready to learn about) an infant's learning and developmental potential until she herself had achieved sufficient maturity to conceive and give birth to an infant of her own. Various authors (Gould, 1975; Maas and Kuypers, 1974) are now suggesting and elaborating upon the developmental stages in the adult life span. One indicates that beyond adolescence humans in the U. S. tend to go "from the confidence and optimism of the 20's through the doubts of the early 30's, the urgencies of the early 40's, and the mellowing and self-acceptance of the 50's" (Gould, 1975, p. 74). Another (McBride, 1973) writes about the growth and development of mothers, pointing out that there are various stages of parenting from the conception to the teenage emancipation of the offspring.

A child who is a bedwetter serves as an example of the interrelationship between learning and development at the lower end of the chronological continuum of human development. He may not be able physiologically to control this function until he has matured or developed further. He may intellectually understand that his parents wish him to stop bedwetting and he himself may dislike the physical discomfort involved, but until he is physiologically (developmentally) ready, he cannot behave in a manner that he perceives (learns) would be more desirable for all concerned. Thus, he understands (has learned) the desirability of not wetting his bed and is keenly motivated to stop it but he does not yet have the developmental capacity to alter his bedwetting behavior. On the other hand, once he gains the physiological capacity to control the previously uncontrollable bedwetting, he may have learned to relish the extraordinary attention he receives for bedwetting, and this previously undesired behavior may now be continued since his perception of its emotional and social value is quite different. He has gained a new perspective and has not changed the behavior in question, even though he is now physiologically ready to bring this function under control.

This child may be the same one who later in school made a puddle on the classroom floor to the utter dismay of the teacher and other pupils; after everyone had closed their eyes, as instructed by the teacher to protect the culprit's tender ego, he was given an opportunity to clean up the puddle without anyone's knowing who did it. Imagine the astonishment of all when they opened their eyes only to see a second puddle and a note on the chalkboard, "The phantom strikes again."

Disabilities in Human Development and Learning—Definitions

The title of this book, *Developmental and Learning Disabilities,* suggests that related disabilities occur in both development and learning. This is consistent with the preceding section which briefly points out the interrelationship between development and learning. Had the title been expressed as *learning and developmental disabilities,* one might conclude that the book only pertains to the effects of developmental disabilities on the learning process, thereby excluding learning disabilities as an interacting set of phenomena. A unique characteristic of this book is that it addresses both learning disabilities and developmental disabilities in order to present the inextricable relationships and simultaneous mutual interaction typically found between the two conditions. For this reason and for the sake of brevity, the phrase *Developmental and Learning Disabilities* is from here on abbreviated DLD. If one were to pronounce the acronym DLD it would probably sound like the word "dulled," which does connote the condition of DLD in children. That is, DLD dulls the normally sharp edge leading a person to the fullest realization of being human.

The problem of definition presents itself every time issues pertaining to DLD are discussed. What is really necessary, however, is to reach some agreement on what is being discussed. After all, communication is largely a function of two or more persons' having identical or at least very similar ideas in mind when they discuss any given concept (an elaboration on the communications theme follows in Chapters 2 and 3) and assumes a common understanding of the definitions of the terms used whether they are written, pictured, gestured, or spoken. Miscommunication frequently occurs when this assumption is not fulfilled either because one or both the sender and receiver of a message attribute a different meaning to the symbols used to express their ideas and feelings. Communication in the scientific community is no exception. When the rigor of precise definition of terms is exercised, new understandings often occur, especially when previous misunderstandings are caused by a lack of definition.

The word *definition* itself has several definitions; it can be a statement of what a thing is or an explanation of what a word or picture means; it can refer to the sharpness or clarity of a visual image or picture; and, in the auditory realm, it can refer to the fidelity of the original or reproduced sounds. For optimum communication, a definition might well employ commonly understood written words, clear pictures if possible, and accurate spoken language. The process of defining is one of determining the boundaries or precise outlines and distinguishing characteristics of a given phenomenon. For purposes of this book, developmental and learning disabilities are considered together as a single, albeit complex, series of interrelated difficulties with multiple manifestations. However, in order to give some idea of the legislative definitions of and distinctions between these two disabilities, a sample definition of each is given below.

First, the Developmental Disabilities Act or Public Law 91-517 of 1970 defined the term *developmental disability* (DD) as "a disability attributable to mental retardation, cerebral palsy, epilepsy, or another neurological condition of an individual found by the Secretary (of the U.S. Department of Health, Education, and Welfare) to be closely related to mental retardation or to require treatment similar to that required for mentally retarded individuals, which disability orginates before such individual attains age eighteen, which has continued or can be expected to contine indefinitely, and which constitutes a substantial handicap to such individual (p. 10—parenthetic item added for clarification)." The 1975 revision of Public Law 91-517 included autism and dyslexia (see Chapter 8 for further discussion). Future revisions may eventually add other specific learning disabilities as additional legitimate DD conditions and further justify the DLD amalgamation presented herein. However, various special interest groups oppose the inclusion of learning disabilities in the DD legislation lest such an inclusion would further dilute the hard won and severely limited funding currently available yet woefully inadequate for the presently included conditions.

Second, a proposed federal bill, which at this writing has not yet been updated or enacted, defined a *learning disability* as "a disorder in one or more of the basic psychological processes involved in understanding or in using language, spoken or written, which disorder may manifest itself in imperfect ability to listen, think, speak, read, write, spell, or do mathematical calculations. Such disorders include such conditions as perceptual handicaps, brain injury, minimal brain dysfunction, dyslexia, and developmental aphasia, but such a term does not include children who have learning problems which are primarily the result of visual, hearing, or motor handicaps, or mental retardation, of emotional disturbance, or of environmental disadvantage" (Senate Bill #2218 from Meier, 1971, pp. 9—10). An essentially identical definition of a learning disability is contained in the aforementioned 1975 revision of Public Law 91-517.

The multiple interrelationships between developmental disabilities and learning disabilities, for which the preceding definitions rather simplistically suggest that the latter is a subset of the former, will become clearer in the remaining discussion about definition and in subsequent chapters of this book. It is hoped that such clarification will help establish broader categories of support for programs serving such DLD children. Definitions are cardinal considerations whenever legislative matters are concerned, since definitions are the hinges upon which funding appropriations swing. The money gate may open for cerebral palsied children whose measured intelligence is less than 80 and abruptly slam closed in the face of those with IQs of 81 or higher.

One definition obviously leads to others and such a discussion could get bogged down in an outwardly spiraling paralysis of analysis. Nevertheless, the difficulties and misunderstandings surrounding definitions and classification of various disorders of child growth and development and the resultant tragedy of misplacement and mistreatment are readily acknowledged and must be avoided whenever possible. This point underscores another feature of definition, namely, that a complete definition should have both inclusive and exclusive stipulations. It should state both what something is and, when it is likely to be confused with something else, what it is not. Since many technical terms are involved in this rather complex discussion, an annotated glossary of terms is included in Chapter 10 of this book to help ensure optimum communication. In order to demonstrate some of the subtleties and complexities of definitions, one example of a DLD, namely, mental retardation, is presented in detail in the next several sections of this chapter. Mental retardation is the DLD selected because it is a bona fide developmental disability by definition and constitutes a severe impairment to learning. Some attention is also given to the prevalence and classification of mental retardation, to show how these considerations depend upon definition.

Definition of Mental Retardation

Some reasonable definition of *mental retardation* is essential for an enlightened and comprehensive discussion of its prevalence and classification. It is critical that those discussing mental retardation share a common definition of the condition or at least fully understand the differences in their definitions, which in turn determine the target population to be served by special programs.

One definition of mental retardation calls it a condition which "refers to significantly subaverage general intellectual functioning existing concurrently with deficits in adaptive behavior, and manifested during the developmental period" (Grossman, 1973, p. 11). This definition, which is widely accepted among clinicians and academicians working with mentally retarded and other DLD persons, is in itself a complex combination of terms filled with potential semantic pitfalls. Nevertheless, the definition represents the distillation of the best thinking of authorities in the field and serves as the basis for this discussion. Moreover, the definition adds the important stipulation regarding concurrent deficits in adaptive behavior, which was not expressly included in previous definitions of mental retardation.

Although the definition of developmental disabilities does shed some light on where mental retardation is thought to fit along the continuum of handicapping conditions, it implies that mental retardation is exclusively a neurological condition. A person who is mentally retarded because of neurological causes would generally fall under the classification of developmental disability, whereas a person whose mental retardation is a function of inadequate environmental enrichment or other deprivations could not legitimately be included within the definition of developmental disability, even though his intellectual functioning might be equally defective.

The preceding definition of mental retardation, therefore, should be construed as a relative definition which is explicitly inclusive and only implicitly exclusive. It states what mental retardation is relative to normal intellectual functioning and adaptive behavior but it does not state which similar conditions are to be excluded. The following three sections address the logical divisions of this definition of mental retardation and further emphasize the importance of accurate and intelligible definitions for clear-cut communication.

Significantly Subaverage General Intellectual Functioning Each of these five polysyllabic words has multiple denotations and connotations but is herein discussed only in relation to mental retardation and in the same order as it appears in the definition. The word *significantly* typically refers to a statistical concept. This concept in turn refers to measured performances which are one standard deviation below the average measured performance of the referent population, in this case groups of normally developing humans in the United States. It has been statistically determined that approximately two-thirds of all persons tested perform within a range of about 30 intelligence points around the preadjusted average of 100 on standardized and commonly used instruments for measuring intelligence, such as the Stanford-Binet or Wechsler tests (see Chapter 10 for listing of evaluation instruments). With reference to the normal distribution curve, this means that nearly 70% of the entire population on which these tests were standardized have intelligence scores between about 85 and 115 ($\pm$ 1 S.D.). It also means that approximately 15% of the population have intelligence scores below 85 (1 S.D. below the mean), which in the past was used as the sole criterion for establishing that a person was mentally retarded. That is, the person's test performance alone indicated that he was significantly less mentally able than the majority of the population. This test result is usually borne out by the fact that such individuals have significant difficulty in benefitting from the standard school program in comparison with their age peers of normal and above normal measured intelligence. In this fashion, such tests of intelligence are said to have predictive validity, within the ecological limitations to be discussed later. Of course, the term "significantly" is in itself relative. If criteria such as school success or performance on intelligence tests are not deemed important in terms of overall human behavior, a cultural phenomenon dealt with below, then the term itself loses much of its significance.

Likewise, the term *subaverage* is relative to what is considered average and depends upon the specific but arbitrary cut-off point below which intelligence scores are designated as subaverage. Actually, the average of 100 is an arbitrary predetermined number around which intelligence scores are statistically adjusted to conform to the mathematically defined normal curve of distribution. This is the case whether the measured intelligence is expressed as a quotient arrived at by dividing the numerical equivalent of one's mental age (in months or years) by his chronological age (in months or years) and multiplied by 100 ($IQ = (MA/CA) \times 100$) or whether it is expressed as a deviation score from the predetermined mean of 100.

It is critical to specify the characteristics of the population on which any given test is normed or standardized. As presently measured, normal or standard intellectual performance among college graduates is typically far superior to that of their impoverished and/or brain-damaged counterparts. In a pluralistic society, with multiple diverse cultural values, it is extremely important to measure intellectual functioning with procedures or instruments which are appropriate to the subject's background and which have been normed on a comparable reference group. A test is, by definition, only a sample of a larger domain of, in this case, so-called intelligent behavior or intellectual functioning. Thus, the test must use relevant and familiar material to accurately assess one's ability to recall what has been learned and to apply this information and skill in solving new problems. It is imperative that the characteristics of the reference population be delineated, since subaverage intelligence compared to a group of geniuses probably constitutes no significant daily living handicap; whereas being 1 S.D. below the average measured ability of a group of retarded persons would constitute a profoundly significant handicap for one who must function in the mainstream of a complex society characteristic of any of the developed countries in the world.

In this respect, it is noteworthy that the increasing complexity of one's environmental requirements demands a concomitantly greater sophistication to successfully cope with daily living demands, which suggests a kind of inflationary factor in measured intelligence. The same intelligence scores, which correctly predicted the ability of a person to get along in a less complex society, may no longer be sufficient in a society which requires increased levels of sophistication and ability to deal satisfactorily with the many abstract and symbol-laden daily problems in most contemporary societies. It can be argued that the prevalence of mental retardation is increasing not only as a result of more persons of significantly subaverage potential being kept alive because of recent medical advances long enough to enter the schools and, in some cases the adult world, but also as a result of there being relatively fewer occupations or life situations in which those with subaverage general intelligence can perform satisfactorily.

The incidence of mental retardation may also be increasing as a result of the relatively larger numbers of persons dropping out of formal schooling, wherein much of the mainstream culture's information and skills are learned. In the United States, this is especially true for those who drop out of school near the sixth grade, since most TV, newspaper, radio, and other mass media do not contain information or vocabulary beyond approximately the sixth grade level. A recent report (Edelmann et al., 1974) reveals that about 20% of U.S. citizens are functionally illiterate, i.e., below fourth grade ability level in reading. There are some exceptional mass media which go beyond sixth grade levels of difficulty, but these are typically referred to as "educational" or "for intellectuals" and are consequently deemed unsuitable for widespread broadcast or dissemination, since they are not consumed and enjoyed by the majority, who either cannot or do not wish to understand or appreciate them.

The word *general* is intended to include only those whose intellectual functioning is impaired across a broad spectrum of cognitive categories and to exclude those who have cognitive deficits in one or two specific domains but are in general intellectually competent. For example, there are many cases reported in the literature of persons with exceptionally high measured intelligence who may have specific intellectual deficits in a verbal domain such as spelling, or a mathematical domain such as solid geometry, or a performance domain such as assembling puzzles. Such DLD persons may have specific learning disabilities and even be legitimately defined as developmentally disabled, yet their overall intellectual functioning would not permit them to be called mentally retarded. On the other hand, there are cases reported of persons, sometimes called "idiot-savants," who exhibit general and severe mental retardation but have developed one or two specific intelligence-related functions to a very high degree of excellence. For example, some of these paradoxical people can read and/or spell very long and tricky words; however, they cannot define or properly use most words in the language. Others may be able to deal with spatial relations problems, such as assembling puzzles, extraordinarily rapidly but cannot abstract or verbalize the underlying cognitive operations, such as the process of elimination, for more general problem-solving applications. Perhaps these persons have fully functioning right hemispheres but dysfunctional left hemispheres in their brain. This will be discussed at length later.

Multiple previous efforts at breaking intellectual functioning into its component factors, such as this chapter is briefly doing, have yielded many different constellations of abilities. As a result, some investigators have charged that current assessments of general intellectual functioning do not represent the full splendor of intellectual functioning, some (Guilford, 1954) positing 120 or more specific composite factors. Others, including the pioneer Spearman (1927), have parsimoniously reasoned that there is one general "g" factor of intelligence with many more specific and less important subfactors. A vocabulary test for example, using carefully selected words, can give a quick assessment of general intelligence which positively correlates quite highly with the overall estimate of cognitive/intellectual functioning derived from more elaborate multifactorial assessments.

The apparent elegance of a single general intelligence score is misleading since it may summarize either a rather flat and even or a widely scattered performance on the subtests which compose it. The analysis of subtest patterns is used to evaluate specific strengths and weaknesses and is thought by some to represent correlates of differential brain development and integrity. There is rising concern with the emphasis placed upon general intelligence as it is now measured since it tends to ignore the creative aspects of human functioning characterized by the divergent thinking necessary to create new ideas and to solve unusual problems. Investigators concerned with fundamental brain electrochemistry (Penfield, 1958) and biophysiology (Pribram, 1971) suggest that rate of responding and quality of responding are not adequately considered in traditional intelligence testing and that some of the currently more elusive functions of the brain, especially those which are hypothesized to largely originate in the nonverbal right hemisphere, are not adequately assessed and yet may be the source of much creative thinking that is not accounted for in current tests of general intellectual functioning. Of course, the society at large has little tolerance for those who do not think convergently, and such divergent responses, if not understood and appreciated by the examiner, might be designated as bizarre and provide a reason for classifying the person as deviant along dimensions of mental illness. This concern plus claims of discrimination against certain subpopulations in a pluralistic society (Mercer, 1972) have made intelligence testing quite controversial, so much so that the less valid and reliable group tests of intelligence have been prohibited from use in some states' public school systems. The reduced validity and reliability for such group tests result from many causes, including the necessary streamlining for group administration, the elimination of one-to-one observation by a clinically sensitive examiner, and inappropriate content and/or norms for the group or individual being tested.

As one might suspect from the preceding discussion, there is no universal agreement about the meaning of *intellectual*. One of the most straightforward operational definitions of intelligence is "that which intelligence tests measure." This equivocal and yet indisputable definition accurately describes the state of the art and knowledge about intellectual functioning, that is to say that there are as many definitions as there are measures, since each measure is designed with a given definition either explicitly stated or implicitly thought. However, the intelligence measures which are widely accepted to sufficiently represent the full domain of intellectual functioning usually include subtests which assess general knowledge, short-term memory, verbal and mathematical problem comprehension and solution, and the coordination of the eye and the hand in various performance tests which presumably also require thinking and planning. Of course, a highly skilled and accomplished musician or artist might do relatively poorly on most of these measures for a variety of reasons and still be referred to by the culture as a genius or an intellectual. There may be more right hemisphere functions not adequately tapped in traditional verbal, left hemisphere-oriented tests of intelligence.

Directly related to the immediately preceding remarks is the word *functioning*, which is inextricably woven into the fabric of intelligence as measured. In fact, the phrase "as measured" relates to this important consideration of function, which is to be differentiated from absolute status. Functional intelligence refers to the contextual or ecological aspects of a person's performance and is frequently qualified by such phrases as "under the circumstances," "all other things being equal," "conditions being what they are," and so forth. The diagnosis of "functional mental retardation" refers to the fact that, on the basis of a person's intelligence test performance, he receives a score which falls in the range of mental retardation, that is, significantly subaverage; however, the word "functional" indicates that there is some doubt as to whether this is an immutable status or a relative function of one or more extenuating circumstances.

If a definition of mental retardation relative to each individual's native or inborn learning capacity is to be accepted, it is quite probable that the majority of persons in the society at large do not realize their fullest capacity for learning and are thus retarded below what they could be if they had the opportunity to fully realize their intellectual capacities. Although intelligence tests purport to measure intellectual capacity, they in fact measure achieved levels of information and skills in the verbal and nonverbal areas. It is then inferred that, based on previous achievements, there is a reasonably high probability that the individual will continue in the future to derive a similar amount from his environment, which includes all of the people, places, and things he experiences in his daily living. Since most individuals do not radically alter their life circumstances, referred to as their ecology, the constancy of their environment tends to ensure that their measured intelligence will not fluctuate appreciably, provided that they continue to function at the same rate of learning and with the same degree of exposure to their environment.

The actual assessment of an individual's ability to learn new skills and to apply this new learning to either old or new problems is rarely done and yet this is what intelligence is allegedly thought to be. Clearly, the person in a deprived environment, regardless of his native intelligence, will be severely limited in the acquisition of new knowledge and the development of new skills. He will probably test as significantly subaverage in general intelligence, remain in or be placed in settings for mentally subaverage individuals, and, in prophecy-fulfilling fashion, continue to perform at a subaverage level on tests of intelligence.

This designation of functional mental retardation further underscores the relativity feature in the currently accepted definition of mental retardation. A person, for example, whose mother tongue is different from that of both the examiner and the test materials will likely function much as a retarded person in attempting to solve verbal problems or to understand verbal directions. In a pluralistic society, the environments in which people are born and reared vary greatly along a continuum from poverty to affluence and typically vary in degree of deprivation to enrichment insofar as the availability of the content of the intelligence tests is concerned. It is, therefore, necessary to take such ecological or environmental factors into consideration before attributing absolute mental retardation to a given individual. The assumption "all other things being equal" is seldom if ever met. If an intelligence test were fundamentally a reflection of the learning on the part of the individual and if the environment in which he grows up were not equal in many of the sources of skill and information enjoyed by the majority, he may also function as relatively mentally retarded, although his basic intellectual capacity and learning ability are equal to that of his peers.

Many subcultures in a pluralistic society have not only different languages but different cultural expectations which may influence a person's general experience, for better or for worse, insofar as his functioning on intelligence testing is concerned. Although most cultural differences are attributed to ethnic differences, there are also different expectations according to socioeconomic status, so much so as to lead one investigator to present the characteristics of the culture of poverty (Lewis, 1970). Such realizations have given rise to euphemisms such as the "six-hour retarded child" (President's Committee on Mental Retardation, 1969) who finds it difficult to function normally in the mainstream school setting, which actually represents a foreign culture, but who functions quite well in the more familiar setting outside of school. Similarly, children of average or above intelligence in mainstream America would have considerable difficulty, especially initially, functioning at the same level of competence in a country where a completely foreign language is used exclusively. Contrariwise, the child who develops language relatively very late or very poorly in his native mother tongue (vernacular), given all of the same opportunities sufficient for his peers to master the language, should be considered to have a communication disorder. If such a child were tested in a different language from his vernacular, his delay may be even more pronounced, but should not be attributed entirely to the unfamiliarity of the new language. A child who has difficulty learning English and displays a significantly subaverage acquisition of speaking and listening vocabulary will likely manifest similar delays in learning "Spanglish," Creole Black dialect, smoke signaling, or other languages, because of a fundamental deficit in language ability. Since expressive and receptive language is critical to intellectual functioning as measured by most current intelligence tests, a child with such a specific language disorder may be assessed as mentally retarded in spite of normal or above normal capacities to learn in nonverbal areas.

Many environmentally deprived or culturally different individuals have intelligence scores which are just below the average level and have in the past been designated as "borderline" mentally retarded. They have been called "slow learners" or "educables" by the mainstream public school system and, until recently, were grouped with others having similar deficits, thereby further depriving them of learning from their more enlightened and able peers. This particular classification has been deleted from the recent classification terminology, since so many of these individuals have demonstrated at least average inherent capacities for learning when given sufficient opportunity to compensate for previous deprivations or differences in experience (Dunn, 1968; Meier, 1970).

Existing Concurrently with Deficits in Adaptive Behavior Continuing the discussion of the generally accepted definition of mental retardation, the phrase *existing concurrently with deficits in adaptive behavior* represents a formal acknowledgment of the fact that a person can demonstrate *significantly subaverage general intellectual functioning* and, at the same time, get along in his social surroundings. The individual who has mastered those behaviors necessary to adapt to his given environment, regardless of how simple or complex it may be, cannot be legitimately labeled mentally retarded. He has, in fact, learned what is necessary to cope with and survive in his own peculiar life situation, which has its own limitations on the extent of information and skills available to be learned. The Eskimo or Tlingit Indian in Alaska, the Amish in the northeastern United States, the coal miner in Appalachia, or the native Hawaiian on the island of Molokai may all test as mentally retarded on the Wechsler or Stanford-Binet tests of intelligence, even if the tests are translated into their vernacular. Nevertheless, they are behaving satisfactorily and normally in their peculiar native environs. And just as the immigrating Puerto Rican may psychometrically test in the mentally retarded range on standard Anglo-American IQ tests, his ability to behaviorally adapt to and satisfactorily function in the Miami or New York City environs speaks well of his mental capacity to learn new information and skills. If an individual cannot satisfactorily behave in his own native environment without extraordinary support from others, he is considered to have deficits in adaptive behavior not only in his native environment but also most probably in any other "normal" situations as well.

The description of deficits in adaptive behavior is more complex than for measured intelligence because of the former's lack of objective measures. Moreover, some or all of the input regarding a person's daily living or adaptive behavior may be from verbal reports of the individual or his primary caregiver and are subject to considerable error and variability. The level of deficiency in adaptive behavior is expressed in four levels which roughly correspond to standard deviation units of measured intelligence (see Table 1). Level I, which is about 2 S.D. below the entire population's average adaptive behavior, represents some noteworthy adaptive difficulties, whereas Level IV represents an almost total lack of adaptive behavior or ability to cope with everyday living demands, including eating, dressing, communicating, eliminating, etc.

The Vineland Social Maturity Scale—supplemented where possible and appropriate by additional developmental assessment from portions of the Gesell (Yale Revised) Developmental Schedules, the Bayley Infant Scales, the Cattell Infant Intelligence Scale, or the Kuhlmann Tests of Mental Development—is recommended for use at the preschool level as a measure of adaptive behavior. During the school-age period, standardized achievement tests serve as an initial index of adaptive behavior, at least adaptation to or coping with the demands of the academic world. Experienced school teachers, who typically have a sort of built-in normative frame of reference, are also good judges of adaptive behavior. The Vineland Scales may have to be used here, as well as with younger children, to differentiate among the lower levels of adaptive behavior characteristically attendant to various degrees of more severe mental retardation. At the adolescent and adult level, adaptive behavior is best seen in social adjustment, but there are few instruments available that adequately assess the quality and quantity of this adjustment. Therefore, the level of social adjustment is frequently determined by the clinician's evaluation of the individual's social and vocational adjustment, often in combination with ratings on such scales as the Alpern-Boll or the American Association of Mental Deficiency's Adaptive Behavior Scales. The overall level of a person's adaptive behavior is expressed in a single score which, like the IQ, is a composite of several measures including self-sufficiency, language, socialization, domestic ability, vocational potential, etc.

> At the present time, the value of a *single score* for adaptive behavior level classification is limited largely to certain administrative purposes and has little diagnostic or program planning import for the individual. Assessment of performance in *specific domains* of behavior, however, can be very useful in identifying deficits and training needs. As with I.Q. scores, individuals who are classified at the same overall level of adaptive behavior may not be "clinically equivalent" in that they may vary significantly in the various domains of behavior that comprise the overall rating (Grossman, 1973, p. 20).

The final clinical judgment as to a person's adaptive behavior level is arrived at only after considering the multiple factors which contribute to the development of adaptive behavior. These must include: repeated observation of the individual in his natural setting by persons trained to make such observations validly and reliably; reports from others, especially caregivers and teachers, who have observed his behavior in other regular settings; recognition of the limitations and opportunities imposed by a given setting, including others in the environment (ecology); and consideration of general intellectual functioning from a more structured test situation. When a deficit in adaptive behavior exists concurrently with inadequate intellectual functioning, a second important criterion of mental retardation is fulfilled. It is noteworthy that the U.S. Office of Education's Project Head Start has chosen to focus on *social competence,* which is defined much the same as the aforementioned adaptive behavior, for assessing program impact on the children.

Manifested during the Developmental Period Since even the term *developmental* can be subject to various and sundry interpretations, possible ambiguities for the term in the definition of mental retardation have been essentially eliminated, although not illuminated, merely by designating the chronological age of 18 as the upper limit of the developmental period. This arbitrary upper limit is regardless of the earlier observation that development is a life-long process. For a person who is over 18 years of age and meets the preceding two main criteria of mental retardation, it is necessary to pursue a thorough history in order to determine whether the condition of mental retardation was manifest in the individual's intellectual functioning and adaptive behavior before the age of 18 years. This history should include pertinent data about: (1) family background (family trees and pedigree charts if readily available); (2) living conditions plus estimate of socioeconomic status; (3) physical characteristics; (4) medical conditions; (5) education and training experiences; (6) academic achievement and skills; (7) several breakdowns of measured intellectual functioning; and (8) several estimates of adaptive behavior. In light of this stipulation, if whatever condition that is responsible for a person's functioning in a mentally retarded or more general DLD fashion occurred after he was 18, he is not technically mentally retarded or developmentally disabled and is classified under some alternative nomenclature.

Current Criteria for Defining Mental Retardation Table 1 summarizes the criteria currently in wide use for defining mental retardation. The preceding discussion has underscored the complexities and controversies involved in the use of these more pragmatic definitional criteria and should be borne in mind as a caution against the indiscriminate application of the criteria. The many intricacies of conducting a sophisticated interdisciplinary evaluation of DLD children, with case study examples, is found in Johnston and Magrab (1975).

Prevalence of DLD

Now that the vicissitudes of definition have been presented for one subset of DLD, the question arises as to how many DLD persons there are.

Table 1. Mental retardation criteria

Adaptive behavior levels	Intellectual functioning deficiency	Approximate percentage		Standard deviation (S.D.)	Measured intelligence score	
		Mentally retarded	Total population		Stanford Binet (S.D.=16)	Wechsler (S.D.=15)
	(Borderline)	67	13	−1.01 to −2.00	68–83	70–84
I	Mild	22	2.7	−2.01 to −3.00	52–67	55–69
II	Moderate	6	0.2	−3.01 to −4.00	36–51	40–54
III	Severe	3	0.1	−4.01 to −5.00	20–35	25–39
IV	Profound	2	0.05	−5.00	20	25

Incidence and prevalence studies which have attempted to document the extent and degree of various subsets of DLD have yielded highly variable results. The wide range of such findings is a function of several inconsistencies or combinations thereof from study to study: (1) variations in the definitions of the various subsets, such as epilepsy, cerebral palsy, mental retardation, autism, and various forms of learning disabilities; (2) variations in tests and procedures used to assess each subset; (3) variations in the characteristics of the population used as a referent group; and (4) other uncontrolled contaminants such as ecological variations.

For example, a marked difference in the estimated prevalence of mental retardation, a DLD subset, would be expected between a study which employed a relative definition and a study based upon an absolute definition of mental retardation. Mental retardation could be defined as any deficiency in mental functioning relative to what could be expected of an individual given full physical integrity and environmental enrichment. This relative definition might legitimately include all persons who have failed to fully realize their presumed potential or whose scores are lower than the highest possible scores in any of several dimensions of mental functioning. This rather extreme possibility is consistent with several definitions of learning disabilities. By this criterion, 99% of the population would appear retarded in physics relative to Albert Einstein, and, surprisingly enough, Einstein himself had what would probably be construed to have been a specific learning disability in conventional mathematical reasoning and did in fact have considerable difficulty in school. It is pointed out in this book that DLD is a relative thing, dependent upon definitions, etc., and the proponent of the theory of relativity serves as a fine example.

Continuing the discussion of prevalence, if individually and competently measured intelligence scores alone were used, approximately 16% of the population would fall at least 1 S.D. below the average or mean of about 100. Using the U. S. population of just over 200,000,000 persons, this would calculate to over 32,000,000 mentally retarded persons (IQ below 85). With the elimination of the "borderline" segment, the estimate dramatically drops to about 3%, or 6,000,000 persons with intelligence scores below 70. It is estimated that at least 0.35% of the population, that is, about 700,000 persons, are moderately to profoundly retarded and would be recognizable in any society as incapable of independent existence, since their adaptive behavior would also be so highly limited. In the milder forms of intellectual deficit and where the environmental demands are relatively simple, a person's adaptive behavior may be adequate to disqualify him from the designation of mental retardation. On the contrary, as suggested in preceding sections, when the environment or culture demands more abstract reasoning skills for successful adaptation, a high prevalence is likely to be quoted. This largely explains why there is a considerably higher estimated prevalence of mentally retarded individuals during school age than for preschool or postschool ages.

Figure 1 shows the prevalence estimates for various subsets of DLD. In a 10-year longitudinal study (Werner, Bierman, and French, 1971), it was revealed that more than 30% of the original 1,300 subjects had some DLD by 10 years of age. It is conceivable that even more of this group would manifest some form of DLD during the following 8 years, when school subject matter becomes more difficult and specific vocational concerns and needs emerge. A discussion of Werner's 18-year follow-up on the original cohort is included in Chapter 9 of this book.

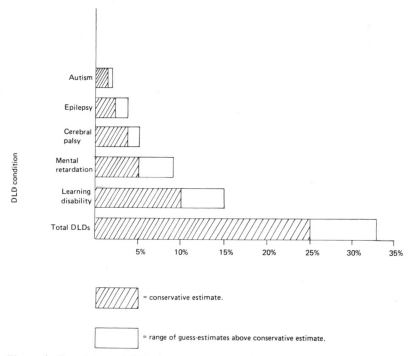

Figure 1. Prevalence of DLD conditions singularly and in combination in general population at 10 years of age (based on Drillien, 1964; Keane, 1972; Lubchenco, 1969; Tarjan et al., 1973; Werner, Bierman, and French, 1971; and others). It has been conservatively estimated that about one-fourth of the 10-year-old population has some form of DLD; liberal guess-estimates place the prevalence as high as one-third of the population. These figures are significantly lower for both preschool and postschool cohorts since academic tasks and tests highlight DLD conditions.

Classification Systems for DLD

Several systems of classification for the various subsets of DLD have been used during the past several decades and some have been alluded to previously in this chapter. Each successive system has usually reflected the advancing state of the art and knowledge with respect to defining such exceptional children. As more is learned about the many complexities of DLD conditions, the classification systems have become increasingly detailed and correspondingly more complex. The inadequacy of earlier classification and labeling systems has been periodically challenged when enough data accumulate to demonstrate that persons have been previously misclassified and, as a result, have endured many inappropriate and inequitable placements in institutions, special classes and programs, sheltered workshops, and the like. The U. S. Department of Health, Education, and Welfare commissioned a task force (Hobbs, 1975a, b) to address the various issues involved in the classification of exceptional children, many of whom fall in one or another DLD subset. This comprehensive and thorough investigation found that many of the past practices of pigeonholing individuals and labeling them with indelible ink has, in the long run, done more harm than good for the individuals and probably for the society.

> Children who are categorized and labeled as different may be permanently stigmatized, rejected by adults and other children, and excluded from opportunities essential for their full and healthy development. *Yet* categorization is necessary to open doors to opportunity: to get help for a child, to write legislation, to appropriate funds, to design service programs, to evaluate outcomes, to conduct research, even to communicate about the problems of the exceptional child.
>
> Children may be assigned to inferior educational programs for years, deprived of their liberty through commitment to an institution, or even sterilized, on the basis of inadequate diagnostic procedures, with little or no consideration of due process. *Yet* we have the knowledge needed to evaluate children with reasonable accuracy, to provide suitable programs for them, and to guarantee them recognized due-process requirements.
>
> Large numbers of minority-group children—Chicanos, Puerto Ricans, blacks, Appalachian whites—have been inaccurately classified as mentally retarded on the basis of inappropriate intelligence tests, placed in special classes or programs where stimulation and learning opportunities are inadequate, and stigmatized. *Yet* these children often do need special assistance to manifest and sharpen their unappreciated competences. Improved classification procedures could increase their chances of getting needed services.
>
> Classification of a child can lead to his commitment to an institution that defines and confirms him as delinquent, blind, retarded, or emotionally disturbed. The institution may evoke be-

havior appropriate to his label, thus making him more inclined to crime, less reliant than he could be on residual vision, less bright than his talents promise, more disturbed than he would be in a normal setting. *Yet* families and communities are not equipped to sustain or contain some children; families require relief, and the child himself may need the protection and specialized services of an institution and the opportunity it presents for instruction and treatment on a twenty-four-hour basis.

We have a multiplicity of categorical legislative programs for all kinds of exceptional children. *Yet* the child who is multiply handicapped, who does not fit into a neat category, may have the most difficulty in getting special assistance.

The juvenile court system was designed to guide and protect the delinquent child, as well as to protect society, with the judge serving a near-parental function. *Yet*, because of inadequate procedural safeguards, children classified as delinquent or in need of supervision may receive harsher treatment than would an adult who had committed the same offense.

Voluntary and professional associations, organized around categories of exceptionality, have effectively pressed for financial appropriations for exceptional children. Funds and services have increased substantially in the past decade. Federal, state, and local bureaus, also organized by categories of exceptionality, are well staffed and busy. *Yet* associations, bureaus, and service agencies compete for scarce resources; there is much duplication of effort; services for children are poorly coordinated; continuity of care is seldom achieved; and children get lost in the system over and over again (Hobbs, 1975a, pp. 3–4).

In addition to the above rather generic concerns about classification, there has been considerable criticism of the use of the traditional medical model for classifying DLD. The medical model focuses upon the diagnosis of the etiology or cause of DLD. This frequently results in parents, educators, and professionals becoming so involved and preoccupied with the origin of a given DLD that they lose sight of the more important treatment planning and actual habilitation for the DLD person. Furthermore, in more than three-fourths of the cases which meet the aforementioned definitional criteria for mental retardation, a clear-cut medical or physical etiology cannot be detected or described. This has given rise to the acronym somewhat euphemistically applied to children for whom no clear diagnosis is forthcoming, namely, *GORK*, which stands for *G*od *o*nly *r*eally *k*nows. It is useful to know the etiology of the DLD in any given individual if there are known treatments which will either cure the condition or prevent further deterioration. In some 10% of mentally retarded persons, a clear-cut organic cause can be found which is amenable to physical, biochemical, or perhaps surgical intervention and arrest. These are quite infrequent yet sufficiently dramatic to maintain a sort of pious hope in the other 90% for whom the strict medical model is inappropriate but who nonetheless chronically and often desperately await similar relatively simple medical cures.

Although research for these cures continues, and occasionally yields new and exciting findings, the vast majority of DLD is caused by far more complex interactions between a person's native endowment and his environmental experiences. Therefore, any classification scheme which is based solely upon the etiology determined by a medical diagnosis is now considered to be naïvely simplistic and usually grossly inadequate for treatment planning. An etiological classification is only useful if it demonstrates the causes of a condition for which there are known cures or, at best, enables one to make accurate predictions about the outcome of the condition.

In spite of the above reservations with respect to the medical model, the clinician is nevertheless encouraged to identify a primary cause and specific disorder whenever possible. These classification schema follow essentially those advanced by the World Health Organization's International Classification of Diseases (1968) and the American Psychiatric Association Diagnostic and Statistical Manual of Mental Disorders (1968), both of which ascribe numerical categories to each condition. It is not within the scope of this discussion to elaborate further on the nomenclature used in the classification of even mental retardation, let alone DLD, according to its many possible causes. Suffice it to say that the causes of mental retardation and other DLDs, regardless of their severity, are grouped under the following main headings: following infection and intoxication; following trauma or physical agent; associated with disorders of metabolism or nutrition; associated with gross brain disease (postnatal); associated with diseases and conditions caused by unknown prenatal influence; with chromosomal abnormality; with gestational disorders; following psychiatric disorder; with environmental influences; and with other conditions.

Under each of the aforementioned headings are numerous highly specific subheadings each having additional qualifiers. For example, in the case of mental retardation caused primarily by an organic cause, an individual may *have* a congenital brain injury with a secondary cranial anomaly such as hydrocephalus *caused by* a chromosomal aberration *resulting in* some impairment of vision, a convulsive disorder of petit mal seizures, and a motor dysfunction of spasticity with mild diplegia. Such a classification of a condition, its cause(s) and results may be derived through careful physical, developmental, and neurological examinations and assigned an impressive multidigit number for the above condition.

However, if the DLD is caused by "environmental influences" or "other conditions," as is true in a majority of the less serious forms of the condition, the classification is not helpful except, perhaps, as it rules out any suspected organic causes.

One of the surest ways of preventing a child's getting an unwarranted and perhaps permanent label is to employ an ongoing evaluation-remediation process of tentatively identifying his strengths and weaknesses and then further refining the assessment of these as the child's ability to profit from trial remediation procedures is observed and evaluated. This approach does not commit the child to a hard and fast label—the hardening of the categories can result in life-long indictments. This scientific model, instead of a medical model, proposes a series of hypotheses about the origins and care for the child's apparent DLD. These hypotheses are confirmed or abandoned as new data are discovered while the child learns and develops, thereby revealing new aspects of his potential. Any classification system which is appropriately linked to remediation postulates only tentative categories of DLD with a common understanding that such a deficit may be temporary, functional, or at least amenable to amelioration. Thus, with the increasing efficacy of intervention/prevention efforts such as those reported by Heber *et al.* (1972), the acceptance of the scientific model of multidetermination and the rejection of the medical model of predetermination characterize the current state of the art and knowledge about classifying DLD. Ironically enough, Heber (1961) authored the first major reference for classification of mental retardation. The definition of DLD is now understood to be complex, relative, and multidimensional, requiring a vast array of interdisciplinary personnel to describe and deal adequately with its many facets.

The commonly used definition of mental retardation, which is one of several DLD subsets, was used in this discussion for purposes of addressing problems of definition illustrating the significance of definition in terms of prevalence and classification of DLD. This knotty problem of definitional integrity, or the untying of the Gordian knots around definition, opens up the whole Pandora's box regarding methods of evaluating and consequent planning of treatment/intervention programs for DLD conditions occurring in children of different ages. Subsequent chapters in this book will clarify these matters or give the reader helpful leads to answers in other sources.

A Decade of Undulating and Incoherent Legislation

This section highlights most of the important legislative milestones regarding DLD matters during the past decade. It does not attempt to recount the inscrutable political intrigue and shrewd maneuvers by various special interest groups and legislative committee members leading up to the enactment of legislation which has had a significant impact on the development of programs for DLD children. For a detailed and knowledgeable account of the blow-by-blow proceedings in federal legislation during the very active period from 1966 to 1971, see Boggs (1972). For an historical picture of mental retardation painted with a much broader brush and including some present and future implications, see Crissey (1975).

Nevertheless, the importance of having a receptive ear in high places can scarcely be overstated when new legislation is being generated and proposed for enactment. A noteworthy example is Public Law 88-164, entitled *Facilities for the Mentally Retarded*. This bill was passed by the 88th U. S. Congress during the presidency of John F. Kennedy. Before his administration, the National Association for Retarded Children (now called the National Association for Retarded Citizens), along with other less well organized or identifiable special interest groups, had lobbied long and hard to establish such a law which, in numerous ways, would advance the cause for handicapped citizens throughout the U.S.A. The Kennedy family knew intimately and felt compassion for the mentally retarded, primarily because one of their own family was afflicted by this condition. President Kennedy not only received many votes from persons and interest groups who were aware of both his concern about mental retardation and the power of a sympathetic president. These persons also began to agitate in Congress with renewed vigor for federal legislation to benefit the mentally retarded. The enactment of Public Law 88-164 is commonly regarded to be a monumental landmark for the participation of the U. S. Federal Government in service, training, and research activities focused on mental retardation.

The succession of President Lyndon B. Johnson and Vice President Hubert Humphrey did not seriously reduce the momentum begun by Public Law 88-164. The fact that the Humphrey family also had a mentally retarded member kept a receptive ear at high levels. Encouraged by the obvious advances being made on behalf of the mentally retarded as a result of Public Law 88-164, encouraged by the parallel claim that a member of President Johnson's family was afflicted with a specific reading disorder called dyslexia, and further encouraged by the entry of massive federal funding into public school special programs, another rather amorphous special interest group of citizens began to take shape and articulate its needs and demands. This group was a rather diffuse and often confused collection of parents whose children were having difficulty learning one or more of the traditional basic school subjects in spite of normal or above normal learning potential. However, since these children by definition could not qualify for the special assistance forthcoming from Public Law 88-164, it became apparent that, if their needs were to be accommodated, it would have to be through other funding channels enacted through additional legislation. Thus, the Association for Children with Learning Disabilities came into existence and continues to grow and develop. To illustrate how this group effected legislative trends without yet getting "its own" proposed legislation enacted, the Elementary and Secondary Education Act, Public Law 89-313, has several titles under which programs for children with various learning disorders might be funded.

Meanwhile, considerable confusion was caused by the nearly simultaneous declaration of the War on Poverty via the Economic Opportunity Act. The confusion stems from the fact that many children from impoverished families were functionally mentally retarded, essentially determined by having a properly measured IQ of less than 85. However, as discussed in previous sections of this chapter, the retardation measured in these children is largely a result of a lack of opportunity to learn the information and skills required to perform normally on test instruments developed for and standardized on the white English-speaking middle-class U. S. population. These children were poignantly and euphemistically called the "six-hour retarded children" (President's Committee on Mental Retardation, 1969) referred to earlier.

Various groups representing each of the above and other special interests, aided and abetted by their professional "spokes-persons," became intensely jealous of their new federal recognition and vied with each other in order to capture the lion's share of funds for their own purposes. Since clear-cut definitions of the children who were or were not eligible to participate in the new programs were nonexistent or only mentioned when advantageous for capturing more funds, the confusion about what particular constellation of factors constituted bona fide DLDs was somewhat counterproductive to maximum progress in new program funding and implementation.

A case in point with regard to the Elementary and Secondary Education Act (ESEA) legislation is that Title 1 authorized funds for establishing special programs for "culturally deprived" children who were having difficulty succeeding in the regular public school program. Title IV of ESEA provided for the establishment of 20 regional educational laboratories, which were charged to do applied educational research and to disseminate the results of their own research and any other germane findings to schools throughout the country. The Rocky Mountain Educational Laboratory (RMEL) was the first to address individual learning disabilities under the direction of this writer. However, RMEL was cautioned to exclude culturally deprived children from consideration, since they were being served by ESEA Title I programs in the schools and by the Office of Economic Opportunity's Project Head Start, and its subsequent upward extension into Follow-Through programs. While serving as a member of President Johnson's Advisory Council for ESEA Title I Programs, this writer was assigned to the southeastern United States, where it was apparent that an alarming amount of ESEA Title I money was ironically being used to perpetuate segregated schools. This presumably inadvertent distortion of intent occurred as a result of trying to improve programs for the culturally deprived population in the "de facto" black urban ghetto and the "coincidental" black rural schools. Title II for improvement of libraries, Title III for innovative programs, and Title VI for handicapped children were equally categorical and, in many instances, illogical with regard to who could and who could not participate in the benefits. Even the then newly established Bureau of Education for the Handicapped was carefully selective in terms of the categories of children's programs and teacher or parent training programs for which it would offer support. In this way, it too perpetuated the status quo regarding segregation along the lines of handicapping condition and/or ethnic group membership.

In the meantime, other more traditional and well established agencies, such as the Maternal and Child Health Administration and the National Institutes of Health, had also turned more of their attention and money toward studying and alleviating certain handicapping conditions. After all, it had been the "in" thing, for the aforementioned political reasons, when the times were relatively good in the U. S. allowing its vigilant and enlightened social conscience to become profoundly aroused by the dramatic domestic inequities among the impoverished and certain ethnic minorities. The gradual enforcement of the school desegregation legislation from 1954 highlighted many grievously inhumane situations throughout America and prompted considerable soul searching among the guilt-ridden "haves" vis a vis the exploited "have-nots."

Again, because of the receptive ear and sympathetic attitude of persons in high places, funds were directed or channeled into programs benefiting children who had the equivalent of DLD. For example, Dr. Gerald Lesser in the Maternal and Child Health (MCH) Administration almost single-handedly enabled the University-Affiliated Facilities (UAF) authorized under Public Law 88-164 to mount and maintain sophisticated interdisciplinary training programs through MCH grants made from Section 511 of the Social Security Act. Moreover, the Public Health Service and the National Institute of Child Health and Human Development, particularly its Division of Mental Retardation, augmented these monies

for training high level service and research personnel from multiple disciplines focused on the mentally retarded population. These agencies also
had the wisdom to support several research centers in order to advance the
state of the art on both a basic and applied level. Thus, rather than having
a number of rather large and elaborate facilities without operational
staffing monies, the University-Affiliated Facilities programs were able to
get launched and into orbit, even with a satellite system included in the
1975 language of the amended Developmental Disabilities Act, Public Law
91-517 (perhaps this explains the confusion expressed by some persons,
when referring to the UAF program, who mistakenly call it the UFO
program?).

   With a change in the national administration, the Office of Child
Development was established during President Richard Nixon's early reign,
allegedly in order to dismember, absorb, and gradually phase out the quite
controversial poverty programs previously located in the Office of Economic Opportunity. At about the same time, the Bureau of Education
Personnel Development emerged in a phoenix-like fashion from the ashes
of the National Defense Education Act and focused on the training of
educators for special education, early childhood education, higher education, vocational education, and other semispecialized areas where trained
personnel were insufficient in numbers and/or inadequately prepared.
Although there were various joint meetings among these various federal
offices, bureaus, and related agencies, the competition among them for the
limited amount of money available prevented very much productive
collaboration and contributed further to the confusion about which child
is eligible for which program or related benefit. Furthermore, many needy
children seemed to either remain unidentified until they later came out of
the woodwork in great numbers or merely continued falling through the
cracks artificially created between the programs supported by various
funding agencies. Many programs were rightly accused of using two or
more sets of definitions and prevalence data in an effort to concentrate the
program's limited funds on a relatively more narrowly defined target group
after the funds had been captured on the basis of promises to serve a much
more broadly and ambiguously defined group.

   In order to protect the citizen from being saddled with inappropriate
or archaic legislation forever, there is typically a kind of self-destruct
feature which requires most legislation to elapse after a given length of
time and be re-enacted and usually amended in order to continue. This
kind of clause also helps to ensure that the provisions will be updated
according to new trends and needs. Such was the case with Public Law
88-164, which was updated and revised in the form of Public Law 91-517,
the Developmental Disabilities Act. As the programs which were initiated

through Public Law 88-164 began to mature and provide services, training, and research primarily for the mentally retarded throughout the U. S., other special interest groups wished to be included. The groups which succeeded in being included in the 1970 Developmental Disabilities Act represented the population of epileptic, cerebral palsied, and related neurologically impaired citizens.

In 1975 President Ford signed into law the Developmentally Disabled Assistance and Bill of Rights Act (Public Law 94-103) which adds autism and dyslexia as additional categories of DLD persons eligible for services through these funds as well as the training of specialized personnel to deal with the conditions. The original definition of developmental disabilities emphasized handicapping conditions which traditionally have been thought to have an organic cause and consequently a medical cure. The inclusion of autism and dyslexia plus a broader interpretation of mental retardation opened the door a bit to less definitively physical conditions. Developmental disability has been redefined to include any other condition found to be closely related to mental retardation because such a condition results in impairment of general intellectual functioning or to adaptive behavior similar to that of mentally retarded persons or requires similar treatment and services. Consequently, the International Association for Children with Learning Disabilities (ACLD) and the many state ACLD chapters also sought to have learning disabilities included in the new version of the Developmental Disabilities Act. They insist that most learning disabilities have some "soft" organic counterparts, such as minimal cerebral dysfunction or genetic anomalies and other inherent predispositions to learning disorders.

This insistence, of course, implicitly sabotaged efforts to include children who are developmentally delayed or learning disabled because of a lack of environmental enrichment, cultural opportunities, or other non-organic factors. In fact, when President Nixon stated a goal of reducing by one-half the incidence of mental retardation in the United States by the year 2,000, he was referring to the mental retardation caused by various organic factors and was not alluding to the aforementioned six-hour retardation found in the six-hour retarded child. The most outspoken and visible group of advocates for mentally retarded and developmentally disabled children are the parents whose children have obvious physical signs of their damaged condition. The damaged children themselves are eloquent testimony to the need for preventive measures since the disfigurement and dysfunction in the more severe cases are indeed pathetic and even revolting to some observers, including those who must live with them in a family or other residential setting. For these reasons, then, the more obvious conditions might first receive attention of this book to repeatedly remind the reader that there is a continuum of DLD and that the prevalence of the milder, less dramatic, and less evident forms is much greater and these subtle DLDs are less well managed than the more severe forms.

There has been no effort herein to recapitulate the many abortive and few successful efforts by states and other smaller population groups to enact legislation in behalf of various and sundry populations of handicapped children and adults. Suffice it to say that the current efforts to decentralize program funding and control from federal levels toward state and local authorities is placing increased importance upon the attitudes and sophistication of state and local authorities to maintain and increase efforts begun through federal laws. An excellent case in point is the Education of All Handicapped Children's Act, which President Ford signed into law in late 1975. This Act (Public Law 94-142), not only authorizes considerable federal support for existing handicapped education programs but it also offers unprecedented monetary incentives for states and local schools to provide equal, appropriate, and free public education to all handicapped children of school age, beginning at 3 years of age.

This past decade of undulating and incoherent legislation has seen several rather specific pieces of legislation enacted in behalf of vulnerable children not the least of which was the Child Abuse and Neglect Act (Public Law 93-247) which President Nixon signed into law in 1974. Moreover, there is some mounting momentum toward getting a more comprehensive bill passed which would provide needed services to all eligible children and families who seek them. Although there is a well-organized and ill-informed small group of opponents to this comprehensive Child and Family Services Act (Senate Bill 626, Mondale et al, 1975), most citizens seem to be in favor of some national provision for the welfare of its many vulnerable children and their families. Such legislation carries a relatively higher price tag than we have been willing to pay, but it becomes very small when one considers that we spend less than 10% of our country's gross national product on 40% of our population (children and youth) who represent 100% of our future. The growing attention and burgeoning federal and state legislation to provide needed services for all citizens, including educational programs for children from birth, whether they be normal or abnormal, augur well for more extensive and intensive programmatic efforts in behalf of all children, including the most promising as well as the most vulnerable. It speaks well for our relatively young nation whose maturity and social consciousness may be measured, as suggested by President Kennedy, in terms of what it is willing to do for its weakest citizens.

chapter 2

Normal Development and Learning

It would be highly presumptuous to attempt to do justice to the detailed presentation of normal, let alone abnormal, human development and learning in a single chapter, when multitudes of ponderous volumes have been written on this topic (see Mussen, 1970, for representative example). This chapter, therefore, presents, once-over-lightly, some of the salient features of human development and learning with particular attention to the preadolescent stages. In order to place early child development and learning in proper perspective as the formative processes for the entire life continuum, Table 2 presents the highlights from several representative systems of normal development and learning. Each of these systems runs the entire gamut or at least the major part of the human life span. There are, of course, many such systems, but the theories selected for Table 2 are those which are referred to frequently within and among various disciplines, are uniquely different one from another, and are of noteworthy stature in the general literature.

Obviously, in such a condensation of any one of the systems, let alone several, only abbreviated samples of each theoretical system can be re-presented. In order to establish and maintain a somewhat parallel presentation of each system in Table 2, the statements in each column are listed under a given authority's name in the approximately appropriate location opposite the chronological age in the far left-hand column. The key word(s) or phrases serve simply as indices to their respective authors. The reader is referred to the corresponding writings of each authority included in this chart. Representative samples of each authority's work are cited in the references and resources in Chapter 10.

Since the most rapid and significant changes in development occur at the earlier formative years, a semilogarithmic chronological age scale is necessary. Because the quantity and quality of changes are progressively

Table 2. Representative systems of normal development and learning

CA	GESELL	FREUD	ERICKSON
	Physical Development	*Psychosexual Stages*	*Psychosocial 8 ages of man*
Birth	Embry-Fetus VISCERAL *INFANCY*	ORAL	TRUST VS.
¼	Ocular control Head balance	*Sensory retentive—*	MISTRUST
½	Grasping	biting	Mom will return
1	Sits, creeps, pokes	sarcasm	Holding on and/or
½	Stands, cruises Larynx-words	expulsive-verbal diarrhea	letting go
2	Walks	ANAL	AUTONOMY vs.
½	Sphincter control	*muscular*	SHAME,
3	Sentences	retentive—stingy, collector "up tight" Expulsive-messy-slob "hangs loose"	SELF-DOUBT Discretion Paranoia
½		PHALLIC	INITIATIVE vs. GUILT
4	Number & Form	locomotor	Superego-introject
½			parental ideals
5	Kindergarten *Childhood*	narcissistic exhibitionist	Rivalry-success/ paralysis
6		Oedipal or	INDUSTRY vs.
7		Electra complex	INFERIORITY
8		LATENCY	recognition from
9	pre-puberty	*homosexual*	products—
10		gang stage	work is pleasure/
11		castration	perceived incompe-
12		anxiety	tence
13			IDENTITY vs.
14	*Adolescence*	PUBERTY	ROLE DIFFUSION
15	sexual potency and secondary characteristics	*heterosexual* Orestes complex	Friends (adult) Ego-integrity/ delinquent dis-integration
20		GENITAL	INTIMACY vs.
	ADULT MATURITY TRAITS (basis):	1) Mutual orgasm	ISOLATION
	1) Motor Charact.	2) Loved person	Freud's genital person/
	2) Personal Hygiene	3) Mutual trust	Frigid impotence
	3) Emotional Expression	4) Share work & procreation	GENERATIVITY vs. STAGNATION
	4) Fears & Dreams	5) Secure offspring nurturance	Next Generation
	5) Self & Sex		Not fear life or death/
	6) Interpersonal	To love & to work	Pseudointimacy
	7) Play & Pastimes		INTEGRITY vs.
	8) School Life		DESPAIR, DISTRUST
	9) Ethical Sense		Complete person

CA	DOLL	HAVIGHURST	PLATO
	Vineland Social Maturity Scale	*Developmental Tasks*	*Philosophical Republic*
	(Items-every fifth) (Score)	(Vocab)	
Birth	1. "Crows" laughs	INFANCY	
¼	5. Rolls over	Dependence vs.	
	10. "Talks," imi-	Independence	
½	tates	Giving & Receiving	
1	15. Stands alone	Affect (3)	
½	20. Masticates		
	food (17)		
	25. Drinks from		
	cup alone		
	30. Knows edibles		
2	35. Asks to	EARLY	State
½	toilet (34)	CHILDHOOD	Nursery
3	40. Dries hands (44)	Relating to chang-	fairy tales
	45. Walks down	ing social	folk-lore
	stairs—one	groups (272)	rhymes
	step per		myths
	tread (50)		
	50. Washes hands		
½		Developing (896)	
4		Greater	
½	55. Uses pencil	Independence (1540)	
5	properly (56)	LATE (2072)	
	60. Trusted with	CHILDHOOD	
6	money (61)	Learning Psycho-	MUSIC &
7	65. Goes to bed (65)	Socio-Biological	GYMNASTICS
8	unassisted (70)	Sex Role (2562)	Harmony
9	70. Cares for		soul & body
10	hair (74)		
11	75. Cares for self		
12	at table (81)		
13	80. Does · remuner-		
14	ative work (84)	EARLY	Read, write
15	85. Plays difficult	ADOLESCENCE	and count
	games	Accepting & adjusting	
	90 Communicates	to changing body	
	by letter	Managing & learning	MILITARY
20	95. Buys all own	motor patterns	TRAINING
	clothing	LATE ADOLESCENCE	PHILOSOPHER
	100. Controls own	EARLY ADULTHOOD	KING (Prep.)
	major expen-	Understand & control	Quadrivium
	ditures	physical world	Philos. Dialect.
	105. Provides for	Develop symbol	& Metaphys.
	future	system	30-35
	110. Promotes civic	MATURITY	World experience
	progress	Relating self to	35-50
	115. Shares com-	cosmos	Elder statesman
	munity re-		Contemplate essence
	sponsibility		of good

Continued

Table 2—Continued

CA	MASLOW	BINET	PIAGET
	Existential Realization	*Mental Age and Intelligence*	*Intellectual Schemata*
Birth	Man is essentially *good*	Bayley Scales of Mental & Psychomotor Development	Acquiring SENSORIMOTOR control
¼			
½			Eye-hand coord.
1	Need potency		Organize percept.
½	hierarchy (throughout life span):	4 parts of body	field into objects
2	1. Physiologic		Extracting concepts
½	(food, drink,	8 pict. vocab.	from experience
3	elimination, re-	4 strung beads	Words for objects &
	production, etc.)	sort buttons in 2	recurring experiences
	2. Safety	minutes	
	3. Belongingness & love		
	4. Self-esteem		
	5. Self actualization		
½	6. Cognitive	2 opp. analogies	Intuitive use of
4	7. Aesthetic	2 build. materials	concepts
½			Accurate perceptions
5	SELF-ACTUALIZED PERSON:	Pict. completion Folding	Superficial gestalts CONCRETE
6	1. Realistic		OPERATIONAL
7	2. Accept self,	5 digits forward	THOUGHT
8	people & world	8 vocab. correct	Information
9	3. Spontaneity		storage re:
10	4. Problem-centered	Making change (2+)	concrete
11	5. Detached	Word naming	imaginary &
12	6. Autonomous	20/min.	anticipatory
13	7. Fresh apprecia-	Verb Absurd IV (2+)	operations
14	tion		FORMAL
15	8. Spiritual peak	5 digits reversed	OPERATIONAL
	experience	Bead Chain	THOUGHT
	9. Identity with	Memory	Operations with
20	mankind	Induction	symbols &
	10. Deep relations	Aver. Adult	abstract ideas
	11. Democratic	Superior Adult III	Logical possiblities
	12. Means not ends	30 Vocab. correct	& multivariable
	themselves	Proverbs (2+)	relations considered
	13. Philosophical	Opp. analog. (2+)	& comprehended
	sense of humor	Directions (2+)	Comparisons &
	14. Creative	Reasoning	deductions made
	15. Resist conformity to culture	Passage II	from information *not* concretely presented

CA	GOODENOUGH	LEWIN
	Draw-A-Man & Intelligence	Phenomenology Cognitive Field
	(Score)	
Birth ¼ ½ 1 ½	Class A Scribbling Some control	Life Perceptual Inner Personal Motor Space
2 ½ 3	Class B Head	Gradually the person differentiates himself (body boundaries) from the life-space.
½ 4 ½ 5 6 7 8 9 10 11 12 13 14 15	Legs Arms (2) Trunk Shoulders (6) Neck, eyes Nose, nostrils (10) Mouth, ears Clothing, hair Thumb, joints (18) Fingers (22) Proportions (26) Eye detail (30) Chin, forehead (34) Dimensions (38) Profile (42)	The person is a differentiated region in the life space: the Foreign Hull represents the rest of the universe not yet perceived or expressed. FOREIGN Life Person Space HULL
20		Adult Increased differentiation and boundary firmness in adult. Greater organization and integration also result from much restructuring in response to cognitive dissonance (Festinger) due to new perceptions & experiences.

John H. Meier, 1964.

diminished with older ages, it is interesting that several of the outstanding authorities in early childhood development and learning have so concentrated their efforts on such small segments of the life span, either prenatal, or the first postnatal year, or first three postnatal years, that they have virtually neglected to include or address the later years and are, therefore, not included in this chart. Nevertheless, they do receive some attention later in this chapter and several subsequent chapters since it is in these very early years that many of the basic patterns of development and learning are determined.

It is important to remember from the preceding chapter that the word *normal* is a relative term based upon a normal curve of distribution. The point at which any developmental phenomenon may be considered sufficiently deviant from average to constitute abnormal is indeed arbitrary, indeed in some cases is culturally determined, and is, therefore, often controversial. The wide range of maturational rates for each developmental domain, within the same child and among different children, indicates that at the same chronological age a wide variety of developmental maturation is typically found within and among children. This suggests an optimum readiness range for learning certain information and skills which must be considered in dealing with the individual child and groups of children. This readiness range is related to the notions of critical periods and so-called teachable moments for developing humans. Nevertheless, norms or standards have been determined for most developmental and learning achievements and serve as useful guides for monitoring a child's progress or signalling a serious lack of progress which may be caused by physical and/or psychic disorders.

In order to give the reader some notion as to the use of Table 2, a 1-year segment from 2–3 years of age (marked off by the dotted line) is selected for commentary.

Beginning at the left, the first authority is Gesell (Gesell and Amatruda, 1947). His principal contributions to developmental theory and fact have derived from a thorough-going study and reporting of physical development in children. As one reads down the Gesell column and comes to the section delineated by the 2- to 3-year chronological age, one sees that three of the most prominent achievements in the normally developing 2-year-old are: (1) ability to walk quite proficiently (and even begin running), (2) the conscious control of bladder and bowel elimination activities, and (3) assuming normal development and adequate language models, an initial use of sentences to express thoughts. The multitudinous subtle specifics of these grossly stated achievements have been parceled out and chronicled in the Revised Yale Developmental Schedule, one of many evaluative procedures mentioned in Chapter 4.

Moving over to the second column, it becomes evident and logical that Freud's (1950) psychosexual theory would place considerable emphasis upon the child's and his caretaker's preoccupation with his anal and bladder sphincter control. Their proximity to the genital anatomy and the association of primary pleasure and pain as a function of such sphincter control give this developmental phenomenon additional psychosexual significance. Because of the intense sensual aspects of this stage in development, it is hypothesized that a significant component of a given individual's personality structure is initiated and reinforced at this stage. It is even postulated that the young child who is strongly reinforced for retaining fecal matter and urine until release in the toilet is also learning certain personality traits of neatness and acquisitiveness. Continued reinforcement from the same caregiving adults who prize and reward this sort of behavior could lead to an extreme fastidiousness and stinginess which might ultimately become excessive and, thus, abnormal. At the other end of the continuum is the child who is ordinarily praised and otherwise rewarded for having regular, albeit uncontrolled, elimination, which may relieve the anxieties of the up-tight parent, particularly when the child has had a history of sickness related to constipation. In this case, it is postulated that the reinforcement of such behavior may result in a child who has a greater tolerance for and experiences unusual pleasure in messy surroundings. Subsequently, one may develop verbal traits euphemistically referred to as diarrhea of the mouth and constipation of the brain. For purposes of classification, then, Freud conceptualized the anal retentive and anal expulsive personality types, which of course seldom exist in their pure form since many other precedent and subsequent events also impinge upon the developing organism and the learned personality. Freud hypothesized that those persons who receive an abnormally large amount of physical and psychic gratification at any one stage in their psychosexual development may tend to fixate at that level and invest a disproportionate amount of their limited psychic and physical energy there, thus having a proportionately lesser amount of energy for investment in subsequent stages. When under considerable stress at later stages, these persons may regress to an earlier and more comfortable stage of development and learning. Moreover, the way in which earlier stages are worked through may profoundly affect subsequent attitudes and behavior so that, for example, the child who considers elimination processes to be filthy and nasty may have a similar attitude about and behavior toward more mature heterosexual genital relationships. To understand the complex integration and interaction of these many phenomena which produce the total behavior and personality constellation of the organism is never simple. For those who become paralyzed or unduly distraught about their personality characteristics, an elaborate process of psychoanalysis or other psychotherapy may be required to learn better (more normal and satisfying) behavior.

The next authority, who addresses the intricacies of human development and learning from a more social point of view, is Erikson (1963). For the 2- to 3-year-old chronological age range he postulates that, in addition to the previously discussed physical and psychosexual phenomena, the child is also learning about his effect on others and vice versa. In this second of the eight hypothetical ages of man, Erikson speaks of the need for the child to develop a sense of autonomy as opposed to a self-concept ridden with shame and doubt about his inability to cope in his peculiar microcosm or life space. Since one of the primary concerns of the caregiver for a child at this age is toilet training, it is suggested that the mastery or lack of mastery of this skill may be very influential. On the one hand, mastery engenders and reinforces feelings of self-reliance and discretion about controlling one's self. On the other hand, failure to master this task breeds feelings of a lack of self-confidence caused by the apparent inability to control primary bodily functions and a concomitant lack of understanding about what is going on behind him, literally and virtually, which is postulated to underly some forms of paranoia in later life. It is at this juncture that the child also learns how better to win the praise of, and perhaps thereby to control, the significant adults in his life. Some children are known to use their conscious (or unconscious) control of bowel and bladder functions to gain greater attention from their parenting ones by either retaining urine and fecal matter to the point of severe bladder distention and constipation or smearing and playing in such excrement. Either behavior may bring about the desired attention, albeit somewhat punitive, from the adults whose personality characteristics are shrewdly perceived by the youngster to be challenged and even threatened by such behavior.

The fourth column presents a sample of the items contained on Doll's Vineland Social Maturity Scale (1966), which is designed to reflect and quantify the degree to which a given child is progressing in the learning of selected developmental tasks deemed important for adequate socialization in our society. The numbers preceding each item correspond to the number of the item on the Vineland Scale; only every fifth item was selected for Table 2. The number in parentheses horizontally directly to the right of any given chronological age indicates the number of items which must be passed in order for an individual to be rated as developing normally. For example, by the time a child is 2½ years of age, he should be able to pass about 34 of the items on the Vineland Scale in order to get a social quotient in the normal range. By the time the child is 3 years of age, he should not only have mastered all of the behaviors around toilet training discussed above, but also use language to express and anticipate such visceral needs. There are some 10–12 other behaviors that are expected of a normally developing 2- to 3-year-old child as sampled by the Vineland Social Maturity Scale but not included in Table 2.

The next authority has conceptualized a series of hierarchically organized developmental tasks, which are hypothesized to be most easily learned at certain readiness ages or teachable moments. These ages or moments are somewhat analogous to the critical period notions being advanced by some child development theorists. Havighurst (1953) called the period beginning at 2 years of age that of Early Childhood and suggests that this is a particularly critical time for children to learn to relate to other individuals, including a variety of new persons and groups. Germane to this ability to relate in our highly verbal society is the ability of the child to express himself through spoken language. The numbers in parentheses indicate approximate numbers of individual vocabulary words which normally developing children typically have in their expressive vocabulary at various chronological ages. Of course vocabulary is not only important for the socialization of the young child, but also for his exchange of ideas and general cognitive development which are reflected in the contents of intelligence tests. These are briefly discussed in later paragraphs of this discussion about Table 2. The ability to accumulate, understand, and use vocabulary to express ideas and perhaps to even think about the real world is in part a function of the richness of the verbal environment in which the child is developing and learning. In this regard, the child's language serves as an index to the quality and quantity of language spoken by the caregiving adults. Tests designed to assess developmental language phenomena, such as Kirk and McCarthy's *The Illinois Test of Psycholinguistic Abilities* (1968), further illustrate the interrelationships among physical, cognitive/intellectual, linguistic, and socioemotional factors in development.

To lend a little more perspective to this presentation of total human development and learning, it seems important to note that even such classical philosophers as Plato, more than 20 centuries ago, advanced notions of the developmental process, albeit with a primary focus on the adolescent and adult years. Nevertheless, Plato did not neglect to point out the importance of early experience with the language and folklore of an individual's culture in order to preserve and advance that belief and behavior system. Many of the pioneers of preschool programs, such as Rousseau, Froebel, Montessori, and Pestalossi, had considerable familiarity with the Greek and Roman philosophers and were undoubtedly influenced by them. From another treatise (Meier, 1973a, Book I), where the Platonic and Aristotelian epistemological systems are described and depicted, it can be legitimately inferred that the importance of early and systematic experience with the real world and the world of ideas was not at all foreign to these philosophical systems (see also Baumrin, 1975).

Another philosophical perspective on the growth and development of the complete man, a theory which is also grounded in current psychological knowledge, is proposed by Maslow (1968). In his heirarchy of needs, the fulfilling of which leads to the fully self-actualized person, Maslow presents the fundamental sequence of developmental needs which, being achieved in proper sequence, enable the human being to fully realize his potential. This hierarchy is consistent with the preceding authorities concerns and reflects the critical interdependence of meeting certain basic needs before the more exquisite and less survival-oriented ones can be addressed and fulfilled. It is submitted that all seven of the needs can and should be met insofar as it is possible to scale them down to the capabilities of the 2- to 3-year-old child being discussed herein as an example. Even a young child has cognitive and aesthetic needs, such as a need for intelligible and pleasant sound as opposed to raucous and unintelligible noise, for ultimate and maximum self-actualization as a human being.

The last four authorities selected for this review focused their attention primarily upon the development of the human intellect, thereby emphasizing the interrelationship between development and cognitive learning.

The first among these is Binet (see Terman, 1916), whose pioneering efforts to measure intelligence resulted in a series of test items or samples of behavior which he demonstrated could be performed by the majority of nineteenth century French urban children at specified ages. His test, which was standardized for American children by Terman and is now referred to as the Revised Stanford-Binet Test of Intelligence (Terman and Merrill, 1961), begins at 2 years of age. At the earlier ages it focuses primarily on vocabulary and motor development. Downward extensions of these scales have been generated by Arthur (1947), Bayley (1969), Cattell (1940), and several others (see Buros, 1972, for additional information on such tests and measurements). The Stanford-Binet Test is an individually administered series of items such as exemplified in the Binet column of Table 2.

From this representative sample of items, it is indicated that at 2½ years of age at least 75% of the children sampled could recognize and name eight pictures of rather common objects, and by the time they are 3 years old they could string four beads of varied shapes in a specific order within a given period of time. Wechsler (1967) developed a similar individual test of intelligence and his Primary and Preschool Scale of Intelligence (WPSSI) is a downward extension of his original Wechsler Intelligence Scale for Children. However, the WPSSI and WISC-R correlate highly enough with the Stanford-Binet that they are used more or less interchangeably and do not warrant separate consideration here. Such standardized intelligence test instruments, although they do predict rather accurately how well a child will do in the mainstream school programs, are the subject of great controversy because they have been standardized on a mainstream and relatively privileged population of children and have been demonstrated to unfairly penalize or discriminate against children not from the mainstream culture. This problem was addressed in Chapter 1 and will recur in subsequent discussions about evaluating a child's progress in learning and development.

What Gesell did for the physical developmental domain, Freud did for the affective domain, Erickson did for the social domain, and Piaget (1963) has done for the intellectual/cognitive domain. His careful studies of the epistemological process have led to a cogent schema of the unfolding intellect and the concomitant cognitive development and learning of a human being. From 2–3 years of age, the child is in the preconceptual or preoperational stage of development, forming the critical foundation for subsequent more complex and abstract thought processes. The primitive labeling of ideas and objects is occurring, and both spoken and nonverbal understanding of the objects in one's environment and his relationships with these objects is taking place. From the relatively simple notion that a previously seen object or person still exists even after it has been moved out of sight, to the relatively more complex notion of conservation of substance or quantity (i.e., the same amount of material such as clay, regardless of whether it is formed into a ball or snake-like form, still has the same amount of matter) are carefully documented and chronicled as indices of cognitive development in children. Once again, although certain ordinal data and expectations do now exist (Hunt and Uzgiris, 1966), the range of variability in achieving these various cognitive levels is very great and dependent to an appreciable extent upon the wealth or dearth of learning opportunities and materials in one's development. Because Piaget has clearly and cogently documented many of these developmental cognitive phenomena, he has given great impetus to a more thorough study of the intellectual/cognitive domain of young human development and learning.

Goodenough (1926) approached the measurement of a child's awareness of his environment and of himself by means of his drawings of a person rather than by means of his verbal communication abilities. This is a correlary technique for estimating a child's attention to and memory of detail, size, and shape relationships, perspective, and related features of the human body and its clothing. The Draw-a-Person technique is another way of estimating a child's ability to accurately perceive, retrieve, and express in two-dimensional representation a given familiar object. At the ages of 2 and 3 years, the child's drawings of a person are typically very primitive and frequently only depict a head and perhaps some notion of eyes, nose, or mouth and rudimentary limbs. At this stage of development, it has been determined that normal children cannot be expected to even draw a circle very well (Beery, 1967). Therefore, the Draw-a-Person technique is not suitable for arriving at any estimate of intelligence or cognitive functioning for children of this age. However, as the child grows older and there are more items to be scored (the number of points credit normally expected at each chronological age is shown in parentheses), this nonverbal estimate of perceptual/cognitive awareness assesses another dimension of learning and development.

A more global and generic approach to human cognitive learning and development is offered by Lewin, who attempts to get inside of the developing person and look at the world through his eyes and perceptions. At the age of 2–3 years, the person is conceptualized as a relatively undifferentiated organism who is still attempting to establish more clearly the real and perceived boundaries between self and nonself. Although it is not explicitly discussed in Lewin's *A Dynamic Theory of Personality Development* (1935), his phenomenological approach offers a helpful conceptual framework for integrating the physical, social, emotional, and intellectual domains of human development and learning into a cohesive theory and system. It is for this reason that his cognitive field system is included as the last column of Table 2 and is further elaborated upon in a subsequent section of this chapter regarding the learning process. As the human being experiences himself and his environment, he progressively refines and differentiates his many perceptions of the world within and around him. It is from within this life space of percepts that he acts upon his environment and interprets the reactions and responses he receives from that environment, which includes the other people with whom he interacts.

This completes a brief description of Table 2, which is offered as a conceptual gestalt and mnemonic chart for placing some of the more prominent theories of normal human development and learning in some meaningful interrelated perspective. By slightly elaborating on one horizontal slice of this chart for the 2- to 3-year-old age group, it should be readily apparent that this chapter scarcely scratches the surface even for this 1-year range, not to mention the conspicuous absence of discussion about the rest of the kaleidoscopic and many splendored phenomena of human development and learning.

SOME PRINCIPLES AND SCALES OF NORMAL DEVELOPMENT

The following dozen principles of normal development are to be borne in mind whenever scales of development are applied to individual children.

1. The sequence of development is, in general, the same for all children, but each child has his own individual rate pattern and ultimate level of development.

2. Individual differences are apparent at an early age and show a high degree of consistency with increasing age.

3. A child progresses step by step through the various stages of development. Each step prepares the way for the one to follow. Regardless of chronological age, an early stage usually has to precede a later development.

4. There is an approximate range at which parents may expect readiness for new learnings of a particular kind. The peak of readiness is often the period when a particular process is most susceptible to either cultivation or damage. The capacity of children to learn is frequently much greater and occurs much earlier than many parents realize.

5. As a child's capacities for doing, thinking, and feeling mature, he has an impulse to use these capacities.

6. There are behavioral cues which the child gives his parents about his individual needs, rhythms, and readiness for something new. Parents can be taught to recognize these periods of readiness. Development progresses best when opportunity is provided for learning when the child is ready. Attempts to push learning and development ahead of readiness are frequently frustrating for both child and parents.

7. Development starts at the head and progresses downward (cephalocaudal). Development progresses from the main axis of the body out (proximodistal).

8. A child does not grow uniformly or all at the same time. The various parts and systems grow at different rates at different times.

NAME _____

UNIT NO. _____

DATE ___ Year ___ Month ___ Date

BIRTH ___ ___ ___

AGE ___ ___ ___

MOTOR SKILLS

	B	6 mos.	1	18 mos.	2	3	4	5	6	7	8
	Follows object	Takes two cubes	Builds tower of 2 blocks	Builds tower of 4 blocks		Builds bridge of 3 blocks	10 pellets in bottle 30 sec.	Catches ball, bounced 2/3	10 pellets in bottle 20 sec.	Rides bicycle	Arranges material neatly
	Rolls over	Sits without support	Walks alone	Walks upstairs		Cuts with scissors	Alternates downstairs	Cuts–follows simple outline	[1]Prints first name	[1]Prints full name	Cuts round outline well
	Grasps object	Walks holding on	Walks backwards	Jumps		Balances on 1 foot 1 sec.	Balances on 1 foot 5 sec.	Balances on 1 foot 10 sec.	Builds steps of 6 blocks	[1]Prints 1-20 few reversals	[1]Prints 1-20 no revs, 1/2 inch
	Bears weight	Stands alone	Stoops and recovers	Throws overhand		Rides tricycle	Hops on 1 foot	[2]Draws Man 4 parts	[2]Draws Man 6 parts	[2]Draws Man 9 parts	Writes full name (cursive)
	Transfers objects	Pincer grasp	Scribbles	[1]Imitates line		Copies circle	Copies cross	Copies square	Copies triangle	Copies vertical diamond	Constructs objects/cooks

[1]On back of this sheet

[2]On back of drawing sheet

COMMUNICATION SKILLS

	B	6 mos.	1	18 mos.	2	3	4	5	6	7	8
	Responds to bell	Says–mama, dada	Plays ball	Show–mouth, eyes, hair, nose 1/4	Show–mouth, eyes, hair, nose 4/4	[2]What do we– 6/7	Made of–car window, dress 2/3	Made of–fork door, shoe 3/3	[2]Names animals 1 min. 9	Names days of week	
	Babbles	Imitates Sounds	Uses 3 to 5 words	Block–on table to me; on floor 2/3	Block–on, under, front, back 2/4	Block–on under front, back 3/4	[2]Completes analogies 2/3	[2]Definitions 6/9	Alike–boat/airplane; hat/shoe 1/2	Tells own address	
	Follows person visually	Responds to no-no, bye-bye	Indicates specific wants	Combines words	Uses plurals	Do–tired, cold, hungry 2/3	Do–cross street	[3]Reads .5 grade level	[3]Reads 1.5 grade level	[3]Reads 2.5 grade level	
	Smiles	Hesitates with strangers	Mimics chores	Brings objects on request	Gives full name	Show–"longer" 3/3 or 5/6	Show–"smoother" 3/3 or 5/6	Show–R-ear L-eye, R-leg L-arm 4/4	When–breakfast, bed, afternoon 3/3	Show–upper R, lower L; middle 3/3	
	Turns to whisper	1 Word–not mama, dada	Solitary play	Parallel play	Cooperative play	Separates–without fuss	Tells age	Plays competitive games	Answers phone–takes message	Plays organized group games	

[2]On back of this sheet

[3]Use WRAT

	B	6 mos.	1	18 mos.	2	3	4	5	6	7	8
SELF-SUFFICIENCY SKILLS	Head upright and steady	Drinks from cup with help	Feeds–scoops with spoon (or fork)	Discriminates edible substances	Feeds–uses fork to spear	Feeds–cuts with fork	Brushes own teeth		Names–penny, dime, nickel 2/3	Spreads own bread	Cuts own meat (knife)
	Recovers toy from chest	Uncovers face	Chews food	Unwraps candy or gum	Blocks–give "just one"	Counts–2 blocks/pellets 2/2	Counts–4 and 3 blocks 2/2		Counts–10 and 8 blocks 2/2	Solves–2+1, 3+2, 5-1 2/3	Solves–8+6 9-5, 7+4 2/3
	Reaches for objects	Works for toy	Drinks without help	Solves pellet bottle	Washes, dries own hands	Ident.–blue, yellow, red, green 3/4	Washes own face		Blows own nose	Bathes self, complete	Buys with money
	Occupies self, unattended	Pulls self upright	Opens closed doors	Goes about house	Avoids danger–street	Cares for self at toilet	Goes about within block		Goes about, crosses streets	Goes to bed unassisted	Tells time, quarter hour
	Feeds self cracker	Gets to sitting position	Removes clothing	Puts on some clothing	Gets own drink	Dresses without help	Buttons–correct, complete		Errands outside home	Ties own shoes	Grooms self

What do we   6/7

play with _____

sit on _____

sleep in _____

ride in _____

eat with _____

cook on _____

sweep with _____

Analogies   2/3

Fire–hot, ice is _____

Mother–woman, dad is _____

Horse–big, mouse is _____

Definitions   6/9

3–4   (What is a . . .)

Ball _____

Lake _____

Desk _____

House _____

Banana _____

Curtain _____

Ceiling _____

Hedge _____

Pavement _____

4–5

Names Animals   6–7

9 in 1 minute _____

_____

_____

_____

5–5

Figure 2. Boyd Developmental Progress Scale. (Reprinted by permission of Dr. Robert D. Boyd.)

9. Progress in development is not smooth and continuous but rather uneven. Children discontinue working on one skill while learning a new one. New skills or learnings may disappear only to reappear later on. A child often regresses under stress.

10. Physical, mental, and emotional forms of development are interrelated.

11. The child's native constitution, the cultural setting, traditions of the family, and community make lasting impressions which influence the process of development and its outcome.

12. Development results both from learning and growth or maturation. Stimulation and struggle are often necessary for optimum human development.

Two of the many scales of early human development are the Boyd Developmental Progress Scale and the Denver Developmental Screening Test (DDST). Since the former was developed by Boyd (1974) to teach child development, it is included here (Figure 2) as a sort of summary of observable behaviors for following a child's developmental progress. The DDST was produced by Frankenburg and Dodds (1967) and is based upon the same developmental phenomena as the Boyd Scale but is designed to screen out young children who are probably not developing normally and is, therefore, included in Chapter 4.

CONTEMPORARY THEORIES OF NORMAL LEARNING

Now that several prominent theories of normal human development have been presented, it is important to consider some representative and prominent counterpart theories of normal learning. As stated earlier, the ability to learn is a function of one's developmental status. More sophisticated learning requires more complex development. The human organism is capable of the most sophisticated learning as a function of its highly developed status especially manifest in its enormously complex central nervous system.

Learning is what education is all about. Anyone working with DLD children should be aware of the contemporary theories regarding how and why human learning occurs. Theories of learning have been advanced for as long as man has recorded his thoughts. The epistemology or learning theory of Piaget (1960 and 1962) synthesizes much of the philosophy of cognitive learning which has accumulated during the past 2,000 years (see Meier, 1973a, Book I, for further elaboration).

There is some controversy among those who work with DLD children as to whether they are *educating* or *training* these children. The former concept commonly implies the process of helping an individual to realize actively his innate talents, as opposed to the latter concept, which has connotations of shaping behavior and imposing ideas on a passive recipient.

A discussion of theories of learning involves issues concerning how humans are to be optimally educated. If individualized learning is a worthy goal for children, is it not an equally desirable goal for adults? This section makes a simplified presentation of two major contemporary theories of learning and their practical application to individualized learning for both children (learners) and adults (development/learning facilitators) who work with them in order to facilitate their development and learning. Within each theory, there are numerous complex refinements which will not be mentioned in this section but can be pursued in most texts of educational psychology and/or theories of learning (e.g., Hilgard, 1964).

Behavioristic Theory

The first major theory of learning is commonly called behaviorism, and, more recent versions, neobehaviorism. A leading contemporary exponent of behaviorism is Skinner. In a renowned book entitled *Walden Two* (1948), Skinner indicated that the stimulus-response and operant conditioning techniques for modifying human behavior are so powerful and predictable that he could develop any kind of person he would wish if he had that person to train or condition from early childhood. He claimed that he could shape human behavior to fit virtually any predetermined mold. The entire behavior modification movement is based on principles originated by Watson and advanced by Skinner and his growing number of disciples. He extended the implications of behavioristic theory to the society at large in a more controversial book entitled *Beyond Freedom and Dignity* (1971).

Skinner's procedures are extensions and revisions of the work originally done by Pavlov in Russia many years ago. Most educators and trainers are familiar with Pavlov's classical conditioning experiments, the most famous of which was his training (educating?) of a dog to salivate in response to the stimulus of a bell by pairing the bell's ringing (conditioned stimulus) with the presentation of meat powder (unconditioned stimulus) until natural salivation (unconditioned response) occurred unnaturally (conditioned response) when the bell was rung in the absence of the meat powder. Figure 3A depicts this classical conditioning learning paradigm, showing a person who has learned to salivate in response to hearing the dinner bell.

In like manner, conditioning applies to learning behavior which can be effectively controlled by pairing an unconditioned aversive stimulus,

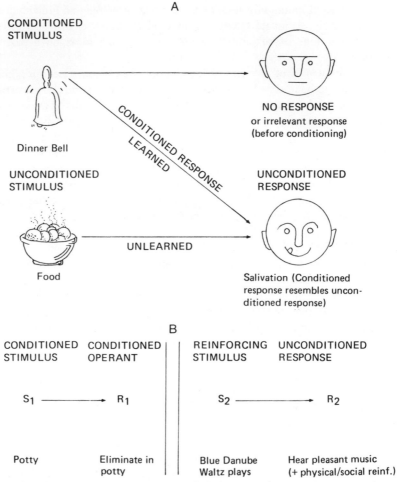

Figure 3. A, diagram of classical conditioning. A ringing bell elicits no specific response until it is paired with food in this instance. Once conditioned, the person may salivate upon simply hearing the ringing bell. B, diagram of operant conditioning. S_2 follows only if R_1 occurs. R_2 does not determine the form of R_1 as it does in classical conditioning above.

such as loud yelling and threats, with a conditioned stimulus, such as a quiet request that the learner turn his undivided attention to learning arithmetic. The teacher knows that after he has yelled loudly enough to engender fear in the learner and perhaps even to inflict auditory pain, the learner will eventually follow the more quiet request, "Please do your arithmetic, or else." In order to avoid such pain and fear, the student responds in the expected fashion.

Thus, the learner learns (is educated, trained, or instructed) to comply properly (conditioned response) with the teacher's soft-spoken requests (conditioned stimulus) in order to avoid the teacher's yelling (unconditioned stimulus) which evokes the same overt behavioral response (unconditioned response) of compliance. However, the teacher may have to remind the learner of the unconditioned stimulus by an occasional additional yelling as the effects of the conditioning gradually wear off.

If the reinforcement for each particular behavior is done somewhat randomly and unpredictably, the conditioned response is more likely to remain longer and stronger because the learner is never quite sure when the learning facilitator might deliver some more of his unconditioned stimuli. If the reinforcement occurs regularly, the learner can predict about when the next unconditioned stimulus is due and anticipate it by behaving acceptably just in the nick of time. Partial or intermittent reinforcement tends to prolong the duration for which a conditioned response is maintained. The influence of appropriate reinforcements is such that the desired behavior persists against many nonreinforcements.

Although the use of threats and punishments (negative reinforcement or avoidance conditioning with aversive stimuli) pragmatically works to control behavior and may be justified to eliminate life-threatening or self-destructive behavior, the use of rewards (positive reinforcement) is far more effective because it indicates what to do rather than solely what not to do. In the complete absence of direction, learners may indiscriminately test the limits of every new unstructured situation. Such a classroom condition, when chronic, can become untenable and cause a high level of anxiety which interferes with optimum learning.

Skinner and his associates found that, when positive reinforcement is presented after a desired behavior is manifest or approximated, another kind of conditioning can be effected. As differentiated from classical conditioning, wherein natural physiological stimulus-response reflexes are typically employed as the unconditioned stimuli and responses, in operant conditioning, a predetermined behavior, for which there is no readily observable or known external stimulus, is awaited. Whenever the learner exhibits this behavior, or some approximation of it, he receives a specified positive reinforcement. For example, in order to help potty-train his granddaughter, it is rumored that Skinner designed a potty that played the Blue Danube Waltz whenever the granddaughter eliminated in it. The unconditioned stimulus of a need to eliminate is paired with the conditioned stimulus of a potty and, when the conditioned operant occurs (eliminating in the potty), a reinforcing stimulus of the Blue Danube Waltz follows. This employs the desire to hear pleasant music, not to mention the sheer pleasure of physical relief and social praise and the absence of discomfort and shame, all as unconditioned responses. It is further rumored that this behavior was so well shaped that even now the adult granddaughter feels compelled to sit down whenever she hears the Blue Danube Waltz, quite the reverse effect that learning the national anthem has on some persons.

If a learner engages in prolonged independent pursuit of a self-selected arithmetic project (assuming this is desirable), the learner might be rewarded with an "OK," "very good," A grade, M & M, marinated olive, tokens to be traded for other goodies, jag of electricity to his brain's pleasure center, or other peculiarly fitting positive reinforcement. Whatever behavior is not desired is simply, but not always so easily, ignored until it goes away (is extinguished), assuming that the undesirable behavior was displayed for adult attention. Even tantrum behavior, for example, which is admittedly difficult to ignore, can be eliminated in this way, if it is displayed to get adult (or peer) attention.

Instead of a learning facilitator's shouting at children to be quiet, she might wait until that occasion when the children are mysteriously silent and reward them with praise or approval—assuming, of course, that the children consider praise from the learning facilitator to be rewarding or satisfying. This in turn requires that praise predictably follows their doing or attempting to do those things which are desirable and that various kinds of punishment, including the conspicuous absence of praise, follow their behaving in an undesirable way. The rewarding effects of praise itself are probably the result of conditioning. Most of us learned that when we "done good" we got rewarded in one way or another. However, simply saying "good" or "OK" in the same monotonous voice loses its effectiveness very quickly; intermittent and varied reinforcement is more effective for enduring results. In order to be an effective learning facilitator one must become expert at catching learners when they are being good, as defined by certain criteria of desirable learning behavior, and appropriately reinforcing this good behavior.

It is possible to explain and manage much of human behavior by means of the classical and operant conditioning techniques. A general principle can be stated that any stimulus can be made reinforcing through association with a reinforcing stimulus. The systematic application of conditioning theory makes it possible to ensure the mastery of an individualized curriculum after the terminal objectives have been determined by a careful analysis of each component task. Such task analysis enables a programmer to lead a learner step by little step to mastery of the terminal behaviors and understandings. Programmed instruction, whether auto-mated or nonautomated, can be a helpful resource to a sophisticated learning facilitator who knows when, how, why, and with whom to use it.

Because the degrees of satisfaction which children receive for various rewards vary, it is important that the learning facilitator identify within each individual learner what are known as high and low probability behaviors (Premack, 1959). A high probability behavior is one which a child very likely would want to do when given a choice from among many alternatives; a low probability behavior is something which a child would not freely choose to do. A high probability behavior (e.g., watching a favorite television program) can be used as a positive reinforcement to induce and reinforce a child's engaging in a low probability behavior. For example, the child is permitted to watch a favorite program on the contingency that he completes his arithmetic homework.

The learning facilitator, in order to manage the contingencies of the learner, has to know the learner's perculiar characteristics so that he can construct a hierarchy of the most effective rewards and punishments for each individual learner. For example, a spelling bee may be fun for a good speller and a miserable experience for the learner who is ridiculed or is otherwise embarrassed by his relative inability to spell. Contingency management is further complicated by the fact that what is rewarding to a learner at one time may be punishing at another. Recess time for a child when he is nauseous or injured may be quite objectionable until he again feels able to participate comfortably or successfully in the required games. By knowing these contingencies and appropriately applying them to rein-force the learner's successive approximations to the educational objectives, the learning facilitator is able to optimize the conditions for learning, regardless of what is to be learned.

The development/learning facilitator must also be aware of any developmental limitations in a given learner, so as not to expect the mastery of tasks beyond his capabilities. One of the most salutory features of the careful and proper application of behavior modification techniques is that capabilities sometime become apparent which would otherwise not have been revealed. The steadily increasing body of knowledge about the assets and liabilities of applied behaviorism in education is generally encouraging (Thoresen, 1973). On the other hand, one of the greatest hazards of the indiscriminate and all-pervasive use of behaviorism to condition learning is that it may result in token learning (Levine and Fasnacht, 1974). In other words, the learner will not apply himself to learning anything without some reward, which is typically external to the learning task. Most behavior modifiers insist that their goal is to help children learn for the intrinsic satisfaction of learning, but few studies demonstrate that this motive lasts for long. Many studies demonstrate the reverse situation, wherein students staunchly refuse to do anything without some contingent reinforcement or external reward. The behavior modifier often presupposes that learning an academic subject, arithmetic in this case, is unpleasant (a low probability behavior) and must be coupled with some pleasant (high probability behavior) to ensure that it will be learned and be firmly stamped into the learner's repertoire. This indeed may be the case for some subjects and some learners at some times. The unrestricted and/or indiscriminate application of behavior modification remains highly controversial, especially when very young children, prisoners, mentally deranged or retarded, or senile persons are involved. Such ethical issues as informed consent and the related human rights of those who may be involuntarily subjected to such procedures loom large in the heated public debate. Stoltz, Wienckowski, and Brown (1975) have placed many of the critical issues in a useful perspective. However, when a society, such as the U.S.S.R., systematically applies behavioristic methods to shape the thoughts and attitudes of its entire population, beginning in infancy, the issues take on much larger and perhaps more ominous significance.

Cognitive-Field Theory

There are other less mechanistic, or, as many behaviorists would say, less realistic, theories of learning which give greater emphasis to the delights of learning for its own sake. The salient considerations of such an alternative theory of learning, a prominent one which is customarily referred to as the cognitive-field theory, also warrant discussion. As the name implies, this learning theory deals principally with the cognitive domain of development. The cognitive-field theory has its roots deep in philosophy, particularly those schools of thought which are categorized as phenomenological. The root word *phenomena* is used in distinction to *noumena*. The latter refers to things as they really are in concrete reality, whereas phenomena are aspects of concrete reality as *perceived by an individual*.

As pointed out earlier, human development proceeds simultaneously in several domains and normally in a reasonably predictable sequence. Although this section is focused upon the cognitive-field theory of learning, it is premised upon the assumption that normal development is occurring concomitantly in the physical, social, linguistic, and emotional domains. The simultaneous mutual interaction among these domains cannot be emphasized enough, since abnormally advanced or delayed development in one domain may accelerate, compensate, or compromise the interdependent development in other domains.

This seems particularly true of cognitive development. Optimum cognitive development requires basic integrity, especially of the central nervous system, since this is the fundamental hardware which receives, processes, stores, and expresses the physical, social, linguistic, and emotional experiences the organism has. An essential characteristic of being human (the principal characteristic according to Descartes) is that of thinking, prompting the Latin phrase, *"Cogito, ergo sum,"* that is, "I think, therefore, I am." The ability to think differentiates mankind from lower animals; thus, the scientific designation *homo sapiens.* Humans are also social beings who think about and rationally plan their societies as well as pass on their own and others' thoughts to succeeding generations. Humans use language to record and communicate their thoughts and some authorities insist that one must have language of some kind in order to think at all. Finally, humans have a wide variety of feelings, some of which motivate them to think, others of which can be so intense that they interfere with rational thought processes. A given human being's thinking, then, depends largely upon his physical, social, language, and affective experiences, which provide the software or programs that determine what the hardware not only thinks about but also how it thinks.

Down through human history some unusually thoughtful persons have thought about how mankind thinks and learns. The cognitive act of thinking about or reflecting upon thinking is peculiarly human. These philosophers advanced many epistemological theories to explain human rational processes. More contemporary theorists, who take into account the multiple advances in the state of the art and knowledge about cognition, have proposed new systems for thinking and talking about cognitive development. The field of developmental psychology has been a fertile breeding ground for new theories and for efforts to empirically validate popular extant theories. A discussion of this evolution, beginning with Plato and Aristotle, or of even the most prominent highlights of it, is beyond the scope of this chapter, but does exist elsewhere (see Meier, 1973a, Book I). Also, the matrix of the more salient features of various modern developmental theories presented and discussed in the immediately preceding section of this chapter should be borne in mind while considering the details of this section.

A pioneer developer of the cognitive-field theory of learning is Lewin (1935), whose theory is briefly presented in the last column of Table 2 since it also has numerous developmental characteristics. A more detailed depiction of his learning and personality development theory is shown in Figure 4. He advanced such notions as the *life space,* which is a peculiarly distinct collection of past and present experiences through which an individual views the world around him. Each person's life space conditions the way in which he perceives the events which he experiences in the present. These idiosyncratic experiences in turn predispose him to the kinds of events to which he will or will not attend in the future.

There are the recognized physiological needs or drives arising from hunger, thirst, etc., which generate a certain tension within the core physical system until these needs are satisfied and homeostasis is temporarily established. In addition, Lewin postulates an analogous tension for cognitive functioning. He states that the intellectual/cognitive domains of man also attempt to maintain a certain balance (homeostasis) among the forces within his understandings. It is herein submitted that a similar phenomenon occurs in the emotional/affective domain and that it is reasonable to postulate an analogous affective dissonance in the realm of feelings (see also Maslow, 1968). For example, in spite of a basic curiosity about novel situations, the human being learns to prefer the status quo in some threatening instances, as opposed to seeking or to allowing new information to enter his life space and consequently upset his current equilibrium. Such new information causes what has been called cognitive dissonance (Festinger, 1957). Presumably there is a corollary condition of affective dissonance elicited by new emotional experiences which the learner must either assimilate and/or accommodate (Piaget, 1962) or reject, suppress, or repress (Freud, 1950). New information or experiences introduce into the cognitive system a usually vague or occasionally intense awareness of disequilibrium which is usually perceived as intellectual and/or emotional tension or anxiety in its nonclinical form. Figure 4 diagrams the way in which new data or relationships enter a person's life space thereby creating disequilibrium in that particular segment of beliefs and behaviors but also spreading to adjacent segments through the semipermeable dividers. Some of these vibrations also penetrate the boundary of the individual and become incorporated as more permanent beliefs and feelings, that is, percepts, about his world (life space). If the foreign hull were thought to be a relatively stable sphere of activity and each segment were like an elastic balloon, then increased pressure in one segment would cause some increases throughout the sphere, even changing the shape of the person within if his boundaries are sufficiently flexible. If the person has an impermeable and inflexible personality boundary or closed segments in his life space, that personality and/or segment will not be modified (informed) by new data or experiences. If too much new data or experience impinges on a segment and stretches its developmental capacity

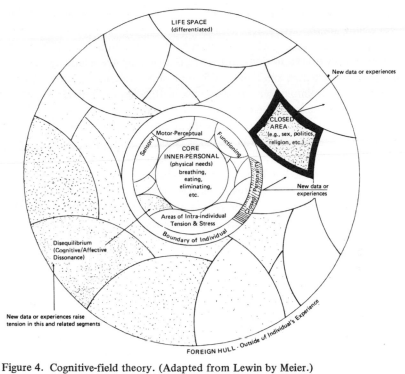

Figure 4. Cognitive-field theory. (Adapted from Lewin by Meier.)

beyond its normal resilience with too much tension and stress, the segment may be exploded and precipitate a breakdown or collapse in the total life space. This traumatic episode may cause a person to become more closed to other, albeit salutory, new data and additional experience.

Most seasoned educators have learned and refined certain cherished beliefs about the management of children in a classroom environment. When these beliefs are seriously challenged by new research findings which indicate that an opposite or very different kind of classroom management is more conducive to optimum learning and development in children, an educator may feel not only that his ideas of discipline are threatened but also that his entire system of beliefs regarding education has been cast into a state of doubt. If this dissonance or disequilibrium is a familiar experience and the educator has what is called an open mind or open personality, he will allow and even welcome these new data and experiences to enter and be assimilated into his dynamic life space or cognitive field. He has learned to be comfortable with this kind of change and has developed a positive attitude regarding innovations and changes in his life space and appropriately accommodates or restructures his behaviors and perceptions. He may relish the opportunity to reconcile new information and feelings with old notions and attitudes. He may even actively seek new data and experiences since they offer not only exciting cognitive/affective challenge and stimulation but also a more fulfilled or satisfied state once they have been experienced and processed. Authorities on stress, including Selye (1974), have modified their generic notions that all stress is harmful to suggesting that some kinds of stress, such as the joyful pursuit of one's very demanding occupation, are benign or even beneficial.

On the other hand, many persons have learned to feel insecure or threatened when such cognitive/affective dissonance is likely to occur and, therefore, they resist the entry of new information or attitudes into their awareness. They may selectively perceive only those parts of any message which are in harmony with their previous beliefs or feelings, thereby minimizing or even eliminating the tension and disequilibrium in their life space. Such a person has a "closed" mind or personality. The closed personality may throw up barriers (like the filters, especially *2e* and *2f*, in Figure 5, Chapter 3) to new developmental and/or learning experiences. Such an educator would not want to be confused with research findings which indicate that his classroom management style is counterproductive, and he would disregard such dissonant ideas. He fears the unknown and resists innovations of any kind. Frequently authoritarian in personality, he has a very low tolerance for ambiguity or uncertainty (Harvey, 1966). Such attitudes are manifest in prejudice or prejudgment, that is, making final judgments before all of the important data are considered.

Various instructional practices apparently engender either a closed-minded attitude or an open-minded attitude in young learners. When children are treated as though they are identical receptacles for the perennial truths and when all questions have single unchanging answers, they will likely develop an attitude that learning is just rote memory work. Consequently, they will avoid situations which require additional learning of what in their opinion are irrelevant and, thus, meaningless facts. Such learners do not have positive feelings about the learning process itself and they find little satisfaction in learning because they have learned to interpret changes in their cognitive field as being uncomfortable and threatening rather than pleasant, exhilarating, and expanding. Regrettably, this negative attitude frequently "is caught" from parents and other significant adults. The selection of appropriate personality types for various occupations, such as education, takes on new meaning when the above variables are considered. For example, to ensure an optimally open classroom where both convergent and divergent (creative or lateral) thinking and feeling are encouraged requires an open educator or learning facilitator, an issue discussed at some length elsewhere (Meier, 1973a, Book III).

It is a mistake to suggest that children willfully refuse or cease to learn. It is more accurate to state that they choose to learn things other than those prescribed for them in school. Such a choice may be misconstrued as a learning disability within the child whereas it is in fact caused by a deficit in the educational ecology discussed in the next chapter. Unfortunately, many who choose education as a career find their satisfaction and success in relatively closed learning systems and then proceed to perpetuate the system for the next generation. One of the most important functions a parent, educator, or other significant person in a child's life can perform is that of personifying and exemplifying an open mind and personality, thereby engendering a zest for discovering new data and experiences and thereby developing new understandings and attitudes. The educator must encourage and reinforce cognitive development for its own sake rather than to please the educator, that is, he should facilitate a love for learning rather than a learning for love (Ekstein and Motto, 1969). To accomplish this function, the educator must have a positive attitude toward his own cognitive growth and development and show a welcoming attitude toward new problems which require new solutions, whether they are matters of classroom management or discipline (disciples are learners or followers) or academic facts and fantasies.

The cognitive-field theory is very much concerned with the intrinsic drives which motivate an individual to behave as he does. It is noteworthy that much behavior modification using external reinforcement is determined by an outside agent, who frequently contributes to the dependency or other-directedness of the relatively passive learner. If children are to develop into independent, inner-directed, self-disciplined learners, it is necessary that they take an active part in determining and pursuing learning because of its intrinsic value found in the sheer joy of cognitive/ affective development and its extrinsic value of enabling them to be masters of their own destinies. This enables them to better cope with an increasingly complex society and its concomitant predictable future shock (Toffler, 1970).

Since each individual has his own cognitive/affective needs and interests, which differ at least in part from those of his peers and elders, the necessity for individually determined educational opportunities and experiences becomes self-evident. Individualized learning must take into consideration how each individual learner perceives the reality about which he is learning. The significance of this reality is relative to each individual's perception of it. A hot, well-prepared school lunch does not mean as much to the well-nourished child who has had a good and large breakfast as it does to the child who has not eaten since yesterday's lunch. Such differences in perception also affect learning motives and styles. Learning to solve various arithmetic problems is probably far more satisfying for the learner who has a basic and perhaps burning curiosity about numbers and quantities than for the child whose all-consuming interest is whether or not his mother will survive a recent accident.

The preceding is not intended to suggest that behavioristic theory does not concern itself at all with intrinsic motivation. Nevertheless, some programmed instruction and most practical behavior modification procedures which are reported in the literature are largely concerned with a child's responding to a stimulus and being reinforced by rewards not inherently related to the task. An M&M or soda pop or an adult's smile has no essential relationship to the completion of 20 arithmetic problems. According to cognitive-field theory, the experience of correctly solving the problems is in itself sufficient reward if the learner finds arithmetic calculations and problem solving in general to be satisfying or meaningful in his life space. If a given skill or understanding which is necessary for "survival" in the academic world is not perceived to be satisfying or meaningful to the learner, it may be necessary to employ contingency management in order to ensure survival. Often, once some success is experienced, the new learning becomes rewarding in itself and the extrinsic reinforcers can be faded out.

A crucial difference between behavioristic and cognitive-field theories is that the former defines and assesses cognitive growth in terms of observable, measurable changes in behavior, whereas the latter defines such growth and development as a change in behavior *and/or perception* which is not always observable or measurable in the customary quantified units of intelligence or achievement. Indeed, a person might continue to behave exactly the same way but for radically different reasons. Of course, the notion of contingency management or operant conditioning can certainly be applied by the individual to himself. Individualized learning should address itself to enabling learners to manage their own educational contingencies.

This would be tantamount to applying intrinsic motivation and the principles of behavior modification to the cognitive-field theory. For example, educators who manage their own contingencies say to themselves, "I will not get up and get a cool drink until I am finished grading these last three papers." A child can also learn this kind of self-discipline and delayed gratification so that he will say to himself, "I cannot go out to recess until I have solved these last two math problems." Although this kind of learning can be taught, much of it is caught by students who observe parents, educators, and other adults more or less effectively managing their own behavior. The principal drawback found in such contingency management is that the reward (some high probability behavior such as drinking cool soda or going out to play) is not an inherently related reward. Thus, there is the danger mentioned earlier that, in certain token economy classroom programs designed ostensibly to promote cognitive growth, only token learning may occur (Levine and Fasnacht, 1974).

A more desirable arrangement obtains when the task itself has properties sufficiently rewarding that it can be pursued for its own inherent value. A task undertaken for its own end is called autotelic (see Meier, 1973a, Book I for a more detailed discussion of this concept). This is what is meant by learning for the sake of learning, for the rewarding experience of mastering new behaviors and changing one's perceptions, the essence of cognitive development.

In order to make individualized learning most effective, the educator is charged with the responsibility of identifying cognitive challenges which contain intrinsic rewards meaningful to the individual learner. However, as stated earlier, each individual has a different hierarchy of behaviors which he would consider to be rewarding or nonrewarding at a given time— "different strokes for different folks." If the educator encourages the learners to become the stimulators and allows his own function to become that of the responder, then response-ability will be measured by his ability to make each learning task meaningful and intrinsically rewarding or autotelic for each individual learner. This reverses the traditional educator-student arrangement in which the educator is the stimulator and the student is the responder. It also rules out much of the standardized curricula, since every individual has his own unique constellation and hierarchy of needs, interests, and abilities. Significant adults then are regarded as facilitators of cognitive development, a very difficult and imaginative professional role to fill. Cognitive activities must then be individually tailored to accomplish an optimum match between the learner, the subject matter, and the method of learning it. When and if this utopian situation obtains universally, many of the so-called learning disabilities will vanish.

Cognition and re-cognition, which is the mental act of retrieving and rethinking past experiences as represented either by abstract symbols, sounds, or by unexpressed memories, are apparently uniquely human functions. They are also quite complex functions which require considerable cognitive/intellectual effort to cogently discuss. Lewin's cognitive-field theory, as modified and interpreted herein clarifies some of the complexities with regard to normal development and learning. A helpful model for further conceptualizing and depicting these complex functions with regard to disabilities in development and learning is to view them as parts of various communications systems, which are presented in the next chapter.

LAMENT OF THE NORMAL CHILD

I was strolling past a schoolhouse when I spied a sobbing lad.
  His little face was sorrowful and pale.
"Come, tell me why you weep," I said, "and why you seem so sad."
  And thus the urchin lisped his tragic tale:

The school where I go is a modern school
  With numerous modern graces.
And there they cling to the modern rule
  Of "Cherish the Problem Cases!"
From nine to three I develop Me.
  I dance when I'm feeling dancy,
Or everywhere lay on with creaking crayon
  The colors that suit my fancy.
But when the commoner tasks are done,
  Deserted, ignored, I stand.
For the rest have complexes, every one;
  Or a hyperactive gland.

Oh, how can I ever be reconciled to my hatefully normal station?
  Why couldn't I be a Problem Child endowed with a small fixation?
Why wasn't I trained for a Problem Child with an Interesting Fixation?

I dread the sound of the morning bell. The iron has entered my soul.
  I'm a square little peg that fits too well
In a square little normal hole.
For seven years in Mortimer Sears has the Oedipus angle flourished;
  And Jessamine Gray, she cheats at play
Because she is undernourished.
The teachers beam on Fredrick Knipe with scientific gratitude,
  For Fred, they claim, is a perfect type
    Of the antisocial attitude.
And Cuthbert Jones has his temper riled
  In a way professors mention.
But I am a Perfectly Normal Child, so I don't get any attention.
  I'm nothing at all but a Normal Child,
    So I don't get the least attention.

The others jeer as they pass me by. They titter without forbearance.
  "He's Perfectly Normal," they shrilly cry,
    With perfectly Normal Parents."

For I learn to read with normal speed. I answer when I'm commanded.
Infected antrums don't give me tantrums.
I don't even write left-handed.
I build with blocks when they give me blocks.
When it's busy hour, I labor
And I seldom delight in landing socks on the ear of my little neighbor.

So here by luckier lads reviled, I sit on the steps alone.
Why couldn't I be a Problem Child with a Case to call my own?
Why wasn't I born a Problem Child
With a
Complex
of my
own?

Phyllis McGinley

chapter 3
Disabilities in Development and Learning

ORIGINS AND MODELS OF
DEVELOPMENTAL AND LEARNING DISABILITIES

Chapters 1 and 2 have defined and described DLDs from the perspective of legislative provisions and normal development and learning. Just as there are numerous definitions and descriptions mentioned in the preceding chapters, there are likewise multiple possible origins of developmental and learning disabilities. Table 3 breaks these origins into two main categories, those occurring within the individual and consequently designated intra-individual (Figure 5) and those occurring as a result of factors outside of the individual or interindividual/extraindividual (see Figures 6 and 7). These two main categories are then each divided into several subheadings. Since each of these subheadings is discussed in considerable detail within its appropriate context throughout the remainder of this book, no further elaboration of the subheadings is presented in this section.

The entire table is included here in order to introduce a gestalt or overview of what is to follow. It is hoped that this framework will be useful for placing the various detailed presentations in their proper perspective. This conforms with proper cognitive-field pedagogy wherein the big picture or gestalt is first given and then progressively finer differentiations follow. The most important percept to be derived from this introductory outline of the origins of DLDs is that by no means are all DLDs to be construed as originating within the individual learner. They may and frequently do originate outside of the learner and may be caused by factors over which the learner has little or no control. It is even more typical for there to be an intraindividual predisposition to DLD, which is evoked or at least exacerbated by extraindividual and interindividual factors.

Table 3. Origins of developmental and learning disabilities

I. Intraindividual
  A. Physical—neurosensorimotor
    1. Neurological immaturity
    2. CNS damage or dysfunction
    3. Sensory defects
    4. Motor deficiencies
  B. Social—linguistic/interactional
    1. Language disorders
    2. Defective adaptive behavior
  C. Emotional—affective/attitudinal
    1. Emotional disturbance
    2. Motivational deficiencies
  D. Intellectual—cognitive/perceptual
    1. Specific learning disabilities
    2. General mental deficiency
II. Interindividual/extraindividual
  A. Ecological—interpersonal/environmental
    1. Experiential ⎫
    2. Parental ⎪
    3. Social ⎬ Deprivation or distortion
    4. Language ⎭

There has traditionally been a predilection to seek, and sometimes at all costs to find, some organic explanation for a DLD within the individual learner without carefully analyzing the many extraindividual and interindividual factors contributing to or causing the DLD. This is still largely the case. The state of the art and science regarding the origins of DLD consequently reflects this predilection to place the blame for disabilities in learning and development exclusively within the individual child. As more is learned about the importance of the ecological factors surrounding the child and either facilitating or debilitating his development and learning, the balance of culprits indicted for causing DLDs may shift remarkably in the direction of inter- and extraindividual dimensions, with corresponding alternatives to intervention (Rappaport et al., 1975). Whenever possible, these will be mentioned as potential contributors to DLDs, much as they have already been alluded to in previous chapters.

Consistent with the concept of intraindividual and interindividual origins of DLDs, the following sections discuss some communication models based upon this breakdown of etiology, cause, source, or origin. Since it is frequently not possible to specify the etiology of many DLDs,

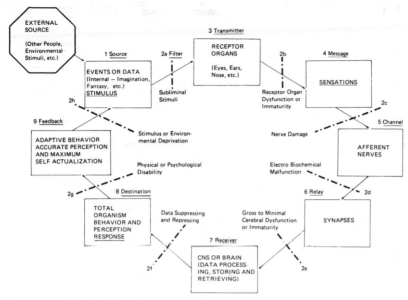

Figure 5. An intraindividual communications system.

the word origin is preferred since that simply suggests that the DLD began at that point insofar as its identification is concerned. It is not necessary to know whether or not there is a cause and effect relationship in order to further deal with the condition.

Since learning involves the communication of information both within an individual and between individuals, the discussion of developmental and learning disabilities is thus clarified by considering such disabilities as malfunctions and/or inadequacies within a communications system or between two or more such systems. In an effort to develop some theoretical rationale for DLD communication malfunctions and to establish a model for evaluating and treating them, two interrelated communication models are presented. The first model is a communication system within one individual and the second model depicts the communication network between two or more individuals.

INTRAINDIVIDUAL COMMUNICATION SYSTEM

The relationship between development and learning within an individual person can be clarified by discussing it in terms of an intraindividual communications system which has several components as shown in Figure 5. This system requires the integrity of each component in the system in order for the individual unit to function optimally. Of course, when the integrity of any single component or group of components is threatened or damaged, the ability to learn, that is, the ability to change perceptions and behaviors, is correspondingly impaired. Thus, if any component fails to develop adequately and commensurately with its companion components, such a disorder results not only in a developmental disability but also in a learning disability, i.e., a DLD.

The developmental status of an organism, which is dependent upon the developmental status of the various components in a communications network, is a precondition for the readiness or ability of the organism to receive, to perceive, to process, and/or to behave differently as a result of the new information or data. Furthermore, in this communication systems approach to developmental and learning disabilities, it is important to consider the accuracy of feedback which the system provides itself in a self-affirming or self-correcting (cybernetic) fashion. Just as the genetic constitution of the organism determines its unfolding as well as sets limitations on its potential for unfolding in the various developmental domains, the actual quality and extent of development within these limitations determine the person's ability or inability to learn.

As an illustration of some of the complexities of DLDs, a child with an apparent hearing disorder can be analyzed in accordance with this model. Of course, any other human communication modality could be selected, including visual, olfactory, gustatory, tactile-kinesthetic, perhaps even extrasensory perception, or some multiple sensory combination of two or more of the above.

As his ears scan the environment for sound, various stimuli from the internal and/or external environment (1) impinge upon the transceiving apparatus (3). If these stimuli are of sufficient intensity, that is, above the threshold to trigger the receptors, a message (4) comprised of a unique sequence and intensity of electrobiochemical impulses is generated. This message corresponds with the air vibrations striking the eardrum and being transmitted through the middle ear into the inner ear, where the physical movements are translated into nerve impulses. Subliminal stimuli (2a) are technically those sound waves which in fact exist in the physical world but are too weak to be sensed either consciously or unconsciously, i.e., they are below the hearing threshold, and that threshold is dependent upon the relative acuity of the receptor ear organs. An inaudible sound is not even received because of the limitations of the ear organ, which has a considerable range among humans and a much greater range throughout the animal kingdom.

The filters (*2a, b, . . .*) shown between all major components represent specific limitations to the quality and quantity of data flowing between any of the two components, which are numbered 1 through 9. These limitations may be genetically determined, experientially acquired, or a combination of both with multiple origins (see Table 3).

For example, there is now a clear case that prolonged exposure to very loud sounds or listening to very loud music can permanently damage the ear's ability to hear relatively soft sounds. The extremely delicate and sensitive receptors are destroyed much as wine glasses were broken by Caruso's strong voice, and are never able to resonate to that particular pitch again even if the volume is reduced later. Such acquired hearing losses may be for only certain frequencies of sound, the higher the frequency, the finer the receptors and the more vulnerable to internal disease or external over-stimulation. Or the loss may be for very soft sounds across a wide range. Or, as is commonly the case, an acquired hearing loss reduces both the frequency range (sensitivity to very low pitched or low frequency sounds through high frequency sounds) and the hearing acuity (sharpness in hearing very soft sounds).

A child may acquire a hearing loss that would render him unable to hear sounds of more than 12,000 cycles/second or of less than 30 decibels in intensity or some combination of the two. A child with both losses (at *2b*) may not be able to hear much of the high frequency sound produced by a violin, piccolo, shrill whistle, or siren, regardless of how loud it is. Nor could he hear any sound, including the human voice, that did not impinge upon his ear with the strength of at least 30 decibels, regardless of how hard he listened or paid attention to its source. Such a dysfunction may also be caused by chronic otitis media, which typically infects and fills the middle ear with foreign substance, thereby severely impairing the ability of the middle ear bone mechanisms to function appropriately.

Since such a condition cannot be "seen" by others nor is it usually "felt" by the child, it may go undetected for days and sometimes for months and years. During this time, the child "hears" only deteriorated, distorted, and diminished sounds, including language. Besides being accused of not paying attention, the younger child may not develop normal language. What he hears is what he attempts to reproduce in spoken language; in computer terminology, this is a GIGO situation—Garbage In Garbage Out, or, for the human computer, "Garbled speech Input results in Garbled Speech Output." A child with an auditory defect may manifest difficulties with speech articulation and occasionally be wrongly placed in speech therapy when his problem is with hearing. On the other hand, there are literally thousands of mentally retarded children whose DLD condition is misclassified as a communication disorder even though their hearing and speech mechanisms are functioning normally. This misclassification may result in misplacement in special classes for children with communication disorders rather than for mentally retarded children.

After a message (4) is sensed, it must flow smoothly through the peripheral channel (5), which is the auditory nerve, and through the relay (6) portion of the central nervous system. Provided that there is no nerve damage (e.g., 2c breakdown at the cochlear analytic level which eliminates high tones or auditory nerve damage caused by myelitis, etc.) nor any electrobiochemical malfunction (e.g., 2d, faulty synaptic transmission, deficiency in ribonucleic acid, nuclei in brain stem damaged by deposits of blood cell pigment in an Rh athetoid condition, reticular activating system disorder, etc.), the message is received by the cortex of the brain (7). However, the auditory cortex may be damaged or immature (2e), thus rendering inadequate or ambiguous the differentiation or discrimination of various electrobiochemical impulse patterns. Such fuzzy decoding necessarily renders the subsequent associating and encoding at least equally fuzzy.

The flood of incoming data—billions of bits per minute—is initially processed in terms of basic survival needs and drives. The individual's cognitive and affective predispositions play a major role in determining which messages are worthy of conscious attention and which are to be ignored, suppressed, and even repressed (2f). Too much cognitive and/or affective dissonance may result in the selective perception of a very limited range of data regarding certain "loaded" messages (Festinger, 1964). Obviously, such preprogramming which automatically "tunes out" certain data, either because the data or events themselves are disquieting or the source(s) of the data is disliked, results in data gaps. Too much threatening data may produce the closed personality described in Chapter 2 during the discussion of cognitive-field theory.

Regardless of the alleged course of data through the learning organism, which has been dismissed as a "black box" by some behavioral scientists, a relationship can be established between a specific input stimulus (1) and an observable output response (8), which is either appropriate or inappropriate in terms of what is commonly construed to be normal behavior (9). Psychoeducational testing typically introduces a controlled stimulus as an external source (1) and measures the corresponding externally observable and measurable responses (8). When the response to a standard stimulus is quite deviant from the normal range of expectations discussed in Chapter 2, some exception is noted and a disorder in the system is inferred.

In order to further clarify the nature of the above communications system model, it is helpful to consider the ordinary radio as an analogy. The source (*1*) is an audio program, e.g., "America the Beautiful" played by the Boston Pops Orchestra. If the orchestra plays loudly enough, its sound is picked up by the transmitter (*3*), which converts the vibrating air impinging upon the microphone into electrical impulses (message, *4*), amplifies these electrical impulses, and transmits them in the form of electromagnetic impulses from an antenna through the air (channel, *5*). Other antennae at the receiving end (relays, *6*) receive the electromagnetic impulses and convert them into electrical impulses (messages, *4*). These are fed into the receiver, which is tuned to allow only one station which is sending the message, "America the Beautiful," to enter the system and screens or filters out all other stations including "noise." The message or program gets to the receiver in the identical form as it was transmitted, provided that all components in the network are sufficiently sensitive and tuned to the desired station that they have an adequate range of *response* (*8*) to the *stimulus* (*1*) of the musical program, and that they are able to screen out competing signals or messages. If, however, the microphone or transceiver circuitry, or antennae systems, or receiver system, or loud-speakers (*8*) are in any way damaged or inadequate for faithful reproduction of the program, it would not be considered a high fidelity product at the feedback (*9*) point, where the original live musical program may be compared to its reproduced version coming out of loudspeakers many miles away.

Therefore, whether parents and teachers say that a DLD child does not listen to what he is told and does not behave appropriately compared with other children, or whether Arthur Fiedler and audiophiles say that the reproduction of "America the Beautiful" is unsatisfactory compared with high fidelity systems, the communication system is not working acceptably. In such a case, a careful checkup on the function of all components is indicated to determine where in the system there is some malfunction. Such a differential diagnosis or troubleshooting effort often requires the expertise of specialists from numerous disciplines in order to rule in or rule out dysfunction of a specific communication system component with which each expert is most familiar.

In many cases more than one component is malfunctioning. Thus, it is generally desirable to synthesize all of the analytic findings into an interdisciplinary summary, which combination frequently is more revealing and instructive for understanding the DLD individual's idiosyncratic behavior than a simple sum of the nonintegrated findings. Several subsequent chapters (especially chapters 4, 6, and 8) address specific screening and diagnostic tests and procedures for differing age groups with reference to the aforementioned communications system model. When a mother suspects some hearing disorder in her newborn child and a nurse, pediatrician, or other specialist confirms this, it is necessary to check out each component with progressively finer diagnostic tests and procedures until the precise nature of the dysfunction is evident. This may involve an audiologist to assess the hearing apparatus much as an electronic technician would check out the studio microphone to determine if it is picking up sound well enough for it to be transmitted accurately. Perhaps the simple accumulation of ear wax or mucous discharge in the ear or dust in the microphone is significantly diminishing or distorting the original signal. Increasingly elaborate testing equipment and procedures may have to be employed by audiologists with additional training to deal with DLD conditions or by other specialists to ferret out all of the dysfunctions at specific points in the system. A few of these will be mentioned in subsequent chapters, but a thoroughgoing presentation of them is not within the scope of this book (see Schiefelbusch and Lloyd, 1974, for such detail).

The preceding intraindividual communication system is helpful not only in determining the likely location of the cause of a DLD but also in determining the appropriate intervention to be instituted for its remediation or compensation. For example, it would be inappropriate to prescribe speech therapy for a child who manifests a language disorder, when his primary problem is that of not hearing well; likewise it would be inappropriate for a radio technician to recommend that a person purchase a new radio receiver when the distortion and static on the present radio's programs are caused by an inadequate antenna.

The communication system analogy is helpful in describing and defining various DLDs such as mental retardation, epilepsy, autism, dyslexia, and other related psychoneurological deficits, hyperkinesis (hyperactivity), perceptual sensory disorders, minimal brain dysfunction, and the neuroses and psychoses. Each of these disabling conditions can be located at one or more filter points on the communications network continuum. It is clear that children with conditions of deafness or blindness require different intervention programs than what is needed for children with normal hearing and vision, as far as their ears and eyes are concerned, but who perceive sounds and/or two- and three-dimensional figures in highly distorted and unreliable ways. Perhaps a child displays autistic-like behavior when confronted with excessive or otherwise debilitating demands for performance in certain learning situations. Frequently, emotional disorders will result from an inability to perform in accordance with expectations which are unrealistic in light of a particular DLD (Alpern, 1967).

It is important to get a sufficient history in each case in order to determine whether major failure or minor difficulties in learning led to a negative sense of self-esteem and consequent other emotional or personal/social disturbances or whether constant put-downs and related accusations led to a child's unwillingness to risk additional failure by further attempts to learn. The communication system forces the clinician to evaluate all possible sources of noise in the individual's learning mechanism going from the most likely to least likely causes, much as a radio technician would do in troubleshooting. By systematically considering various aspects of DLDs, as represented in Figure 5, it is possible to rule in or rule out the likelihood of deficits at these various filter points.

INTERINDIVIDUAL COMMUNICATIONS NETWORK—
FROM LABORATORY TO CLASSROOM

If there is no evidence of deficits at any of the filter points shown in Figure 5, and yet the individual is not developing and/or learning as well as is reasonable to expect of a child with his apparent inherent capacities, it is recommended that the evaluator take an equally careful look at the elements in the *inter*individual communication network shown in Figure 6. This schema depicts what goes on when two or more individuals (intraindividual communication systems) attempt to communicate. As an example of getting two or more of these systems to "talk" or interface with each other, the steps required for communicating a new treatment technique are shown. The same fundamental components of a communications model are represented in Figure 6 as are found in Figure 5. However, the interindividual communication network in Figure 6 identifies the steps to be taken in implementing research findings regarding efficacious intervention methods and materials for various DLDs.

The principal investigator for research and development projects is in fact the transmitter (*3*) of whatever methods and materials he has developed and tested to his own satisfaction. Of course, what might be satisfactory to one investigator/designer might be quite unacceptable to another. Thus, filter *2a* enters in as a bias, which must be taken into consideration when any intervention methods or materials are used. This is why each person in an interindividual communications system is shown outlined by an octagon which represents the eight possible sources of miscommunica-

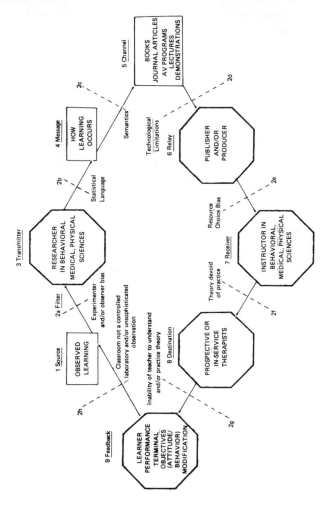

Figure 6. An interindividual communications network.

tion depicted in the boxes outlining the components within each individual (Figure 5) in the network. The description of the intervention methods and materials constitutes the message (4), which can be clouded by complex and obscure statistical language and figures (filter 2b) presented in a way to best reflect the biases of the investigator/designer. Moreover, as this message is disseminated through various channels such as books, journal articles, audio-visual programs, lectures, demonstration workshops, conferences, and so forth, communication disorders may occur (filter 2c) because of the misunderstandings which frequently result from semantic differences in word meanings. The relay in this communication network may be a book publisher, an audio-visual program producer, a conference program organizer, a talent broker for consultative services, universities, colleges, and other preservice and inservice training and technical assistance entities, all of which serve to help disseminate the message to various and sundry consumers. However, limitations in either funds or the state of the dissemination technology art (filter 2d) may produce distortions or noise in the system either by omission or commission. Component 7 is the receiver in the network and might be any one of several facilitators of optimum development and learning; these would include teachers, parents, child development specialists, and any other caregivers who have primary relationships with the learner for whom the intervention program is intended.

Just as the investigator/designer of an intervention program has certain biases with respect to how development and learning occur and are facilitated, the development/learning facilitator also has biases about the developmental and learning processes. He is likely to select only certain aspects of a given intervention program or may only select certain intervention programs in preference to others because of their format, theoretical underpinnings, or even lesser rational reasons. This choice of selective bias may also be caused by the availability of a program which is a function of the dissemination process; nevertheless, this choice bias (filter 2e) does influence which programs are attempted and may in fact effect their efficacy, depending on whether the development/learning facilitator is favorably or unfavorably biased toward a particular program which he is expected to implement.

If the intervention program is accurately and happily received by the development/learning facilitator, he then serves as an external source of stimulus to the individual learner, represented in Figure 5. Of course, it may turn out that the entire intervention program, which is compellingly written and reasoned through, does not work in practice. Or it may be that the development/learning facilitator is not sufficiently well grounded in the application of such programs, although he fully understands the rationale for them. He therefore fails to implement them in an appropriate and effective way. Thus, the destination (8) may be receiving a stimulus which is improperly presented and, in spite of the integrity of the intra-individual communication network, the raw data with which the DLD child has to deal are misleading, incomplete, or in some other way externally distorted. This may be revealed in the feedback (9), wherein specific changes in either development and/or learning in the specific areas for which the intervention program is designed to effect positive change in fact are not happening or do not meet designated standards of expectation. This may be caused either by the misunderstanding and misapplication of the intervention program (filter 2b) or it may be the result of the extenuating circumstances in the home, the nursery, or the classroom, which are admittedly not as controlled (filter 2h) as those in the original experimental circumstances wherein the intervention program was developed.

FROM LABORATORY TO HOME

In order to give another example, Figure 7 depicts the process by which a child and his caregiver develop verbal language, which is an extremely important index of developmental and learning ability or, when subnormal, an index of DLD. The practical implementation of a research finding about the importance of early language input is discussed below, along with the many potential sources of miscommunication (Figure 7, filters 2a through 2h).

Research evidence derived from studies by Heber et al. (1972), Levenstein (1970), and others indicates that intensive and extensive talking to preverbal infants favorably effects their subsequent vocabulary size several months later when they begin to say words. These findings were derived from studies controlled under relatively refined laboratory conditions and were set up to investigate a bias (2a) that early language input is an important part of infant stimulation and will enhance subsequent child growth and development in the language and related cognitive and social domains. From this source (1) of information, the researcher in the field of psycholinguistics (3) has a message (4) which he or she wishes to transmit to colleagues and practitioners working with infants. However, the message is largely derived from an interpretation of statistics and the researcher's interpretation may or may not (2b) be totally warranted by

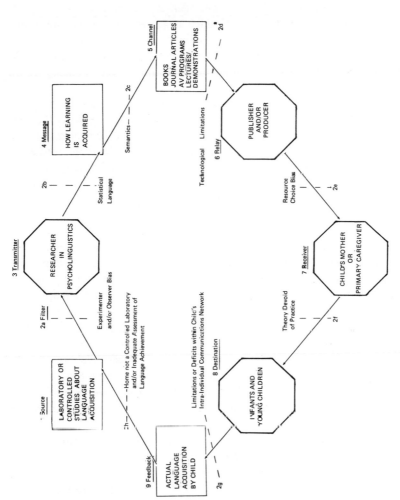

Figure 7. An interindividual communications network.

the raw data; moreover, when it is discussed in narrative form it may become further confused or misleading as a result of semantic difficulties (*2c*).

Such research findings are customarily reported by means of scholarly books, journal articles, lectures, demonstrations, as well as more popularized public media, all of which have various built-in limitations (*2d*) in terms of accurately and adequately conveying the entire content and spirit of the message. Thus, the channel (*5*), which is restricted by the capabilities of the relay (*6*), may limit or distort the integrity of the message. Furthermore, if the relay does not connect with the receiver (*7*), either because the material is not aimed at the appropriate target or the appropriate target is not tuned in to that particular channel, then the information will not be received (*2e*) by the intended consumer, namely, mothers or primary caregivers for infants. For example, if the message is conveyed through the channel of written literature and it is expected to reach illiterate mothers or caregivers, it is obvious that the message will not get through to the intended target.

Assuming that the findings do get properly articulated for the receiver, and she understands the message, an additional breakdown (*2f*) may occur if the theory being proposed has not been properly reduced to practical application. In this case it will not have the desired impact (*8*) upon the destination, which in this case is the infant and young child. If the procedures have been appropriately debugged for practical application and have been empirically demonstrated to work with normally developing infants, they may not have the desired effect on infants who have abnormal limitations or deficits within their intraindividual communications network. An example of this possibility has already been elaborated in the preceding discussion about an auditory disorder depicted in Figure 5.

The feedback (*9*), which in this case would be a measure of the actual number of vocabulary words acquired, must pass through the last filter (*2h*), which in this case suggests that the home environment is not a controlled laboratory and/or the assessment of language achievement in terms of vocabulary may not have satisfactorily standardized assessment procedures.

GENERAL BEHAVIORAL INDICES OF DLDs

Although subsequent chapters will deal with much more specific criteria for various DLD conditions, it is appropriate to present some general indices at this point. Table 4 presents a summary of behavioral development, indicating many observable behaviors which are either normally

Table 4. Behavioral development

Age	Normal	DLD symptoms and/or coping
Birth	"Normal autism" (0–3 mo); anticipation of feeding	Birth defects Feeding disorders: colic, regurgitation, vomiting, rumination, refusal
3 mo	Symbiosis (4–18 mo)	Extreme stranger anxiety
6 mo	Stranger anxiety (6–10 mo)	Absence of stranger anxiety
9 mo	Separation anxiety (8–24 mo)	Sleep disturbance: resistance or over-response to stimulation
1 yr	Self-feeding	Extreme separation anxiety
	Oppositional behavior	Interaction disorder—refusal to be held, rigidity
	Messiness	Bronchial asthma
	Exploratory behavior	Pica—eats everything
	Thumb sucking strong, with or without an accessory object; occurs in daytime, just before sleep and during the night	Teeth grinding Pseudoretardation
	Transient and somewhat accidental stool smearing	Temper tantrums, negativism
	Presleep rocking in crib, bed shaking, head banging or head rolling	Very difficult to quiet Severe and prolonged loss of appetite
	Handling genitals and some masturbation	
	Crying	

Continued

Table 4—*Continued*

Age	Normal	DLD symptoms and/or coping
18 mo	Thumb sucking reaches a peak Rocking, bed shaking, head banging or head rolling may occur Occasional episodes of stool smearing Sit down temper tantrums—fleeting Tears books or wallpaper	Excessive head banging, apparently for stimulation Prolonged temper tantrums Obsessive smearing Violent destructiveness of environment, others, self
21 mo	Tears bedding apart Removes clothes and runs around unclothed	
2 yr	Parallel play Pleasure in looking at or being looked at Beginning self-concept Thumb sucking less during the day May be some stool smearing Rocking, bed shaking, bouncing, head banging, or head rolling Many presleep demands Left alone in a room, removes everything from drawers and cupboards	Toilet training disturbances: severe constipation and/or diarrhea Excessive feeding, frustration, fatigue Many normal fears may become excessive (phobias): auditory—trains, air planes, trucks, thunder, flushing of toilet, vacuum cleaner, sirens; visual—dark colors, large objects like trucks approaching; personal—mother's departure or separation from her at bedtime, going down the drain; Other fears—heavy rain and wind, animals (especially "wild" animals, quick movements)

Rocking, head banging in some
Some masturbation
Stuttering may come in with high-language children
Tears wallpaper, digs into the plaster
Completely disrupts playroom, both large and small objects
Sudden aggressive attacks—may "sock" a stranger

3 yr
Temper tantrums more controlled
Beginning self-concept expression
Orderliness,
disgust,
curiosity, some
masturbation,
Cooperative play beginning
Fantasy play, imaginary companions
Thumb sucking at night or occasionally in the daytime
May wander around house during night

3½ yr
Thumb sucking at night with accessory object, can suck when awake daytime without object
Spitting

Elaborate bedtime and toilet rituals
Speech disorders; delayed elective mutism, stuttering
Petit mal seizures
Extreme separation anxiety
Excessive thumb sucking
Pronounced immaturity in motor, sensory, and affective development
Nightmares, night terrors
Phobias and marked fears of strangely colored or wrinkled people, masks, "bogeyman," policemen, burglars, the dark, animals
Obsessive thumb sucking "all the time"
Serious clumsiness, awkwardness, and "accidents"

Continued

Table 4—*Continued*

Age	Normal	DLD symptoms and/or coping
	Considerable stuttering Nose picking, fingernail biting Hands may tremble and child may stumble and fall Whining	
4 yr	Thumb sucking only as goes to sleep Out-of-bounds behavior: motor—runs away, kicks, spits, bites fingernails, picks nose, grimaces; verbal—calls names, boasts and brags, silly or playful use of language Nightmares and fears Needs to urinate in moments of emotional excitement Pain in stomach and may vomit at times of stress	Unusual food rituals and fads
5 yr	Tasks completion Rivalry with parents of same sex Fears are more realistic—bodily harm, falling, mean dogs Hand to face: nose picking, nail biting Thumb sucking before sleep or with fatigue	Sleepwalking School phobias Excessive lags and/or spurts in cognitive functions, psychosexual, and emotional development Pronounced and persistent fear of animals, bad people, "bogeyman," and other unreal creatures, the dark, that mother will not return home

6 yr	Eye blinking, head shaking, throat clearing, especially toward end of day—peak at dinnertime Games and rules, full cooperative play Problem-solving Achievement Voluntary hygiene Competes with partners	Tics Psychoneuroses Enuresis, soiling and excessive masturbation Schizophreniform psychotic disorder Very fearful: doorbell, telephone, static, ugly voice tones, flushing of toilet, insect and bird noises, supernatural ghosts and witches, someone is hiding under the bed, fire, water, thunder, lightning, sleeping alone in a room, or of being only one on a floor of the house, mother will not be home when he arrives home, something will happen to her, or she may die, others will hit him, splinters, little cuts, blood, nose drops Nail-biting constantly Learning problems in regular school subjects
7 yr	Hobbies Ritualistic play Mild fears—some new ones from reading, TV, movies	
8–11 yr	Relatively quiet and pleasant period Rational attitudes about foods, fears	Psychophysiologic disorder, such as ulcers Personality disorders: compulsive, hysterical, anxious, overly dependent,

Continued

Table 4—*Continued*

Age	Normal	DLD symptoms and/or coping
	Companionship sought and maintained Invests in: community leaders, teachers, impersonal ideals, heros	oppositional, overly inhibited, overly independent, isolated and mistrustful personality, and sexual deviations Predelinquent violent/aggressive patterns Phobias persist: animals, especially snakes and wild animals, high places, fires and criminals or "killers" or burglars
12 yr	Heterosexual interests rekindled	Legal delinquency Anorexia nervosa Dysmenorrhea
13 yr	"Revolt"	Sexual promiscuity
14 yr	Loosens tie to family Cliques	Excessive masturbation Pseudopsychotic regressions
15 yr	Responsible independence Work habits solidifying	Suicidal attempts Acute confusional state
16 yr		
17 yr	Heterosexual activities predominate	Schizophrenic disorders (adult type)
18 yr	Recreational activities Preparation for occupational choice Occupational commitment	

present or are presented by the DLD child as manifestations of his efforts to cope with his disabilities. This table should be considered together with Table 2 and with the *Boyd Developmental Progress Scales* in Chapter 2, since serious and persistent deviations from these normal developmental milestones serve as indices to probable DLDs. An important part of a professional's training to work with children is to become a sensitive "suspectician" who can pick up these deviations as a sort of gut-level, clinical intuition stemming from a built-in normal frame of reference.

Although many of the observable behaviors listed in Table 4 under the heading "DLD Symptoms and/or Coping" are occasionally found in normally developing children, they differ in both quality and quantity when arising from DLD origins. These behaviors are the feedback shown as 9 in Figure 5 and, when they are widely discrepant from the norms of one's culture and peer group, they are regarded as maladaptive. If they are numerous, severe, and endure for unusually long periods of the person's life, they interfere with effective behavior and general adjustment and, therefore, contribute to or are manifestations of various DLD conditions. The well trained clinician is able to sense and distinguish normal from abnormal frequency, intensity, and duration of these behavioral criteria. Moreover, the actual diagnosis of a given DLD is contingent upon the ruling in or ruling out of various physical indices, many of which will be addressed in the section immediately following this one.

GENERAL GUIDELINES FOR PHYSICAL EVALUATION OF DLDs

When a child is too young to yield an adequate language sample, general physical development may be used to predict later development and learning. The resultant developmental quotient (DQ) correlates highly and positively with later IQ or learning ability for most individuals. However, this is not a cause and effect relationship, as evidenced by some well coordinated children who are aphasic or of subnormal intelligence, as well as by some congenitally crippled children who are highly articulate and of above average intelligence. Furthermore, the concept that DQs and IQs are stable arises not so much from an individual's stable rate of development and learning but more often from the persistence of his environmental conditions as depicted in Figures 6 and 7.

With present diagnostic sophistication, a clear-cut organic cause can be determined in only 20–30% of cases of DLDs. Furthermore, most organically caused DLDs are irreversible. This places the professional in the uncomfortable position of having to admit ignorance about the causes of disabilities in specific cases and having to explain that the DLD is chronic and that there is little chance of totally normal learning and development, i.e., the child will probably continue to develop and learn more slowly or less well than his age mates.

There are several objectives for the physical evaluation of a child who has been referred as suspect for DLD conditions. First, one must determine whether or not the child is actually DLD, as defined in Chapter 1. Second, one must attempt to determine the origin of the DLD (Table 3) if possible, being careful not to overlook those physical causes that are treatable, for example, hydrocephalus, cretinism, subdural hematoma, certain inborn errors of metabolism, and malnutrition. Genetically determined disorders are of particular interest for genetic counseling of the parents, who will want to know the probability of any subsequent child's being similarly affected (chromosomal abnormalities, metabolic errors, tuberous sclerosis, Hunter's syndrome, and others). Third, one should attempt to determine the extent and degree of the DLD in order to generate some predictions of the probable course of the condition in the immediate and long-range future. Fourth, based upon this predictive information, the professional can derive a meaningful and feasible management plan for the DLD individual.

DLDs having physical intraindividual (Figure 5) origins are associated with many diseases and related organic conditions. During the last decade, for example, at least 50 new inborn errors of metabolism have been described. The following classification system is intended only as a broad outline of categories with a few examples listed for each. These examples are those which are commonly mentioned, although some may be unfamiliar medical terms; the glossary in Chapter 10 of this text defines many of the less technical ones. There are, of course, many more technical and detailed sources for further elaboration and clarification of diagnostic and treatment procedures for some of the more rare DLD conditions (Johnston and Magrab, 1975; Kempe, Silver, and O'Brien, 1974; Meier and Martin, 1974). This classification system is a modified version of the system recommended by the American Association for Mental Deficiency (Grossman, 1973) and, as modified herein, is quite appropriate for the broader category of DLDs. The previous cautions about classifying exceptional children (Hobbs, 1975a) still obtain, but it is necessary to systematize and standardize the language about DLD conditions in order to facilitate valid and reliable communication among those who are involved.

A) Infection: prenatal—rubella, syphilis, toxoplasmosis, cytomegalic inclusion and other viral diseases: perinatal, postnatal—type II viral disease, meningitis, brain abscess, encephalitis.
B) Intoxication: toxemia, hyperbilirubinemia, poisoning.

C) Trauma or physical agents: birth injury, postnatal injury, with description as contusion, hemorrhage, vascular occlusion.

D) Metabolism: galactosemia, phenylketonuria, cerebral lipidosis, lysosomal dystrophies, porphyria, gargoylism, hypoglycemia, malnutrition.

E) Growths: tuberous sclerosis, neoplasm, neurofibromatosis.

F) Chromosomal aberrations or syndromes: Turner's, Klinefelter's, trisomy 13-15, trisomy 17-18, trisomy 21 (Down's), Cri du Chat.

G) Unknown prenatal influence: anomalies of brain, craniosynostosis, primary microcephaly, hydrocephalus, intra-uterine growth retardation.

H) Associated or causative psychological problems: psychosis, neurosis, reactive disorder, deprivation, neglect or abuse, other emotional disturbances.

I) Familial-Cultural: although cultural or familial patterns, particularly for poverty or minority groups, are often strikingly different and may be deficient relative to majority cultural patterns, polygenic inheritance of low intelligence may also account for some of the cases in this category. Moreover, consanguinity increases the probability of uncommon recessive traits being inherited by the child.

J) Miscellaneous and unknown: This and the preceding category account for at least two-thirds of cases of DLD, thereby underscoring the importance of the inter/extraindividual origins (Figure 7) likely in many cases.

The following evaluative procedure serves to force the professional to attend to the multiplicity of origins of DLDs (Table 3), some management recommendations, and the interrelationships between evaluation and management considerations.

The physical examination must emphasize the neurological function of the individual suspected to be DLD. Head circumference, transillumination of the skull, and ophthalmoscopic examination through dilated pupils must be included. Investigation for soft signs not historically considered as part of a classical neurological examination, e.g., subtle abnormalities in grasping patterns, quality of motor performance, and reflex development, may be helpful in leading to other problems, but are not ordinarily sufficient in themselves to classify a person as DLD since those signs are often found in normally developing and learning persons (see later section on minimal brain dysfunction). Developmental screening in children under age 5 and intelligence screening in older children are part of the functional assessment and can be readily and rapidly administered by trained personnel. More about this in subsequent chapters.

Hearing and vision must be assessed more carefully than in a normally developing child. If there are any doubts, specialist help should be obtained. Auditory disorders often mimic some DLDs; high frequency hearing deficits are particularly difficult to detect and, when suspected, should be investigated with special audiological testing. Associated defects of sensory organs must be diagnosed and treated. Figure 8 is a useful scheme for depicting the various neural mechanisms which must be evaluated when an intraindividual DLD is suspected. This also relates to the components of the intraindividual communications system (Figure 5), as noted on the right-hand side of the page.

Laboratory evaluation should include a complete blood count and urinalysis, including a check for galactosuria and phenylketonuria, amino acid and organic acid chromatography, and a copper oxidase screen. If there is more than one DLD individual in the family, the mother should have a similar biochemical evaluation. Some clinics routinely order bone age films, PBI determinations, serological tests for syphilis, and an electro-encephalogram (EEG), but the yield of useful information from these procedures is quite low, suggesting that they only be required when specific questions have arisen from preceding data.

Electroencephalography, for example, while not specifically diagnostic of DLDs, is indicated if trauma or a seizure disorder seems likely or if localized neurological findings exist; the EEG is perhaps the most overprescribed procedure since it is both inconclusive and frequently yields abnormal patterns in otherwise normal populations. Skull films are indicated if the child is microcephalic, if prenatal infection seems likely, or if the head is abnormally shaped. Chromosomal analysis is necessary for any disabled child who has peculiar facial features or multiple congenital anomalies or in the child with Down's syndrome born to a mother less than 30 years of age. When specific diagnoses, for example, neuromuscular disorders, cerebral anomalies, errors in metabolism, congenital heart disease, etc., are associated with various DLDs, additional specific laboratory evaluations may be indicated.

Attention must be given to salient events in the individual's past medical history such as the pregnancy, labor, and delivery, including such factors as excessive or minimal weight gain, exposure to radiation, infections, medications, threatened or attempted abortion, toxemia, inadequate prenatal care, excessively rapid or prolonged labor, heavy sedation, and abnormal fetal presentation. A history of the newborn period reveals the baby's sleep pattern, feeding history, and energy level as signs of early central nervous system (CNS) damage, as well as any specific neonatal difficulties. Following the newborn period, a history of unexplained high fevers, trauma, infections, inadequate nutrition, or any other medical problem deserves attention.

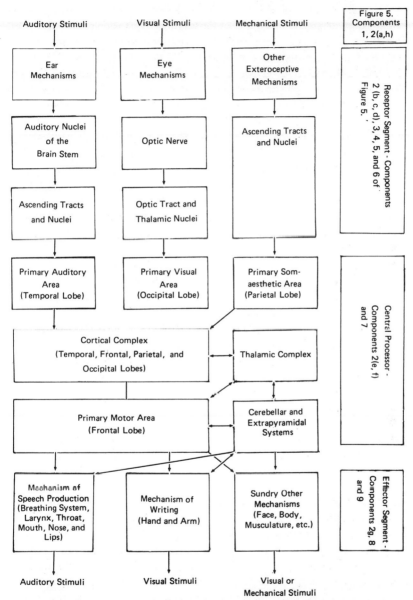

Figure 8. Schematic diagram of neural mechanisms for human communication. (Reprinted from *Human Communication and Its Disorders—An Overview*, 1970, National Institute of Neurological Disease and Stroke, U.S. Government Printing Office, Washington, D.C., and Crowell, 1972.)

Family history of any condition or disease associated with DLD(s) should be ascertained. From a genetic standpoint, it is helpful to know of siblings, uncles, aunts, or cousins of the parents who were stillborn or died in infancy before a diagnosis of incipient DLD could be made. Complete obstetric information about the mother is essential, including data about previous abortions, relative infertility, and difficulties with previous pregnancies—all of which suggest impaired ability to give a pregnancy adequate biological support. If the child were born prematurely, subtract the weeks he is born prematurely from his chronological age in determining any age norms applied to the child's functional and adaptive behavior.

A retrospective recall, insofar as possible, of prior developmental progress helps to clarify the degree of DLD. Regression or changes in the rate of development may indicate the time of a postnatal neurological insult. It is helpful to see the individual's baby book and any baby pictures in order to assess more objectively early developmental landmarks such as smiling, reaching, and turning over. Prenatal and nursery records on mother and child often point to etiological factors not elicited through recall, which by itself is notoriously unreliable. Apgar scores, length of gestation, newborn head circumference, and nurses' observations of the newborn are important facts parents can rarely recollect. In older children, records from other preschool experiences should be requested and should include reports of teachers' observations and the results of any testing done. Any evaluation by other professionals should be reviewed. A history of frequent illness, debilitation, or prolonged hospitalization including the causes, course, and outcome of each illness should be carefully documented and evaluated.

Particularly in the first 18 months of life, when the major developmental milestones are motoric, the child with altered muscle tone or coordination may appear to be developmentally disabled. If mentally retarded, neuromuscular disorders, such as cerebral palsy or hypotonia, make it difficult to assess the degree of retardation.

If any question remains concerning the child's developmental status, formal testing by a developmental psychologist or developmental pediatrician is in order. This is particularly germane when adoptibility status is being determined, school placement is an issue, or development has been erratic or variable. A discussion of some of the more useful standardized developmental and learning screening instruments and tests for children of various ages follows in later chapters.

A physical, psychosomatic reaction to some stressful situation resulting in excessive fear, anxiety, or illness may interfere with a child's activity and test performance. Intelligence and/or developmental tests merely sample behavior. When behavior is transiently altered, test results will reflect this. This is most striking during hospitalization or serious family disintegration, when behavioral regression is typically present. The history taken from the parents or a reassessment of the child at a later time allows a more valid estimate of the child's status.

If DLDs related to childhood psychoses or autism are suggested, the individual may appear retarded, but usually manifests other unusual or bizarre behavior. Nonetheless, the characteristics of severe mental retardation and autism are sufficiently similar to make a clear-cut differential diagnosis very difficult in some cases. With less serious disturbances such as reactive disorders or neurosis, it is more common for individual functions to be variably normal and retarded. Behavior problems and altered peer or parent-child relationships are usually seen in DLDs having a primary emotional basis.

The evaluator also needs to know how the family views the child, what their questions are, how they perceive DLDs, and how the family functions in relation to the child—especially if the family sees the child as completely normal or just "lazy, clumsy, uncooperative," etc. There are many misconceptions about DLDs, such as that all mentally retarded children should be institutionalized, that they will sexually act out, will be delinquent, or will cease learning anything at some specific age. Unspoken concerns about inheritance, the part either parent may have played in etiology, and the effect on the siblings are frequent. The child development specialist must anticipate, be sensitive to, and answer unspoken questions and must determine whether the parents need more extensive counseling to assist them in accepting their DLD child and in planning constructively for his care now and in the future.

MINIMAL BRAIN DYSFUNCTION—MYTH OR MYSTIQUE

The rather ill-defined syndrome of minimal brain dysfunction (MBD), which some clinicians believe is a myth and others use to explain everything that is otherwise inexplicable, is characterized by often inscrutable combinations of the following findings: neurological signs such as poor coordination, atypical associated movements, exaggerated reflexes, tight heel cords, poor eye-tracking, incomplete or mixed brain dominance, drooling, fine tremors, and impaired ability to carry out fine motor tasks. Other findings include wide scatter on subtests of intelligence or psycholinguistic ability, noteworthy learning disabilities in specific school subjects (dyslexia, dysgraphia, dyscalculia, etc.), emotional lability, distractibility, hyperactivity, decreased attention span, "borderline" EEG, "perceptual deficits," history of slow language development, and poor sequential auditory and/or visual memory. Insofar as MBD can be identified, it legitimately constitutes or at least contributes to mild DLDs which are frequently manifest as learning disorders in school subjects. Insofar as MBD is illegitimately used to explain away extraindividual/ecological origins of DLDs, the unfortunate and misleading mystique that all learning disorders originate and remain within the learner is perpetuated.

LEARNING DISORDERS IN SCHOOL

One of the most common problems brought to the child development specialist is the child whose school performance is unsatisfactory to teachers, parents, and/or the child himself. The role of the professional is the same as when the preschool child is brought to his office with concerns about delays in learning, motor, or speech skills. One must first determine the presence or absence of a variety of biological and psychological bases for the child's DLD, such as: (1) mental retardation; (2) sensory handicap(s); (3) central nervous system dysfunction or immaturity; (4) brain injury; (5) chronic illness; (6) inappropriate or inadequate instruction; (7) emotional disorder and/or motivational deficiency; (8) family dysfunction; and (9) social-economic-cultural deprivation or debilitating differences.

Before seeing the child, the child development specialist should obtain a signed permission for release of information from the parents and all pertinent data should be gathered from the school if the child has attended school. In most school settings, it is standard protocol, if not just courtesy, to clear everything through the school principal first. School-related information should include records of any and all testing which has been done, data from the school nurse and/or school social worker, and the impressions and observations from the child's teacher. Inasmuch as the teacher will be reluctant to share sensitive information in writing, a telephone conversation or interview with the teacher will elicit information which may not be obtained in any other fashion. In an interdisciplinary clinic, it is especially salutory to have an educator as a member of the team in order to serve as an informed relay (Figure 6, 6) between the school and the clinic to ensure accurate and amicable communication.

The second step is to obtain a careful developmental history from parents when the child is not present. Parents may need to be interviewed separately. One must elicit the ideas of the parents as to the basis for the DLD, always bearing in mind that even the best intentioned parents consciously or inadvertently exaggerate or understate historical information for various reasons. The third step is to examine the child without the parents present. It is during this examination that one can make an assessment of the child's general intelligence and emotional status. Sensory handicap and chronic illness, while suggested by the history, will be confirmed by a physical/neurological examination, preferably done by a developmental pediatrician, who is more sensitive to the subtle soft signs often characteristic of mild DLDs.

Dysfunction or immaturity of the central nervous system is the one basis for school learning disorder which must be most carefully investigated by the physical/neurological examiner since he alone will be able to make this diagnosis. In addition to a careful neuropsychiatric history, 30 minutes can well be spent in a detailed neurological examination (Brazelton, 1973). The most frequent indications of central nervous system dysfunction adversely affecting school learning are as follows: (1) poor coordination of gross or fine motor skills; (2) delay in motor skill acquisition; (3) poor ability to plan and execute a motor task (dyspraxia); (4) impaired ability to inhibit movement, noted by associated movements, mirroring, fidgeting; (5) immature neurological signs such as a persistent tonic neck reflex, poor equilibrium, and righting reactions; (6) impaired somatosensory perception, as noted on tests of proprioception, stereognosis, two-point tactile discrimination, graphesthesia (drawing on skin of child), on finger identification when touched; (7) poor visual-motor integrative skills, assessed by having the child draw geometric forms, playing catch with a ball, imitating gestures of the examiner; (8) poor understanding and processing of auditory input, assessed informally or by having the child repeat digits or nonsense sounds; (9) a driven hyperactivity, not related to stress or the situation, which the child is unable to control; (10) mild hemiparesis, easily overlooked, suggested by difference in skill with left and right side, or when there is lack of lateral preference by age 5 or lack of lateral dominance by age 7; (11) hyperactive deep tendon reflexes, tight heel cords, clonus in ankles; (12) poor eye-tracking, poor control of tongue or oropharyngeal musculature; (13) symptoms or signs which are not peculiar to central nervous system dysfunction but must be differentiated as to whether they manifest emotional disturbance, e.g., impulsivity, distractibility, emotional instability, poor attention span, history of delayed language development, etc.

A comprehensive evaluation of the DLD child often requires an interdisciplinary approach in order to clarify fully all of the complex factors affecting the functioning of the child and his family. This requires consultation and cooperation among numerous professionals to determine optimal management. These may include professionals from early childhood special education, pediatrics, psychiatry, neurology, psychology, nursing, social work, nutrition, speech and hearing, and occupational and physical therapy. These additional resources are often available in special clinics and university-affiliated child development centers. Figure 9, shown below, shaped like a circle, depicts a partial array of the possible management techniques which a given DLD child and his family might receive if he is evaluated by one or more of the professional specialists mentioned. The goal of the interdisciplinary process is to orchestrate these many virtuosi and, thereby, enable the DLD child to be put together better than any one specialist could do it. The process should prevent the DLD child's being passed and kicked around or pushed off the edge of one discipline like Humpty-Dumpty to fall and shatter between some cracks in

Figure 9. The interdisciplinary ball game—getting the child back together instead of passing him around.

the evaluation and service delivery system. Further insights into this interdisciplinary process can be obtained from Johnston and Magrab (1976), Krajicek and Tearney (1976), and Meier (1973a).

BEYOND THE PARALYSIS OF ANALYSIS

This chapter has briefly presented many of the things that can go wrong in the developmental and learning process. However, it must be hastily added that it is not enough to simply know what is wrong and why there is malfunctioning. It is necessary to go beyond this analysis, which can indeed be overwhelming and temporarily paralyzing in some complex cases, and to intervene with efficacious remedial or preventive procedures as outlined in the next chapters. The professional developmental specialist attempts to diagnose or rule out a variety of biological and many of the psychogenic bases for the child's DLDs. Ultimately, the school staff and the parents are responsible for the child's learning and for the design and support of an appropriate educational program for the child.

The developmental specialist may not infrequently come to the end of his evaluative investigations having eliminated many origins, especially intraindividual ones, for the child's DLD condition, but without any clear understanding of the cause of the still present difficulties. In these instances, the examiner has completed his task and it is now time for the educator to seek alternative, often modified, interindividual solutions. The discipline of education is responsible for understanding learning and the best modern methods for facilitating it. The examiner must not be deluded, even by himself, into assuming proficiency in educational theory or technique that he does not have. His knowledge of the personality and neurological function of the child and of the child's family functioning, enhanced by the interdisciplinary enlightenment from other examining professionals, is invaluable when transmitted to an aware and competent educational staff. This staff must then translate these findings and recommendations into daily learning activities, whether for an infant or a teenager.

This chapter indicates that regardless of how much is known about development and learning and the causes of DLDs, the accurate communication of such knowledge is very difficult. Although there are many research findings which suggest how some mental retardation may be prevented by active and appropriate intervention (Meier, 1975a), the communication of the efficacious procedures to the proper implementors seldom occurs satisfactorily because of their own cognitive inaccessibility, rigidity, or deficiency as depicted in Figure 4. It is hoped that this book will successfully identify and bridge some more of the communication gaps which now yawn within and between individuals and disciplines.

21 MEMOS FROM YOUR CHILD

1. Don't spoil me. I know quite well that I ought not to have all I ask for. I'm only testing you.
2. Don't be afraid to be firm with me. I prefer it; it makes me feel more secure.
3. Don't let me form bad habits. I have to rely on you to detect them in the early stages.
4. Don't make me feel smaller than I am. It only makes me behave stupidly "big."
5. Don't correct me in front of others if you can help it. I'll take much more notice if you talk quietly with me in private.
6. Don't make me feel that my mistakes are sins. It upsets my sense of values.
7. Don't protect me from consequences. I need to learn the painful way sometimes.
8. Don't be too upset when I say, "I hate you." It isn't you I hate but your power to thwart me.
9. Don't take too much notice of my small ailments. Sometimes they get me the attention I need.
10. Don't nag. If you do, I shall have to protect myself by appearing deaf.
11. Don't make rash promises. Remember that I feel badly let down when promises are broken.
12. Don't forget that I cannot explain myself as well as I should like. That is why I'm not always very accurate.
13. Don't tax my honesty too much. I am easily frightened into telling lies.
14. Don't be inconsistent. That completely confuses me and makes me lose faith in you.
15. Don't put me off when I ask questions. If you do, you will find that I stop asking and seek my information elsewhere.
16. Don't tell me my fears are silly. They are terribly real and you can do much to reassure me if you try to understand.
17. Don't ever suggest that you are perfect or infallible. It gives me too great a shock when I discover that you are neither.
18. Don't ever think that it is beneath your dignity to apologize to me. An honest apology makes me feel surprisingly warm toward you.
19. Don't forget how quickly I am growing up. It must be very difficult for you to keep pace with me, but please try.
20. Don't forget I love experimenting. I couldn't get on without it, so please put up with it.

21. Don't forget that I can't thrive without lots of understanding love, but I don't need to tell you, do I?

(Source unknown)

CHILDREN LEARN WHAT THEY LIVE

If a child lives with criticism,
    He learns to condemn.
If a child lives with hostility,
    He learns how to fight.
If a child lives with ridicule,
    He learns to be shy.
If a child lives with tolerance,
    He learns to be patient.
If a child lives with encouragement,
    He learns confidence.
If a child lives with praise,
    He learns to appreciate.
If a child lives with fairness,
    He learns justice.
If a child lives with security,
    He learns to have faith.
If a child lives with approval,
    He learns to like himself,
If a child lives with acceptance and friendship,
    He learns to find love in the world.

Dorothy Law Nolte

THE POOR SCHOLAR'S SOLILOQUY

No, I'm not very good in school. This is my second year in the seventh grade, and I'm bigger and taller than the other kids. They like me all right, even if I don't pay much attention in the schoolroom, because outside I can tell them how to do a lot of things. They tag me around and that sort of makes up for what goes on in school.

I don't know why the teachers don't like me, they never say very much. Seems like they think you don't know anything unless you can name the book it comes out of. I've got a lot of books in my own room at home . . . books like Popular Science, Mechanical Encyclopedia, and the Sears' and Ward's catalogues, but I don't very often just sit down to read them through like they make us do at school. I use my books when I want to find something out, like whenever Mom buys anything second hand, I look it up in Sears' and Ward's first and tell her if she is getting stung or not. I can use the index in a hurry to find the things I want.

In school, though, we've got to learn whatever is in the books and I just can't memorize the stuff. Last year, I stayed after school every night for two weeks trying to learn the names of the Presidents. Of course, I know some of them like Washington and Jefferson and Lincoln, but there must have been thirty altogether and I never did get them straight. I'm not too sorry, though, because the kids who learned the Presidents had to turn right around and learn the Vice-Presidents. I'm taking seventh grade over, but our teacher this year isn't so interested in the Presidents. She has us trying to learn the names of the great inventors. The kids seem interested.

I guess I just can't remember names in history. Anyway, this year I've been trying to learn about trucks, because my uncle owns three and he says I can drive one when I'm sixteen. I already know the horsepower and number of forward and backward speeds of twenty-six American trucks, some of the Diesels, and I can spot each make a long way off. It's funny how the Diesel works. I started to tell my teacher last Wednesday in science class when the pump we were using to make a vacuum in a bell jar got hot, but she said she didn't see what a Diesel engine had to do with our experiment on air pressure, so I just kept still. The kids seemed interested, though. I took four of them around to my uncle's big garage after school and we saw the mechanic Gus, tearing a big Diesel truck down. Boy, does he know his stuff.

I'm not very good in geography, either. They call it economic geography this year. We've been studying the imports and exports of Chile this week, but I couldn't tell you what they are. Maybe the reason is I had to miss school yesterday because my uncle took me and his big trailer truck down state about two hundred miles and we brought back ten tons of stock to the Chicago market. He had told me where we were going and I had to figure out the mileage. He didn't do anything but drive and turn where I told him to. Was that fun! I sat with a map in my lap and told him to turn south or southwest or some other direction. He made seven stops and drove over five-hundred miles round trip. I'm figuring how much his oil cost and also the wear and tear on the truck—he calls it depreciation—so we'll know how much we made.

I even write out all of the bills and send letters to the farmers about their pigs and beef cattle bought at the stockyards. I only made three mistakes in seventeen letters last time, my aunt said—all commas. She's been through high school and reads them over. I wish I could write school themes that way. The last one I had to write was on "What a daffodil thinks of spring," and I just couldn't get going.

I don't do very well in arithmetic, either. Seems I just can't keep my mind on the problem. We had one the other day like this: If a 57-foot telephone pole falls across a cement highway so that $17^1/_6$ feet extends from one side and $14^9/_{17}$ feet from the other, what would be the width of the highway? That seemed to me like an awfully silly way to get the width of a highway. I didn't even try to answer it because it didn't say whether the pole had fallen straight across or not.

Even in shop, I don't get very good grades. All of us kids made a broom-holder and a bookend this term and mine was sloppy. I just couldn't get interested. Mom doesn't use a broom any more with her new vacuum cleaner and all of our books are in a bookcase with glass doors in the parlor. Anyway, I wanted to make an endgate for uncle's trailer but the shop teacher said that meant using metal and wood both and I'd have to learn how to work with wood first. I didn't see why but I decided to keep still and made a tie rack at school and the tailgate after school at my uncle's garage. He said I saved him $10.00.

Civics is hard for me, too. I'm staying after school trying to learn the "Articles of Confederation" for almost a week because the teacher said we couldn't be good citizens unless we did. I really tried because I do want to be a good citizen. I did hate to stay after school, though, because a bunch of us boys from the south end of town have been cleaning up the old lot across from Taylor's Machine Shop to make a playground for the little kids from the Methodist Home. I made the jungle gym from old pipe and the guys made me Grand Mogul to keep the playground going. We raised enough money collecting scrap this month to build a wire fence clear around the lot.

Dad says I can quit school when I'm fifteen, and I'm sort of anxious to because there are a lot of things I want to learn to do, and, as my uncle says, I'm not getting any younger.

Stephen M. Corey
University of Michigan

A CURRICULUM FABLE

Once upon a time, the animals had a school. The curriculum consisted of classes in running, climbing, flying, and swimming. All the animals were required to take all the classes.

The duck was a good swimming student—better, in fact, than the instructors. He made passing grades in flying, but was particularly hopeless in running. Because he was low in the subject, he was made to stay in after school and drop his swimming classes in order to practice running. He kept this up until he was only average in swimming. But as educators, we all know that average is acceptable, so no one worried much about it. No one—but the poor duck.

The eagle was considered to be a problem pupil and was always being disciplined severely. He beat all others to the tops of the trees in climbing classes—but he had used his own way of getting there.

The rabbit started out at the head of the class in running; but he had a nervous breakdown and dropped out of school because of so much makeup work in swimming.

The squirrel led the class in climbing, but his teacher made him start his flying lessons from the ground up rather than from the top of the tree down. The poor thing developed charley horses from over-exertion at takeoff and began getting failing grades in both climbing and running.

The practical prairie dogs apprenticed their offspring to a badger when the local school board refused to add digging to the school curriculum.

At the end of the school year, the abnormal eel that could swim, walk, run, climb, and fly was given the honor of being made valedictorian of the class (Benjamin, *The Cultivation of Idiosyncrasy*).

"TEACHERS' TRANSLATIONS"

Parents, are you bewildered by those comments the teacher writes on your youngster's report card? With the help of college professors and the school janitor, I succeeded in translating them. Following are typical teacher comments and their translations:

Michael does not socialize well.

> This means that Mike is always beating some other kid's brains out.

John is progressing very well for him.

> Don't feel so happy, Pappy. This means Johnny is a dope. He's twelve years old and has just learned 2 and 2 make 4, which, as teacher points out, is progress—for him.

Frank's personality evidences a lack of social integration.

> This is a nice way of saying Frank is a stinker.

Oscar shows a regrettable lack of self-control.

> This means Oscar doesn't do what teacher wants. Self-control means how much control the teacher has over Oscar.

Jerome participates very fully in class discussion.

> This may be good or bad. It means that Jerry never shuts his big yap. Perhaps he'll grow up to be a salesman.

David does not harmonize well with his peer group.

> This has nothing to do with his voice. Teacher means that he doesn't get along with his classmates. Or—everybody in the class is out of step but Davey boy.

Richard's work indicates a lack of mastery in the upper ranges of the combinations necessary for computation.

> Don't rush to a psychiatrist. Just teach Dick his 7, 8, and 9 tables.

Nathan's lack of muscular coordination prevents him from participating fully in body-building activities.

> Cut down on the calories, Ma. Nat's too fat to play games.

Robert is a well-adjusted, wholesomely integrated individual.

> Jackpot, brother, you're in. Bobby is teacher's pet (Phi Delta Kappan, "Alpha Newsletter," May, 1958, pp. 2, 9).

chapter 4

Detection and Evaluation of Developmental and Learning Disabilities for Infants and Toddlers

This chapter is an abbreviated and updated version of a much more extensive monograph (Meier, 1973b), which addresses the state of the art and science regarding operational or proposed methods and materials for the developmental screening and assessment of children from conception to 3 years of age. It is focused on a selected and representative sample of extant contemporary techniques and instruments (Table 5) for the early detection and evaluation of children who have various DLDs or are at considerable risk of later experiencing them. It mentions most and discusses some of the literature reporting sundry related, but hitherto isolated, efforts at detecting, assessing, evaluating, and classifying the developmental status of young children. The evaluation and classification occur after a DLD has been detected and assessed, thus forming the bases for intervention and remediation with existing DLDs and/or the prevention of probable ones.

To categorize neatly and consistently everything germane to the aforementioned is virtually an impossible task. Nevertheless, this chapter sets a point of departure for subsequent more comprehensive and sophisticated endeavors and also serves to prevent any unnecessary duplication of such summary reviews or related efforts caused by ignorance of what has been accomplished. This chapter presents and addresses the rudiments

Table 5. Annotated index for selected developmental screening tests and procedures

Developmental Domain	Page[1]	Test or Procedure	Developer(s) Author(s)	Age Range[2]	Reliability[3]	Validity	Time[5]	Cost per Child[6]	Administration[7]	Recommended Stage[8]
PHYSICAL	30	Automated Multiphasic Health Testing Services	Collen & Cooper	Over 4 yr.	A[3]	A	70	30[5]	Mix	Ter.
	34	Biochemistry & Cytogenetics	Guthrie	5-3 mo.	A	A	U[4]	<1	LT&EE	Sec.
	38	Amniocentesis	O'Brien	C-B	A	A	60	20	P	Sec.
	40	Metabolic	Howell, Holtzman & Thomas	B-3 mo.	A	A	<30	2	LT&EE	Sec.
	41	Ultra-Micro Automated System	Ambrose	B-3 mo.	A	A	60	1	Mix	Sec.
	42	Nutritional Status	Fomen	B-30 mo.	A	U	20	1	PP	Sec.
	44	Gestational Age	Lubchenco	B-1 mo.	A	A	5	2	PP	Sec.
	49	Statistical Mortality Morbidity	MCH	B-12 mo.	A	A	Neg[v]	Neg	P	Pre-Pri
	51	Statistical Epidemiology	Tarjan, et al.	Pre-B	A	A	Neg	Neg	P	Pre-Pri
	55	Data System	Scurletis, et al.	Pre-B	A	A	Neg	Neg	PP	Pri
	57	Prevention	de la Cruz & LaVeck	Pre-C	U[4]	U	U	U	P	Pri & Pre-Pri
	58	Apgar Rating	Apgar	B	A	A	6	1	P	Pri
	59	Vision	Press & Austin	Over 30 mo.	U	U	Neg	Neg	PP	Pri
	61	Eye Screening	Barker & Hayes	B-5 yr.	A	U	Neg	<1	PP	Pri
	62	Electro-Oculograph	Petre-Quadens	1-6 yr.	A	U	120	10	LT&EE	Ter.
	64	Hearing High-Risk Register	Hardy	C-3 yr.	A	U	Neg	Neg	PP	Pri
	67	Hearing Screening	Young; Downs & Silver	9-12 mo.	A	A	5	2	PP	Pri
INTELLECTUAL/ COGNITIVE	71	Potential Battered Children	Kempe & Helfer; Walworth & Metz; Gil	C-2 yr.	U	U	U	U	P	Sec.
	73	Vocalization Analysis	Filippi & Rousey	B-12 mo.	A	U	40	20	PP	Ter.
	75	Behavioral & Neurological Assessment Scale (I)	Brazelton	B-3 yr.	A	U	40	30	P	Ter.
	75	Neuro-Developmental Observation	Ozer & Richardson	Over 5 yr.	U	U	20	15	PP	Sec.
	80	Attention to Discrepancy	Kagan	B-12 mo.	A	U	30	20	LT,EE	Ter.
	83	Ordinal Scales of Cognitive Dev.	Uzgiris & Hunt	B-3 yr.	U	U	60	30	PP	Sec.
	86	Infant Intelligence Scale (CIIS)	Cattell	B-30 mo.	A	A	25	15	P	Sec.
	86	Bayley Scale of Infant Dev.	Bayley	B-30 mo.	A	A	45	25	P	Sec.
	88	Kuhlmann-Binet Infant Scale	Kuhlmann	B-30 mo.	A	A	30	15	P	Sec.
	88	Griffiths Mental Dev. Scale	Griffiths	B-4 yr.	A	A	30	15	P	Sec.
	89	Gesell Developmental Scale (Revised Scale)	Gesell, et al.	B-5 yr.	A	A	40	30	P	Sec.
	92	Ivanov-Smolensky	Luria	B-24 mo.	A	U	20	15	LT	Sec.
	93	Habituation	Lewis, et al.	B-18 mo.	A	A	30	15	PP	Sec.
	93	Psychophysiological	Crowell	B-3 mo.	A	A	80	Mix	Mix	Ter.
LAN- GUAGE	98	Playtest	Friedlander	3-12 mo.	A	A	50	25	LT,EE	Ter.
	99	Infant Cry Analysis	Ostwald, et al.	B-3 mo.	A	U	30	15	LT,EE	Ter.
	104	Expressive Language	Reyes, et al.	2-4 yr.	A	A	40	20	PP	Sec.
	108	Receptive Language	Marmor	1-3 yr.	A	U	30	15	PP	Sec.
	108	Early Language Assessment Scale	Honig & Caldwell	3-48 mo.	A	U	30	15	PP	Sec.

Category	No.	Instrument	Author(s)	Age					Min.	$		Stage
SOCIAL/EMOTIONAL	114	Behavioral & Neurological Assessment Scale (II)	Brazelton, et al.	B-3 yr.	A	U	A	U	30	15	PP	Sec.
	114	Behavior Problem Checklist	Quay & Peterson	B-4 yr.	U	U	U	U	30	20	P	Sec.
	116	Rimland Diagnostic Check List	Albert & Davis	B-4 yr.	A	U	A	U	30	20	P	Sec.
	116	Behavior Checklist	Ogilvie & Shapiro	3-6 yr.	A	A	U	U	45	30	P	Sec.
	117	Quantitative Analysis of Tasks	White & Kaban	1-6 yr.	U	A	A	U	60	30	PP	Sec.
	118	Behavior Management Observation Scales	Terdal, et al.	B-4 yr.	U	U	U	U	60	20	PP	Sec.
	118	Vineland Soc. Maturity Scale	Doll	B-18 yr.	A	A	A	A	25	10	PP	Pri/Sec.
	118	Preschool Attainment Record	Doll	B-7 yr.	A	A	U	U	30	15	PP	Pri/Sec.
	119	Behavioral Categorical System	DeMyer & Churchill	2-5 yr.	A	U	A	U	30	20	P	Sec.
	125	Psychological Assessment: Functional Analysis	Bijou & Peterson	B-Adult	A	A	A	U	U	U	P or PP	Ter.
COMPREHENSIVE SYSTEMS	128	First Identification of Neonatal Disabilities (FIND)	Wuikan	B-12 mo.	U	U	U	U	U	U	U	All
	128	System of Comprehensive Health Care Screening & Service	Scurletis & Headrick	C-4 yr.	A	A	U	U	U	U	Mix	All
	132	Preschool Multiphasic Program	Belleville & Green	B-4 yr.	A	U	A	U	U	U	Mix	All
	136	Pluralistic Assessment Project	Mercer	5-11 yr.	U	U	U	U	U	U	U	Sec.
	140	Pediatric Multiphasic Program	Allen & Shinefield	Over 4 yr.	A	A	A	A	120	30	Mix	All
	143	Rapid Developmental Screening Checklist	Giannini, et al.	B-5 yr.	A	A	A	A	5	1	PP,P	Pri
	143	Guide to Normal Milestones of Development	Haynes	B-3 yr.	A	A	A	U	15	5	PP,P	Pri
	150	Developmental Screen, Inventory	Knobloch, et al.	5-18 mo.	A	A	A	A	20	10	PP,P	Pri
	153	CCD Develop. Progress Scale	Boyd	B-8 yr.	A	A	A	A	30	15	PP	Pri
	156	Denver Develop. Screening Test	Frankenburg & Dodds	B-6 y.	A	A	A	A	30	15	PP	Pri
	16	At Risk Register	Alberman & Goldstein, Sheridan; Oppe; Walker	Pre-C to 12 yr.	A	A	Neg	Neg	Neg	Neg	PP,LT	Pre-Pri.
	19	Risk Factors (Kauai Study)	Werner, Bierman & French	Pre-C to 12 yr.	A	A	Neg	Neg	Neg	Neg	PP	Pre-Pri.

NOTES: 1. Number of first page discussing topic in *Screening and Assessment of Young Children at Developmental Risk* (by Meier, J. H., Wash., D.C., Gov't. Printing Office, 1973).

2. C=Conception; B=Birth.

3. A=Adequate, i.e., >.75, when reported or estimated (only concurrent and face validity — not predictive).

4. U=Unknown — in any category indicates that data are either unavailable, too variable, or sparse.

5. Minutes required for administration and interpretation — estimated average with normally developing child.

6. Estimated total in dollars including time and materials under optimum conditions.

7. P=Professional trained to administer test(s); PP=ParaProfessional properly trained; LT=Laboratory Technician; EE=Elaborate Equipment (in laboratory and usually not portable); Mix=Combination of preceding. A trained professional is required to interpret test results.

8. Recommended stage in Screening System — Pri=Primary; Sec.=Secondary; Ter.=Tertiary; Pre=Before.

9. Neg.=Negligible amount of time or cost per child.

necessary for establishing and implementing a massive screening and evaluation system to detect infants and children at risk of being or becoming DLD, while they are very young and presumably most amenable to treatment and habilitation.

Significant advances have been made beyond both the Procrustean notion of making all individuals fit a predetermined ideal human mold, and the Spartan notion of gross screening by throwing infants into cold water and keeping only those who can save themselves. This chapter is concerned with the reverse side of the coin, that is, with the early detection of those individuals who are likely to sink unless they are either taught to swim in a complex world or properly protected from a fatal total immersion and at least enabled to crawl, walk, or run on land.

The advances have prompted the 1967 amendments to Title XIX of the Social Security Act which provides for Early and Periodic Screening, Diagnosis and Testing (EPSDT) for all children of welfare-eligible mothers. Guides are now available for health screening (Frankenburg and North, 1974) and for dental screening (Lindahl and Young, 1974) under the Medicaid regulations for reimbursement. Guides for other types of screening are in preparation but are inherently more difficult to delineate and promise to be more controversial, especially in the developmental domains of social, emotional, and intellectual functioning. Such a massive screening program promises to reveal those factors which contribute to DLD risks in varying degrees and, thereby, to allow them to be weighted in terms of their relative contribution to DLD conditions. This in turn will facilitate the prevention of more serious DLDs which reportedly can be prevented, eliminated, or at least better compensated by early detection and appropriate intervention. Moreover, the appropriateness and efficacy of various intervention/prevention methods and materials can be empirically determined by carefully monitoring their results when they are applied to given DLDs. Figure 10 presents a partial flow chart for a massive screening system, depicting the course for children developing abnormally or normally through the first 3 years of life. Table 6 in the next chapter carries this flow chart on into the intervention programs, which should be instituted as early as possible and appropriate.

Also, the results from such massive screening and assessment procedures systematically applied to a representative sample of the population will help to document more thoroughly and accurately the prevalence of various incipient and full-fledged DLDs. Such information is needed to calculate the cost/benefit estimates for large-scale identification/intervention programs, after pilot programs have been designed, debugged, fully implemented, and the power of the respective identification/intervention

Figure 10. Massive screening system flowchart.

PRECONCEPTION

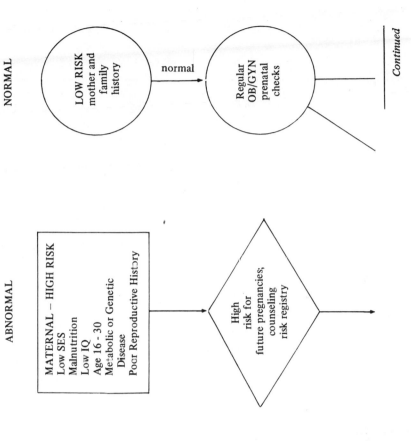

ABNORMAL

NORMAL

MATERNAL – HIGH RISK
Low SES
Malnutrition
Low IQ
Age 16 - 30
Metabolic or Genetic
    Disease
Poor Reproductive History

High
risk for
future pregnancies;
counseling
risk registry

LOW RISK
mother and
family
history

normal

Regular
OB/GYN
prenatal
checks

Continued

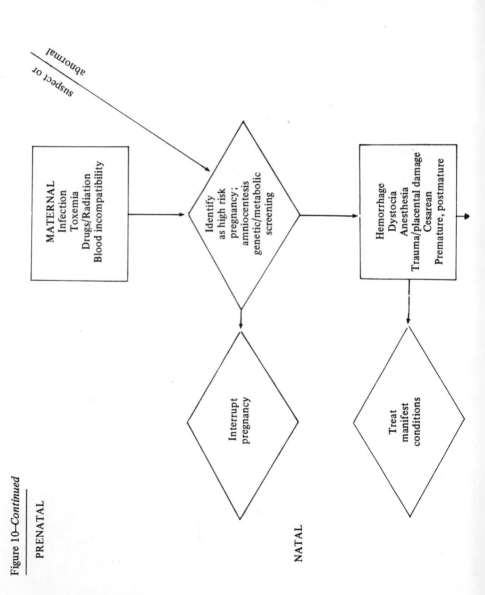

Figure 10—*Continued*

PRENATAL

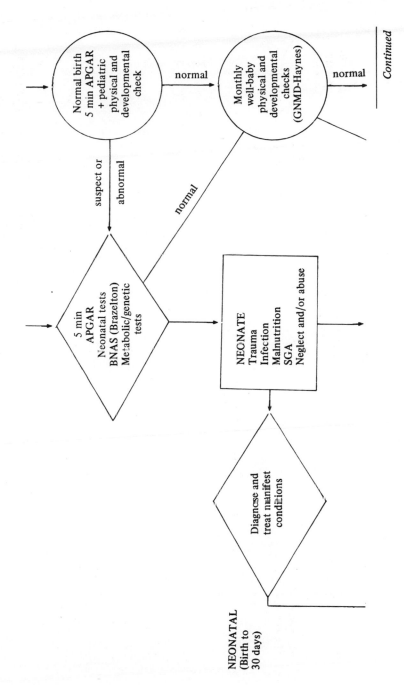

Continued

NEONATAL
(Birth to
30 days)

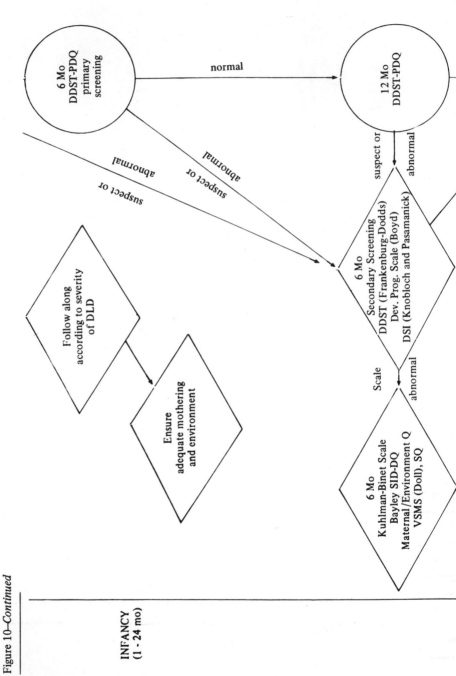

Figure 10—*Continued*

**INFANCY
(1 - 24 mo)**

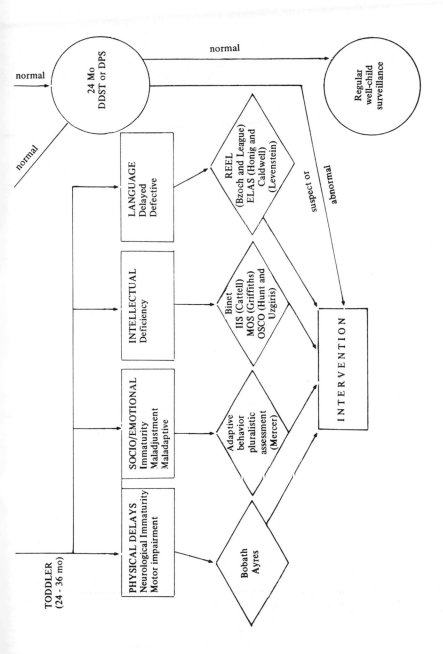

techniques has been demonstrated. In spite of the many promising features of the U. S. Congress's first major program for comprehensive health care to needy children, the ambiguities in the EPSDT administration seriously delayed and impaired its implementation (Foltz, 1975).

Each of the next four main sections is concerned with a given developmental domain describing a variety of potential problems (sources of noise in the communications systems) which lead to DLDs. The last section mentions some comprehensive approaches to early screening and evaluation of DLDs in young children. Each section only skims the cream from the far more thorough discussions contained in the aforementioned monograph (Meier, 1973b) and its respective references. Proportionately more attention is given to the various physical factors since this domain is the most usefully assessed during the first few years of life and it consequently receives less emphasis in the remaining chapters of this book.

> The state of knowledge varies with general areas of human growth, development, learning and behavior as well as within areas. For example, more is known about the chemistry of growth than about the chemistry of learning. More is known about cognitive development than about social-emotional development, and more is known about language development than cognitive development, More is known about physiological development than learning behavior and more is known about disease than personality. Within any given area the same pattern is found. Thus, in learning, more is known about associative learning than logico-mathematical processing in learning. In language, more is known about vocabulary development than about concept development. In social-emotional development, more is known about aggressive behavior than withdrawal behavior and more about competition than cooperation and more about peer assessment than self-concept (Grotberg, 1975).

Especially germane to the state of the art and science of early screening and evaluation is the statement in footnote 3 of Table 5 which points out the inadequacy or absence of predictive validation for most extant tests and procedures used singly and only one time. This deficiency is somewhat attenuated by the fact that predictive screening must be accomplished with a comprehensive battery of screening instruments and procedures whose most valid portions are extracted and the composite of which will be more accurately predictive than the sum of the parts. Moreover, the age-appropriate procedures would have to be readministered periodically to improve the reliability and the validity of the evaluation and to take into account the inevitable changes naturally occurring as a result of passing time.

PHYSICAL FACTORS

Streamlining Routine Physical Exams and Lab Procedures

To gain some perspective on and appreciation for the multiple factors involved in physical screening, the Automated Multiphasic Health Testing and Services (AMHTS) program (Collen et al., 1970) is exemplary. A Pediatric Multiphasic Program for children 4 years and older, which is patterned after the AMHTS, includes several behavioral parameters as well. It is briefly described in a later section of this chapter as an example of a promising Comprehensive Early Screening System, provided that data collection techniques, valid predictive developmental indices, and computer-mediated analytic programs can be extended downward to birth.

Potentially DLD infants and very young children are even more difficult to screen and assess definitively due to both the wide normal range of inter- and intraindividual variations as they rapidly grow and develop and also to their inability to communicate their more subtle sensations and perceptions, although physical screening is often thought to be the most definitive of the developmental domains, because of the precision of the measuring units and procedures for some parameters. However, as pointed out by Williams (1970), even laboratory reports on such measures as blood sugar level are approximate. Rather than being reported as a single number, say 125, laboratory results should be reported to reflect the range of analytical deviation, thus 125 ± 10.

Automated medical examinations are now becoming fairly well debugged and widespread throughout the U.S. Therapy programs are being linked to them in many instances. A modern health maintenance center functions like a luxurious assembly line and, with the assistance of paramedical personnel, analyzes all of the factors now known to be important in the adult patient's physical functioning. Such a process has promise for infant and child evaluations but will require considerable modification to use data from the relatively nonverbal and unsophisticated infant or reports from the child's primary caregivers.

Genetics and Amniocentesis

Guthrie (1972), a pioneer in the development and use of bacterial inhibition tests for phenylketonuria (PKU), makes an eloquent case for not only continuing present neonatal screening procedures but also for expanding and further streamlining them. He writes from a knowledgeable and vast experience about several of the cardinal issues in mass screening, including yield, the economics of regional versus local analytical laboratories, automation, simultaneous multiple screening for approximately 40 detectable inherited anomalies, cost/benefit ratios, and the practical application of recent advances.

Another kind of screening automatically occurs when parents give birth to a child with any one of a variety of congenital defects, since both the parents and the physician are then alerted to the possibility of subsequent defective offspring. A Committee Work Group on Research and Prevention issued a report for the President's Committee on Mental Retardation (1972b), the bulk of which is a series of fact sheets which are organized with a synopsis of the condition, the population at risk, current technology, cost/benefit estimates, current needs, and recommendations for preventive intervention. The various conditions described as contributing to organic mental retardation and amenable to preventive procedures include narcotic addiction in pregnancy, maternal rubella, maternal diabetes, prematurity, lack of prenatal care, maternal iron deficiency, maternal malnutrition and protein deficiency, and adolescent or elderly mothers.

O'Brien (1971) has indicated that there are 27 or more neurological diseases involving severe mental retardation, which can now be identified and diagnosed during the 4th and 5th months of pregnancy. This is early enough for the safe termination of the pregnancy, if so desired, and it is crucial to alleviate the often unwarranted anxiety in a pregnant woman who has some increased likelihood of bearing a genetically anomalous DLD child. O'Brien pointed out that each of the diseases is individually very rare but taken together they represent a noteworthy proportion of the organic causes of DLDs. An example is Tay-Sachs disease, with many of the symptoms described and the manner in which it is inherited explained. Insofar as screening for this disease is concerned, it is possible to detect adult carriers of the recessive and debilitating genes by a simple blood test or skin test. O'Brien stressed the importance of amniocentesis, a procedure which is still in its early stages of widespread utilization but is nevertheless a reliable and accurate technique for identifying several types of suspected anomalous conditions in the developing fetus. The ethical necessity for the physician to tell the parents what he knows and to involve them in any decisions to interrupt the pregnancy is poignantly presented by Etzioni (1973).

A helpful booklet (Howell, Holtzman, and Thomas, 1969), excerpted from a thorough laboratory procedures book, is suggested for the biochemical screening for potential DLDs. The booklet focuses only on those tests which are simple and practical to do on large numbers of patients and excludes tests which are routinely done in most hospital central laboratories. The tests include: ferric chloride, qualitative dinitrophenylhydrazine, excessive concentration of urinary cystine and homo-cystine, nitrosonaphthol for increased urinary concentrations of "para-hydroxyphenyl catabolites," acid mucopolysaccharides, single dimension chromatography for serum amino acids, amino acid electrophoresis-chromatography, thin layer chromatography of sugars in urine, and assays for aryl sulfatase A activity in urine. There are some other promising ultramicro automated procedures for quickly and easily identifying new-born infants with a high probability of being or becoming DLD because of organic causes (Mental Retardation News, 1971).

The primary difficulty does not lie in administering the tests which were selected but rather in coming up with a valid interpretation of their results. Differing levels of sophistication are necessary at different levels of the screening and assessment process. This chapter does not attempt to give a detailed account of the administration and/or interpretation of each test mentioned, but rather to note its existence as a potentially good candidate for a screening system. Moreover, once a high risk or at-risk pregnancy is detected or even suspected at various stages of screening, the far more complex and sophisticated assessment (O'Brien, Ibbott, and Rodgerson, 1968) for confirming the suspicions and differentially diag-nosing their nature is beyond the scope of this book. Nevertheless, Ham-bracus and Holmgren (1974), Holtzman (1973), Milunsky (1975), Nitow-ski (1973), and Summer (1974) all address the rapid advances in the state of the art and science regarding early screening for genetic and metabolic errors and underscore its feasibility and desirability for the prevention or at least better study of the processes leading to DLDs.

Nutrition

Multiple studies demonstrating the importance of adequate nutrition for optimum growth and development have emerged (Brockman and Ricciuti, 1971; Chase and Martin, 1970; Lester, 1975; Neligan, 1974). A report by Fomon (1971) illustrates the importance of knowing not only the child's nutritional status but also the community's nutritional characteristics (e.g., racial and ethnic food preferences, availability of vitamin-fortified bread and milk, iodized salt, and fluoridated water). He identifies routine phys-ical examination and laboratory indicators of nutritional risk, which are spelled out in great detail and constitute little additional investment of time or money when done routinely. In addition, a relatively simple food intake questionnaire and rationale for certain laboratory procedures are presented in terms of massive screening. Although there are now relatively high awareness and consequent prevention of the brain damage attribut-able to the ingestion of lead from eating lead-based paint, a related problem of lead in the human system is due to the rising levels of ambient lead from automobile exhausts, which may be inhaled or ingested from foods grown in close proximity to major highways.

Gestational Age and Birth Weight

Lubchenco (1970), a pioneer investigator of the effects of prematurity, addresses the difficulties of assessing gestational age and development at birth and expresses hope that a more precise laboratory estimate of gestational age will soon be forthcoming. In spite of the relative imprecision of identifying and describing the small-for-dates infant, various developmental charts depict the course of the postnatal growth of premature infants compared to their intrauterine growth. These charts indicate that the notion that these children "grow out" of their retardation, including retarded size and weight, is not supported by the data. In fact, in an earlier article by Lubchenco et al. (1963), many other sequelae to premature birth are identified as developmentally hazardous and manifest in DLD conditions, such as social and emotional problems and school learning disabilities. These findings should underscore the importance of identifying premature infants as being at risk for many different DLDs and of following them closely because of the increased probability of their developing DLDs whose severity is typically inversely proportional to their birth weight. In a corroborating study, significantly more educational and psychological problems were found among 7-year-olds who were low birth weight or small-for-dates than found among their full birthweight full-term controls (Rubin, Rosenblatt, and Balow, 1973).

Statistical Mortality and Morbidity Risk Indicators

In order to increase the yield of any massive screening system, it is possible to do some preliminary screening by means of various census data. It is suggested that initial screening systems should concentrate on the populations from the highest risk locations which can be identified statistically because they produce the largest percentage of stillborn or defective children per 100,000 pregnancies, etc. Such references as the *MCH Exchange* (Pratt et al., 1972, pp. 37 and 48) and other compilations of national health statistics are very helpful in this determination. The Collaborative Study of Cerebral Palsy, Mental Retardation, and Other Neurological and Sensory Disorders of Infancy and Childhood contains vast amounts of data which have only partially been marshalled and rendered intelligible (Chipman et al., 1966). Further elaboration on the use of various demographic data to plan a comprehensive screening system for a hypothetical representative U. S. community of 100,000 is presented in a later section of this chapter.

After a given subset of the entire population is delineated for probable high yield, it is possible to zero in further on other factors which are highly correlated with children at risk of DLD. By studying the characteristics of the birth and death population of a previous year, the characteristics of the high risk group can be established by asking each woman of childbearing age the following six critical questions:

1. What is your age?
2. How many years of education have you completed?
3. What is your marital status?
4. How many pregnancies have you had?
5. Have you had a previous fetal death?
6. Have you had a previous child born alive who is now dead?

The responses to these questions will classify each woman with respect to risk of fetal, neonatal, and postneonatal death. In order to apply such a system effectively and ethically, one should have a systematized concept of service which includes an effective outreach and follow-up program (Scurletis and Headrick, 1972).

Besides corroborating the aforementioned statistical approach, de la Cruz and LaVeck (1970) summarize the preconceptual, prenatal, natal, and postnatal known causes of DLDs. After discussing these conditions and suggesting some modern management techniques, they proceed to address some challenging and broadening prevention considerations, which are germane to the central theme of this chapter. They point out that the advances in medicine and improved health practices in the general population are reducing the demands for crises treatment and increasing the emphasis on the growth and development of the total person.

The entire effort to identify the infant who is unusually vulnerable or at risk of subsequent DLDs is fraught with difficulties. Nevertheless, the numerous predisposing biological and environmental factors are being gradually identified and reported (Hunt, 1975; Parmelee and Haber, 1973; Sameroff and Chandler, 1975; Tjossem, 1975). The Brookline Early Education Project is concerned with assessing at-riskness for DLDs.

> The planning of appropriate preventive developmental intervention necessitates some assessment of a child's potential educational capacity. The determination of "at-riskness" for ineffective learning is an important part of this assessment. The measurement of relevant health factors constitutes one element in the determination

of such "at-riskness." It should be evident to the reader that data used to support the role of various early events in the pathogenesis of developmental dysfunction is in relatively short supply. What studies have been done are often conflicting and inconclusive. Our at-risk guidelines must remain tentative.

If life begins with a conceptus of definite genetic potential for developmental attainment and if that conceptus is destined to be born into a home of predetermined intellectual, cultural, socioeconomic, and psychological level, what medical events will modify his educational destiny? The conceptus is faced with the ever present threats of hypoxia, metabolic imbalance, malnutrition, physical or toxic damage, infection, capricious malformation, and early discharge from the security of the womb. The true toll of these hazards is what is so difficult for us to measure. Their role as part of a "continuum of casualty" has been mentioned. But casualties may occur that we cannot even appreciate, much less measure. The results of such casualty may be even less measurable, especially since we have no way of judging the original potential of the conceptus.

Accepting our limitations, we are obligated to measure at-riskness and to keep revising our gauges in accordance with the state of the art. Medical at-riskness, taken with other parameters of both nature and nurture, must have its own development as a concept needed to individualize the early education of children (Levine, 1973, p. 39).

One of the most thoroughgoing and promising studies designed to reveal the salient risk factors is not sufficiently well along at this writing to report any conclusions, but is described as follows:

We have two primary purposes for our assessment system: one is to identify infants at high risk for later developmental disability with greater accuracy than has been possible in the past, and the other is to define the areas of deficit with greater specificity.

To do this we have designed a cumulative risk system that features the use of multiple measures. We expect that the most valid predictions will be made using clusters of these measures. The strength of the approach used is that it will make possible the identification of the contributions made by the various measures independently and in combination. With this information it may be possible to design a more effective system either by eliminating certain measures or utilizing a weighting system. In addition, the strength of the various components of each measure can be evaluated in relation to risk score and later performance so the individual measures can be improved. We anticipate that the risk score system will be applicable for infants identified as at risk for developmental disabilities due to environmental and/or biological factors (Parmelee, Kopp, and Sigman, 1975, p. 24).

Vision

One of the more comprehensive and thorough earlier studies of vision screening was reported by Savitz, Reed, and Valadian (1964). Among many other conclusions and recommendations, they, and more recently Lin-Fu (1971), discuss the difficulties inherent in coordinating the several levels and kinds of agencies, personnel, etc., for successfully mounting a massive vision screening program for very young children. One way in which a large group of paraprofessionals might become involved in the early screening of children's vision is suggested in a proposal that parents do the preliminary screening. Although some studies which were conducted using parents who were in middle and upper class socioeconomic strata seemed to work out reasonably well (Lin-Fu, 1971, p. 16 seq.), it is imperative that such studies be conducted in poverty populations, since they are the ones least likely to have other contact with health professionals and paraprofessionals. Nevertheless, the results of some of these preliminary studies are instructive and warrant further consideration and replication.

One vehicle for communicating screening procedures to large numbers of middle and upper class parents was successfully demonstrated in the area of visual screening by Boehm (1973), who used the *Reader's Digest* to help parents make preliminary identification of such visual defects as amblyopia, popularly known as the lazy eye. Another promising procedure using a simple stereopsis device for amblyopia screening has been developed by Simons and Reinecke (1974). Incidentally, Charles Schultz who produces the *Peanuts* comic strip also alerted his wide readership to this condition. Shortly before its demise, *Life Magazine* ran a special double issue concentrated on children and containing an information tear-out section (Pines, 1971) for parents to use for better understanding and following of their children's growth and development.

The careful study of the infant's visual behavior is beginning to yield some important leads to the dynamics of interaction with his caregivers. Simply monitoring infant gaze behavior (Friedman, 1974) has shown that inconsistent and erratic visual perceptions may trigger inappropriate caregiver responses, thereby starting a vicious cycle of communication breakdown or sources of noise in the interindividual system (Figures 6 and 7).

The chronic quest for physiological indices to intellectual functioning is somewhat encouraged by the correlations reported (Petre-Quadens and DeLee, 1970) between eye movements during sleep, recorded by an electro-oculographic instrument, and learning capacities. Of course it is realized that electro-oculographic recording requires some sophisticated apparatus and trained technicians to operate it, thereby ruling it out as a primary screening procedure. Nevertheless, such physiological indices, if proved to have a high predictive value in terms of learning capability (and, in this case, endocrine activity as well), might be routinely employed as secondary or tertiary screening procedures on children who are being evaluated in controlled situations for other conditions, since it is possible to make these recordings in the home as well as in a clinical setting. The developmental nature of this phenomenon is clearly illustrated by the large discrepancies shown between various age group clusters.

Data such as the above, along with electroencephalographic indices, promise to yield very early clues to central nervous system integrity, which undoubtedly has a high relationship to higher cortical and presumably cognitive functioning. Along these lines, Crowell (1973) has come up with some promising findings relating electroencephalographic data to visual, auditory, and tactile stimulus-response parameters in infants, which is suggestive of even more sophisticated early estimates of CNS functioning. Early visual dysfunction has also been investigated in relation to subsequent emotional disorders since it serves as an index to faulty neurological integration and there is evidence that poor integration in infants makes them more vulnerable later to schizophrenia and related psychic disorders (Fish and Hagin, 1972).

Hearing

Perhaps an even more elusive index to DLDs is auditory functioning, which is one reason that this area was discussed in reference to the Intraindividual Communication System (Figure 5). In an article on selective hearing loss and some clues for its early identification, Holm and Thompson (1971) describe the diffficulties of picking up selective hearing loss in a very young child. They cited one typical case:

> The child in this report was thought at various times to be mentally retarded, emotionally disturbed, and brain damaged before his selective hearing loss was discovered at age 5¼ years. He had developed puzzling behavior secondary to the confusing verbal messages he received and his unpredictability in turn had had a disturbing effect on his environment (p. 451).

In such cases, a high risk register may obviate the pernicious sequelae described above. Some fairly general observations about the benefits of a high risk register plus some specific findings and advantages from the use of such an approach are reported by Bergstrom, Hemenway, and Downs (1971) with reference to hearing loss and deafness which may be affecting as many as 100,000 children of school age in the United States. Along with the familiar litany of developmental red flag phenomena, they cite some which are peculiar to deafness or hearing loss. It may soon be practical to assess the neonate's movements in relation to the adult speech he hears since the synchronous quality of this behavior seems to be an important prelinguistic activity, perhaps beginning in utero (*Science,* 1974).

Of course, one of the primary reasons for undertaking early screening is to reduce the time intervening between the onset of a potential DLD condition and the beginning of some appropriate treatment or prevention of further deterioration. One of the most impressive achievements of the risk register and subsequent screening and assessment is stated by Bergstrom, Hemenway, and Downs (1971). They report the magnificent accomplishment of diagnosing and fitting children with hearing aids an average of 16 months earlier as a result of the register. The technology using impedance audiometry for screening for middle ear problems is also rapidly advancing to where it can be used widely (McCandless and Thomas, 1974). Moreover, simplified techniques for tympanography with very young children are being perfected for widespread use in hearing screening.

Abused and Neglected Children

Another group of children which should be screened as "at risk" are those who have a high probability of being abused or neglected (Helfer and Kempe, 1968). The battered child syndrome has gained enormous visibility lately and numerous centers, such as the one established in 1973 at the University of Colorado Medical Center under Kempe's direction, are investigating its causes, management, and prevention (Hurt, 1975). Studies to determine predictors of probable abusing or neglecting mothers, based on the mother's claiming versus disclaiming behavior toward her newborn infant in the delivery room, are among the more promising efforts in terms of early screening. Martin and Beezley (1974) have carefully and comprehensively followed a cadre of abused children to determine deleterious developmental sequelae and have, thereby, revealed additional prognosticators and associated factors. The U. S. Office of Child Development (OCD) has also focused its attention on child abuse and neglect and now sponsors many related scientific investigations; OCD devoted an entire and most informative issue of *Children Today* (1975) to the topic of child abuse and neglect. The Children's Bureau of the OCD has established a National Center for Child Abuse and Neglect from which several additional publications on the topic have been issued and are listed in the Resources section of Chapter 10.

According to a preliminary report (Walworth and Metz, unpublished), it does seem possible to identify children who are likely to suffer psychosocial or medical problems arising from often undetected physical abuse or less flagrant forms of parental mistreatment such as neglect, excessive pressure, cruel ridicule, etc. Using two new parent questionnaires as a part of the procedures for the Pediatric Multiphasic Examination, these investigators checked out parent satisfaction with the behavior of their child and the child's family background as it might relate to his emotional and physical well being. The preliminary questionnaire findings are such that replication studies with larger numbers of subjects are certainly warranted, since they do predict children who are very likely to suffer various kinds of parental mistreatment. Although no actual cases of child battering are reported, an identifiable group of subjects had a much higher incidence of accidental injuries, poisoning, or swallowing of foreign objects, poor parental discipline, probable psychosomatic reactions, parent or teacher dissatisfaction, doctors' notations of parental neglect, and indications of the need for counseling. The parents of these children also reflected dissatisfaction with their children's behavior on the behavior questionnaire. If these findings are replicated in a larger and more carefully controlled study, such high-yield questionnaire items would certainly be important to include in the initial interview in a detection regimen for potential DLDs. Smith, Hanson, and Noble (1973) have identified young (mean age 21) neurotic mothers of lower SES and borderline IQs (mean of 80) married to psychopathic fathers to represent a constellation of factors likely to produce DLD conditions. Kempe (1975) has enumerated various additional behaviors and attitudes which are useful in detecting parents who are at high risk of abusing and/or neglecting their youngsters. Included are: (1) the inability of the mother to find any physical or psychological attribute in her infant which she values in herself; (2) either parent was repetitively beaten or severely deprived as a child; (3) parents had no pets as children; (4) parental record of serious mental illness or repeated difficulties with the law; (5) abuse or neglect of parents' siblings or extended family members; (6) violent parental temper outbursts; (7) serious marital discord or generally chaotic life; (8) parents socially isolated; (9) rigid and unrealistic parental expectations for child; (10) evidence of harsh or unusual punishment already inflicted on child; and (11) parents do not want child for a variety of reasons.

Using an historical/sociocultural, as opposed to a clinical, approach to physical child abuse, DeMause (1975) and Gil (1971) reveal the traditions behind the use of force in childrearing, which they compellingly contend lies at the base of physical abuse of children. Gil then places the issue of child abuse in the much larger ecological or extra-individual perspective, which is what makes massive and comprehensive screening so important and at the same time so enormously complex.

> It is important to keep in mind that physical abuse committed by individual caretakers constitutes a relatively small problem within the array of problems affecting the nation's children. Abuse committed by society as a whole against large segments of the next generation through poverty, discrimination, malnutrition, poor housing and neighborhoods, inadequate care for health, education and general well-being are far more dangerous problems that merit the highest priority in the development of constructive social policies (Gil, 1971, p. 394).

On the other side of the coin is an effort to identify children who are prone to violent behavior, which in itself may be the manifestation of a DLD and may precipitate abuse or neglect in reaction to the expression of such violent tendencies. For example, the child who is violence prone and expresses this through uncontrollable and destructive temper tantrums at an early age may become the subject of parental abuse and consequent additional handicaps. One novel way of detecting such children is related to deviations from normal speech sounds, which difficulties seem associated with certain aberrant personality characteristics (Filippi and Rousey, 1971). Although such a relatively simple and brief procedure speaks primarily to one particular behavioral pattern of proneness to violence, it does seem to be a promising technique for screening, particularly if the yield in terms of other personality and health factors can be determined and reliably and validly elicited. The authors go on to point out that this relatively simple and nonthreatening procedure using speech sound findings as indicators for potential behavior should never be a substitute for comprehensive diagnosis but only as one of a series of indications that further evaluation and subsequent intervention be undertaken. It is also noteworthy that one enduring sex difference between boys and girls is that boys are more aggressive (MacCoby and Jacklin, 1974). Moreover, more boys than girls are victims of child abuse and neglect, suggesting another interactive factor in the syndrome.

One of the great unchartered frontiers is that of clearly delineating criteria for child neglect. This less dramatic and more subtle passive aggression toward helpless children can be even more debilitating to their subsequent development. Since the neglect may arise either out of ignorance or frank frustration, it seems doubly important that prospective parents be better prepared to provide at least a minimally acceptable environment for childrearing. More about this preparation for parenthood is in Chapter 9.

Neurological Screening

The state of the art and science for screening and assessing the integrity of the nervous system in infants and toddlers is itself in need of considerable refinement. The multiple and complex interrelationships between neurological dysfunction and behavior disorders in early childhood are eloquently presented by Touwen and Prechtl (1970). These same distinctions are equally germane to the contents of all subsequent sections in this chapter, which emphasizes the necessarily and inextricable intersystem and interdisciplinary nature of any comprehensive screening endeavor.

Although the aforementioned book goes into great detail for doing a sophisticated differential diagnosis of hard and soft signs of neurological dysfunction, Brazelton (1973) has systematized and somewhat simplified the heart, or nerve, of the matter. The first page of his Behavioral and Neurological Assessment Scale is largely historical and organic in content, except for the optional "Descriptive Paragraph" section, whereas the second page is more concerned with the rating of observable behaviors in response to various intraindividual and extraindividual stimuli, some of which may be construed as being primarily cognitive, linguistic, and/or socioemotional in content and implication. This further emphasizes the importance and perhaps real feasibility of synthesizing a comprehensive multiple purpose developmental screening system yielding maximum information with a minimum of redundancy. The data required for the completion of even the top of the first page and all of the second page of this Behavioral and Neurological Assessment Scale are germane to several of the preceding and subsequent developmental factors mentioned in this chapter.

Indicative of the neurological/behavioral interface is the Neuro-Developmental Observation (NDO) procedure presented by Ozer and Richardson (1974), who are taking a highly pragmatic approach to learning developmental disabilities. Their success in using this problem-solving model is leading them to extend it downward for use with younger children. The 15-minute protocol, which in part has grown out of prior efforts to standardize neurological testing, makes use of interdisciplinary health personnel, parents, and teachers in the process of diagnosing and communicating what the child can do.

It is conceivable that the standardized collection of such data on all infants, with the addition of several other heavily weighted prognostic factors described throughout this chapter, would constitute a primary screening of young children at developmental risk, and could probably be accurately collected by trained paraprofessionals. The addition of these items to existing screening devices, none of which now includes them all, or the creation of supplementary scales, all of which would have to be standardized, is a next logical step.

Of course, secondary and tertiary screening and assessment of those children who emerge as borderline or worse would have to be carried out by progressively more sophisticated personnel and procedures. For example, an abnormal rating on several of the items which are highly related to seizure disorders could lead to the more salutory earlier neurological assessment and diagnosis of these conditions.

> Adequate medical concepts exist in the literature which, if understood by physicians and parents, indicate that neurologic screening can detect, at the least, a suspicion of the presence of a seizure disorder in a child. In short, medical knowledge does exist, but the fact remains that screening doesn't exist . . . (Arangio, 1972, p. 8).

Other more sophisticated secondary and tertiary screens might include developmental EEG's to determine fatigue times for visual and auditory stimuli and infant sleep pattern aberrations (Anders and Hoffman, 1973) which are proving to be precursors to DLDs. The procedures being refined by Crowell (1973) for assessing CNS integrity in infants by use of the EEG are mentioned in a previous section on vision screening and a subsequent section on cognitive functioning dealing with infant state and response rate. Further discussion of the EEG for assessing CNS function is contained in Chapter 6. Rosenstein (1974) has demonstrated that abnormal neurological status is related to dental abnormalities, which may be subsequently interacting with nutritional difficulties. Valid and reliable screening procedures for these DLD potential indices do not yet exist but are being vigorously sought.

INTELLECTUAL/COGNITIVE FACTORS

The study of intellectual and cognitive functioning has been reserved for older children by the majority of investigators. This has been the prophecy-fulfilling result that most studies of intellectual and cognitive functioning have not focused on infants and toddlers because they presumably are preoccupied with simply reacting to sensory stimuli with their motor apparatus without thinking about the relationships between the stimulus and response events. Abstract thought processes cannot be observed nor can infants and toddlers with minimal language give much verbal hint to the intervening processes which may be mediating their rather predictable responses to a controlled series of stimuli as depicted in Figures 5 and 8 of the preceding chapter.

Historically, homo sapiens was not regarded to be very wise, much less able to reason, until approximately the age of 7 years. Several developmental theories (see Chapter 2) postulate that the early stages of development are exclusively sensorimotor with essentially no cognitive functioning worthy of investigation occurring until sufficient language capacity has been achieved. In fact, the controversy continues to rage about whether or not an individual can think without having the necessary language to label and represent those events or phenomena about which he is thinking. Of course, this chapter cannot treat the numerous subtle nuances of these esoteric debates, but they do serve to point up once again the inextricable interrelationships among physical, intellectual/cognitive, language, and social-emotional factors.

Despite the many preconceived notions about infant growth and development, several investigators on the cutting edge of this intellectual/ cognitive area of inquiry have recently generated some evidence which is contrary to many earlier fatalistic anachronisms. A decade ago a rash of factor analytic studies (Meier, 1965) attempted to ferret out the salient dimensions of intellectual and related functions partly in the parsimonious interest of consolidating and simplifying the assessment of these functions within and across various age and ability subgroups. Another interest was that of creating more accurate assessment instruments and procedures for progressively younger children. An article of the same vintage acknowledged the agonizingly tedious process of teasing out the factors which would be included in a comprehensive screening system.

> As to next steps, it is believed that the factor content of existing scales has been nearly milked out, that further effort will have to be in the direction of hypothesizing and instrumenting for different groups and different levels, the directions guided by previous studies and adult models. Until it is possible to know what factors exist in continuity, they cannot be placed into age scales designed to reveal them longitudinally. Until more is known about emergence, no comparison of emergence can be accomplished. There is, in short, much to be done (Meyers and Dingman, 1966, p. 25).

Infant Cognition

Kagan (1972) reported a series of experiments, the result of which can be legitimately interpreted to substantiate that infants demonstrate considerable cognitive or hypothesis-forming abilities even before they are 1 year old. After marshalling a great deal of supporting evidence from other laboratories and presenting a compelling synthesis of results from his own investigations, Kagan concluded the article with some implications and suggestions related to early screening. He indicated that, contrary to the prevalent views of child developmentalists during the past 20 years, an infant may be quite thoughtful and able to resolve various discrepancies and even to solve problems.

> . . .For example, the eminent Swiss psychologist Jean Piaget has argued that during the first 18 months of life an infant knows the world only in terms of his sensory impressions and motor activities. Cognitive development, says Piaget, begins after the sensorimotor period ends. These results provide a mild challenge to his view. The infant may be more thoughtful than most psychologists have surmised (1972, p. 81).

Kagan also promulgated claims about a carefully studied sample of Guatemalan Indian children reared in extreme environmental deprivation who, despite uniform retardation of about 4 months in cognitive and affective development during the first year and a half of life, at 11 years of age performed at levels comparable to American children on some very specific tests of recall and recognition, memory, perceptual and conceptual inference, and analysis. These findings (Kagan, 1973) led him to assert a much greater resiliency in cognitive development than he and most other child developmentalists have acknowledged and they suggest major discontinuities in early cognitive development that interfere with any attempts to predict later ability from early testing.

In contrast is the study reported by Heber et al. (1972) in which more than 20 infants at high risk of becoming functionally retarded received a thoroughgoing intervention program and at age 7 not only have avoided becoming retarded, as their matched controls have become (mean IQ in the 70's), but have achieved and maintained a mean IQ in the 120's. Besides standard measures of intelligence, this study has given rise to and employed several new measures of cognitive and linguistic development which seem to have good predictive validity. When the study is adequately replicated with better controlled and described procedures and measures, there is hope that the empirically validated intervention/prevention portions can become a part of a comprehensive screening system followed by appropriate remedial/preventive methods and materials specifically keyed to individual DLDs. More about this Milwaukee Study is contained in subsequent chapters since it makes such an encouraging case for early intervention with potentially DLD children and their families.

In articles reviewing various intervention efforts throughout the United States and their results, Bronfenbrenner (1970), Caldwell, Bradley, and Elardo (1975), Meier (1975c), and Starr (1971) emphasize the importance of assessing not only the individual infant but also the context within which he is growing and developing in order to arrive at a contextual and more valid prediction of whether or not he stands some risk of DLDs.

> Historically, developmental psychology has dramatically turned in the last ten years from the maturational viewpoint of development espoused by Gesell and others toward a view which has varied between strict environmentalism and moderate interactionism. In general, psychologists have been most interested in environmental effects given the genetic status of a particular individual with whom they are dealing. Within this context they must assess the effects of environment and, if possible, eliminate deleterious environmental effects while providing appropriate experience (Starr, 1971, p. 153).

Infant Test Instruments and Procedures

The literature makes increasingly frequent reference to Uzgiris and Hunt's instrument for assessing psychological development in infants and toddlers. This instrument was originally conceived to study the effects of specific environmental experiences on the rate and course of development in a group of experimental infants. Discussions by Uzgiris and Hunt (1966) illustrate the complexity and partial ordinality-ambiguity of interaction between individual infants and their environments. Some of the semantic nuances become evident when one takes Kagan's notions of representation and attention to discrepancy in infants plus his aforementioned challenge to Piaget and compares them with Uzgiris and Hunt's interpretation of Piaget's notions of representation. Since a number of the behaviors which must be observed and interpreted are subtle and time-consuming to elicit, this instrument would presumably be a secondary or tertiary stage in the total screening and assessment process and applied only to those children who demonstrated developmental discrepancies on earlier more gross screens. Furthermore, the carefully sequenced and detailed approach to Uzgiris and Hunt, in spite of the controversies about semantics and ordinality of developmental unfolding, has lent itself very nicely to the assessment of growth and development during experimental studies on intervention.

Nevertheless, in the interest of equitable treatment and in light of important challenges such as Kagan's, it seems imperative that any studies investigating the salient factors in the cognitive growth and development of infants and toddlers cannot be restricted to the theoretical frame of reference espoused by any one investigator when there is sufficient evidence supporting other equally important factors in the behavioral repertoire of the human subjects under study. A theoretically and practically balanced and comprehensive consideration of all intellectual/cognitive factors is needed, regardless of whether the concern is for screening and assessing children at risk of developmental disabilities or for evaluating the results of a carefully designed and implemented intervention and/or prevention program for DLDs.

There are numerous other instruments which might well serve as the primary, secondary, or tertiary levels of screening for development in this realm (see Thomas, 1970). One of the main difficulties with infant tests of intellectual/cognitive functioning is that most of the items for the infant and toddler have traditionally been based on and consequently biased toward sensorimotor functioning (reflecting the aforementioned controversial theories) and are, therefore, more highly related to subsequent sensorimotor development than to intelligence. Because of this, the predictive validity of such tests has been so low that the results have routinely been regarded with well advised skepticism in terms of their ability to predict the level of intellectual functioning during later childhood, adolescence, and adulthood.

Two infant tests which have been subjected to extensive standardization procedures and have been used in secondary stages of screening and assessment are the Cattell Infant Intelligence Scale (Cattell, 1940) and the Bayley Scales of Infant Development (Bayley, 1969). One study by Erickson, Johnson, and Campbell (1970) investigated the interrelationships among scores on these infant tests when used with children who appeared to be having DLDs.

> Results indicated that the scores on the two infant tests were so similar and highly correlated that they might be considered interchangeable in diagnostic settings. Clinically, the Bayley presented advantages of a greater variety of items and separate mental and motor scales, while the Cattell took less time to administer and could be combined with the Stanford-Binet (p. 102).

From the above study it was clear that: (1) the Cattell Infant Intelligence Scale does not have satisfactory predictive validity for normal children or even for those referred through screening tests; (2) 2-year-old children seem to be more easily examined than 3-year-old children partly because of their increased emotional instability during the third year; and (3) as Wechsler (1966) pointed out in defense of his intelligence scales when they were being challenged and ultimately dismissed in the New York school systems, IQ stability is very probably in large part a function of environmental stability and in no way predicts how an individual might do when the environment is radically modified toward greater enrichment or deprivation. Although frequently mentioned as being of great usefulness for following the impact of intervention efforts with developmentally disabled infants, the Kuhlmann-Binet Infant Scale (Shotwell, 1964) and the Griffiths Mental Development Scale (Lally, 1968) also suffer from a lack of predictive validity.

Prediction of Later Intellectual/Cognitive Functioning

In an article which might legitimately have been included in the later section dealing with social/emotional factors, since it also brings out their importance, Holden (1972) reported a study dealing with the prediction of mental retardation in infancy. His discussion concludes by reiterating the difficulties of using a single predictive factor such as the relatively primitive estimates of intellectual/cognitive functioning now available for infants.

Holden makes the point and backs it up with several studies, including his own data, that prediction of a group's mean intelligence from infant test results is far better than prediction of an individual's intelligence from his infant performance on intelligence tests. He quoted Bayley, whose developmental scales he employed in his own study, which was part of the Collaborative Study of Cerebral Palsy, Mental Retardation, and Other Neurological and Sensory Disorders of Infancy and Childhood, supported by the National Institute of Neurological Diseases and Stroke.

> Early studies of mental development in normal infants have demonstrated little or no relationship between mental ability in infancy and intelligence at a later age (Bayley, 1949). Nancy Bayley went so far as to say, "it is now well established that we cannot predict later intelligence from the scores of tests made in infancy" (Bayley, 1955, quoted in Holden, 1972, p. 28).

In contrast to the above, Holden presented more encouraging findings. Similar findings from subsequent studies, such as by Birns and Golden (1972); Broman, Nichols, and Kennedy (1972); Knobloch and Pasamanick (1963); Van der Veer and Schweid (1974); Werner, Honzik, and Smith (1968); and Willerman and Fiedler (1974), showed that Bayley's undertaking of the development and standardization of the elaborate scales bearing her name, in spite of her aforementioned reservations, was not all in vain even in terms of predicting later intellectual/cognitive functioning.

The problem of accurate prediction of mental development in normal infants has often been controversial. Out of a population of 2,875 infants in the Child Development Study at Brown University, 230 subjects were followed to age four and 115 to age seven. Each child was 1 month or more below average on the Bayley Scales of Mental or Motor Development at age 8 months. At both ages four and seven, mean I.Q. scores were significantly lower than a control group of 150 children (Holden, 1972, p. 28).

Even the Gesell Developmental Scale (Gesell and Amatruda, 1947) works relatively well for differentiating infants in terms of their neuro-motor development, aberrations of which are frequently correlated with organic causes of mental retardation.

> There has been much controversy concerning the usefulness of the Gesell Developmental Scale. By showing the discrepancy between Down's syndrome children and normal children our results confirmed Illingworth's view (1966) that the Gesell schedules have great value in demonstrating the presence of mental retardation in early childhood. The fact that the normal group showed the expected steady rate of development points furthermore to the usefulness of these scales for assessing development in young children (Dicks-Mireaux, 1972, p. 31).

Holden further complicates the matter by noting that additional factors, such as socioeconomic status of the family and its members' emotional stability, often contribute substantially to the accuracy of predicting DLDs, particularly in borderline cases (see Social-Emotional Factors).

Using a principal-components factor analysis of infant test scores, McCall, Hogarty, and Hurlburt (1972) continued to trace a path of predominant skills through infancy, suggesting that this path may represent the developmental progression of skills culminating in childhood intellectual skills. A developmental trend is identified as proceeding from "manipulating objects that yield perceptual consequences" to "social imitation of fine motor and verbal behavior" to "verbal labeling and comprehension" to "verbal fluency and grammatical fluency." The authors conclude their thoroughgoing analysis of the apparent futility of attempting to predict childhood intelligence from scores on extant infant tests by offering several observations which seem germane to the design of screening and assessment procedures for greater predictive validity. Many others (Bersoff, 1973; Grotberg, 1975; Keniston, 1974; Keogh and Becker, 1973; Lewis, 1973; and Meyers, 1973, to name a few of the representative and relatively balanced discussions) have investigated the issues involved in early psychometric prediction of later intellectual functioning and offer many helpful cautions and constructive recommendations for this applied science.

As the child gets older, and the number and complexity of tasks to be mastered become more numerous and more like those which adult intellectual/cognitive functioning involve, it is easier to screen and assess reliably and validly those who seem to be lagging behind normal expectations. In a search of the literature dealing with assessment of young children, practically all of the 115 annotated references dealing with preschool tests, screening procedures, and standardized examination methods and materials dealt with children 3–6 years old. The listings ranged from standardized procedures for assessing self-concept to standardized neurological examinations and numerous related inventories. This is also true of the listings found in Buros (1965 and 1972), but the reader is nevertheless referred to these classic references for further information. The *Head Start Collection* (E.T.S., 1973), *CSE-ECRC Preschool/Kindergarten Test Evaluation* (Hoepfner, Stern, and Nummedal, 1971), and a chapter by Gallagher and Bradley (1972) all provide information about instruments for those engaged in research or the direction of projects involving this older age group (3–6 years) with which Chapters 6 and 7 deal in greater detail.

Changes in Infant State and Response Rate

In an effort to get at sheer intellectual/cognitive functioning in infants, Garber (1971) relates some of his experience with a promising Ivanov-Smolensky technique which simply requires the subject to squeeze a rubber bulb to register his response. He also mentions some of the problems encountered in testing cognitive functioning in very young children with the suggestion that some screening application be made of this technique after it has been further refined. Lewis, Goldberg, and Campbell (1969) have also attempted to obtain a "purer" measure of infant cognitive development and have also been influenced by Russian research, primarily that of Sokolov (1963). They argue that the rate of habituation of attentional responses to a repeatedly presented signal provides an index of cognitive development. Specifically, more rapid habituation is interpreted to mean that the infant is processing information more effectively, forming a representation or schema of the event more rapidly, and, thus, is cognitively advanced compared with an infant who habituates more slowly. The authors present a variety of evidence in support of this hypothesis, e.g., more rapid habituation among infants with Apgar scores of 10 than among infants with scores less than 10, and correlations between rate of habituation at 1 year of age and Stanford-Binet IQ at 44 months (r = 0.46 for girls, 0.50 for boys). Friedman's work (1974), mentioned in the earlier section on visual factors, corroborates these findings on habituation.

In an effort to analyze the biological substrate which is an essential precursor of cognitive functioning, Crowell (1973) has been gathering and interpreting heart rate and electroencephalographic data on several hundred newborns during the past decade. He has clearly demonstrated the relationship between central nervous system integrity and these data, as affected by carefully controlled auditory, visual, and tactile stimuli. Although such sophisticated procedures require elaborate and expensive equipment and trained technicians, they would seem quite appropriate for tertiary stage screening and assessment of infants whose sensory sensitivities and reflex systems seem below normal expectations on other more gross behavioral levels. These psychophysiological precursors of intellectual/cognitive capacity are promising, but have not been universally supported for accurately predicting mental ability in children (Davis, 1971).

Of course, such efforts as the ones which have been described in this section require a certain amount of instrumentation and additional studies to streamline the administration for screening and to establish more firmly their validity and reliability. The difficulties in obtaining meaningful behavior of an intellectual/cognitive kind from infants are attested to by all investigators in the field and underlie the fact that most infant screening and assessment procedures focus primarily on the more easily elicited, observed, and measured sensorimotor factors.

As pointed out in Chapter 3, the fact that such sensorimotor development does statistically correlate rather highly with subsequent cognitive functioning, when the data for large groups of normally developing children are reviewed, contributes to a great deal of the confusion in the field, since an illicit conclusion is frequently drawn from such a seductive relationship, namely, that a statistical correlation is the same as a cause and effect relationship. Although difficulties and/or delays in eye-hand coordination, basic reflexes, or achievement of gross and fine motor developmental milestones may in some instances reflect disturbance not only of lower brain functions but also of higher cortical functioning, it is quite possible for an individual with severe sensorimotor problems to have totally intact higher cortical processes. This is demonstrated by an intellectually bright quadriplegic or even a cerebral palsied child. Conversely, a given child may be seriously intellectually impaired but be physically well coordinated and up to par in his gross and fine motor milestones; the all brawn-no brain syndrome is an exaggerated description of this. Much intense controversy has arisen and continues to rage around the issues of sensorimotor training to enable or facilitate intellectual/cognitive development. The tenor of the arguments is contained in an exchange between Zigler and Seitz (1975) and Neman (1975).

This discussion of screening and assessment of early cognitive development should not close without an additional cautionary note. The state of the infant at the time of testing, that is, the degree of wakefulness and alertness, is an important confounding factor in practically all screening and assessment efforts and has frequently been overlooked. Thus, it is possible that a low score on some screening or assessment procedure may *not* be a function of some real deficiency, but rather a function of the infant's being in a state inappropriate for that assessment at that time (Hutt, Leonard, and Prechtl, 1969).

LANGUAGE FACTORS

Receptive Language Development

As stated in the section dealing with intellectual/cognitive factors, in the past a child was not considered to be a thinking person until he had begun to express his thoughts in a verbal way. In fact, for several centuries it was believed, and still is by many, that the age of reason does not arrive until 7 years of age. Within recent years, however, investigators have developed increasingly accurate and ingenious equipment and procedures for evaluating receptive language in infants and young children. After giving some notions of the state of the art and science regarding the testing of a young child's ability to process auditory stimuli, Friedlander (1971) goes on to explain the value of his automated evaluation techniques for assessing selective listening in infants and young children.

> The principal results show that the two groups of normal children were more and more decisive in their rejection of the degraded sound tracks as the noise interference increased in intensity. However, the language-impaired children listened to both the normal and the increasingly incomprehensible sound tracks with almost identical degrees of attention. Furthermore, these children's total listening response time was just as high as that of the normal children, emphasizing the difference between them (p. 9).

Butterfield and Cairns (1974) go beyond the assessment of a neonate's ability to discriminate speech and ask how impaired ability affects abnormal language development. They proceed to ask whether infants can be trained in speech discrimination and suggest that further experiments are needed to determine whether language intervention programs could be improved by training infants to discriminate speech. If not, why screen for such problems?

Once again the utilization of rather sophisticated apparatus is required to assess the selective listening patterns of infants, and even more elaborate instrumentation is required to get at the integration of sound with sight experiences and the interpretation of these by normal and abnormal infants. Nevertheless, the screening, at perhaps the tertiary level, of infants in terms of their ability to relate what they see to what they hear would certainly provide a meaningful assessment and prediction of likely learning disabilities in subsequent years. The synchronized movement of the neonate with adult speech is eloquent body language (*Science*, 1974) telling us that receptive language begins very early, perhaps in utero, and suggests the critical importance of the first couple of years for later intellectual/linguistic development (Dennis, 1973).

Diagnostic Significance of Infant Cry

Ostwald, Phibbs, and Fox (1968) present a review of published infant cry studies along with some of their own laboratory findings, which all tend to indicate that the very crying of infants has diagnostic value when subjected to careful analysis. Indeed, the infant cry is the individual's first expressive language and has real meaning and communication value. Of the 24 studies they report from 1838 to 1967, 22 of them have been done since 1927, and over half since 1960. However, more definitive sonographic studies of normal and abnormal vocalization patterns during the first 6 months of life are necessary for satisfactory predictive screening and assessment.

Expressive Language Development

A technique of assessing expressive language development for 2- to 4-year-old children is that of a sentence repetition task, such as the one developed by Reyes, Garber, and Heber (1972). This technique, plus several others developed to assess the impact of a thorough intervention program (Heber et al., 1972), has considerable empirical validation in the sense that the experimental groups, which experienced considerable language enrichment, predictably and empirically performed better than their control counterparts on various and sundry receptive and expressive language assessments. It does seem from the data reported that, although there is yet much to learn about factors of length in syntactic complexity, the results of the sentence repetition test may be used as a reasonable estimate of children's language functioning and, because of its straightforward and simple administration, it might actually serve as a part of a screening battery. In addition to the standardized technique of sentence repetition for assessing expressive language development, it is also considered important to determine how well an individual can produce speech in a free and open situation. Bernard, Thelen, and Garber (no date) have demonstrated some promising approaches to this problem with the same population as was involved in the Heber study and their findings corroborate the developmental trends evident in other psycholinguistic studies.

Language Tests and Scales

Marmor (1971) has developed a manual for testing the receptive language ability of 1- to 3-year-old children. The portion of the test for 1- to 2-year-old children measures their ability to understand vocabulary words and to follow verbal instructions by responding to simple object labels and to more difficult labels for classes of objects by identifying their reference object. The instructions require the child to follow simple familiar commands and progress to the more difficult phases of carrying out more complex sequences and language comprehension tests. The manual instructs the examiner in specific scoring procedures using the materials to assess receptive language ability. The final score for the 2- to 3-year-olds is expressed as a developmental age equivalent and the reliability of interobservers in all cases exceeded 0.90, but the instrument still requires additional validation on the basis of longitudinal data before it can be used confidently in any massive screening and assessment project.

Another effort along these lines is found in the Early Language Assessment Scale developed by Honig and Caldwell (1966, Part I) and Honig and Brill (1970, Part II). These scales, complete with instructions and scoring or rating sheets, tap both the receptive and expressive language of infants and toddlers. It is evident from reviewing the reports on the scales that they can be administered and scored rather easily by trained paraprofessionals and might serve as a good secondary stage of language development screening.

Language Screening—An Interdisciplinary Process

It has been repeatedly stated or implied that screening is a multi-stage procedure and Grewel (1967) makes a cogent case for both an interdisciplinary and differential diagnosis.

> . . . It is not sufficiently realized that many developmental delays in children must be regarded as belonging to developmental neuropsychology. Speech and language disorders in children confront us with a special aspect of neurology and neuropsychology.

The study of these disorders requires thorough knowledge of speech and its disorders, articulatory as well as verbal. Whereas the neurological symptoms must be ascertained, phonetic as well as linguistic analysis of the symptoms is necessary, whereas the relation or correlation with psychological delay or deterioration must be studied. Differential diagnosis is necessary (Grewel, 1967, p. 864).

From the foregoing very cursory and incomplete review of some language factors, it should be clear that there is much more to receptive language in infants than their ability to hear sound and there is more to their expressive language than the neurophysiological and anatomical integrity of the speech mechanisms (see Berry, 1969; McNeill, 1970; Schiefelbusch and Lloyd, 1974; and Travis, 1971, for a much more extensive and intensive treatment of the acquisition of and anomalies in language as explained by various developmental approaches). Also, implicit throughout all of the comments about screening for DLDs associated with receptive and expressive language, it must be remembered that various associative processes are also inferred from the findings on studies of language input and output (remember the intraindividual communication system in Figure 5 and the related schema in Figure 8). The actual integrity of the central nervous system in processing the linguistic input properly, i.e., in efficiently categorizing, storing, retrieving, and associating data, is still not systematically and scientifically measurable. It is nevertheless conceivable that certain neurophysiological and electrobiochemical indices to central nervous system integrity and overall efficiency will be forthcoming in the future. Studies such as Crowell's (1973), reported in the previous sections, are continuing to investigate these brain-behavior relationships, and it is anticipated that they will shed additional light on the process of language acquisition.

Moreover, the interaction between heredity and environment in terms of language development and its importance for optimum intellectual/cognitive functioning lead to the next section dealing with the social and emotional manifestations which are equally complex and interdependent with the other factors. This makes comprehensive and massive screening and assessment of children at risk for any of the vast range of DLDs an extremely complex process.

As in other previously described sophisticated measures of fine phenomena, rather elaborate instrumentation is required simply in order to properly analyze the characteristics of infant cries, for example. A properly designed combination screening console may very well allow much of the salient detection data from the several domains described in this chapter to be collected and analyzed quite efficiently.

SOCIAL-EMOTIONAL FACTORS

Mother-Infant Attachment Dynamics

At a national conference on early screening and assessment, Starr (1973) summarized his thorough review of literature and synthesis of current knowledge about the social-emotional developmental factors from birth to 2 years. He stated, "At the present time there are few methods available which are useful in assessing social and emotional development during the first years of life" (Starr, 1973, p. 45). He went on to point out the multiple methodological and ethical difficulties involved in doing basic research on such clinical phenomena in very young children.

Germane to the social-emotional issues of early screening and assessment is a paper presenting a neonatal behavioral assessment scale by Brazelton et al. (no date). Although this particular paper is addressed primarily to the neurological "state" of the infant, its intent is to predict his later personality development, which is regarded, for purposes of this chapter, as largely social-emotional in nature. The first page of the rating scale, which is entitled *A Neonatal Behavioral Assessment Scale* (1973), is almost exclusively physically oriented, and the behaviors to be rated on the second page are largely sensorimotor; thus, some discussion of the scale is in the preceding section regarding physical factors. Nevertheless, the scoring sheet also rates such things as cuddliness, consolability, smiles, and general activity level, all of which may be variables contributing to the "sending power" (Murphy, 1968) of the infant and the consequent quality of interaction between him and his mothering one(s). The reactions which the neonate engenders in his caregivers seems to be quite predictive of later personality and social development (Kennell et al., 1974; Lewis and Rosenblum, 1974; Rutter, 1970) and even of abuse and neglect (Martin and Beezley, 1974). This example also serves to emphasize the difficulty of separating many of the screening procedures which overlap several developmental domains.

Structured Parental Observations of Children

An alternative to observing infants and toddlers in order to screen and assist their socioemotional developmental status is to rely upon the principal parenting adult in the child's life as an informant for completing various questionnaires, checklists, or inventories. One such instrument is a behavior problem checklist (developed by Quay and Peterson, 1967) which has been used with a wide variety of child samples and whose results have been replicated many times in spite of somewhat less than desirable interrater correlations. With regard to the interrater correlations, which are highly variable, and the fairly extensive literature which implies that parental recall is rather unreliable, Speer (1971) makes some pragmatic observations based on a combined ecological and phenomenological rationale (Figure 4) justifying a wide variability in data for a screening collection system and advocates a circumstantial analysis of any data gathered in this fashion. It may be more important to know how the parent perceives his DLD infant than to know the exact details of the child's feeding behavior. It would, indeed, complicate the process of selecting children at risk, since the degree of their risk estimate would be a function of idiosyncratic perceptions on the part of those reporting about them. In a prophecy-fulfilling manner, parents spontaneously interact less effectively with children they perceive to be damaged than with those they perceive to be developing normally, thus setting up another pernicious interactive cycle (Denenberg and Thoman, 1974).

Such an approach might prove enlightening to such findings as those reported by Albert and Davis (1971) regarding the Rimland diagnostic checklist on which the discrimination of autistic, normal, and schizophrenic children is quite cloudy and, in some instances, contradictory. It may be that the discrepant results on such checklists are to be expected and dealt with in a constructive fashion as representing differences in general perceptions of a child, not only by parents of both sexes, but also by any other caregiving adults who have primary relations with the child in varying circumstances. They assume that it is more reasonable to ascribe behavioral discrepancies to the reality of qualitative and quantitative differences in interaction patterns caused by the phenomenologically perceiving and reporting adult than by misperceptions on the part of that adult, since it is readily acknowledged that individuals, including children, perform differently in different situations with different people (Gergen, 1972).

Social Adaptation, Maturity, and Achievement Ratings

A somewhat more complex checklist for assessing the social abilities of 1- to 6-year-old children has been developed and is in the process of being refined by Ogilvie and Shapiro (1969). The content of the checklist is quite appropriate for a screening system. However, it probably would be very difficult to train paraprofessionals to use this checklist reliably and validly in its current form. An overall correlation coefficient of 0.87 was computed on paired ½ hour observations of 20 children, age 3–6, in seven preschools. This approach is desirable in the sense that it samples current behavior and does not rely upon recall by parents or other caregiving individuals. However, it does require a structured setting and well trained observers in order to get valid and reliable data. The *Camelot Behavioral Checklist* (Foster, 1974) falls in the same category of promising but unsatisfactorily validated instruments.

Another approach toward analyzing behavior of 1- to 6-year-old children is in White and Kaban (1971). This systematic approach requires that the observer adopt the child's orientation in order to describe the purpose behind a wide variety of the child's efforts. The manual delineates and exemplifies the highly specific scoring criteria and cites several examples of various kinds of social tasks such as to please, cooperate, gain approval, procure service, achieve social contact, gain attention, maintain social contact, avoid unpleasant circumstances, reject overtures, experience pure contact, avoid attention, annoy, dominate, direct or lead, compete, gain status, resist domination and assert self, enjoy pets, provide information, converse, and verbalize.

Some other measures of social adaptation, maturity, and achievement behavior have been organized and annotated by Mercer (1971a). Three of these seem to offer promise in use at the primary or secondary levels of screening. The first was developed by Terdal (1970):

> ... Specifically, it relates to behavior management and describes standard observational techniques to be applied in evaluating mother-child interactions that may form a basis for teaching "alternative repertoires" for handling retarded children. Laboratory observations are suggested in addition to interview-based information. Two types of coding sheets are presented which take the form of a matrix coding system. Each employs a time-sampling technique, and taps the child's behavior as well as the parent's response to the child (p. 1).

The other instruments mentioned by Mercer, which are complementary and obviously extend into several of the preceding developmental domains, are the *Vineland Social Maturity Scales* (Doll, 1966b) and the *Preschool Attainment Record* (Doll, 1966a). Emmerich's (1969) Parent Role Questionnaire also has the potential of being useful in this regard. However, the instrument has not yet been used, let alone validated, with other than middle class parents. The flexibility of being able to rely upon both informant and subject is helpful but would have to be controlled in any standard screening and assessment situation where comparable data are being collected. Many of the items would be quite appropriate for inclusion in any primary screening questionnaire.

Perhaps the best instrument for placing and following a child with rather severe DLD is the *Adaptive Behavior Scales* (Nihiria et al., 1969) which have been officially adopted by the American Association of Mental

Deficiency. However, in spite of the recognition of the scales and the implicit acknowledgment that adaptive behavior is an important dimension, physicians and psychologists still tend to rely almost exclusively upon estimates of intelligence to make major decisions about the lives of severely DLD children (Adams, 1973).

Prediction of Childhood Psychosis

It seems ironic that a conference concerned with high risk factors predictive of childhood schizophrenia was being held at the same time as the Boston Early Screening and Assessment Conference (President's Committee on Mental Retardation, 1972a). The irony lies in the fact that the schedulers for both conferences attempted to avoid as many potential conflicts for likely participants as possible and yet these two certainly competed, especially for some of the behaviorally oriented members of the community of scholars. It is no great consolation to learn from several who attended the conference on schizophrenia that their collective conclusion was that there really are no valid and reliable predictors of schizophrenia for very young children. Regardless of the rather seductive, overly simplistic theories, ranging from sheer organic etiopathogenesis (Mandell et al., 1972) to purely environmental causes (such as the schizophrenogenic mothering syndrome), childhood schizophrenia is evidently not yet satisfactorily predictable from early infancy. One statistical curiosity is that significantly more schizophrenic, manic depressive, and mentally retarded persons seem to be born during the first quarter of the year than during any other quarter of the year (Hare, Price, and Slater, 1974). The researchers suggest that this is explained by an increased risk of nutritional deficiencies and infections which may damage the constitution and enable these conditions to be more readily expressed in those genetically predisposed to them.

Nevertheless, progress is being made in separating young children into at least the more gross categories of psychotic versus nonpsychotic, which is a major task of a screening system. The differential diagnosis of psychotic conditions seems to hinge upon definitions, which in turn influence diagnostic systems and scales as reported by DeMyer et al. (1971).

The pendulum does seem to be swinging back in the direction of biophysiological substrates for many psychotic conditions in early childhood. Early screening systems will have to make provision for testing and monitoring the infant or child's reactions to challenge in both behavioral and physiological parameters (Alpern, 1967; Small, DeMeyer, and Milstein, 1971). Even the schizophrenogenic mother myth may be partially exploded on the basis of the maternal age factors; this appears to be the most salient finding in a study of parents of psychotic, subnormal, and normal children (Allen et al., 1971). Holding all other variables constant, parents of normals were significantly younger at the child's birth, which was an unexpected finding implying a neurological and/or genetic link between autism and subnormality. A genetic predisposition to schizophrenia has also continued to receive support in recent studies (Clausen and Huffine, 1974).

Functional Analysis for Intervention

In a summary at the end of their paper, Bijou and Peterson (1970) weave together a number of the loose ends from the preceding commentaries on various screening and assessment instruments and procedures. Their remarks are not exclusively related to social-emotional factors. Although their emphasis on follow-up may not be appropriate to screening itself, it is extremely important in the evaluation of whether or not a screening and assessment procedure is leading to accurate identification of children in such a way that description of their problems is sufficient for instituting remediation and/or prevention. This can only be determined on the basis of the efficacy of the treatment program, which is presumably matched to the diagnosis. Capute and Biehl (1973) echo the importance of doing a thorough functional developmental evaluation as a prerequisite to effective treatment planning and habilitation of DLD children.

COMPREHENSIVE DEVELOPMENTAL SCREENING SYSTEMS

Early Identification and Intervention

This section is primarily concerned with ongoing or proposed endeavors to identify children at developmental risk in a systematic and comprehensive way. The preceding four sections have each, for the most part, included only a limited domain of growth and development and generally excluded the others so that no one of them addressed the entire range of vicissitudes experienced by the developing human being.

> The ways of recognizing congenital handicaps are changing, and the act of diagnosis which depended on the recognition of fully developed clinical syndromes has been increasingly superseded. More and more often handicaps are recognized at routine examinations during infancy or because patients are considered to be "at risk" of suffering from them, and so are followed up (Ingram, 1969, p. 279).

A fairly simple beginning approach to what is being said by Ingram is referred to as the *First Identification of Neonatal Disabilities* (F.I.N.D.)

program in Arizona described by Wulkan (no date) and primarily focused on organically retarded children and their families.

Screening as Part of Total Service System

A somewhat more advanced conceptualization of the problems involved in a screening system and some suggested solutions are offered by Scurletis and Headrick (1972). Their *System of Comprehensive Health Care Screening and Service for Children* employs different levels of screening throughout and is designed to reach out and identify the high risk child and family in North Carolina and to introduce them into the appropriate service system. The use of the system has helped to define many of the characteristics of mothers and families who produce children at high risk for DLDs.

A preschool multiphasic screening program in rural Kansas is described by Belleville and Green (1971). This system, which is sponsored by the Kansas State Department of Health, was designed to help get planned well-child care to the widely scattered rural population. After getting promising results from a preliminary pilot program to identify vision and hearing problems in 3- to 5½-year-old children and receiving endorsement from the appropriate community agencies, the program has continued to grow. It now serves more counties and has broadened its goals to detect deficiencies of all the senses, mental retardation, emotional and/or behavioral disorders, and physical, nutritional, social, and economic deprivation. Other representative exemplary screening programs as parts of comprehensive service systems are described by Battle and Ackerman (1973) for the State of Illinois, the Governor's Council on Developmental Disabilities (1973) in California, and Lipscomb (1973) in Texas.

Screening in a Pluralistic Society

Although intended for purposes other than the design and development of a screening and assessment system and focused on children 5–11 years of age, Mercer (1972) has a number of enlightening findings and caveats for consideration before instituting any massive screening system. The study was fundamentally an epidemiological one to determine the prevalence of mental retardation in Riverside, California. She distinguished between clinical versus social system perspectives and statistical versus pathological models for defining normal. Warren (1973) added an engineering model for defining normal when discussing normalization and deinstitutionalization. Some of the ethnic implications of screening systems were also pointed out in Mercer's study. In addition to offering some answers to numerous questions about the interaction of ethnicity and sociocultural and socioeconomic factors with performance on intelligence tests, this

study is producing several other results relevant to screening and assessment programs in a pluralistic society.

As the pluralistic assessment project generates the products and
answers the questions it is designed to address, the results will have many
applications to earlier screening and assessment efforts as well. One of the
issues which repeatedly surfaces in such discussions and conferences is that
of labeling and classification of DLD children. Hobbs (1975b), Mercer
(1973), Samuda (1973), and Trotter (1975) all seem to concur with the
notion that most labeling as now practiced does more harm than good for
the DLD child and his family. They all acknowledge the theoretical value
of labeling for communication among researchers and practitioners, the
legislative value for designating who should and who should not receive
additional support, and the practical value for grouping recipients of
services in clusters most appropriate for a given intervention. Nonetheless,
the resultant compromises and complications of labels, especially when
wrong or misunderstood, are more often than not deleterious to the
DLD individual and his family in U.S. society. The pluralistic considerations for fairly interpreting these data number some 520 items in
the *Adaptive Behavior Inventory for Children* (Mercer, 1971a). As listed,
they would not be appropriate for infants and toddlers and a downward
extension of some of these items would not be feasible, but they do
illustrate some other family, neighborhood, and community dimensions
which must be taken into consideration. The proceedings from a conference sponsored by Educational Testing Service (1973) squarely or at least
obliquely faced many of the current social issues in testing. The interpretation of all screening data obtained from minority ethnic groups and lower
socioeconomic status populations will have to be weighted in accordance
with the relative contributions to the variance which are attributable solely
to the environment and which exercise considerable influence on subsequent adaptive behavior.

Multifactorial Developmental Screening Techniques

Since nearly all comprehensive and massive screening programs contain
provisions for assessing the developmental progress of children, it is important that some consideration be given to the current status of the multifactorial measuring instruments, methods, and materials now available for
doing this. Some of the more familiar tests and scales devised by Bayley,
Binet, Cattell, Doll, Gesell, Griffiths, Wechsler, and others are briefly
mentioned in previous sections of this chapter. However, each tends to
concentrate its in-depth assessment on only one or two factors of the
developmental domain and requires considerable time and training to

administer properly, thereby disqualifying each as a primary screen. At least five instruments warrant exposition and consideration as primary or secondary level screening instruments. These include *The Rapid Developmental Screening Checklist* (RDSC), *Guide to Normal Milestones of Development* (GNMD), *The Developmental Screening Inventory* (DSI), the *Boyd Developmental Progress Scale* (BDPS), and the *Denver Developmental Screening Test* (DDST).

A very simple and straightforward checklist consisting of 40 items covering the age range from 1 month to 5 years of age was developed by the Committee on Children with Handicaps of the New York Chapter of the American Academy of Pediatrics (Giannini et al., 1972). Called *The Rapid Developmental Screening Checklist,* this 1-page instrument has some brief instructions at the top and is designed to be used by a physician or aide. Once the norms are better established and appropriately adjusted, it might serve as a primary stage screening instrument for a widespread canvassing of a large population in a massive screening and assessment program.

An ingenious device called a *Guide to Normal Milestones of Development,* originally designed by Haynes (1967) for use by nurses dealing with infants and newborn children, serves as a handy reference and perhaps the basis of a primary screening system.

> The wheel consists of two discs fastened at the center so that they can be rotated one upon the other. A wedge-shaped opening in the top disc permits a view of a section of the bottom disc. On the top disc are listed basic reflex patterns. The bottom disc is divided into 11 wedge sections—one each for the 1st, 2nd, 3rd, 4th, 6th, 9th, 12th, 15th, 18th, 24th, and 36th months of age. As the wheel turns, symbols appear on the bottom disc next to the names of the reflex patterns printed on the top disc; these symbols indicate whether the reflex is present (+), absent (0), evolving or diminishing (±) at that particular stage of development (p. 55).

Also appearing in the wedge-shaped windows are abbreviated statements of some of the major milestones of development for that age.

A more thorough version of a developmental screening instrument, divided into 21 4-week periods spanning approximately 18 months of age, was created by Knobloch, Pasamanick, and Sherard nearly a decade ago and reported by Haynes (1967). The *Developmental Screening Inventory* breaks each 4-week segment into adaptive, gross motor, fine motor, language, and personal-social categories. Provision is made for recording responses as present, absent, or unknown and whether based upon observation or a caregiving adult's report.

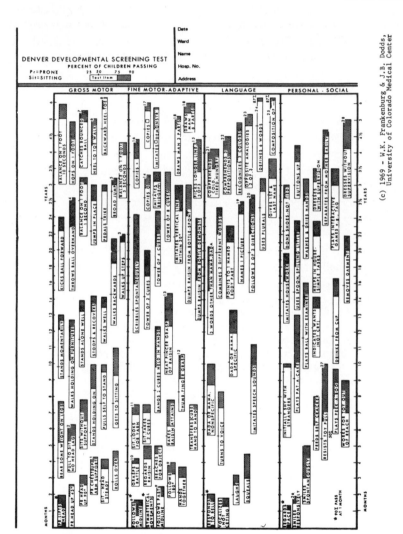

Figure 11. Denver Developmental Screening Test. (Reprinted with permission from Frankenburg and Dodds, 1969.)

Figure 11. Key to DDST.

1. Try to get child to smile by smiling, talking or waving to him. Do not touch him.
2. When child is playing with toy, pull it away from him. Pass if he resists.
3. Child does not have to be able to tie shoes or button in the back.
4. Move yarn slowly in an arc from one side to the other, about 6" above child's face.
   Pass if eyes follow 90° to midline. (Past midline; 180°)
5. Pass if child grasps rattle when it is touched to the backs or tips of fingers.
6. Pass if child continues to look where yarn disappeared or tries to see where it went. Yarn
   should be dropped quickly from sight from tester's hand without arm movement.
7. Pass if child picks up raisin with any part of thumb and a finger.
8. Pass if child picks up raisin with the ends of thumb and index finger using an over hand
   approach.

| 9. Pass any enclosed form. Fail continuous round motions. | 10. Which line is longer? (Not bigger.) Turn paper upside down and repeat. (3/3 or 5/6) | 11. Pass any crossing lines. | 12. Have child copy first. If failed, demonstrate |

When giving items 9, 11 and 12, do not name the forms. Do not demonstrate 9 and 11.

13. When scoring, each pair (2 arms, 2 legs, etc.) counts as one part.
14. Point to picture and have child name it. (No credit is given for sounds only.)

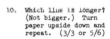

15. Tell child to: Give block to Mommie; put block on table; put block on floor. Pass 2 of 3.
    (Do not help child by pointing, moving head or eyes.)
16. Ask child: What do you do when you are cold? ..hungry? ..tired? Pass 2 of 3.
17. Tell child to: Put block on table; under table; in front of chair, behind chair.
    Pass 3 of 4. (Do not help child by pointing, moving head or eyes.)
18. Ask child: If fire is hot, ice is ?; Mother is a woman, Dad is a ?; a horse is big, a
    mouse is ?. Pass 2 of 3.
19. Ask child: What is a ball? ..lake? ..desk? ..house? ..banana? ..curtain? ..ceiling?
    ..hedge? ..pavement? Pass if defined in terms of use, shape, what it is made of or general
    category (such as banana is fruit, not just yellow). Pass 6 of 9.
20. Ask child: What is a spoon made of? ..a shoe made of? ..a door made of? (No other objects
    may be substituted.) Pass 3 of 3.
21. When placed on stomach, child lifts chest off table with support of forearms and/or hands.
22. When child is on back, grasp his hands and pull him to sitting. Pass if head does not hang back.
23. Child may use wall or rail only, not person. May not crawl.
24. Child must throw ball overhand 3 feet to within arm's reach of tester.
25. Child must perform standing broad jump over width of test sheet. (8-1/2 inches)
26. Tell child to walk forward, heel within 1 inch of toe.
    Tester may demonstrate. Child must walk 4 consecutive steps, 2 out of 3 trials.
27. Bounce ball to child who should stand 3 feet away from tester. Child must catch ball with
    hands, not arms, 2 out of 3 trials.
28. Tell child to walk backward, toe within 1 inch of heel.
    Tester may demonstrate. Child must walk 4 consecutive steps, 2 out of 3 trials.

DATE AND BEHAVIORAL OBSERVATIONS (how child feels at time of test, relation to tester, attention
span, verbal behavior, self-confidence, etc,):

The *Boyd Developmental Progress Scale* (BDPS; Boyd, 1974) consists of 150 items, some of which are immediately and directly observable and measurable and others of which are ascertained through parent interview (see Figure 2 in Chapter 2 for illustration of the BDPS). It is not intended to measure all developmental units but is focused on practical and useful developmental skills which are known to emerge at a given age and are related to daily living or are related to subsequent efficacy of adaptive behavior. It is one of several efforts stemming from the early 1960's to describe developmental progress graphically, thus avoiding the errors and misinterpretations involved in age equivalents or quotient scores.

> The *Boyd Developmental Progress Scale* is a screening device and may be given by any discipline among the helping professions (assuming reasonable care in following the directions). The results are combined in one visual report pictorialized on one page. Follow-up treatment can focus on the *development of desirable next step or remedial behaviors*. In short, the results should lead to meaningful action—whether more precise diagnosis, more realistic expectations, or more meaningful treatment or training (Boyd, 1974, p. 3).

A review of the literature indicates that validity and reliability studies done on developmental scales have not been widely undertaken or reported and the results are frequently not impressive. An exception to this is the *Denver Developmental Screening Test,* which has been subjected to relatively extensive and intensive reliability and validity studies (see Figure 11 for illustration of the DDST).

> Tester-observer agreement and test-retest stability of the Denver Developmental Screening Test (DDST) were evaluated with 76 and 186 subjects, respectively. The correlation coefficients for mental ages obtained at a 1-week interval were calculated for 13 age groups between 1.5 months and 49 months. Coefficients ranged between .66 and .93 with no age trend displayed (Frankenburg et al., 1971, p. 1315).

Of course, regardless of how reliable and easily administered a test is, it is far more crucial to be certain that it is measuring what it claims to be measuring and is therefore valid.

> In view of the widespread use of the Denver Developmental Screening Test (DDST) for screening the development of preschool aged children, a study was undertaken to evaluate the validity of the DDST. 236 subjects were evaluated with the DDST and the following criterion tests: Stanford-Binet, Revised Yale Developmental Schedule, Cattell, and the Revised Bayley Infant Scale. Correlations

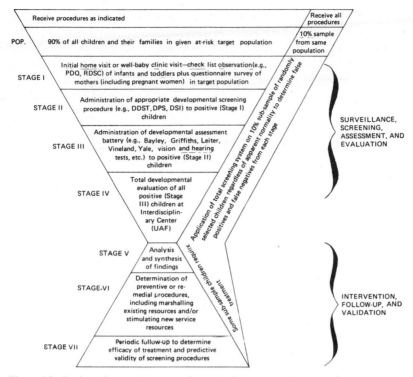

Figure 12. Design of screening research study. One suggested approach.

of mental ages obtained with the DDST and the criterion tests varied between .86 and .97. Scoring the DDST as normal, questionable, and abnormal agreed very highly with IQs or DQs obtained on the criterion tests (Frankenburg, Camp, and VanNatta, 1971, p. 475).

Most studies conducted which employed the DDST are generally supportive of the instrument in terms of face and concurrent validity even though some items are questioned in terms of familiarity to some groups. For example, vocabulary words like "hedge" and "pavement" are deemed inappropriate for many low SES minority ethnic children's experience. A Parent Developmental Questionnaire (PDQ) version of the DDST has been released subsequently (Frankenburg and Camp, 1975), but required more validation before massive application. However, in line with some of the preceding remarks in this and earlier sections, concern was expressed about its predictive validity, particularly with minority ethnic groups in poverty settings (Sandler et al., 1970 and 1972). One large study (Black, 1971) involved 1,629 preschool children, about equally distributed in age from early infancy through 5 years, with a significant skew toward children from lower SES environments, as determined by Hollingshead's *Two Factor Index of Social Position* (1957), which takes both income and educational level of parents into consideration. This study also partially questions the validity of the DDST as normed and scored for this population.

> According to the President's Committee on Mental Retardation (1969), three-fourths of the nation's mental retardation is found in rural and urban low-income, disadvantaged areas. Only 6 percent of the children in the study showed less than normal development as determined by the DDST. This is perhaps less than what one would expect for a population of children having approximately 80 percent in social classes IV and V . . . (Black, 1971, p. 58).

The validation of screening instruments and systems has been undertaken with older preschool and elementary school children (Bakalis, 1972; Denhoff, 1969; Hoffman, 1972; Meier, 1971; Sandler, 1972; Wyatt, 1971) and might prove instructive for designing validation studies for screening tests and procedures to be used with infants and younger children. Figure 12 depicts a design which would enable a longitudinal validation of some screening efforts. It can be readily determined from Table 5 of the preceding narrative that there are very few, if any, adequate single instruments for primary or subsequent screening and evaluation of young children at developmental risk. However, a careful combination of such instruments at appropriate stages and chronological ages promises to comprise a satisfactory comprehensive detection system leading to appropriate comprehensive interdisciplinary evaluations and intervention plans drawn from programs such as described in the next chapter.

chapter 5

Prevention/ Intervention Procedures for Developmental and Learning Disabilities in Infants and Toddlers

The title of this chapter suggests that DLD conditions can be prevented. If they originate within the individual, that is, are intraindividual in nature (see Table 3 and Figure 5), the most parsimonious and perhaps heroic preventive approach is that of preventing the conception of any individual who would be at high organic risk of being or becoming DLD. Remember that a truly comprehensive human development course runs the full gamut beyond womb to tomb to between erection and resurrection. Advocates of this preconceptual intervention are seeking fail-proof prevention of DLD individuals, at least those whose DLDs clearly have their origins within the skin of the individuals themselves.

The preceding chapters in this book have briefly mentioned the multifaceted aspects of the genetic and other related organic factors responsible for DLDs during the largely invisible but critical first 9 months of life in the mother. Other books, such as the one edited by Milunsky (1975), give an informed and contemporary account of advances in cyto-genetics and related disciplines contributing to enlightened genetic counseling and other helpful early intervention. It would be redundant to elaborate here upon the controversial issue of discouraging conception

between high risk procreative partners as the earliest and surest intervention procedure for many probable cases of DLD. Such primary prevention is an ideal that is seldom realized and that is fraught with moral
and ethical dilemmas, even for the most well informed and well intentioned
procreative partners. And even then, contraception against wanted children is accomplished only with considerable skepticism, usually after
having had at least one seriously impaired youngster, whose impairment is
clearly of genetic or other constitutional origin and which has a significantly better than chance probability to be repeated in any future children. Besides the private dilemmas faced by those intimately involved in
such family decision making, the controversy is raging in the more public
domain where members of groups such as the Right to Life movement
bitterly oppose members of the Planned Parenthood or National Organization of Women in terms of whose prerogative it is to decide whether or not
a potentially DLD child should be conserved or subsequently born.

In addition to not adequately employing the increasingly sophisticated technology now available for shooting some of these DLD anomalies
out of the saddle before they get a foot in the stirrup, there is an
increasing number, both absolutely and relatively, of DLD children. Many
more children who have been born with various degrees of DLDs are
surviving the previously fatal vicissitudes of infancy and early childhood.
They are entering and remaining in school, and some are subsequently
seeking employment and the good life, insofar as they are able to pursue
and enjoy it. It is neither humane nor prudent from the larger societal and
even legal point of view to assume the posture that the advent of a
handicapped child is simply the parents' tough luck. It has become even
more important and is becoming more widely mandatory through new
right to treatment and normalization legislation to program even the most
limited computers (human brains) to utilize their maximum capacities. To
assess the capacity of a computer, one of the first questions asked is about
the size of its core storage. That is, how many bits of information can it
store for later retrieval and processing? Likewise, in the human brain it is
very important to maximize the capacity of this human computer to
ensure that it gets rich data from birth when it is developing most rapidly
(North, 1968).

Until genetic counseling, prenatal diagnosis, and perhaps genetic
engineering or eugenics are more widely and efficaciously practiced, and
also fully accepted in the general public's ethics and attitudes as well as in
legislative governmental policies, it is obvious that there will continue to
be malfunctioning and limited computers produced. Since the vast majority of DLDs have no clear-cut etiology, it is exigent to employ the best

that is known in the current state of the art and science regarding early intervention programs beginning at birth for any individual at risk of DLD. Moreover, it is becoming increasingly apparent that many, perhaps the majority of DLD conditions, do not have their origin within the individual but are a function of the individual's environment, including other significant persons. It is apparent that, like the proverbial farmer who knows how to farm much better than he practices, most DLD conditions with intraindividual and/or extraindividual origins could and should be prevented if only what is now known were used (Begab, 1974; Gold, 1968; Goodman, 1972; Milunsky, 1975). The aforementioned irony of increasing numbers of DLD persons, both absolutely and relatively, suggests that the prevention of DLD is also a relative phenomenon in the sense that the prevention of further disability through early intervention is still prevention of otherwise inevitable further deterioration, although the total DLD may not be fully ameliorated or compensated. The specific genetic inheritance or other congenital idiosyncracies of a DLD person may establish certain ceiling limitations for growth and development but even these lowered ceilings will probably not be reached without appropriate intervention.

This chapter is divided into two main sections. The first section addresses the rationale for instituting intervention efforts early. For this book, early means starting at birth, since other books discuss preconceptual and prenatal intervention which is deemed to be beyond the purview and practice of most readers of this book. The first section reviews some of the representative recent and relevant literature about early intervention programs for both normally developing and DLD infants and toddlers. The second section presents and discusses a suggested schema for early intervention built upon the foundation of several representative and exemplary intervention programs.

The effectiveness of several efforts to systematically intervene in the lives of children from the culture of poverty with compensatory educational programs has been obscured by the largely negative and extremely controversial reports about the efficacy of massive intervention programs. However, positive acknowledgment has been accorded several small, well designed and carefully implemented compensatory preschool educational programs (White and Watts, 1973). This chapter makes no attempt to enter the impassioned polemics about why or in what way various large scale compensatory programs have allegedly failed. This chapter is concerned with a consistently strong thread woven through the blanket statements about preschool educational intervention, namely, that it should begin as early as infancy.

A conviction about early intervention prompted the Office of Child Development to launch, in 1967, as a logical downward extension of the popular Head Start Program, the original 36 experimental Parent and Child Centers, each serving about 100 children 3 years and younger, plus their generally impoverished families. Later, encouraged in part by the apparent success of the OCD efforts, the Bureau of Education for the Handicapped has seeded more than 100 infant intervention projects in its national First Chance Network.

This chapter presents a review of the relevant recent literature regarding infant education, marshals reasons for developing a systematic infant education program, and makes some suggestions as to how this might be accomplished, including recommendations for the empirical validation of an infant curriculum.

RATIONALE FOR EARLY INTERVENTION

Last Two Dynamic Decades

Intervention programs for young children did not develop overnight but rather over a period of many centuries, a history of which has been traced elsewhere (Braun and Edwards, 1972; Meier, 1973b). The foundations of early childhood intervention programs are, therefore, set upon deep and strong caissons of experience and theory from several interdisciplinary sources which collectively have withstood the shifting sands of fad and fantasy and act as a firm footing for more recent approaches.

As the American economy and its populace recovered from the military drain of World War II, the U. S. regained much of its domestic stability which had been shaken by the broken families in war and the baby boom shortly thereafter. Many insightful social critics again began to prod the social conscience of America. Examples were cited of children and their parents who were starving to death in the midst of unprecedented affluence and high average standards of living scarcely dreamt of a generation before. Coincidentally, but not accidentally, scholars in the field of child development, early childhood education, developmental psychology, academic pediatrics, and several other related disciplines were publishing findings which underscored the plasticity and educability of the human being. These discoveries served as cogent rationale for early intervention into the lives of children whose estimated intellectual potential would never be realized unless some compensatory experience was provided during the most modifiable first 5 years of his life (White and Watts, 1973).

During the past two decades, a significant portion of developmental research has been directed toward studying the effects of various high risk situations on the developing organism. Attention has been focused primarily on two high risk groups: the child with socioeconomic deprivation (extraindividual DLD), and the infant with high potential for organic damage (intraindividual DLD). The premature or low birth weight baby makes up a large proportion of this latter group. In considering the outcome statistics of this research, it seems that experiential deprivation, whether determined extrinsically (extraindividual/exogenous/ecological) or intrinsically (intraindividual-endogenous/organic), is the predominant contributing factor to DLD in the society today. If this factor can be eliminated or minimized by furnishing potentially handicapped children with more appropriate and therapeutic experiences throughout infancy and early childhood, it is believed that these disabilities can be minimized or prevented.

According to the Mental Retardation Clinic statistics published by the U. S. Department of Health, Education, and Welfare for the fiscal year 1968, 76% of the DLD population fell into these two categories of experiential deprivation. About one-third of this 76% was functioning as DLD, presumably caused by environmental factors alone, with no organic manifestations detected on routine examination. The remaining two-thirds of the group had organic manifestations frequently associated with histories of pre- and perinatal insults. Caution must be exercised in rigidly establishing a cause and effect relationship between the neurological manifestations and historical/obstetrical incidents which may, but may not, have caused the damage (Bowes et al., 1970). Other causes of neurological damage such as infection, injury, etc., were classified separately. The reader is reminded that these statistics are misleading in terms of the incidence of retardation, since one of the characteristics of members of the culture of poverty is that they do not know how to avail themselves of such services as mental retardation clinics and consequently are not reflected in the above statistics.

Further analysis of the HEW statistics, with regard to supplementary classification, revealed that 30% of the handicapped population has significant learning disability and an additional 25% falls into the category of minimal cerebral dysfunction. According to the government task force definition of minimal cerebral dysfunction, academic disability with normal or near normal intelligence is a major criterion of diagnosis. When one considers the etiological studies of children with minimal cerebral dysfunction (studies admittedly retrospective), the majority of cases have histories of pre- or perinatal insult and/or environmental deprivation. In essence, the intrinsically insulted baby and the extrinsically threatened infant are both at extreme statistical high risk to become DLD.

The reader should not ignore the potential overlapping of groups: when statistics are reported from clinics, professionals must categorize children according to predominant factors (see Figure 1, Chapter 1 for "combination" DLDs). In truth, the two high risk situations frequently co-exist. It is well known that poor prenatal care and prematurity are most prevalent in lower socioeconomic groups; by the same token, Drillien's (1964) follow-up study of prematures has shown that the "outcome" (in terms of IQ, school problems, etc.) of prematures is significantly poorer in those infants reared in lower socioeconomic homes than in those reared in middle class homes (see also Golden and Birns, 1971; Wachs, Uzgiris, and Hunt, 1971; Willerman, Broman, and Fiedler, 1970). It is a frustrating realization and exasperating feeling to consider an 8-year-old ghetto child, born prematurely, whose unwed teenage mother had no prenatal care, and to try to decide if his severe DLD is predominantly the product of his environment or his damaged nervous system. We are frequently forced into using classification systems which limit decisions in seeking and in applying appropriate intervention. Such hardening of the categories causes almost interminable arguments, and occasional misplacements, which is precisely why the Hobbs (1975b) report is so important.

In analyzing existing intervention systems, several shortcomings are immediately evident, which also interfere with the adoption of sound treatment procedures. These may be summarized as follows: (1) A preventive approach is rarely taken; when it is, it is at an age too late to be most effective. (2) Treatment is initiated after the handicap has severely disabled the child, and secondary complications have arisen. (3) Treatment focuses on only one aspect of the multiple problems presented, and the attempts to alleviate one symptom before others are attacked often result in incomplete or unsatisfactory results.

These shortcomings inhibit carrying out the interdisciplinary efforts expended in the comprehensive evaluation. Such inappropriate practices exist not only in the community, but also in clinical research facilities where the efficacy of one treatment approach is being compared to others (Komich et al., 1973). In order to facilitate the optimal development of any DLD child's potential, a comprehensive program must be implemented and consist of interdisciplinary (Figure 9) multiphasic intervention, where the various phases of the program occur simultaneously (Miller and Goldberg, 1975). Optimal programming can occur only if it is initiated at as early an age as is possible, especially if it has as its goal the prevention of additional secondary disability.

The efficacy of early intervention has been established by numerous research studies (see Ambrose, 1969; Ball, 1974; Beller, 1973; Bobath, 1967; Caldwell and Richmond, 1968; Denenberg, 1970; Fowler, 1972; Gordon, 1969; Horowitz, 1968; Illingsworth, 1973; Keister, 1970; Painter, 1969; Parker, 1973; Robinson and Robinson, 1971; Swartz, 1974; Westinghouse Report and Ohio University, 1970; White and Watts, 1973). Nevertheless, the problems of getting to these at risk populations at appropriately early ages are tremendous and need to be recognized in criticizing past and existing programs. Harkening back to the HEW statistics, it is found that less than 3% of the developmentally suspect population was referred under 12 months of age, and that less than 15% was referred under 3 years of age. Literally no reported cases were discussed prenatally in terms of high risk or preventive intervention. This lack of referral of young infants and children, even to highly specialized facilities, is most striking when one considers that 97% of developmentally handicapped children are not even detected during their first year, the most critical period for efficacious intervention. It is clear that serious attention must be given to gaining access to this population. Even with the best of community screening and early detection devices, valuable time may be lost before diagnosis is confirmed and intervention is begun. Children with milder disabilities may be missed until they are of school age.

With the valuable information from various outcome and prospective studies (Drillien, 1964; Lubchenco, 1969) and with statistical risk figures for many situations available, populations significantly at risk can be identified with relative ease. Therefore, the primary effort should be toward detecting the high risk situation, whenever possible, in the prenatal period (Richards and Roberts, 1967, and Rogers, 1968). Subsequent postnatal evaluation can then become an integral part of the intervention program. Such a situational evaluation will set the framework upon which a truly preventive intervention program can be built, one which is specifically designed to provide an optimal developmental environment for each child it serves. The more recently acquired higher cortical functions such as language, refined visual and auditory perception and discrimination, and abstract problem solving seem to be the more vulnerable to such insults. These more subtle distinctly human capabilities are typically the first to be impaired and unfortunately the last to be detected in infant assessment. The slight consolation given by the belief that early brain damage could be more readily compensated both physiologically and experientially, because of the greater plasticity of the developing brain, has now been disputed by Isaacson (1974). In reconsidering his data and lengthy experience with brain damaged infants, he concluded that the brain damage sustained by very young infants has more pervasive, diffuse, and pernicious effects on higher cortical functions than originally believed. Furthermore, Purpura (1974) has determined that the human brain is a good deal more mature at birth than previously believed, rendering it somewhat less amenable to intervention intended to capitalize on the plasticity phenomenon advanced by others (Sperry, 1958; White, 1967).

DLDs of Intraindividual Origins

The neurologically high risk infant has attracted a great deal of attention during the past decade. The thrust of this attention has been in two directions—first, to improve methods of perinatal care by the establishment of intensive care units for these babies in larger teaching hospitals and medical centers. There is no question that infant mortality has decreased as a result of this improved care. Second, the question of "intactness" of infant survivors has been exhaustively reviewed in various follow-up studies. There is no doubt that the high risk situation ultimately poses its greatest threat to the central nervous system of a developing infant and that, if permanent damage occurs, it is this system that bears the brunt of the insult on a long-term basis (Ireton, Thwing, and Graven, 1970).

Most of the infants considered to be of high risk are low birth weight, and, hence, most follow-up studies deal with outcome of these groups. Less information is available regarding follow-up of normal birth weight babies with perinatal complications which place them at significant risk. Although this latter group represents a relatively small percentage of the intensive care nursery population, they must be considered at significant high risk and are usually suffering from disorders similar to the complications of prematurity that do lasting damage. They are frequently infants with birth injury and hypoxia, respiratory distress, transient metabolic, hematological, and/or infectious problems, all of which can permanently insult the nervous system.

Much more specific information is available concerning the outcome of the low birth weight infant. Virtually all follow-up studies have shown a striking excess in proportions of dull and retarded children in low birth weight follow-up groups (Drillien, 1961 and 1964). Even in the best environments, the proportion of children considered below average at 2 and 4 years of age directly increases as birth weight decreases. Because the general outcome for the larger low birth weight infant differs in characteristics from the smaller infants, that is, those infants of less than 1,580 g (3 lb., 8 oz.), they will be discussed separately in the following section.

When one considers the very small premature (less than 1,580 g), literally all statistics agree on a poor prognosis regarding future development (Drillien, 1964; Lubchenco, 1969; Parmelee and Haber, 1973). Lubchenco reports on incidence and severity of DLD, within this group, which is inversely related to birth weight. Her findings are corroborated by Drillien (1964), Knobloch et al. (1956), and others, all of whom report an overall incidence of DLD in approximately 65% of the samples studied. In Lubchenco's population, 48% of the mentally retarded children had associated findings of cerebral palsy. Of additional interest was the fact that, of the 35 children followed with normal intelligence in this very low birth weight group, 20 were experiencing difficulty in school characterized by significant underachievement, problems in speech, reading, math, and behavior. And so the DLD plot or rationale thickens!

In low birth weight infants with birth weights greater than 1,580 g, less severe, but significant, defects in intellectual development are also shown. The incidence of actual DLDs in these larger preemies reared in enriched environments is only slightly increased over that of the full-term population, whereas the DLD incidence doubles when the matched low birth weight population is reared in deprived environments. When one disregards the extraindividual factors, it has been demonstrated that most of these low birth weight infants performed significantly below their siblings from the same biological parents and reared in nearly identical environments.

> From the findings reported so far, it seems likely that a combination of inferior genetic endowment, a poor environment, and restricted opportunity has a more marked effect on development in those who were small at birth than on maturely born children from a similar background (Drillien, 1964, p. 188).

It must be pointed out that an IQ of 100 in a child of a middle or upper class home, where parents and siblings are of above average or superior intelligence, may represent a relative DLD to that family. Again, the finding was prevalent that, of the small infants who did score within the average range of intelligence at ages 2 and 4, there is subsequently an increased incidence of learning disability and school maladjustment (Drillien, 1964).

All low birth weight infants are not premature, and further unpublished data from Lubchenco (1969) indicate that any infant that is small for gestational age is at statistical high risk when compared to infants of similar gestational age but appropriately sized for his/her gestational age. This impression of Lubchenco's is corroborated by Van den Berg (1968).

Twinning may represent another example of small for gestational age infants, as most will fall into this category when compared with singleton birth weight infants. Statistics also indicate that twinning involves some additional high risk (Drillien, 1964; Mehrotra and Maxwell, 1949). Premature twins show a significantly poorer outcome than paired singletons of like birth weight. There are many theoretical explanations for this: the intrauterine environment is not as optimal in terms of nurturance and mechanical factors; there is a higher incidence of birth trauma; there is a higher incidence of psychological problems in early childhood. The poor outcome for premature twins as compared to matched singletons is probably caused by a combination of the above factors.

While the incidence of mild brain damage and consequent learning disability is significantly high in all of the aforementioned follow-up studies, there are few prospective data to assist in determining the natural history of these disorders. The diagnosis is made when the child gets to school, and follow-up studies regarding this disorder are mostly retrospective. The aforementioned (Chapter 4) Werner, Bierman, and French (1971) 10-year study of the children in Kauai, Hawaii and the Brookline Early Education Project (Pierson, 1974) are outstanding exceptions to be discussed in more detail later in this and other chapters. In addition to lack of prospective data, there is an associated lack of supportive pathological data, e.g., supportive of the fact that these children are indeed mildly damaged.

Some animal experimentation is greatly illuminative, however. In the controlled asphyxia experiments reported by Windle (1969), all asphyxiated rhesus monkeys had striking pathological findings. There was marked depletion of nerve cell populations, not only in the cortex, but also in the brain stem, thalamus, dorsal spinal columns, and basal ganglia.

> The main structural defects involve centers that process signals from the environment and others that control association and integration of information (Windle, p. 83).

When one associates these pathological findings with the clinical findings in the same monkeys of transient neurological symptoms and later defects in memory and learning (5 and 10 years later in some instances), it represents the experimental model of perceptual dysfunction with mild organic damage, albeit in the monkey. It is not surprising that scholars like Lubchenco have found that 34% (or more) of high risk infants with normal intelligence are school underschievers with multiple problems with learning.

Environmental manipulation and stimulation programs (other than intensive medical care nurseries) are only recently being comprehensively tested for these neurologically high risk populations and the longitudinal data have not been adequately marshalled yet to make a clear case for optimum procedures. Some practical nursery procedures, such as parent counseling programs and consistent mothering from nursing personnel, have been incorporated into intensive care as well as normal newborn nurseries. In infant intensive care units across the country now, foster grandmothers are frequently employed to give loving attention to "sick" newborn infants like any sick child. Sensory stimulation projects for premature nurseries have been reported to have a beneficial effect on both growth and development of the infants studied (Barnard, 1973; Powell, 1974; Scarr-Salapatek and Williams, 1973; Solkoff et al., 1969). Earlier studies by Hasselmeyer (1964) and Freedman (1966) demonstrated beneficial immediate effects of sensory stimulation and rocking in the nursery. Leboyer (1974) is advocating a much gentler and more humane series of procedures in the delivery room to reduce the trauma of birth which he contends does untold psychic if not physical damage to the newborn person. The previous rigidly enforced "hands off" policies of premature nurseries are disappearing for various reasons (Kennell et al., 1974). When one considers that an infant might spend his first 3–6 months in an isolated environment with a dearth of stimulation, the possible DLD effects of such austere sensory and affective deprivation are frightening.

Workers in the field of cerebral palsy have been able to demonstrate impressive successes with high risk infants and have shown the salutory significance of early intervention (Bobath, 1963). While the effects of specific physical therapy on the neurologically handicapped population have been demonstrated to be efficacious, it remains to be shown that comprehensive, coordinated stimulation and therapeutic intervention will affect the long-term outcome of these neurologically high risk infants.

Maturation and Critical Periods

In a different tradition from the aforementioned studies of the effects of early experience, the work of Piaget (1962) has equally important theoretical significance. The relevance of Piaget's work for the present discussion lies in its emphasis on the critical importance of the earliest learning experiences. His work clearly implies that the later expression of intelligent behavior has its roots in the schemata laid down during the earliest months and years of life. Piaget's observations on the continuity of development point to the cumulative nature of intelligent behavior, which he conceptualized as a sequential unfolding process. Although he did not discuss the effects of deviant environmental circumstances, such as deprivation, on cognitive development, one can infer that without intensive exchange between the infant and his environment during the sensorimotor period (the first 18 months), there will be impairment of later adaptation and intellectual growth.

Piaget and Inhelder (1958) take an essentially maturational position and argue that specific levels of cognitive development must be achieved before certain conceptual strategies can be learned. Piaget's view is that the more new things a child has seen and heard, the more he wants to see and hear; the broader the child's repertoire (developed by experience), the more new relationships he can discover. Intelligence incorporates all the given data of experience within its framework; thus, the greater variety of experience to which the child has been exposed, the greater his capacity for coping with new experiences. This would be true of cognition as well as of sensorimotor intelligence. He feels that, in every case, intellectual adaptation involves an element of assimilation. But "assimilation can never be pure, because by incorporating new elements into its early schemata the intelligence constantly modifies the latter in order to adjust them to new elements" (Piaget, 1962, p. 6). The elements in the environment to which the child attends depend on his prior experience, and he learns only from that experience to which he attends.

Piaget, in stressing the importance of introducing learning based on the natural stages of the child's interaction with the environment, alludes to the problem of "appropriate match" between the new encounters and the earlier schemata already assimilated into the individual's repertoire. This principle of the match seems to be of great significance in both motivational and intellectual development, since a teacher or parent must match the learning encounter to the critical period of development of the child in which there is maximum capability for and interest in the learning of that particular material.

DLDs of Extraindividual Origins

Research on the determinants of functional retardation has revealed that more than two-thirds of "slow learners" and "school failures" are retarded on the basis of experiential deprivations frequently associated with the "culture of poverty," which have left their scars before the child enters school (Bloom, 1964; Hunt, 1961; Masland, Sarason, and Gladwin, 1958; Riessman, 1962). The apparent irreversibility of the effects of early deprivation makes it evident that social planning in the area of DLDs must include prevention as a first priority. Although the culturally determined

DLDs being considered here have no demonstrable organic correlates, they are as real and disabling to the individual as are the more grossly identifiable DLDs caused by brain damage and chromosomal defects. With the knowledge that preventive environmental measures are possible, it is necessary to discover the most effective ways to intervene in this problem which affects at least 5% of children entering school.

A primary thrust of the U. S. Government's interventions in the poverty cycle has been the early childhood education efforts of Project Head Start. While it is recognized that the Head Start Program has promoted the socialization and emotional development of most of the children involved, recent evaluations have suggested that some basic research and reorganization are necessary before this program can be of maximum benefit in facilitating intellectual growth and development (Beller, 1973; Bronfenbrenner, 1974). One of the major recommendations growing out of the Westinghouse Learning Corporation's assessment of Head Start (1970) was that intervention must begin before the preschool period of development in order to be maximally effective. This articulation requirement gave rise to various downward (Parent and Child Development Centers), upward (Follow Through and Developmental Continuity), and lateral (Home Start) efforts with some programs combining them all into a continuum of services for children 0–9 years old and their families. The notion of education during the first 3 years of life is not a new one, and it receives support from knowledge of the critical significance of this developmental period for later learning and adjustment.

The literature on the effects of socioeconomic class on development is uniform in its conclusion that there is strong, positive correlation between environmental deprivation and intellectual deficit (Deutsch and Brown, 1964; Heber, Dever, and Conry, 1968; Masland, Sarason, and Gladwin, 1958). This, of course, is what led Heber et al. (1972), Meier (1970), and others (Williams, 1972 and 1974) into developing compensatory programs for low SES children and their families. Although it has been demonstrated repeatedly that low SES children are at least equal to middle SES and upper SES children in sensorimotor abilities very early in life, by 18 months of age the adverse effects of environmental deprivation manifest themselves in the measured intellectual inferiority of the low SES child. From that point on, the curves of normal intellectual growth for low SES versus environmentally enriched children show a continuing divergence (Bayley, 1965; Deutsch, 1967; Knobloch and Pasamanick, 1953). In fact, Kagan (1968) has found that, as early as 4 months of age, babies in low SES homes vocalize significantly less than do babies in upper middle SES homes. Sears, Maccoby, and Levin have hypothesized that the fundamental difference between lower and middle class childrearing practices lies in the variable of "access to information." Bernstein (1961) has made a similar suggestion in his formulation of the linguistic difference between the classes. He suggests that communication in lower class families is marked by an absence of verbal elaboration and language-mediated internal cues, as contrasted to the highly elaborated nuances of communication found in the verbal transactions of middle class families. This reliance of lower class families on nonverbal and implicit modes of communication results in a lack of stimulating verbal input which is so necessary to the development of language in young children.

Since verbal facility has been shown to be the best predictor of later intelligence (Bayley, 1968), it is evident that ways must be found of providing children in the culture of poverty with models for language development in the earliest months of life. Developmental services, including day care programs for infants and toddlers, have become a central part of the compensatory intervention efforts, for example, the federally sponsored Parent and Child Centers and Community Coordinated Child Care (4-C) centers. The preponderance of proposed federal legislation, such as the Child and Family Services Act of 1975 (Mondale, S-626, 1975), maintains an emphasis on very young children and their parenting ones. These programs provide a convenient means for implementing language programs for disadvantaged children. Another method of stimulating language development is instructing parents to set aside some time each day for reading to their infants. Irwin (1960) did an experiment in which lower class mothers read to their infants for 10 minutes a day, beginning at 13 months of age. When tested after 7 months of this treatment at 20 months of age, the experimental infants were found to be superior to a control group in all language functions.

Parental Extraindividual Influences

Bruner (1966), using Piaget's work as a cornerstone, has used a wide variety of experimental techniques and takes as one of his major themes the impact of culture in the nurture and shaping of growth. His view is that cognitive growth occurs as much from the outside in as from the inside out, which reinforces the previous statements regarding the nature/nurture issue and intraindividual/extraindividual origins of DLDs.

Freiberg and Payne (1967), in a review of parental influence on cognitive development in early childhood, report a mounting evidence for the potency of early environment in shaping later cognitive abilities. They note that the early learning deficiencies and the "cumulative deficit" resulting from a deprived environment have been identified as DLD origins by many researchers. They cite Zingg's classic study (1940) to point out that there appear to be extremes of social and cultural deprivation resulting in a cumulative deficit for which compensatory training provides only limited benefit. They conclude that "the formation of cognitive and intellectual skills can be reasonably conceived of as developmental in nature and modifiable by variation in the environment" (p. 68). If human cognitive development is to be enhanced through early environmental enrichment or other intervention, then the home or other preschool program must be recognized as the beginning educational unit (Caldwell, 1970a; Kohlberg, 1968; Schaefer and Aaronson, 1972; Yarrow, 1968)— not the traditional school. Gray (1971) states that the mother plays a key role in providing environmental control conducive to learning in the child's early years. Rolcik (1965) found a significant relationship between scholastic achievement and parental interest in the child and in his education. Shaw and White (1965) concluded that the child-parent identification bore a relationship to school performance, while Norman (1966) found that the parent value system influenced academic achievement. Hess and Shipman (1965), who assessed interaction patterns of mothers and children from several socioeconomic classes, argue that cognitive growth is dependent on the cognitive meaning in the parent-child communication system, and that the mother's pattern of interaction and communication with the child tends to determine whether the child later will actively participate in formal educative processes and other basic institutions of society. Other studies underscoring the importance of the interaction patterns between infants and mothers (Ainsworth, 1969; Beckwith, 1971; Carter, Rheingold, and Eckerman, 1972; and Lewis, 1972) as well as fathers (Baumrind, 1971; Kotelchuck, 1973; Pederson and Robson, 1969; Rebelsky and Hanks, 1971) are being reported with increasing frequency and cogency.

Renewed interest is being focused on the interaction between the family and the infant at risk (Beckwith, 1974). Siqueland (1973), for example, found that intervention with premature infants in the first few weeks of life changed the infants so that they thereby evoked more responsive interaction from the mother. Similarly, Beckwith (1972), Falender (1973), and Saltz (1973) found that intervention produced more talkative children who asked more questions and made more requests which in turn provoked more verbal interaction from the mother. This view suggests the possibility that the timing of various accomplishments, such as mother-infant coupling immediately after birth (Kennell et al., 1974), might be important insofar as it influences the mother's subsequent interaction with her child. Moreover, projects such as the Office of Child Development's Project Homestart and Meeting Street School's home-based program (Denhoff et al., 1974) exemplify the emphasis again being placed on intervening with the parents and families of DLD children and have reported considerable success in counseling with and otherwise involving parents in the care of their DLD infants and toddlers.

Fowler (1962) summarized a large body of research done by educators and psychologists who have evaluated techniques applied to children during their preschool years in order to accelerate intellectual growth. Fowler felt that Gesell (1954) and McGraw (1939), who attempted to support a maturational point of view, often de-emphasized the fact that "specific training invariably has produced large gains regardless of whether training came early or late in development." In this same review, studies on verbal memory and language improvement point to the advantages of early verbal stimulation provided by oral, written, and dictational material, as well as to the general experience gained in making observations and learning to discriminate between objects.

Bloom (1964) studied all of the available data published from a number of longitudinal studies carried out over the last half-century. He concluded that "the introduction of the environment as a variable makes a major difference in our ability to predict the mature status of a human characteristic" (p. 184). Furthermore, he suggested that "in terms of intelligence measured at age 17, about 50% of the development takes place between conception and age 4, 30% between ages 4 and 8, and about 20% between ages 8 and 17" (p. 88).

Caldwell and Richmond (1967), who performed a systematic study of the environments of infants of varying SES backgrounds, stressed that it is as important to measure the environment or ecology in which a child's growth and development are occurring as it is to measure the developmental processes themselves. Bayley studied the relationships between infant development and SES; in 1965, she published standardization data on a sample of 1,409 children. At all assessment points up to 15 months of age, there were no significant differences as a function of sex, birth order, parental education, etc. Coleman (1966) found that as early as first grade most groups of children from lower SES backgrounds and most children representing minority groups tended to score significantly lower than the national average on most measures of school achievement and, thus, lower than children from high SES backgrounds. These deficits increased as the children progressed through the typical school experience. Caldwell noted that lower SES homes varied greatly in their stimulation value and that SES alone failed to discriminate low SES children with favorable environments from those with unfavorable environments.

The heterogeneity of home stimulation among lower SES families is also supported by Werner, Bierman, and French (1971), who found that their educational stimulation scale was much more predictive of later school success than was any SES variable. The following presents and discusses a few of the noteworthy findings from their study entitled *The Children of Kauai*. This was a longitudinal study of children from the perinatal period through age 10 from a wide range of ethnic and socioeconomic backgrounds, all living on the Island of Kauai, one of the Hawaiian Islands. In retrospect, it was discovered that for each 1,000 live births, an estimated 1,300 pregnancies were required because of early and late fetal deaths. Of the 1,000 live births, about 850 children at 2 years of age remained free of any observable physical defect or serious developmental disability. By the time they were 10 years old only two-thirds of the original 1,000 children were considered to be functioning satisfactorily in school and having no recognizable physical, intellectual, or behavioral problem. During the period from conception to 10 years of age about one-half of the subjects either died or had some handicap. Many of the handicaps were the more diffuse ill-defined minimal cerebral dysfunction manifestations or the sort of things seen in the deaf-blind rubella child or the child who has sensory impairment problems for other reasons.

This Kauai study analyzes a great deal of data and demonstrates some very meaningful relationships between various environmental predictions of handicap. For example, the structured family interview item dealing with an educational stimulation rating predicted IQ 10 years later better than parental socioeconomic status, education, occupation, or intelligence. Environmental casualties are shown to take a much greater toll than hereditary factors, underscoring the urgent need for prevention and intervention programs beginning at conception or before. Werner (in press) has now completed an 18-year follow-up analysis on the children in the Kauai study; these findings are reported and discussed in Chapter 9 and which further corroborate the notions of environmental casualties *vis à vis* DLDs in adolescence.

One of the greatest contributors to the wide heterogeneity of the home environment, regardless of social class, is the wide variety of parenting behaviors. The type of concern shown for the child in terms of fostering either dependency or independency is often crucial (Bayley and Schaefer, 1964; Hess and Shipman, 1965; Lorr and Jenkins, 1953). Some parents exercise a kind of democratic guidance and enjoy a pleasant harmony with the child whereas others are at best benevolent authoritarians in their parenting styles, which has been shown to have a profound influence on the child's development (Baumrind, 1971; Bing, 1963; Shaeffer, 1971). Parenting behavior is also reflected in the general home organization, which also impinges upon the child (Baumrind and Black, 1967; Bayley and Schaefer, 1964; Honzik, 1967a; Lesser, Fifer, and Clark, 1965; Moore, 1967). Although these studies were done on parenting behaviors as related to normally developing children, the dynamics also obtain and the negative interaction cycles may even be exacerbated if the child has an intraindividual DLD condition. On the other hand, the parenting behavior itself may be so debilitating as to precipitate and maintain a DLD condition in the child. Clarke-Stewart (1973) reported that an infant's intellectual and social development during the first two years of life is optimally facilitated if his mother or primary caregiver provides varied stimulation, shows affection, and responds fairly quickly and consistently to his signals.

One of the most influential and timely publications during these dynamic decades was *Intelligence and Experience* (Hunt, 1961), which marshalled all of the existing evidence into an overwhelmingly compelling argument that the experiences derived from one's environment during the early years of life have a profound and irreversible impact upon his subsequent level of intellectual functioning. Hunt (1961) presented evidence dissonant with the assumption of fixed intelligence in pointing to research showing that: (1) IQs of identical twins reared apart are lower than the IQs of identical twins reared together (Newman, Freeman, and Holzinger, 1937); (2) IQs of infants obtained at successive stages show considerable variation (Bayley, 1940); (3) IQ rises with nursery school experience of foster home children; and (4) orphanage-reared children score lower on tests than do children reared in foster homes (Skeels and Dye (1939). The combination of the scholarly work by such renaissance thinkers and investigators as Bloom (1964), Bruner (1966), Denenberg (1963), Deutsch (1967), Fowler (1962), Gray (1966), Hess and Shipman (1965), Lewis (1964), Murphy (1968), and many others, plus the political wisdom of providing the American public with a respectable cause tantamount to making the world safe for democracy or protecting innocent countries from ruthless aggressors, resulted in the mid-sixties declaration of a national War on Poverty.

The Supreme Court decision of 1954 also served as a catalyst for polarizing scholars who had for years been waging battles about the relative importance of heredity and environment on human growth and development. This centuries-old nature/nurture controversy was highlighted by the recurring phenomenon of newly integrated low socioeconomic status children from black and Chicano homes into the view and very lives of the more advantaged. Ethnic minority children were more readily identifiable by virtue of superficial traits of skin pigmentation and/or characteristic surnames than were their equally deprived Anglo counterparts, all of whom were failing in competition with age mates who came from more enriched and privileged backgrounds.

In spite of the failure syndrome stereotypically attributed to and perhaps prophesy fulfilling (Rosenthal, 1966) for children of low SES and ethnic minority status, existing research data failed to support any pervasive genetic determinants to account for their persistent low quality performance when confronted with the academic demands placed upon them in middle and upper class school programs. Adding fuel to the perennially raging fire of the nature/nurture controversy was a report issued by Jensen (1969), which in itself was a scholarly contribution, but which lent itself to volatile interpretations causing a great deal more heat than light. Marshalling the evidence from numerous studies, he cogently demonstrated that better than half, in some cases up to 80%, of the variability in children's performance on intelligence tests was attributable to inherited capabilities. However, Jensen's over-zealous disciples neglected to point out the corollary that environmental influences are accountable for 20–50% of the variability, and that many children were being nurtured in very limiting, indeed intellectually and otherwise crippling, environments. Furthermore, the modifiability of intelligence was becoming more clear in such intervention studies as the efforts by Heber and associates (1972) discussed in a later section of this chapter.

Two Assumptions Discredited

From before the turn of the twentieth century through the 1940's, there were two basic, long entrenched assumptions which influenced both the science and the practices of childrearing: "fixed intelligence" and "predetermined development." These two assumptions suggested that intelligence and other developmental abilities are functions of an inherited capacity which increases at a fixed rate to a predetermined level. The intelligence quotient, which adjusts the estimate of intellectual functioning to one's chronological age, accordingly remains constant throughout life. This point of view overlooked the corollary findings that deprivation of experience caused marked retardation in the rate at which the infant developed intellectually and otherwise.

Wellman (1940) conducted another study through the Iowa Child Welfare Research Station and compared the spring and fall test performance of 652 children who had enrolled for one academic year in the nursery school. Spring tests, after a year in nursery school, averaged 7.0 IQ points higher than those which had been given the previous fall. For 228 children who had 2 years of nursery school experience, there was a gain of 4.0 for the second year. For the 67 children who attended nursery school for a third year, the mean gain was 8.0 for the first year, 4.0 for the second year, and 2.0 points for the third year. These children were matched with a control group which showed that between the fall and spring testings the schooled group gained 7.0 points, while the unschooled group lost an average of 3.0 points.

The pioneer studies of Spitz (1945, 1946a, 1946b) have had great influence in establishing the notion that intelligence is not fixed but plastic and modifiable and that adequate mothering is crucial for optimal growth and development during the first year of life. One of Spitz's studies was concerned with infants from a foundling home, where the infants received very little attention of stimulation after being weaned from their mothers at 3 months of age. The other infants were in a nursery attached to a penal institution for delinquent girls where the mothers were allowed to play with and attend their children every day throughout the first year. The foundling home children came from well adjusted mothers whose only handicap was that they could not support themselves or their children. The nursery children were mothered mostly by delinquent minors, some of whom were physically defective, psychopathic, and criminal. The mean developmental quotient for the 61 children in the foundling home dropped progressively during the first year of the infant's life from a starting level of 131 to a final level of 72. On the other hand, the nursery children rose from 97 to 112 by months 4 and 5, remained level to months 8 and 9, then dropped to 100 for months 10 and 12. The mean for the first 4 months was 101.5 and for the last 4 months 105. Unfortunately, these findings were explained and rationalized away for a long time. The belief that development is entirely predetermined and intelligence fixed was advocated by G. Stanley Hall, who communicated the belief to his students and to the child study associations of America. Consequently, the belief was widely held, even though compellingly contradictory evidence existed. This is a good example of selective perception described in Chapter 2 and depicted in Figure 4.

Importance of Environmental Enrichment—Animals and Humans

Hebb (1949) concluded that experience is an essential requirement for the formation of so-called cell assemblies, since it is the mediator of neural connections. Thus, it is the earliest experience of primary learning input which forms much of the pattern for later information-processing capability in the system and which serves as the initial software program for the human computer hardware and, thus, the interdependency between intra-individual and extraindividual functions.

Gray and Miller (1967), in reviewing the literature on cognitive development, point out that early experience has four dimensions: the nature of the experience itself, timing in the developmental period, duration, and intensity. Each dimension may differentially affect cognitive structure and development. Studies of lower animals are noteworthy, but the scope of this chapter only permits the brief mention of a few.

Rats reared in darkness take longer to learn pattern discrimination than those reared in light, and rats handled as pups give birth to more adaptive pups (Denenberg, 1963). Rat pups of handled or generally more stimulated mothers are more active and alert than offspring of less stimulated mothers (Denenberg and Thoman, 1974). Pets (cats and dogs) reared in a home with more attention and stimulation do better in learning situations than laboratory-reared animals (Scott, 1958; Scott, Fredrickson, and Fuller, 1951). Studies by Denenberg (1964), Harlow (1963), and Levine (1960), with various kinds of laboratory animals, have all led to the conclusion that close physical contact and stimulation are essential for adequate physiological, emotional, and adaptive development. Some other investigations (Bennett et al., 1964; Krech, Rosenzweig, and Bennett, 1962; Purpura, 1974; Wallace, 1974) have shown that rearing in enriched environments produces anatomical as well as biochemical differences in the brains of rats; not only were the experimental animals more proficient on problem-solving tests, but also they were found, on autopsy, to have more of an enzyme (acetylcholinesterase), which is associated with synaptic transmission of neural messages (data processing) in their brains.

The research relevant to infant intervention using human subjects has been mainly concerned with the consequences of maternal deprivation and institutionalization, and the developmental effects of handling and physical contact. The earliest carefully conducted and reported studies on the effects of maternal deprivation (Bowlby, 1951; Spitz, 1946a) were alarmingly grim in their description of the devastating and lasting consequences of early lack of mothering. Subsequent investigations (Dennis and Najarian, 1957; Goldfarb, 1955; Provence and Lipton, 1962) have led to similar, although perhaps less extreme, conclusions. In essence, they have shown that children deprived of a consistent mothering figure in early life are significantly behind normal children on almost all measures of growth and development. The most strikingly deficient areas are language behavior and social competence.

Since neither institutionalization nor mothering is a pure or unitary variable, subsequent investigations have endeavored to isolate the factors in the mothering process which are crucial for the infant's development. One such factor which is now known to be basic is the handling of the infant. Brody (1951) reports that visual attentiveness in infants is highly correlated with the amount of handling provided by the caregiving person. Studies by Casler (1965), Rheingold (1961), and White, Castle, and Held (1964) have shown that additional handling of and attention to institutionalized infants facilitate their development and increase their alertness. Spitz has suggested in his formulation of the "cradle of perception" that the infant can only begin to see and learn about the environment through her/his close physical relationship with his/her mother. Along these lines, Korner and Grobstein (1967) recorded the visual scanning behavior of 12 neonates, and observed that their eyes were open 90% of the time when being held, and only 25% of the time when either left unhandled or moved to a sitting position. Clearly, this finding suggests that the development of early visual-motor schemata is facilitated by handling, since it is known that the child even at this young age can discriminate between visual cues (Fantz and Nevis, 1967). Yarrow (1963) found a similar result in a study of children in foster care. He discovered a significant correlation between developmental test scores at 6 months and ratings of amount and appropriateness of maternal handling. Rubenstein (1967) reported a significant positive relationship between ratings of maternal attentiveness and measures of exploratory behavior and preference for novel stimuli in 5-month-old infants.

INTERVENTION PROCEDURES AND MODEL PROGRAMS

Beyond Paralysis of Analysis

When a satisfactory comprehensive developmental screening system has been field tested and thoroughly debugged as suggested in Chapter 4, it is only useful for DLDs if it is matched with practical intervention programs. Otherwise, the child gets caught in a paralysis of analysis, wherein his DLD is analyzed incessantly and no synthesis or plan of intervention is ever formulated, much less tried. Several successful intervention procedures and model programs have been reported in the literature, a representative sample of which is briefly reviewed herein.

Table 6 presents a matrix of screening, evaluation, and intervention considerations in a composite and essentially self-explanatory format. It is beyond the purview of this chapter to elaborate upon all of the various procedures, instruments, and model programs mentioned or implied at various points in the matrix. Several of the programs mentioned in the preceding rationale section are slightly elaborated upon to form a better base for the suggested model infant education system and curriculum. It is most desirable for any child in this system to begin and remain normal, thus progressing down column II. However, for those who yield positive screening results (column III) and are subsequently found to have bona fide developmental delays or disabilities (column IV), the sooner that they are identified and placed in properly matched remediation/prevention programs (examples of which are mentioned in column V), the better it is for the child, the professional, and the society. Since individual subjects and individual professionals and paraprofessionals bring various requirements to each case, several options are mentioned in the evaluation and intervention columns.

This entire chapter, therefore, based upon the current state of the art and knowledge, suggests what must be done to approach optimum matches among the most efficacious approaches to screening, evaluation, and intervention for young DLD children or for those at risk of DLD. Many of the answers are not available yet, and it is hoped that several heuristic issues have been or will be raised to prompt further research.

Preconception through Newborn Intervention Suggestions

It is, of course, rare that an opportunity presents itself for preconceptual screening and risk assessment regarding the likelihood of a DLD child's being conceived, especially if it is to be the first child of the potential parents. This is a strong argument for courses and other educational programs aimed at adolescents in junior and senior high school to inform them about the various risk factors and the means for either preventing pregnancy in the first place or ensuring as many positive conditions as possible for a planned pregnancy. One promising movement in recognition of this need is the National Consortium on Early Childbearing and Child-rearing, which sponsored state-wide conferences throughout the United States to address these critical issues in consort not only with school board, school administration, health care, and other establishment representatives, but also with the cooperative planning of pregnant and frequently unwed teenage mothers (and occasionally fathers). These young parents historically have been systematically discriminated against, ridiculed, and maintained in a state of ignorance and shamefulness by a punitive puritanical system, all of which serve to seriously exacerbate the debilitating features of the typically unwanted pregnancy and attendant responsibilities.

In addition to the obvious necessity for good prenatal, perinatal, and postnatal care, another promising avenue for prevention of DLDs, whose cause can be traced to chromosomal or genetic aberrations, is genetic counseling. Several DLDs have been linked to specific chromosomal or genetic anomalies. Thus, the probability of recurrence of DLDs in the

TABLE 6
SCREENING, EVALUATION, AND INTERVENTION
FOR YOUNG CHILDREN AT DEVELOPMENTAL RISK*

I Age	II Satisfactory Progress If not ⟶	III Screening and Risk Assessment If screening results or risk factors are positive ⟶	IV Evaluation, Close Observation and Diagnosis to ⟶	V Intervention and Follow-Along ⟶
PRE-CONCEPTUAL	Intent to Conceive Adaptive & Physiological Readiness (Normal Maternal & Family History)	Presence of One or More Maternal Risk Factors: Physical/Medical 1. Malnutrition 2. Age < 16 or > 35 3. Poor Reproductive History 4. Suspect Metabolic and/or Genetic Disease Social/Behavioral 1. Low SES 2. Sixth Grade Education 3. Functionally Illiterate 4. Low Adaptive Behavior Rating	Nutritional/Metabolic Tests Derive Genetic Pedigree Literacy/Educ. Tests Adult Adaptive Behavior Rating (Nihira)	Genetic Counseling (Sterilization) Diet Therapy Contraceptive Counseling (Planned Parenthood) Maternal Training (Jr. & Sr. High School)
PREGNANCY (first 3 mo)	Request for Service (suspected pregnancy confirmed) Regular OB/GYN Checks Normal Progress	Complications During Pregnancy: 1. Infections 2. Rubella 3. Toxemia 4. Drug Overuse 5. Radiation 6. Blood Incompatibility 7. Malnutrition 8. Maternal Psychosis 9. Unwanted Pregnancy	Appropriate Medical Tests to Evaluate Maternal & Embryo Condition Amniocentesis Social/Behavioral Tests of Maternal Ability and Attitudes	Counseling Therapeutic Abortion Psychotherapy
PREGNANCY (last 3 mo)	Regular OB/GYN Checks Normal Progress	Above First Request for OB/GYN Services	Evaluation of Maternal and Fetal Condition	Counseling Positive Attitude (Natural Childbirth)
NEWBORN (first month)	Hospital Admission Normal History of Pregnancy and Routine OB/GYN Checks Uneventful Delivery	Complications During Delivery: 1. Hemorrhage 2. Dystocia 3. Excessive Anesthesia 4. Trauma 5. Placental Damage 6. Cesarean 7. Premature (SGA) 8. Postmature 9. Hospital Admission with no Prior OB/GYN Checks	Appropriate Medical Tests to Evaluate Maternal & Infant Condition	Necessary Procedures to Insure Maternal and Infant Viability
INFANCY	Normal Neonatal Growth & Development	Pediatric Physical and Developmental Exam: 1. Apgar (5 min.) 2. Metabolic/Genetic Screens (e.g., PKU) 3. Trauma 4. Infection 5. Malnutrition 6. Head Circumference 7. Guide to Normal Milestones of Development (@ 1 mo.)	Behavioral & Neurological Assessment Scale (Brazelton & Horowitz, @ 1 mo.) Environmental Quality Maternal Attitude & Aptitude (Below for Specifics)	Sensory Stimulation Behavior Modification Environmental Enrichment Maternal Training (Below for Specifics)

	II	III	IV	V
Age	Satisfactory Progress If not ⟶	Screening and Risk Assessment If screening results or risk factors are positive ⟶	Evaluation, Close Observation and Diagnosis to ⟶	Intervention and Follow-Along ⟶

I — INFANCY

Monthly Well-Baby, Physical and Developmental Checks (1st year)	Physical: 1. Trauma 2. Infection 3. Diseases 4. Malnutrition 5. Vision 6. Hearing 7. Maternal Postnatal Depression/ Rejection, Neglect and/or Abuse 8. Prolonged Separation of Infant from Mother	**DQ** — Albert Einstein Scales of Sensori-Motor Development; Fantz-Nevis Visual Preference Test; White-Held Visually-Directed Prehension Test; Gesell Developmental Scale; Bayley Scale of Infant Development
		Cognitive Q — Ordinal Scales of Cognitive Development; Griffiths Mental Development Scale; Kahn Intelligence Tests; Infant Rating Scales (Hoopes); Kuhlman-Binet Infant Scale; Infant Intelligence Scale
Normal Progress Bi-Monthly Physical and Developmental Checks (2nd year)	Developmental 1. Rapid Developmental Screening Checklist (@ 6 mo and 1 yr) 2. Developmental Screening Inventory (@ 18 mo) 3. Developmental Progress Scale (@ 12, 18, 24 mo) 4. Denver Developmental Screening Test (@ 12, 18, 24 mo) 5. Behavior Problem Checklist (@ 24 mo)	**Environ./Parent Q** — Caldwell (A Procedure for Patterning Responses of Adults and Children – APPROACH); Parental Attitude Research Instruction; Parents' Attitude Scale; Wechsler Adult Intelligence Scale (WAIS)
		Language Q — Irwin Speech Sound Development Test; Prelinguistic Infant Vocalization Analysis (Ringwell, et al.); Shield Speech and Language Development Scale; Early Language Assessment Scale (Honig); Receptive-Expressive Emergent Language (REEL, Bzoch)
		Ach. Q — Preschool Attainment Record (Caldwell)
		P/N Q — Psychophysiological/Neurological Maturity (Brazelton, Crowell)
		Soc./Behav. Q — Vineland Social Maturity Scale (Doll); Emotional Maturity Adaptive Behavior Scales (Nihira); Pluralistic Assessment (Mercer)

Intervention and Follow-Along (Column V for Infancy):
Bobath & Ayres (Physical Therapy)
Gordon (Home Learning Center – Florida)
Gray et al. (DARCEE)
Heber & Garber (Milwaukee Project)
Keister (North Carolina Infant Day Care)
Lally & Honig (Syracuse Infant Project)
Levenstein (Mother-Child Home Program)
Parent-Child Center Programs (Costello, Holmes)
Meier et al. (Education System for High-Risk Infants)
Robinson (Frank Porter Graham Infant Project)
Weikart & Lambie (Ypsilanti-Carnegie Infant Education Project)
White & Kaban (Brookline)
Haynes (United Cerebral Palsy Assoc. Infant Stimulation Projects)
Bureau of Education for the Handicapped, First Chance Network

TODDLER – EARLY CHILDHOOD

| Periodic Physical and Developmental Checks (approximately every 6 mo.) | Pediatric Physical Exams (see above considerations) Developmental Screens (Nos. 4–6 above); Peabody Picture Vocabulary Test; Goodenough-Harris Draw-A-Person | Preschool Inventory (Caldwell) Leiter International Performance Scale Slosson Intelligence Test Raven's Coloured Progressive Matrices Stanford-Binet Intelligence Scale Developmental Articulation Test (Hejna) Illinois Test of Psycholinguistic Abilities (Kirk & McCarthy) Verbal Language Development Scale (Mecham) Developmental Test of Visual-Motor Integration (Beery) Developmental Test of Visual Perception (Frostig) Detroit Tests of Learning Aptitude Minnesota Preschool Scale IPAT Test of G-Culture Fair (Cattell) Arthur Point Scale of Performance Tests California Tests of Mental Maturity and Personality Metropolitan Readiness Test Oseretsky Tests of Motor Proficiency Weoman Auditory Discrimination Test | Model Preschool Programs (by last names of developers – for designation, see sources below). Anderson & Bereiter Blank Hooper Kamii Karnes, Zehrbach, & Teska Meier Miller & Camp Montessori Nedler Nimnicht Palmer Robison Shaeffer & Aaronson Weikart Whitney & Parker |
| Normal Progress | | | |

*Developed by Meier for California Governor's Conference on Prevention of Developmental Disabilities, 1973, pp. 23–24.
SOURCES: Battle and Ackerman (1973); Guthrie and Horne (1971); Hoepfner, Stern, and Nummedal (1971); Meier (1973a and 1973b); Parker (1972); and Williams (1972).

offspring can be communicated to parents contemplating more children. Ideally, all couples who have histories of DLDs in their families should obtain genetic counseling and understand the risks involved before conceiving children or consider the appropriateness of a therapeutic abortion. On the other hand, many of these DLDs are both rare and recessively inherited, so that parents can often be reassured that the chances of giving birth to another DLD child are relatively slight. Now that the procedure of amniocentesis has been perfected, it is desirable to do it when the risk is high that the developing fetus is destined to be DLD because of some detectable chromosomal anomaly.

Although prenatal causes of DLDs are multifactorial, early and comprehensive prenatal care should significantly lower the incidence of DLDs. The goals include adequate maternal nutrition, prevention of prematurity, prompt treatment of maternal infections, expert management of diseases such as diabetes and eclampsia, and avoidance of radiation and rubella. Rubella immunization of all children is critically important in draining the reservoir from which pregnant mothers contract this developmentally crippling fetal disease. Other viral diseases have recently been indicted as contributing to the incidence of DLDs. The physician who is going to be responsible for the physical care of the child should see the mother during pregnancy and consult with her obstetrician. No drug should be taken by pregnant women except on urgent medical indication.

The results of investigations now under way promise to help to clarify which perinatal factors most seriously affect subsequent development. Smith et al. (1972) have reported some very encouraging findings along this line. Anoxia, hemorrhage, trauma, hyperbilirubinemia, and hypoglycemia have been shown to result in brain damage to animals and humans. Improved obstetrics and newborn care can prevent some of these insults. The sensory and maternal deprivation many premature and sick infants experience should be avoided. Sensory and emotional stimulation can often be provided by handling the child, holding him during feedings, and assigning a foster grandmother to infants who must undergo long-term immobilization or isolation from their primary caregivers.

The President's Committee on Mental Retardation and other epidemiological studies have shown that 50–75% of retarded children come from the lower socioeconomic level, and that the developmental problems of a majority of children appear to be related to poverty. Although polygenic inheritance of subnormal intelligence remains a possibility, increasing data indicate that the causes of DLDs in this large group of children are largely environmental and preventable. It is not the traditional role of physicians to engage in social reform, but their success in recognizing venereal disease and tuberculosis as social problems led to effective intervention and prevention. The examiner who takes a similar view of DLDs should advocate better nutrition, early and periodic screening, individualized preschool enrichment experiences through improved and more numerous day care centers and nursery schools, family planning, universally available prenatal care, and better medical care for children by whatever means may be required to minimize the incidence of children with damaged or poorly functioning nervous systems and diminished learning ability.

Since the physician or other health care specialist is frequently the first to examine a child, it is important to be alert to detecting conditions which are conducive to DLDs. These conditions include metabolic errors, endocrine dysfunction, cerebral anomalies, and many others. Similarly, specific treatment of associated problems such as seizure control, management of strabismus, and therapy for cerebral palsy are available elsewhere. Circumstances leading to brain damage or dysfunction must be prevented or promptly treated. Examples include accidents, poisoning, child battering, CNS infections, electrolyte disturbances, inadequate nutrition, and anesthesia. Prompt treatment of infections, assistance in feeding and diet, medications for organically caused hyperactivity, and management of associated medical problems, while they do not constitute specific treatment of DLDs, are important in the general care of the child. For detailed accounts of evaluations and care for various pediatric problems see Kempe, Silver, and O'Brien (1974).

Parents of a DLD child need periodic discussions about their child regarding diagnosis, etiology, prognosis, home management, educational placement, plans for the future, and progress. When the detection of a DLD is first determined, the impact of having a DLD child may be overwhelming and the parents may selectively perceive only what they wish to hear, requiring repetition several times to get the entire message. Thereafter, interviews with the responsible professional should be scheduled at regular intervals (i.e., every 6–12 months) to discuss the child's current status, problems, and questions which inevitably occur as the child matures. It is important that the parents realize that physicians and allied health professionals are interested and willing to talk with them about their DLD child. Occasionally, parents who are having an unusually difficult time understanding and accepting their child's DLD condition may require referral to a psychiatrist, psychologist, or social worker. Assistance from a public health nurse or visiting nurse is often helpful; problems stemming from feeding, toileting, and general home management are best handled by means of home visits by such nursing or parent education personnel.

Local chapters of organizations, such as the National Association for Retarded Citizens, the Association for Children with Learning Disabilities, the National Cerebral Palsy Association, and the Epilepsy Foundation of America, are helpful to many parents. Sharing of common problems, parent education, information about resources and new developments, and a forum for community action to improve services for DLD children are available through such organizations. Sometimes the severity of a DLD condition raises the question of whether or not a child should be placed in a residential institution. Placing a DLD child in an institution involves the parents in difficult, emotion-laden decisions which may require considerable help. Even severely DLD children should be kept at home for at least the first 3 years of life if possible and if the caregivers are willing and competent, because the nondeprived and supportive home environment has proved to be more beneficial than an institution for most young severely DLD children. The decision to institutionalize is typically a last resort and should be the least restrictive setting for the severely DLD child. When other reasonable options have been exhausted, one should seek placement in an institution where the children are happy, self-sufficient, show intellectual growth, manifest minimal stereotypy (such as rocking), and manifest no excessive need for social reinforcement. Considerable parental counseling is generally required to facilitate the placement and to prevent later resentment and guilt. Some of the bases for institutionalization are as follows: (1) more nursing care is needed than the parents can provide; (2) the family is unable to accept the child in the home; (3) the community lacks day care educational or training facilities; and (4) disintegrated or negligent family circumstances make it impossible to provide an enabling home for the child.

In abnormal development, many professions have specialized knowledge which may be useful in evaluating an incipient DLD. If the child's behavior seems unusual or bizarre, consultation with a child psychologist or psychiatrist should help determine whether or not a psychic disturbance is the basis for aberrant development. Social workers and visiting nurses are particularly helpful in the assessment of complex families in determining etiological factors as well as providing assistance in treatment. Besides these nonmedical personnel, neurologists, orthopedists, ophthalmologists, psychiatrists, developmental pediatricians, physical and occupational therapists, and public health nurses are but a few of the specialists who can help in evaluating and managing the disabled child. Consultation with a comprehensive child development clinic or center is sometimes indicated, particularly where multifactorial causation makes it necessary to obtain the help of many interdisciplinary professionals (see Figure 9).

Some Infant and Toddler Intervention Models

Specific instructional techniques to be used by parents to assist the young child's optimum development are becoming available from multiple sources. McCandless (1961) reported a study by Irwin (mentioned earlier) indicating that working class mothers who spent 10 minutes per day reading to their child, from 12 months to about 20 months of age, achieved improvement in all phases of language acquisition. Fowler (1962), in his surveys of gifted children, one of whom was his daughter, indicates that these children were generally exposed to instructional techniques developed by a parent, and many learned to read by age 3. Meier (1970), Moore (1961), and Nimnicht (1967) reported encouraging results from using a nonautomated "talking typewriter" system for enabling very young preschoolers to learn to read, among many other accelerated "academic" achievements. These procedures and concepts were then formulated into an autotelic responsive environment (Meier, 1973a) for widespread implementation described in detail in Chapter 7.

One concern which is inevitably raised in discussion of group day care for infants has to do with its effects on mother-child attachment. A report by Caldwell, Heider, and Kaplan (1968) compared a group of home-reared 30-month-old children with a group of children of the same age who had been enrolled in an infant day care program in regard to patterns of child-mother and mother-child attachment. No differences were found. There was an association, however, between strength of attachment and amount of stimulation and support for development available in the home. A related issue has to do with the effects of multiple mothering. On the basis of the results of Rheingold (1961) and Caldwell and Hershel (1964), it seems that the presence of more than one mothering person has no ill effects if all the "mothers" are good and are working together. What is known about the development of children raised in the Russian children's collectives (Bronfenbrenner, 1970) and the Israeli kibbutzim (Spiro, 1958) gives no reason to believe that there is anything detrimental about multiple mothering. The whole gamut of variables currently perceived to be most important for facilitating optimum child development in center-based day care, such as adult/child ratios and training of the caregivers, is being carefully investigated in a massive study under the auspices of the Office of Child Development. Unfortunately, it is too early at this writing to report any findings, but some of the preliminary results will probably affect the modified version of the Federal Interagency Day Care Regulations scheduled to be released in 1976.

Weikart and Lambie (1968) stated that the proliferation of pre-schools may be attacking the problem of enhancing educational opportunity of the disadvantaged child in the wrong way. Perhaps amelioration of his learning deficits might be made more effective by retraining the parents. The Perry Project uses weekly home visits to provide direct instruction to the child, to share with the mother information about the educative process, as well as to encourage her to participate in the actual teaching of her child. The home visitor's demonstration of child-management techniques indirectly teaches the mother the most effective ways of handling her children.

Another project which was established to meet the needs of children from homes lacking so-called mainstream cultural and economic advantages is a research and demonstration unit started by Caldwell and Richmond (1968). Their educationally oriented day-care program for children from 6 months to 5 years of age had as basic program goals: (1) to create an atmosphere in which infants and children can grow happily; (2) to be a bridge between whatever culture the parents offer to the culture of a larger world; and (3) to provide specific learning experiences for stimulating cognitive growth of the infants and children. Staff of the unit, which is part of a larger research project on patterns of learning during the first years of life, included educators, nurses, social workers, researchers, and pediatricians. In the first year, the IQs of the 29 children who attended the center for 3 months or more showed average increases of 5.5 points, while the control group showed a downward drift. In general, when the child's environment, including the parents, was seriously deficient in cognitively enriching opportunities, the IQ of the potentially bright control children dropped as much as 20 points in the period between the ages of 6 months and 24 months.

Children from enriched and stimulating home environments gain substantially more intellectual power and potential, as measured in IQ points, than do their control counterparts from less stimulating homes. The environmental deprivation found in the homes of many children attending central day care programs may constitute a fundamental limitation of day care in counteracting the effects of an unstimulating home environment (Wachs, Uzgiris, and Hunt, 1971). Consequently, recent efforts are increasingly directed toward intervention efforts delivered in the home (Wright, Lally, and Dibble, 1970).

Although the curriculum of many intervention programs is highly structured and theoretically oriented, the aforementioned home-based intervention studies of Gordon (1969), Palmer and Rees (1969), and Weikart and Lambie (1969) showed that the specific curriculum may not be as important to the success of the program as the method by which any well conceived regimen for stimulation is carried out. When the stimulation is parent-child centered and somewhat playful, with emphasis on the existing strengths of the child, parents tend to maintain the stimulation regimen between sessions and even after the termination of home visits. Both the Gordon and Weikart programs showed gains before 12 months of age. Palmer and Rees showed substantial gains between 24 and 36 months of age. Grim (1974) has produced a useful compilation of annotated references to books, articles, films, and other materials about facilitating parent involvement in such programs.

Schaefer and Aaronson (1972) also proposed a carefully structured approach to curriculum and emphasized the need for careful training of intervention personnel. They noted the lack of response of some mother-infant dyads to the intervention program and stated that mothers who scored high on hostility were associated with hostile infants who subsequently had depressed mental test scores at 36 months. Experimental group infants who showed the greatest gains had mothers who had flexible, spontaneous, and pleasant relationships with them. The importance of the quality of the caregiver/child interaction, especially where DLD children are concerned, has gained renewed emphasis in the studies reported by Beckwith (1974) and Denenberg and Thoman (1974).

The home-based program of Levenstein (1970) has shown some of the most impressive gains in IQ scores during and following the 2-year program which typically began at 20 months of age with children of apparently normal potential. The explicit purpose of the home visits is for the "toy demonstrator" to model verbal stimulation techniques for the mother through the medium of a prescribed sequence of books and toys. The mother is encouraged to take over the toy demonstrating as she becomes more familiar with the materials and procedures. Levenstein (1971) has shown a cost/benefit advantage over other home-based programs in that the volunteers and mothers who have been through the 2-year program with their own children have become effective toy demonstrators themselves. Moreover, of great significance to early home intervention efforts, reports show that gains made by the early intervention children have been maintained into the first grade.

In other studies, when the experimental subjects have "regressed" toward the control group, they have done so following too early termination of a program (Weikart and Lambie, 1969; Gordon, 1969; Levenstein, 1970; Caldwell and Richmond, 1967) and because the program failed to involve the parents to a degree sufficient to alter the home environment (Starr, 1971). Levenstein attributes the unusual holding power of her program's effects to having influenced the mother's childrearing habits as well as to continuing the intervention intensively for 2 years during the most critical period for language development. Lane (1968) states that the mother is a small child's most important teacher. The staff, in order to influence the mother's style of teaching, has devised different tasks such as games, puzzles, walking boards, and so forth. These materials are then left in the home for 1 or more weeks, after their use has been explained in detail and understood by the mother, who becomes responsible for educating her child, influencing his attitudes toward learning by stimulating curiosity, etc., all through the use of prescribed tasks.

The next noteworthy demonstration project is the Milwaukee Project (Heber et al., 1972). Besides being mentioned in numerous technical and research-oriented journals, it has received acclaim in several more popular magazines such as *American Education* which recently ran a feature article about the Milwaukee Project entitled, "Can Slum Children Learn?" The answer is a very strong yes. The results of a survey (Heber, Dever, and Conry, 1968) revealed that children whose mothers are retarded have a 14 times greater chance of being retarded or DLD themselves. Consequently, an experimental intervention program was launched to determine whether or not some of the retardation and related DLDs can be prevented. A highly structured program was designed to greatly enrich the early environment of these children. The Milwaukee Project started with newborn infants in their homes for the first year of life and then brought them into a center for 5 days a week of various structured and unstructured experiences. Unfortunately, the specific curriculum used with each infant was not carefully documented, although considerable information does exist about the overall program. It is now exigent that replication studies document very carefully every part of the intervention program and its differential impact on each child because the children in the Milwaukee Project made remarkable gains which have held extremely well. Experimental children have maintained a mean IQ of 120, independently assessed in second grade, as compared to a mean IQ of 80 in controls, whose IQ is still dropping.

The Office of Child Development has sponsored 36 experimental Parent and Child Centers across the country. These are each designed to provide comprehensive services to approximately 100 children, 0–3 years of age, who are euphemistically described as disadvantaged, environmentally deprived, culturally different, low SES, ethnic minority members of the culture of poverty. The 36 programs, three of which are highly research oriented, bring these young children and their parents into centers for various and sundry services including cognitive stimulation. Although conclusions from preliminary findings are guarded and premature in terms of positively influencing later performance of the infants, the results are very encouraging from programs which have been in operation for several years (Costello, 1970; Holmes, 1972; Johnson et al., 1973; Rafael, 1973).

The Parent and Child Centers (PCC) also take ideas and materials into the homes of the participating infants and toddlers. Several beginning guides for infant curriculum, such as the booklet by Segner and Patterson (1970), were forthcoming from these PCC Programs. The guidelines describe the kinds of things a mothering person might do with an infant, including illustrations, some rationale, written procedures, and lists of necessary equipment, which are very simple and readily available. To ensure easy and correct use of each learning episode, the La Junta, Colorado PCC staff (Cranson, 1970) placed the pieces of equipment for each episode in separate cloth bags on which the instructions for their use were written in outline form.

The aforementioned three highly research-oriented Parent Child Development Centers (PCDCs) have also begun to yield some very promising results (Robinson, 1975). First, they have been able to retain high percentages of both the random control and the experimental groups, which have also remained essentially equal across all salient matching variables, including SES. Second, there has been nearly a 12-point mean difference in cognitive development in favor of the experimental groups at 3 years of age and as much as 20 points difference by 4 years, i.e., 1 year after leaving the enrichment program. Third, measures of mother/child interaction show changes among the experimental mothers toward styles of interaction that are supported by theory and research to be facilitative of superior infant development along social, emotional, and cognitive dimensions. Fourth, data now show that the positive short range effects on children are being retained and even extended by the effects of increased competence among the experimental mothers, which argues very well for a truly preventive model. Fifth, the general success of the PCDC models has led to the initially modest replication of three more centers, made possible by the unprecedented combination of federal (OCD) and foundation (Lilly) support. The nearly exclusive dependence upon the child's mother as the primary intervention/prevention agent in the PCDC model offers a significant and considerably more cost/beneficial alternative to the Milwaukee Project's replacement of the mother and home for the critical early years.

Changes in mothers' child-rearing behaviors, skills, and attitudes vary somewhat between models, but are significant in all three programs. The program effects on participating mothers are especially notable because they are congruent with the whole body of research and theory dealing with the relation of mother characteristics that are causally linked with high early and sustained levels of child development. Some of the most important changes in participating mothers, in comparison to control mothers, are as follows: (1) more sensitive to childrens' social, emotional, intellectual, and developmental needs; (2) more accepting of children; (3) more affectionate, warmer, use less punishment, praise more; (4) more aware of causes of child distress, more skillful in allaying distress, comforting child; (5) more aware of range of individual differences between children, place less value on stereotypic expectations for children; (6) use more and more complex language with child, encourage child verbalization more; (7) reason more with children, use less punishment, place less emphasis on authority as shaper of desired behaviors, praise child initiatives more, encourage exploratory behaviors more; (8) feel less restricted by child-rearing and home-making tasks, find children more interesting and enjoyable; (9) pursue own educational development more; and (10) use community agencies more skillfully to meet family and child needs.

Both pre-post and group comparisons show the following evidence of program impact on target children compared to control children: (1) greater attentiveness, awareness, and response to new and discrepant experiences in first year, followed by more exploratory behaviors in second and third years; (2) greater vocalization in early months, more and more complex language skills achieved earlier in second and third years; (3) significantly higher general cognitive development as measured by Bayley at 20+ months, and by Stanford-Binet at 36 months (gains are retained or extended at 48 months, whereas controls (except Mexican-American) lose); (4) earlier and stronger attachment to mothers, followed by earlier and stronger explorativeness, greater capacity to relate to strangers in second and third years; (5) social interactions with mother richer in texture, in vocalization, touching, smiling, proximity, seeking to share discoveries, more eye contact and verbalization from distances, etc.; and (6) more and richer play behaviors and fantasy, sharing first with mothers, and then with other adults. In later cohorts where mothers' changes emerge earlier and stronger, developmental differences between experimental and control infants emerge earlier and stronger.

The Portage Project (Shearer and Shearer, 1972) is one of the most successful of the more than 100 First Chance Programs sponsored by the Bureau of Education for the Handicapped. It initially served 75 preschool multiply handicapped children aged 0–6 years, was conducted exclusively in the children's homes, and has developed a library of curriculum cards each containing one of a series of sequential learning episodes. It has subsequently enjoyed widespread replication throughout the U. S. based upon results such as are mentioned in the following citation.

> The average IQ of the children in the project was 75 as determined by the Cattell Infant Test and the Stanford-Binet Intelligence Test. Therefore, it would be expected that on the average, the normal rate of growth would be 75 percent of that of the child with normal intelligence. Using mental ages, one would expect that the average gain would be about 6 months in an 8 month period of time. The average child in the project gained 13 months in an 8 month period; he gained 60 percent more than his counterpart with a normal intelligence (Shearer and Shearer, 1972, p. 216).

A comparison was made between randomly selected children from the Portage Project and randomly selected children attending local classroom programs for culturally and economically disadvantaged preschool children. The Stanford-Binet Intelligence Scale, the Cattell Infant Scale, and the Alpern-Boll Developmental Skills Age Inventory were given as pre- and post-tests to both groups. In addition, the Yale Revised Developmental Schedule was given as a post-test to both groups. The Portage Project children made significantly greater gains in the areas of mental age, IQ, language, academic development, and socialization, as compared to the group of similar underprivileged children receiving typical classroom instruction.

Many experienced nonworking mothers acknowledge and complain that, although they had lots of time for their first child and really showered all kinds of attention on him or her, with each subsequent child they had correspondingly less time to interact. It is easier to neglect the little one than it is to ignore the ones who can talk and make their demands known, so that the younger ones tend to get progressively less adequate interaction with adults. Studies about superior intelligence, including such classics as Terman's *Genetic Studies of Genius* (1925), indicate that it is the firstborn who typically tends to grow and develop in the cognitive area most fully and rapidly. Some of the recent birth order studies also support this notion (Zajonc, 1975).

Various crib apparatus are now being explored, not to substitute for human mothering, but rather to supplement the interaction which an infant has with his environment during those many alert moments he otherwise spends staring into space in a relatively sterile and unresponsive environment. A truly responsive environment for infants very likely facilitates their developing a sense of control over their destiny which is closely linked to competence (Baumrind, 1970; White et al., 1972). Such competence enables a person to move easily into new situations, to deal efficiently with vast amounts of new tentative data, to be comfortable in complex situations, to have a relatively high tolerance for ambiguity in such situations, in short to have effective coping behavior which is essential to avoid Toffler's *Future Shock* (1970).

For the past decade, the writer has been actively involved in developing responsive environment preschools (Meier, 1970; Nimnicht and Meier, 1966). More recently, he has extended the principles of an autotelic responsive environment to the first extrauterine learning environment of the infant, namely, the crib environment. The resultant supercrib allows the infant as young as 3 months old: (1) to summon the adults by sounding a buzzer or bell; (2) to operate a videotape playback unit for replaying appropriate portions of such programs as Sesame Street as well as various face schema and other audiovisual materials; (3) to control a continuous loop film projector for movies on the ceiling; (4) to control flashing lights strung around the periphery of the ceiling; (5) to control an audio tape playback unit with music and/or language programs on it; (6) to control a vibrator, which burps the baby out of both ends, or a heartbeat simulator, both of which have a very quieting tactile-kinesthetic effect; and (7) to control the room illumination with an easily manipulated dimmer.

Several of the items are on time-delay switches so they go off automatically and must be reactivated for another cycle. Other apparatus can be controlled to alter additional features of the environment, including heaters, fans, etc. A long arm supports a manipulandum which the baby can grab or just hit with fisted swiping and cause a motorized mobile hung up above on another arm to rotate. The experimental version also has several event and time unit counters to record the number of times and duration various items are operated in order to give some index to their autotelic properties, that is, how intrinsically interesting they are to an infant. It is too early yet to draw any conclusions about the efficacy of these supercribs; the number of infants receiving such experiences is so small to date that any conclusions will be tenuous. The children who experienced such responsive environments in their infancy several years ago are extraordinarily competent and well adjusted at this writing. Caplan (1973) has pursued the creation of similarly enriched infant environments and reports favorable results not only for the children involved but also for the quality and quantity of concomitant caregiver/infant interaction.

A longitudinal study of Negro males in New York City was reported by Palmer (1969), in which the experimental infants were given two 1-hour education sessions a week in a one-to-one situation. There were two types of training: "concept training," which included systematic instruction; and "discovery," in which the same play materials were presented, but with no instructions. After 8 months of such training, which was begun at age 2, both experimental groups were superior to controls on such diverse tasks as the Stanford-Binet Intelligence Test, language comprehension and use, perceptual discrimination, motor behavior, delayed reaction, and persistence at a boring task. This superiority of the treated groups was still present on retesting 1 year later. Palmer proposed four factors to account for this effect: (1) the regularity of exposure to a structured learning condition; (2) the affective relationship between instructor and child; (3) the uninterrupted nature of the instructor-child interaction; and (4) the increasing realization by the child that he could respond to educational experiences and be rewarded for his response.

Probably the largest scale and most thoughtfully planned infant education project undertaken to date by a single investigator is the one at the University of Florida under the direction of Gordon. This program utilizes disadvantaged women to train other disadvantaged mothers in techniques of infant stimulation used at home. A report (1969) of Gordon's findings indicates that, at the end of the first year of the project, the children whose mothers had been given instructions in infant education were superior to control children on the Griffiths Mental Development Scales (useful for longitudinal follow-along since the scales have a range of 0–8 years of age). At the end of the second year, the same differences obtained for those children who had been in the program from 3 months to 24 months of age, as well as for those who had participated from 12 months to 24 months of age. However, those children who were enrolled only from 3 months to 12 months of age were not significantly different from their controls, which suggests that the "headstart" gained during the first year is lost unless the education program continues during the second year of life. It is interesting to note that there was a language lag on both the Griffiths and Bayley Scales for those children enrolled in the education program, as well as for the controls. This suggests that the language deficits in the environment of these children were not completely offset by the stimulation program. However, the fact that the developmental quotients of the "educated" children were elevated in comparison to controls gives encouragement for developing more effective programs.

Although demonstration projects (Caldwell, 1967b; Gordon, 1969; Keister, 1969; Palmer, 1969) have shown that education experience in the first 3 years of life can enhance intellectual development, there has been no systematic evaluation of the effectiveness of various approaches to stimulating the infant. It is now known that infant education is efficacious, but little knowledge exists as to when and how to intervene with what experiences for maximal benefits. It is clear that projects are needed which have the primary goal of developing a detailed curriculum of materials which follows a hierarchical sequence and corresponds with existing knowledge about learning and development in the first 3 years of life (Meier, Segner, and Grueter, 1970). Based on the assumption that DLDs can be prevented in children at risk for sociocultural or organic reasons through systematic programs of early intervention, there is a need for a cohesive series of learning episodes and related curriculum materials which can be easily communicated to nonprofessionals and parents. Some promising beginnings toward this end are evolving (Haynes, 1974; Honig and Lally, 1972; Kamii, 1972; Meier, 1975a; Restaino et al., 1971; Shearer and Shearer, 1974; Tronick and Greenfield, 1973).

Infant Education Curriculum

As implied in the preceding rationale section, there are several assumptions underlying the notion that systematic education of infants facilitates their optimal development. A basic assumption is that the developmental process occurs as the result of a simultaneous mutual interaction between biological mechanisms and environmental factors (Bigge and Hunt, 1962). That is, the organism does not develop without use. Secondly, it is assumed that the infant actively seeks the experiences required for his optimal growth and development. A third assumption is that information is processed for meaning, and the infant develops cognitively only when he performs certain learning acts within certain kinds of surroundings. A fourth assumption, suggested by Bloom (1964), is that the first 3 years is a critical period for intervention and "feeding" emerging abilities, because of the unparalleled growth of cognitive/intellectual functioning during this period. The fifth assumption is that a disproportionate amount of DLDs in high risk children is caused by either inadequate or inappropriate educational experiences during the earliest years of life. Finally, the present thesis is that compensatory measures can be implemented with these high risk infants to prevent subsequent DLDs.

The findings from early efforts to train indigenous paraprofessionals to assist parents in helping their infants to achieve the various prescribed developmental milestones have been encouraging (Caldwell, 1967; Gordon, 1969; Gray, 1967; Weikart and Lambie, 1968). There are many opponents to such intervention, and many others who are either lukewarm to the idea or feel ill-prepared to implement such programs and, thus, remain adamantly uncommitted to any specific formulation of an individualized curriculum. Some of the reluctance on the part of the child development specialists is caused by a genuine, albeit romantic, appreciation for the pristine innocence of the infant. Some already harassed parents prefer the greater convenience of having a more passive infant, and of not having to busy themselves about the additional task of tending to educational experiences for infants whose toileting, feeding, and sleeping needs are already too much for the harried parenting ones to accomplish. The reticence frequently is also a function of the lack of familiarity with even the rudimentary requirements of curriculum building.

Several years ago, Barsch (1967) wrote a chapter in a book about exceptional infants which he entitled "The Infant Curriculum—A Concept for Tomorrow." The chapter was the last of a series of contributions from experts of many disciplines writing in regard to the exceptional or DLD infant. A second volume of this series (Friedlander, Sterritt, and Kirk, 1975) reflects some of the many advances in the detection and intervention with DLD infants made during the past decade. It seemed quite fitting, after having presented the multiplicity of problems which occur in very early childhood from the viewpoint of numerous disciplines, that some prescription for the amelioration or, even better, the prevention of such disabilities be offered. Certainly Barsch's interest and sophistication in the perceptual-motor development of the human organism qualified him to make informed recommendations about the optimal development of the human organism, particularly where efficient perceptual-motor functioning is concerned. However, as a reflection of the state of the art, Barsch admittedly had precious few empirically validated methods and materials to offer in behalf of the education of infants. Nevertheless, he suggests what tomorrow's infant curriculum should be:

> The sequences of stimulation should be precisely described in handbook style as a ready reference for any parent or clinician who wishes to pursue the same course with a given infant. It should be possible, perhaps, to have developed this curriculum to such a point of clarity that specific sequences might have been studied in each perceptual mode so that remedial sequences might be strategically employed to the benefit of those infants who have suffered specific losses or impairments. Unfortunately, the concept of infant curriculum is far from such an advanced stage of development (Barsch, 1967, p. 553).

In order to construct the infant curriculum which will produce an infant education system capable of simple, but highly specific, application, a basic structural framework must exist. This framework should contain six essential major parts. First, the entire system must be built from a solid conceptual rationale—one which supports the idea that the measurements, activities, and environmental manipulations in the system will validly indicate and foster optimum development. Second, there should be an inventory of infant development which will assess each infant's existing skills or entry behaviors, his readiness to accomplish new tasks, and his environmental situation by using validated instruments of assessment and skilled observations. Third, there should be a systematic method of training those who will teach parents and infants to use the infant educational system which will enable the least sophisticated or least skilled learning facilitator to implement the curriculum and administer and interpret the progress inventory. Fourth, there must be a detailed curriculum of sequential and hierarchical experiences to carry out with the infants; this curriculum should reflect the aforementioned conceptual framework at its core and be continually guided by the progress inventory. Fifth, there must be an additional system of remediation which can be added to the core program when the inventory indicates a discrepancy in either terminal behavior performance or in the environment that necessitates special techniques of intervention. Sixth, techniques must exist to evaluate the effectiveness of such programs so that objective evidence of their efficacy can be presented and they can be replicated by others at a future date (Simeonsson and Wiegerink, 1975).

In developing an infant education system, the development of the child during the first 3 years of life has been conceptualized according to Piagetian theory. Piaget described six basic stages of development within the sensorimotor period. Using the theoretical framework of these stages, a hierarchy of behaviors and skills has been drawn up which utilizes not only Piagetian observations, but also infant developmental milestones as described or suggested by Gesell and Amatruda (1941), Havighurst (1953), Stott and Ball (1965), Uzgiris and Hunt (1966), and others. In other words, the hierarchy of skills and behaviors described by these workers has been translated into the Piagetian theoretical framework, and serves as a basis for the educational activities contained in an infant educational system.

The adoption of Piaget's theory of development as a rationale for a curriculum is desirable for two reasons. First, Piaget and his associates have formulated a learning or epistemological theory in which the nature of the entire developmental process is the primary concern (Chapter 2 shows some of the principles of Piagetian theory alongside other developmental theories). Thus, curriculum sequences can be based on a dynamic rationale, the nature of which is explainable in terms of the unfolding human. Secondly, Piaget describes the process of development, neither exclusively as a predetermined sequence of events nor as solely a biological maturation, but as a vital continuous interaction between an individual and his environment.

> . . .Intelligence does not therefore appear as a power of reflection independent of the particular position which the organism occupies in the universe but is linked, from the very outset, by biological a priori's. It is not at all an independent absolute, but it is a relationship among others, between the organism and things. If intelligence thus extends an organic adaptation which is anterior to it. . . . From this point of view, physiological and anatomical organization gradually appears to consciousness as being external to it and intelligent activity is revealed for that reason as being the very essence of the existence of our subjects (Piaget, 1932, p. 19).

Using this theory as a point of departure for curriculum development, the appropriate manipulation of the environment in terms of both stimulation and interaction can be conceptualized as influencing the dynamic chain of events which is critical in human development. Once a curriculum is developed, based on this rationale, it is possible to assign specific meanings to curriculum tasks, thus giving the tasks (activities) a defined representational role in the total schema of human development.

Within the first 3 years of life, Piaget describes two periods of development: that of sensorimotor development and the early phases of preoperational thought which encompass the child's preschool and early educational years. Although the ordinality and duration of Piaget's postulated stages have generally held up when replication studies have been conducted, exceptions do occur (Kagan, 1972), and some modifications are necessary when DLD children are being programmed into the system. Within the sensorimotor period, covering approximately the first 18 months for normally developing children, Piaget describes seven stages of development.

Stages I and II These stages generally deal with elementary sensorimotor adaptations and show early progression from automatic or reflexive behavior to a modification and differentiation of these responses. Stages I and II normally occur during the first 4 months of life. The final four stages of development deal generally with intentional sensorimotor adaptations and their refinement.

Stage III (4–8 months) The infant begins to make intentional adaptations toward various goals. "Intention" is primarily a generalized response directed toward maintaining or reproducing a pleasurable or stimulating experience.

Stage IV (8–12 months) The infant actively anticipates the goals, and consequent activity becomes less generalized and more specifically goal directed, or intentional.

Stage V (12–18 months) Active exploration and experimentation become evident, and experimentation itself becomes goal oriented.

Stage VI (18 months to beginning of subperiod of preoperational thought) The final stage of the sensorimotor period involves the use of inventiveness and creativity in goal-directed behavior, and the consequent transition into preoperational thought.

Final Stage VII (age 2–3) This stage encompasses the early phase of the subperiod of preoperational thought described by Piaget as existing in the child from age 2 until around age 7. During this period of time, the child learns to utilize his multiple sensorimotor adaptations from previous periods, and moves toward internalization of cognition and symbolic manipulation of reality. Using what is known about these seven stages during an infant's first 3 years, activities can be planned, in a learning sequence fashion, which will not only provide appropriate stimulation, but will also facilitate the generally expected development of that period.

Developmental Inventory—Profile and Base for Curriculum Planning

The Bayley Infant Scales for Psychomotor and Mental Development (1969), the corresponding Ordinal Scales by Uzgiris and Hunt (1975), the Revised Yale Developmental Schedules (Knobloch and Pasamanick, 1974) and the more gross screening devices such as the Boyd Developmental Progress Scales (1974) and the Denver Developmental Screening Test (Frankenburg and Dodds, 1967) all indicate that there are specific behaviors and capabilities which are expected of children at various chronological ages. Administration of these types of tests to an infant not only gives one an accurate picture of the infant's present development, but also serves as a guide to the systematic education of infants as specified by various authorities of early childhood development (see Chapters 2 and 3 for more details). As a matter of fact, the entry and terminal behaviors, particularly in the realm of sensorimotor/perceptual functioning, have already been rather thoroughly delineated by the observable behaviors enumerated in the aforementioned infant appraisal instruments (Chapter 4).

In considering, for example, the evolution of standing and walking skills as delineated by a composite of these tests, a "learning sequence" can be designed by interjecting a hierarchy of precursor skills between an accomplished "entry behavior" and a projected goal—"terminal behavior." As illustrated by sample E in Figure 14, item 42 on the Bayley Infant Scales for Psychomotor Development specifies that a child should be able to walk, with help, within the age range of 7–12 months (mean 9.6 months). A stimulation-learning sequence is suggested to enable an infant to develop the sensorimotor/perceptual skills requisite in walking without someone's holding one hand. The inventory is administered until the infant's highest point of mastery of a precursor task in this sequence is established. This accomplishment is considered an entry behavior if passed with a qualitative criterion performance. From this point of mastery, perhaps item 40 (stepping movements) or item 38 (stands up by furniture), to that of the achievement of the terminal behavior, an orderly step-by-step sequence of training is instituted and practiced until mastery of the underlying skills and understandings is accomplished. Once the terminal behavior is accomplished at criterion level, it may well become an entry behavior for a related and more advanced sequence.

The appropriateness of items on standardized test instruments is challenged by many defenders of the culture of poverty. If these items are being challenged as valid test items, they will equally well be challenged as accepted items in learning sequences in an infant education curriculum. Wechsler makes a cogent reply to this criticism.

> The I.Q. has had a long life and will probably withstand the latest assaults on it. The most discouraging thing about them is not that they are without merit, but that they are directed against the wrong target. It is true that the results of intelligence tests and of others, too, are unfair to the disadvantaged, deprived, and various minority groups, but it is not the I.Q. that has made them so. The culprits are poor housing, broken homes, a lack of basic opportunities, etc., etc. If the various pressure groups succeed in eliminating these problems, the I.Q.'s of the disadvantaged will take care of themselves (Wechsler, 1966, p. 66).

A history of the intelligence testing movement clearly demonstrates that standardized tests comprise a distillation of those skills and abilities which are most validly and reliably assessed and most of which have been replicated by other investigators. Therefore, it is unnecessary to be apologetic or surreptitious about employing the current and rather well conceptualized series of behaviors contained in various infant assessment instruments, at least as the skeletal framework for an infant curriculum. Although this procedure involves educating youngsters to successfully perform on test-like items, there is nothing inherently wrong in this, provided that the items sample behaviors which are universally recognized as essential indices of normal infant growth and development and constitute critical experiences in optimal human development. Although addressing their concern to school-age children, Karp and Sigel (1965) make a

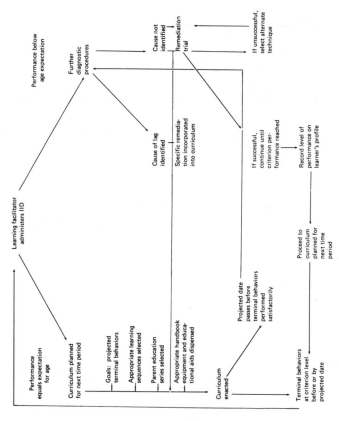

Figure 13a. Infant education system flowchart.

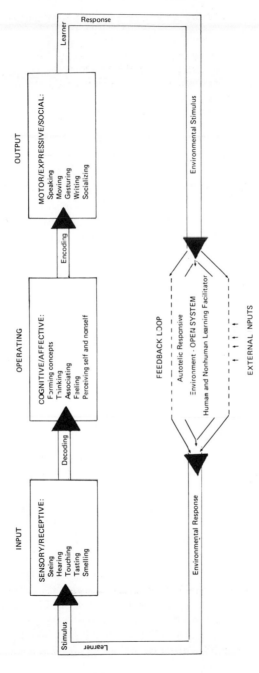

Figure 13b. Information processing model underlying infant education system.

strong case for a test's truly reflecting a desired constellation of terminal behaviors.

> . . . tests and trained observations should take on new meaning and different diagnostic significance. In addition to appraising learning difficulty, measurement and observation should lead to remedial and compensatory techniques which can be incorporated readily into the curriculum and translated easily into work in the classroom. Psychoeducational appraisal of the disadvantaged pupil confronts us anew with the need to develop assessment procedures that both clarify the mechanisms by which learning occurs and guide the teaching-learning process (Karp and Sigel, 1965, pp. 409–410).

It has been stated that the behavioral series contained in infant assessment instruments will comprise not only an initial profile of the child but also a skeletal framework for the infant curriculum. In order to initiate curriculum planning, other factors must be taken into consideration. The fleshing out of such a curriculum is a function of the individual infant whose idiosyncratic style of dealing with his environment requires an equally individual match of educational experiences suitable to his learning style, so that these individual idiosyncrasies must be observed in a skilled way and taken into consideration in planning. Furthermore, the infant's existing environment must also be assessed as it is his interaction with this environment which is critical in development. In other words, both intraindividual and interindividual factors must be considered. Much as a curriculum is based upon accepted sequences of performance, an environment may be assessed and manipulated in accordance with the infant's needs.

A Suggested Infant Education System

A general procedural flow chart depicting a suggested Infant Education System (IES) is provided by Figure 13a. As illustrated by this chart, the system is self-perpetuating if the infant responds according to expectations. If he does not, as is often the case with DLD children, further evaluation and modified intervention techniques must be designed and incorporated into the core curriculum for a given time period. Figure 13b depicts an information processing model which is used to rationalize and organize a large series of learning episodes for infants, toddlers, and preschoolers (Meier, 1975a). It represents a simplified version of the communications systems presented and discussed in Chapter 3. The curriculum may include therapeutic techniques, additional parent counseling, environmental manipulation, or whatever is required to make an appropriate response to the individualized needs of the infant as delineated by the

Figure 14. Infant education system curriculum samples.

A.   The following sequence demonstrates the evolution of sensorimotor skills involved in maintaining sitting with good posture and stability. The learning situation is combined with several "game" situations: foot play, mirror play, and the removal of obstacles (diaper over face), and incorporate play, object and self-concept into activity.

Motor Skills
(Supine and Sitting)

Midposition of head and symmetrical posture in supine	Regards feet (sit)	Regards self in mirror
Sits propped forward with head steady	Lifts legs high in extension (supine)	Motor approach to mirror image
Pulling to sit — no head lag	Grasps foot (supine)	Smiles at mirror image
Head erect and steady when sitting	Terminal behavior	Terminal behavior
Assists with arms when pulled to sit	Foot play mouthing	Playful response to mirror image mouthing touching vocalizing
Pull to sit: helps lift head		
Sits with support with trunk steady and erect		
Removes diaper from face (supine)		
Lifts head and shoulders in effort to sit		
Sitting — props forward with hands		
Erect momentarily without support		
Terminal behavior Sits alone steadily		

Can stabilize sitting to engage in play: feet, mirror, toys, with good coordination; removes diaper from face in sitting position.

A. Activities: A general description.

All practice of motor skills will be associated with game or play situations so that they are more enjoyable for mother and/or facilitator and baby, and so that

Continued

Figure 14—*Continued*

emerging skills in the areas of play, object and self-concept, space concept, and time both are reinforced and reinforce the sensorimotor development. Motor activities stress reinforcement and stimulation of righting, propping, and equilibrium responses necessary in maintaining head and trunk stability. A colored scarf is used in the beginning to cover the face and eventually it will be used to hide objects, progressing from perceptual freeing of the face toward recovering of partially hidden objects.

B. The following sequences deal with stimulation of motor activities in prone and standing positions. Activities are reinforced with object and personal play. Conceptual development with respect to object and space are both reinforced and reinforcing.

Entry behaviors:

1. Head extended, weight on forearms, sustained in prone position; legs extended or semi-extended.

2. Attempts rolling to prone.

3. Brief supporting reaction — standing.

1. Rolls to prone.

2. Scratches platform and uses hands in prone.

3. Can support weight on hands, arms fully extended.

1. Removes diaper from face in prone.

2. Bears large fraction of weight — standing.

3. Bounces in standing.

1. "Works" motorically (creeps, scoots, etc.) toward object out of reach in prone.

2. Early reciprocal stepping movements in standing position (with trunk support).

Terminal behaviors:

1. Prone — pivots toward object.

2. Standing — maintains full weight briefly, hands held.

3. Can be pulled to full stand by facilitator — traction on hands.

B. Activities to stimulate this series will be facilitated by use of a toy object, personal (affectionate) reinforcement, and nursery rhymes and songs. Use of the latter facilitates early development of rhythmic, sequenced motor activity. Generally, the infant will initiate the desired motor activities as he progresses from:

Secondary **circular** reactions. The consolidation by repetition of certain motor habits leading to effects in the milieu which are of interest to the infant (effects — desirable toy play, social reinforcement, and auditory reinforcement).

↓

Recognitory assimilation (recognition of the desired effect is acted out motorically).

↓

Generalized assimilation — the act becomes represented in thought and is utilized toward a variety of objects (without recognition of novelty) in an effort to make interesting sights last. Motor schemas become progressively more complex.

C. The following sequences deal with the acquisition of language skills and imitation skills involved in language development. Early indication of auditory perceptual skills are included in the sequences.

Entry behaviors:

1. Differentiation of vocalization from cry.

2. Excites, breathes heavily, strains.

3. Laughs.

4. Turns head to sound.

↓

1. Responds with mouth movements, smile, or vocalization to familiar sounds.

2. Squeals.

3. Vocalizes to toys, mirror image.

4. Vocalizes attitudes — pleasure, satisfaction, etc.

↓

1. Uses sound to localize in turning head after falling object.

2. Grunts and growls.

3. Bangs objects in play.

4. Reflects a facial mimic.

↓

1. Interest in sound production (object).

2. Vocalizes four syllables.

3. Lip closure; vocalizes — m-m-m cry.

4. Polysyllabic sounds — vowels.

↓

Continued

Figure 14—*Continued*

Terminal behaviors:

    1.   Vocalizes similar sounds in response to familiar sounds.

    2.   Attends (quietens, decreases activity) to unfamiliar sounds – may vocalize.

    3.   Says da-da or equivalent (ba-ba, ma-ma).

    4.   Listens selectively to familiar words (name, baby, bottle, etc.).

C. Activities center around auditory stimulation with visual and tactile reinforcement. Development of imitation begins with sounds already in the infant's repertoire with reinforcement of any attempt to imitate. Auditory skills of localizing, association, early discrimination are stimulated and reinforced. Investigatory mouth play and sensory stimulation around mouth are utilized.

D. The following sequences deal with the acquisition of fine motor and visual motor and conceptual skills regarding objects, space, and causality.

Entry behaviors:

    1.   Anticipates trajectory of moving objects.

    2.   Activates arms or hands with visual identification of stimulus object.

    3.   Retains object in hand and takes to mouth.

    4.   Hands together in midline.

    5.   Glances from hand to object and object to container.

    6.   Regards (visually) small objects.

    1.   Precarious grasp of object, especially when near hand.

    2.   Visual pursuit of lost object.

    3.   Bilateral approach.

    4.   Sustained inspection with manipulation of object.

    1.   Exploitation of objects (string, paper), using more complex motor schemas.

    2.   Palmar grasp.

    3.   Displeasure at loss of object; searching prehensory pursuit of lost object.

    4.   Playful responses to objects, people.

    1.   Radial-palmar grasp of larger objects.

    2.   Unilateral approach to objects.

3. Visual rediscovery and anticipation of whole object after seeing part.

4. Transfers adeptly.

5. Imitates knocking with hand, banging toys on table top.

Terminal behaviors:

1. Raking approach to small objects.

2. Retains two objects.

3. Holds object, regards container.

4. Exploitation more goal-oriented:

    Retrieves partially hidden toy.
    Resists toy pull.
    Pulls string and secures tied toy.
    Motorically works to get toy out of reach.
    Manually rotates objects to get to desired portion of object (flashlight, bottle, etc.).

E. The use of play objects to stimulate the motor behaviors listed will also stimulate the transition from simple motor schema development (e.g., standing) to that of more complex motor schemas (e.g., standing and cruising in order to obtain desired object).

Entry behavior:	Source
Stands up by furniture	
Pulls to stand	
1. Supports full weight on legs (holding rail for stabilization, not using arms for support)	Bayley-item 38 Yale-Gesell

Learning sequence:	
2. Lifts and replaces foot — standing at rail	Yale-Gesell
3. Stepping movements and reciptoral leg movements with two hands hold	Yale Bayley-item 40
4. Cruises at rail	Yale Yale

Terminal behavior:	
5. Walks forward and walks with help with one hand held	Yale Bayley-item 42

diagnostic profile. In these cases, the learning facilitator may need ongoing consultation and perhaps assistance from other professionals. For example, the infant with a motor developmental lag may need a physical therapy home program incorporated into the overall development program; thus, a physical therapy consultant may work closely with the learning facilitator to plan appropriate curriculum and deliver it expertly to the infant or toddler.

Finally, Figure 14 illustrates some details of the curriculum for infants between 4 and 8 months of age, corresponding to Piaget's sensori-motor stage III. This curriculum is an example of the type of basic procedures which would be implemented at other stages of development and is offered as illustrative only. By study of the given sequences and sequence goals, it may be seen how validated landmarks of development are incorporated into the Piagetian framework and how suggested activities would educate and stimulate an infant in such a way as to foster optimum development and learning regardless of the presence of DLDs. The System for Open Learning (Meier, 1975a) Series of Learning Episode for Infants and Toddlers is a much simplified source of numerous separate activities for parents and paraprofessionals to use in promoting an individual child's optimum growth and development.

chapter 6

Detection and Evaluation of Developmental and Learning Disability Conditions for Preschool Children

As indicated in previous chapters, in order for intervention efforts to be effective, it is essential that they be properly matched with whatever DLD condition may exist. Since there is a long tradition of seeking and often finding, in a prophecy-fulfilling way, the causes of all DLDs exclusively within the individual, it is necessary to repeatedly underscore the importance of alternative ways of interpreting many DLD conditions. The customary accusation of the victim as being solely responsible for his DLD condition is no longer warranted, especially in those cases where the principal villain is the social system or milieu (Rappaport et al., 1975). It is for this reason that this chapter's title speaks of evaluating DLD conditions *for* preschool children rather than *in* preschool children since a DLD condition may originate outside of a given child (see Table 3). Although the manifestation of the DLD condition is usually first noticed in a child, it should be understood that whenever the term "DLD child" is used in this text the condition does not necessarily have its origin from within the child.

This is not intended to deny the importance of checking out the intraindividual components in accordance with the classical medical model for their possible contribution to and perhaps even cause of given DLD conditions. The intraindividual considerations (Figure 5) of a differential diagnosis are quite necessary and, in some cases, are even sufficient for detecting and evaluating DLD conditions whose origins and extent are essentially restricted to the internal functioning of the individual's organism. In fact, in many cases, such conditions are simpler to evaluate, to accurately predict their course, and to be more confident in their intervention prescriptions as compared to the far more complex DLD conditions whose origins lie outside of the individual or are some intricate combination of intraindividual and extraindividual influences.

As the individual grows older chronologically, simply because of the passage of time, there is a greater probability for extraindividual influences to impact upon and generally exacerbate conditions which might have originally been more simply restricted to the intraindividual and physical domain of development. Although considerable discussion has already been presented in preceding chapters, with regard to physical developmental aberrations in infants and toddlers (see especially Chapter 4), there are various DLD conditions which have physical counterparts that are not readily detected during the first 3 years. This detection is difficult because either the DLD conditions are not sufficiently manifest during these early years to be detected by existing tests and procedures or perhaps the DLD conditions are not even present during the first 3 years of life. This chapter is concerned with the salient factors which should be considered for detecting and evaluating DLDs in 3- to 6-year-old children in addition to the factors which have already been mentioned in Chapter 4.

PHYSICAL FACTORS

Pediatric Screening and Evaluation

With increased sophistication among both the lay and professional communities regarding DLD conditions, a concomitantly greater amount of attention is being focused on preschool identification of children at risk of subsequent school learning disabilities. One of the terms frequently used by physicians to refer to the constellation of symptoms presented by a child who is likely to have some difficulty in learning is the generic term minimal brain dysfunction (MBD). This term has enjoyed rather wide circulation since it was coined several years ago and took its place among the litany of other terms bandied about by various disciplines and the persons within them. Some other terms found under the MBD umbrella are: chronic brain syndrome, diffuse brain damage or dysfunction, hyperkinetic behavior disorder, mild neurosensory deficit, minimal or minor brain injury, minimal neurological dysfunction, minimal cerebral damage or dysfunction, perceptually impaired or handicapped, psychoneurological disorder or delay, sensorimotor perceptual deficit or delay. The use of so many different terms to describe a single syndrome connotes considerable confusion or communication disorder among those in the various disciplines concerned with DLDs. Moreover, the MBD syndrome has not been universally accepted or even acknowledged by most members of the medical community. However, MBD must have some communicative validity since it is sufficiently popular to serve as the syndrome around which several articles and books have evolved (e.g., Clements, 1966; Ferinden and Van Handal, 1971; Myklebust and Boshes, 1969; Peters et al., 1973a,b; and Wender, 1971).

It is interesting to note that the book by Peters et al. (1973b), which is designed to serve as a handbook for physicians to screen for MBD, does not delve into any in-depth psychoeducational testing procedures nor does it engage in the extensive theoretical controversies in the DLD field. Instead, it serves as a highly practical guide to the practicing physician who hitherto has largely ignored the subtleties of MBD, which are frequently the precursors of subsequent school learning and behavior problems. It does, however, emphasize the assessment of an individual's language functioning. Historically, it has been unusual for physicians to show much concern for language development, but there is a slowly growing trend to familiarize physicians, pediatricians in particular, with ways of assessing development in the "nonphysical" domains as an integral part of a total evaluation. For example, in England, an additional year of interdisciplinary training for pediatricians has been added to the traditional training experience. This year is dedicated to learning developmental pediatrics, which demands an increasing amount of time to answer the greater number of questions which now arise in most private pediatric practices. The necessity for this additional training in developmental pediatrics is also becoming more widely accepted throughout the United States. More than 30 university affiliated facilities have been established at medical schools across the U.S. to offer postdoctoral pediatric fellowships in comprehensive interdisciplinary DLD evaluation and treatment programs. The much briefer book by Ferinden and Van Handal (1971) is useful in training the nonmedical and some paraprofessional disciplines in the rudiments of evaluating children for DLD conditions.

Denhoff (1969) has been pleading with his physician colleagues for many years now to incorporate in their routine preschool medical examinations various screening tests designed to detect deficits and delays in sensorimotor, perceptual, and language functioning which have any probability of subsequently interfering with satisfactory academic performance. In his work at the Meeting Street School, Denhoff has analyzed many of the more prominent indices of risk for academic failure and synthesized these into some screening and evaluation techniques which he advocates as an integral part of the preschool medical examination, especially for the 5- to 7-year-old child who is being checked out before entering the formal traditional school system. Denhoff's concern is with what he refers to as "neurological inefficiency," and the Meeting Street School Screening Test (MSSST) (1969) assesses this parameter by tapping such neurologically mediated functions as balance, eye-hand coordination, stereognosis, gross and fine motor synchronization, fine pattern movements, perceptual-motor functioning, extraocular motility, sensory integration, language skills, and complex integrative skills. As numbers of subjects and other related data accumulate, the MSSST is gaining in normative comparisons and acceptance among those physicians who do the bulk of medical examinations for children before entry into school. The MSSST is now available in a readily useable form and has proved to be quite helpful in alerting physicians and primary school personnel to fullblown or incipient DLD conditions requiring various kinds of individual intervention methods.

Another screening test similar to the MSSST and designed for physician use with kindergarten children to detect those who are at risk for various DLDs is the Neurological Screening Test (NST), by Thomas et al. (1973). This test assesses the child's laterality, sense of direction, some cranial nerve functions, fine and gross motor coordination, and certain sensory functions deemed to be of special importance in this age group of children. It is interesting to note that Thomas et al. acknowledged the fact that about 30% of the children whom they diagnose as learning disabled have significant language and/or speech problems, which they are now suggesting should be more carefully assessed and, therefore, incorporated into the anticipated improved version of the NST. They have been able to establish some concurrent and limited predictive validity for the NST, in terms of its correlation with the Metropolitan Readiness Test (1969) and the Vane Kindergarten Test (1968), across several socioeconomic levels and ethnic groups.

EEG and CNS Assessment

One very attractive, yet still pious, hope is that some relatively simple and clear-cut measurement of neurological functioning will surface as the single index to central nervous system integrity and overall functional capacity of the intraindividual communications system. One such assessment procedure which recurrently holds out this promise, as various new findings emerge and additional doubts are dispelled about its validity and reliability, is the measurement of electrical activity in the brain and the interpretation of the patterns of this activity (electroencephalography, EEG). As the EEG instrumentation is refined, much more sophisticated print-outs can be generated by linking up the multiple EEG channel outputs to computers preprogrammed to highlight certain functional parameters. The computer-like brain of the electroencephalographer programs an electronic computer to help him to analyze and to interpret the electrical activity from the computer-like brain of another human. Thus, computer technology, which used the human brain as an analogue in its early development, now provides an important link in the scientific study of the very organ it was originally conceived to imitate and supplement.

The fact that various central nervous system disorders frequently have typically pathological EEG patterns encourages the unrelenting quest for the more subtle indices to so-called "soft neurological signs," which are thought to be related to milder DLDs. However, the wide range of EEG tracings, which are now accepted as falling within normal limits, presently defies the establishment of a sufficiently clear-cut normal standard against which questionable EEG tracings might be compared and accurate judgments of higher cortical dysfunction might be accurately made. This variability is especially true in the rapidly developing brain which produces somewhat erratic electrical activity during the first 6 or 7 years of life. Nevertheless, there are some EEG indicators, such as spikes of 6 to 7 and 14 cycles per second as well as slow waves, especially if the latter have a rhythmical pattern of long bursts with a frequency under four cycles per second, which seem to be abnormal at any age (Hughes, 1967). If nothing else, these post-temporal slow waves, which sometimes subsequently disappear as the child grows older, may at least serve as an index to neurological immaturity.

As more is learned about the significance of these tracings and as the technology allows new combinations and permutations of this complex electrical activity to be teased out and longitudinal developmental research is advanced (Crowell, 1973; Davis, 1971), the EEG will probably become an increasingly useful instrument for assessing and predicting future CNS function. Although the average incidence of EEG abnormalities in mental deficiency has been shown by many studies to exceed 60% of the cases, the definitive use of the EEG for evaluating intraindividual learning disabilities, particularly with young persons who have normal IQs but difficulty in integrating information or in other ways processing it efficiently, is still an area requiring a great deal of further research.

The specialty area of pediatric neurology has necessarily addressed the issues of DLDs since it is frequently the last resort in the medical sciences for ferreting out the presumed organic cause and electrobiochemical characteristics of mild DLDs. In a useful and nearly classic general reference regarding learning disabilities (Myklebust, 1967), a pediatric neurologist (Vuckovich, 1967) reviewed the state of the art and science in terms of what pediatric neurology had to say about learning disabilities and the same facts continue to pertain at this writing. Once more, much as revealed in the previous discussions about neurological screening devices, concern is expressed about the narrowness and even irrelevance of classical neurological assessment of DLD conditions for preschool children. Once again, the various developmental aspects of a neurological examination are emphasized. In addition, such matters as mother-child interaction and a plea for more standardized neurological evaluation procedures, such as those advanced by Brazelton (1973) and Ozer (1966), are sought in order to give some coherence and consistency to the endeavor of identifying the child who is at neurological developmental risk.

Since it takes some 15 years for final neurophysiological maturity to be achieved, the developmental chronicling of maturational stages by Gesell (1947) and others, now updated in the Yale Revised Developmental Scales (Knobloch and Pasamanick, 1974), is suggested by Vuckovich (1967) as a useful guide. Once again the importance of language in the 3- to 6-year-old as a primary behavioral index of neurological integrity is mentioned. Thus, even though 90% of the brain growth is achieved normally during the first 5 years of life, the finalization of other more subtle cellular and biochemical refinements continues to influence CNS function as manifest in the higher order cortical processes. These processes are assessed customarily by tests of intelligence and tend to plateau at around 16 years of age. Vuckovich goes on to delineate many of the behavioral symptoms of neurological immaturity which are relative to age and, although they commonly occur in all children, if they persist and are more pervasive and numerous than is normal for that age, such a combination may indicate the presence of at least a mild DLD. Such behavioral signs also become the basis for comprehensive screening instruments, some of which are discussed in the last section of this chapter.

It would be an oversight not to mention the widely publicized notions of Delacato (1963) regarding the amelioration of DLDs through the establishment of neurological laterality. Many studies have now been completed to discount this claim, all of which basically conclude that: (1) creeping is not related to reading performance; (2) reading performance in lateralized subjects does not differ from normal controls; (3) neurological organization does not affect reading more than arithmetic; and (4) groups exposed to neurological organization did not exhibit more consistent cerebral dominance than the controls (Robbins, 1967). However, the controversy over the efficacy of patterning has not ended, as shown in the argument raging between the National Association for Retarded Citizens (1973), Neman (1975), and Neman et al. (1975), who claim some significant positive benefits from the method, versus the American Academy of Pediatrics (1968) and Zigler and Seitz (1975), who vigorously and compellingly deny such claims.

Visual/Auditory Indicators

The interaction between the visual and auditory systems has been highlighted, especially with reference to difficulties in reading. The complexity of interrelations between various areas of the brain and the visual and auditory mechanism has been addressed by ophthalmologists and otolaryngologists for many years (Rychener, 1948). Most ophthalmologists are persuaded that reading disabilities are not caused by an inability to see the written characters and words but rather are caused by an inability to interpret them in a meaningful way. That is, the difficulty is not one of sensory integrity and acuity but rather one of perceptual and cognitive dysfunction. It appears that amblyopia and strabismus do not affect the interpretation of two-dimensional written symbols. Convergence insufficiency and a weak binocular status may cause fatigue and slow reading, but will not retard mastery of the process itself.

Frank and Levinson (1974) have advanced the notion that organically caused dyslexia may be the result of some yet unexplained defect in the nerve pathways between the inner ear, which helps to control balance, and the cerebellum, the part of the brain that controls coordination. It is as though the individual experiences a sort of chronic motion sickness which may in fact confuse and scramble the incoming visual information that he is receiving and/or perceiving. A relationship between the inner ear and visual motor processing of information has been further supported by Bizzi (1974). He has demonstrated that efferent or incoming signals arising from the sensitive receptors of the vestibule of the inner ear are solely responsible for modulating the amplitude of eye movements, referred to as saccadic movements. The saccadic eye movements are critical for targeting the eyes on whatever written material might be intended by the individual for reading or inspection. These scanning left-right activities are obviously critical for reading the written word in proper sequence and for not getting lost on a page or feeling dizzy and sometimes nauseous when attempting to read, as is the case with some children and adults with primary dyslexia.

There is evidence emerging that visual-perceptual difficulties underlying reading disabilities and related learning disabilities may have some genetic etiology. However, since the symptoms of the disability have not traditionally been noted until school age when reading is required, they have typically been falsely designated as exclusively developmental or environmental in origin. Hallgren (1950) and Hermann and Norrie (1958) marshalled evidence to demonstrate a high probability that many specific reading disabilities and other similar DLDs may very likely have their origin in some genetic predisposition to difficulties in carrying on complex visual-perceptual functions in the higher centers of the brain. Since visual refractive and eye muscle imbalance problems have no greater prevalence in dyslexia than found in control groups of competent readers, the notion that dyslexia is seated in the higher cortical area is further supported. Goldberg and Drash (1968) make a concerted plea for the interdisciplinary team approach to the reading-disabled child since the reasons for his difficulty are frequently very complex. Even if the etiology is fundamentally hereditary, the secondary emotional and social effects must also be carefully dealt with, and the pedagogical procedures for remediation must be carefully determined. Martin (1971) summarized the state of the art as follows:

> In summary, reading disability is a term that is used to describe children who are reading very poorly for their age, grade level and intelligence. A small percentage of these children have poor vision that can be corrected by the ophthalmologist. While some of these children will have poor coordination of their eyes, there is considerable data to indicate that poor eye coordination, poor ability to converge one's eyes and discrepancy between one's dominant eye and one's dominant hand or leg are not significantly related to reading disability and when present, are not the basis for the poor reading . . . (p. 471).

Although language delay is perhaps the most frequent reason for referral to a child development specialist, the sheer fact that a DLD child does not talk is alarming. It is important to rule out any auditory dysfunction as suggested in Chapter 3, since frequently the most obvious intervention such as speech therapy is incorrectly prescribed. Failure to speak may in fact be caused by an auditory dysfunction such as prolonged otitis media or serous otitis media. Friedman (1975) has reviewed the many reasons why a young child does not talk and makes several helpful suggestions for the evaluation and management of such cases. It may be necessary to perform certain surgical operations or institute other medical interventions before beginning speech therapy in order to ensure that the individual is accurately receiving the auditory information. For example, it may be necessary to perform bilateral tympanotomies and to insert tubes for the relief of the effects of a bilateral serous otitis media in order to bring the tympanic membranes back to normal functioning. This procedure must be done either before or in conjunction with a speech therapy regimen, since speech therapy alone would not be effective until the child is able to hear adequately.

Nutritional Factors

Not only is there a great deal of agitation from the self-styled nutritional purists who insist upon organically grown foods and naturally produced foods, but also there is concern being raised by members of the scientific community regarding the effects of nutritional imbalances or deficiencies on development and learning. One of the prime exponents of the notion that malnutrition causes difficulties in development and learning is Wunderlich (1973). He makes a cogent argument regarding the deleterious effects of nutritional imbalance which may underlie a lack of oxygen-carrying ability of the blood and its subsequent effects on such things as eye function. Of course, other considerations such as the effects of low-grade lead poisoning on brain function, of insufficient vitamin C on synaptic transmission, and of various food additives on other developmental and/or learning functions may also be important. He is concerned that every cell be optimally nourished in order to maintain physical and mental health as well as to provide resistance to ordinary disease and to the more subtle nutrition-related deficiencies in DLDs. Although nutritional concerns have not been a regular part of evaluating DLDs, they are becoming an increasingly acceptable area for investigation. Wunderlich has written many articles and books about his concerns, most of which are summarized in his book about the prevention and treatment of learning problems in children (1970).

One of the few carefully documented longitudinal studies of the effects of severe malnutrition in infancy on subsequent school performance reported a significant relationship between the two (Richardson, Birch, and Hertzig, 1973). A group of Jamaican school boys who had been severely malnourished during infancy were carefully examined during their first year in school for performance on academic tasks. Compared with their classmates of the same age and sex, they did significantly less well on the Wide Range Achievement Test, their grades for academic performance, and other teacher nongraded evaluations of their general academic functioning. Thus, even the early evaluation of school performance may be adversely affected by malnourishment in infancy. This study, among others, suggests that malnutrition may be one of several causes of subsequent cognitive dysfunction, which in turn leads to various other behavioral disorders in reaction to failure in the learning setting. If one considers that development and general learning potential begin at conception, then such DLDs can have deep and long-standing roots in one's developmental history, which makes it very difficult to uproot, prune, and replant an individual's abilities in more productive and fertile soil.

Systematic Assessment

In addition to the various procedures and tests already mentioned in the preceding sections and in Chapter 4, there are various checklists which are useful for 3- to 6-year-old children for evaluating their physical integrity. The use of the Problem-Oriented Record (Weeds, 1974) is a promising method adaptable for all ages for keeping the examiner's attention on the doughnut instead of the hole. Most standardized tests, or the parts of them regarding physical functioning, assess sensorimotor development and functioning. Of course, because of the necessity of having to deal with the entire organism, as represented by an intraindividual communications network (Figure 4), any given assessment stimulus must pass through the central nervous system which involves perceptual/cognitive processes, at least to a limited extent. Therefore, just as it is very difficult to assess the functioning of any single developmental domain to the total exclusion of other domains, the simultaneous mutual interaction among these various domains requires a systematic approach to assessment in order to not overlook some crucial variable in the complex origins of a given DLD condition.

COGNITIVE/INTELLECTUAL FACTORS

The primary DLD condition in the cognitive/intellectual domain of development is reflected in mental retardation or deficiency. With the 3- to 6-year-old age group, there are a fairly large number of reasonably well standardized tests and procedures for evaluating mental functioning (see Chapter 10). Since there is a vast literature on various tests of mental ability (Buros, 1965 and 1972), no effort will be made herein to evaluate the numerous materials in this realm. Nevertheless, one noteworthy instrument, which was published too recently for review in the latest Buros at the time of this writing, is the *McCarthy Scales of Children's Abilities* (1970). This instrument is designed to assess verbal functioning, perceptual functioning, quantitative abilities, general cognitive ability, memory ability, motor ability, and laterality. There are 18 subtests which are designed to assess these various functions and many practicing clinicians who are evaluating DLD children for difficulties in school performance find the McCarthy Scales to be quite useful. From a research point of view, the data gathered on large numbers of children who are followed longitudinally will be useful in determining the relative efficacy of the various subtests for predicting subsequent learning ability. For example, the still controversial notion that laterality plays a significant role in learning ability will be further documented one way or the other if sufficient data are gathered and analyzed in conjunction with the other subtests on the McCarthy Scales when correlated with later school achievement. However, McCarthy even had the informed judgment to keep the laterality assessment separate from the other indices of children's abilities.

As mentioned in an earlier section, it is not sufficient to get a measurement of an individual's intellectual level through an intelligence test in order to determine placement in special programs, since even the definition of mental retardation includes an assessment of adaptive behavior. Christian and Malone (1973) reported a relationship among scores on the Wechsler Intelligence Scales for Children, the Stanford-Binet, the Wide Range Achievement Test, and the Adaptive Behavior Scales, but they further state that no one score was adequate for making the judgment about placement in special education. They advocate the use of the Adaptive Behavior Scales as an important supplement for making these decisions. Moreover, modified versions of the Adaptive Behavior Scales for use in school settings, as opposed to strictly institutional settings, were reported by Lambert et al. (1975). As assessment of how well an individual can maintain himself independently in daily living and the extent that he has mastered other daily living skills is an important consideration in his school placement. Since good adaptive behavior for one's chronological age can and often does mask the degree of mental deficiency present, it is important to study this interaction in greater depth. Heber, Dever, and Conry (1968) suggested that this interaction would be a fruitful area of research in their survey of the influence of various environmental and genetic variables on intellectual development. Subsequently, they undertook the aforementioned revealing and somewhat revolutionary approach to the prevention of cultural/familial or functional mental retardation.

In addition to the McCarthy Scales, four of the old standbys for evaluating cognitive/intellectual processes in children 3–6 years old are as follows: the Revised Stanford-Binet Intelligence Scale; the revised Wechsler Intelligence Scale for Children (WISC-R); the Wechsler Preschool and Primary Scale of Intelligence (WPPSI); and the Griffiths Developmental Scales. Some innovative adaptations of various assessment procedures and tests for disadvantaged preschoolers were devised by Caldwell (1967a), Meier (1967), and others. As testimony to the multiple origins of DLDs and especially to the importance of extraindividual influences, it is noteworthy that Caldwell, Bradley, and Elardo (1975) report a high predictive value of a systematic rating of the child's home environment and his later school performance.

SOCIAL-EMOTIONAL FACTORS

Most workers in the field of DLD subscribe to the notion that standardized testing has reached the point of diminishing returns in terms of assessing problems in children, whether they are characterized by low IQs, MBD, dyslexia, hyperkinesis, low SES background, emotional disturbance, etc. Once again, the plea is issued that more attention be given to the ecology, or sociocultural surround, in which the child is developing and learning and which may predispose the child to DLDs. For example, a number of researchers are concerned with the large gray area between the battered child with broken bones or parent-inflicted burns and the well functioning child who seems to have it all together. Less dramatic, but still pernicious, there is emerging a kind of syndrome which might be referred to as the over-punished/over-pushed child whose behavior seems to be unusually danger oriented, tense and guarded, visually hyperalert, unable to deny unpleasantness, limited and inflexible in his cognitive functioning (closed personality), and frequently occurring in a disorganized home. Corporal punishment and threats of the same are frequently used to control the behavior of the 3- to 6-year-old child, who is still small enough to be readily punished by physical means and, at least superficially, responds as desired by the punishing adults. This syndrome is becoming more clearly delineated (Kempe and Helfer, 1972) and will undoubtedly lead to further knowledge about both active battering and the more insidious and difficult problems of child neglect.

Keniston (1974) traces the history of some of this phenomenon, stating that Americans previously valued a child as a producer on the farm and in the factory but are now shifting this value to the child's productivity in the school. He suggests that it is time for the American society to value children for such qualities as playfulness, imagination, and love rather than their brawn power, brain power, and productivity. He envisions a society that would be concerned about the optimal unfolding of each individual child's inherent talents through nurturing families, neighborhoods, and child care programs designed to cultivate the humanistic values in the nation's children. However, he states that this would require a radical restructuring of a society which, for all intents and purposes, evidently does not really care about its greatest potential resource—its children.

Various mental health disciplines such as child psychiatry, developmental pediatrics, developmental psychology, and social work are pooling their perspectives on the social-emotional antecedents of DLD and shedding greater light on the entire subject.

> Progress in understanding the significance of emotional factors in children with learning disabilities cannot be subsumed under a single heading: psychiatrists have finally learned, with a humble perception, that children with learning disabilities are a powerful interdisciplinary catalyst (Giffin, 1967).

The importance of drawing upon the insights of many disciplines and evaluating the psychoneurotic underpinnings or overlays of various DLDs cannot be overstated. As stated by Rabinovich, "No single disciplinary approach to learning problems is valid; neurological, psychological, psychiatric and educational emphases must be brought together without preconceived bias in both clinical and research work" (1959, p. 58).

Because of the debilitating effects that anxiety and other intense emotional states may have on learning efficiency or deficiency, it is critical that the possible emotional origins as well as their secondary effects be carefully evaluated or ruled out regarding DLDs. Abrams (1973) goes into considerable detail with respect to the evaluation of a child who has a learning disability. He enumerates the various areas of personality factors which must be assessed in determining the emotional features of a learning disability. This assessment is necessary to determine which factors may be either causative or may be secondary and sustaining to any given DLD. It is essential to ensure a DLD child the use of his full intellectual capacity to focus upon specific tasks instead of being so overwrought with anxiety and related feelings that he is unable to marshal sufficient psychic energy for learning. The multiplicity of factors which impinge upon this ego function are reviewed and discussed illustrating how some may obscure the DLD, whereas others may be causing or exacerbating the fundamental DLD. Depending upon the evaluation of the DLD dynamics, different treatment regimens are indicated.

In the area of emotional development, the traditional Rorschach Ink Blot (or Paint Blot) Test and the Children's Apperception Test are traditional in the repertoire of the clinician. The Vineland Social Maturity Scale and Adaptive Behavior Scales are fairly commonly accepted instruments regarding social competence. However, they are frequently supplemented with such additional instruments for assessing the affective domain as the Cassel Developmental Record, the California Preschool Social Competency Scale, the Primary Academic Supplement Scale, the California Test of Personality, Child Behavior Rating Scale, the Bristol Social Adjustment Guide, and the Cain-Levine Social Competency Scale. These instruments are listed in resource Chapter 10 and are criticized in Hoepfner, Stearn, and Nummedal (1971). Walker (1973) has also reviewed many of the social/emotional measures for preschool and kindergarten children and shares some helpful hints for selecting the appropriate measure for a given situation.

LANGUAGE FACTORS

By the time the child reaches 3 years of age, he is normally able to communicate with other human beings quite effectively. By the age of 6 years the normal child's expressive vocabulary exceeds 2,000 words, and his receptive vocabulary is even larger. He is usually able to carry on extensive conversations about daily events with peers and adults. The child's linguistic performance then becomes one of the most useful dimensions of behavior for evaluating his overall development.

Each of the preceding developmental domains can be assessed in part through language development. Since language is mediated by cortical neurophysiological development and since the human cortex is one of the latest evolutionary refinements of the developing human brain and consequently is also one of the most vulnerable and typically first aspect to manifest damage, language disorders are often attendant to physical insults to the human cortex. As a child reaches the age of expressive speech, assessment of cognitive/intellectual functioning relies increasingly upon the child's expression of what he is thinking or what he knows about whatever stimulus is presented to any of his sense modalities. Likewise, in the social/emotional domain, the child verbally interacts with his elders and peers. His expression of his feelings and his verbalized perceptions of social expectations are most important in assessing his overall social/emotional developmental maturity.

As in the other developmental domains, a great deal has been written and said about the importance of the early detection of language disabilities in children (Bannatyne, 1971; Berry, 1969; Mecham, Jones, and Jex, 1973; Garvey and Gordon, 1973; Freston and Drew, 1974; and Downing and Oliver, 1974). These pleas for early detection (between 3 and 6 years of age) are based upon the generally accepted theory that the most efficacious time for intervention is between the ages of 4 and 8 years when there is optimum response to language facilitation (Bannatyne, 1971; Berry, 1969; Lenneberg, 1967; McNeill, 1970; Menyuk, 1971; Smith and Miller, 1966). As with the other domains of development, since the administration of a full language survey to every child would be difficult and time consuming, various screening tests have been developed which seem to have succeeded in reducing the examiner time and sophistication yet yield satisfactory results.

One promising language screening device, the Utah Test of Language Development (UTLD) (Mecham, Jones, and Jex, 1973) is an instrument constructed to assess both the onset and the progressive maturation of a number of developmental milestones in children's language. Although it was originally designed as a screening instrument which would assess a child's total language competence, the approximately half-hour administration time seemed too long. Consequently, Beckstead (1972) analyzed various combinations of reduced numbers of items for the UTLD requiring less time for massive screening. The resultant short versions of the UTLD, comprised of various clusters of items appropriate for different ages, correlates well with the total test, which in turn correlates well with the ITPA. Another widely used instrument for quickly assessing a young child's language development is the Test for Receptive-Expressive Emergent Language by Bzoch and League (1970).

Some light has been shed on the obscure enterprise of determining whether impaired verbal performance is a function of cognitive/intellectual retardation or vice versa by Freston and Drew (1974). They indicated that the recall performance of learning disabled children as a function of the organization or disorganization of the input is not determined so much by the organization of the input as by the input's level of difficulty and, therefore, is presumably a function of cognitive/intellectual functioning. This question also impinges upon the highly controversial and complex issue of whether or not language is necessary for cognitive functioning and whether or not a complex of innate ideas is available to be tapped for cognitive/intellectual processes, regardless of the sophistication of language development (Chomsky, 1974). The screening and assessment problems this issue raises are profound but cannot be adequately dealt with in the scope of this chapter.

Reading—End of Language Rainbow

Reading is defined as the active intentional processing of the written word and the general understanding of written symbols. As Myklebust has shown in his hierarchy of language development (1965a), reading is the ultimate in language achievement. It is in the written word that experiences are preserved for posterity and, like a great pot of gold in the rainbow of human experience, the best recorded source of these is found in written or other symbolic form. Therefore, the ability to read has for several centuries been deemed essential for becoming an educated person. Indeed, the traditional notion of teaching children to read when they reached 7 years of age was thought to coincide with the onset of rationality in the human species. Seven was, therefore, the appropriate age for the developing person to begin reading the Bible and other sources of moral wisdom. The Age of Rationality also lays at the base of the universal compulsory education to promote functional literacy within a society of people who had to make informed judgments based upon information found and promulgated in written form throughout the democratic society. Because reading has been for several hundred years the touchstone for optimum language and concomitant cognitive/intellectual development, children who are unable to read and seem unable to learn the process by 7 years of age become serious concerns of parents, teachers, relatives, and, ultimately, themselves. Despite the advanced standard of living and universal compulsory education in the U.S., a 4-year study supported by the U.S. Office of Education revealed that about one-fifth of the nation's adult population—some 23 million persons—are functionally incompetent to cope with the complexities of modern living (National Assessment of Educational Progress, 1973). More than one-third of the population just gets by in terms of functional competency and more than one-tenth cannot read or write at the 5th grade level—defined as functional literary (see Chapter 8 for more discussion on reading).

The entire process of reading has been subjected to numerous research studies, each attempting to identify the essential factors to ensure one's learning to read. From these studies have emanated various tests and other measures of skill levels in order to determine an individual child's readiness to begin the formal process of reading instruction. One such study (Hammill and Larsen, 1974) reviewed the extensive literature on the relationship between reading skill and measures of auditory discrimination, memory blending, and auditory-visual integration. At the conclusion of their review, they stated that the aforementioned auditory skills were not sufficiently highly correlated to the ability to read to be pragmatically useful in school determinations of readiness to read, or for improving reading ability. The authors suggested that the teaching of children to associate letter sounds with their graphic representations, long claimed to be an essential skill for reading preparation, may not be as important as had been thought. There are currently a number of remedial reading programs which devote considerable time and expense to auditory training, but this review of the literature reveals that particular auditory skills as measured are not essential to the reading process. In fact, the authors point out that a large percentage of the children who have difficulty learning to read perform adequately on tests of auditory perception, whereas an equally impressive percentage who do poorly on these auditory-perceptual tests have no problem in learning to read. By differentially eliminating any suspected problems with the specific factors in visual and auditory perception which are critical for reading ability, and given adequate environmental and instructional opportunities, it is reasonable to suggest that an individual's inability to read is very likely a function of brain immaturity or inefficiency.

Satz and Friel (1974) report one phase of a longitudinal project designed to identify the precursors of developmental dyslexia. A preliminary 2-year follow-up of nearly 500 male kindergarten children, who were previously given a developmental and neuropsychological test battery, showed that the battery predicted with 90% accuracy those children who subsequently did or did not learn to read satisfactorily. One of the suggested reasons for various test instruments and procedures not being valid and reliable across a wide age range is that the maturational lags of the brain delay differentially skills which are in primary ascendency at different chronological ages. Therefore, those skills which evolve earlier during childhood, such as visual perception, auditory perception, and cross-modal integration are more likely to develop ontogenetically earlier and are, therefore, more likely to be delayed in younger children who have DLD or a propensity for DLD. Thus, deprivations or disturbances in the intraindividual and interindividual communication systems will have their greatest quantitative effect on whatever characteristic is at its most rapid period for change and will have their least effect on the characteristic which is at the time going through its least rapid period of change. Using this frame of reference, instead of expecting difficulties and delays in the aforementioned developmental skills, it is more reasonable to find lags and distortions in language (and Piagetian formal operations) in older children who are neurologically immature.

It is interesting to note that in the Satz and Friel (1974) study the test of the single variable of finger localization revealed the highest discriminable ranking and accounted for 76% of the total correct predictions. Recognition-discrimination, date of testing, and alphabet recitation ranked second, third, and fourth, respectively. When all of these variables were put together the hit rate for predicting reading failure was increased to 82% accuracy. All of these variables load on a first factor derived from a previous factor analysis (Satz and Friel, 1974) which was defined as a general measure of sensory-perceptual-motor mnemonic ability. These findings highlight the usefulness of developmental notions for creating predictive instruments that are based upon appropriate antecedents of later reading and learning ability or disability.

Certain perceptual skills have been considered crucial to the early phases of reading by Gibson (1968) and Luria (1966a) and are similar to the skills comprising a factor discovered in a large sample of kindergarten children using results derived from the deHirsch Predictive Battery (Adkins, Holmes, and Schnackenberg, 1971). Measures of perceptual motor functioning during the first grade seem quite sensitive to school achievement at the end of third grade, whereas skills which have a much earlier rate of development, such as balance and motor coordination, correlate with academic aptitude and achievement in younger first grade boys but not in older third grade boys (Chissom, 1971). Results of such research studies are important when an early detection system identifies a child at risk of later reading disability, and appropriate intervention techniques must be instituted at that time. It is especially important because the intervention techniques might well be different for different developmental stages and, to be maximally efficacious, may have to focus on ameliorating and accelerating those behaviors which are predictive of the subsequent handicap but not focus on the handicap itself. To date, a cause and effect relationship between reading disability and inadequate perceptual skills has not been established, but the correlational studies and inferential statistics are becoming more and more convincing.

Another promising effort at predicting reading failure by means of a screening battery to be used on kindergarten children assigned the children (some 725 in number) to six diagnostic categories based on their performance on the Slosson Intelligence Test (SIT) (Slosson, 1963), the Bender Visual-Motor Gestalt Test (Koppitz, 1964), and the Metropolitan Readiness Test (Hildreth, Griffiths, and McGauvran, 1969). The predictive power of this battery of tests, in terms of second grade reading progress, was found to be 95% accurate. The screening procedure was tiered or cascaded by first administering the Metropolitan Readiness Test; and for those whose scores indicated potential difficulties, administering the SIT; and, finally, the Bender Visual-Motor Gestalt Test for those showing difficulty on the SIT. The six diagnostic categories which had various cut-off points for performance on the various tests seemed to be quite discriminative and would suggest that existing instruments do predict subsequent reading failure when properly administered in meaningful combinations and their resultant patterns aptly interpreted.

It is also possible to use more elaborate individually administered ability tests but to score them in special ways to ferret out those children who are most likely to have difficulty in reading. For example, Rugel (1974) reviewed 25 studies which reported WISC subtest scores of disabled readers. These scores were reclassified into categories labeled spatial, conceptual, and sequential. The disabled readers were ranked according to their relative strength or weakness in each of these three categories. Several disabled readers had their highest performance in the spatial category, did less well in the conceptual category, and did most poorly in the sequential category. This suggests that disabled readers are relatively stronger in the visual-spatial skills and weaker in the short-term memory processes and sequential processes, which are at the automatic level in one psycholinguistic model (Kirk and Kirk, 1971). Bannatyne (1971) and Meier (1970) also emphasized the importance of sequencing difficulties in dyslexic children. The Rugel study also suggests that there may be different subgroups of disabled readers, some of whom have a characteristic DLD pattern of genetic dyslexia and others whose reading difficulties are apparently caused by neurological dysfunction as discussed earlier and referred to as MBD. Similar efforts at ferreting out the factors responsible for reading failure have been undertaken with similar findings by Farrar and Leigh (1972), wherein delayed neurological maturity, third or later in birth order, low socioeconomic status, and other lesser factors were found to play an important role in failure to read as expected.

At the same time, studies are investigating the validity of some of the traditional tests themselves. For example, the construct validity of the ITPA was investigated by factor analyzing the subtests with 20 other criterion tests. These tests were designed to match the ITPA subtests on each psycholinguistic variable but either vary in content or relate to a different channel of communication while matching in all other respects (Newcomer et al., 1975). It has been established that many of the existing tests do not in fact measure what they purport nor do they measure discrete abilities with each subtest as falsely claimed for the five subsets of the Frostig Developmental Test of Visual Perception (1964a). On the other hand, in the case of the ITPA, the subtests proved to be relatively discrete and valid for the items and abilities they purported to measure. The channel of communication and especially the visual modality subtests were shown to be the weakest parts of the ITPA in this empirical validation study. Such a study is important to persons interested in designing intervention programs since there are now many remedial programs which are intended to match specific learning episodes to weaknesses found on the various subtests of instruments such as the ITPA. The results of this study enable the clinician to feel relatively secure in interpreting specific subtest results and matching intervention procedures in accordance with findings of strengths and weaknesses in the individual child's performance. Since some of these subtests do tap sequencing ability, which has been shown to predict problems in reading, then it is important that appropriate prevention procedures be generated from these subtests and employed to improve sequencing ability in all modalities when weaknesses in this developmental phenomenon are detected.

Thus, such books as those dealing with diagnosis and remediation of learning disabilities (e.g., Kirk and Kirk, 1971), which are based upon assessments shown to be valid, can enable teachers in special schools and assessment units to more fully understand children's strengths and weaknesses and to guide more effectively the child's formal and informal learning in the most beneficial ways. The large variety and number of useful tests for language and reading assessment for 3- to 6-year-old children preclude mentioning them here, but they are listed in Chapter 10.

COMPREHENSIVE ASSESSMENT TESTS AND PROCEDURES

Developmental Screening of Children 3–6 Years of Age

As noted in Chapter 4, several of the existing developmental screening inventories have age ranges from birth to 6 years of age. Moreover, those which do contain items for the 3- to 6-year-old child are much more predictive for the older age group since a greater variety and number of academically relevant behaviors can be tapped in older children. There is now available a fairly extensive variety of screening instruments and procedures for the identification of children in the 3- to 6-year-old range who are at risk of one or another DLD. Five of the more prominent instruments were reviewed by Thorpe and Werner (1974). All five were compared on relevant, technical, and practical criteria, and each revealed its peculiar limitations especially in terms of incomplete information about reliability and validity. Thorpe's review addressed the Denver Developmental Screening Test, the Head Start Developmental Screening Test and Behavior Rating Scale (HSTS), the Cooperative Preschool Inventory (CPI), the School Readiness Survey (SRS), and the Thorpe Developmental Inventory (TDI). Although the article seems most favorably disposed toward the

TDI, it concludes by observing that any developmental screening inventory is only as good as the personnel using it. The five inventories reviewed, and several others which are available, all proved to be useful for certain applications, but all need further standardization and debugging before wholesale use on all preschool children.

Comprehensive Systems

It is interesting to note that, in a review of infant and preschool mental tests by Stott and Ball (1965), there was no mention of any of the five preceding screening tests, since the general screening effort was just beginning to unfold at that time. In fact, the state of the art and knowledge of a decade ago was quite primitive by comparison with the present. During the past 10 years much of the information contained herein was thus giving rise to the necessity for this and other books on the subject of DLD.

Other efforts at the early identification of children with potential DLDs are those produced by Anderson (1971), Mann and Suiter (1974), Mardell and Goldberg (1975), Medvedeff (1974), Peters et al. (1973b), Petersen (1970), and Wyatt (1971), to mention a few of the more noteworthy ones. These efforts at designing valid instruments, procedures, and batteries for screening children 3–6 years of age have been produced by a variety of persons from a variety of disciplines for use by persons working with actually or potentially DLD children. Figure 9 depicts the interdisciplinary ball game in which each of the aforementioned plus many other unmentioned investigators look at the child from a slightly different vantage point and assess his growth and development accordingly. Moreover, as might be expected, the prescriptions forthcoming from such a variety of perspectives are also varied and, in the eyes of someone looking at the child through another discipline's lenses, would probably seem incomplete or even totally off target. Nevertheless, these various identification systems are mentioned in this section on Comprehensive Systems since each of them purports to assess the growth and development of the whole child.

Some of the issues surrounding the early identification of children with DLDs are cogently addressed in a monograph produced by Keogh et al. (1969) as proceedings from a germinal conference about DLD conditions. This and other such volumes served as a stimulus to the burgeoning research and critical literature that has subsequently evolved. Such issues as physical-motor factors, perceptual-motor factors, cognitive and language factors, and emotional-social factors were summarized and discussed at the conference which was primarily focused on special education for identified DLD children. Repeatedly, the clarion call was issued for more longitudinal validation of existing detection methods and materials, which in turn has resulted in the issuance of more studies and more publications both in the professional and commercial literature.

A useful reference on many of the traditional and some relatively new preschool and kindergarten tests was edited and prepared by Hoepfner, Stern, and Nummedal (1971). This reference evaluates, in accordance with each respective publisher's claims, more than 100 tests, including over 600 subtests, categorized as either preschool (30–59 months) and/or kindergarten (60–72 months). Each test and subtest is evaluated in order to identify and ultimately endorse those measures which are most appropriate, effective, and useful in assessing programs or children. Each test or subtest was assigned to an appropriate category and evaluated in accordance with a relatively objective point ranking system. There is a special evaluation form used in order to evaluate each test in accordance with: (1) its measurement validities; (2) the examinee appropriateness; (3) its administrative usability; and (4) its normed technical excellence. Each test or subtest received a "G" if it was good in a given category, an "F" if it was fair, and a "P" if it was poor in accordance with the criteria specified. One of the most salutory aspects of this entire reference is that it "grades" a number of evaluation instruments and willingly runs the risk of doing some critical violence to venerable old tests instead of allowing such instruments perennially to be misused or misinterpreted and, thereby, do untold violence to children whose fate may hinge on the results. It is indeed sobering to peruse the total grades for these tests and subtests and to realize how few "G's" are awarded. Frost and Minisi (1975) also produced an annotated list of early childhood assessment instruments and procedures, some of which are not included in the above reference by Hoepfner et al.

In spite of the rather sad report card for most extant evaluation instruments, programs for DLD children must continue to be launched and augmented if the numbers of eligible children are ever to be adequately served. One of the most comprehensive programs for the early detection and evaluation of DLDs in preschool children is the Brookline Early Education Project (BEEP). This program is a joint venture between the public schools of Brookline Massachusetts and the Children's Hospital Medical Center in Boston and Harvard University. Its primary goal is the provision of the opportunity for optimal physical and intellectual growth during the preschool years; consequently, no child involved in the project should enter kindergarten with an undetected DLD. There are approximately 280 children and their parents participating in the program. These children live in the Brookline area and in the black and Spanish-speaking communities in neighboring Boston.

An earlier phase of the project (see Figure 15) monitored the growth and development of the participating children during the first 3 years of their lives. The BEEP program subsequently provides a prekindergarten program at an educational center for children who are participating in the project once they reach the age of $2^{1}/_{2}$ years. BEEP is assessing the impact of various special educational and health services on children and is measuring the varying affects produced by different amounts of contact between program staff and the families. By means of this carefully designed and evaluated assessment procedure, it is hoped that communities interested in tax-supported preschool programs will be given an opportunity to choose the model which is most effective in relation to cost and to the local educational resources available to them. Table 7 shows the schedule of diagnostic and evaluation procedures being used or being considered for use in the BEEP project.

Since the projected duration of this project includes the last group of BEEP subjects who will be eligible for public school kindergarten in 1979, it is not now possible to report all of the longitudinal findings anticipated from this demonstration project. A second year progress report (Pierson, 1974) gives the results of some of the diagnostic examinations conducted on the BEEP infants and toddlers; these examinations are being used for referring the children with suspect findings to appropriate intervention procedures. It is hoped that the longitudinal follow-up on these children will reveal patterns of borderline findings which ultimately prove predictive of later DLDs. Moreover, it is probable that some of the suspect findings will subsequently prove to have no lasting significance; whereas children falling completely within the normal limits on early exams may subsequently develop suspicious and debilitating findings as a function of increased age and experience. Of the 362 examination findings reported for March of 1973 through April 1974, 188 fell within normal limits, 131 revealed new suspicious findings, and 43 revealed the continued presence of the suspicious findings. As a result, 47 referrals were made to family physicians, community health centers, Children's Hospital, and appropriate social service agencies. Several case studies are reported to illustrate the procedures followed in this project. There are also guides for teacher training and general project administration and dissemination of findings. Since several levels of service are being explored in the BEEP

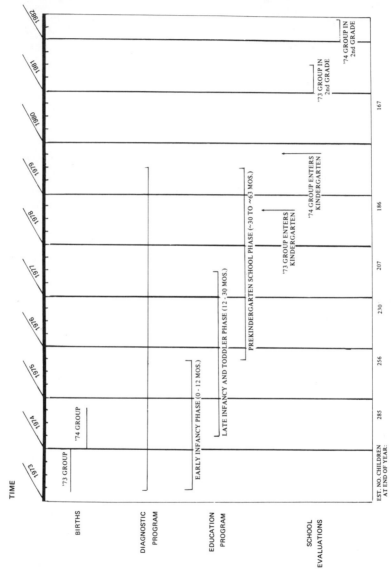

Figure 15. Time span of the BEEP programs. (Reprinted from Pierson, 1974, p. 7.)

Table 7. Diagnostic and evaluation procedures

24 Months	30 Months[a]	42 Months	54 Months	Entering kindergarten[a]	Mid second grade[a]
Health					
Physical examinations					
Medical event record					
Hearing and speech questionnaire					
Hearing evaluation					
Vision evaluation					
Neurological examination					
Orthopedic examination					
Dental examination					
Developmental					
Bayley Scales of Infant Development	Stanford-Binet Intelligence Scale	McCarthy Scales of Children's Abilities	Stanford-Binet	McCarthy Scales	California Achievement Tests[b]
Mental					
Motor	Harvard Test of Abstract Abilities			General information inquiry	Short form, academic aptitude[b]
Denver Developmental Screening Test					

Continued

Table 7—*Continued*

24 Months	30 Months[a]	42 Months	54 Months	Entering kindergarten[a]	Mid second grade[a]
Selected developmental items—to assess gross motor development	→				
Social competency rating	→————→				
Harvard Preschool Project language exam	→				
			Language sample[b] (exploratory) →————→	Language sample[b] (exploratory)	
					Writing sample[b]
				Circus[b]	
				Teacher ratings	
				Observations of task competence and social skills	

From Pierson, 1972, p. 55.
[a]Major evaluation points—examinations to be conducted by independent evaluators.
[b]Procedures under consideration.

program, it promises to reveal the most cost-effective combination of early detection, evaluation, and intervention tests and procedures for ensuring optimum growth and development in preschool children.

An integral part of the BEEP project is the assessment of organic predisposition to DLD. Since this was mentioned in Chapter 4, it does not seem necessary to elaborate here on the medical at-risk inventories developed by Levine (1973) for the BEEP Project. It will be of great interest to see which of the multiple at-risk inventory items has consistently predictive value for subsequent school functioning, whether this functioning is normal or is exceptional at either end of the continuum.

Interdisciplinary Child Development Evaluation

Repeatedly throughout this book, a plea is made for comprehensive interdisciplinary evaluations and management planning, if not the treatment itself. This is to ensure that no significant stone is left unturned when attempting to understand and remedy a given DLD condition. To give the reader some idea of the process, Figure 16 presents a flow system for clients undergoing an interdisciplinary developmental evaluation and management planning process in a typical university affiliated facility. This chapter is primarily concerned with the various activities numbered 1.1–3.13. Following the heavy dark arrow, the client is led through various intake procedures (1.1–2.0), to acceptance of the case (2.1), to assignment of discipline tasks (2.4), and to the accomplishment of each discipline's evaluation of the client based upon all of the information available (3.13). Chapter 7, which deals with the intervention process, takes the client from the point at which the case review commences (4.1) until the actual management recommendations are forthcoming from the interdisciplinary deliberations and summaries (5.1–5.12) and interpretations are sent to appropriate referral persons and agencies (6.2). Similarly, in Table 6, columns I through IV are concerned primarily with evaluation, with column V addressing or listing various intervention procedures mentioned in Chapter 5 for ages 0–3 years of age and in Chapter 7 for ages 4–6 years of age.

If the entry criteria specified by a particular learning and developmental evaluation center are met, then the intake worker will send the necessary forms to obtain signed releases of information from hospitals, agencies, and practitioners who have already seen the child. It is also useful to obtain as much preliminary information from the parents as possible. Table 8 presents an abbreviated version of a quite detailed questionnaire which is sent to the child's parent(s) or primary caregiver to be completed

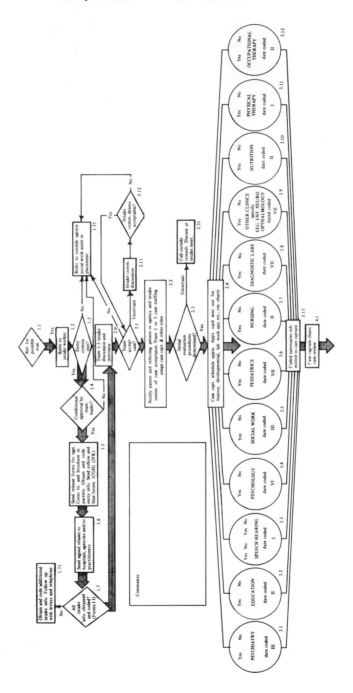

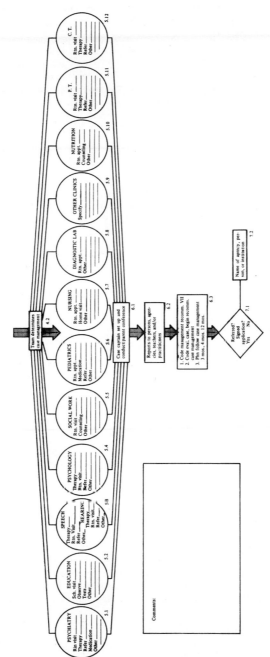

Figure 16. Child development center client flow system.

Table 8. Parent/guardian questionnaire (abbreviated sample)

This questionnaire concerns your child and his problems. Some of the questions may puzzle you because you may not remember the answers. Some of the information can be found by looking through baby books, calling your physician, or writing and talking to relatives. If you still do not know the answers, leave the questions blank.

Some of the information requested herein may not seem related to your child or his problems, but often seemingly unrelated data becomes very important to our study of the child. It also helps in making decisions as to how to best help your child. Therefore, please try to answer as many of the questions as possible.

If there is not enough space to answer a question, use the back of the sheets or write on paper of your own and clip it to the sheet where the question is found. (Note: in this abbreviated sample, all writing space has been eliminated and is indicated by a colon.)

General information
   Child's name: Birthdate: Sex: Home Address: Phone:
   Father's name: Birthdate: Occupation: Religion: Ethnic background: Years of schooling: Health:
   Mother's name: Birthdate: Occupation: Religion: Ethnic background: Years of schooling: Health:
   Previous marriage of either parent, and if so, date and to whom:
   Who referred you here for evaluation: What is it about your child which concerns you: When was it first noticed:
   How do you think that we might be able to help you: Please be specific.
   Whom have you seen: when and what were you told with regard to the problems:

X-Ray history
   X-rays in mother of child (include number, types and dates): X-rays in father of child (include number, types, and dates):

Pregnancy history
   Past pregnancies in this marriage: Number of times pregnant: Live births: Stillborn: Miscarriages:
   List dates of past pregnancies; indicate if there was a miscarriage; threatened miscarriage (bleeding); premature birth; twins; deformity or other difficulty with live-born children; or any other complication: Please list any birth defects however unimportant you consider them:
   Birthdate: Name: Birth weight: Condition at birth:
   Indicate how the above listed children are doing at the present time:
   Name: Present health: Grade in school: Any school problems:
   Are the mother and father cousins, or in any other way related:
   Mother's pregnancies before this marriage (include miscarriages and stillborn):

Continued

Table 8—*Continued*

Birth date: Name: Birth weight: Condition at birth:
Indicate how the above listed children are doing at the present time:
Name: Present Health: Grade in school: Any school problems:
Father's children before this marriage (include miscarriages and still-born):
Birth date: Name: Birth weight: Condition at birth:
Indicate how the above listed children are doing at the present time:
Name: Present health: Grade in school: Any school problems:

Family history
Please indicate if any of the persons listed below have the same problem for which you are seeking counseling. Also indicate for each of these persons all serious, chronic or recurrent illnesses or abnormalities such as birth defects, miscarriages, known sterility, diabetes, allergies, convulsions or epilepsy (fits), mental or emotional disorders, slow development, mental retardation, school problems, cerebral palsy, muscular disorders, cancers, leukemia, thyroid disease (goiter), deafness, or blindness. List all causes of death, if known, and age at time of death.
Mother of child^a: Birthplace: Father of child^a: Birthplace: Children:
Mother's relatives: Mother's sisters: Mother's brothers:
Maternal grandmother of child: Birthplace: Maternal grandfather of child: Birthplace: Maternal grandmother of mother: Birthplace: Maternal grandfather of mother: Birthplace: Mother's aunts on maternal side: Mother's uncles on maternal side: Mother's nieces and nephews: Mother's cousins on maternal side: Paternal grandmother of mother: Birthplace: Paternal grandfather of mother: Birthplace: Mother's aunts on paternal side: Mother's uncles on paternal side: Mother's cousins on paternal side: Mother's relatives, other:
Father's relatives: Father's sister: Father's brothers:
Paternal grandmother of child: Birthplace: Paternal grandfather of child: Birthdate: Maternal grandmother of father: Birthplace: Maternal grandfather of father: Birthplace: Father's aunts on maternal side: Father's uncles on maternal side: Father's nieces and nephews: Father's cousins on maternal side: Paternal grandmother of father: Birthplace. Paternal grandfather of father: Birthplace: Father's aunts on paternal side: Father's uncles on paternal side: Father's cousins on paternal side: Father's relatives, other:
Are there any marriages between cousins in any of these families:
Additional information that you think would be of value:

Pregnancy
Questions refer to the pregnancy for the child whose problem has caused you to seek assistance:
Did you have any problems getting pregnant: During which month did

Continued

Table 8–*Continued*

you start prenatal care: Where: Weight before pregnancy: Weight gain: Any weight loss in any part of pregnancy: Medicines taken and when (include all, such as vitamins, birth control pills, etc. Include aspirin if taken frequently): Did you smoke during the pregnancy: How many cigarettes a day: Have you ever smoked: How many years: Number of cigarettes/day: Any narcotic drugs during or prior to this pregnancy: Any illnesses or fever: X-rays during or shortly before pregnancy: Vaginal bleeding: Much morning sickness: Much swelling: High blood pressure: Hospitalizations: Operations: Accidents: Unusual worries: Special diet: When did you first feel the baby move: How were the baby's movements during pregnancy: Stronger than expected; weaker than expected; about the same as expected: How was the pregnancy confirmed: examination by doctor; urine sample; pills; hormone injection; other, describe: When, to the best of your recollection, was the pregnancy confirmed: Please indicate the number of weeks after the first day of the last menstrual period: Other comments or remarks that you think might be of importance.

Birth history
Questions refer to the child whose problem has caused you to seek assistance. Hospital of birth and address: Was the baby born on time, early or late: Any stimulation of labor used: type: Length of labor in hours: Length of hard labor: Length of time before delivery that bag of waters broke: Type of Anesthesia or pain relief: Sedative; Shot for pain relief; Spinal or caudal; Gas or Pentothal: Were you awake when the baby was born: Type of delivery: Natural: Breech: Cesarean section: Forceps: Mother's Blood Group (ABO): Mother's Rh factor: Baby's Blood Group (ABO): Baby's Rh factor: Infant's condition: Breathed immediately: Cried immediately: Required oxygen: Apgar score (1 minute): (5 minute): Length of stay in nursery: Problems during the first week (i.e., incubator; yellow skin, feeding difficulties, etc.): Baby's birth weight: Birth length: Birth head circumference: Later hospitalizations of child: Reason: Date: Hospital:

Environment, health, and development

Environment
Living Conditions
Who lives in home besides child, parents, brothers and sisters? List age, relation—if any, and health: List members of the family not living at home, where living, and reason:
Date of marriage of child's parents: Father's annual salary: Mother's annual salary: Home: Rent or own: No. of rooms: No. of bedrooms:

Continued

Table 8—*Continued*

Health

Past history of the child

Breast or bottle fed: Did child eat well: Childhood diseases: list age and anything unusual about any of them: Mumps: 3-day or German measles: Chicken pox: 7-day or red measles: Roseola: Scarlet fever: Whooping cough: Immunizations: dates or ages received—and any unusual reaction: DPT series: Smallpox: DPT booster: Measles: Polio (oral): Polio (shots): Rabies: Other:

If your child has had any of the following, please indicate and explain details: Accidents: Operations: High fever, unknown cause: Pneumonia: Anemia: Urine infection or disease; Constipation: Vision Problems: Crossed eyes: Speech problems: Hearing problems: Frequent ear infections: Foot problems (any special shoes, braces, etc): Skin disease or abnormality: Allergies: Birthmarks: Seizures or convulsions: Unusual fears: Sleeping difficulties and night terrors: Head banging: Breath holding: Temper tantrums: Discipline problem: Ingestion of toxins or poisons such as drugs, cleaners, etc.: Other illnesses:

Dental history

Has your child ever been examined by a dentist: For what reason: When was his last visit to the dentist: Name and office address of your child's dentist:

Development (See Giannini, et al., 1972, The Rapid Development Screening Checklist.)

Schools

List schools (with dates) that child has attended: Has child ever been in Special Education—if so, when, where, and what kind: Has child ever been in remedial classes—if so, when, where, and by whom: Has child ever been in special tutoring—if so, when, where, and by whom: Has child ever received speech therapy—if so, when and where: Has child ever received any other type of therapy: Has child ever been in preschool classes—if so, when and where:

Additional information that you think would be of value:

Miscellaneous

What things does your child like to do: What things does your child do well: Does your child ever eat nonfood items: If yes, please describe: Describe play indoors: Describe play outdoors: How does your child play and/or get along with other children: Has your child been separated from the family: (age, duration, and reason): Please indicate any recent major family events or problems, such as a death, serious illness or accident: Give a detailed description of an average day:

Continued

Table 8—*Continued*

In order to have a better understanding of your child's particular needs, it is important to gather background information from the following places and persons. Please list their names and addresses and complete and sign the authorization for release of information forms enclosed: Doctor who delivered child—Name: Address: City: State: Hospital where child was born—Name: Address: City: State: Places where child has received care: Hospitals—Name: Address: City: State: Agencies (welfare, visiting nurse service, speech, occupational or physical therapy, psychiatric, etc.): Name: Address: City: State: Physicians who have cared for your child—Name: Address: City: State: Schools: (Pre-school, nursery) Kindergarten—Name: Address: City: State: Grade School—Name: Address: City: State: Special school—Name: Address: City: State:

Signature: Relationship: Date:

---

[a]A release of information form is enclosed with questionnaire.

and submitted to the child development center before the appropriate disposition of the case can be determined. In some cases, the additional information indicates that the child should be referred to a more appropriate outside agency (Figure 16, 1.31), but if the intake committee and the evaluation team decide that the case is appropriate (2.1), the parent or primary caregiver is notified of the case acceptance (2.2). The initial evaluation procedures then are determined (items 3.1–3.12) in order to identify whatever DLD conditions are present according to the several disciplines listed in Figure 16 (and also in Figure 9 of Chapter 3).

The various conditions which are found are classified as shown in Table 9, which is one page of a more lengthy classification schema and annual reporting form developed by the U. S. Maternal and Child Health Division to be used by a national network of child development centers located in university affiliated facilities. These various problems are then collected together, summarized, and coded for subsequent presentation at a full case review where the interaction of these many problems is discussed and placed in proper perspective for arriving at management intervention/prevention recommendations (6.3). A national client-tracking and data base system has been created to pool these data from the nearly 40 centers serving DLD children (Mayeda, 1973). This reservoir of client data will facilitate making accurate estimates of national incidence and prevalence of various DLD conditions plus providing a great deal of readily retrievable data for many applied clinical research studies. This process of

Table 9. Classification schema for DLD conditions, using mental retardation as example

PART IV. CLASSIFICATION OF NEW PATIENTS
A. MEDICAL CLASSIFICATION OF MENTALLY RETARDED PATIENTS BY PRIMARY ETIOLOGY

Code	Category	Patients	Code	Category	Patients
.0	TOTAL NEW PATIENTS ON LINE IIB, 2a		.33	Cerebral white matter, degenerative	
	INFECTIONS AND INTOXICATIONS		.34	Specific fibre tracts or neural groups, degenerative	
.01	Prenatal infection		.35	Cerebrovascular system	
.02	Postnatal cerebral infection		.39	Other (including .38)	
.03	Intoxication		.4	UNKNOWN PRENATAL INFLUENCE	
.031	Toxemia of pregnancy		.41	Cerebral malformation	
.032	Other maternal intoxications		.42	Craniofacial anomaly	
.033	Other maternal disorders, not PKU		.43	Status dysgraphicus	
.034	Hyperbilirubinemia		.44	Hydrocephalus	
.035	Lead		.45	Hydranencephaly	
.036	Post immunization		.46	Multiple malformations	
.039	Other (including .038)		.47	Single umbilical artery	
.1	TRAUMA OR PHYSICAL AGENT		.49	Other (including .48)	
.11	Prenatal injury		.5	CHROMOSOMAL ABNORMALITY	
.12	Mechanical injury at birth		.50	A Group	
.13	Perinatal hypoxia		.51	B Group	
.14	Postnatal hypoxia		.52	C Group	
.15	Postnatal injury		.53	D Group	
.2	METABOLISM OR NUTRITION		.54	E Group	
.21	Neuronal lipid storage diseases				
.22	Carbohydrate disorders				

Continued

Table 9—Continued

Code	Category	Patients	Code	Category	Patients
.23	Amino acid disorders		.55	F Group	
.231	Phenylketonuria		.56	G Group	
.239	Other (*including .238*)		.57	X Chromosome	
.24	Nucleotide disorders		.58	Y Chromosome	
.25	Mineral disorders		.59	Chromosomal abnormality, other	
.26	Endocrine disorders		.6	GESTATIONAL DISORDERS	
.261	Thyroid dysfunction		.61	Prematurity	
.269	Other (*including .268*)		.62	Small for date	
.27	Nutritional disorders		.63	Postmaturity	
.29	Other (*including .28*)		.69	Other (*including .68*)	
.3	GROSS BRAIN DISEASE (POSTNATAL)		.7	FOLLOWING PSYCHIATRIC DISORDER	
.31	Neurocutaneous dysplasia		.8	ENVIRONMENTAL INFLUENCES	
.311	Neurofibromatosis		.81	Psychosocial disadvantage	
.312	Trigeminal cerebral angiomatosis		.82	Sensory deprivation	
.313	Tuberous sclerosis		.89	Other (*including .88*)	
.319	Other (including .318)		.9	OTHER CONDITIONS (*include 317*)	
.32	Tumors		V	TOTAL MENTALLY RETARDED (sum of items with single digit code)	
			W	NOT MENTALLY RETARDED	
			XX	NOT DETERMINED (not evaluated) (include 318)	
			Z	TOTAL NEW PATIENTS (same as Part IIB, Item 2a)	

B. MEDICAL CLASSIFICATION OF MENTALLY RETARDED PATIENTS BY ADDITIONAL IMPAIRMENT

TOTAL NEW MENTALLY RETARDED PATIENTS

(See IV A, Line V) (Total of positive and negative cases in each group below)

Code	Category	Patients	Code	Category	Patients
0	MINIMAL CEREBRAL DYSFUNCTION		6	PSYCHIATRIC IMPAIRMENT, NOT IN .7 CODE	
00	No minimal cerebral dysfunction		60	No other psychiatric impairment	
1	GENETIC COMPONENT		6x	Impairment not further specified	
10	No genetic component		61	Psychosis, hallucination, delusion, disorientation, etc.	
2	SECONDARY CRANIAL ANOMALY		62	Neurosis, severe anxiety, tension, phobia	
20	No secondary cranial anomaly		63	Character	
3	IMPAIRMENT OF SPECIAL SENSES		64	Psychophysiologic disorder, i.e., psychogenic (e.g., flushing, sweating, vomiting)	
30	No impairment of special senses		69	Other	
3x	Impairment not further specified		7	MOTOR DYSFUNCTION	
31	Deaf (i.e., 95 decibel loss in best ear)		70	No motor dysfunction	
32	Hearing handicapped, include partial hearing (i.e., 30–95 decibel loss in best ear)		7x	Dysfunction not further specified	
33	Blind (i.e., 20/200 in best eye)		71	Ataxia	
34	Visually handicapped (i.e., 20/40 to 20/200 in best eye) Includes partial blindness, blindness in one eye, hemianopia, etc. Exclude correctable refractive error		72	Hypotonia	
			73	Choreoathetosis	
35	Deaf-blind		74	Dystonia	
36	Blind and hearing handicapped		75	Rigidity	
37	Deaf and visually handicapped		76	Tremors	
38	Hearing and visually handicapped		77	Spasticity	
39	Other (specify)		79	Other (including mixed)	

Continued

Table 9—*Continued*

Code	Category	Patients	Code	Category	Patients
4	DISORDERS OF PERCEPTION AND EXPRESSION		8	OTHER CONGENITAL ABNORMALITIES	
40	No disorders of perception and expression		80	No other congenital abnormalities	
4x	Disorder not further specified		8x	Abnormality not further specified	
41	No speech		81	Of circulatory system	
42	Motor disorder of speech		82	Of digestive system	
43	Perceptual disorder (sensory cortical)		83	Of genito-urinary system	
49	Other		84	Of bone, joint, skin, and muscle	
5	CONVULSIVE DISORDER		85	Of respiratory system	
50	No convulsive disorder		86	Of blood and blood-forming organs	
5x	Disorder not further specified		87	Of endocrine system and metabolic diseases	
51	Akinetic seizures		89	Other	
52	Autonomic seizures		9	ACADEMIC RETARDATION IN SCHOOL GRADE	
53	Focal seizures		90	No academic retardation in school grade as pupil in school; or not in school	
54	Major motor seizures		91	Retention in grade (repetition of grade)	
55	Myoclonic seizures (*includes infantile spasms*)		92	Placement in grade lower than normal for chronological age of patient	
56	Petit mal seizures		XX	OTHER (conditions not covered by above categories 0 to 9)	
57	Psychomotor seizures		XO	No other conditions	
59	Mixed, unclassifiable, other		XI	Other conditions, specify (attach sheet if you wish)	

"getting it all together" is arduous and time consuming, but is believed to be most efficacious in the long run. Such information will be especially important in the planning of subsequent phases of national programs of early periodic screening, diagnosis and treatment plus the development of the subsequent intervention programs in conjunction with such early identification.

chapter 7

Prevention/ Intervention Procedures for Developmental and Learning Disabilities In Preschoolers

THE PRESCHOOL MOVEMENT–THE PENDULUM SWINGS

Various persons addressing the area of preschool intervention programs for DLD children are asking whether the movement is a brilliant star or glaring copout (McCulloch, 1975) or panacea or portent (Moore and Moore, 1972)? An article which characterized the learning-disabled child as the latest victim in education (Divoky, 1974b) elicited a heated exchange among the readers of *Learning* magazine. Divoky indicated that the LD (and, by association, the DLD) movement is based on very shaky information about neurological functioning, a lot of semantic games, and numerous unvalidated identification, evaluation, and intervention procedures. She cogently challenged the traditional medical model, which tends to promote the notion that DLDs are exclusively intraindividual and that the victims should, therefore, be treated as standard patients for whom specialized prescriptive therapy is to be ordered.

Before that, Divoky (1974a) had taken on the entire field of early childhood education and suggested that it was fading because of its failure to live up to its overzealous promises. The pendulum seemed to be swinging for several reasons, two of which were: (1) the overwhelming difficulty of organizing the unwieldy federal and state bureaucracies to mount coherent and effective programs and (2) the mounting evidence that many programs which promised to reap major benefits for children were later shown to have a marked washout effect, where most of the gains disappeared after the programs were discontinued or the children graduated. Zigler (1973), past director of the U. S. Office of Child Development, identified early childhood education's benefits primarily as a respite for mothers from the tough task of mothering, employment for teachers of Head Start, and an opportunity for the participating children to improve their social interacting skills and to enjoy an interesting and happy experience. The reintroduced versions of federal child care legislation (e.g., The Child and Family Services Act—SB-626—by Senator Mondale et al., 1975) tend to place greater emphasis on family revitalization as a means of ensuring optimum child development rather than removal of the child from his home and placing him in large day care centers as was previously advocated.

> . . . The child who thus develops values of responsibility, neatness, promptness, etc., becomes a self-respecting creature. This translates into self-discipline and intrinsic motivation of a high order.
> . . . To the extent that we can support this family integrity, by hewing as close as possible to the home ideal, the child will not only be a better social and emotional creature, but also a better intellectual person, with all the mental stimulation that may be appropriate for his age (Moore and Moore, 1972, p. 15).

The various criticisms and outright dismissals of early childhood special education for DLD children, as defined in this book, have not gone without equally vigorous and compelling reactions. As might be expected, reactions came from the various state associations for children with learning disabilities, from authorities in the field of learning disabilities, as well as from editors of the various journals addressing developmental and learning disabilities. Since a substantial part of Chapter 5 addresses the general rationale for early intervention and prevention procedures, including early childhood special education, it is redundant to repeat that rationale here. Besides, each of the multiple programs which have had some desirable impact on children, their families, and the larger society has its own rationale which should be understood in order to appreciate the idiosyncrasies of each intervention/prevention effort. Regardless of the pendulum's present swing in the direction of fashionable disfavor toward prevention/intervention procedures, the empirically substantiated positive impact of some programs is impressive (Bronfenbrenner, 1970; White and Watts, 1973). The first half of this chapter briefly presents several major programmatic issues and a representative sample of the more efficacious programs, which are listed in column V of Table 6 and are useful in counteracting various DLD conditions. The second half of this chapter presents one programmatic approach in considerable depth and, finally, discusses some of the accountability issues attendant to all prevention/intervention efforts.

DELIBERATE SHAPING OF BEHAVIOR

The use of behavior modification in the education of young children in general and DLD children in particular has been addressed in detail elsewhere (Thoresen, 1973). Much of the pioneering in the applied use of behavior modification principles to human beings occurred in residential institutions for seriously handicapped individuals, in order to help them learn fundamental daily living skills and thereby become more independent. As the power and efficacy of these principles were empirically validated in many clinical settings, the techniques spread to application with more normally developing adults and children in more everyday settings (Bassin, 1975; Hewett, 1968).

Behavior modification is now being used for shaping the behavior of parents of children who already have or are at risk of subsequently developing behavior problems (Eyberg and Johnson, 1974). The parents were placed on a behavior modification regimen, and those who were subjected to this process became significantly superior in coping with their children's problems, were more highly regarded by the therapists working with their children, and were far more diligent in completing various assignments they received. A review of the application of behavior therapy to children's problems, where parents themselves carry out the intervention program, suggests that there are mixed results in these efforts because of multiple variables, some of which are very difficult to control in a practical daily living situation. In addition to the difficulties encountered when applying the principles of behavior modification to any individual in a natural setting, these difficulties become even more numerous and more difficult to overcome when applied to populations larger than one in natural settings (Reppucci and Saunders, 1974).

> For example, there is nothing in behavior modification that guides us in answering these questions: Where should one seek to enter a setting? Where will the points of conflict arise? What will constitute a viable support system? What is a realistic time perspective for change? From one standpoint, these can be viewed as "practical" questions. From the standpoint of the organizational or systems theorist, these are questions that are basic in that how one

answers them reflects the level of one's sophistication about complex social organizations. When behavior modification confronts its
theoretical limitations, it will be on its way to a new stage of growth
(Reppucci and Saunders, 1974, p. 660).

Recognition of the natural and theoretical limitations of behavior
modification when applied to more than one person at a time brings it
back to the reality sarcastically suggested by the frequently quoted statistical over-generalization, "All Indians walk single file; at least the one I saw
did." Although behavior modification theory and application have their
limitations, nevertheless, a burgeoning number of prevention/intervention
programs are employing them in the home, the school, and various other
residential and/or institutional settings. It has been reported in multiple
studies that children's learning is increased significantly by the application
of behavior modification, but at some hitherto untold expense, such as
implied in the phrase, "A token economy may result in token learning"
(Levine and Fasnacht, 1974).

It is heartening to realize that the relatively new technology of
behavior modification and its underlying rationale have reached sufficient
maturity to become introspectively self-critical and can more objectively
report their limitations, failures, and casualties as well as their successes.
All sorts of guides, handbooks, and related materials are being produced to
help teachers, parents, and employers shape up their respective charges to
behave as they wish them to behave. Corsini and Painter (1975) have
published a book aimed at parents to enable them to change their family
life in a more desirable direction by instituting such a disciplinary system.
They indicate that in order to be a successful parent the mother or father
must learn certain attitudes and behaviors when dealing with their children. Parents are counseled to stop over-protecting, over-estimating, and
over-supervising children. Instead, parents should express confidence in the
children's ability to care for themselves and to behave in a way that will
justify further confidence in them. These authors dismiss punishment
because it does not logically connect with whatever offense is being
punished and because it does not tell the child what to do but only what
not to do. Physical punishment also tells the child that power is what
counts; eventually, the physical size of the child is going to prevent
physical punishment, or turn the punisher into the punishee.

Such advice as letting natural consequences, when they are not
harmful or dangerous, teach the child to seek some experiences and to
avoid others, has been quite effective. Corsini and Painter discuss the use
of logical consequences and the setting up of contingencies when the
natural consequences are ineffective or harmful. The following brief

examples illustrate this commonsense application. If a child does not behave in a restaurant, he is taken home (presuming he prefers to be in the restaurant); if he loses money, he does not get more; if he breaks a window playing ball, he has to pay for the replacement; if he spills something, he has to clean it up, and so on. They even suggest a "bathroom technique" by which the mother or primary caregiver, when she reaches her wit's end, can literally have a time-out period locked in the bathroom, where she remains until she gains composure and the child has had a chance to understand that the mother expects the child to rectify his behavior and she is withdrawing from the situation until he does so. This is an interesting reversal of the more traditional time-out procedure of confining the child to his bedroom, closet, or strait-jacket. Another reportedly effective technique is that of waking a child during his sleep to fulfill a task that he has been assigned and has repeatedly neglected to do during his ordinary waking hours. Of course, if the neglectful behavior persists on the part of the child, and the adult must continue to awaken the child to do his chores, it becomes moot as to who is the shaper and who is the shapee.

The successful efforts of Premack (1959) to condition DLD preschool children to read and to do other academic tasks by use of high probability and low probability rooms led to the token economy principles and procedures reported in many articles and books. In his pioneering research laboratories, a high probability room was developed, which had all kinds of materials and activities available which children typically had a high probability of wanting to do. Down the hall was a low probability room containing various tasks and materials which were important for the child to master but for which most children would have a low probability of preference compared to those things in the high probability room. Various activities in the high probability room were illustrated on a "menu" and the child could choose from among these offerings one or more which he wished to do contingent upon his satisfactorily working on or completing a task assigned to him in the low probability room. Such behavior modification systems and principles have led to numerous programs throughout the world and the reports on their efficacy are indeed encouraging with respect to this powerful technique of managing and shaping the behavior and consequent development of normal and DLD children. However, limitations, such as the techniques not always working satisfactorily in nonlaboratory settings or abuses such as the overzealous use of aversive stimuli when other approaches work as well or better, must be considered. These precautions must be borne in mind to prevent the indiscriminate or inappropriate use of behavior modification, which abuse only serves to discredit the whole procedure (Meier and Weaver, 1974).

The theoretical limitations of behavior modification alluded to above by Reppucci and Saunders (1974) are quite real. Nonetheless, when the "natural setting" is sufficiently modified, the efficacy of the procedure is most impressive, if not alarming, as in Skinner's *Walden Two* (1948) and *Beyond Freedom and Dignity* (1971). When a dozen of us visited the U.S.S.R. in 1975 to conduct in-depth seminar exchanges with our counterpart Soviet scholars in child development and early childhood education, we were duly impressed by the systematic application of neobehaviorism (Figures 3A and 3B in Chapter 2) to the upbringing of Soviet infants, toddlers, and young children (*see also* Bronfenbrenner, 1970). The utter flatness of affect apparent on the faces of 1-year-old children, who silently and solemnly "played" various highly programmed games designed to stamp in certain moral qualities, was alarming. The precise and highly disciplined performances of 6-year-old children in language, art, and dance fundamentals were impressive. The apparent absence of spontaneity and creativity in their rather mechanistic and rote performances made many humanistic qualities conspicuously absent and depressive if not oppressive of their individual human spirits.

MEDICAL/PHYSICAL MODIFICATION TECHNIQUES

In those instances where a DLD apparently has its origin within the individual (intraindividual), it is sometimes necessary to intervene with various physical or chemical agents. In some instances the condition might respond to the singular application of occupational or physical therapy. Some language disabilities can be largely remediated through speech and physical therapy. However, the DLD field is filled with concerns about brain dysfunction which have led to the application of various forms of drug therapy and occasionally to even more heroic and radical neurosurgical procedures. The role of the physician in dealing with DLD children is a growing one which is inversely related to both the decline of serious and infectious disease and other acute childhood problems as well as to an increasing identification of the more subtle problems such as minimal brain dysfunction. In medical parlance, it is legitimate to refer to the DLD condition as a "syndrome," implying that there are multiple symptoms characteristically associated with it. Moreover, there are many DLD children with milder forms of DLDs who do not even demonstrate any of the traditional signs of organic insult to their brain or nervous system. Thus, the physician must be increasingly alert to the sorts of symptoms and soft signs which were outlined in Chapter 5 and are now included in various tests and procedures for screening and evaluation purposes. Such symptoms as hyperactivity, distractability, short attention span, emotional lability, and low frustration tolerance seem to be commonly experienced singly or in various combinations by DLD children and are thought to be the result of some brain dysfunction. As might be suspected, this dysfunction of the brain changes the perceptions the child has of his environment and frequently results in various behavioral disorders and emotional handicaps requiring considerable additional counseling and even psychotherapy.

One of the most widely discussed soft neurological signs of MBD is the one referred to as hyperactivity, hyperkinesis, or, simply, over-activity. This behavioral manifestation of a DLD condition is only one of the many soft signs, but, since space does not permit an account of the myriad other indicators of MBD, a more detailed discussion of hyperkinesis, including a wide variety of perspectives, is given here as an example of the range of opinion among the experts. Hyperkinesis seems to be a "driven" kind of behavior consisting of constantly nongoal-directed movement that is not under the conscious control of the DLD individual. Therefore, medical or chemical intervention may be required as would be the case with any other otherwise uncontrollable medical condition.

A hot debate rages around the advisability of administering psychoactive medications (the word "drugs" is generally no longer used in this context because of its bad connotations) to help manage such behavioral symptoms as hyperactivity and its attendant short attention span. The alleged paradoxical effect of certain stimulants calms the driven overactivity of these MBD DLD children with reportedly fewer undesirable side effects, such as the counterproductive drowsiness, caused by various tranquilizers (e.g., Phenobarbital or Dilantin). Much of the controversy stems from the growing impression that such medications have a different biochemical effect on immature developing brains than they do on behaviorally hyperactive DLD children. At this writing, the stimulants methylphenidate (Ritalin) and dextroamphetamine (Dexedrine) reportedly have been effective in reducing the hyperactivity and impulsitivity while increasing the attention span and acuity for two-thirds to three-fourths of those DLD children who are defined as behaviorally hyperactive. Since the child spends approximately one-seventh of his time in school each year, school is thus one place where intervention can be instituted and, in some cases, rendered more effective by the prudent use of stimulant medication. Medicating of DLD children in school is instituted not only to help the child to cope better in the present, but also to prevent the subsequent development of significant psychiatric and social problems in adolescence and later life as stated before. These problems include antisocial behavior, serious academic retardation, juvenile delinquency, dropping out, and depression in adolescence, or alcoholism, sociopathy, hysteria, and possibly even psychosis in adulthood (see Chapter 9 for further discussion).

In addition to discussing the pros and cons of medical intervention, Wunderlich (1970) discusses and diagrams the interaction between the brain and the environment. He makes various other suggestions for control of hyperkinesis which include training parents to be more understanding of overactive behavior; training parents to be more supportive of temporary chemotherapeutic intervention; and the gradual independent control of his own behavior on the part of the individual through various behavior modification applications.

Howell, Rever, and Scholl (1972) tend to take a more ecological approach, especially with regard to hyperactivity which they contend is secondary to other problems. The authors state that drug treatment alone is unsatisfactory and, in fact, may be a detriment insofar as it interferes with the individual's learning ability. They point out that the higher activity level in itself may not be a handicap and need not be regarded as maladaptive, although in many school settings it is in fact discouraged and suppressed. When the child seems to be learning according to his potential and is enjoying satisfactory social relationships, it may be more important to alter the attitudes of the adults and the arbitrary demands of the environment in order to permit the child to be his more active self. Of course, it is recognized that there is a point of diminishing returns beyond which true hyperactivity cannot be allowed to go. This led to Chess's description of some hyperactive children as "mother killers" caused by not only a fundamental mismatch between parent and child temperaments but also by a critical drain on the physical and psychic energy of the mother or principal caregiver (Thomas, Chess, and Birch, 1968). In this same intensive prospective study of the behavior of 136 children, 30% of the children designated hyperactive at 2 and 3 months of age and characterized as very intense, persistent, and adapting poorly to new situations developed behavioral problems in later life. However, there were other comparison children with similar characteristics who later developed satisfactorily. It seems that the critical variable in the psychic and social development of the children was the quality of the interaction pattern between the child's behavior and the parent's response. Management for such children, then, is not only in the realm of chemotherapy but may also require parent and/or teacher training in order to help them become more comfortable in dealing with such a child in the home and/or classroom.

A noteworthy example of unifying the medical, behavioral, and social science knowledge for the condition of hyperactivity is reflected in the report by Schmitt et al. (1973). This report discusses the various possible origins for hyperactivity, including developmental origins, neurological origins, and psychogenic origins. Moreover, besides discussing the differential diagnosis of the hyperactive child, a systematic analysis of various treatments of different kinds of hyperactivity is presented (see Table 10). Besides presenting this treatment matrix, certain procedures for modifying behavior of hyperactive children are given and include: (1) setting realistic goals; (2) giving outlets for the release of excess energy; (3) rewarding nonhyperactive behavior ("catch 'em being good"); (4) structuring the home existence and making it more predictable; (5) establishing rules to prevent harm to the child and others; and (6) designating an isolation or time-out room to "cool off." Hyperactivity is one of the more frequently mentioned symptoms of mild DLD conditions by exasperated parents and teachers and is, thus, discussed at some length herein. For a more complete discussion of the issues involved with hyperactivity, the reader is referred to the following references: Battle and Lacy (1972); Connors (1969); Keogh (1971b); Minde et al. (1971); Pope (1970); Stewart and Olds (1973); and Walker (1974).

Regardless of the nature or extent of a given DLD, it is disturbing to the child who experiences uncontrollable and inexplicable handicapping phenomena, such as the hyperkinesis discussed above as one of many possible examples. There is an increased vulnerability to emotional and personality problems for the DLD child who is continuously aware of the fact that he is different from most of his peers. The way in which caregiving and professional adults relate to DLD children is quite important in enabling them to make optimum adjustment to their DLD conditions. McDermott and Atina (1972) address this issue and suggest a new kind of "developmental specialist" whose training includes a knowledge of physical therapy, special education, psychology, social work, and speech therapy. This interdisciplinary training would help to integrate rather than to separate the physical, emotional, and intellectual parts of these DLD children. Such an individual would be the personification of the interprofessional about which Meier (1973a) writes in relation to the product of an interdisciplinary training program. One of the primary motivating factors for the production of this text is that of getting all of this sort of thing together in one place for use in interdisciplinary training programs. Although it is unlikely that this ideal interprofessional single individual will emerge in such programs, it is quite realistic to expect trainees in various specialty disciplines to become sufficiently familiar with the underlying principles and axioms of other disciplines so as to better understand their

Table 10. Treatment of the hyperactive child

	Label	Home management instructions	Medical/chemical therapy	Referral for learning problems	Additional referrals
Neurological Chronic	"Brain injury"	+	+	+	Occupational therapy
Acute	Depends on etiology	+	–	+	Neurosurgeon, etc.
Mental retardation	M.R.	+	Variable	+	Preschool stimulation program
Developmental	"Immature energy control center"	+	Usually not	Usually not	–
Psychogenic Mild	Hyperactivity from being under pressure	+	–	Not unless school is the source of anxiety	–
Severe	"Important emotional problems"	Won't work alone	After referral	Usually present	Needs mental health referral

own limitations and to better appreciate and use the resources available from other professionals specialized in other disciplines (see Figure 9 in Chapter 3).

EDUCATION MODIFICATION TECHNIQUES— SOME EXEMPLARY PRESCHOOL PROGRAMS

As shown in column 5 of Table 6 (Chapter 5), there are numerous preschool programs or approaches to intervention with the DLD child in his preschool years of 3–6 years of age. Moreover, the list of intervention models contained in Table 6 is merely representative of the wide diversity available, and the following citations are a slightly expanded list designed to include a larger variety. Each of these representative programs is amply described elsewhere, and it would be both redundant and beyond the scope of this text to attempt herein to describe each. Consequently, a citation of each follows in order to lead the reader to those programs or approaches which may be most suitable for a given child and set of circumstances, that is to say, the best intraindividual/extraindividual match. Since it is practically impossible to cluster these programs according to similarities and differences without doing violence to one or the other, they are simply cited in alphabetical order by author or sponsor organization. The entire title of one representative reference for each is given in Chapter 10 to at least provide some clues to the gist of its contents. *Appalachia* (1972); Ball (1974); Bereiter and Engleman (1966); Blank and Solomon (1968); Caldwell (1967a and b); Cruickshank et al. (1961); Delacato (1963); Frostig (1968); Getman and Kane (1964); Hooper (1968); Kamii and Radin (1970); Karnes and Zehrbach (1972); Kephart (1960); Lane (1971); Meier (1970); Miller (1968); *Minimal Brain Dysfunction Compendium* (1974); Montessori (1965b); Nedler (1972); Nimnicht, McAfee, and Meier (1969); O'Keefe (1973); Palmer (1969); Robison and Wann (1967); Schaefer and Aaronson (1972); Thompson (1972), Weikart (1971), Whitney and Parker (1972). White et al. (1973) produced a four-volume comprehensive report on federal programs for young children which very well represents the state of the art and knowledge regarding preschool education in the U. S. and which discusses many of the aforementioned programs.

RATIONALE FOR OPEN PRESCHOOL EDUCATION

Systematic Approach to Optimum Development and Learning

Educators are frequently asked why they are supporting and participating in their particular program. Their answers typically range from statements that it is the program mandated by the director, principal, or dean to carefully considered reasons as to why one kind of program seems better for them and the children than other programs. Whether the educators are, or could be, absolutely right or wrong is not as important as the fact that they know why they are doing what they are doing, that is, they have a rationale or set of interconnected reasons for their commitment and daily function. This section is concerned primarily with the theoretical under-pinnings for open systems in general and their implications for optimal learning and development in particular. The following section briefly describes the characteristics of an autotelic responsive environment—an open education system rooted in a theoretical rationale and body of re-search regarding open systems and, thus, serving as a prototype approach to intervention.

A system for open learning (SOL) is one concept of a comprehensive preschool educational system. This rationale section of the SOL program unravels the salient threads of several theoretical constructs from various disciplines and reweaves them into a meaningful rubric to be used as an umbrella over the SOL. The theses from several disciplines are presented, original quotations cited to augment authenticity, briefly analyzed, and synthesized into an overall gestalt which enables the SOL facilitator or critic to see the many faceted SOL program in its kaleidoscopic perspectives. At the risk of sounding overly dramatic, the interdisciplinary ration-ale is the heart which pumps life through and is inspirational for the establishment of a new, dynamic system for open learning. The SOL acronym can also be understood to stand for student-oriented learning, or changed to SOLE to emphasize the individualized features which are quite consistent with a system for open learning which is discussed in greater detail elsewhere (Meier, 1973a). The word "sol" means "sun" in several languages and lends connotations of enlightenment and warmth to any description of the learning environment. Moreover, it is submitted that an open learning environment is conducive to the optimum development of the individual when it enables the individual to progress in all develop-mental domains at his own rate and readiness levels. Although the follow-ing discussion is focused upon open learning, it is nonetheless referring to optimum development and is, thus, advanced as a useful prevention/inter-vention procedure for many preschool DLD conditions.

There are numerous kinds of systems contained within general systems theory (Buckley, 1968). Within the hierarchical skeletal structure of general systems theory (and above the static framework, predetermined clockwork, and mechanistic cybernetic systems) is found the separate classification of an *open* system which is a live, dynamic system that reproduces and maintains itself in the midst of various "throughputs" and has the evolutionary and survival properties required to adapt to novel and changing surroundings (Boulding, 1968).

Allport (1960) addressed himself to open systems in personality theory. He states that all living organisms are open systems and that all personality theories, although differing widely, are more or less open systems with certain characteristics.

> If we comb definitions of open systems we can piece together four criteria: there is intake and output of both matter and energy; there is the achievement and maintenance of steady (homeostatic) states, so that the intrusion of outer energy will not seriously disrupt internal form and order; there is generally an increase of order over time, owing to an increase in complexity and differentiation of parts; finally, at least at the human level, there is more than mere intake and output of matter and energy: there is extensive transactional commerce with the environment (Allport, 1960, p. 345).

One of the inherent characteristics of a system for open learning and development is that, within its structure, there are an indefinite number of learning episodes or throughputs, which can contribute to the growth-provoking learning and development of a person who has an open orientation toward himself (intraindividual), toward others in the human environment (interindividual), and toward the physical environment (extraindividual).

The episodic nature of learning has been discussed by Kohl (1969), when he presents the nature of curriculum in an open classroom:

> This matter of breaking down the tyranny of the "curriculum" is one of the most difficult problems facing teachers who are trying to develop open classrooms. Even though the texts are senseless and the children restless and bored, teachers still develop feelings of guilt that they are not "teaching" their students what they're supposed to know. Actually, the whole notion of there being an "orderly sequence" to learning is fallacious. Children's learning is *episodic* rather than vertical or linear. One can think of it as a spider web rather than as a staircase. Happily, more recent studies by psychologists and other experts are beginning to point this out (pp. 53–54).

The ideal content of a program for open learning and optimum development is comprised of a large and varied repertoire of learning episodes offered in an environment which is open and responsive in meaningful ways to the individual. The episodic nature of learning does not contradict the fact that learning episodes must be matched to the learner's ability and interest level, which is dictated by his developmental maturity. This is true whether the learning environment is designed for preschool children or postdoctoral graduate students. The rationale of the SOL program is integrally related to the open systems concepts in personality theories preposed by Allport (1960), Combs and Snygg (1959), Harvey (1966), Harvey, Hunt, and Schroder (1961), Lewin (1935 and in Chapter 2), and others who have addressed themselves to the critical issue of what kind of people our educational system must help to produce for optimum participation in our society.

One theory proposes a continuum of personality types ranging from System 1 to System 4 types.

> System 4 functioning, the more abstract end of the continuum, is viewed as the consequence of childhood freedom to explore both the social and physical aspects of one's environment, to establish and rely upon values derived from one's own experience and thought, and to solve problems and evolve solutions without fear of punishment for deviating from established truth. The System 4 representative who is the recipient of diversity along with stability as a developing child, and who is of high perceived self-worth despite momentary frustrations and deviation from the normative, comes to have a highly differentiated and integrated cognitive structure and consequently to be more flexible, more creative and more relative in thought and action . . . (Harvey, 1966, p. 46).

This theory of personality systems, which enables various personality types to be quite reliably and validly identified, is an encouraging development and enables those operating a SOL program to select staff whose personalities are compatible with the overall rationale. Of course, this theory requires considerable additional validation, but it is a step in the direction the SOL program is heading. Allport indicates that such validation may be a while in coming. However, an open approach to personality theory adds to the controversy about the nature of humanity; the resultant multiple and highly divergent assumptions are unfortunately not cumulative.

> Theories, we know, are ideally derived from axioms, and if axioms are lacking, as in our field, they are from assumptions. But our assumptions regarding the nature of man range from the Adlerian to the Zilborgian, from the Lockean to the Leibnitzian, from the Freudian to the Hullian, and from the cybernetic to the existentialist. Some of us model man after the pigeon; others view his potentialities as many splendored. And there is no agreement in sight.
> . . . Among our students, I trust, there will be many adventurers. Shall we not teach them that in the pastures of science it is not only the sacred cows that can yield good scientific milk? (Allport, 1960, p. 350)

It is possible to engage further in lengthy discourse and analysis of current educational and societal systems as well as theories of personality. Suffice it to say that at this juncture the accumulated empirical evidence and theoretical bases for the desirability of implementing a SOL program as an exemplary kind of prevention/intervention procedure for preschool DLDs are quite compelling and gradually accumulating (Miller, 1975; Rayder and Body, 1975; and Stallings, 1974).

In some aspects, the philosophical and psychological underpinnings of the SOL program can be traced historically to the writings of such American philosophers as Dewey (1916), Kilpatrick (1914 and 1916), and others identified with the progressive education movement several decades ago; it is noteworthy that a 1970 conference on early childhood education, entitled "Open Education," was subtitled "Legacy of the Progressive Movement." Other early childhood education pioneers such as Comenius (1896a and b), Gesell (1924), Froebel (1912a and b), McMillan (1920), Montessori (1964, 1965a and b), Pestalozzi (1894 and 1898), Rousseau (cf. Boyd, 1911), and others are all in one way or another identified with the open system of learning.

Now there are students of human development and learning, such as Bruner (1960 and 1966), Gordon (1962 and 1965), Holt (1964 and 1967), Piaget (1932 and 1960), Weber (1971), and others, suggesting that optimum learning occurs under conditions consistent with a SOL program. However, because of the spontaneity of learning which typically occurs in a SOL program, the learning facilitator, who is no longer called a teacher, must be trained to function in a spontaneous and response-ably resourceful fashion. This is borne out in the realm of psychotherapy as well, where the leader's style for group therapy and presumably the therapist's style for individual therapy get best results from response-able persons.

> If we want to be helpers, counselors, teachers, guiders, or psychotherapists, what we must do is to accept the person and help him learn what kind of person he is already. What is his style, what are his apititudes, what is he good for, what can we build upon, what are his good raw materials, his good potentialities? We would be nonthreatening and would supply an atmosphere of acceptance of the child's nature which reduces fear, anxiety and defense to the minimum possible. Above all, we would care for the child, that is enjoy him and his growth and self-actualization (Maslow, 1968, p. 693).

The curriculum for such a learning facilitator becomes a series of learning episodes, which can be extemporaneously introduced into any appropriate set of circumstances and modified to meet the individual and active learner's current interests and developmental capacity. The revised and enlarged *System for Open Learning: Learning Episodes,* Book II (Meier, 1975a), is comprised of more than 200 sample learning episodes for adaptation to any given preschool responsive environment and is mentioned simply as one example from among many available quasicurricula.

A spontaneous and appropriate response to a learner's inquiry and discovery behavior is a problem for many learning facilitators to resolve; it has been described by Hunt (1961 and 1964) as the "problem of the match" between a learning facilitator's and a learner's styles. The problem of the match is discussed in somewhat different terminology by Montessori (1965b) in her description of spontaneous learning in the classroom. Such a SOL program fosters creative thinking which seems to get snuffed out by traditional school programs.

> Many youngsters in the beginning year of junior high school express concepts about creative problem solving and self concepts that would seem to limit seriously their ability to learn on their own and solve problems. Many of them apparently feel rather keenly that their ideas are not given serious consideration by classmates and are likely to be ridiculed. Many seventh graders are handicapped by beliefs in one best answer to all problems, the authority of the peer majority, an aversion to new and divergent ideas, suppression of ideas, the innateness of problem-solving ability, and the unresponsiveness of these abilities to practice and education. Fortunately, however, many of these attitudes and concepts are amenable to change through preventive and remedial projects (Torrance, 1965, p. 85).

The majority of informed persons in an open society are painfully aware of the rapidly accumulating stockpile of factual knowledge and the equally rapid rate at which many preconceived and sacred ideas undergo radical change as new information is accumulated (Toffler, 1970). As a result of this rapid turnover in factual data, it is predictable that much of the factual information one learns in any given year will be obsolete in a matter of 5–10 years in the future. This short half-life of factual information has given rise to a re-examination of the kind of end-product the society should attempt to produce in its educational system. As the eternal verities shrink in number, and since much of the information considered sacred today can be expected to lose much of its utility by tomorrow, a shift in the focus of education is occurring. The shift is away from the rote memorization of factual information, which is only tentative, to a focus upon the process of learning. In short, the emphasis is shifting to learning how to learn.

Consistent with the notion that one learns by doing, if a person is learning to learn, the best way to do so is to practice learning. Although this may sound like circuitous reasoning, it is merely suggesting that learning how to learn is best accomplished in an environment which is structured so that it is open and responsive to each individual's efforts to master himself (intraindividual) and his extraindividual environment, whether it be impersonal or interindividual. Ideally, the individual learns to master as many facets of himself and his environment as possible besides developing the wisdom to know what is impossible to control and how to cope with it (analogous to the slogan of Alcoholics Anonymous). Thus, the learning facilitator or DLD manager structures the environment in such a way that the DLD child, regardless of what he chooses to invest his time and interest in, inevitably encounters and experiences learning and development. Moreover, the child develops an inner-directedness (Riessman, 1962) or internal locus of control (Rotter, 1967) as he acts as the independent variable in each learning experiment. This is in clear distinction to the dependent, other-directed, externally controlled learner who passively waits to be stimulated by the people and things in the environment and often meets with sheer boredom and/or feelings of alienation toward the establishment which traditionally perpetrates a sterile and stifling milieu.

In keeping with the technocracy and its many recent advances, a SOL program relies to some extent upon technological facilitation of learning. A pervasive belief among traditional school authorities is that the teacher-to-child ratio is an extremely crucial consideration in determining a quality program. However, it can be argued that one caring and competent learning facilitator can do more good for 50 children than 5 uncaring and incompetent taskmasters can do harm. In the traditional sense of the word *education,* meaning to draw out or lead out, the student or pupil is to a large extent the passive recipient of information from the teacher. Or, he is the subject from whom the teacher draws out information which, according to some Socratic theorists, is innate and according to other didactically oriented theorists has been taught into the student. Thus, the stimulus-response paradigm (see Chapter 2 for a brief explanation of this learning theory) is that of an adult teacher and school system stimulating a student or pupil, who, it is hoped, will respond in the desired fashion and not rebel.

The SOL program reverses this stimulus-response paradigm and places the joy of learning directly in the learner and considers the learner as the stimulus in the environment; the external environment, both interindividual and extraindividual, becomes the responsive element in the learning process.

> The shift in point-of-view—to set the antitheses sharply—has been from the child who is a passive receptacle, into which learning and maturation pour knowledge and skills and affects until he is full, to the child as a complex, competent organism who by acting on the environment and being acted on in turn, develops more elaborated and balanced ways of dealing with discrepancy, conflict, and disequilibrium. This shift, I believe, is of incalculable implication and seems to have been accepted to some degree by almost all students of children. Bowlby emphasizes the control by the child in crying and smiling; psychoanalytic theory makes more space for autonomous ego functions; child psychologists dedicated to a learning analysis speak of the child as active; and I suspect Piaget thinks of how he knows it all the time (Kessen, 1963, p. 92).

The human (interindividual) and nonhuman (extraindividual) response-ability becomes the criterion upon which the quality of any learning or developmental program is judged. In some instances, educational technology, such as "teaching" machines, which tirelessly and reliably respond to a learner's inquiries and explorations, are employed to supplement the more versatile and creative human components of the system, thus freeing these learning facilitators to engage in more creative interaction with learners. The technology of self-correcting teaching machines (more properly labeled learning machines) and educational (learning) games can reduce the demand upon the adult learning facilitator, whose role in a traditional, relatively barren, learning environment is one of maintaining the attention and interest of all the learners all the time they are within his/her control. In the SOL program, the learners are free to interact with their peers, with the learning facilitators, and with their physical environment in practically any way or combination they choose. The properly chosen physical components of the enriched preschool learning environment bear a great deal of the minute-by-minute burden of meaningful interaction between the learner and the entire learning environment. Thus, the SOL environment fosters the individual learner's quest for competence because of its *effectance* or intrinsically attractive (autotelic) properties.

> We are no longer obliged to look for a source of energy external to the nervous system, for a consummatory climax, or for fixed connection between reinforcement and tension-reduction. Effectance motivation cannot, of course, be conceived as having a source in tissues external to the nervous system. It is in no sense a deficit motive. We must assume it to be neurogenic, its "energies" being simply those of the living cells that make up the nervous system. External stimuli play an important part, but in terms of "energy" this part is secondary, as one can see most clearly when environmental stimulation is actively sought. Putting it pictur-

esquely, we might say that the effectance urge represents what the neuromuscular system wants to do when it is otherwise unoccupied or is gently stimulated by the environment (White, 1959, p. 316)...

... White is saying that, given a situation of mild arousal, the child will engage in a wide variety of activities because it is satisfying to him to deal effectively with his environment. He will seek out the more complex tasks over the simpler ones he can already perform.

Simple observation of children on the street or playground shows this: the youngster who has mastered the elements of bike riding tries to do it with "no hands," the prospective little league star chides the novice with the cry that "two hands are for beginners," and the adolescent with the newly acquired driving license is not content merely to drive, but engages in "drag races" and games of "chicken." The adult, in turn, climbs Mount Everest "because it's there" (Gordon, 1965, p. 67).

This emphasis on the learner in no way depreciates the value of the human learning facilitator who is always present and available to the learner as needed. In fact, to be an effective learning facilitator for a group of children, especially if several are DLD children, requires an extraordinarily alert and resourceful person who can spontaneously orchestrate and even create learning episodes for a wide variety of matches. The focus on the learner emphasizes that, when a learner is interested in drawing upon the rich resources of the human learning facilitators, they will be ready to respond in a fashion that is far more significant to the learner. After the learning facilitator becomes aware of the greater efficacy of this approach, it enhances his/her self-esteem since he/she is able to perform the role of facilitating learning and development in a far more meaningful and satisfying way than the traditional teacher.

As discussed in Chapter 5, an enriched environment significantly increased the cell density and connective tissue complexity for animals and, by inference, has a similar salutary effect on the human computer. The complexity of a computer's circuitry and the extent of its storage capacity determine its ability to deal with complex data. The SOL program is premised upon the transactional model of man, which, among other nuclear age notions, postulates a computer brain (Table 11, number 3). The SOL program is designed around the contemporary behavioral science findings listed in the right-hand column of Table 11 as a basis for a unique preschool experience for all involved.

The curriculum for a SOL program is a many splendored, evolving creation. Multiple learning episodes are suggested for the SOL facilitator's repertoire (Meier, 1973a, *Facilitator's Handbook II*). However, the total curriculum cannot be written down in a series of daily lesson plans since

Table 11. Two models of man

Linear causation model man (a mechanistic, fixed, closed system, characterized by:)	Transactional model man (an open-energy, self-organizing system, characterized by:)

1. Development as orderly unfolding
   a. Physical-physiological-genetic
   b. Socioemotional: antecedent-consequent
   c. Intellectual-fixed
2. Potential as fixed, although indeterminable
3. A telephone switchboard brain
4. Steam engine driven motor
 	
5. Inactivity until engine is stoked
6. Additive collection of past
7. Uniqueness essentially genetic
	1. Development as modifiable in both rate and sequence
	   a. Genetic-experiential
	   b. Socioemotional: field transactional
	   c. Intellectual-modifiable
	2. Potential as creatable through transaction with environment
	3. A computer brain
	4. A nuclear power plant energy system
	5. Continuous internal flow of activity
	6. Organization into a system
	7. Uniqueness continuously evolving from organism-environment transactions

From Gordon, 1965, p. 50.

learners are, fortunately or unfortunately, depending upon one's viewpoint, not sufficiently predictable as groups to allow for anything but an authoritarian classroom to keep them all in their places with bright shiny faces and to prevent them from moving at their own rate with a curriculum which they find relevant to their interests at the time.

The obsolescence of certain pedagogical notions derived from the linear causation model of man (left-hand column of Table 11) is underscored by Elkind (1969), who is a renowned Piagetian exponent:

> In this essay I have discussed four of the arguments for introducing an academic curriculum into preschool education. These arguments were that academic instruction is: a) more economical; b) more efficient; c) more necessary, and d) more cognitively stimulating than the traditional preschool. I have tried to show that each of these arguments are weak at best and that there are stronger arguments yet for not having an academic preschool at least for the middle class child. There is no preponderance of evidence that formal instruction is more efficient, more economical, more necessary or more cognitively stimulating than the traditional preschool

program. Indeed, while there is room for improvement in the traditional preschool, it already embodies some of the most innovative educational practices extant today. It would, in fact, be foolish to pattern the vastly expanded preschool programs planned for the future upon an instructional format that is rapidly being given up at higher educational levels. Indeed, it is becoming more and more apparent that the usual formal instructional program is as inappropriate at the primary and secondary levels of education as it is at the preschool level (pp. 13—14).

The SOL program is also suitable for children whose DLDs are caused by extraindividual origins and it seeks out and welcomes individuals from all economic and ethnic strata of this pluralistic society. Nevertheless, the creative resourcefulness of the learning facilitator is necessary to appropriately modify the learning episodes to match each learner's abilities and interests.

> ... The application of pedagogical concern, competence and skill to the improved education of the disadvantaged is forcing education to give more serious attention to some of the basic problems of teaching and learning. Reduced to its essence, the crucial pedagogical problem involved is that of understanding the mechanisms of learning facility and learning dysfunction and applying this knowledge to the optimum development of a heterogeneous population characterized by differential backgrounds, opportunities, and patterns of intellectual and social function (Gordon, 1970, p. 1).

Training of learning facilitators consists of alerting and sensitizing them to opportunities for entering into meaningful interactions with learners without being intrusive. This includes knowing when not to interfere with a learner who is interacting with other parts of his environment. It may entail the acquisition of a more humble and real understanding of the learning process on the part of those who are wont to be the dispensers of all wisdom and depended upon as authorities with all the information. In fact, the learning facilitator must master the process of learning for himself/herself so that he/she not only learns about the environment as he/she facilitates learning, but he/she also learns about each individual learner with all of his idiosyncrasies and capabilities. It is under these conditions that optimum learning circumstances obtain and the whole process and program take on an open, free, and enjoyable spirit which permeates its every participant and generates its own momentum for renewed learning activities as old ones are mastered and abandoned.

The SOL curriculum, then, is a flexible and, in many respects, unpredictable phenomenon. The SOL curriculum is a skeleton which is fleshed out by the simultaneous mutual interaction (Bigge and Hunt, 1962) between an enriched preschool environment and an emancipated learner. The daily program lends some structure to the availability of certain opportunities for learning, but beyond that does not pretend to prescribe precisely what will be occurring on a given date at a given time as do many lesson plans. To be sure, there will be many times when the learning facilitator will see an opportunity to clarify misunderstandings of a group of learners and have them all gathered around, sharing their thoughts and feelings and receiving clarifying feedback to help them to clarify their understanding of and attitudes about mechanical, musical, artistic, linguistic, and other learning experiences. When possible, the clarification will be in concrete terms; however, the SOL program allows ample room for abstract thinking (see also Moore and Anderson, 1968).

> While direct impression has the advantage of being first-hand, it also has the disadvantage of being limited in range. Direct acquaintance with the natural surroundings of the home environment, as a means of making real ideas about portions of the earth beyond the reach of the senses and as a means of arousing intellectual curiosity, is one thing. As an end-all and be-all of geographical knowledge it is fatally restricted. . . . Just as the race developed special symbols as tools of calculation and mathematical reasoning, because the use of the fingers as numerical symbols got in the way, so the individual must progress from concrete to abstract symbols—that is, symbols whose meaning is realized only through conceptual thinking (Dewey, 1916, p. 315).

There will be ample time for creative learning facilitators to introduce games, songs, stories, etc., to groups of children which vary in size and composition, depending upon the learners' interests or investment and the availability of other perhaps more attractive options. These times also allow the charismatic learning facilitator to do his/her things with learners who can elect to leave when the charisma is exhausted for them. The SOL program is in many respects a nondirective, gentle approach to learning which has an unconditional positive regard (Rogers, 1951) for the learner and enables and facilitates his understanding and mastery of the SOL environment including himself, his peers, his elders, and his physical surroundings.

A PROTOTYPE OPEN PRESCHOOL PROGRAM

Although prototype programs for a SOL preschool were established at least a decade ago, numerous variations have subsequently developed. The rationale and procedures have been applied to programs for normal and exceptional infants, children, and adults in locations throughout the world. This section briefly presents the characteristics of an open preschool and discusses four objectives related to a learning environment, with particular reference to the DLD learner.

An entire preschool program may be organized as an autotelic responsive environment (ARE) as Moore and Anderson (1968) have defined it. The ARE principles are compatible with the SOL philosophy, which is a logical extension of many of the ARE's, underlying concepts and practices. Thus, the following discussion of an ARE preschool program serves as the SOL prototype. The reader who is familiar with early childhood education will note that many outstanding nursery school programs in the United States have been operated more or less as responsive environments without the label. Nevertheless, it is essential to state the underlying principles explicitly because of their importance in formulating curricula and procedures and in evaluating the results.

Definition of Autotelic

An activity is autotelic if the activity is done for its own sake rather than for obtaining rewards or avoiding punishments that have no inherent connection with the activity itself. An ARE is one which satisfies the following conditions: (1) it permits the learner to explore freely; (2) it informs the learner immediately about the consequences of his actions; (3) it is self-pacing, i.e., events happen within the environment at a rate determined by the learner; (4) it permits the learner to make full use of his capacity for discovering relations of various kinds; and (5) its structure is such that the learner is likely to make a series of interconnected discoveries about the physical, cultural or social world (Moore, 1964, p. 89).

The definition of an ARE/SOL program points out important differences between it and the behavior modification approach briefly described earlier in this chapter. There is an emphasis on free exploration and discovering relationships. The learner's behavior is not shaped to perform a given task. The objective is not to teach the learner something step by step, but to place him in a situation where he can make his own discoveries. This aspect of the ARE is submitted to be more important for the preschool learner's overall development in the long run than the fact that he also usually learns to read and write, unless, of course, the DLD condition is quite severe. This hypothesis is, of course, speculative at this time, but there is limited and growing evidence to support the contention. In spite of the lack of emphasis on academic subjects, the SOL preschool program graduates are accelerated beyond their matched peers in reading and writing skills, and this successful advantage holds for several years at least (Meier, 1970).

Objectives

There are four primary objectives of the ARE/SOL preschool program. These were selected on the basis of various studies which indicate that DLD children do not develop in certain respects to the extent that one would expect of normally privileged learners. The objectives are: (1) to developmental domains discussed in previous chapters, social/emotional, physical, language, and cognitive/intellectual, respectively. The satisfactory meeting of these objectives enables the learner to gain the functional competency mentioned in Chapter 6 or the social competence now declared to be the overall goal for Head Start children.

Positive Self-Image   Learners at the ages of 3 and 4 are beginning to develop a sense of self-awareness, frequently called a self-concept, and an awareness of ethnic and racial differences. The way a person views himself tends to affect the way he behaves. Frequently, members of the culture of poverty have an inferior image of themselves and their ability to cope with the everyday problems of existence in a hostile society. DLD children often have poor self-images because of additional perceived inadequacies; moreover, a disproportionate number of them come from the culture of poverty, which may cause or at least compound their DLDs.

The families in poverty settings may be larger than most, living on the borderline between cohesiveness and disintegration as a family unit. They may be headed by defeated and often mentally ill or otherwise functionally incompetent adults. If the father is in the family, his position may be insecure; perhaps he cannot guarantee support for his wife or food for his children. The mother is often more likely than the father to obtain employment, which takes her out of the home with no one to replace her, and no labor-saving devices to help when she comes home. The problems of the adults are passed on to the children. A tired, worried mother has little time and energy to give to a child, regardless of how much she might love him. Each child compounds her problems, and the child misses the attention the mother should provide for his optimum development. Soon he learns that his very existence only creates problems. The first requirement in a school for environmentally deprived DLD children, therefore, must be to help each child to develop a positive self-image. The younger the child is when this process begins, the better. The entire SOL preschool program should be organized to foster a positive self-concept.

The SOL environment itself contributes to the development of a positive self-concept. The learner is free to explore and use anything within his sight or reach. Since the environment is self-pacing and noncompetitive, he is not compared unfavorably with someone who can speak better or build bigger and better block structures. Instead, he is free to do those things he can do and do them as long as he likes. It is the response-ability of the SOL learning facilitator to know a learner's strengths and weaknesses well enough to provide attractive learning episodes to help the child, especially a DLD child, to overcome or cope with his weaknesses. This often requires considerable planning and ingenuity on the part of the learning facilitator. Some people express the logical concern that this is an unreal situation and, therefore, may be harmful. Nevertheless, the SOL rationale is designed to partially compensate for the fact that the world offers an over-abundance of opportunity for a DLD child to discover that the world is ruthlessly competitive. What he and all normally developing children need most is to experience as much success as possible during the formative years when fundamental affective attitudes are developing.

In a SOL environment, the learner is placed in a situation where he can make discoveries about his physical and social world. This also means that real opportunities exist to praise the learner and his accomplishments when he makes these discoveries. This may sound inconsistent with the concept of autotelic activities because praise for an activity is generally extrinsic to the activity. The crucial point is that participation in the activity is not dependent upon external rewards or punishments, but is done because it is intrinsically interesting. For example, in truly amateur sports, the athlete does not participate because of the rewards or punishments, but because he likes the game. Competence, however, occasionally does receive praise or applause, in addition to its inherently satisfying feedback. This point may seem to be a fine one, but it is important in developing and establishing activities which are truly autotelic and do not depend upon extrinsic motivation.

The general rules concerning adult-child relationships are designed to aid in developing the learner's positive self-image. For example, adult-initiated conversations are too often demeaning or threatening. The typical adult-child conversation frequently starts off with, "My name is John. What's yours?" It continues with "What are you playing?" "Are you having fun?" etc. Whereas in a child-initiated conversation, the child will start with, "My daddy is going to Arizona," or "I saw a policeman yesterday," or "Our dog died." The simplest question asked by an adult, such as "What is your name?" can be threatening because it requires a response. "Hello" is better, just as "Good morning" is better than "How are you today?" Allowing and encouraging the learner to initiate the conversation also have the effect of saying to him, "What you have to say is important—you're important!"

Learning games and refreshment are usually limited to five or six learners at a time rather than to all 15 at once. With five or six learners and one facilitator at a table, conversation among all of the learners and the facilitator is possible, whereas with 15 learners only a few can participate. Another general rule is that the facilitators use the learner's name when speaking to him and write the learner's full name on all of his paper products. Facilitators play many games with the learners to help them learn their names. Another specific technique to build a positive self-image is simply to have a cubicle or "cubbie" for each learner where he keeps his coat, overshoes, and products. In each cubicle, the learner's photograph is placed so he might think, "That's me," "My place," and "My picture."

Sensory and Motor Development Such materials as pegs and pegboards, color cones, nesting cups, depth cylinders, Cuisenaire rods, puzzles, alphabet boards, and other manipulative toys are used to develop greater sensorimotor skills and perceptual acuity. Of course, numerous items can be effectively used in a SOL preschool program to meet this objective, and these are examples only. *System for Open Learning, Facilitator's Handbook II* (Meier, 1973a) contains more than 200 episodes for sensorimotor, affective/attitudinal, linguistic/interactional, and perceptual/ cognitive development, with entry and terminal behaviors, explanations and related details to ensure the effective application of each learning episode. The sensorimotor learning episodes are specifically designed to help the learner discover certain concepts about the physical world through structured play. As he puts together, takes apart, stacks, matches, nests, groups, and rearranges, he not only observes physical relationships, but participates in the physical manipulation of these materials.

Recent research has focused upon the importance of input to the senses, all the senses, in the development of perceptual/cognitive/ intellectual abilities. These studies have particular relevance for those concerned with the education of the preschool DLD child, since they emphasize the importance of the selection and use of equipment the learner can look at, feel, listen to, and manipulate.

The more privileged and normally developing child is surrounded by words and experiences, and, as he grows, he sorts out these experiences and generates workable concepts to deal with them. The casual observer, who observes this process by which most children develop and learn in such a "natural" way, may be inclined to believe that it happens automatically as a result of development or maturation alone. Until the last decade, even among teachers and researchers, there has been a tendency to stress the importance of development and maturation and to overlook the developmental impact of differences in environment. A 4-year-old without the richness and variety of experience customarily available to his normally developing and privileged peers, and without a vocabulary to think or talk about his experience, is in a different situation. He needs a period of time to work (play) with suitable manipulative toys and to have ample verbal interaction with the responsive facilitator and other learners who provide symbols (words) for what he is doing, has done, or expects to do. The experience alone is not enough. Simply placing the 3-, 4-, or 5-year-old DLD child in an enriched environment will not, by itself, make up for what he did not have at 1, 1½, or 2 years of age. The timing is wrong, and the supporting elements (speech and encouragement) were missing. Heber et al. (1972) and Robinson (1975) have demonstrated the importance of early and continuous intervention by systematically enriching the language environment of DLD-risk children whose mothers are functionally incompetent or retarded and whose cognitive and affective development consequently was dramatically accelerated beyond their matched controls, who received no such systematic intervention.

Language Development The development of language in young learners is crucial if they are going to be able to communicate and generally interact with other humans effectively. But, of equal importance is the internal use of language in the thought process. Language is required to progress from labels for things, such as oranges, apples, peaches, potatoes, carrots, peas—to categories such as fruits, vegetables, or food—to concepts such as nutrition, survival, life. "Over," "under," and "between" are relational concepts that can only be thought of in some language. Thus, developing receptive and expressive language skills is a prerequisite for most complex concept formation and problem solving.

Learning to speak and understand a language is one of the most difficult learning and developmental tasks confronted by young humans. It usually occurs before a learning facilitator can simplify the task by breaking it down into small logical steps as is done with reading and arithmetic. Since language develops in the preschool years, the naïve observer might think that it occurs almost by osmosis. However, careful observation shows that, even under the best of circumstances, acquiring a language is a long and tedious process of trial-and-error. Some of the trial-and-error slowness can be eliminated by applying knowledge derived from a careful analysis of what is involved in learning a language. The fact that a child comes from an impoverished and crowded home increases the chances that: (1) he receives less adult attention; (2) most of the language he hears is adult-to-adult conversation or television programs, both of which are difficult for the beginner to understand; and (3) there is more distracting unintelligible noise. The first assumption means that he is not listened to, praised, and corrected as much as a child from a more privileged situation. The next two assumptions mean that he does not have an opportunity to sort out words (labels) and attach them to the correct object or activity, and that he tends to tune out the noise and meaningless conversation, that is, he simply stops listening (Deutsch, 1963). This sequence partially accounts for the assertion that, even if children are cheaper by the dozen in a family, they are also dumber by the dozen (Zajonc, 1975).

The more opportunities the learner has to be talked to and listened to with the appropriate adult interaction, the more likely he is to develop adequate language skills. The child naturally develops language that is appropriate for his use in his home environment, and it is undesirable to create the impression that his native domestic language is wrong. One does not improve the learner's self-image by constantly correcting his native spoken language. Also, there is always some risk of creating psychological distance between the learner and his family, which is in itself undesirable and is often educationally counterproductive. In a SOL preschool, one major goal is to develop a second language, the language of the school, regardless of what the first language might be.

It follows, then, that the facilitator never corrects the learner's native language. The facilitator either says, "This is what we say in school," or echoes the statement using the correct school form and construction. As a general rule, the facilitator should not initiate a conversation, but wait until the learner initiates the conversation. This refers back to developing a positive self-image, as well as to giving the learner every opportunity to speak and to be heard. Of course, in the case of a child with a language DLD, the response-able learning facilitator may judge that it is necessary to initiate conversation, especially when the child is too embarrassed or disabled to make an attempt.

The clearer the reference points are in developing verbal skills, the more likely the learner is to make the correct association and to learn something correctly the first time, eliminating the problem of unlearning-relearning. The implications of this proposition are clear. Adjectives should not be used as nouns. If you say, "Hand me the red," instead of "Hand me the red paper," the learner may not be sure of the name for paper and think that it is "red." A good example is the learner who said "Teacher, I want more yellow," and when the facilitator handed him the yellow paint, he said "No, that yellow," and pointed to the blue paint. For similar reasons, one is advised to use a specific noun instead of a pronoun. For example, one should say, "The paper is red, the cloth is velvety, and wood is smooth," instead of "This is smooth, this is velvety," etc. To make certain that a reference is initially clear, whenever possible, the language should be related to real objects or actions instead of to pictures or illustrations. To teach the concepts of *on, under, between,* etc., start with something like a ball. "The ball is *on* the table," "The ball is *under* the table," "The ball is *between* the books." Illustrate each statement by placing the ball in the correct position. After many experiences with the real object, pictures and finally word-labels can be used. The facilitator should also avoid ambiguous expressions such as "big" and "little," when "short" and "tall" or "shortest" and "longest" or "smaller" and "larger" are more correct.

Children appear to learn nouns more easily than verbs, so when the facilitator is helping a learner to learn verbs, the facilitator should be certain that the learner already knows the nouns. A good method to introduce action verbs in a specific way and to eliminate ambiguity is to tell a learner what he is doing on the playground. "Juanita *walks* on the board," "Jessie *jumps* down," "Mary *rides* a play horse," and finally, "Juanita *will walk* on the board. Juanita *is walking* on the board. Juanita *walked* on the board."

The learner needs specific assistance in learning how to listen. This means presenting sounds in clear, unambiguous ways and training learners to listen for specific sounds such as their names in a song or the bark of a dog among many animal sounds.

Problem Solving and Concept Formation The growing evidence indicates that early deprivation prevents optimum cognitive development. However, some individuals within and outside of the field of early childhood education resist the idea of intentionally providing any experiences specifically for developing the cognitive/intellectual abilities of young learners. One reason for their resistance is the notion that early training is wasted effort, that the preschool child has not reached the level of maturation when he is ready for such learning. Another notion is that efforts to provide cognitive activities for young learners are inherently harmful.

An example of the maturation fallacy is a study completed at the New Nursery School on the ability of learners to make the sounds of the consonants and certain digraphs such as "th" and "sh." According to the norms provided with the tests, certain digraphs are usually not mastered by learners until they are 7 or 8 years old. Actually, it would not make much difference if these norms were set at 5 and 6 years or 3 and 4 years. It was found that, among three groups of learners (middle class Anglo, lower class Spanish-surnamed, and lower class Anglo), there was a wide variation in the ability to make certain sounds. The assumption that middle class Anglo learners as a group have a faster rate of maturation than lower class Spanish-surnamed learners who, in turn, mature faster than lower class Anglos, seems to be an untenable hypothesis. A far more reasonable hypothesis, which was subsequently empirically supported, is that there are differences in the environments of the three groups which account for a major part of the variability in making certain sounds correctly.

Other findings raise serious questions about establishing the mental or chronological ages when certain cognitive tasks can be performed without specifying the enviromental conditions. This has been pointed out regarding infants and toddlers in earlier chapters, and applies here as well. Normally developing, privileged children usually do not read until after they are 6 years old, but under special circumstances 3- and 4-year-old children learn to read in a matter of months, and kindergarten learners are capable of publishing their own newspaper (Moore, 1964). Recent studies confirm that early training in cognitive development is probably worthwhile for all learners, and essential for DLD learners in order to partially compensate for their existing and anticipated intraindividual and/or extra-individual deficits.

The notion that early teaching of cognitive activities is inherently harmful probably stems from the emphasis upon teaching rather than learning and the inclination of parents and educators to ignore the significance of maturation. If it is true that 20% of the middle class learners in the study quoted earlier have not reached the level of physical maturation to enable them to make the blend sounds, then early instruction in blending based upon extrinsic rewards and punishments (including grades) can be harmful, and the net results will probably be that 20% of the learners find the experience distasteful and try to avoid it in the future. For 20% of the learners to pay such a price for early instruction makes the price too high, and such teaching should be postponed until all learners are likely to be successful. But this is based upon the erroneous assumption that the approach must emphasize teaching with external rewards and punishments, and that all learners must be taught the same thing at the same time. If this procedure is reversed, placing the emphasis upon learning through autotelic activities and making the learning self-paced, there is no fear of trying to make learners learn something that is beyond their maturational level; opportunities for a variety of levels are present, and the response-able facilitator is challenged and obliged to discover empirically what a learner can and will learn or not learn under certain environmental conditions.

Many studies indicate that young learners can and do learn many cognitive skills in addition to speech, and the relationship between early cognitive development and school success is rather well established (Hunt, 1961). The assumption made in advocating education for 3- and 4-year-old learners is that education has worth—it is better to read than not to read; it is better to have a skill than not to have a skill. Only when an individual possesses a skill can he choose to use it or not to use it, or choose how it will be used. The cogent case for feelings of competence as an important aspect of positive self-image, motivation, and improved performance bolsters the validity of this assumption.

Memory is the ability to recall something that has been learned previously. Learners can develop memory in two ways: through learning to remember specific things (that is, exact recall) and through remembering in a more general way, not involving exact recall. Exact recall of specific information is usually associated with rote learning or drill, while general recall is associated with meaningful learning that enables the learner to arrive at a fact without specifically remembering it. Learning multiplication tables is an illustration of the two approaches. Specific recall can be achieved by constant drill until the learner will automatically think "72" when someone asks, "What is 9 times 8?" This can be learned without any clear notion of why 9 times 8 equals 72. To learn the multiplication tables in a meaningful way, the learner would first have to understand that adding up nine 8's equals 72. After that, he might memorize the fact, for the sake of efficiency, through drill, or he might rely upon his general knowledge of addition and multiplication to figure out the answer. For example, when he is asked what 9 times 8 equals, he might think, "I don't know, but 8 times 10 equals 80, so 9 times 8 is 8 less than that and, therefore, must equal 72." On the other hand, the resourceful preschooler might simply whip out his pocket calculator and obtain the answer.

There are some facts preschool learners need to remember, such as the names of the colors, names of letters of the alphabet, numbers up to 100, etc. With these facts the learner has the tools to learn by listening to records or playing with the Language Master or using other self-instructional methods and materials. Beyond this, learners are enabled to learn how to arrive at facts without memorizing them. Categories and classification systems are obviously related to this kind of mental operation.

Problem solving refers to a variety of cognitive activities. Problems can be classified as physical, interactional, and affective. Physical problems are those that deal with the physical world. Puzzle solving, learning to eliminate wrong responses to arrive at a correct answer, learning to discover the rules of a game, and learning how to extend a geometric pattern are different kinds of physical problems. The most common kind of interactional problems involves two or more people who interact with each other. When an interactional problem has emotional overtones, it is also an affective problem. Most of the interactional problems which preschoolers must learn to solve are affective, for example, finding a place in the group, getting along with the adult facilitators, and learning to take turns are all interactional interindividual problems with emotional overtones.

Classroom Activities

By ensuring that all activities are autotelic and by avoiding unrelated rewards or punishments, the autotelic classroom enables each learner to do something because he wants to and not because an adult is applying pressure to have him accomplish some task that the adult has decided the learner is ready to do. This means that, in observing the learner's behavior in the classroom, one sees the learner make choices and carry out certain activities that are not pressed upon him by adults. Moreover, curriculum development and the relationship between maturation (including high and low probability behaviors) and learning can be studied without fear of pushing the learner beyond his capacity.

The notion of a responsive environment is equally important. Learning facilitators decide what materials to place in the classroom. Once the learner enters the room, he is free to explore. He can spend as much time on any activity as he likes; no one will ask him to stop one activity to begin another. This has some interesting consequences. For example, the concept of normal attention span for various ages must be modified. Children do have a short attention span if they are required to do what the adult wants them to do when the adult wants them to do it. But when the learners are allowed to choose their own activities, this no longer holds. Many learners have been read to for 1½ hours. One learner painted 25 pictures without stopping. Another spent the whole 3 hours, except for time out for refreshments, playing a game which required him to recognize and match pictures. Some learners will spend over half of their time, particularly at the beginning of the year, playing with the blocks. Of course, if the adult believes that the DLD child's prolonged attention is a form of perseveration caused by organic brain damage, it would require some gentle leadership from the adult to interest the child in alternative activities.

As the year progresses, their activities become more varied and they spend more time in the reading corner, the listening corner, or the manipulative toy area. There are group activities, such as singing and story-telling, but no learner is required to take part. At the beginning of the year, several (five or six out of 15) will choose not to come to the group, but day by day they move closer until they have joined the group. After that, it is a rare occasion when a learner chooses not to partici- pate in the group activities which also take on autotelic qualities as he succeeds in them.

The notion that the environment informs the learner immediately about the consequences of his actions determines the kind of equipment that is used, the way it is used, and the behavior of the learning facilita- tors. The learner is informed either by the self-correcting toys, machines, other learners, or the adult learning facilitator(s). Most of the manipulative toys are self-correcting. The nesting and stacking toys go together or stack in only one way; the puzzles are the same. Concentric circles, squares, or rectangles must fit inside each other to complete the pattern, and so forth.

The Bell and Howell Language Master is an example of a machine that tells the learner about the consequences of his actions. The Language Master records and plays back sound recordings on two channels on magnetic tape located across the bottom of cards that vary in size from $8\frac{1}{2}$ inches by 11 inches to 3 inches by 6 inches. One can write or draw on the card so that a learner sees and hears something at the same time. The learner can operate the machine without assistance, and he is free to play with it. For example, on a single red card, the word "red" is written and the statement, "This color is red," is recorded on the instructor channel for the learner to see and hear; the learner can also record his own language samples on the student channel and compare his language with the facilitator's. The learner is free to spend as much time playing with the colors as he wants, or if he wants to know the name of a specific color, he can go and find out—the machine will give him the necessary feedback. A modified juke box provides a simple random access information-retrieval system by which learners can hear books read to them, songs sung to them, or other auditory input which they select and in some cases have recorded themselves.

The learning facilitator(s) is(are) another source for the learner to use in finding out the consequences of his acts. The important thing for facilitators to remember is that they, too, are a part of a responsive environment and must respond to the learner as he spontaneously encounters and manipulates his surroundings—they do not teach, they facilitate children's learning. The notion of a learning facilitator captures the essence of response-ability in teaching.

Most of the learner's time in school is spent in self-directed activities such as painting, working puzzles, looking at books, dressing up, building with blocks, and a host of other activities. About 15 minutes a day in a typical half-day program are devoted to group activities, such as singing, listening to a story, or participating in planned lessons. If a visitor were to walk into the school as the learners are arriving in the morning, he could expect to see one or two learners go immediately to paint or play with clay, three or four learners settle down in the block corner, two or three learners head for the listening corner to listen to a record that they select on the remote controlled juke box or to play with the Language Master, three or four learners select a manipulative toy, the alphabet board, or a wood insert puzzle to play with, one learner asks to be read to, and one or two learners ask to use the typewriters. At midmorning, several of the learners will likely be at the same activities. Others, perhaps five or six, will be gathered around a facilitator playing some lotto game or learning other simple concepts. Some learners will be joining the group while others are going to another activity. When the learners have lost interest, the facilitator will introduce a new game or proceed to another familiar game. Late in the morning or afternoon, weather permitting, most of the learners go outside, one or two might still be in the same room with a facilitator, and one might be in the typing booth or later called the learning booth.

Learning Booth   Since many of the principles of the ARE/SOL program are derived from the empirical results of creating learning episodes using a nonautomated "talking typewriter" (Pines, 1965), it is instructive to briefly present what happens in the typing booth as a concrete example of SOL methodology, whether or not a typewriter is used at all in the program. Once each school day, a learning facilitator asks a learner if he would like to play with the typewriter. If he says, "Yes," the facilitator takes him to a small room equipped with an electric typewriter. The learner is allowed to play with the typewriter for as long as 20 minutes. The learner begins by simply playing with the typewriter. The facilitator answers his questions and names the symbols he strikes such as "x," "a," "y," "comma," "space," and "return." The learner moves on to typing words and eventually to dictating stories to the facilitator who transcribes the stories. Finally, the learner will transcribe his own stories.

Moore (1964); Nimnicht, McAfee, and Meier (1969); and others have had remarkable success in enabling 3- and 4-year-old learners, including DLD children, to read using such procedures. Nevertheless, this ARE/ SOL program is not so concerned about preschool children's learning to read at an early age as with the mental process involved in discovering such relationships as the association of sounds with symbols and the discovery of the rules for a new keyboard game as one moves from one learning phase to the next. Obviously, if the learner can see a form such as *A* on a piece of paper, find the same form on the keyboard of a typewriter, and hear a facilitator say "A," at least one of the prime objectives is being met, namely that of helping the learner to perceive different forms and discriminate among sounds.

The booths are used for a variety of other autotelic activities, which are not described here. Some rules for the learner's use of the typing booth include: (1) saying that: "Now it is *your* turn to play with the typewriter"; (2) he need not come to the booth if he refuses; (3) he can leave whenever he wishes; (4) he must leave when his time is up (20 minutes maximum stay to allow time for other learners); (5) he need not explain his coming or going; (6) if he says he wants to leave, or starts to leave, he may come back again the next day, but not the same day; (7) a learner is asked only once a day if he wishes to come to the booth; if, after refusing, the learner later asks to come, he is allowed to do so; (8) he is never asked to come to the booth if he is obviously involved in another activity; (9) the booth facilitator is a part of the responsive environment and only *responds* to the learner, that is, he answers questions, announces letters as the learner strikes them, etc.; while the facilitator should be friendly and responsive, he does not direct or teach the learner—the learner is allowed to discover and learn for himself; and (10) the *only* punishment used in the booth is to say, "I'm sorry, your time is up," at which time the learner is taken back to the main room. Chapter 8 presents one of the more advanced learning episodes (Figure 21) for the learning booth emphasizing reading skills.

Evaluation of ARE/SOL Program

The notion of the learner's freely exploring a self-pacing environment, where he learns immediately about the consequences of his actions, is meaningless unless he discovers worthwhile things about himself and his physical, cultural, and social world. The evaluation of this aspect of the ARE/SOL program is addressed in great detail elsewhere (Meier, 1970 and 1973a). In view of the disastrous consequences of being caught up in the poverty cycle and a commitment to early education intervention as an antidote, it is exigent to devise a responsive preschool environment which enables each learner to begin to become as fully self-actualized and competent to cope with his world as possible. The aforementioned objectives and concomitant procedures provide a cogent basis for a set of criteria, including observable behavioral outcomes, against which any given learner's present state of functional competence, self-actualization, or emergence from his defeating and debilitating DLD condition can be evaluated. This competence or emancipation is the ultimate criterion of the ARE/SOL program's success.

So far, the short-term results have been most encouraging. As sophistication in creating an ARE/SOL program increases, an even better performance on the part of the graduates can be anticipated. At this writing, they have done significantly better than their matched controls on standardized tests, and do better in school in the opinion of kindergarten, first, and second grade teachers (Nimnicht, Meier, and McAfee, 1967). According to probabilities based upon the history of groups of similar learners, several of the experimental group should have been placed in special education for educable mentally handicapped children; although several of the matched controls have been so classified, none of the experimental group has yet met this fate. Other controlled studies investigating the relative efficacy of various intervention programs, including the ARE model, are yielding additional insights (Cheever, 1975; Rayder and Bödy, 1975; Rayder, Bödy, and Abrams, 1975; Stallings, 1974). Such studies are being conducted throughout the country with groups of learners having various DLD characteristics. However, because of the longitudinal nature of the program's objectives, it is too early yet to draw any firm conclusions about the overall or comparative efficacy of this early educational intervention program for preventing, or at least partially compensating for, the undesirable effects of various DLD conditions in young children.

Furthermore, the efficacy of an ARE/SOL program for effecting optimum learning and development among normal and exceptionally well-endowed children warrants further research and evaluation. It would be highly provincial for this writer to draw any conclusions from the small numbers of cases, including his own three children, who were at least normal middle class children and are currently doing extraordinarily well in junior high and late elementary school in terms of general achievement, functional competence, and self-actualization. In addition to evaluating the longitudinal effects of the overall ARE/SOL program, it is important to evaluate the curriculum itself. As pointed out in several other chapters of this book, as well as witnessed by the proliferation of articles and books in the professional literature, DLDs are highly complex. It follows then that the development and evaluation of the curriculum are at least an equally complicated process. A point of departure might be to adapt

Guilford and Hoepfner's (1966) factor-analytic conceptualization of the structure of intellect which is schematically depicted in a three-dimensional cube having numerous composite cells (5 X 6 X 4=120) representing various combinations of intellectual functions; this is one way to graphically portray the complex interrelationships within a multifactorial function or process (of course, the cognitive/intellectual domain is only one of several facets for most DLD conditions). A similar graphic depiction is offered by Peter (1965) to illustrate a model for translating diagnostic findings into a prescription for an individual child's learning. Another approach might be to generate a taxonomy of learning abilities (coordinated with Bloom's *Taxonomy of Educational Objectives,* 1954) and then to assess the learning episodes in terms of their value for facilitating development and learning or for ameliorating a DLD condition. The *Handbook on Formative and Summative Evaluation of Student Learning,* by Bloom, Hastings, and Madaus (1971), is a commendable, but somewhat limited, step in this direction.

In order to account more satisfactorily for the numerous variables which typically interact in any learning situation and consequently interact in any effort to remediate or prevent a DLD, a more complex multidimensional model is herein presented to ensure that all parameters are taken into consideration when evaluating any given remedial/preventive curriculum or learning episodes. The word-combination *remedial/ preventive* is used herein since an intervention technique which is appropriate for *remediating* a learning disability in one child might be equally appropriate for *preventing* that disability in a younger or less advanced learner.

A cube has six facets which must all be present in order to fulfill the definition of a cube; that is, each side or facet is necessary and has a specific interrelationship with each other facet of the cube. There are at least six facets to be considered in evaluating the efficacy of a remedial/ preventive curriculum: (1) the individual learner's intraindividual characteristics (Figure 5); (2) the extraindividual learning environment itself (Figure 6); (3) the origin of the DLD (Table 3); (4) the behavioral manifestations of the DLD (Chapters 4 and 6); (5) the selection of remediation/prevention curriculum or learning episodes (Meier, 1973a, Facilitator's Handbook II); and (6) the application and follow-up of the remediation/prevention curriculum (Figure 13). Thus, in order to evaluate the efficacy of any given remediation/prevention curriculum, multifaceted interactions between the individual's idiosyncrasies, the learning milieu or ecology, the origins and characteristics of his particular DLD conditions, and the selection and application of remedial regimen must be considered.

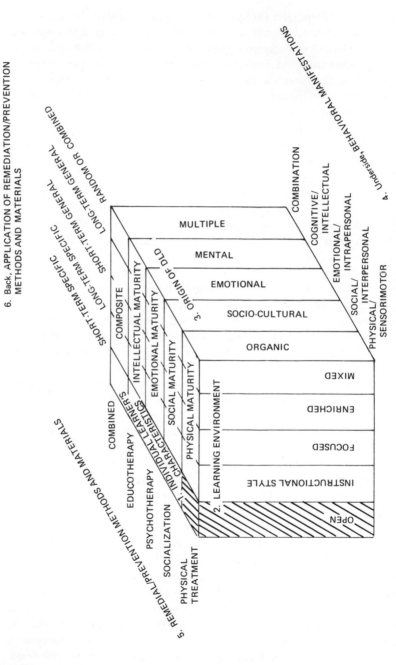

Figure 17. Matrix of multifaceted considerations for evaluation of remediation/prevention methods and materials.

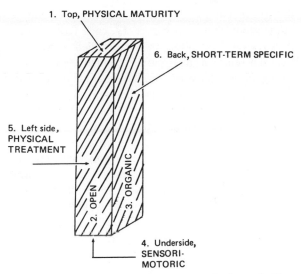

Figure 18. A single unit from the lower left of the matrix shown in Figure 17.

These factors must be taken into account both statistically, insofar as they are quantifiable, and observationally, insofar as qualitative differences can be perceived. Figure 17 depicts 25 of the salient components of the entire DLD intervention matrix of possible remediation/prevention combinations. Figure 18 illustrates the complex of considerations for a single six-faceted cube. Figure 18 extracts the shaded single unit on the lower left of the multifaceted rectangular cubes which represent the important dimensions to be accounted for in evaluating any given remediation/ prevention methods and materials. Figure 18, for example, indicates the interrelationships among: a case of delayed or deviant physical maturation (*1,* individual learner's characteristics); manifest in an open classroom (*2,* learning environment); with an organic origin (*3,* origin of DLD); revealed in sensorimotor dysfunction (*4,* behavioral manifestations); treated with physical therapy (*5,* remediation/prevention methods and materials); and specifically prescribed over a short period of time (*6,* application of remediation/prevention methods and materials). Figure 17, as it now stands, does not allow for substituting, in the above example, a focused learning environment (*2*), nor a multiple origin (*3*), nor perceptocognitive behavioral manifestations (*4*), nor combined physical and psychotherapy methods for remediation (*5*), nor prolonged general application (*6*) of remedial methods.

In order to account for all possible combinations and permutations within the dimensions shown in Figure 17, each facet would have to be divided both ways by 5, resulting in 5 multiplied to the sixth power or 18,725 cubes, each representing a unique combination. Only the 25 more commonly occurring combinations are shown in Figure 17. Figures 17 and 18 are provided to assist the reader to comprehend several rather complicated interactions. Any attempt to depict visually all possibilities would go beyond the point of diminishing returns even for the visually oriented genius. If empirical data were gathered and reported, or its absence clearly noted, with regard to remediation/prevention methods and materials tested under even the 25 combinations shown it would be unprecedented. However, if four conditions produce favorable results and six do not, the consumer would not only know that, but he would also know that in the other 15 possible conditions, he is dealing with unevaluated methods and materials and should carefully monitor each step to be sure that desired results are occurring.

chapter 8

Developmental and Learning Disability Conditions in the Elementary School

By the time a child is 7 years of age, the simultaneous mutual interaction between his natural endowments and environmental opportunities has fairly well shaped his personality, his learning style, his basic physical features, and, in fact, his entire being. A child during the elementary school years, from approximately 7 through 12 years of age, is indeed the father of the man or mother of the woman. Thus, it becomes both increasingly more easy to predict how an individual is likely to grow and develop in the future with a minimum of 6 years of historical prologue to draw upon, and increasingly more difficult to effectively intervene and radically alter any DLD conditions which have become established during these formative years. During the first three grades of school, sometimes called the primary school years, when children are 6–10 years of age, the basic foundation of what is euphemistically referred to as the "three R's" is being laid down. This is also a time when much of the child's attitude toward formal academic learning is being established.

This chapter is divided into two main sections: (1) the first is concerned with screening and identification of elementary school children with fully expressed or incipient DLD conditions; (2) the second is concerned with some of the existing methods and materials which might be used to supplement or replace the regular elementary school curriculum to enable children with various DLD conditions to better cope with their difficulties.

DETECTION AND PREVALENCE OF DLD CONDITIONS

Pediatric Screening and Evaluation for School Entry

Most school systems require a physician's examination of all children who are entering school for the first time. This is an excellent opportunity, albeit several years too late for some conditions, to screen children for hitherto undetected DLD conditions as they enter kindergarten or first grade. An exemplary pediatric multiphasic program (Allen and Shinefield, 1969) for children over 4 years of age is designed to administer a series of screening tests in a single visit and has been conducted by the Permanente Medical Group at the Kaiser Foundation Hospital in San Francisco since 1967. The pediatric multiphasic examination requires about 1½ hours and very systematically obtains data in the following parameters: electrocardiogram; blood pressure and blood pulse; bone age by wrist roentgenograms; anthropometry including various bone diameters, height, and weight; visual acuity; respirometry, including spirometry tests for which adaptations for younger children are now being made; audiometry; intelligence tests, including screens for various learning disabilities; drawing tests, including the Draw-a-Person and Bender-Gestalt to look for perceptual-motor and conceptual deficiencies; tuberculin tine test; throat and nose cultures for streptococcus; blood tests using an automated blood analyzer; urine tests allowing some prospective studies; neurological maturity scale; and a behavior inventory, which is responded to by the parent and addresses the areas of sensorimotor development, learning, communication skills, social rapport, interests, creativity, responsibility, and symptomatic behavior. One month after all of the multiphasic testing is completed, the parent returns for interpretation of the results and physical examination of the child by a pediatrician who now has all of the data analyzed by a computer.

When comprehensive screening and assessment systems are planned, there are many helpful considerations contained in the *Provisional Guidelines for Automated Multiphasic Health Testing and Services,* Volume 2, Operational Manual, in which several quality control suggestions are contained. For example, the selection of tests for the physical factors (or any other developmental domain) must be in keeping with several clear-cut criteria.

> (a) Consideration of reproducibility or precision (consistency of repeated measurements); accuracy or validity (true measurement); sensitivity (percent of true positives); and specificity (percent of true negatives).

(b) Yield rate (of previously unknown, or known but uncontrolled conditions) sufficient to provide an acceptable cost per positive case.

(c) Minimum physician time for processing.

(d) Acceptable to the patient (harmless; reasonable time).

(e) Useful for medical care, or research.

(f) Completeness (adequately comprehensive to satisfy users' needs (two or three phases, or a clinical chemistry panel of tests alone, is not an acceptable AMHTS) (Collen in Collen et al., 1970, pp. 6–7).

A problem commonly raised in most discussions of massive screening is that a standard method is needed for examinee identification which is unambiguous, immutable, and relatively simple. This becomes particularly critical when automation plays an increasingly larger role in the retrieving and processing of data for a large number of relatively mobile infants and toddlers at random intervals.

An example of the use of automation and rather sophisticated instrumentation for screening at the secondary or tertiary level which is applicable to young children is a technique referred to as phonocardiography, which is actually more accurate than its nonautomated counterpart. Nevertheless, the limitations of automated interpretations of electrocardiographs and vectorcardiographs is acknowledged and cited as an area where more adequate computer programs must be developed. Other comments relevant to massive screening in general are contained in the aforementioned operational manual as specifically related to visual acuity, hearing acuity, and anthropometry.

Some of the best developed and empirically validated patient data coding and retrieval forms have also been composed for the Permanente Medical Group's Pediatric Multiphasic Testing Program. These forms are workable data-gathering instruments and enable computer print-outs from the correlated storage and retrieval systems to be used and interpreted by a wide variety of appropriate professionals and paraprofessionals. The standardization of data recording across multiple parameters, some of which are digital and others nondigital, is a slow process. Once meaningful and helpful data are at the fingertips of those desiring it, their subsequent cooperation in collecting data in a standard form is markedly improved.

Judging from the efficacy of many early intervention programs (Heber et al., 1972; White et al., 1973), which have the benefit of early differential diagnosis of developmental disabilities, the attendant cost in design and development of such instrumentation would be very small compared to the savings in human functional competence. Cost/benefit analyses may likely indicate that only a few regional screening centers be established for conducting the tertiary stage screening and assessment and for coordinating the primary and secondary stage screening. Some members of the network of university affiliated facilities would be eminently well qualified to serve in this capacity.

Detection of DLDs in Elementary School

It is in the elementary grades when DLDs become especially evident and pronounced. This is the first time when children are systematically dealt with, and compared to, and evaluated against their peers, in terms of their ability to cope with the formal academic curriculum of reading, writing, and arithmetic. Insofar as probable ability to cope with school is concerned, it will be relatively clear whether or not a child is going to be able to normally benefit from regular school learning opportunities and instruction by the end of the first grade or the middle of the second grade. Since personality factors and related interindividual variables can significantly alter a child's initial adjustment and consequent performance in the early school years, it seems ill-advised to draw many conclusions from the results of his first year of "academic" experience whether this occurs in preschool, kindergarten, or first grade.

It seems more appropriate to see how well the child progresses during his second year of academic experience before making the judgment that a school-related DLD condition is present in either the child or the larger school system environment. This provides an opportunity for whatever resilience there may be within the child or for whatever flexibility there is within the school system to make adjustments for what may have been an unsatisfactory beginning or general mismatch between child and program. This is not to say that obvious mismatches should be allowed to continue in order to test the child's mettle or to test the belief that the system, including the teacher, is self-correcting. The delay in jumping to conclusions simply allows the tincture of time and the new mix of peers, teachers, and perhaps learning environments to give the child a second chance to succeed. And, if he fails to progress as expected during the second year, there is sufficient reason to find out exactly why.

Prevalence of DLD Conditions in Second Grade Children

This section presents some findings from two studies of the prevalence and characteristics of learning disabilities as found in a total of 110 second grade classrooms located in eight Rocky Mountain states. Although the studies were focused solely upon learning disabilities, these conditions typically had their origins in the same developmental phenomena as other

DLDs. However, by this age and within the school context, greater emphasis was placed upon learning abilities than upon developmental achievements. Thus, the definition of DLD obtains throughout this discussion.

The first exploratory prevalence study was conducted by the writer in early 1967 in all 30 of the second grade classes of the Greeley Public Schools in Greeley, Colorado. This study was conceived subsequent to a 1966 national tour of representative programs for dyslexic children. The second prevalence study was conducted in early 1968, using instruments and procedures which were developed for the previous study but somewhat refined as a result of the analysis of the original study and the related inputs solicited from numerous experts in the DLD field. The second study, reported here in detail, was an integral part of the Individual Learning Disabilities Program begun under the auspices of the Rocky Mountain Educational Laboratory and was initiated and directed by Meier (1971). In order for the reader to understand better where these studies fit into the development of a comprehensive instructional system for DLD children, Table 12 is included to give an overview, since the scope of this section precludes detailed explanation of every stage of development.

Preliminary Study   The preliminary study conducted in Greeley, Colorado in early 1967 was designed to establish the prevalence of specific reading disabilities manifested in second grade children in all Greeley public schools. Thirty classes, each comprised of about 30 children, constituted the population. Approximately 100 children of average and above average intelligence were identified as being at least 1 year retarded in reading. This 11% figure was obtained in spite of the fact that Greeley has outstanding public schools, a special education program, relatively little cultural or environmental deprivation, and is an academically oriented college community. Moreover, the criterion of 1 year's retardation is quite rigorous when applied to second graders—it is more appropriate with, say, fourth graders who have had 2 more years for the cumulative deficit phenomenon (Deutsch, 1967) to be fully expressed. On the basis of this finding, supported by the growing international literature regarding the pervasiveness and severity of these conditions, further research and development in the more general field of learning disabilities were initiated.

Eight-State Study   This second study was undertaken to determine with greater precision the nature and extent of DLDs in eight Rocky Mountain states. Estimates stated that from 4–40% of children in regular primary school classrooms have learning disorders of one sort or another. Much of the variation in these estimates is caused by a problem of communication among authorities who have not clearly defined or delim-

Table 12. Stages in the development of a comprehensive system for DLD[a]

Year	Funds[b]	Stage	Description
1966	Ford	I	National tour to determine state of the art in dealing with dyslexic children
1967	PERI	II	Development and exploratory application of Classroom Screening Instrument (CSI) using 30 second grade classes and approximately 900 children in the Greeley school system
1968	RMEL	III	Refinement of CSI on basis of exploratory application of findings and 16 national experts' opinions
1968	RMEL	IV	Use of refined CSI with 80 second grade classes and approximately 2,400 children selected on stratified random sampling basis in eight Rocky Mountain states
1968	RMEL	V	Identification of DLD children (N=284) and differential diagnosis of language (ITPA, Templin-Darley, Audiometry) and psycho-educational functioning (WISC, DTVP, VMI, WRAT, Durrell-Spache)
1968–1969	RMEL	VI	Organic functioning of children with most severe DLD (N=134) determined by thorough medical evaluation
1968–1970	NDEA and EPDA	VII	Development and downward extension of System for Open Learning (SOL) Programs and coordinated series of learning episodes designed to remediate and/or prevent most prevalent DLDs in 2- to 8-year-old children

1969–1975	EPDA	VIII	Training of Learning Facilitators (teachers, USDA county extension agents, and parents) to implement and manage SOL
1970–1975	EPDA and MCH	IX	Widespread dissemination of field-tested components of SOL materials with continued up-grading and elaboration based on R & D feedback plus provision of consultation clinic for extreme DLD cases
1975	EPDA	X	Seven-year follow-up on sample of children involved in 1968 CSI study and downward extension of SOL curriculum to include learning episodes for normal and DLD children from birth to 2 years of age

[a]No endeavor of this magnitude and duration could be accomplished without a great deal of professional and financial support. The writer acknowledges the support of the Psycho-Educational Research Institute (PERI) in conducting the first exploratory prevalence study. The writer, as president of PERI, extends thanks to L. Triplet, Ed.D., Assistant Superintendent for Instruction, for permission to work in the Greeley, Colorado Public Schools.

The support of the Ford Foundation and the interest of G. Nimnicht, Ed.D., Director of the Ford Program at the University of Northern Colorado, enabled B. Barnes, dyslexia project assistant, and the writer to visit with: M. Brutten, Ph.D. (Director, Vanguard School in Philadelphia); L. Eisenberg, M.D. (Pediatric Neurologist at Johns Hopkins University); R. Adams (Director of Reading Research for the U. S. Office of Education); F. McGlannan at the McGlannan School in Miami; M. and C. Goodwin, M.D.'s (Pediatricians at Cooperstown Hospital); M. Ozer, M.D. (Pediatric Neurologist at Children's Hospital in Washington, D. C.); M. Rawson (Executive Director of the Orton Society); and L. Waites, M.D. (Pediatric Neurologist directing a dyslexic center at Scottish Rite Memorial Hospital in Dallas).

The following consultants assisted in augmenting the content validity of the Classroom Screening Instrument: B. Bateman, Ph.D.; D. Carline, Ph.D.; K. de Hirsch, F.C.S.T.; M. Frostig, Ph.D.; J. Irwin,

Continued

Table 12—*Continued*

Ph.D.; J. Isom, M.D.; A. Keeney, M.D.; J. Lampe, M.D.; J. Money, Ph.D.; G. Schiffman, Ph.D.; G. Spache, Ed. D.; and E. Zedler, Ph.D. Numerous teaching-training ideas were obtained from the following consultants: W. Cruickshank, Ph.D.; G. Della Piana, Ph.D.; S. Englemann, B.A.; R. Hagin, Ph.D.; F. Hewett, Ph.D.; D. Johnson, M.A.; J. Mednick, M.D.; M. Rawson, M.A.; R. Saunders, M.A.; G. Schiffman, Ph.D.; G. Wyatt, Ph.D.; and N. Zigmond, Ph.D.

Grateful acknowledgment is given to the 15 professional members of the Field Evaluation Teams, and to the local school officials and teachers throughout the Rocky Mountain area for their helpful cooperation in the Level II survey. Special thanks are due to Jean McMahon, M.D. and her staff at Denver Children's Hospital for their very competent collaboration in the Level III medical diagnoses.

The salvaging of the salient remnants from the RMEL involvement was in part due to the help of V. Cazier, Ed.D., M. Giles, Ed.D., and J. Scott, Ed.D., all of whom were graduate assistants in the RMEL Individual Learning Disabilities project under the writer's direction.

Although the several collaborators on the production of the S.O.L. materials are appropriately acknowledged within those materials, especial thanks are due to both B. Borthick, M.A., who has helped keep the NDEA and EPDA efforts alive for the past 7 years, and O. Every, who has typed, retyped, reproduced, and disseminated the NDEA/EPDA products thousands of times for nearly a decade.

[b] Abbreviations for funding sources: Ford, Ford Foundation; PERI, Psycho-Educational Research Institute; RMEL, Rocky Mountain Educational Laboratory; NDEA, National Defense Education Act; EPDA, Education Professions Development Act; MCH, Maternal and Child Health.

ited what they mean by the term "learning disability." It was mandatory that a relatively more definite estimate of prevalence be established before any grand schemes for remediation or prevention were launched. The following sections describe the procedures and salient findings of this study.

Subjects In order to obtain a representative, stratified random sample of children, the following procedures were employed: first, a representative proportion of population distribution was determined on the basis of three population groupings, namely: (1) cities of 15,000 citizens or more; (2) cities of 5,000–15,000 citizens; and (3) towns or rural areas of less than 5,000 people. A proportionate number of population groups, which is representative of their relative occurrence in the selected eight-state Rocky Mountain region, was determined. Then, using a table of random numbers applied to a Rand-McNally 1967 atlas, an initial 20 such locations were identified with an additional 20 alternates. It was then determined on the basis of information from the State Departments of Education from the eight states involved and from a Rocky Mountain Educational Laboratory baseline data study what the proportion of public to private schools in the Rocky Mountain region is; on this basis, a representative proportion of private schools was also determined for inclusion in the study.

Next, letters were sent to the superintendents of school districts representing the cities and towns which were identified by the stratified random procedure. These superintendents identified either one, two, or three teachers in their district who met the criterion of at least 1 year's satisfactory experience as a second grade classroom teacher. In several instances, the superintendent was asked to select an elementary art or elementary physical education teacher in addition to, or in lieu of, the second grade classroom teacher. It should be noted that these procedures were used primarily to identify 60 experimental and 20 control teachers for some specialized professional development; a part of their development was their administration of the Classroom Screening Instrument, which constituted Level I of the Eight-State Study. Therefore, the teacher-selection process also served indirectly to identify the child population to be included in the study.

Three Levels of Diagnosis

Level I: Classroom Screening Each of the 80 teachers received a packet of materials for screening children in their own classroom in accordance with procedures and instruments devised by the writer. Twelve experts in the field of learning disabilities (see acknowledgments at end of

Table 12) augmented the face validity of the instruments by providing a critique and making recommendations as the Classroom Screening Instrument was being developed. Each teacher was instructed to identify in his/her classroom those children whom he/she thought were having unusual difficulty in learning. This was done after the teachers had administered a uniform spelling test, a pupil productions fill-in sheet, and a design-copying test. The Goodenough Draw-a-Person test was also completed by each of the more than 2,000 children. The teacher was instructed to rank the children in order of the difficulty they were having learning, with the child who had the most difficulty being placed first. Considerable confidence was placed in the judgment of seasoned classroom teachers, who develop a sort of normal frame of reference, and have demonstrated their ability to ferret out fullblown or potential DLD children as well as or better than psychometrists (Feshbach, Adelman, and Fuller, 1974). Then, each teacher proceeded to check the 80 observable behavioral indices listed on the Classroom Screening Instrument (CSI). Each behavior was checked as present (+), absent (−), or no opportunity to observe (0).

The teacher also completed a form containing related information about the child's school achievement and some information about the family background. This information was used to determine which of the children warranted the Level II Differential Diagnosis and which were to be excluded from this next step. Some children were excluded from Level II testing because they were evidently working up to their expectancies as revealed in the related information, pupil productions, and teacher comments forms. Other children were excluded from the Level II testing if a combination of parental occupation and related teacher observations indicated that the child's reduced learning was evidently because of the deprivation of the environment in which she was living; culturally disadvantaged children were excluded by definition from this particular study. Thus, the judgment to exclude or include any child whose name was submitted by his/her teacher on the Classroom Screening Instrument was based on the intrainidividual model for DLD for this study.

The CSI and several pieces of supplementary written material, such as directions for its administration, some history of its development, and related forms (including a consultant fee form by which each teacher received $25.00 for doing the task) were distributed to 80 teachers either by mail or in person during the month of April, 1968. Completed instruments were returned to the writer's headquarters within a 2-week period after their receipt, and all instruments with complete data were received by the middle of May, 1968.

The 80 teachers had a mean class size of approximately 30 children;

class size ranged in number of children from 12–46. Children's ages ranged from 7–11 years. It is estimated that approximately 2,400 children attended the second grade classes which were screened by their teachers. There were 478 potentially DLD children's names identified. The number of names listed by teachers on the CSIs varied from 1–12 (12 children was the maximum number that could be listed by any single teacher without using a second set of forms, which was never requested). Using the criteria described earlier in this report, 117 names were eliminated from consideration for the Level II differential diagnosis. There were 361 children selected for Level II evaluation from the original sample population of approximately 2,400 children in 80 regular second grade classrooms scattered throughout the eight-state region (Arizona, Colorado, Kansas, Montana, Nebraska, New Mexico, Utah, and Wyoming).

The most noteworthy data regarding the CSI were the number of times the teachers checked the various behavioral indices for the 284 children who subsequently were diagnosed as bona fide DLD cases. For a list of behavioral indices and the frequency counts for each index, see Table 13.

It is evident that some of the behavioral indices were checked far more frequently than others for the 284 DLD children in 80 regular second grade classrooms. Thirty-six of the indices were checked for more than one-third of the DLD children; 13 were checked for more than one-half; and only three were checked for more than two-thirds of the DLD group. It was retrospectively discovered that the behavioral indices, especially those checked for one-third or more of the DLD children, have concurrent validity with poorer school achievement and a significantly lower learning quotient than obtained by normally learning peers. Thus, the 80 CSI behavioral indices might well be reduced to about two-thirds as many, using those indices which teachers find meaningful and descriptive of DLD children and which they would seldom check for children who are developing and learning normally.

Level II: Differential Diagnosis This testing was conducted by an interdisciplinary field evaluation team in each child's home area, usually in a school centrally located in the district where the child was attending school. The following battery of tests was administered to all children in Level II work-ups: The Wide Range Achievement Test (WRAT); a combination reading-achievement test made up of subtests from the Durrell Reading Achievement Analysis Test (oral reading) and the Spache Reading Test (silent reading and listening comprehension); the Wechsler Intelligence Scale for Children; the Beery Visual Motor Integration Test (VMI); the Frostig Developmental Test of Visual Perception (DTVP); the Illinois

Table 13. Classroom screening instrument: 80 behavioral indices and the frequencies checked for DLD children ($N = 284$) by their second grade teachers

	Behavioral indices	Frequency
1.[a]	Holds book too close (6 inches or less)	49
2.[a]	Avoids work requiring concentrated visual attention	112[b]
3.[a]	Head forward or tilted to one side (more than 15°) when reading or engaged in other tasks	52
4.[a]	Moves head or trunk excessively during visual task (instead of moving eyes)	55
5.[a]	Uncontrollable rapid jumping of eyes	
6.[a]	Rubs eyes often when reading or engaged in other visual tasks	41
7.[a]	Facial contortions with visual tasks (including squint)	73
8.	Seems to have pop-eyes	8
9.	Eyes are crossed	7
10.[a]	Unable to learn the sounds of letters (can't associate proper phoneme with its grapheme)	117[b]
11.[a]	Doesn't seem to listen to daily classroom instructions of directions (often asks to have them repeated whereas rest of class goes ahead)	173[c]
12.[a]	Can't correctly recall oral directions (e.g., item 11 above) when asked to repeat them	153[c]
13.	Doesn't seem to comprehend spoken words (may recognize the words separately but not in connected speech)	59
14.[a]	Can't name letters when they are pointed to	36
15.[a]	Can't pronounce the sounds of certain letters	95[b]
16.[a]	Mild speech irregularities (can't pronounce common second grade words)	67
17.[a]	Immature speech patterns (still uses much baby talk)	47
18.	Lips apart when at rest (mouth breathing)	52
19.	Tongue thrust forward between teeth and often beyond lips (especially when using hands for writing, cutting, etc.)	53

20. Unable to correctly repeat a 7–10 word statement by the teacher (omits or transposes words) .... 124[b]

21. Errors in oral expression—confuses prepositions such as over, under, in, out, etc.) ("Put water under a fire to boil it.") 71

22.[a] Transposes sounds in words (says "nabana" instead of "banana") 40

23.[a] Can't recite the days of the week in correct order 70

24.[a] Underactive "seems lazy, couldn't care less) in classroom and on playground 72

25.[a] Is slow to finish work (doesn't apply self, daydreams a lot, falls asleep in school) .... 160[c]

26.[a] Overactive (can't sit still in class–shakes or swings legs, fidgety) .... 96[b]

27. Tense or disturbed (bites lip, needs to go to the bathroom often, twists hair, high strung) .... 101[b]

28. Occasional lapses of contact with classroom activities (has "spells" when hands and/or body shakes, eyes blink or don't seem to see) 37

29. Very small for age (less than 36 inches tall at age 7) 22

30. Misses school frequently (average 5 days a month) because of illness 18

31. Poor coordination (can't skip or hop on one foot more than 3 times) 69

32.[a] Fingers tremble when hands held forward and arms supposed to be steady 37

33. Accidentally breaks and tears things (clumsy, awkward) 73

34. Unusually short attention span for daily school work .... 190[d]

35. Easily distracted from school work (can't concentrate with even the slightest disturbances from other student's moving around or talking quietly) .... 187[d]

36.[a] Mistakes own left from right (confuses left-hand with right-hand side of paper) .... 111[b]

37.[a] Often begins tasks with one hand and finishes with the other 19

38.[a] Can't tie shoes and/or hold scissors properly 34

39.[a] Loses way in school (gets turned around and doesn't know which way to go) 15

40. Improper pencil grasp (clutched in fist, held too lightly or presses so hard as to break lead and tear paper) 77

41. Draws circles clockwise 78

Continued

Table 13—Continued

	Behavioral indices	Frequency
42.[a]	Poor drawing of diamond compared with peers' drawing	102[b]
43.[a]	Poor drawing of crossing, wavy lines compared with peers' drawing	131[b]
44.[a]	Poor drawing of a man compared with peers' drawings	121[b]
45.[a]	Poor handwriting compared with peers' writing	147[c]
46.	Reverses and/or rotates letters, numbers and words (writes "p" for "q," "saw" for "was," "2" for "7," "16" for "91") far more frequently than peers	148[c]
47.	Does very poorly in written spelling tests compared with peers	183[c]
48.[c]	Unable to learn the forms of letters (can't recognize letters when they are named)	43
49.[a]	Reverses and/or rotates letters and numbers (reads "b" for "d," "u" for "n," "6" for "9") far more frequently than most peers	135[b]
50.	Reverses and/or rotates words and numbers (reads "tac" for "cat," "left" for "felt," "327" for "723") far more frequently than peers	79
51.[a]	Can read better when print is upside down	8
52.	Loses place more than once while reading aloud for one minute	107[b]
53.	Omits words while reading grade-level material aloud (omits more than one out of every 10)	126[b]
54.[a]	Reads silently or aloud far more slowly than peers (word by word while reading aloud)	194
55.[a]	Points at words while reading silently or aloud	140[c]
56.[a]	Substitutes words which distort meaning ("when" for "where")	200[d]
57.[a]	Can't sound out or "unlock" words	182[c]
58.[a]	Can read orally but does not comprehend the meaning of written grade-level words (word-caller)	123[b]
59.[a]	Can't follow written directions, which most peers can follow, when read orally or silently	186[c]

60.[a]	Reading ability at least ¾ of a year below most peers	180[c]
61.	Tells barren or incoherent stories (they don't even make sense to peers)	49
62.[a]	Has trouble telling time	175[c]
63.[a]	Doesn't understand the calendar (what day follows Wednesday, etc.)	79
64.	Difficulty with arithmetic (e.g., can't determine what number follows 8 or 16; may begin to add in the middle of a subtraction problem)	132[b]
65.[a]	Cannot apply the classroom or school regulations to own behavior whereas peers can	105[b]
66.	Excessive inconsistency in quality of performance from day to day or even hour to hour	121[b]
67.	Has trouble organizing written work (seems scatterbrained, confused)	159[c]
68.	Seems very bright in many ways but still does poorly in school	141[b]
69.	Repeats the same behavior over and over	159[c]
70.[a]	Doesn't get along with most peers (can't make or keep friends, is picked on, wants to change rules, poor loser)	91
71.	Shows excessive affection toward peers or adults in school or playground	47
72.[a]	Unusually aggressive toward peers or adults in school or playground	52
73.[a]	Unusually shy or withdrawn	59
74.[a]	Cries easily or often for no apparent reason	28
75.[a]	Afraid of many things which most peers don't fear	21
76.[a]	Explodes for no apparent reason	38
77.[a]	Demands unusual amount of attention during regular classroom activities	110[b]
78.	Seems quite immature (doesn't act his/her age)	122[b]
79.	Seems insensitive to others' feelings	59
80.[a]	Objects or refuses to go to school either for no apparent reason or because of fear of failure	9

[a] Item remaining in reconstitution of CSI by Beatty (1975).
[b] Checked for at least ⅓ of DLD children.
[c] Checked for at least ½ of DLD children.
[d] Checked for at least ⅔ of DLD children.

Test of Psycholinguistic Abilities (ITPA—experimental edition); the Templin-Darley Articulation Test; and a standard pure-tone audiometric screening. (See Chapter 10 for more information on these tests.)

Since an important function of the Level II and Level III information is its use in validating the CSI, portions of the Level II battery were administered to all children in four randomly selected classes from throughout the region; this total class testing was done to determine whether any false negatives were occurring in the classroom screening procedures. For the total class screening at Level II, the Wide Range Achievement Test, the ITPA, the Templin-Darley Articulation Test, an audiometric test, and the WISC were administered; when indicated, the remainder of the battery was also used. The entire Level II battery of tests was administered to at least five randomly selected average or better than average learners in each of the aforementioned four classes. These children served as controls, but were not originally identified as such, for the Level III testing and had complete work-ups and were otherwise treated the same as the suspected DLD children.

All of the totals from the various tests mentioned, such as perceptual age (Frostig), language age (ITPA), mental age (WISC), and so on, were included in an analysis which generated learning quotients for each tested behavioral dimension in accordance with Myklebust's formula (1968). This formula was designed to take into account the child's mental age, his chronological age, and his school experience in order to arrive at an expectancy age. In turn, the expectancy age may be divided into the child's performance age for various specific behavioral dimensions, such as spoken language, reading, spelling, arithmetic, perception, visual-motor integration, performance and verbal intelligence, and so forth. In order to determine those children who warranted the Level III medical diagnosis, the computer print-out of overall learning quotients and other quotients for specific behavioral dimensions was inspected. Every child whose overall learning quotient (average of eight specific learning quotients) was below 90 or who had learning quotients below 85 in two or more specific behavioral dimensions was included in the Level III group.

An advance representative of the DLD program preceded the field evaluation teams into each school district and made preliminary arrangements with the school officials, in some instances with the child's teacher, and in every instance with the child's parents in order to establish a receptive attitude toward the Level II diagnosis. This person also helped to schedule the five three-member interdisciplinary teams of field diagnosticians in order to ensure that they would work with maximum efficiency and convenience. Before any testing on the part of the field evaluation team, written release of information regarding the child was signed by a parent or other responsible adult. Written clearance was obtained from each State Department of Education with regard to the field evaluation team members, all of whom met minimum state requirements for administering the tests for which they were responsible. Although children were typically transported to the site of testing by their parents, or by a responsible adult, in some instances the child's teacher, a member of the field evaluation team, or a taxi delivered a child to the testing site and/or returned him home. Children on vacation or who had moved from the area were not sought out, and their absence in the study was considered to be random and noncontaminating. All tests were scored and doublechecked by the field evaluation team members who administered them, and the data were recorded on forms specially designed to expedite the keypunching of data processing cards and subsequent analysis in accordance with specific predetermined computer programs.

Of the 361 children who were selected for Level II testing, 284 were actually available and tested with the entire test battery. The 76 children who were not tested were unavailable because they were out of town, because they had moved from the area, or, in two of the locations, because the school administration and school board refused to allow the Level II testing for the 18 children scheduled for it.

The refusal for testing was reportedly based upon the belief that such testing would arouse the anger of the community and the child's parents in particular. This assumption was in turn based on a quite hostile reaction on the part of some parents in those locations toward some other allegedly unscrupulous testing which had been attempted earlier that same year. These were the only two locations where the DLD program's advance representative met with anything less than gracious and willing cooperation. Omission of these 18 children who were not allowed to be tested is not thought to create a substantial problem with the data, since the number of children omitted is small and similar communities were represented elsewhere in the sample.

Table 14 includes the means and standard deviations for the Level II experimental and control groups. Inspection of the data reveals several important relationships.

It can be seen, for example, that the DLD children in this study performed, on the average, considerably better in articulation (Templin-Darley) than in general language (ITPA). Not only is the mean articulation score for the DLD children closer to that for the normal controls, but the variability is less than that found in the areas of language or visual-motor integration. Additional variables, which were not entered into the calcula-

Table 14. Level II findings by interdisciplinary field evaluation teams

Variable	Mean		Standard deviation		Correlation with learning quotient	
	Exp.[a]	Control[b]	Exp.	Control	Exp.	Control
Chronological age (months)	101.95	101.51	7.32	6.06	−64	−0.84
Grade age (months)	96.00	96.00	0.00	0.00	0.00	0.00
Mental age (CA × IQ)	97.43	102.00	9.80	10.63	−0.02	−0.23
Expectancy age (MA + GA + CA/3)	98.50	99.86	4.08	4.42	−0.41	−0.57
Test administered						
1. Perceptual quotient (DTVP)[c]	89.48	104.94	12.45	14.82	0.55	0.31
2. Language quotient (ITPA)[c]	90.73	99.00	9.25	8.65	0.27	0.65
3. Cognitive quotient (WISC)[c]	97.52	100.74	11.15	9.02	0.53	0.52
4. Visual-Motor quotient (VMI)	99.34	110.05	23.54	15.53	0.36	0.44
5. Articulation quotient (Temp-D)[c]	103.70	106.85	5.22	5.18	0.36	0.51
6. Reading quotient (WRAT)[c]	90.32	105.79	11.31	16.70	0.55	0.51
7. Spelling quotient (WRAT)[c]	88.38	99.03	8.21	11.98	0.61	0.75
8. Arithmetic quotient (WRAT)[c]	90.30	94.95	9.30	6.99	0.52	0.61

Results

Spatial score $\dfrac{(PC + BD + OA)}{3}$	96.01	100.69	21.71	18.84	0.26	-0.04
Conceptualizing $\dfrac{(comp + sim + voc)}{3}$	102.29	103.53	26.63	22.72	0.17	0.05
Sequencing $\dfrac{(DS + PA + coding)}{3}$	89.98	101.80	17.51	18.97	0.21	0.24
Learning quotient = $\dfrac{(\text{sum of } 1-8)/8.00}{\text{expectancy age}}$	94.79	101.60	10.34	9.25	1.00	1.00
Verbal IQ	97.43	100.56	12.74	11.93	0.22	0.28
Performance IQ	96.10	101.23	11.84	10.70	0.19	0.08

[a] Experimental $N = 284$.
[b] Control $N = 87$ (total classes tested).
[c] These tests were administered to 19 children randomly selected from the Level II total class control [b] groups.

tion of the overall learning quotient, are those suggested by Bannatyne (1968) and are referred to as conceptualizing, spatial, and sequential skills; these are derivatives from subtest scores taken from the WISC. It is noteworthy that children in this study performed considerably better in the conceptual and spatial realms than they did in the sequential realm. This is consistent with findings reported by Doehring (1968), who addresses the associated neuropsychological phenomena, and by Rugel (1974), who reanalyzes and summarizes the findings from 25 studies reporting WISC subtest scores with regard to DLD children. The above findings suggest some skills which may be crucial for prevention and/or remediation of DLD conditions in children.

The high negative correlations between chronological age and learning quotient and between expectancy age and learning quotient are most probably explained by the fact that the children who were older (ages ranged from 7–11 years in the population), but still in second grade at the time of testing, had experienced greater difficulty in learning and had often been retained once or twice in the same grade.

Level III: Medical Evaluation This part of the study was designed to thoroughly evaluate the child's physical development and functioning in order to ascertain either the specific types of physical abnormalities which may be related to his DLD or to rule out any physical malfunctioning as a possible explanation for his DLD. This evaluation was done in a central location at the Children's Developmental and Evaluation Clinic at Children's Hospital in Denver, Colorado. The Level III work-up consisted of a medical history, a social history, pediatric, neurological, ophthalmological, otolaryngological, metabolic, chromosomal (buccal smear), electroencephalographic (awake and asleep) examinations, standard blood and urine laboratory tests, psychological, and occupational therapy evaluations. The neurological examination was done in accordance with a standardized procedure developed by Ozer (1966). The otolaryngological examination included quite sophisticated audiometric testing to further validate the free-field hearing screening done in Level II. The occupational therapy evaluation involved administration of the Southern California Tests (Ayres, 1966) and the Purdue Perceptual-Motor Survey (Roach and Kephart, 1966). In those cases where a child's functioning seemed to be seriously impaired by emotional disturbance, a staff psychiatrist or psychologist at the clinic was asked to examine the child and give an opinion as to the etiology of the emotional disturbance and whether or not it was primarily or secondarily related to the child's inability to learn. The Level II field evaluation team members were also alerted to manifest signs of emotional disturbance and asked to remark about such signs in their anecdotal record of the child's behavior during the testing session.

Medical Findings   Among a wealth of data, there are a number of highlights from the clinical findings which warrant mention in this paper. These data were collected on 101 DLD children and their families plus 19 controls. There was a larger percentage of subclinical ("soft") neurological signs manifest among the experimental group (about 90%) as compared to the controls (about 75%) or "normal" children in general. Soft signs refer to difficulties in integrating and processing neurological inputs and to general fine motor functioning, as opposed to "hard" signs of tumors or cerebral palsy. About 95% of the DLD children were classified in the organic brain syndrome category, compared to about 5% of the controls. Several causes of hearing problems, such as chronic middle ear infections, were discovered; these probably accounted for some of the behavior problems among children who "never paid attention" when their teacher was talking, perhaps because they could not hear adequately. Very few uncorrected visual problems were detected. Considerable numbers of elec-troencephalographic abnormalities were recorded in both the DLD and the control groups; the percentages of epileptiform tracings (about 20%), slow and poorly organized tracings (about 10%), 14-6 spikes (about 8%), and other EEG anomalies (about 15%) were about the same in both groups, whereas convulsive-type tracings were not found in the controls but were evident in about 10% of the DLD children. In terms of overall develop-ment, the DLD children had more (about 25%) lags in physical and language development as well as various congenital abnormalities (about 10%) compared to the controls (about 5%).

The medical histories revealed chronic illnesses, including those occurring during pregnancy, to be more prevalent in the mothers of DLD children (about 15%) compared to controls (3%). There was a considerably higher incidence of premature births (less than 5½ pounds) among the DLDs (about 20%) than the controls (5%); about 15% of parents were over 40 years of age when their DLD child was born, compared to no parents over 40 in the control population. Miscarriages had been experienced by about one-fourth of both parent populations. There was some evidence of genetically based abnormalities, based on pedigree studies (such as mental and neurological retardation of development), in more than three-fourths of the DLD children's families and in about one-half of the control families. However, about one-half of the DLD children showed actual signs of genetic anomalies, whereas none of the control children did.

Other Findings in Level III Evaluation   The social/behavioral his-tories revealed family irregularities (divorce, stepchildren, and emotional instability) in about 20% of the DLD children's families as contrasted with less than 5% in the control families. For these DLD children referred for psychological examinations, it is noteworthy that about 20% of them were found to be hyperactive, irritable, withdrawn, self-deprecating, and aggressive; about 40% were labeled general behavior problems, and about 65% were referred to as emotional and easily upset ("high strung"), whereas essentially none of the controls showed these behaviors to the same pathological degree. It is also interesting that at least half of the DLD children's parents were not made aware of their child's learning and behavioral disorders until 2 years of schooling had been completed.

The DLD group performed considerably less well than controls on the Peabody Picture Vocabulary Test (Dunn, 1965); the mean IQ was 93 for DLDs compared to 104 for controls. The DLDs also did far less well on all parts of the Picture Story Language Test (Myklebust, 1965b), especially on the Total Words Subtest (DLD mean score of 26 to control score of 49) and on the Abstract-Concrete Rating (9 to 13). These specific language deficits were further corroborated and more clearly delineated by a Test of Concept Utilization (Crager and Spriggs, 1970) which was administered to 20 of the DLD children. In comparison to the norm group of the same ages (8–10 years old), a significantly greater proportion of the DLD children had *unusual* (possible within reality, yet a rather farfetched or contrived commonality or relationship not typical of the two objects and not regarded as *creative*) and *affective* (carrying heavy emotional, sexual, and/or aggressive connotations) responses, suggesting some additional bases for the disordered communication in DLD children.

There were no data on the Southern California or Purdue tests which warrant mentioning, since DLD and control children performed about equally well on these.

Refinement of CSI for Widespread Use   Several steps were taken in order to determine the reliability and validity of the CSI which, next to determining the prevalence of DLD conditions in second grade children, was a principal object of this study:

1. As previously mentioned, the content validity, in keeping with the state of the art and knowledge, was augmented by 12 highly reputed consultants regarding DLD conditions, who provided a critique of the various rough drafts of the CSI as it evolved.

2. Once a satisfactory compilation of behaviors had been determined, the pilot study version of the CSI was devised and its reliability checked by having several groups of teachers apply it to a series of videotape-recorded vignettes of classroom behaviors which were representative of DLD children; the reliability coefficient exceeded 0.85, which was judged adequate to proceed with its use.

3. When the CSI forms were completed and returned, all of the responses were tallied on data processing forms and keypunched on data processing cards. In order to get a better understanding of the composition of the

CSI, factor analysis and cluster analysis procedures were applied to the correlation matrix generated by the 80 variables. The resultant 80 × 80 correlation matrix was factor analyzed, using a varimax orthogonal rotation program, to determine to what extent the behavioral indices tended to group statistically within the categories logically ascribed to them. Subsequently, original and redefined cluster analyses were performed to further clarify the CSI composition. An inspection of the factor loadings revealed that the original categories held up quite well in most instances. Some rearrangement of certain indices was indicated; several indices had no loadings above 0.30 and have been eliminated from the next version of the CSI. Some categories were complex and broke out into two or more factors which are logically consistent.

4. A fourth generation ILD/CSI (Meier, Cazier, and Giles, 1970) was designed to take all of the aforementioned findings into account. At least two independent research studies have been conducted to further analyze the CSI. Beatty (1975) collected data from 400 primary children (grades 1 through 3) on the CSI and subjected the data to a very thorough factor analysis. Of the original 80 items, 48 (asterisked in Table 13) were found to be loading on 10 factors. The original CSI for second grade children had 8 subscales including: visual, auditory, speech, body/motoric, drawing/writing, reading, relational/conceptual, and social/emotional. The proposed revision for the primary version of the CSI has 10 factors including: speech/auditory disability, hyperactive/aggressive, reading disability, drawing/writing disability, anxiety, visual disability, conceptualization incompetencies, inactivity/lack of concentration, and laterality/disability. Bowen (1974) conducted a study with several hundred elementary school-aged boys in private schools in the eastern United States to determine the comparative efficacy of three screening instruments for identifying DLD children. The Pupil Rating Scale (Myklebust, 1971), the Rhode Island Pupil Identification Scale (Novack, Bonaventura, and Merenda, 1973), and the CSI were used. At this writing, the data from the multiple external criteria, similar to those described in Level II above, were regrettably not yet available, and thus the results of this study cannot yet be reported.

Individualized Instructional System A series of appropriate remedial techniques are currently being field-tested in classrooms to determine their efficacy in overcoming various DLD conditions. Figure 19 presents a CSI-based intervention system flowchart which shows how the individualized learning episodes are selected.

Certain clusters (descriptors) of checked behavioral indices (2.2) retrieve a series of keyed remedial procedures (2.3) from which the classroom teacher can select until a particular procedure is found to work

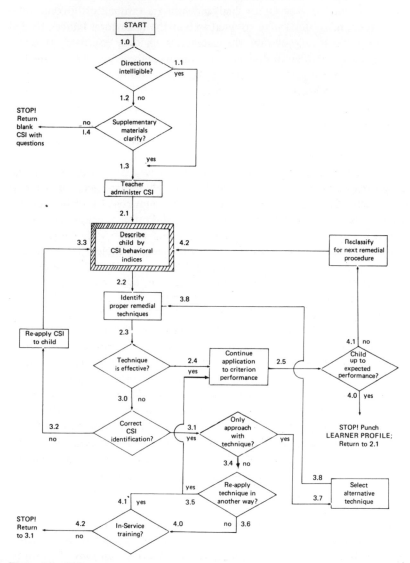

Figure 19. CSI-based intervention system flowchart.

best with a given DLD child (4.0). Therefore, the CSI is designed to become an aid to a teacher for individualizing instruction or for appropriate intervention with validated procedures and materials.

Although some few DLD children might benefit from chemotherapy and psychotherapy, they still have academic deficits which must be remediated by individualized educotherapy. Of course, in addition to treatment of DLD, prevention is an even greater challenge, and efforts along these lines are reported earlier, especially in Chapters 5 and 7.

As stated throughout this volume with regard to numerous points, DLD conditions are multifaceted phenomena whose causes and characteristics are kaleidoscopic. It should by now be obvious that they are important contributors to many school failures, whether the communication network breaks down within a learner (intraindividual) or between the learner and her/his instructor (interindividual) or his/her environment (extraindividual origins of DLD). This section has presented two studies which, among other findings, reveal several characteristic aspects of DLDs and a skeletal outline for their remediation. A disability in receiving, processing, storing, retrieving, and/or expressing data in proper *sequence* seems to characterize a large proportion of DLD conditions. This was apparent within and across all sensory modes and was characteristic of a large percentage of DLD second grade children, who comprised about 15% of the population in 110 regular classes randomly selected from throughout eight Rocky Mountain states.

In order to avoid the paralysis of analysis, it is suggested that teachers and parents can remediate and, more importantly, prevent many such disorders by careful planning and providing for, for example, SOL learning episodes designed to develop and perfect sequencing abilities. Numerous methods and materials for doing this are becoming available, several of which are mentioned in the following section and in Chapter 10. Although some physical complications may make this training more difficult, the preliminary evidence does not indicate insurmountable organic barriers to ordered communication in DLD children. Although there were numerous physical findings regarding the DLD children, there were similar findings for many children who were judged to be learning normally well.

A computer observer's acronym is applicable here—GIGO—which stands for Garbage In Garbage Out; thus, garbled input to any of the components of the communications networks (Figures 5–8) inevitably results in garbled output. Troubleshooting such malfunctions requires systems analysis techniques which can test each link in the network, identify the "noise" and eliminate it, thereby enabling the individual or group of individuals to engage in undistorted communication and learning.

Other Procedures for Detecting Readiness to Learn and to Read   As mentioned previously in several different places in this book (especially Chapters 4 and 6, and the first section of this chapter), the identification of children involved in DLD conditions or with a high probability of subsequent DLD involvement is fraught with problems and promises. In addition to the CSI detection procedure described above, a large number of other screening devices subsequently have been introduced. For example, the number of reading readiness tests cited in Buros (1965) test reference was eight as compared to 29 in Buros (1972). This increase is not only caused by the arousal of greater general interest in early detection endeavors, but also is caused by the national agitation by various special interest groups for proposed pieces of national legislation, as well as their state and local legislative counterparts. The burgeoning numbers of early detection tests and procedures are to one degree or another premised on the incidence, prevalence, and early detection and intervention for DLD conditions.

Conners (1973) reviewed several of the most widely used and acceptable rating scales for children's behavior available at that time. Although his primary concern was with recording the effects of medications on DLD children and evaluating these effects for several biometric studies (see Chapter 7), he cited several scales for use in psychiatric and elementary classroom settings. His observations are paraphrased and abbreviated in the following several paragraphs.

Cattell and Coan (1957) gave a 38-item trait list of bipolar items to teachers of 198 first and second grade pupils. This list was compiled to include the major "markers" from other personality research, as well as useful indicators of personality disturbance.

Peterson (1961) used the referral problems of 427 cases at a guidance clinic to select the 58 most common symptoms. The list was given to teachers of 831 kindergarten through sixth grade pupils for rating. Two major factors, conduct problem and personality problem, emerged with considerable consistency across the whole age range. Quite similar factors have engaged in a number of studies by Quay (1964) and other researchers for various populations from sources as disparate as case history ratings, questionnaires, standard ratings, and via a variety of factor extraction methods.

The Devereux Elementary School Behavior Rating Scale (Spivack and Levine, 1964) is a 47-item anchored scale for teachers with items easily grouped into 11 behavior factors. Normative data are available on 809 normal children in kindergarten through sixth grade. The factor structure is quite similar across grade levels. In general, the scale meets most of the requirements for an instrument in drug studies, although there is no known demonstration that shows that it is "drug sensitive." This scale has a high priority for use as a standardized data-gathering instrument.

A 39-item teacher questionnaire originally developed by Eisenberg and his colleagues has been used in several drug studies and has been factor analyzed by Conners (1969). The five factors were labeled "aggressive conduct," "day-dreaming-inattentive," "anxious-fearful," "hyperactivity," and "sociable-cooperative." A newer, slightly modified form has been developed which contains 10 items that overlap with the symptom checklist for parents and is described below. This allows one to compare ratings from both sources on a common core of items.

Sprague, Wherry, and Christiansen (1972) compared normal school children and children diagnosed as hyperkinetic and found that all five factors significantly discriminated between the groups. Interestingly, he found that, for some factors, the differences were of the order of 2 S.D., suggesting that the scales could be quite useful for individual diagnosis as well as for measures of change.

Three other excellent teacher scales should be mentioned. The first two are more appropriate for identification of learning disorders and for children with developmental deviations than for measuring change. Nevertheless, in view of the likelihood of increased interest in drug studies of learning disorders, the scales are important to keep in mind where large scale screening may be needed to identify potential candidates for drug studies. The first is a 24-item anchored scale by Myklebust (1971). The items are grouped into five areas: auditory comprehension and learning, spoken language, orientation (time, space, and relationship), behavior, and motor. The scale was used to identify children with minimal cerebral dysfunction in a sample of 2,767 third and fourth graders. Excellent discriminative power and validity were shown with the scale.

Secondly, a very thorough study of teacher ratings was published by Miller (1972). Using a modification of the Pittsburgh Adjustment Survey, five factors were extracted from a pool of 94 items and standardized on a sample of over 5,000 normal children, representative of the school population in IQ and socioeconomic status.

Finally, the CSI (above, Meier, 1971) was described as most promising for eliciting teacher judgments validly and reliably regarding children's classroom behavior. A number of studies of the dimensions of symptom behavior in young children as rated by parents or adults have been made during the past several years. Jenkins (1966) identified five clusters which he labeled "shy-seclusive," "overanxious-neurotic," "hyperactivity with poor concentration," "undomesticated," and "socialized delinquent." These clusters fell into two broad categories of inhibited and aggressive children. Peterson (1961) identified two dimensions from parent and teacher ratings which he labeled "conduct disorder" and "personality disorder." These patterns have emerged in several other studies by Borgatta and Fanshel (1965), Dreger et al. (1964), and Quay (1964).

An anchored rating scale for nonprofessionals was developed by Spivack and Spotts (1966) at the Devereux Foundation. Good norms are available for the 17 subscales of the 97-item scale. Like the teacher's version, this scale is thoroughly researched, easy to use and score, and covers a broad range of psychopathology.

The Missouri Children's Behavior Checklist (Sines et al., 1969) is a similar 70-item, yes-no checklist of symptoms. The factors of aggression, inhibition, activity level, sleep disturbance, somatization, and sociability have odd-even reliabilities ranging from 0.67–0.86. Interparent agreement on individual items ranged from 53–94%. Validity studies of clinic clients versus controls showed significant discrimination of all factors except somatization and sleep disturbance.

Conners (1970) has described a 93-item parent symptom checklist that was validated on 316 clinic patients (between the ages of 6 and 14 years) and 367 normal controls of the same age. Twenty-four categories of symptoms, such as problems of sleep, learning, and sociability, were factor analyzed. Six factors were identified by principal components analysis and were labeled aggressive conduct disorder, anxious-inhibited, antisocial, enuresis-encopresis, psychosomatic, and anxious-immature. Discriminant function analysis showed that 83% of controls and 70% of clinic patients could be correctly classified from factor scores. Neurotic and hyperkinetic children were also correctly identified in 77 and 74% of the cases, respectively.

One drawback of the scales described here is that none includes symptoms of severe psychopathology such as psychotic manifestations. A rather extensive study on children's psychiatric symptoms by Achenbach (1966) includes more such symptoms. The large, first principal component factor appeared to be a bipolar "internalizing versus externalizing" factor, and the second large component was identified as a unipolar "diffuse psychopathology" factor. Eight rotated factors were identified as: somatic complaints (delinquent behavior, obsessions, compulsions, and phobias), sexual problems, schizoid thinking, unsocialized aggression, hyperactivity, and one minor factor. The main problem with this scale is that it is designed for professionals or semiprofessionals, so that various items, such as diplopia and compulsions, would be difficult for parents to use. This is an excellent list, however, for the rating of case records or other symptom rating in a clinical context.

For more severe degrees of retardation, one should consider using the Children's Behavior Inventory by Burdock and Hardesty (1964), a 139-item, yes-no scale with items grouped by age-appropriateness. Extensive reliability and validity studies have been done, and the results indicate sufficient discriminative power and stability to warrant using the inventory in settings where a moderate amount of training of observers is possible. The items are rationally grouped into categories of vegetative function, appearance and mannerisms, speech and voice, emotional display, socialization, and thought processes.

There are several noteworthy studies either introducing additional tests and procedures or reporting evaluation studies completed on previously developed assessment devices. The similarities among the various old and new devices are far greater than the differences. As experience and data accumulate on the use of each device, various modifications and refinements are typically indicated. Usually the modification of format, the wording of some items, and other minor changes are sufficient to bring the procedures up to acceptable standards for a given application. In other cases, the data indicate that the device should be completely revamped or discarded. However, some commercial entrepreneurs continue to push their below standard products on an often unsophisticated consumer, giving rise to the recommendation that there be a national bureau of standards for psychoeducational measuring devices (Hobbs, 1975 a and b), presumably to enforce such standards as promulgated by the American Psychological Association. Maitland, Nadeau, and Nadeau (1974) took some consolation in the fact that, in spite of the proliferation of school readiness tests, the old standby Metropolitan Readiness Test (1969) was used by most school districts for kindergarten and first grade, and reportedly was an effective predictor of daily school achievement (Lessler and Bridges, 1973; Severson, 1972). However, Badian and Serwer (1975) found the venerable old Metropolitan Readiness Test wanting as an external selection criterion for subsequent early school performance. They found that a kindergartner's understanding of number concepts was a good predictor (corroborated by Hagin, Silver, and Corwin, 1971; Kingston, 1962; Searls, 1971) and visual-motor skills were not. The whole area of visual-perceptual problems and the policy of remediation through perceptual training as related to reading disability was seriously and cogently questioned by Black (1974):

> The learning problems of children with normal visual percep-
> tion appear as common and as severe as those of children with
> significant visual-perceptual problems. The placement of children
> with learning disabilities in programs for remediation should be
> based upon the presence and nature of the achievement problem,
> not upon the presence or absence of a concomitant factor such as
> visual-perceptual dysfunction, as defined in this study. Once placed
> in remedial programs, the emphasis for these children should be
> upon good teaching of reading and related academic skills, rather
> than on remediation of concomitant splinter skills. The most effi-
> cient way to remediate reading problems would seem to be the
> teaching of reading (Black, 1974, p. 64).

Camp (1973) had concluded that perceptual deficiencies, such as
low visuomotor functioning and auditory-visual integration, were not
related to learning rate or achievement, nor did they predict response to a
remedial program (Cohen, 1969). As further testimony to the controversy
surrounding the training of perceptual skills to enhance learning ability,
Mann (1971) asserted that perceptual training is essentially a farce equivalent to training nothing at all, whereas Gersten et al. (1975) reported
favorable results from a program which trained paraprofessionals who in
turn offered perceptual training to children with learning disabilities. In
order to best predict likely DLD children, Colligan and O'Connell (1974)
opt for psychometric and general developmental screening as part of the
pediatric preschool examination, and Haring and Ridgway (1967) suggest
that general language ability is the most important developmental criterion.

Ozer and Richardson (1974) have collaborated on an improved
version of the neurodevelopmental observation approach, which is a process approach designed to determine how a given child might be helped to
overcome difficulties from a structured observation of his learning and
problem-solving behavior.

> . . .The teacher has the opportunity to view a child with whom
> she has had problems in a context in which a set of possible
> solutions are illustrated. The strategies demonstrated are well within
> her repertoire. It is their application to that specific child in her
> specific classroom that is the objective of the diagnostic evaluation.
> The child is considered not only in terms of what he is but what he
> might become. The diagnosis is not of a learning problem but of the
> conditions under which such problems may be solved (Ozer and
> Richardson, 1974, p. 33).

Other promising early detection tests and procedures for elementary
school DLDs include: Erickson's (1975) statistical approach; Gearhart's

(1973) behavioral approach; Bower's (1969) scale for identifying children likely to have or develop emotional handicaps; Blom and Jansen's (1974) international comparative approach; Kosc's (1974) or Sanday's (1974) ecological approach; Bannatyne's (1975) psychometric approach; and the genetic/pedigree approach of Foch, DeFries, and Singer (1974).

Dyslexia—First Learning Disability Wedge into DD

As pointed out in Chapter 1, the official definition of developmental disabilities in the 1975 revised version (Public Law 94-103) of the original 1970 Developmental Disabilities Act (Public Law 91-517) has been expanded to include dyslexia. During the lengthy deliberations held to resolve differences and construct an improved version of the DD Act, there were persons who were actively seeking the inclusion of the entire range of learning disabilities in the DD defintion. However, groups of persons representing the developmental disabilities which were included in the original definition opposed the addition of more disabilities. Their opposition was largely because funds appropriated for the DD Act had not been increased during the previous years and would probably not be increased in the immediate future, thus spreading the limited and inadequate funding over a broader range of conditions.

One proposed compromise qualified learning disabilities by allowing only "severe specific learning disabilities." However, even this qualification was difficult to adequately define and would make it difficult to fund any activities focused on such an ambiguous target population. Naming the specific learning disability of dyslexia seemed to be the most acceptable compromise since such an impaired ability to read does constitute a severe handicap in our culture and since dyslexia is widely believed to have its origin in intraindividual neurophysiological damage or dysfunction. In fact, the conditions of dyslexia and alexia have been part of the neurology discipline's terminology for years since these are conditions frequently associated with central nervous system (CNS) damage or dysfunction.

Several national conferences and task forces of authorities on reading disorders have been held (see Templeton, 1969), and some of their salient findings and recommendations are discussed elsewhere in this section. As shown in Chapter 9, there is a high relationship between the inability to read adequately and various forms of juvenile delinquency. Such social implications provided incentive to solve the problems of illiteracy by preventing it. A decade ago, when the youth revolution was especially exploiting the concomitant sex revolution, one conference participant was prompted to write the following limerick:

There once was a boy with dyslexia,
Who met a young girl with dyspepsia.
His trouble was books, her trouble was cooks,
So they dehorned their dilemma with sexia.

The effort to find hereditary causes of dyslexia and related learning disabilities is an unrelenting but thus far inconclusive quest (Owen, 1971; Preston, 1974; Sklar, Hanley, and Simons, 1972; and Sladen, 1970). There is some evidence that it runs in families, but the dilemma of intraindividual versus interindividual origins comes up since parents and older siblings who have difficulty reading are less likely to read to the younger children in the family or to set an example that reading is a desirable skill. And, thus, the child who may have the neurophysiological integrity required for reading may not have sufficient motivation to master this critical skill.

Intervention

As discussed in previous sections of this book, the interdisciplinary approach to evaluating and intervening with DLDs is generally more efficacious than unidisciplinary efforts, primarily because most DLD conditions are sufficiently complex to require the expertise of more than one specialist for satisfactory resolution. It is important to involve mental health personnel in dealing with the DLD child, since it is practically inevitable that there will be social-emotional complications as secondary effects of a DLD, if indeed they are not a major part of the primary origin of the DLD condition.

The immediately preceding section indicated that school psychologists must broaden their understanding and approach to DLD conditions. The same advice is clearly directed to psychiatrists by Nichol (1974), whose findings very likely pertain to other mental health professionals dealing with children having DLD conditions as manifest in academic difficulties. The Commission on Emotional and Learning Disorders in Children (CELDIC), as well as such leaders as Eisenberg (1961), have encouraged psychiatrists to collaborate closely with the schools in seeking appropriate evaluations and intervention strategies for DLD children. In a 5-year follow-up study on the utility of a psychiatric consultation to children's teachers and its effects on children's subsequent progress in school, Nichol found that in only 40% of the cases were the psychiatric findings even made available to school personnel. There were over 200 children in the sample who were referred for a psychiatric evaluation of their academic problems, which incidentally comprises more than one-fifth of a child psychiatrist's typical caseload. There were neither the psychiatric findings themselves nor any evidence that such an evaluation had been performed in the school records of more than half of the children who had been evaluated 5 or more years previously. In less than 25% of the cases evaluated for academic difficulties were the findings of psychiatric evaluation judged by the teachers to be useful in their work with the children involved. Remedial education of one form or another was given to more than 90% of the DLD children during the 5 years of follow-up, in distinction to less than 25% who received continuing psychiatric care.

Clearly then, the school carries the remedial burden with precious little useful assistance from other specialists. Moreover, the psychiatric diagnosis, which was reported by teachers to be generally incomprehensible and which only categorized various symptoms and restated the presenting problem, was far less satisfactory than a more detailed evaluation of the child's perceptual, conceptual, language, motor, emotional, and social abilities. It is the preceding kind of data which supports the alleged futility of the school's bringing in outside consultation teams. It is hoped that with modifications in the training of such specialists, including some practicum experience in interdisciplinary consultation with the schools and feedback on the efficacy of their efforts, such specialist consultation and intervention will become more useful to the classroom teacher.

As the germane disciplines become increasingly interested in DLD conditions, they issue professional guides which are useful to teachers and parents who are attempting to better understand DLD conditions and to more satisfactorily intervene with them. The guides developed by Williams (1971), The American Occupational Therapy Foundation's publication describing and discussing the child with MBD (1974), the discussion of minimal cerebral dysfunction by Ferinden and Van Handel (1971), and physicians' guides (e.g., Peters et al., 1973b) are examples of some simplified versions of descriptive materials related to DLD conditions.

The greatest effort to date to provide compensatory intervention programs for DLD children, or at least children whose environmental circumstances place them at high risk of DLD conditions, was the combined efforts of Title I of the Elementary and Secondary Education Act and Project Follow-Through. Project Follow-Through (now authorized under Title V of the Community Services Act of Public Law 93-644) was launched in school year 1967–1968 as a research and development program to sustain and expand upon the gains made by disadvantaged children who had attended Head Start or similar preschool programs and would presumably profit from a smoother articulation into the public school primary program. This writer assisted in getting the western United States Follow-Through efforts launched in Greeley, Colorado. In the school year 1967–1968, there were 40 pilot projects throughout the

United States, and by school year 1971–1972, there were more than 78,000 kindergarten through third grade children in more than 150 Follow Through programs. The ethnic distribution of children was approximately 1/2 black, 1/3 white, slightly more than 1/10 Chicano, and less than 1/10 Indian. The Follow-Through program was designed to be comprehensive in scope. It included not only improvement of academic classroom activities, but also the provision of medical, dental, nutritional, psychological, and social services to the children and their families. It also included inservice training and career ladders for the professional and paraprofessional staff who by 1971 numbered more than 10,000 people. Because of its experimental nature, Follow-Through used a wide variety of sponsors who provided multiple educational approaches. The following assumptions underpinned the program: (1) service to children and research and development can be combined effectively; (2) the child's "life chances" must be improved, not merely his chances to succeed in school; (3) the involvement of parents and other community members in program planning and operation is essential; (4) a variety of educational approaches must be tested to determine the most effective ways to meet the needs of disadvantaged children; (5) a multi-approach Follow-Through program is required because of varying local needs; and (6) Follow-Through is a continuing effort with specific outputs and plans for successive years.

Some of the noteworthy findings reported in a study of Follow-Through (Applied Urbanetics, Inc., 1972) were as follows: (1) Follow-Through children made greater gains in achivement than did non-Follow-Through comparison children; (2) gains were greatest for children from identified poverty families; (3) Follow-Through children made greater positive gains in attitudes toward school and learning than did non-Follow-Through children; (4) these attitude gains were also greatest in children from identified poverty families; (5) carefully administered classroom observation of a sample testing of all grade levels showed that Follow-Through children display more self-expression, ask more questions, and display considerably more self-directed learning than non-Follow-Through children; and (6) the teachers in the same classrooms responded more often, expressed praise more frequently for the children's work, displayed negative behavior toward the children less often, and asked more thought-provoking questions.

There were some 178 Follow-Through projects, at least one in each of the 50 states, sponsored by a wide diversity of model programs and located in both rural (40%) and urban (60%) areas. The more than 20 sponsors offered a wide variety of educational approaches, from which a community was encouraged to choose the one with which it felt most comfortable. Even though all the sponsors differed considerably among themselves in terms of their approach to helping these primary children succeed in school, they were all dedicated to improving the learning abilities, feelings of self-esteem, motivation, autonomy, and general functional competence of the educationally disadvantaged children. About half of the Follow-Through children had previous Head Start experience, whereas nearly one-third had no preschool experience, and about 20% had experienced some other preschool activities before entering Follow-Through programs.

The Office of Education had strengthened the impact of the Follow-Through Program by relating it more closely to the ESEA Title I program through shared funding provisions. By 1972, several of the larger urban compensatory education projects were deriving nearly half of their support from Title I funds. A cost-effectiveness effort resulted in an attempt to reduce the additional yearly compensatory funding from $600 to $900 per child down to $400 per child, and yet maintain the quality of service. In the years following 1972, the levels of funding for Follow-Through programs have been progressively reduced, causing some programs to go out of existence, especially where they had not demonstrated sufficient efficacy for the local school system to come up with the required supplemental funding. Nevertheless, the ripple effect of successful Follow-Through/Title I projects has produced positive changes for disadvantaged children, including many DLD children, in many educational systems throughout the United States.

Various evaluation efforts have been undertaken to assess the impact of these programs which had the primary goal of raising the academic achievement of elementary school children, regardless of socioeconomic class, ethnic group, or other characteristics. In attempting to review the effectiveness of compensatory Follow-Through projects in the primary grades, there were several limitations within the existing data: (1) the project descriptions were often vague and too general, (2) evaluation measures were primarily limited to the cognitive realm, i.e., to IQ and achievement tests; (3) statistically significant gains observed were not always of educational significance; (4) most evaluations measured the effects of projects over only 1 year rather than assessing the longitudinal impact; and (5) very few projects followed the children for longer than 1 year beyond the third grade.

The impact on actual classroom processes and school organizational changes was even more difficult to assess. Findings from large scale evaluations of Title I offer little evidence of a positive overall impact on the eligible and participating children, with some exceptions in a small proportion of projects. The Follow-Through evaluation information is equally disappointing, with some few exceptions. The exceptional projects which did report successful intervention were those which had: (1) clearly stated academic objectives; (2) small group or individualized instruction; (3) extensive parent involvement; (4) teacher training in the methods of the project together with careful planning for implementation; (5) directly relevant and intensive instruction; (6) high expectations for the children; and (7) a positive and relatively structured learning environment. However, once again, the evaluation focus was primarily on measured achievement and intelligence, both of which require sustained input in order to remain the same during subsequent years and are, therefore, quite susceptible to the washout effect which occurs when enrichment input is terminated. A more encouraging evaluation of compensatory and enrichment efforts was reported by Stallings (1974) and Rayder and Body (1975), who separately have demonstrated that measured growth has also been obtained along other dimensions, such as motivation, self-concept, problem-solving, and question-asking, in a number of the less structured and more open Follow-Through/Title I endeavors.

Since there are so little reliable incidence and prevalence data on DLD conditions (see Chapter 1), as found in the elementary schools, it is not possible to assess to what extent Follow-Through/Title I programs have reduced DLD conditions, especially those attributable to extraindividual origins. Nonetheless, it is hoped that the collective experience from these several massive intervention efforts, described by one HEW Follow-Through official as "the largest, most expensive social experiment ever launched," will result in an even more massive modification of the school program to better meet the individual needs of all children, especially those with various DLD conditions. The Follow-Through/Title I joint efforts were experiencing progressive phase-out at this writing. For example, there were $35 million available for Follow-Through efforts in school year 1975–1976, including 153 programs and serving some 38,000 children in second and third grades, as compared to the 1972 fiscal year when $63 million were being used in 155 programs to serve 84,000 children in grades kindergarten through third. As further evidence of the perennial capriciousness of federal funding patterns, the U. S. Congress approved the extension of Project Follow-Through for 3 more years, 1975–1978, and authorized $60 million for each year, which, of course, does not actually appropriate that much money but does offer some hope for the continuation of the program.

As one might expect, the number and variety of prevention/intervention procedures and programs for children with DLD conditions in the elementary school are far more numerous and have considerably greater empirical history. During the primary grades, the greatest concern is with reading, and, hence, most methods and materials are focused on this specific academic ability. The ability to read in practically any advanced society is essential for independent survival. For everyone with sufficient vision to see the printed word, even if it has to be enlarged, it is highly desirable that he become at least functionally literate, which in the United States is regarded as roughly the equivalent of fourth to sixth grade reading ability.

The National Assessment of Educational Progress Program, which is a project of the Education Commission of the States, has revealed that a sizable proportion of the population, and especially those in the low income brackets, have difficulty with the basic academic skills.

> Three major studies which have pinpointed reading deficiences include: A national assessment of educational progress (NAEP) survey of reading achievement that shows 20–30 percent of the U.S. young people, ages 9, 13, 17 and 26–35, cannot complete satisfactorily various reading tasks that range from understanding words and word relationships to critical reading. The U.S. survey also shows a correlation between reading achievement and socio-economic background, parental education, sex, race, and region of the country.
>
> Estimates based on the results of a 1970 Lewis-Harris Poll indicate that 19 million U.S. adults are functionally illiterate, and that 7 million people under age 16 will become functionally illiterate adults.
>
> Further, the Harris findings show "the practical literacy in the United States decreases in direct proportion to income." The range of illiteracy for persons with annual incomes of $5,000 or less is 5–18 percent, compared to a range of 1–7 percent for income groups at or above $15,000.
>
> An international survey shows that U.S. 10-year-olds perform less well in tests of reading comprehension than 10-year-olds in nine other countries; U.S. 14-year-olds perform less well than their peers in three other nations; and at the end of the secondary level, U.S. students' achievement falls below that of students in 12 other countries (NAEP, 1973, p. 1).

As a result of these and similar findings from other studies, a strong focus has now been placed on reading as a top educational priority in the United States, and has led to a major U. S. Office of Education endeavor entitled "The Right to Read Program," which is aimed at ending illiteracy in the United States by 1980. This was also the focus of the program, under the direction of the writer, sponsored by the Rocky Mountain Educational Laboratory (Meier, 1968). As stated in earlier chapters, one of the primary reasons for compulsory schooling was originally to ensure that all the citizens in a democracy would be functionally literate, and, therefore, able to play their appropriate role as informed participants in their own government. Before that, most formal education was designed to give persons the ability to read and understand the Bible and other sources of moral enlightenment. In this modern era, in a developed contemporary society, reading has taken on the dignity of a survival skill, since even daily living is dependent upon one's ability to read the written word, whether it be for shopping in a supermarket, understanding highway maps and signs, finding palatable food, observing safety warnings, or following other directions which typically cannot be presented in any other than written form. Therefore, the child who is unable to learn to read represents a major concern to his parents, teachers, and any other caregivers who have a concern for his welfare and functional competence.

Reading Process and Prevention/Remediation of Its Disorders

The heavy emphasis on the ability to read has given rise to a commensurately large number of methods and materials for both initially teaching children how to read and/or for subsequently providing children who do not learn to read through one approach an opportunity to learn through an alternative approach. As illustrated in Myklebust's proposed continuum (1965a), reading is the final and presumably most difficult state of language development, depending upon all other receptive, associative, and expressive language functions being previously established (Figure 20). The readiness to learn to read is highly and positively correlated with general cognitive/intellectual development, since recognition and comprehension of words which are read are a function of the size of a person's receptive vocabulary, which in turn is highly correlated with verbal intelligence, which in turn is a function of the richness or paucity of one's verbal environment, and so forth. The controversy regarding readiness to read in part revolves around notions of overall developmental and learning maturation. Various techniques have been developed to teach or enable young children to learn to read single words and some simple primers as young as 3 years of age (Engelmann, 1966; Meier, 1970; Moore, 1964; Nimnicht, 1967). Apparently very young children can and do master the reading process whether as a result of formal instruction or simply from observing television commercials. Programs such as Sesame Street and the Electric Company have enabled young children to read who have very little written material in their homes or who have no adults who care to help them learn to read.

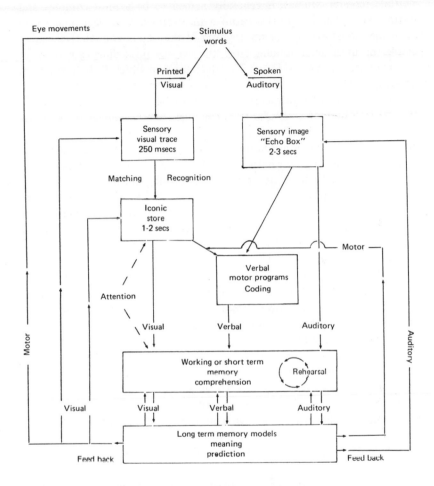

Figure 20. Model of reading process. The visual stimulus (letter, word, picture, etc.) leads to a sensory trace which is matched with a memory trace and causes recognition of familiar stimuli or short-term memory of unfamiliar stimuli. The data in short-term memory are processed in various ways by feedback from long-term memory and may be stored or forgotten. In reading, the written word is first matched to a stored visual pattern, then coded into speech motor programs, and finally comprehended by comparison with mental models (Mackworth, 1972, p. 710). The importance of stimulus trace was corroborated by Meier (1965) for differentiating mentally retarded children, whose stimulus trace functioning was defective, from emotionally disturbed children.

Nevertheless, the process of reading, which has been the subject of multiple research studies, is generally agreed to be a most complex and abstract skill. The progression from a three-dimensional real object to a two-dimensional drawing or photograph of the object is a relatively more simple transition than jumping from the two- or three-dimensional object to some abstract symbol for it. To select the one which is different from among several drawings of cats or dogs or balls or other familiar objects, especially when he has just learned to abstract "catness" from a number of pictures of different cats, is difficult enough for the individual. Then he must select the cat which is different from an array of several cats when the difference is simply a function of which direction the odd one of four identical cats is facing, or whether or not it has a tail or both ears, etc. This discrimination and choice are similar to identifying the difference between a "b" and a "q" or a "d" and a "p" or an "N" and a "Z," all of which are not rotated versions of the same form or configuration. The addition or elimination of small elements which convert an "F" to an "E," or an "n" to an "m" or an "O" to a "Q" add to the confusion and further violate the laws of constancy of shape, size, form, etc.

Although it is asserted that there are only 26 letters to the Roman alphabet, when one considers the varieties introduced by capital and small letters (upper case and lower case), font styles, printed versus cursive manuscript, and other combinations and permutations, it is clear that there are easily more than 100 standard varieties of the basic 26 letters and many idiosyncratic variations on the standard varieties. Moreover, the sounds represented by some of these individual letters and by various combinations of these letters are irregular in that they "say" different sounds in different words or when preceded or followed by various letters. For example, the word *enough* could be spelled "enuf," "enouf," "einough," "enouph," "enauph," "inuf," "ynouf," etc.

In order to simplify the understanding of the various letter combinations, one reading system (Gategno, 1962) assigned particular shades of color to all of the letter combinations which make the sound of a long "e," and a different shade of color to those combinations making the sound "uf." Thus, the word *enough,* regardless of how it is spelled, would always have the same color pattern, which was thought to be helpful in learning to read. In another effort to introduce regularity into the sound equivalence of various letter combinations, an initial teaching alphabet was devised (Pitman, 1961) which had 42 letter characters instead of 26, and every character always said the same thing. This variation on the traditional orthography (TO) or standard Roman alphabet was called the Initial Teaching Alphabet, and was thought to simplify the learning of reading.

Unfortunately, these two systems, plus several others which enjoyed even less success, have never demonstrated consistently their superiority over the traditional alphabet for learning to read and sometimes the transition has further complicated the mastery of reading "everyday" regular writing.

It is popularly believed that many children can be classified in accordance with their strongest learning modality, which is to say that some children may be considered to be primarily visual learners, others to be primarily auditory learners, and some to be primarily tactile-kinesthetic learners. The olfactory and gustatory (and extrasensory perceptual) modalities have not received much attention in the DLD literature to date, but may in the future. One reason why reading is such a complex process is that it usually involves at least the visual and auditory modalities and requires crossing over between these modalities for comprehension. When oral reading is considered, there is the additional operation of the motor/ speech modality. It seems reasonable that the child who learns best through the auditory modality should begin reading by means of a phonics approach, just as the more visually oriented learner might benefit most from a whole word approach.

Following the above logic, and in an effort to involve as many of the sense modalities as seemed reasonable, Fernald (1943) also involved the tactile-kinesthetic sense modality. This required a beginning reader who was having difficulty recognizing letter and word forms to trace with his finger or hand enlarged versions of these letters and words which had roughened or otherwise tactilely different surfaces representing the letter or word shapes. This tactile-kinesthetic involvement in learning letter and word forms, in conjunction with pronouncing the letter's name or sound, and visually seeing it, seemed to be a useful approach (sometimes referred to by the acronym VAKT for the combined visual, auditory, kinesthetic, and tactile technique) for some children who were not learning to read through regular instructional procedures. However, this rather tedious process has not been well researched and critics suggest that the attendant one-to-one tutorial situation, the greater attention the child must pay to the task of learning to read, plus other factors may explain much of the favorable results which are reported.

Another technique for involving multiple sensory modalities in the habilitation of reading was proposed by Heckelman (1962) and experimentally implemented by Gardner (1965). This technique was referred to as the Impress Method and was premised on the notion that if learning to speak and understand the spoken word is an inherent human capability, then also learning to read and write the language is an inborn capacity. The Impress Method is described as follows: the disabled reader and his teacher read the same materials in unison with the voice of the teacher directed into the ear of the student at close range. The learner is expected to slide his finger along the line of written material which is being read aloud, and his finger must be at the location of the spoken word at all times. The reading is spontaneous and as few pauses as possible are made during the process. The teacher does not teach sounds of the words or word recognition or pay attention to any pictures or content of the story itself. There are no comprehension question-and-answer sessions afterward. The child is permitted to volunteer any information or questions he may have about the material they have just read, and the teacher generally reinforces the child's growing ability to read.

In an experimental application (Gardner, 1965) of the Impress Method, a total of 49 learners were involved in a reading research program which entailed severely retarded readers. After working with the students using the method for 10 minutes a day for a 6-week period, there was a significant gain in their reading abilities. The implication of the beneficial results for this total of 5 hours of accumulated instruction in the habilitation of severely retarded readers is clear. The fact that these children made an average gain of 3.2 months in reading ability was doubly significant in view of their past history of regressing in reading ability with the passage of time. This Impress Method was sufficiently impressive to warrant further research and development. As a result, Meier and Scott (1967) developed a filmed version of the story "Androcles and the Lion" which presented the words and sounds simultaneously on an 8-mm film loop for the learner to watch and listen to as many times as he wished. This Automated Impress Method (AIM) has not been further explored because of the loss of funding for the sponsor program, but, in this writer's estimation, it still warrants further investigation. The advance in technology permits the production of such training techniques with accelerated auditory material (using compressed speech technology) and should be the next generation beyond controlled readers and tachistoscopic presentation of symbolic material for the amelioration of certain reading disorders.

Regardless of all that has been said about matching reading instruction to the specific perceptual modality that is strongest in the learner, the results of this are also still confounding. For example, when Sabatino and Dorfman (1974) tried such curriculum matching with 77 mild DLD children, they failed to get any significant interactions when using the Sullivan Programmed Reading Series, which emphasizes the visual modality, and the Distar Reading I Program, which emphasizes the auditory modality.

Of course, for the DLD child who is deaf and/or blind, the development of the ability to read is a much more difficult endeavor. The child who sees things routinely or erratically in a distorted manner because of visual dysfunction(s) may have great difficulty associating various letter combinations he "sees" with sound combinations he hears. Furthermore, the sound combinations may not be heard in the same way from one time to the next or may be routinely distorted or incomplete because of one or another kind of hearing impairment. In such a case, the amplification and/or correction of what is heard as the spoken word is necessary before receptive language can be sufficiently accurate and sophisticated to permit reading subsequently to occur.

For those who do not see adequately and whose vision cannot be corrected satisfactorily, it may be necessary to employ Braille, which is another way of using the tactile-kinesthetic sense modality for processing symbolic language. McCoy (1975) reported the successful use of the Braille technique with a DLD (severely dyslexic) teenager, perhaps opening another way, albeit a kind of last resort, for helping DLD children with reading disorders. Using touch as an alternative neural pathway to processing coded language was further supported by Doehring (1973), who found that, of 109 measures used to statistically compare normal readers with retarded readers, the reading retardation group showed a significant superiority to the normal reading group on five measures, four of which were tests of tactile ability.

Cases have been reported of persons with various genetic defects, such as Turner's syndrome, which may in fact impair their ability to copy certain figures. For example, one girl 12 years of age, with an IQ of more than 130, had extreme difficulty in accurately perceiving and copying some simple forms such as found in the Beery (1967), Bender (1962), or Frostig (1964a and b) tests. Furthermore, she had considerable difficulty in learning to read, since she was unable to perceive accurately more complex forms of written language. This was in spite of her obviously good verbal understanding of the spoken word, her ability to express her thoughts, and her demonstrated comprehension of complex ideas.

Practically all children, during the development of their reading skills, rotate, invert, and otherwise distort written and heard symbols as they begin to read. Many humorous stories are told about children who scramble sounds and words while they are learning to talk. However, some children continue to have these difficulties long after their peers have mastered the underlying skills and understandings. Whether they are called late-bloomers, underachievers, educationally handicapped, significantly learning-impaired children (SLIC), or DLD children, they are educationally handicapped despite their normal or above normal intelligence. They have difficulty distinguishing the word "saw" from the word "was" or the phrase "sacred god" from "scared dog." They may also find it difficult to always move their eyes smoothly from left to right in reading the English language. They not only reverse the direction of reading for certain letters and words, but may even reverse direction for whole lines; there are examples of children learning numbers up to 100 who wrote 1 through 10 from left to right, then down one space from right to left wrote the numbers from 11 to 20, then down one space going left to right wrote 21 to 30, etc., which is a logical but not acceptable approach in the English language and Arabic numeration system. These DLD children probably would have difficulty with even simple arithmetic calculations wherein they might not only reverse numbers (4,856 instead of 6,584), but they might also inadvertently shift processes, such as suddenly beginning to subtract in a multiplication problem. When correcting their papers, they may hear one number and see a different one and be uncertain as to which is right and which is wrong.

These DLD children do not perceive the world the way most people do, and this is also manifest in such an apparently simple task as drawing a person. When such drawings are significantly less well executed than those of the majority of children for a given age, this may indicate some degree of neurological immaturity. When general immaturity is the principal reason for a child's academic delays relative to his peers, a simple solution is to give him an extra year in a transition class (deHirsch, Jansky, and Langford, 1966) whereby the tincture of time may remedy the potential DLD. Otherwise, the DLDs resulting from the maturational delays will probably carry over into other areas of school performance, such as handwriting, where reversals, rotations, transpositions, and other kinds of errors frequently contribute to miserable spelling. For a child whose intelligence is normal or better, and yet whose academic function is impaired with one or another DLD condition, it is no surprise that considerable emotional disturbance might become an additional symptom and require counseling in addition to whatever educational therapy is instituted. This gives rise to the term "psychoeducational" therapy.

There are many other remedial reading procedures, most of which are adaptations of the standard instructional techniques, but are broken down into smaller steps and presented to the DLD child at a slower pace, and frequently from 1 to 4 years later than normally developing children received reading instruction and mastered the process. Various programs, instruction manuals, and other guides have been developed for such remedial procedures (Chapter 10 lists several). One noteworthy approach, which was designed to facilitate the learning of children at risk of DLD conditions caused by environmental differences and deprivations, employed the use of an automated or nonautomated "talking typewriter." Although this procedure was perfected for use with younger, normally developing but deprived children (see Chapter 7 for more details), it has also been used with primary school children with considerable success.

> The Learning Booth may be located in or outside the classroom—even in a small trailer. It is manned by a booth attendant and equipped with an electric typewriter. It is a place children can explore freely, a place where they can solve problems on their own. Most problems are about reading, but teaching reading is *not* the main purpose of the booth. The main purpose is to teach a child to solve problems and find answers himself. A child who depends on himself to learn has learned how to learn. If he also learns to read, that is a bonus.
>
> A child will learn how to learn if a booth attendant does not question, but answers questions and *responds* to exploration. In this way, children are likely to make discoveries about the typewriter and letters and numerals.
>
> The booth is called a *responsive environment* because the typewriter *shows* and the attendant *says* what the child does (Nimnicht et al., no date, p. 7).

To give a more concrete example of how the booth learning activities are programmed, Figure 21 depicts a flow chart to be followed by the booth attendant during one of the most advanced phases of learning to read and write. Although developed for use with potentially DLD disadvantaged preschool children, the process has been employed successfully with older DLD children.

One of the most highly touted remedial reading approaches is that developed by Orton (1964) and his followers. This approach, besides using the various techniques of phonics, appeals to the logical nature of symbolic language, which Orton considered to be a sign or a series of sounds which have come to serve as a substitute for an object or a concept and can thus be used as a means of transferring ideas. Orton studied various language disabilities, and coined the term "strephosymbolia," which literally means "twisted symbols," and applied this term to language problems which involved reading, writing, spelling, speaking, and calculating difficulties. As a result of Orton's pioneering work (1937), an Orton Society was formed and attracted a number of DLD therapists into its folds. These persons have enlarged the Orton Society (1963) and promulgated the various reading remediation techniques explored and refined by Orton

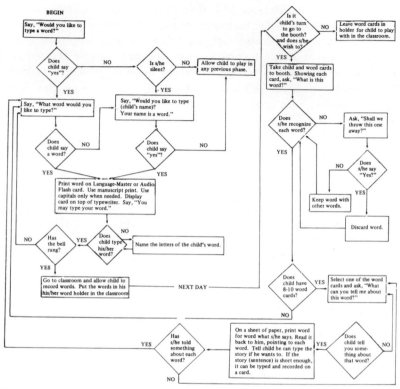

Figure 21. The learning booth; phase IV—words and stores. (Reprinted from Nimnicht et al., no date, p. 59.)

(1964) and by Gillingham and Stillman (1960), two educational therapists affiliated with Orton's early work. Their rather intellectual approach to reading, which involves the understanding of the roots of words, including their Latin derivation, appeals to and works with many of the brighter dyslexic children.

One of the few well documented longitudinal studies of the efficacy of remedial procedures is that reported by Rawson (1968), wherein she describes successful intervention efforts using much of the Orton approach with a number of dyslexic children whom she followed for 30 years. Various case histories reveal that her students had learned to compensate for their difficulties and to reason their way through some of their reading disabilities into becoming physicians, lawyers, other professional persons, as well as successful businessmen and otherwise skilled employees and productive citizens.

One promising approach to preventing DLD conditions which have their origins in different cultural values, customs, and languages is that of bicultural/bilingual school programs. In the U. S., these programs typically attempt to integrate either the Black or Spanish-speaking ethnic traditions with those of the predominantly Anglo traditions. This is accomplished through multi-ethnic books and related curriculum materials, bilingual/ bicultural teachers, and other arrangments designed to maintain and increase the minority child's sense of positive self-esteem. Using methods and materials which have relevance to a child's experience, including the Anglo child from the culture of poverty, is becoming more popular among academicians and voting citizens alike. The U.S. Office of Child Development has sponsored the production of numerous bilingual/bicultural materials and even some tests (especially the CIRCUS battery), largely for Spanish-speaking children (see Chapter 10 for examples). The existence of the "Six-Hour Retarded Child" (President's Committee on Mental Retardation, 1969) may be substantially reduced by such modified school programs. To date very little has been done for Indians, Eskimos, Hawaiians, or Portuguese minority groups in terms of modified curriculum and general school programs.

Although the preceding literature discussion of DLD conditions in elementary school children focused almost exclusively upon reading ability in the primary grades, Goodstein and Kahn (1974) have pointed out that computational disabilities are separate and distinct from deficits in reading and are not even measured well in most tests of intelligence. They consequently advocate that any screening process for identifying DLD children should include assessment of arithmetic computational skills and that arithmetic remedial programming should be an integral component of any intervention program. It is clearly stated that negligence to assess academic functioning in all three of the "R's" has led to the mistaken belief that concentration upon reading remediation is sufficient in the case of a DLD child, whereas at least writing skills and arithmetic computational skills should round out the three "R's" when intervention programming is being designed.

Although Dunn (1965) challenged the whole notion of segregated special education for the mild DLD child, the consequent effort to mainstream as many children as possible, including mild DLD cases, is only gradually being realized. Careful efforts to place elementary children classified as mentally retarded and living in an economically depressed area into regular classroom programs have been tried in many settings for various scientific and humanitarian reasons (see Hobbs, 1975a and 1975b, for an updated and detailed explanation of these reasons). However, the careful monitoring of the progress of such replaced children is rare, and it is, therefore, difficult to determine how effective this mainstreaming effort has been.

One notable exception to this characteristic lack of hard data about the effects of mainstreaming was that reported by Haring and Krug (1975). These investigators began with 48 elementary school-aged DLD children whom they had randomly selected from a larger population and subsequently divided into matched experimental and control groups for placement in four classrooms of 12 students each. They wished to determine the efficacy of an experimental individualized instructional program designed to facilitate the return of special education elementary children to regular classroom programs. After a year of carefully managed intervention using precision teaching techniques, 13 students from the experimental group were placed in regular classes. A year later a follow-up study was conducted to determine how well these 13 students had adapted to the regular classroom program, both academically and socially. The 1-year follow-up study on the 13 students who had been placed in the regular class milieu indicated that they could acquire basic skills at a rate to allow their continued regular class placement. The other 11 students in the experimental group were also followed; with some additional special intervention time, five of them had moved into the regular program. Thus, in this single small study, with appropriate educational priming, a total of 18 out of 24 mild DLD children were mainstreamed successfully. However, of the 24 control children who received no special intervention to prepare them for mainstreaming, only three were successfully moved into the regular classroom program, and 21 had to be retained in special classes to meet their special academic and behavioral needs. The importance of such a study is that it suggests that there are many children in special education programs who are capable of being satisfactorily mainstreamed when they are properly prepared academically and socially before re-entry. This finding places a significant value upon special education programming, which might assume as one of its primary objectives that of self-destructing by providing the intensive individualized instruction necessary to prepare children with various fundamental DLD problems or conditions for entry or re-entry into the regular school program, where they might be expected to function satisfactorily in larger groups of normally developing and learning peers.

Moreover, this suggests that the preparation of personnel working in special programs should include the thorough understanding of individualized learning, using such techniques as precision teaching (Kunzelman et al., 1970; Peter, 1965). Such an approach allows the teacher and other school program specialists, such as the school psychologist, to systematically modify the learning setting by altering one condition at a time until the individual child begins to make satisfactory progress. Expanded understanding and competencies in special school personnel, such as school psychologists, are advocated not only by the psychologists themselves, but also in the professional literature (Cassel, 1973). Indeed, the growing awareness that professionals working with DLD children require training in intervention models from various disciplines was underscored by Hagin (1973). After reviewing intervention projects described in 306 papers appearing in the educational and school psychology literature for a 6-year period, several trends and common characteristics were identified. She identified a shift from unidisciplinary rather restricted interpretations of DLD conditions originating almost exclusively within the individual (intra-individual deficits, Figure 5) to an interdisciplinary synthesis of possible origins and appropriately matched intervention strategies. This represented a move from the more traditional pathological model and the concentration on reading and learning processes to a greater emphasis upon a kind of educational mismatch model, which takes into consideration all the possible combinations and permutations of the origins of DLDs shown in Table 3.

The preceding does not suggest that the search for malfunction within the individual be abandoned, but strongly indicates that, regardless of whether a DLD's origins are found to be partially explainable by intraindividual conditions, the examiner is obliged to also evaluate the interaction of the interindividual and extraindividual dynamics for any given DLD condition, in order to determine the optimum intervention approach (Scott, Kell, and Salisbury, 1970). This trend, of course, serves to underscore the importance of comprehensive interdisciplinary evaluation of DLD conditions, which in turn must be carried out by persons trained in the interdisciplinary and interprofessional settings such as those provided by the university affiliated facilities network throughout the United States (AUAF, 1974).

chapter 9

Developmental and Learning Disability Conditions during Adolescence

According to some authorities who have investigated human growth and development from a cross-cultural vantage point, adolescence is a creation of contemporary society. It is a term describing the period of time which varies in length in different societies during which persons are considered to be neither adults nor children. As societies become more advanced, requiring longer and more specialized preparation of their citizens to become acceptably productive, the phenomenon of adolescence becomes more universal. As a consequence, many new scholarly and popular treatises on adolescence are produced. Conger's (1973) contemporary version seems to be the most definitive and comprehensive. Typically, the more advanced the culture, the longer the time period required for becoming an adult and, thus, being an adolescent. Much of the time during adolescence is set aside for teenagers to master the necessary skills of functional competence to become productive citizens in their respective societies. Table 15 is included to illustrate a cross-section of the dynamic developmental phases normally encountered in adolescence. The developmental phases shown in Table 15 are practically self-explanatory, but a thorough discussion of each one is found in Erikson (1959). The teenager with a DLD condition is especially disadvantaged since it is necessary for both the skills and the developmental stages of adolescence to be mastered from formal school instruction and from less formal life experiences, a doubly difficult demand for one who is not developing "normally."

Table 15. Erikson's epigenetic chart of developmental phases[a]

Age (yr)		Infancy	Early childhood	Play age
0–2 Oral Zone	I. Infancy	Trust vs. mistrust		
2–4 Anal	II. Early childhood		Autonomy vs. shame, doubt	
4–6 Oedipal	III. Play age			Initiative vs. guilt
6–12	IV. School age			Industry vs. inferiority
13–20+	V. Adolescence	Time perspective vs. time diffusion	Self-certainty vs. identity consciousness	Role experimentation vs. negative identity
	VI. Young adult VII. Adulthood			
	VIII. Mature age			

School age	Adolescence	Young adult	Adulthood	Mature age
	Unipolarity vs. premature self-differentiation Bipolarity vs. autism Play identification vs. (oedipal) fantasy identities Work identification vs. identity foreclosure			
Anticipation of achievement vs. work paralysis	Identity vs. identity diffusion Solidarity vs. social isolation	Sexual identity vs. bisexual diffusion Intimacy vs. isolation	Leadership polarization vs. authority diffusion Generativity vs. self-absorption	Ideological polarization vs. diffusion of ideals Integrity vs. disgust, despair

From Erikson, 1959, p. I.1.

The awkwardness of a rapidly growing and changing body coupled with an increased self-consciousness about one's growth and development, intensified by a growing concern over one's peer-group acceptance, plus the growing expectations of one's elders for adult behavior and competence are enough to make this period of adolescence a most stressful one. Ironically enough, as the adolescent does master the skills of independent adult living, he is kept relatively dependent upon parents and other elders, often until well into his twenties if college and advanced degrees or training are pursued. In the United States, then, the ambiguous period of adolescence may last 10–15 years during which multiple roles, values, life styles, and fads are tried. The typical adolescent's experiments with various identities are often perplexing and exasperating to the responsible caregiving people and agencies. If some combination of disabilities in learning and/or abnormalities in development is added to this complex and volatile period, the stage is certainly set for all sorts of weird hangups.

This chapter addresses some of the ways in which DLD conditions can be detected in adolescence and discusses a few of the procedures for preventing and/or remediating these DLD conditions. Moreover, since many parents are adolescents and most adolescents eventually become parents, it seems important to include some discussion about the effects of DLD conditions on the family whether the DLDs exist in the parents themselves or are found in their offspring. Most of the DLD children described earlier grow older, develop sexually, and frequently marry and bear children. Formal preparation for such parenting in our society is seldom provided, and the general dissolution of the extended family, which in the past served as an informal educational network and sort of fail-safe, now leaves adolescent parents and their children quite vulnerable to many problems, including DLD conditions, which might have been avoided in the past. Thus, although this chapter falls at the older end of the DLD continuum, it comes full circle to address some of the parental, societal, and cultural origins of DLDs (Table 3).

Just as adolescents frequently find themselves on the horns of a dilemma regarding whether to behave as adults or children, the literature on adolescence is often ambiguous. Since the scope of this book is already quite extensive, the writer resolved most of such literary ambiguities by not citing much of the adult literature, leaving that for other treatises. Furthermore, since the quality and quantity of authoritative treatises on DLD conditions in adolescence are relatively sparse, this chapter is correspondingly shorter, thereby reflecting the current state of the art and science.

DETECTION OF DLDs IN ADOLESCENTS

One of the most revealing and pernicious indicators of DLD conditions during adolescence is the school dropout rate. Furthermore, the numbers of children and teenagers who are simply not attending school for multiple questionable reasons is an alarming and related statistic (Edelman et al., 1974). Several investigators have reported a high and positive relationship between dropping out of school and having a DLD condition.

Once a DLD adolescent has dropped out (or been pushed out) of school and typically is unable to find time and energy-consuming employment, the idle time weighs heavily on his active mind and body. He may become severely depressed and/or turn to socially deviant occupations to pass the time. The more civilized and lawful his environment, the less tolerance there is for asocial behavior; his malaise and resentment, in a vicious cycle, may lead to fullblown juvenile delinquency. This link between delinquency and DLDs has been noted by several authorities: Jorgensen, Bangsgard, and Glad (1968) relate it to general learning disorders; Keldgord (1968) and Tarnopol (1970) relate it to brain damage; Jacobson and Ekanger (1968) and Rousy and Cozad (1966) to speech and hearing disorders; Harrower (1964) and Mulligan (1969) to reading retardation or dyslexia; and Harrington (1935), Hershkovitz, Levine, and Spivak (1959), and Petric, McCullough, and Kazdin (1962) all relate delinquency to mental deficiency.

> In the last few years, a significant amount of evidence has been published verifying the relationship between learning disabilities and delinquency. In 1972, Anderson reported EEG abnormalities in 50 percent of adult female prisoners. In the same year, Berman found that 60 percent of delinquents have auditory problems which would impair learning, and Walle found speech and hearing problems in 48.3 percent of a delinquent population. Dzik, in an earlier study, found visual perceptual problems in 53 percent of delinquents (Jacobson, 1974, pp. 193–94).

All too often the academically defeated adolescent resorts to nonproductive, then delinquent, and then criminal activities, since these may represent achievements the DLD youth can do as well as his peers. It is widely recognized that as many as 90% of delinquent youth and school dropouts have one or more DLD conditions. The converse is likely to be nearly as high a relationship, that is, that most children/youth with DLD conditions sooner or later at least drop out of school before completing high school and, depending upon their home environment and the nature of the DLD condition, there is a substantially increased probability for their becoming socially deviant. In fact, the observable behaviors and related symptoms ascribed to DLD conditions in adolescence are very similar to many of the predictor variables for youth at high risk of becoming juvenile delinquents, or at least school dropouts. Although the term "dropout" is euphemistically the popular jargon or nomenclature used by school authorities, many experts who fully appreciate the dynamics of why children and youth fail in school and drop out of school suggest that the term "pushout" is more accurate.

With the increased interest in crime prevention and an enlarging appreciation for the persistence of some DLD conditions whose origins were in early childhood but whose presence may continue to impair the individual's functioning through adolescence, increased energy and resources are being extended to identify the adolescent who has a DLD condition and who might benefit from certain intervention procedures. Since the schools are allegedly designed to prepare students for life, it is readily understandable why a youth who is repeatedly failing to perform satisfactorily in a situation where everyone is competing for a limited number of rewards, much as is true in life, should drop out of this defeating situation and pursue some other avenue for a sense of worth and achievement. Until the past decade or so, it was more possible for DLD female adolescents to "save face" and remain in school, taking largely nonacademic domestic subjects. Women's liberation and equal opportunity (as well as equal expectations) in the world of work no longer permit the frustrated DLD teenage young lady to prove herself by learning homemaking skills or perhaps becoming pregnant. Thus, adolescent girls are not only entering most of the major sports previously restricted to boys but also are entering the ranks of the violent teenage delinquent.

It may be presumptuous to consider it necessary to alert the experienced educator to symptoms for recognizing adolescents who are prone to subsequent academic failure and the downward spiral to desperate delinquency. Their past performance in elementary and early junior high school has already probably documented this proneness. Nevertheless, there are adolescents who have mastered various social graces plus the related adaptive behaviors and have developed some deliberate camouflaging techniques which effectively mask the existence of their DLD conditions. Some DLD youngsters employ their average or above average general intelligence to adequately compensate for real deficiencies in one or more academic functions. The youth with extraordinary social awareness may relate extraordinarily well with his teachers and other adult authority figures so as to create a kind of halo effect around himself or herself, thereby nearly always receiving the benefit of the doubt and social promotions, until the point of diminishing academic returns is too severe to be overlooked. Others may deliberately learn to write sloppily so as to cover up their spelling disability. There are still others who, by dint of sheer perseverance, including spending twice as much time in learning academic subject matter, manage to get by or even to do well compared to their ordinarily endowed peers, especially those who do not fully use their normal abilities.

The behavioral indices for the detection of elementary school DLDs have counterpart behavioral indices for identifying the adolescent who may be experiencing and even deliberately disguising a DLD condition. Giles (1973) has modified the Individual Learning Disability Classroom Screening Instrument (ILDCSI) discussed in Chapter 8 to produce a version of the ILDCSI suitable for use with the adolescent age group. Some of the noteworthy additional behavioral indices included in the adolescent version, in addition to many academically related ones from the elementary ILDCSI, address the functional categories dealing with vocational attributes, social adjustment, and emotional characteristics. Thus, even though standard visual, auditory, motor, and integrative abilities must be checked out, perhaps with more difficult and sophisticated learning tasks, other useful indices include: poor response to career guidance, unrealistic vocational ambitions, general irresponsibility, inability to make and keep friends, seeing school as "kid stuff," rebelliousness against all authority, undue self-criticism, imagining peer persecution, general avoidance of academic learning tasks, and so on.

The most difficult aspect of detecting DLD conditions in adolescence is the typically heavy secondary overlay of emotional disturbance (Lehtinen, 1971). As stated earlier, these adolescent years are ones characterized by new and deeper layers of emotion unfolding in a most fresh and volatile form. If emotion were expressed in the same way and same degree by individuals who were either younger or older than what is traditionally thought to be adolescence, they likely would be construed as emotionally disturbed. However, during adolescence, a much wider tolerance for emotional instability is normally accepted and, thus, for example, the depression attendant to academic failure caused by a DLD condition may be misinterpreted as just another adolescent phase. It is at this time that communication breakdowns frequently occur. The accusation by adolescents that nobody understands them is often the projection of their own inability to understand what's going on inside and around themselves. The detection of DLD conditions in adolescents requires an extremely sensitive sleuth who is able to discern unusual and counter-productive ripples in a normally wind-swept sea of emotion.

Mohr and Despres (1958) discuss multiple aspects of emotional disturbance in adolescence. They point out the developmental aspects of much adolescent emotional disturbance and suggest that many DLD precursors may underly the emotional disturbance which becomes manifest during the stressful and unstable period of adolescence when compensatory strengths are not within the individual, his family, or the environment. Various forms of neurotic, passive-dependent, rebellious, passive-aggressive, and compulsive-obsessive behaviors are illustrated with exemplary case studies. The development of more severe psychotic conditions is also presented with the hopeful note that these are frequently transitory or are a function of nonrecurring trauma, and, in some instances, hormonal imbalances during this physical adjustment period. They also elaborate upon the psychological aspects of health problems in adolescence and poignantly point out how hypersensitive teenagers are to their rapidly changing bodies, and that any unusual health handicap can be doubly debilitating during these years. The characteristic resilience of most adolescents preserves the hope that, with appropriate intervention, their physical and psychic health can be restored, in spite of what might be overwhelming odds to older people.

INTERVENTION FOR DLDs IN ADOLESCENCE

Generally speaking, the techniques for helping adolescents overcome or cope with DLD conditions are largely derived from the same techniques alluded to in the intervention section of the preceding Chapter 8. However, it is usually necessary to alter the content of various elementary remedial activities in order to make them more appealing to the interests of the teenage population. For example, high interest/low vocabulary materials are available from many sources, some of which are listed in Chapter 10. It should be obvious from the preceding section that a good deal of the effort in intervening effectively involves counseling with the DLD adolescent to enable him to better cope with his feelings about failure, inadequacy, and hopelessness, to name a few perceptions. Copeland (1974) elaborates on the psychopathology of adolescence and how it can be treated. The careful searching for areas of strength and interest, upon which remedial procedures can be based, is an important part of arriving at an effective intervention regimen. It may require the adaptation of materials about such topics as auto mechanics, dating, cooking, or skiing in order to capture and hold the interest of a teenager who is having difficulty in one or more of the academic areas.

If the DLD condition is such that it severely limits the individual's potential for completing high school, let alone entering and finishing college, additional vocational counseling is in order to prepare the individual for entering various careers in the world of work which do not require such academic credentials. Besides enabling the DLD adolescent to do as well as possible on basic academic tasks, the major intervention effort generally concentrates on optimizing interindividual and extra-individual dynamics within the family, the school, and his overall environment. The DLD adolescent's employment as a helping resource for younger children is another possibility for improving his self-concept (Irving, 1975).

PARENTS AND THEIR DLD OFFSPRING

The discussion has now come full circle to consideration of the attitudes of parents toward their DLD children, and, subsequently, to the preparation for DLD adolescents for possibly becoming parents themselves. The growing concern about establishing criteria for optimum parenting attitudes and skills is at least partially a result of the increased contemporary focus upon neglected and abused children. It is also the result of efforts to establish minimum standards for day care centers or normalization standards for institutions which somehow must supply adequate parenting. Some efforts are now coming to fruition to identify competency-based personnel credentialing systems, such as for the Child Development Associate (Klein and Weathersby, 1973) who works in day care centers or early childhood education programs. There are also controversial discussions regarding certifying or licensing prospective parents as having minimal parenting competencies before they are allowed to procreate children (McIntyre, 1974).

Parents who give birth to a child with severe DLD intraindividual deficits have received more attention in the literature than have the parents whose child later is found to have various but milder forms of DLD conditions of mixed or unclear origins. The child who is organically damaged, and looks and behaves that way, usually receives more positive nurturance and succor from parents than the child whose obnoxious or incompetent behavior is apparently willful and diabolical with no evident organic origins. The states of adjustment through which parents typically go after giving birth to a severely damaged child have been likened to those which people commonly experience around the death of a loved one. Periods of denial followed by resentment and anger and grief and ultimately, it is hoped, some realistic acceptance of and adjustment to the condition and its implications, are customary. However, some parents do not gracefully pass through each of these stages. Some parents become relatively fixed at one or another of the earlier stages, and behave accordingly toward the child, toward the DLD condition, and toward other professional or para-professional adults who become involved in their attempts to cope with the child. Primarily for this reason, a great deal of time and attention must be given to the family unit in order to deal with the dynamics which may either lead to further interindividual complications of the DLD condition or, when dealt with successfully, may in fact attenuate significantly the effects of the intraindividual deficits. The major part of intervention with DLD children and adolescents is necessarily expended upon effecting optimum dynamics within the family or its substitute organization.

Some of the more perplexing cases for parents to comfortably deal with are those DLD conditions which do not become manifest until their child is an adolescent or teenager. Even though there may have been some parental and professional suspicion that the child's behavior and development were somewhat below par, by sheer dint of everyone's cooperating and trying a little harder, the child may have gotten by, in spite of mild forms of various DLD conditions. These conditions are seldom cured, but some DLD individuals do learn to compensate quite well for their deficits (Masland, 1969). However, when the relatively well compensated child reaches the teens, the advent of the peculiar combination of physiological and anatomical changes associated with puberty, school changes associated with moving into high school, and overall higher expectations for more adult-like behavior may precipitate some of the intraindividual breakdowns mentioned in the first section of this chapter.

Such unanticipated collapses of physical and psychic integrity may be met with attitudinal reactions of a milder form than those experienced by parents of young children with more severe DLDs. Now, however, the youngsters have adult-sized bodies and strength and, if sufficiently emotionally disturbed, they present significant threats to the parenting ones. This growth and development may provoke their removal to an institutional or residential placement as a last and desperate resort by fearful parents who were previously able to cope with school failure and noncompliance. Personal experience of this writer with such programs verifies this evolution. For example, it was found that a residential program, established for boys who were emotionally disturbed with other DLDs, which was originally designed for 10- to 14-year-olds was very seldom sought out or seriously considered by parents until their boys reached the adult physical stature and strength sufficient to produce a real physical threat to parents and other authority figures. In short, parents were customarily reluctant to place their DLD youngster outside of their home as long as they believed they could physically control him. However, once he had been involved in various acts of life-threatening violence, such as assault and armed robbery and rape, acts which were sometimes prompted by and directed toward the parents themselves, then the parents were suddenly ready to relinquish their teenagers and willing to pay the rather heavy fee (sometimes referred to as guilt money) for full-time out-of-home psycho-educational placements.

The foregoing delayed reaction seems analogous to the child abuse and neglect phenomenon whereby the parents are not indicted, nor are their battered children removed from their custody, until the parents have been proved to be unfit. Typically, proof consists of physical evidence of damage which the parents have inflicted upon their child. The other side of this coin is now evident; parents are unwilling to relinquish their youngster until the interaction between them has a high probability of physical harm to one or the other.

Open to conjecture is the vast area of psychological battering. By its very definition, it is unlikely to have any physical signs. Only those psychosomatic conditions which might logically be attributed to the pathological interaction between parents and offspring could evidently and objectively indicate psychological battering. Unfortunately, the psychological battering by parents of their child or by a teenager toward his parents is frequently an agonizing precursor to the subsequent physical battering resulting from such psychic abuse and/or neglect. Moreover, the physical and psychological battering sustained by one generation may be passed on, like senseless fraternity hazing, to succeeding generations. Unfortunately also, is the fact that the state of the art and knowledge regarding reliable and valid psychological predictors for later physical onslaughts is not sufficiently refined to allow its systematic application in the early identification and prevention of such violence on a wide scale.

The whole study of the origins of violence and contributors to it is still fraught with controversy, in spite of rather elaborate studies of such things as the effects of observing violent acts in the media and the subsequent effect on behavior. Therefore, much of the counseling between parent and teenager may be devoted to evaluating the proneness to physical violence of the parents involved and appropriately intervening to prevent it from occurring whenever possible. Perhaps equally important in this regard is attention to identifying proneness to nonphysical but equally violent and insidious punishments of a psychological nature inflicted by one on the other.

Another area of considerable concern is that of heterosexual activity between adolescents in general and DLD adolescents in particular. The normalization principle (Wolfensberger, 1972) would support the notion that DLD youngsters should enjoy, insofar as possible, the same opportunities for sexual expression which teenagers normally experience. This opportunity, of course, deeply concerns the parents of DLD adolescents, and sometimes re-awakens many of their uncomfortable feelings about having a DLD child. During the DLD child's early years parents often begin to speculate that their child will inevitably grow older and their DLD teenager may give birth to additional children who, the parents presume, have a greater probability of also being mildly or severely DLD. Instead of genetic counseling for the parents of a DLD infant to arrive at estimates of the likelihood of producing another DLD child, the focus now shifts to the parents of the DLD adolescent who wish to know the probabilities of their DLD teenager's giving birth to additional DLD offspring. And, of course, the genetic counseling can only address a small percentage of the factors leading to DLD conditions. Those teenagers who become pregnant, live in poverty, are unmarried, do not want to have children, and do not know how to give appropriate care to them, also present a high risk situation for reproduction of more DLD conditions, regardless of the genetics involved.

The growing numbers of teenage pregnancies have prompted the Child Welfare League of America, with the support of the U. S. Office of Child Development, to form a Consortium on Early Childbearing and Childrearing, which has sponsored numerous publications and a number of symposia throughout the United States dealing with adolescent birth planning and prevention. The entire issue of *Psychiatric Opinion* (1975) discussed various aspects of teenage pregnancies from abortions, informed consent, contraception, and developmental motivations to a long historical overview. In spite of the many clichés about America's being child-centered, the fact is that this is a myth which has led to a kind of complacency regarding the preparation of the next generation to bear and rear children (Casady, 1975). Various promising efforts to help bridge the gap of knowledge and skill which used to be bridged by the extended family are being explored and experimented with on a small scale throughout the United States.

Two efforts to reach out to the potentially childbearing youth population of childbearing age, and to prepare them for responsible parenthood or to prevent their becoming parents until they are ready, warrant mention. The first noteworthy effort is offered by the Girl Scouts of America to introduce much of the salient current information about childbearing, childrearing, and pregnancy prevention into their standard program of learning. Another effort, which has been aimed more at rural American youth, involves the training of United States Department of Agriculture County Extension home-visiting personnel to more fully understand child growth and development, to recognize signs of abnormality, and to disseminate this understanding to the rural homes of America (Meier and Borthick, 1975).

The dissolution and even disappearance of the more traditional nuclear family of a mother, father, and several children growing and developing together in reasonable proximity to the extended family of grandparents and other elders, who served as information and training resources, has left a great void. As a result, there are now increasing numbers of parents, single or married, who are confronted with the task of childrearing without any real preparation or understanding of what is required of them. This ignorance alone can lead to frustration, which in turn breeds anger and possibly violence toward oneself, if one is intra-punitive, or toward others, including one's offspring, if one is extra-punitive.

Caplan (1973), Cooper (1974), Stowitschek and Hofmeister (1975), Weigle (1974), Williams (1974), and others have done a great deal to accumulate information about infant development and parenting techniques for optimizing it. Nevertheless, in spite of all that is known and available, very little of this information is properly and effectively communicated to young mothers (and young fathers to a lesser degree) who are isolated and even expelled from the mainstream society while they attempt to bear and rear an illegitimate and/or unwanted child, who in turn is at an increased risk for various DLD conditions.

Although this discussion has surfaced concerns about parents neglecting and abusing their children, and adolescents neglecting and abusing their parents, it seems appropriate to also suggest that the professional community has neglected, if not abused, parents. This seems especially true regarding those teenaged mothers who are either unknown or avoided, or have been so alienated that they refuse to seek help. An entire issue of the journal, *Exceptional Children* (1975), addresses the importance of the parent-professional partnership and contains articles ranging from such concerns as being a parent of a handicapped child to being a brain-damaged parent. The journal entitled, *Exceptional Parent*, is another indication of a growing concern that information and attitudes be disseminated to individuals who have in the past been essentially neglected by the professional community.

One of the prime targets for the aforementioned Consortium on Early Childbearing and Childrearing and other groups is the members of school boards and school administrations throughout the United States. This focus was established in order to bring about a more enlightened approach to teenage pregnancy which affects so many high school students. In many cases, the school and related community institutions also are instituting a variety of parent education experiences for junior and senior high school students, in addition to the more traditional sex education and social problems courses. The U. S. Office of Child Development has sponsored the production of an *Education for Parenthood* series (see Chapter 10), which has enjoyed enormous popularity throughout the U. S. junior and senior high school systems. These child development sequences are frequently coupled with practicum experiences with infants and young children to give the prospective parents some real hands-on learning opportunities under competent supervision, which is analogous to what grandmother did in the so-called "good old days." These efforts are meeting with enthusiastic response from the teenage population. Many young people genuinely hope to bear and raise a family. Others are learning that such an aspiration is to be tempered with the realities of childrearing, which are not exclusively sweetness and light. The reality of childrearing responsibilities may serve as a deterrent to early parenting by those who previously had little or no appreciation for the many demands offspring make upon their parents.

Adolescence certainly seems to be a bona fide developmental stage, and is at least a convenient and descriptive term for the tumultuous teenage transition time from childhood to adulthood. It is certainly a critical and formative time in a person's life, when multiple attitudes about becoming an adult are formed and largely confirmed. Before the teen years, most of a person's referents for self-concept and societal expectations were a few significant adults. During adolescence the prospects of the adult world of work and love become quite imminent as physical growth and sexual maturity elicit expectations from adults for the adolescent to gradually, but not too rapidly, assume this more mature role in the society. Perhaps the closest thing we have to the more primitive puberty rites is that of graduation from grade school, which in the past was typically the eighth grade and now is the sixth grade or about 12 years of age. This coincides with the earlier onset of puberty, and probably even earlier beginnings of sexuality among the more developed and well nourished countries of the world.

The frequently rapid oscillation between being child-like and adult-like often results in many approach-approach and approach-avoidance conflicts, consequently manifest in unpredictable behavior, which perplexes not only those observing it but even the adolescent individual himself. The prolongation of this adolescent period, during which the teenager is expected to master the necessary skills for becoming a self-sufficient and productive member of the society, only serves to prolong the agony, with very little ecstasy, of growing through this period of perennial preparation to take one's place in the real world. The increased complexity of many professions and specialties in this nuclear age presents dilemmas which are almost the reverse of those confronted by a young DLD child who is not yet ready to perform a task in spite of his chronological age. In the latter stages of adolescence, the individual in his late teens or his early twenties is very much ready for procreative and other grownup activities, which are traditionally and even legally tantalizingly held out of the teenager's reach. Or, in the case where two teenagers engage in sexual intercourse and produce offspring and neither is able to financially support themselves or their children, their lives become very complicated, dependent upon others, and frustrating.

With all of the foregoing hazards of attempting to survive adolescence when one's growth, development, and learning are proceeding normally, it should be readily understood that the adolescent who is also experiencing one or more DLD conditions has a very rocky road to travel indeed. Ironically enough, the prolongation of the adolescent period does allow a greater period of catch-up time for those DLD conditions which are a manifestation of delayed growth and development. This partially explains why the incidence and prevalence data on DLD conditions vary rather dramatically from one age group to another, with the largest numbers falling in the preteen years. This variance is even true with relation to mental retardation, since the adaptive behaviors required for functioning adequately in the adult society can be learned, although over a longer period of time for the retarded individual. Once the requisite social skills are learned, that DLD individual no longer fulfills the full definition for mental retardation, even though his intelligence quotient remains significantly below the average general population's mean intelligence. Thus, the gradual acquisition of daily living skills and their habituation frequently does obtain in cases where individuals remain deficient in verbal and other related intellectual functioning. On the other hand, since the advancing technocracy is displacing more and more persons whose work can be done as well or better by machines, the numbers of unemployed among the DLD population are enlarged since they are often the first to fall victim to unemployment. Moreover, the combination of efforts at de-institutionalization, training the handicapped for various kinds of skilled employment, and the overall high levels of unemployment, and the technological displacement of menial laborers with machines, all contribute to making the plight of the DLD adolescent a difficult one at best.

One of the most impressive longitudinal studies of development and learning, which also clearly delineates the causes and evolution of corollary DLD's, is reported by Werner (in press). She followed a cohort of more than 600 children and youth for nearly two decades from their prenatal period to 18 years of age. The 10-year follow-up (Werner, Bierman, and French, 1971) is presented briefly in Chapter 3; 90% of the original cohort, comprised of seven distinct ethnic groups from a wide range of SES, participated in the 10-year follow-up. An astounding 88% of the original cohort was involved in the 18-year follow-up. Although the study was conducted on the Hawaiian island of Kauai, many of its findings are instructive and applicable to other U. S. communities and their children and youth. The vast amount of data have been deeply mined by Werner (in press) and only a few of the gems can be mentioned herein.

About 3% of the 1955 cohort had been diagnosed in need of placement in a learning disability class at age 10 on the basis of serious reading and communication DLDs (in spite of normal intelligence), visual-motor impairment, hyperactivity, and difficulties in attention and concentration. Twenty percent of this group had physical evidence of "organicity" on pediatric-neurological examinations. For the overwhelming majority in this group serious problems persisted throughout adolescence. Agency records for 80% indicated continued academic underachievement confounded by absenteeism, truancy, and a high incidence of repetitive impulsive acting-out behavior that led to problems with law enforcement agencies for the boys and sexual misconduct for the girls, as well as other mental health problems less often recognized and managed. Rates of contact with community agencies were 9 times as high for the experimental group as for the control subjects matched by age, sex, socioeconomic status, and ethnicity.

Group tests at age 18 showed continued perceptual-motor problems for most as well as deficiencies in verbal skills and serious underachievement in reading and writing. Self-reports revealed a pervasive lack of self-assurance and interpersonal competency and a general inadequacy in utilization of intellectual resources. High "external" scores on the Locus of Control Scale were indicative of the youths' feeling that their actions were not under their own control; this is reflective of the same characteristic found prevalent among adults in the culture of poverty discussed in earlier chapters of this book.

Predictions of serious learning and behavior problems in childhood and adolescence from data at birth, infancy, and early childhood were consistently higher for children from poor homes, and tended to be more accurate for the girls than for the boys. The following 11 items proved to be key early predictors of subsequent serious DLDs: (1) moderate to marked degree of perinatal stress; (2) presence of cogenital defects; (3) very high or very low levels of infant inactivity; (4) Cattell IQ score below 80 by age 2; (5) low Primary Mental Abilities IQ score; (6) moderate to marked degree of physical handicap; (7) recognized need for placement in a learning disability class; (8) recognized need for more than 6 months of mental health services by age 10; (9) low level of maternal education; (10) low standard of living at birth, age 2, or age 10; and (11) low family stability at age 2.

These key predictors, which serve as high risk factors for DLD conditions, were also studied for the cumulative frequency with which they appeared among DLD children and youth. The presence of three or more of these predictors in early childhood and of five or more factors in middle childhood proved to be a reasonable cut-off point. For example, three or more predictors were found in 88–100% of those who were mentally retarded, learning disabled, or mentally disturbed by age 10 and who were delinquents or experiencing serious mental health problems by age 18. Werner acknowledges the need to replicate and cross-validate her study across a wider SES range and across other ethnic groups but nonetheless draws encouragement from such data as those found in the Collaborative Project in New Orleans with black children (Smith et al., 1972) and preliminary data from a welfare sample of black, Caucasian, and Spanish-speaking children in New York City (Langer, 1974) which have shown a dramatic increase in predictive power of psychological assessment if biological and sociological variables are taken into account. Once again the interactive and interdisciplinary theme ringing throughout this book is struck with great resonance.

Some of the other salient highlights from the 18-year follow-up are the following. (1) DLDs which persist into young adulthood have strong biological and temperamental origins which should be prime targets for early intervention; (2) although low SES increased the likelihood of DLD, the combination of biological stress and environmental deprivations, especially family instability, led to greatest risk of subsequent serious and persistent DLDs in both lower and middle class children; (3) the quality of parent-child interaction plays a pervasive role in the origins of DLDs, especially among unwed teenage mothers who are not prepared physically, phychically, or fiscally for adequately rearing their offspring; (4) the role of the father seemed quite crucial as a DLD factor, especially as related to learning disabilities among sons and teenage pregnancies among daughters; (5) major factors contributing to the improvement for some DLDs included the youth's sense of competence and perceived internal locus of control as well as the ability to read and write standard English; (6) risk factors for likely subsequent mental health problems are taken least seriously early, yet the results become most problematic later; and (7) both the natural resiliency in children and youth to cope with various DLD conditions and their ability to benefit from intervention, especially if it is early and appropriate, are impressive and heartening.

In order to ensure periodic and adequate DLD screening programs and to avoid many of the pitfalls inherent in some proposed approaches, Werner recommends four critical time periods and the concomitant sources of information: (1) hospital, birth, and physicians' records containing information about the newborn which should be available to community agencies for utilization and planning with the family for the special needs of the high risk infant; (2) developmental screening examinations in the second year of life that include information on the physical development, sensorimotor, language, and social development of the child and observations on temperamental characteristics and patterns of mother-child interaction (these could be administered by preschool staff, day care center staff, and various home visitors such as nurses, social workers, county extension home consultants, etc.); (3) another round of screening in the beginning grades (1–3) that could be incorporated into the routine school program and should include a profile of cognitive skills in both the language and nonlanguage areas (verbal, reasoning, perceptual, spatial) and a measure of perceptual-motor development, as well as behavior checklists filled out by teachers and parents; and (4) a measure of self-concept and/or locus of control that could be filled out by the youths themselves around the age of their puberty and might spot any emergent problems in adolescence. And thus we come full circle to the original premise of this book, namely, that development and learning are inextricably interrelated.

chapter 10

Developmental and Learning Disability: References, Resources, and Glossary

There are many resources available for DLD children, adolescents, their parents, and the multiple professionals who work with them. It is extremely difficult to classify these many different resources in a logical and useful way for such a wide variety of persons. Some resources address issues which cross over a number of possible classification categories and would have to be listed several times in each respective appropriate category. Other more general references address virtually all of the categories and would either have to be repeatedly mentioned in each category or clustered together in a general bibliography. Moreover, many of the references used in the preceding nine chapters of this text are relevant resources for one or more of the resource categories.

This chapter of DLD references, resources, and glossary is divided into three major sections or categories. The first major section is the list of references, which contains all of the references cited in the preceding nine chapters; if a reference is listed in this first section, it will not be listed again under any of the subsequent resource categories, even though it might belong in one or more of them. The second major section is that of DLD resources. The general bibliography and readings are in addition to the DLD references that are found in the preceding section of Chapter 10. This general bibliography provides the person who wishes to pursue any topic in greater depth with a wealth of resources to investigate. Following that is a listing of commentaries on evaluation instruments, tests, and scales for DLD conditions. Included are some references discussing the pros and cons of evaluation, not only of DLD children and their families, but of programs serving them. Then comes a listing of commonly used evaluation instruments, tests, and procedures for assessing DLD conditions. The next subsection includes a number of reports and guides regarding intervention procedures with DLD conditions, such as curriculum guides, and commentary about the efficacy of certain intervention procedures. The next subsection lists a representative sample of the intervention materials available in various formats. The last subsection contains resources for and about parents of DLD children and may be used by both parents and professionals working with the families wherein DLD children grow and develop. The third and last major section is a glossary of terms to help the reader better understand some of the more technical jargon contained in this and other texts. For a more clinically oriented glossary, the reader is referred to the aforementioned companion text by Johnston and Magrab (in press). A listing of tests used to assess sensorimotor function is provided in Table 16.

REFERENCES

Abrams, J. C. 1973. Learning disabilities. *In* S. L. Copel (ed.), Behavior Pathology of Childhood and Adolescence, pp. 300–323. Basic Books Inc., New York.

Achenbach, T. M. 1966. The classification of children's psychiatric symptoms: A factor analytic study. Psychol. Monogr. 80(6):33–34.

Ackerman, P. R., and M. G. Moore. 1974. The delivery of educational services to preschool handicapped children in the U. S.: The state of the art. (Mimeographed paper.)

Adams, J. 1973. Adaptive behavior and measured intelligence in the classification of mental retardation. Am. J. Ment. Defic. 78(1):77–81.

Adkins, P. L., G. R. Holmes, and R. C. Schnackenberg. 1971. Factor analyses of the de Hirsch predictive index. Percept. Motor Skills 33:1319–1325.

Ainsworth, M. D. S. 1969. Object relations, dependency, and attachment: A theoretical review of the infant-mother relationship. Child Dev. 40:969–1025.

Albert, R. S., and A. J. Davis. 1971. A reliability study of interparental agreement on the Rimland Diagnostic Checklist. J. Clin. Psychol. 27:499–502.

Allen, C. M., J. R. Metz, and H. R. Shinefield. 1971. Test development in the Pediatric Multiphasic Program. Pediat. Clin. Am. 18(1):169–178.

Allen, C. M., and H. R. Shinefield. 1969. Pediatric multiphasic program. Preliminary description. Am. J. Dis. Child. 118:469–472.

Allen, J., M. DeMyer, J. A. Norton, W. Pontius, and E. Yang. 1971. Intellectuality of parents of psychotic, subnormal and normal children. J. Autism Child Schizo. 1(3):311–326.

Table 16. Matrix of tests commonly used to assess sensorimotor functioning[a]

| Author | Test | Sensory modality | | | | | | |
		Visual	Tactile	Proprio-ceptive	Vestibular	Auditory	Visual-motor accommodation
Ayres	Southern California Battery	X	X	X	X		X
Beery	Developmental Test of Visual-Motor Integration						X
Bender	Bender-Gestalt						X
Benton	Left-right discrimi-nation and finger localization		X	X			
Berges	Imitation of gestures			X			X
Denhoff	Meeting Street School Screening Test	X	X	X		X	X
Egan	Developmental screening				X	X	X
Fiorentino	Reflex testing		X	X	X		X

Continued

Table 16—*Continued*

		Sensory modality					
Author	Test	Visual	Tactile	Proprio-ceptive	Vestibular	Auditory	Visual-motor accommodation
Frostig	Developmental test of visual perception	X					X
Goodenough	Draw-a-Person	X					X
Kephart-Roach	Purdue Perceptual-Motor Survey						X
Kirk	I.T.P.A. (Parts)					X	X
Lincoln-Oseretsky	Motor Development Scale						X
Pasamanick-Knobloch	Yale Revised Developmental Schedules (Gesell)					X	X
Prechtl	Neurological examination of full-term newborn		X	X	X		X
Reitan-Halstead	Impairment Index (Parts)	X	X			X	X
Wechsler	WISC-R						X

[a] Such a display is helpful in designing a comprehensive screening battery comprised of the most appropriate portions of existing instruments for a given developmental domain.

Allport, G. H. 1960. Personality and Social Encounter. Beacon Press, Boston.

Alpern, G. D. 1967. Measurement of "untestable" autistic children. J. Abnorm. Psychol. 72(6):478–486.

Ambrose, A. 1969. Stimulation in Early Infancy: Proceedings of the Center for Advanced Study in the Developmental Sciences. Academic Press, Inc., New York.

American Academy of Pediatrics. 1968. Statement on the Doman-Delacato treatment of neurologically handicapped children. J. Pediatr. 72:750–752.

American Psychiatric Association. 1968. Diagnostic and Statistical Manual of Mental Disorders. Committee on Nomenclature and Statistics, Washington, D. C.

Anders, T. F., and E. Hoffman. 1973. The sleep polygram: A potentially useful tool for clinical assessment in human infants. Am. J. Ment. Defic. 7(5):506–514.

Anderson, E. D. 1971. Preschool screening: A program for detecting learning disabilities. North Carolina J. Ment. Health 5(3):49–54.

Appalachia. 1972. Vol. 6, No. 2, October-November. Available from the Appalachian Regional Commission in Washington, D. C.

Applied Urbanetics, Inc. 1972. A Mini-Guide to Follow Through. U. S. Office of Education, Washington, D. C.

Arangio, A. 1972. A working paper on adequate neurological examination of all preschool age children. Epilepsy Foundation of America, Washington, D. C. (Unpublished.)

Arthur, G. 1947. A Point Scale of Performance Tests. Psychological Corporation, New York.

Association of University Affiliated Facilities (AUAF). 1974. Program Descriptions. AUAF Executive Office, Washington, D.C.

Ayres, A. 1966. Southern California Test Battery. Western Psychological Services, Los Angeles.

Badian, N. A., and B. L. Serwer. 1975. The identification of high-risk children: A retrospective look at selection criteria. J. Learn. Disab. 8(5):283–286.

Bakalis, M. J. 1972. Illinois program for screening for learning disabilities. Interim (Fall) 3:1–2,

Ball, T. S. 1974. Note on "Effect of Motor Development on Body Image Scores for Institutionalized Mentally Retarded Children." Am. J. Ment. Defic. 79(2):225–226.

Bannatyne, A. 1968. Diagnosis and remedial techniques for use with dyslexic children. Acad. Ther. Quart. 3:75–91.

Bannatyne, A. 1971. Language, Reading, and Learning Disabilities. Charles C Thomas, Springfield, Ill.

Bannatyne, A. 1975. Bannatyne System: Early Screening and Diagnostic Tests Phase One. Learning Systems Press, Lafayette, La.

Barnard, K. 1973. A program of stimulation for infants born prematurely. Paper presented at the meeting of the Society for Research in Child Development, March, Philadelphia.

Barsch, R. 1967. The infant curriculum, a concept for tomorrow. In J.

Helmuth (ed.), Exceptional Infant, Vol. 1, pp. 541–568. Special Child Publications, Seattle.

Bassin, A. 1975. Psychology in action: Red, white, and blue poker chips. Am. Psychol. 30(6):695–696.

Battle, C. U., and N. C. Ackerman. 1973. Early identification and intervention programs for infants with developmental delay and their families—A summary and directory. National Easter Seal Society for Crippled Children and Adults, Chicago.

Battle, E. S., and B. Lacy. 1972. A context for hyperactivity over time. Child Dev. 43:757–773.

Baumrin, J. M. 1975. Aristotle's empirical nativism. Am. Psychol. 30(5): 486–494.

Baumrind, D. 1970. Socialization and instrumental competence in young children. Young Child. 26:104–119.

Baumrind, D. 1971. Harmonious parents and their preschool children. Dev. Psychol. 4:99–102.

Baumrind, D., and A. E. Black. 1967. Socialization practices associated with dimensions of competence in preschool boys and girls. Child Dev. 38:291–328.

Bayley, N. 1935. The development of motor abilities during the first three years. Monogr. Soc. Res. Child Dev. 1(2).

Bayley, N. 1940. Mental growth in young children. Yearbook Nat. Soc. Study Educ. 39:11–47.

Bayley, N. 1949. Consistency and variability in the growth of intelligence from birth to 18 years. J. Genet. Psychol. 75:165–196.

Bayley, N. 1955. On the growth of intelligence. Am. Psychol. 10:805–818.

Bayley, N. 1965. Comparisons of mental and motor test scores for ages 1–15 months by sex, birth order, race, geographical location and education of parents. Child Dev. 36:379–411.

Bayley, N. 1968. Behavioral correlates of mental growth: Birth to 36 years. Am. Psychol. 23(1):1–17.

Bayley, N. 1969. Infant Scales of Psychomotor and Mental Development. Psychological Corporation, New York.

Bayley, N., and E. S. Schaefer. 1964. Correlations of maternal and child behaviors with the development of mental abilities: Data from the Berkeley growth study. Monogr. Soc. Res. Child Dev. 29(97).

Beatty, J. R. 1975. The analysis of an instrument for screening learning disabilities. J. Learn. Disab. 8(3):180–186.

Beckstead, M. G. 1972. Determining discrimination power of selected items on the Utah test of language development for establishment of efficiency in potential screening procedures. Unpublished Master's thesis, University of Utah, Salt Lake City, Utah.

Beckwith, L. 1971. Relationships between attributes of mothers and their infants' IQ scores. Child Dev. 42:1083–1097.

Beckwith, L. 1972. Relationships between infants' social behavior and their mothers' behavior. Child Dev. 43:397–411.

Beckwith, L. 1974. Caregiver-infant interaction and the development of the at-risk infant. University of California, Los Angeles. (Mimeographed paper.)

Beery, K. 1967. Developmental Test of Visual-Motor Integration: Administration and Scoring Manual. Follett Educational Corp., Chicago.

Begab, M. J. 1974. The major dilemma of mental retardation: Shall we prevent it? Am. J. Ment. Defic. 78:519−529.

Beller, E. K. 1973. Impact of early education on disadvantaged children. *In* S. Ryan (ed.), A Report on Longitudinal Evaluation of Preschool Programs. Office of Child Development, U. S. Department of Health, Education, and Welfare, Washington, D. C.

Beller, E. K. 1973. Research on organized programs for early education. *In* R. Travers (ed.), Handbook of Research on Teaching. Rand-McNally, Chicago.

Belleville, M., and P. B. Green. 1971. Preschool multiphasic screening programs in rural Kansas. Presented at the American Public Health Association Annual Meeting, School Health Section, October 13, 1971, Minneapolis.

Bender, L. 1956. Psychopathology of Children with Organic Brain Disorders. Charles C Thomas, Springfield, Ill.

Bender, L. 1962. The Bender Visual Motor Gestalt Test for Children. Western Psychological Services, Los Angeles.

Bennett, E. L., M. C. Diamond, D. Krech, and M. R. Rosenzweig. 1964. Chemical and anatomical plasticity of the brain. Science 146:610−617.

Bereiter, C., and S. E. Englemann. 1966. Teaching Disadvantaged Children. Prentice-Hall, Englewood Cliffs, N. J.

Bergstrom, L., W. G. Hemmenway, and M. P. Downs. 1971. A high risk registry to find congenital deafness. Otolaryng. Clin. North Am. 4(2):171−184.

Bernard, M. E., M. O. Thelen, and H. L. Garber. (No date.) The Use of Gross Features Tabulation for the Analysis of Early Language Development. University of Wisconsin, Madison, Wisc.

Bernheimer, L., J. Keaster, and F. J. Linthicum, Jr. 1972. Neonatal hearing screening. Calif. Med. 116:1, 5−8.

Bernstein, B. 1961. Social class and linguistic development: A theory of social learning. *In* A. Halsey, J. Floud, and C. Anderson (eds.), Education, Economy and Society, pp. 288−314. Free Press, Glencoe, Ill.

Berry, M. F. 1969. Language Disorders of Children. Appleton-Century-Crofts, Inc., New York.

Bersoff, D. N. 1973. Silk purses into sow's ears—the decline of psychological testing and a suggestion for its redemption. Am. Psychol. 28(10): 829−899.

Bigge, M., and M. Hunt. 1962. Psychological Foundations of Education. Harper and Row, New York.

Bijou, S. W., and R. F. Peterson. 1970. The psychological assessment of children: A functional analysis. *In* P. Reynolds (ed.), Advances in Psychological Assessment. Vol. II. University of Illinois, Urbana, Ill.

Bing, E. 1963. Effect of child rearing practices on development of differential cognitive abilities. Child Dev. 34:631−648.

Birns, B., and M. Golden. 1972. Prediction of intellectual performance at 3 years from infant tests and personality measures. Merrill-Palmer Quart., 18:54–58.

Bizzi, E. 1974. Visual motor processing–inner ear: The coordination of eye-hand movements. Sci. Am. 231:100–106.

Black, F. W. 1974. Achievement test performance of high and low perceiving learning disabled children. J. Learn. Disab. 7(3):60–64.

Black, R. B. 1971. Final report: Early identification of and intervention for handicapped children. Appalachian Regional Commission, Project FY-70, Ohio University, Athens, O.

Blank, M., M. Koltuv, and M. Wood. 1972. Individual teaching for disadvantaged kindergarten children: Comparison of two methods. J. Spec. Educ. 6(3):207–219.

Blank, M., and F. Solomon. 1968. A tutorial language program to develop abstract thinking in socially disadvantaged preschool children. Child Dev. 39:379–389.

Blatt, B., and F. Kaplan. 1966. Christmas in Purgatory. Allyn and Bacon, Boston.

Blom, G. E., and M. Jansen. 1974. A gross national study of factors related to reading achievement and reading disability. Comparative Education, Part I. Presented at the 5th IRA World Congress on Reading, August 14, 1974, Vienna, Austria.

Bloom, B. S. 1954. Taxonomy of Educational Objectives. Longmans, Green & Co., Inc., New York.

Bloom, B. S. 1964. Stability and Change in Human Characteristics. John Wiley & Sons, Inc., New York.

Bloom, B. S., J. T. Hastings, and G. F. Madaus. 1971. Handbook on Formative and Summative Evaluation of Student Learning. McGraw-Hill Book Co., New York.

Bobath, B. 1963. Treatment principles and planning in cerebral palsy. Physiotherapy 49:122.

Bobath, B. 1967. The very early treatment of cerebral palsy. Dev. Med. Child Neurol. 9(4):373–390.

Boehm, G. A. W. 1973. Play the "pointing E." Reader's Digest. July, pp. 41–44.

Boggs, E. 1972. Federal Legislation 1966–1972. In J. Wortis (ed.), Mental Retardation, Vol. 4. pp. 165–206. Grune & Stratton, Inc., New York.

Borgotta, E. F., and D. Fanshel. 1965. Behavioral Characteristics of Children Known to Psychiatric Outpatient Clinics. Child Welfare League of America, Library of Congress 65-19746, Washington, D. C.

Boulding, K. 1968. General Systems Theory–The Skeleton of Science. In W. Buckley (ed.), Modern Systems Research for the Behavioral Scientist, pp. 3–10. Aldine, Chicago.

Bowen, L. F., Jr. 1974. In-class diagnosis of learning disabilities–proposal for experimental research. Gilman School, Balitmore.

Bower, E. M. 1969. Early Identification of Emotionally Handicapped Children in Schools (2nd Ed.). Charles C Thomas, Springfield, Ill.

Bowes, W. A., Y. Brackbill, E. Conway, and A. Steinschneider. 1970.

Obstetrical medication and infant outcome: A review of the literature. Monogr. Soc. Res. Child Dev. 35(4, whole no. 137).

Bowlby, J. 1951. Maternal Care and Mental Health. World Health Organization, Geneva, Switzerland.

Boyd, R. D. 1969. CCD Developmental Progress Scale, Experimental Form, Manual, and Directions. University of Oregon, Eugene, Ore.

Boyd, R. D. 1974. The Boyd Developmental Progress Scale. Inland Counties Regional Center, Inc., San Bernardino, Calif.

Boyd, W. 1911. Educational Theory of J. J. Rousseau. Appleton, London.

Braun, S. J., and E. P. Edwards (eds.). 1972. History and Theory of Early Childhood Education. Charles A. Jones Co., Worthington, Ohio.

Brazelton, T. B. 1973. Neonatal Behavioral Assessment Scale. J. B. Lippincott Co., Philadelphia.

Brazelton, T. B., D. G. Freedman, F. D. Horowitz, B. Koslowski, H. Ricciuti, J. S. Robey, A. Sameroff, and E. Tronick. (No date.) Neonatal behavioral assessment scale. Harvard University, Cambridge, Mass. (Mimeographed paper.)

Bricker, D. D., W. A. Bricker, and L. A. Larsen. 1968. Operant audiometry manual for difficult-to-test children. Institute on Mental Retardation and Intellectual Development. Papers and Reports, Vol. V, No. 19.

Brockman, L. M., and H. N. Ricciuti. 1971. Severe protein-calorie malnutrition and cognitive development in infancy and early childhood. Dev. Psychol. 4:312–319.

Brody, S. 1951. Patterns of Mothering. International Universities Press, Inc., New York.

Broman, S. H., P. L. Nichols, and W. A. Kennedy. 1972. Precursors of low I.Q. in young children. Proceedings of the 80th Annual Convention, American Psychological Association, pp. 77–78.

Bronfenbrenner, U. 1970. Two Worlds of Childhood: US and USSR. Russell Sage Foundation, New York.

Bruner, J. 1960. The Process of Education. Random House Vintage Books, New York.

Bruner, J. 1966. Toward a Theory of Instruction. Harvard University Press, Cambridge, Mass.

Buckley, W. (ed.). 1968. Modern Systems Research for the Behavioral Scientist. Aldine, Chicago, Ill.

Burdock, E. L., and A. S. Hardesty. 1964. A children's behavior diagnostic inventory. Ann. N. Y. Acad. Sci. 105:890–896.

Buros, O. K. (ed.). 1965 and 1972. The Sixth and Seventh Mental Measurements Yearbook. Gryphon Press, Highland Park, N. J.

Butterfield, E. C., and G. F. Cairns. 1974. Discussion summary—Infant perception research. In R. L. Schiefelbusch and L. L. Lloyd (eds.), Language Perspectives—Acquisition, Retardation, and Intervention, pp. 75–102. University Park Press, Baltimore.

Bzoch, K. R., and R. League. 1970. The Receptive-Expressive Emergent Language Scale for the Measurement of Language Skills in Infancy. Tree of Life Press, Gainesville, Fla.

Caldwell, B. M. 1967a. Descriptive evaluations of child development and of developmental settings. Pediatrics 40:46–54.

Caldwell, B. M. 1967b. What is the optimal learning environment for the very young child? Am. J. Orthopsychiat. 37:8–21.

Caldwell, B. M. 1970a. The Preschool Inventory. Educational Testing Service, Princeton, N. J.

Caldwell, B. M. 1970b. The Rationale for Early Intervention. Except. Child. 36:717–726.

Caldwell, B. M., R. M. Bradley, and R. Elardo. 1975. Early stimulation of the mentall retarded. In J. Wortis (ed.), Mental Retardation, pp. 149–187. Grune & Stratton, Inc., New York.

Caldwell, B. M., J. Heider, and B. Kaplan. 1968. Inventory of home stimulation. Unpublished manuscript. Syracuse University, Syracuse, N. Y.

Caldwell, B. M., and L. Herscher. 1964. Mother-infant interaction during the first year of life. Merrill-Palmer Quart., 10:119–128.

Caldwell, B. M., and J. B. Richmond. 1967. Social class level and stimulation potential of the home. In J. Helmuth (ed.), Except. Infant, pp. 455–466. Special Child Publications, Seattle, Wash.

Caldwell, B. M., and J. B. Richmond. 1968. The Children's Center in Syracuse, New York. In L. L. Dittman (ed.), Early Child Care: The New Perspectives, pp. 326–358. Atherton, N. Y.

Camp, B. W. 1973. Psychometric tests and learning in severely disabled readers. J. Learn. Disab. 6(7):512–517.

Cantwell, D. P. 1974. Early intervention with hyperactive children. Presented at the Symposium Sponsored by the Section of Child Psychiatry, November, 1974, pp. 56–67. University of Missouri, Columbia, Mo.

Caplan, F. (ed.). 1973. The First Twelve Months of Life. Grosset & Dunlap, New York.

Capute, A. J., and R. F. Biehl. 1973. Functional development evaluation—prerequisite to habilitation. Pediat. Clin. N. Am. 20(1):3–26.

Carter, C. M., H. L. Rheingold, and C. O. Eckerman. 1972. Toys delay the infant's following of his mother. Dev. Psychol. 6:138–145.

Casady, M. 1975. Society's pushed-out children—We must combat the myth that we are a child-centered society. Psychol. Today 6:57–62, 65.

Casler, L. 1965. The effects of extra tactile stimulation on a group of institutionalized infants. Genet. Psychol. Monogr. 22:135–175.

Cassel, R. N. 1973. Types of cases referred and recommended program for school psychology preparation. Prof. Psychol. 10:377–385.

Cattell, P. 1940. The Measurement of Intelligence of Infants and Young Children. The Psychological Corporation, New York.

Cattell, R., and R. Coan. 1957. Child personality structure as revealed by teacher's behavior ratings. J. Clin. Psychol. 13:315–327.

Champney, H. 1941. The measurement of parent behavior. Child Dev. 12:131–66.

Chase, P., and H. Martin. 1970. Undernutrition and child development. New Eng. J. Med. 282:933–939.

Cheever, J. (ed.). 1975. The responsive education program. Far West Laboratory for Educational Research and Development, San Francisco.

Children Today. 1975. Child abuse and neglect. Vol. 4, No. 3, pp. 1–44.

Chipman, S., A. M. Lilienfeld, B. B. Greenberg, and J. F. Donnelly (eds.).

1966. Research Methodology and Needs in Perinatal Studies. Charles C Thomas, Springfield, Ill.

Chissom, B. S. 1971. A factor-analytic study of the relationship of motor factors to academic criteria for first- and third-grade boys. Child Dev. 42:1133–1143.

Chomsky, N. 1974. Recent contributions to the theory of innate ideas. In S. G. Sapir and A. C. Nitzburg (eds.), Children with Learning Problems, pp. 99–108. Brunner/Mazel, New York.

Christian, W. B., and D. R. Malone. 1973. Relationships among three measures used in screening mentally retarded children for placement in special education. Psychol. Rep. 33(2):415–418.

Clarke-Stewart, A. 1973. Interactions between mothers and their young children: Characteristics and consequences. Mongr. Soc. Res. Child Dev. 38(6).

Clausen, J. A., and C. L. Huffine. 1974. Living with mental illness: Some preliminary findings of a twenty-year follow-up. Unpublished manuscript. University of California at Berkeley.

Clements, S. D. (ed.). 1966. Minimal Brain Dysfunction, Terminology and Identification. U. S. Government Printing Office (PHS 1415), Washington, D. C.

Cohen, B., S. Bala, and A. G. Morris. 1975. Do hyperactive children have manifestations of hyperactivity in their eye movements? Presented at Biennial Meeting of the Society for Research in Child Development, April 10–13, 1975, Denver, Colo.

Cohen, H. J., H. G. Birch, and L. T. Taft. 1970. Some considerations for evaluating the Doman-Delacato "patterning" method. Pediatrics 45:302–314.

Cohen, S. A. 1969. Studies in visual perception and reading in disadvantaged children. J. Learn. Disab. 2:498–507.

Coleman, J. S. 1966. Equality of Educational Opportunity. U. S. Government Printing Office, Washington, D. C.

Collen, M. F., R. Feldman, J. Barbaccia, J. Dunn, R. Greenblatt, and A. Mather. 1970. Introductory Statement, Provisional Guidelines for AMHTS. U. S. Government Printing Office, Washington, D. C.

Colligan, R. C., and E. J. O'Connell. 1974. Should psychometric screening be made an adjunct to the pediatric preschool examination? Clin. Pediat. 13:29.

Colman, A., and J. Boren. 1969. An information system for measuring patient behavior and its use by staff. J. Appl. Behav. Anal. 2:207–214.

Combs, A., and D. Snygg. 1959. Individual Behavior. Harper & Row, New York.

Comenius, J. A. 1896a. In Keatings (ed.), Great Didactic. Black, London.

Comenius, J. A. 1896b. In W. Monroe (ed.), School of Infancy (1628). Heath, Boston.

Conger, J. 1973. Adolescence and Youth: Psychological Development in a Changing World. Harper & Row, New York.

Conners, C. K. 1969. A teacher rating scale for use in drug studies with children. Am. J. Psychiat. 126:884–888.

Conners, C. K. 1970. Symptom patterns in hyperkinetic, neurotic, and normal children. Child Dev. 41:667–682.

Conners, C. K. 1973. Rating scales for use in drug studies of children. Psychopharmacol. Bull. (special issue):24–84.

Cooper, G. C. 1974. Parenting Curriculum (6 booklets). Consortium on Early Childbearing and Childrearing, Washington, D. C.

Copeland, A. D. 1974. Textbook of Adolescent Psychopathology and Treatment. Charles C Thomas, Springfield, Ill.

Corsini, R., and G. Painter. 1975. Marvelous new way to make your child behave. In R. Corsini and G. Painter (eds.), ABC's of Child Discipline, pp. 25–37. Harper & Row, New York.

Costello, J. 1970. Review and Summary of a National Survey of the Parent-Child Center Program. Prepared for the Office of Child Development, U. S. Department of Health, Education, and Welfare, August, 1970.

Crager, R. L., and A. J. Spriggs. 1970. The Development of Concepts. Western Psychological Corporation, Los Angeles, Calif.

Cranson, M. 1970. H.O.M.E. Infant Stimulation Program. LaJunta Parent and Child Center, Otero Junior College, La Junta, Colo.

Crissey, M. S. 1975. Mental Retardation: Past, Present, and Future. Am. Psychol. 30:800–808.

Crowell, D. H. 1973. Screening and assessment in the cognitive/intellectual area. In J. H. Meier (ed.), Background Papers of the Boston Conference: Screening and Assessment of Young Children at Developmental Risk, pp. 18–35. U. S. Government Printing Office, Washington, D. C.

Cruickshank, W. 1967. The Brain-Injured Child in Home, School, and Community. Syracuse University Press, Syracuse, N. Y.

Cruickshank, W. M., F. A. Bentzen, F. H. Ratzeburg, and M. T. Tannhauser. 1961. A Teaching Method for Brain-Injured and Hyperactive Children. Syracuse University Press, Syracuse, N. Y.

Dave, R. H. 1963. The identification and measurement of environmental process variables that are related to educational achievement. Unpublished doctoral dissertation, University of Chicago, Chicago, Ill.

Davis, F. B. 1971. The Measurement of Mental Capacity through Evoked Potential Recordings. Educational Records Bureau, Greenwich, Conn.

de Hirsch, K., J. J. Jansky, and W. S. Langford. 1966. Predicting Reading Failure: A Preliminary Study of Reading, Writing, and Spelling Disabilities in Preschool Children. Harper & Row, New York.

Delacato, C. H. 1963. The Diagnosis and Treatment of Speech and Reading Problems. Charles C Thomas, Springfield, Ill.

de la Cruz, F. F., and G. D. LaVeck. 1970. Mental retardation: A challenge to physicians. W. Virginia Med. J. 19:145–153.

DeMause, L. 1975. Our forebears made childhood a nightmare. Psychol. Today, April, pp. 85–87.

DeMyer, M. K., D. W. Churchill, W. Pontius, and K. M. Gilkey. 1971. A comparison of five diagnostic systems for childhood schizophrenia and infantile autism. J. Autism Child. Schizo. (1)2:175–189.

Denenberg, V. H. 1963. Early experience and emotional development. Sci. Am. 208(6):138–146.

Denenberg, V. H. 1964. Critical periods, stimulus input and emotional reactivity: A theory of infantile stimulation. Psychol. Rev. 71: 335–351.

Denenberg, V. H. (ed.). 1970. Education of the Infant and Young Child. Academic Press, Inc., New York.

Denenberg, V. H., and E. B. Thoman. 1974. From animal to infant research. Presented at the National Conference on Early Intervention with High Risk Infants and Young Children, May 5–8, 1974. University of North Carolina, Chapel Hill, N. C.

Denhoff, E. 1969. Detecting potential learning problems at preschool medical examinations. Texas Med. 65:56–59.

Denhoff, E., N. B. D'Wolf, A. K. Cassidy, A. B. Brindle, E. Danella, A. Gang, T. Maloney, E. Lieberman, and I. Hyman. 1974. Parent Programs for Developmental Management. Presented at the Conference on Early Intervention for High Risk Infants and Young Children, May 5–8, 1974. University of North Carolina, Chapel Hill, N. C.

Dennis, W. 1973. Children of the Creche. Appleton-Century-Crofts, Inc., New York.

Dennis, W., and F. Najarian. 1957. Infant development under environmental handicap. Psychol. Monogr. 71(7).

Deutsch, M. 1963. The disadvantaged child and the learning process. In A. H. Passow (ed.), Education in Depressed Areas, pp. 163–179. Bureau of Publications, Teachers College, Columbia University, New York.

Deutsch, M. 1967. The Disadvantaged Child. Basic Books, Inc., New York.

Deutsch, M., and B. Brown. 1964. Social Influence in Negro-White intelligence differences. J. Soc. Iss. 32:24–35.

Dewey, J. 1916. Democracy and Education. Teacher's College Press, New York.

Diagnostic and Statistical Manual of Mental Disorders. 1968. 2nd Ed. American Psychiatric Association, Washington, D. C.

Dicks-Mireaux, M. J. 1972. Mental development of infants with Down's syndrome. Am. J. Ment. Defic. 77(1):26–32.

Divoky, D. 1974. Education's latest victim: The "LD" kid. Learning 3: 20–25.

Doehring, D. G. 1968. Patterns of Impairment in Specific Reading Disability: A Neuropsychological Investigation. Indiana University Press, Bloomington, Ind.

Doll, E. A. 1966a. Preschool Attainment Record. American Guidance Services, Inc., Circle Pines, Minn.

Doll, E. A. 1966b. Vineland Social Maturity Scales. American Guidance Services, Inc., Circle Pines, Minn.

Downing, J., and P. Oliver. 1973–1974. Linguistic concepts: The child's conception of a "word." Reading Res. Quart. 9(4):568–582.

Dreger, R. M., M. P. Reid, P. M. Lewis, D. C. Overlade, T. A. Rich, C. Taffel, K. S. Miller, and E. L. Fleming. 1964. Behavioral classification project. J. Consult. Psychol. 28:1–13.

Drillien, C. M. 1961. A longitudinal study of the growth and development of prematurely and maturely born children. Arch. Dis. Child. 36:233.

Drillien, C. 1964. The Growth and Development of the Prematurely Born Infant. The Williams & Wilkins Co., Baltimore.

Dunn, L. 1965. Peabody Picture Vocabulary Test. American Guidance Services, Circle Pines, Minn.

Dunn, L. 1968. Special education for the mildly retarded—Is much of it justifiable? Except. Child 35:5–22.

Edelman, M. W., M. Allen, C. Brown, and A. Rosewater. 1974. Children Out of School in America. Children's Defense Fund, Cambridge, Mass.

Educational Testing Service. 1973. Assessment in a Pluralistic Society. Princeton, N. J.

Eisenberg, L. 1961. The strategic development of the child psychiatrist in preventive psychiatry. J. Child Psychol. Psychiat. 2:229–241.

Ekstein, R., and R. Motto. 1969. From Learning for Love to Love of Learning. Brunner/Mazel, New York.

Elkind, D. 1969. Preschool Education—Enrichment or Instruction. Childhood Educ. 14:321–328.

Emmerich, W. 1969. The parental role: A functional cognitive approach. Monogr. Soc. Res. Child Dev. 34(132).

Engelmann, S. 1966. Give Your Child a Superior Mind. Simon & Schuster, New York.

Erickson, M. T. 1969. MMPI Profiles of Parents of Young Retarded Children. Am. J. Ment. Defic. 73(5):728–732.

Erickson, M. T. 1975. The Z-score discrepancy method for identifying reading disabled children. J. Learn. Disab. 8(5):308–312.

Erickson, M. T., M. M. Johnson, and F. A. Campbell. 1970. Relationships among scores on infant tests for children with developmental problems. Am. J. Ment. Defic. 75:102–104.

Erikson, E. H. 1959. Identity and the life cycle. Psychol. Iss. 1(1):1–67.

Erikson, E. H. 1963. Childhood and Society. W. W. Norton & Co. Inc., New York.

Etzioni, A. 1973. Doctors know more than they're telling you about genetic defects. Psychol. Today, November, pp. 26–37.

Exceptional Children. 1975. May, Vol. 41, No. 8. Council for Exceptional Children, Reston, Va.

Eyberg, S., and S. M. Johnson. 1974. Multiple assessment of behavior modification with families: Effects of contingency contracting and order of treated problems. J. Consult. Clin. Psychol. 46:594–606.

Falender, C. 1973. Mother-child interaction and the child's participation in the Milwaukee Project: An experiment in the prevention of cultural-familial mental retardation. Presented at the Society for Research in Child Development Meeting, March, 1973, Philadelphia, Pa.

Fantz, R. L., and S. Nevis. 1967. Pattern preferences in perceptual cognitive development in early infancy. Merrill-Palmer Quart. 13:77–108.

Farrar, J. E., and J. Leigh. 1972. Factors associated with reading failure: A predictive Tasmanian survey. Soc. Sci. Med. 6(2):241–51.

Ferinden, W. E., and D. C. Van Handal. 1971. Minimal Cerebral Dysfunction: Diagnosis, Management and Remediation. Remediation Associates, Inc., Linden, N. J.

Fernald, G. M. 1943. Remedial Techniques in Basic School Subjects. McGraw-Hill Book Co., New York.

Feshbach, S., H. Adelman, and W. W. Fuller. 1974. Early identification of children with high risk of reading failure. J. Learn. Disab. 7(10):639–644.

Festinger, L. 1957. A Theory of Cognitive Dissonance. Row, Peterson, Evanston, Ill.

Filippi, R., and C. L. Rousey. 1971. Positive carriers of violence among children—detection by speech deviations. Ment. Hyg. 55:157–161.

Fish, B., and R. Hagin. 1972. Visual-motor disorders in infants at risk for schizophrenia. Arch. Gen. Psychiat. 27(5):594–598.

Foch, T., J. C. DeFries, and S. M. Singer. 1974. Specific reading disability: A family study. Presented at the Fourth Annual Meeting of Behavior Genetics Association, June 6–8, 1974, Boulder, Colo.

Foltz, A.-M. 1975. The development of ambiguous federal policy: Early and periodic screening, diagnosis and treatment (EPSDT). Health and Society, Winter.

Fomon, S. J. (ed.). 1971. Screening Children for Nutritional Status. Report of Maternal and Child Health Services, Department of Health, Education, and Welfare, U. S. Government Printing Office, Washington, D. C.

Foster, R. 1974. Camelot Behavioral Checklist. Camelot Behavioral Systems. Arizona State University Press, Tucson.

Fowler, W. 1962. Cognitive learning in infancy and early childhood. Psychol. Bull. 59:116–152.

Fowler, W. 1972. A developmental learning approach to infant care in a group setting. Merrill-Palmer Quart. 18:145–175.

Frank, J., and H. Levison. 1974. Medicine. Time, May 13, p. 64.

Frankenburg, W., and B. W. Camp. 1975. Pediatric Screening Tests. Charles C Thomas, Springfield, Ill.

Frankenburg, W., B. W. Camp, and P. A. VanNatta. 1971. Validity of the Denver Developmental Screening Test. Child Dev. 42:475–485.

Frankenburg, W., B. W. Camp, P. A. VanNatta, and J. A. Demersseman. 1971. Reliability and stability of the Denver Developmental Screening Test. Child Dev. 42:1315–1325.

Frankeburg, W., and J. Dodds. 1967. The Denver Developmental Screening Test. J. Pediat. 71:181.

Frankenburg, W., and J. Dodds. 1975. The Denver Developmental Screening Test—Revised. LADOCA, Denver, Co.

Frankenburg, W., and A. F. North. 1974. A Guide to Screening for the EPSDT Program under Medicaid. Social and Rehabilitation Services, Department of Health, Education, and Welfare, Washington, D. C.

Freedman, D. G. 1966. Effects of Kinesthetic Stimulation on Weight Gain and on Smiling in Premature Infants. Presented at the Meeting of American Orthopsychiatric Association, April, San Francisco.

Freiberg, S., and D. T. Payne. 1967. A survey of parental practices related to cognitive development in young children. Child Dev. 38:65–87.

Freston, C. W., and C. J. Drew. 1974. Verbal performance of learning disabled children as a function of input organization. J. Learn. Disab. 7(7):424–428.

Freud, S. 1950. The Ego and the Id. Hogarth, London.

Friedlander, B. Z. 1971. Automated evaluation of selective listening in language-impaired and normal infants and young children. Matern. Child Health Exchange 1(5):9–12.

Friedlander, B. Z., G. M. Sterritt, and G. E. Kirk (eds.). 1975. The Exceptional Infant: Assessment and Intervention. Vol. III. Brunner/ Mazel, New York.

Friedman, R. J. 1975. The young child who does not talk: Observations on causes and management. Clin. Pediat. 14:403–406.

Friedman, S. 1974. Infant Habituation: Process, Problems and Possibilities. Presented at the Symposium on Aberrant Development in Infancy, March, 1974, Gatlinburg, Tenn.

Frierson, E., and W. Barbe (eds.). 1967. Educating Children with Learning Disabilities. Appleton-Century-Crofts, Inc., New York.

Froebel, F. 1912a. Education of Man. Published in 1826; translated by Hailmann. Appleton-Century-Crofts, Inc., New York.

Froebel, F. 1912b. Pedagogics of the Kindergarten. Translated by Jarvis. Appleton-Century-Crofts, Inc., New York.

Frost, R. 1955. Stopping by Woods on a Snowy Evening. In O. Williams (ed.), The New Pocket Anthology of American Verse, p. 202. Pocket Books, Inc., New York.

Frost, J., and R. Minisi. 1975. Early childhood assessment list. Bureau of Education for the Handicapped, Washington, D.C.

Frostig, M. 1964a. Developmental Test of Visual Perception. 3rd Ed. Consulting Psychologists Press, Palo Alto, Calif.

Frostig, M. 1964b. The Frostig Program for the Development of Visual Perception. Follett Publishing Co., Chicago, Ill.

Frostig, M. 1965. Corrective reading in the classroom. Reading Teacher 18:573.

Frostig, M. 1967. Testing as a basis for educational therapy. J. Special Educ. 2(1):15–34.

Frostig, M. 1968. Education for children with learning disabilities. In H. Myklebust (ed.), Progress in Learning Disabilities. Grune & Stratton, Inc., New York.

Furunu, S. 1973. Enrichment Project for Handicapped Infants. University of Hawaii, School of Public Health, Honolulu, Hawaii.

Gallagher, J. J., and R. H. Bradley. 1972. Early identification of developmental difficulties. In I. Gordon (ed.), Early Childhood Education. University of Chicago Press, Chicago, Ill.

Garber, H. L. 1971. Measuring differential development in young children. Paper presented at the American Educational Research Association Meeting, February, New York.

Gardner, C. 1965. Experimental Use of the "Impress Method" of Reading Habilitation. U. S. Department of Health, Education, and Welfare, Office of Education Cooperative Reading Project S-167, Washington, D. C.

Garvey, M., and N. Gordon. 1973. A follow-up study of children with disorders of speech development. Brit. J. Disord. Commun. 8(1):17–28.

Gategno, C. 1962. Words in Color. Learning Materials, Inc., Chicago, Ill.

Gearhart, B. R. 1973. Learning Disabilities: Educational Strategies. C. V. Mosby Co., St. Louis.

Gergen, K. J. 1972. Multiple identity. Psychol. Today, May, pp. 33–35.

Gersten, J. W., K. B. Foppe, R. Gersten, S. Maxwell, P. Mirrett, M. Gipson, H. Houston, and B. Grueter. 1975. Effectiveness of aides in a perceptual motor training program for children with learning disabilities. Arch. Phys. Med. 56:104–110.

Gesell, A. 1924. The nursery school movement. School Soc. 20:644–52.

Gesell, A. 1954. The Ontogenesis of infant behavior. In C. Carmichael (ed.), Manual of Child Psychology. John Wiley & Sons, Inc., New York.

Gesell, A., and C. Amatruda. 1941. Developmental Diagnosis. Paul B. Hoeber, Inc., New York.

Gesell, A., and C. Amatruda, 1947. Developmental Diagnosis. 2nd Ed. Paul B. Hoeber, Inc., New York.

Getman, G. N., and E. R. Kane. 1964. The Physiology of Readiness: An Action Program for the Development of Perception for Children. P.A.S.S., Inc., Minneapolis, Minn.

Giannini, M., et al. 1972. The Rapid Developmental Screening Checklist. American Academy of Pediatrics, New York.

Gibson, E. J. 1968. Learning to read. In N. S. Endler et al. (eds.), Contemporary Issues in Developmental Psychology. Holt, Rinehart and Winston, Inc., New York.

Giffin, M. 1967. The role of child psychiatry in learning disabilities. In H. R. Myklebust (ed.), Progress in Learning Disabilities, Vol. 1, pp. 75–97. Grune & Stratton, Inc., New York.

Gil, D. G. 1971. A sociocultural perspective on physical child abuse. Child Welfare 50(7):389–395.

Giles, M. T. 1973. Individual Learning Disabilities Classroom Screening Instrument: Adolescent Level. Learning Pathways, Inc., Evergreen, Colo.

Gillingham, A., and B. W. Stillman. 1960. Remedial Training for Children with Specific Disability in Reading, Spelling, and Penmanship. 6th Ed., Education Publication Service, Cambridge, Mass.

Gold, E. M. (ed.). 1968. Proceedings of the National Conference for the Prevention of Mental Retardation through Improved Maternity Care. U. S. Government Printing Office, Washington, D. C.

Goldberg, H. K., and P. W. Drash. 1968. The disabled reader. J. Pediat. Ophthalmol. 8:11–24.

Golden, M., and B. Birns. 1971. Social class, intelligence, and cognitive style in infancy. Child Dev. 42:2114–2116.

Goldfarb, W. 1955. Emotional and intellectual consequences of psychological deprivation in infancy: A re-evaluation. In P. Hock and J. Zubin (eds.), Psychopathology of Childhood, pp. 105–119. Grune & Stratton, Inc., New York.

Goodenough, F. 1926. Measurement of Intelligence by Drawings. World Book Co., Yonkers-on-Hudson, N. Y.

Goodman, S. I. 1972. Some advances in the prevention of mental retardation. In I. Schulman (ed.), Advances in Pediatrics, Vol. 2. Yearbook Medical Publishers, Chicago, Ill.

Goodstein, H. A., and H. Kahn. 1974. Pattern of achievement among children with learning difficulties. Except. Child. 17:47–49.

Gordon, I. 1962. Human Development: From Birth through Adolescence. Harper & Row, New York.

Gordon, I. (ed.). 1965. Human Development: Readings in Research. Scott, Foresman, Chicago, Ill.

Gordon, I. 1969. Early Childhood Stimulation through Parent Education. Final report to the Children's Bureau, Social Rehabilitation Service, Department of Health, Education, and Welfare, PHS R-306, June, Washington, D. C.

Gordon, I. 1970. Baby Learning through Baby Play. St. Martin's Press, New York.

Gould, R. 1975. Growth toward self-tolerance. Psychol. Today, pp. 74–78.

Governor's Council on Developmental Disabilities. 1973. Report on the Governor's Conference on Prevention of Developmental Disabilities, December 2–4, 1973. Newport Beach, Calif.

Gray, S. 1966. Before First Grade. Teacher's College Press, New York.

Gray, S. 1971. The Child's first teacher. Childhood Educ. 48:127–129.

Gray, S., and J. O. Miller. 1967. Early experience in relation to cognitive development. Rev. Educ. Res. 37(5):48–112.

Grewel, F. 1967. Differential diagnosis of disorders in the development of language and of speaking. Acta Neurol. Belg. 67:861–866.

Grim, J. 1974. Training Parents to Teach: Four Models: First Chance for Children. TADS, Vol. 3. University of North Carolina, Chapel Hill, N. C.

Grossman, H. J. (ed.). 1973. Manual on Terminology and Classification in Mental Retardation. Revised. Garamond/Pridemark Press, Baltimore.

Grotberg, E. H. 1975. Identification of preschool learning disabled children—Is it possible? Presented at 1973 International Conference Association for Children with Learning Disabilities, February 26, 1975, New York.

Guilford, J. P. 1954. Psychometric Methods. 2nd Ed., McGraw-Hill Book Co., New York.

Guilford, J., and R. Hoepfner. 1966. Structure of Intellect Factors and Their Tests. Report from University of Southern California. No. 36. Los Angeles, Calif.

Guthrie, R. 1972. Mass screening for genetic disease. Hosp. Practice 16:93–100.

Hagin, R. A. 1973. Models of intervention with learning disabilities: Ephemeral and otherwise. School Psychol. Monogr. 8:1–24.

Hagin, R. A., A. A. Silver, and C. G. Corwin. 1971. Clinical-diagnostic use of the WPPSI in predicting learning disabilities in grade one. J. Spec. Educ. 5(3):221–232.

Hainsworth, P. K., and M. L. Siqueland. 1969. The Meeting Street School Screening Test. Crippled Children and Adults of Rhode Island, Inc., Providence, R. I.

Hallgren, B. 1950. Specific dyslexia ("congenital word-blindness"): A clinical and genetic study. Acta Psychiat. Neurol. Scand. (Suppl. 65).

Hambracus, L., and G. Holmgren. 1974. Urinary metabolic screening in children with psychoneurological diseases. Upsala J. Med. Sci. 15:1–23.

Hammill, D. D., and S. C. Larsen. 1974. The relationship of selected auditory perceptual skills and reading ability. J. Learn. Disab. 7(7): 429–435.

Hare, E., J. Price, and E. Slater 1974. Mental disorder and season of birth: A national sample compared with the general population. Brit. J. Psychiat. 124:81–86.

Haring, M. G., and D. A. Krug. 1975. Placement in regular programs: Procedures and results. Except. Child. 41:413–417.

Haring, M. G., and R. W. Ridgway. 1967. Early identification of children with learning disabilities. Except. Child. 33:387–395.

Harlow, H. F. 1963. The maternal affectional system. In B. M. Foss (ed.), The Determinants of Infant Behavior, pp. 3–33. John Wiley and Sons, Inc., New York.

Harrington, M. 1935. The problem of the defective delinquent. Ment. Hyg. 19:429–438.

Harrower, M. 1974. Who Comes to Court? Presented at the American Orthopsychiatric Conference, San Francisco.

Harvey, O. J. 1966. Experience, Structure, and Adaptability. Springer-Verlag, New York.

Harvey, O. J., D. E. Hunt, and H. M. Schroder. 1961. Conceptual Systems and Personality Organization. John Wiley & Sons, Inc., New York.

Hasselmeyer, E. G. 1964. The premature neonate's response to handling. Am. Nurses Assoc. 11:15–24.

Havighurst, R. J. 1953. Human Development and Education. Longmans, Green & Co., Inc., New York.

Haynes, U. 1967. A Developmental Approach to Casefinding with Special Reference to Cerebral Palsy, M. R., and Related Disorders. U. S. Government Printing Office, Washington, D. C.

Haynes, U. 1974. A Nationally Organized Collaborative Project to Provide Comprehensive Services to Handicapped Infants and Their Families: An Overview, April, 1974. (Mimeographed paper.) United Cerebral Palsy Association, New York.

Head Start Test Collection Report. 1973. Self-Concept Measures: An Annotated Bibliography. ERIC Clearinghouse on Early Childhood Education, University of Illinois, Urbana, Ill.

Hebb, D. O. 1949. The Organization of Behavior. John Wiley & Sons, Inc., New York.

Heber, R. 1961. A Manual on Terminology and Classification in Mental Retardation. American Association on Mental Deficiency, Washington, D. C.

Heber, R. F., R. B. Dever, and J. Conry. 1968. The influence of environmental and genetic variables on intellectual development. In H. J. Prehm, L. A. Hamerlynck, and J. E. Crosson (eds.), Behavioral Research in Mental Retardation. University of Oregon, Eugene, Ore.

Heber, R., H. Garber, S. Harrington, C. Hoffman, and C. Falender. 1972. Rehabilitation of families at risk for mental retardation. University of Wisconsin, Madison, Wisc.

Heckelman, R. G. 1962. Using the neurological impress remedial reading technique. Acad. Ther. Quart. 1:235–239.

Helfer, R., and C. H. Kempe. 1968. The Battered Child. University of Chicago Press, Chicago, Ill.

Hellmuth, J. (ed.). 1965–1971. Learning Disorders, Vols. 1–4. Special Child Publications, Seattle, Wash.

Hermann, K., and E. Norrie. 1958. Is congenital word-blindness a hereditary type of Gerstmann's Syndrome? Mschr. Psychiat. Neurol: 36 59–73.

Hershkovitz, H., M. Levine, and G. Spivak. 1959. Antisocial behavior of adolescents from higher socio-economic groups. J. Nerv. Ment. Dis. 125:467–76.

Hess, R. D., and R. M. Bear (eds.). 1968. Early Education. Aldine, Chicago, Ill.

Hess, R. D., and V. C. Shipman. 1965. Early experience and socialization of cognitive modes in children. Child Dev. 36(4):869–886.

Hess, R. D., and V. C. Shipman. 1968. Maternal attitudes toward the school and the role of the pupil: Some social class comparisons. In A. H. Passow (ed.), Developing Programs for the Educationally Disadvantaged. Teachers College, Columbia University, New York.

Hewett, F. 1968. The Emotionally Disturbed Child in the Classroom. Allyn & Bacon, Boston, Mass.

Hildreth, G. H., N. L. Griffiths, and M. E. McGauvran. 1969. Metropolitan Readiness Tests. Harcourt, Brace and Co., Inc., New York.

Hilgard, E. 1964. Theories of Learning and Instruction, Part I. University of Chicago Press, Chicago, Ill.

Hobbs, N. (ed.). 1975a. The Classification of Exceptional Children. Jossey-Bass, Inc., San Francisco, Calif.

Hobbs, N. (ed.). 1975b. The Futures of Children: Categories, Labels and Their Consequences. Jossey-Bass, Inc., San Francisco, Calif.

Hoepfner, R., C. Stern, and S. G. Nummedal. 1971. CSE-ECRC Pre-school/Kindergarten Test Evaluations. University of California, Los Angeles, Calif.

Hoffman, M. S. 1972. "Slide-rule" for catching potential learning disorders early. Expectations 1(8):2.

Holden, R. H. 1972. Prediction of mental retardation in infancy. Ment. Retard. 12:28–30.

Hollingshead, A. B. 1957. Two-factor index of social position. (Mimeographed paper.)

Holm, V. A., and G. Thompson 1971. Selective Hearing Loss: Clues to Early Identification. University of Washington, Seattle, Wash.

Holmes, D. 1972. Report on Preliminary Impact Data from a National Survey of the Parent-Child Center Program. Center for Community Research, New York.

Holt, J. 1964. How Children Fail. Dell, New York.

Holt, J. 1967. How Children Learn. Pitman, New York.

Holtzman, N. A. 1973. Prevention of retardation of genetic origin. Pediat. Clin. N. Am. 20(1):151–158.

Honig, A. S., and S. Brill 1970. A Comparative Analysis of the Piagetian

Development of Twelve Month Old Disadvantaged Infants in an Enrichment Center with Others Not in Such a Center. Enlarged version of a paper presented at the Annual Meeting of American Psychological Association, September, 1970. Miami. Syracuse University, Syracuse, New York.

Honig, A. S., and B. M. Caldwell. 1966. Early Language Assessment Scale. Syracuse University Children's Center, Syracuse, New York.

Honig, A. S., and J. R. Lally. 1972. Infant Caregiving. Media Projects, Inc., New York.

Honzik, M. 1967a. Environmental correlates of mental growth: Prediction from the family setting at 21 months. Child Dev. 38:337–364.

Honzik, M. 1967b. Prediction of differential abilities at age 18 from the early family environment. *In* Proceedings of the Seventy-Fifth Annual Convention of the American Psychological Association, Vol. 2, pp. 151–152. American Psychological Association, Washington, D. C.

Hooper, F. H. 1968. Piagetian research and education. *In* I. E. Sigel and F. H. Hooper (eds.), Logical Thinking in Children: Research Based on Piaget's Theory, pp. 423–434. Holt, Rinehart, and Winston, Inc., New York.

Horowitz, F. D. 1968. Infant Learning and Development: Retrospect and Prospect. Merrill-Palmer Quart. 14:101–120.

Howell, M. C., G. W. Rever, and M. L. Scholl. 1972. Hyperactivity in children. Clin. Pediat. 11:30–39.

Howell, R. R., N. A. Holtzman, and G. H. Thomas. 1969. Selected Screening Tests for Genetic Metabolic Diseases. The Johns Hopkins School of Medicine, Baltimore.

Hughes, J. 1967. Electroencephalography and learning. *In* H. Myklebust (ed.), Progress in Learning Disabilities, pp. 113–146. Grune & Stratton, Inc., New York.

Hunt, J. McV. 1961. Intelligence and Experience. Ronald Press, New York.

Hunt, J. McV. 1964. How children develop intellectually. Children 11(3): 496–517.

Hunt, J. McV. 1975. Environmental risk in fetal and neonatal life and measured infant intelligence. *In* M. Lewis (ed.), Infant Intelligence. Plenum Press, New York. (In press.)

Hunt, J. McV., and I. C. Uzgiris. 1966. Scales of perceptual cognitive development. (Unpublished manuscript.) University of Illinois, Urbana, Ill.

Hurt, M. 1975. Child Abuse and Neglect: A Report on the Status of the Research. U. S. Department of Health, Education, and Welfare No.(OHD) 74-20. George Washington University, Washington, D. C.

Hutt, J. S., H. G. Lenard, and H. F. R. Prechtl. 1969. Psychophysiological studies in newborn infants. *In* L. Lipsitt and C. Spiker (eds.), Advances in Child Development and Behavior. Academic Press, Inc., New York.

Illingsworth, R. S. 1966. The diagnosis of cerebral palsy in the first year of life. Dev. Med. Child Neurol. 8:178.

Illingsworth, R. S. 1973. The Development of the Infant and Young Child. The Williams & Wilkins Company, Baltimore.

Ingram, T. T. 1969. The new approach to early diagnosis of handicaps in childhood. Develop. Med. Child Neurol. 11:279–290.

Ireton, M., E. Thwing, and H. Graven. 1970. Infant Mental Development and neurological status and intelligence at age four. Child Dev. 41:937.

Irving, J. E. 1975. Friends unlimited: Adolescents a helping resource. Children Today 4:14–17.

Irwin, O. C. 1960. Infant speech: Effect of systematic reading of stories. J. Speech & Hearing Res. 3:187–190.

Isaacson, R. L. 1974. Recovery "?" from early brain damage. Prepared for the National Conference on Early Intervention with High Risk Infants and Young Children. University of North Carolina, May 5–8, 1974. Chapel Hill, N. C.

Jacobson, F. N. 1974. Learning disabilities and juvenile delinquency: A demonstrated relationship. In R. E. Weber (ed.), Handbook on Learning Disabilities, pp. 189–216. Prentice-Hall, Inc., Englewood Cliffs, N. J.

Jacobson, F., and C. Ekanger. 1968. The Model School Project. Englewood Public Schools, Englewood, Colo.

Jenkins, R. 1966. Psychiatric syndromes in children and their relation to family background. Am. J. Orthopsychiat. 36:450–457.

Jensen, A. R. 1969. How much can we boost I.Q. and scholastic achievement? Harv. Educ. Rev. 39:1–123.

Johnson, D. L., H. Leler, L. Rios, L. Brandt, A. J. Kahn, E. Mazeika, and B. Bissett. 1973. The Houston Parent-Child Development Center: A Parent Education Program for Mexican-American Families. Later version of a paper presented in symposium at the Meeting of the Society for Research in Child Development, March 1973, Philadelphia.

Johnston, R., and P. Magrab (eds.). 1976. Developmental Disorders: Assessment, Treatment, Education. University Park Press, Baltimore.

Jorgenson, E., O. Bangsgard, and T. Glad. 1968. Adolescent psychiatry in a private Danish institution. J. Learn. Disab. 1:38–41.

Kagan, J. 1968. On cultural deprivation. In D. Glass (ed.), Proceedings of the Conference on Biology and Behavior, pp. 211–250. Rockefeller University Press, New York.

Kagan, J. 1972. Do infants think? Sci. Am. 40:74–82.

Kagan, J. 1973. Cross-cultural perspectives on early development. Am. Psychol. 28:947–961.

Kagan, J., and M. Freeman. 1963. Relation of childhood intelligence, maternal behaviors and social class to behavior during adolescence. Child Dev. 34:899–911.

Kamii, C. 1972. An application of Piaget's Theory to the conceptualization of a preschool curriculum. In R. Parker (ed.), The Preschool in Action, pp. 91–131. Allyn and Bacon, Boston, Mass.

Kamii, C. K., and N. L. Radin. 1970. A framework for a preschool curriculum based on Piaget's theory. In I. J. Athey and D. O. Rubadeau (eds.), Educational Implications of Piaget's Theory. Ginn-Blaisdell, Waltham, Mass.

Karnes, M. B., and R. R. Zehrback. 1972. Flexibility in getting parents involved in school. Teaching Except. Child. 5(1):6–19.

Karp, J., and I. Sigel. 1965. The psychoeducational appraisal of disadvantaged children. Rev. Educ. Res. 35(5):401–412.

Kass, E. R., M. Sigman, R. Bromwich, and A. H. Parmelee. 1976. Educational Intervention with High-Risk Infants. *In* T. J. Tjossem (ed.), Intervention Strategies for High Risk Infants. University Park Press, Baltimore.

Kazdin, A. E. 1973. Issues in behavior modification with mentally retarded persons. Am. J. Ment. Defic. 78(2):134–140.

Keister, M. E. 1969. A Demonstration Project: The Good Life for Infants and Toddlers. Presented at a symposium sponsored by the Day Care Council of New York, Inc., New York.

Keister, M. E. 1970. A Demonstration Project: Group Care of Infants and Toddlers. Final report submitted to the Children's Bureau, Office of Child Development, June, U. S. Department of Health, Education, and Welfare.

Keldgord, R. 1968–1969. Brain damage and delinquency: A question and a challenge. Acad. Ther. 4:93–99.

Kempe, C. H. 1975. The Armstrong Lecture: Predicting and Preventing Child Abuse: Establishing Children's Rights by Assuring Access to Health Care Through the Health Visitors Concept. Paper read before the Annual Meeting of the Ambulatory Pediatric Association, June 9, 1975, Toronto, Canada.

Kempe, C. H., and R. E. Helfer. 1972. Helping the Battered Child and His Family. J. B. Lippincott Co., Philadelphia.

Kempe, C. H., H. Silver, and D. O'Brien. 1974. Current Pediatric Diagnosis and Treatment. Lange Medical Publications, Los Altos, Calif.

Keniston, K. 1974. "Good Children" (Our Own), "Bad Children" (Other People's), and the Horrible Work Ethic. Yale Alumni Magazine, Vol. 37, No. 7.

Kennard, M. A. 1969. EEG abnormality in first grade children with "soft" neurological signs. Electroenceph. Clin. Neurophysiol. 24:544–549.

Kennell, J. H., R. Jerauld, H. Wolfe, D. Chesler, N. C. Kreger, W. McAlpine, M. Steffa, and M. H. Klaus. 1974. Maternal behavior one year after early and extended post-partum contact. Dev. Med. Child Neurol. 16:172–179.

Keogh, B. K. 1971a. A compensatory model for psychoeducational evaluation of children with learning disorders. J. Learn. Dis. 4:544–548.

Keogh, B. K. 1971b. Hyperactivity and learning disorders: Review and speculation. Except. Child. 37:101–107.

Keogh, B. K., and L. D. Becker. 1973. Early detection of learning problems: questions, cautions, and guidelines. Except. Child. 39:5–11.

Keogh, B., M. Leydorf, R. Schain, K. Wedell, J. Switzer, M. Faust, C. Stern, J. D. Call, L. Liverman, and M. H. Jones. 1969. JSE Monograph No. 1: Early Identification of Children with Potential Learning Problems. Proceedings of a conference held at University of California, May, Los Angeles,

Kephart, N. 1960. The Slow Learner in the Classroom. Charles Merrill, Columbus, O.

Kessen, W. 1963. Research in the psychological development of infants: An overview. Merrill-Palmer Quart. 9:83–84.

Kilpatrick, W. H. 1914. The Montessori System Examined. Houghton, Boston, Mass.

Kilpatrick, W. H. 1916. Froebel's Kindergarten Principles Critically Examined. The Macmillan Co., New York.

Kingston, A. H. 1962. The relationship of first-grade readiness to third- and fourth-grade achievement. J. Educ. Res. 56:61–67.

Kirk, S., and W. Kirk. 1971. Psycholinguistic Learning Disabilities: Diagnosis and Remediation. University of Illinois Press, Urbana, Ill.

Kirk, S., and J. McCarthy. 1968. The Illinois Test of Psycholinguistic Abilities. University of Illinois Press, Urbana, Ill.

Klein, J. W., and R. Weathersby. 1973. Child Development Associates: New Professionals, New Training Strategies. Children Today 9:2–6.

Knobloch, H., and B. Pasamanick. 1953. Further observations on the behavioral development of Negro children. J. Genet. Psychol. 83: 137–157.

Knobloch, H., and B. Pasamanick. 1963. Predicting intellectual potential in infancy. Am. J. Dis. Child. 106:43.

Knobloch, H., and B. Pasamanick (eds.). 1974. Gesell and Amatruda's Developmental Diagnosis: The evaluation and management of normal and abnormal neuropsychologic development in infancy and early childhood. Harper & Row, New York.

Knobloch, H., R. Rider, P. Harper, and B. Pasamanick. 1956. Neuropsychiatric sequelae of prematurity: A longitudinal study. J. A. M. A. 161:581–585.

Kohl, H. R. 1969. The Open Classroom. Random House, Inc., New York.

Kohlberg, L. 1968. Early Education: A Cognitive-Developmental View. Child Dev. 39:1013–1062.

Komich, M. P., A. Lansford, L. B. Lord, and A. Tearney. 1973. The sequential development of infants of low birthweight. Am. J. Occup. Ther. 27(7):396–402.

Koppitz, E. M. 1964. The Bender-Gestalt Test for Young Children. Grune & Stratton, Inc., New York.

Korner, A., and R. Grobstein. 1967. Visual alertness as related to soothing in neonates: Implications for maternal stimulation and early deprivation. Child Dev. 13:867–876.

Kosc, L. 1974. Developmental dyscalculia. J. Learn. Disab. 7(3):164–177.

Kotelchuck, M. 1973. The nature of the infant's tie to his father. Presented at the Meeting of the Society for Research in Child Development, March 1973, Philadelphia, Pa.

Krajicek, M. J., and A. Tearney (eds.). 1975. Reference Guide for Community Nurses and Other Health Care Professionals: Detection of Developmental Problems: Screening and Intervention. (In preparation.) University Park Press, Baltimore, Md.

Krech, D., M. R. Rosenzweig, and E. Bennett. 1962. Relations between brain chemistry and problem-solving among rats raised in enriched and impoverished environments. J. Comp. Physiol. Psychol. 55:801–807.

Kunzelman, H. P., M. A. Cohen, W. J. Hulten, G. L. Martin, and A. R.

Mingo. 1970. Precision Teaching: An Initial Training Sequence. Special Child Publications, Seattle, Wash.

Lally, J. R. 1968. A study of the relationships between trained and untrained twelve month old environmentally deprived infants on the "Griffiths Mental Development Scale." (Unpublished paper.) Presented at the American Educational Research Association Meeting, February 1968, Chicago.

Lambert, N. M., M. Windmiller, L. Cole, and R. A. Figueroa. 1975. Standardization of a public school version of the AAMD Adaptive Behavior Scale. Ment. Retard. 3–7.

Lane, M. B. 1968. Consultation to the campus planning committee of the Parent-Child Educational Centers of Litchfield Park Area, Arizona, February, Arizona State University, Tempe, Arizona. (Unpublished.)

Lane, M. B. 1971. Nursery schools in the service of mental health. *In* J. Segal (ed.), Mental Health Program Reports, Department of Health, Education, and Welfare Publication 1724-0176, U. S. Government Printing Office, Washington, D. C.

Langer, T. S. 1974. Family Research Project: Welfare (AFDC) Sample. Year 1 Data: Summary of findings and comparison with cross-section sample. Columbia University, New York. (Unpublished.)

Leboyer, F. 1974. Pour une Naissance sans Violence. Paris, France.

Lehtinen, R. L. 1971. How do we teach him? *In* I. E. Schloss (ed.), The Educator's Enigma: The Adolescent with Learning Disabilities. Academic Therapy Publications, San Rafael, Calif.

Lenneberg, E. 1967. Biological Foundations of Language. Wiley, New York.

Lesser, G. S., G. Fifer, and D. Clark. 1965. Mental abilities of children from different social-class and cultural groups. Monogr. Soc. Res. Child Dev. 30(4).

Lessler, K., and J. Bridges 1973). The prediction of learning problems in a rural setting: Can we improve on readiness tests? J. Learn. Disab. 6(2):90–94.

Lester, B. M. 1975. The consequences of infantile malnutrition. *In* H. E. Fitzgerald and J. P. McKinney (eds.), Developmental Psychology: Studies in Human Development. Revised edition. Dorsey Press, Homewood, Ill.

Levenstein, P. 1970. Cognitive growth in preschoolers through stimulation of verbal interaction with mothers. Am. J. Orthopsychiat. 40:426–432.

Levenstein, P. 1971. Manual for replication of the mother-child home program. (Mimeographed version.) Family Service Association of Nassau County, Inc., New York.

Levine, F. M., and G. Fasnacht. 1974. Token rewards may lead to token learning. Am. Psychol. 29:816–817, 819–820.

Levine, M. D. 1973. The assessment of medical predisposition to educational dysfunction. (Mimeographed paper.) Brookline Early Education Project, Brookline, Mass.

Levine, S. 1960. Stimulation in infancy. Sci. Am. 202(5):80–86.

Lewin, K. 1935. A Dynamic Theory of Personality Development. McGraw-Hill Book Co., New York.

Lewis, H. 1970. Culture, class, poverty and urban schooling. *In* A. H. Passow (ed.), Reaching the Disadvantaged Learner. Columbia University, Teachers College Press, New York.

Lewis, M. 1972. State as an infant-environment interaction: An analysis of mother-infant interactions as a function of sex. Merrill-Palmer Quart. 18:95–122.

Lewis, M. 1973. Infant intelligence tests: Their use and misuse. Hum. Dev. 16(1):108–118.

Lewis, M., S. Goldberg, and H. Campbell. 1969. A developmental study of information processing in the first year of life: Response decrement to a redundant signal. Monogr. Soc. Res. Child. Dev. 34(9, serial no. 133).

Lewis, M., and L. A. Rosenblum (eds.). 1974. The Effect of the Infant on Its Caregiver. John Wiley & Sons, Inc., New York.

Lewis, O. 1959. Five Families. Basic Books, New York.

Lewis, O. 1964. Pedro Martinez: A Mexican Peasant and His Family. Random House, New York.

Lindahl, R. L., and W. O. Young. 1974. A Guide to Dental Care for the EPSDT Program under Medicaid. Social Rehabilitation Services, U. S. Department of Health, Education, and Welfare, Washington, D. C.

Lin-Fu, J. S. 1971. Vision Screening of Children. U. S. Department of Health, Education, and Welfare, Maternal and Child Health Service, U. S. Government Printing Office, Washington, D. C.

Lipscomb, H. S. 1973. Overview: Health Screening–Experience to Date. Institute for Health Services Research, Baylor College of Medicine, Houston, Tex.

Lorr, M., and R. L. Jenkins. 1953. Three factors in parent behavior. J. Consult. Psychol. 17:306–308.

Lubchenco, L. 1969. High Risk Infant Follow-Up Study. (Unpublished progress report.) University of Colorado Medical Center, Denver, Colo.

Lubchenco, L. 1970. Assessment of gestational age and development at birth. Pediat. Clin. N. Am. 17(1):125–145.

Lubchenco, L., F. A. Horner, L. H. Reed, I. E. Hix, D. Metcalf, R. Cohig, H. C. Elliott, and M. Bourg. 1963. Sequelae of premature birth. Am. J. Dis. Child. 106:101–115.

Luria, A. R. 1966a. Higher Cortical Functions in Man. Basic Books, New York.

Luria, A. R. 1966b. Human Brain and Psychological Processes. Harper & Row, New York.

Maas, H. S., and J. A. Kuypers. 1974. From Thirty to Seventy. Jossay-Bass, San Francisco.

Maccoby, E. E., and C. N. Jacklin. 1974. The psychology of sex differences. Stanford Press, Palo Alto, Calif.

Mackworth, J. F. 1972. Some models of the reading process: Learners and skilled readers. Reading Res. Quart. 22:701–73..

Maitland, S., J. B. E. Nadeau, and G. Nadeau. 1974. Early school screening practices. J. Learn. Disab. 7(10):55–59.

Mandell, A. J., D. S. Segal, R. T. Kuczenski, and S. Knapp. 1972. The search for the schizococcus. Psychol. Today, October, pp. 68–72.

Mann, L. 1971. Perceptual training revisited: The training of nothing at all. Rehab. Lit. 32:322–327, 335.

Mann, P. H., and P. Suiter. 1974. Teacher's Handbook of Diagnostic Screening. Allyn and Bacon, Boston.

Mardell, C., and D. Goldenberg. 1975. For prekindergarten screening information: DIAL. J. Learn. Disab. 8(3):140–147.

Marmor, J. 1971. Manual for Testing the Language Ability of 1- to 3-Year-Old Children. Preschool Project. Laboratory of Human Development, Harvard University, Cambridge, Mass.

Martin, H. P. 1971. Vision and its role in reading disability and dyslexia. J. School Health, Vol. XLI, No. 9, November.

Martin, H. P., and P. Beezeley. 1974. Prevention and the consequences of child abuse. J. Operat. Psychiat. 41(1):68–77.

Masland, R. L. 1969. Children with minimal brain dysfunction—A national problem. In I. L. Tarnopol (ed.), Learning Disabilities: Introduction to Educational and Medical Management. Charles C Thomas, Springfield, Ill.

Masland, R. L., S. B. Saranson, and T. Gladwin. 1958. Mental Subnormality. Basic Books, New York.

Maslow, A. H. 1968. Toward a Psychology of Being. Van Nostrand-Reinhold Co., New York.

Mayeda, T. 1973. Data Collection and Utilization in University Affiliated Facilities. Association of University Affiliated Facilities, Washington, D. C.

Mazurkiewicz, A. J. 1964. The Initial Teaching Alphabet. New Perspectives in Reading Instruction. Pitman, New York.

McBride, A. B. 1973. The Growth and Development of Mothers. Harper & Row, New York.

McCall, R. B., P. S. Hogarty, and N. Hurlburt. 1972. Transitions in infant sensorimotor development and the prediction of childhood IQ. Am. Psychol. 27:728–748.

McCandless, A., and G. K. Thomas. 1974. Impedance audiometry as a screening procedure for middle ear disease. Trans. Am. Acad. Ophthal. Otolaryng. 78:98–102.

McCandless, B. 1961. Child and Adolescent Behavior and Development. Holt, Rinehart and Winston, Inc., New York.

McCarthy Scales of Children's Abilities. 1970. Psychological Corporation, New York.

McCoy, L. E. 1975. Braille: A language for severe dyslexics. J. Learn. Disab. 8(5):288–292.

McCulloch, F. (ed.). 1975. The LD movement: Brilliant star or glaring copout? Learning, 2:26.

McDermott, J. F., and E. Atina. 1972. Understanding and improving the personality development of children with physical handicaps. Clin. Pediat. 13(3):130–134.

McGraw, M. B. 1939. Behavior of the newborn infant and early neuro-muscular development. Res. Publ. Assoc. Nerv. Ment. Dis. 19:244–46.

McIntyre, R. 1974. Licensing parents to have children. Psychol. Today, pp. 25–31.

McMillan, M. 1920. Nursery Schools: A Practical Handbook. John Bale, London.

McNeill, D. 1970. The Acquisition of Language. Harper & Row, New York.

Mecham, M. J., J. D. Jones, and J. L. Jex. 1973. Use of the Utah test of language development for screening language disabilities. J. Learn. Disab. 6(8):524–527.

Medvedeff, E. 1974. The Preschool Early Identification Screening Inventory. Westinghouse Learning Corp., Iowa City.

Meeting Street School Screening Test. 1969. Crippled Children and Adults of Rhode Island, Providence, R. I.

Mehrotra, S. N., and J. Maxwell. 1949. Intelligence of twins: A comparative study of eleven year old twins. Pop. Stud. 3:295.

Meier, J. H. 1965. An Exploratory Factor Analysis of Psychodiagnostic and Case Study Information from Children in Special Education Classes for the Educable Mentally Handicapped. (Dissertation.) University Microfilms, Ann Arbor, Mich.

Meier, J. H. 1967. Innovations in assessing the disadvantaged child's potential. In J. Helmuth (ed.), Disadvantaged Child, Vol. 1, pp. 173–199. Special Child Publications, Seattle, Wash.

Meier, J. H. 1968. Programs for disabled readers. Int. Reading Assoc. J. 21(8):712–716.

Meier, J. H. 1970. An autotelic nursery for deprived children. In J. Masserman (ed.), Current Psychiatric Therapies, Vol. X, pp. 30–45. Grune & Stratton, Inc., New York.

Meier, J. H. 1971. Prevalence and characteristics of learning disabilities in second grade children. J. Learn. Disab. 4:1–16.

Meier, J. H. 1973a. System for Open Learning. Facilitator's Handbook I: Foundations and Rationale; Facilitator's Handbook II: Learning Episodes; Facilitator's Handbook III: Staff Development and Program Implementation.

Meier, J. H. 1973b. Screening and Assessment of Young Children at Development Risk, U. S. Government Printing Office, Washington, D. C.

Meier, J. H. 1973c. Learning disabilities found in elementary schools. In P. Satz (ed.), The Disabled Learner: Early Detection and Intervention, pp. 101–120. University of Rotterdam Press, Netherlands.

Meier, J. H. 1975a. System for Open Learning: Learning Episodes. Book II enlarged and revised. John F. Kennedy Child Development Center, Publishers Press, Denver, Colo.

Meier, J. H. 1975b. Mental retardation—Definition, incidence, and classification. In B. Wolman (ed.), International Encyclopedia of Neurology, Psychiatry, Psychoanalysis, and Psychology. (In preparation.)

Meier, J. H. 1975c. Early intervention in the prevention of mental retardation. *In* A. Milunsky (ed.), The Prevention of Mental Retardation and Genetic Disease, pp. 385–409. W. B. Saunders Co., Philadelphia.

Meier, J. H. 1976. Cognitive Development: Mental Retardation: *In* R. Johnston and P. Magrab (eds.), Developmental Disorders: Assessment, Treatment, Education. University Park Press, Baltimore.

Meier, J. H., and W. A. Borthick. 1975. Remote Microtraining. John F. Kennedy Child Development Center, Denver, Colo.

Meier, J. H., V. O. Cazier, and M. T. Giles, 1970. Administration, Scoring, and Interpretation Manual for the ILD/SCI. Learning Pathways, Inc., Evergreen, Colo.

Meier, J. H., P. J. Malone, and W. A. Borthick. 1975. Systems for Open Learning, Book II-R (enlarged and revised ed.). John F. Kennedy Child Development Center, Denver, Colo.

Meier, J. H., and H. P. Martin. 1974. Developmental and learning disabilities. *In* C. Kempe, H. Silver, and D. O'Brien. (eds.), Current Pediatric Diagnosis and Treatment 22:580–587.

Meier, J. H., and J. Scott. 1967. Automated Impress Method of Reading Remediation. (Unpublished.) Greeley, Colo.

Meier, J. H., L. L. Segner, and B. B. Grueter. 1970. Early stimulation and education with high risk infants: A preventive approach to developmental and learning disabilities. *In* J. Helmuth (ed.), The Disadvantaged Child, Vol. 3, pp. 405–444. Brunner/Mazel, Inc., New York.

Meier, J. H., and N. Weaver. 1974. Reward and Punishment. Book Forum, Vol. 1, No. 3, pp. 409–411, 413.

Mental Retardation News. November 3, 1971, p. 3.

Menyuk, P. 1971. The Acquisition and Development of Language. Prentice-Hall, Inc., Englewood Cliffs, N. J.

Mercer, J. R. 1971a. Adaptive Behavior Scales and Bibliography. University of California, Riverside, Calif.

Mercer, J. R. 1971b. Sociocultural factors in labeling mental retardates. Peabody J. Educ. 48:188–203.

Mercer, J. R. 1972. The Origins and Development of the Pluralistic Assessment Project. University of California, Riverside, Calif.

Mercer, J. R. 1973. Labeling the Mentally Retarded. University of California Press, Richmond, Calif.

Metropolitan Readiness Tests. 1969. Harcourt, Brace and Co., Inc., New York.

Meyers, C. E. 1973. Psychometrics. *In* J. Wortis (ed.), Mental Retardation, Vol. V, pp. 25–54. Brunner/Mazel, New York.

Meyers, C. E., and H. F. Dingman. 1966. Factor analysis and structure of intellect models in the study of mental retardation. Am. J. Ment. Defic. 70(4):7–25.

Miller, J. D. 1968. Cultural deprivation and its modification: Effects of intervention. *In* H. C. Haywood (ed.), Proceedings of Conference on Social-Cultural Aspects of Mental Retardation. George Peabody College for Teachers, Nashville.

Miller, L. B. 1975. Situational Determinants of Behavior in Preschool

Classrooms. International Society for Study of Behavioral Development, Guilford, England.

Miller, L. C. 1972. School behavior checklist. J. Consult. Clin. Psychol. 38:134.

Miller, T. G., and K. Goldberg. 1975. Sensorimotor integration. Phys. Ther. 55(5):501–504.

Milunsky, A. (ed.). 1975. The Prevention of Genetic Disease and Mental Retardation. W. B. Saunders Co., Philadelphia.

Minde, K., D. Lewin, G. Weiss, H. Lavigueur, V. Douglas, and E. Sykes. 1971. The hyperactive child in elementary school: A five-year, controlled follow-up. Except. Child. 37:215–221.

Minimal Brain Dysfunction. 1974. The Child with Minimal Brain Dysfunction. American O. T. Foundation, Inc., Rockville, Md.

Mohr, G. J., and M. A. Despres. 1958. The Emotionally Disturbed Adolescent. *In* G. Mohr and M. Despres (eds.), The Stormy Decade of Adeolescence, pp. 159–180. Random House, New York.

Mondale, W. F., et al. 1975. Senate Bill S-626: Child and Family Services Act of 1975. U. S. Senate, Washington, D. C.

Money, T. (ed.). 1966. The Disabled Reader. Johns Hopkins Press, Baltimore.

Montessori, M. 1964. The Montessori Method. Schocken Books, New York.

Montessori, M. 1965a. Dr. Montessori's Own Handbook. Schocken Books, New York.

Montessori, M. 1965b. Spontaneous Activity in Education. Schocken Books, New York.

Moore, O. K. 1964. Autotelic responsive environments and exceptional children. *In* J. Hellmuth (ed.), The Special Child in Century 21, pp. 87–138. Special Child Publications, Seattle.

Moore, O. K., and A. R. Anderson. 1968. Some principles for the design of clarifying educational environments. *In* D. Goslin (ed.), Handbook of Socialization Theory and Research. Rand McNally, Chicago.

Moore, R. W., and D. R. Moore. 1972. The pre-school movement: Panacea or portent? Paper available from Hewitt Research Center, Detroit, Mich.

Moore, T. 1967. Language and intelligence: A longitudinal study of the first eight years. Part I: Patterns of development in boys and girls. Hum. Dev. 10:88–106.

Mulligan, W. 1969. A study of dyslexia and delinquency. Acad. Ther. 4:177–87.

Murphy, L. B. 1968. Child development—then and now. Children Educ. 44(5):302–306.

Mussen, P. (ed.). 1970. Carmichael's Manual of Child Psychology, Third Edition, Vols. 1, 2. John Wiley & Sons, New York.

Myklebust, H. 1965a. Development and Disorders of Written Language. Grune & Stratton, Inc., New York.

Myklebust, H. 1965b. Picture Story Language Test. Grune & Stratton, Inc., New York.

Myklebust, H. 1967. Learning disabilities in psychoneurologically disturbed children: Behavioral correlates of brain dysfunctions. *In* P. Hoch and J. Zubin (eds.), Psychopathology of Mental Development. Grune & Stratton, Inc., New York.

Myklebust, H. R. (ed.). 1968. Progress in Learning Disabilities, Vol. I. Grune & Stratton, Inc., New York.

Myklebust, H. 1971. The Pupil Rating Scale, Screening for Learning Disabilities. Grune & Stratton, Inc., New York.

Myklebust, H. R., and B. Boshes. 1969. Minimal Brain Damage in Children. Northwestern University, Evanston, Ill.

National Assessment of Educational Progress. 1973. Reading Becomes Top Educational Priority. September, Vol. VI, No. 7. Education Commission of the States, Denver.

National Association for Retarded Citizens. 1973. Results of sensorimotor training study announced: Reported programs show positive benefits. Ment. Retard. News 22:4.

Nedler, S. 1972. A development process approach to curriculum design. *In* R. K. Parker (ed.), The Preschool in Action, pp. 59–89. Allyn & Bacon, Boston.

Neligan, G. A. 1974. Brain–Vulnerable stages. Dev. Med. Child Neurol. 16(5):677–678.

Neman, R. 1975. A reply to Zigler and Seitz. Am. J. Ment. Defic. 79:493–505.

Neman, R., P. Roos, B. M. McCann, F. J. Menolascino, and L. W. Heal. 1975. An experimental evaluation of sensorimotor patterning used with mentally retarded children. Am. J. Ment. Defic. 79:372–384.

Newcomer, P., B. Hare, D. Hammill, and J. McGettigan. 1975. Construct validity of the Illinois Test of Psycholinguistic Abilities. J. Learn. Disab. 8(4):220–231.

Newman, H., F. N. Freeman, and K. J. Holzinger. 1937. Twins: A Study of Heredity and Environment. University of Chicago Press, Chicago.

Nichol, H. 1974. Children with learning disabilities referred to psychiatrists: A follow-up study. J. Learn. Disab. 7(2):64–68.

Nihira, K., R. Foster, M. Shellhaas, and H. Leland. 1969. Adaptive Behavior Scales: Manual. American Association on Mental Deficiency, Washington, D. C.

Nimnicht, G. 1967. Low-cost typewriter approach helps preschoolers type words and stories. Nation's Schools 80:34–37.

Nimnicht, G., B. Barnes, R. Warner, and B. Rogers. (No date.) Manual for Learning Booth Attendants. Far West Laboratory for Educational Research and Development, San Francisco.

Nimnicht, G., and J. A. Johnson. 1973. Beyond "Compensatory Education"–A New Approach to Educating Children. U. S. Government Printing Office, Washington, D. C.

Nimnicht, G., O. McAfee, and J. Meier. 1969. The New Nursery School. General Learning Corp., New York.

Nimnicht, G. P., and J. H. Meier. 1966. A first year partial progress report of a project in an autotelic responsive environment nursery school for environmentally deprived Spanish-American children. J. Res. Serv. 5:2, 3–34 (University of Northern Colorado, Greeley, Colo.)

Nimnicht, G., J. Meier, and O. McAfee. 1967. Nursery school education today. J. Res. Serv. 3:33–39. (University of North Colorado, Greeley, Colo.)

Nitowski, H. M. 1973. Prescriptive screening for inborn errors of metabolism: A critique. Am. J. Ment. Defic. 77(5):538–550.

Norman, R. D. 1966. The interpersonal values of parents of achieving and non-achieving gifted children. J. Psychol. 64:49–57.

North, A. F., Jr. 1968. Preventing mental impairment—How can the pediatrician help? Clin. Pediat. 7(11):670–675.

Novack, H. S., E. Bonaventura, and P. Merenda. 1973. The Rhode Island Pupil Identification Scale. Rhode Island College, Providence.

O'Brien, D., F. Ibbott, and D. Rodgerson. 1968. Laboratory Manual of Pediatric Micro Biochemical Techniques. 4th Ed. Harper & Row, New York.

O'Brien, J. S. 1971. How we detect mental retardation before birth. Med. Times 99:103–108.

Ogilvie, D., and B. Shapiro. 1969. Manual for Assessing Social Abilities of One-to-Six-Year-Old Children. Preschool Project, Harvard University, Cambridge, Mass.

O'Keefe, R. A. 1973. Home start: Partnership with parents. Children Today 2(1):12–16.

Orton, S. T. 1937. Reading, Writing, and Speech Problems in Children. W. W. Norton & Co., Inc., New York.

Orton, J. L. 1963. The Orton Story. Bull. Orton Soc. 13:1–6.

Orton, J. L. 1964. A Guide to Teaching Phonics. Salem College, Winston-Salem, N.C.

Ostwald, P. F., R. Phibbs, and S. Fox. 1968. Diagnostic use of infant cry. Biology of the Neonate 13:68–82.

Owen, F. W. 1971. Learning disorders in children: Sibling studies. Monogr. Soc. Res. Child Dev. (Serial no. 144), 3:4.

Ozer, M. N. 1966. Neurological Evaluation. Children's Hospital of D. C., Washington, D. C.

Ozer, M. N., and H. B. Richardson. 1974. The diagnostic evaluations of children with learning problems: A "process" approach. J. Learn. Disab. 7(2):30–34.

Ozer, M. N., H. B. Richardson, M. T. Tannhauser, and C. D. Smith. 1970. The diagnostic evaluation of children with learning problems: An interdisciplinary model. Children's Hospital, Washington, D. C. Clin. Proc. 26(6):497–513.

Painter, G. 1969. The effect of a structured tutorial program on the cognitive and language development of culturally disadvantaged infants. Merrill-Palmer Quart. 15:279–294.

Palmer, F. H. 1969. Learning at two. Children 16:55–57.

Palmer, F. H., and A. H. Rees. 1969. Concept training in two year olds: Procedures and results. Presented at the Meeting of SRCD, Santa Monica, Calif.

Parker, R. K. (ed.). 1973. The Preschool in Action. Exploring Early Childhood Programs. Allyn and Bacon, Boston.

Parmelee, A. H., and A. Haber. 1973. Who is the "risk infant?" Clin. Obstet. Gynec. 16:376–387.

Parmelee, A. H., C. B. Kopp, and M. Sigman. 1976. Selection of developmental assessment techniques for infants at risk. In T. J. Tjossem (ed.), Intervention Strategies for High Risk Infants. University Park Press, Baltimore.

Parmelee, A. H., M. Sigman, C. B. Kopp, and A. Haber. 1974. Diagnosis of the Infant at High Risk for Mental, Motor, or Sensory Handicap. Presented at the Conference on Early Intervention for High Risk Infants and Young Children, May 5–8, Chapel Hill, N. C.

Pederson, F. A., and K. S. Robson. 1969. Father participation in infancy. Am. J. Orthopsychiat. 39:466–72.

Penfield, W. 1958. The Excitable Cortex in Conscious Man. Liverpool University Press, Liverpool, England.

Pestalozzi, J. H. 1894. How Gertrude Teaches Her Children. (Published in Burgdorf, 1801; translated by Holland Turner.) Bardeen, New York.

Pestalozzi, J. H. 1898. Letters on Early Education. (Written to J. Greaves, 1818.) Bardeen, New York.

Peter, L. J. 1965. Prescriptive Teaching. McGraw-Hill Book Co., New York.

Peters, E., R. A. Dykman, P. T. Ackerman, and J. S. Romine. 1973a. The special neurological examination. In Research on Minimal Brain Dysfunction, Excerpta Medica, Princeton, N. J.

Peters, J., J. S. Davis, C. M. Goolsby, S. D. Clements, and T. J. Hicks. 1973b. Physician's Handbook Screening for MBD. Ciba, Summit, N. J.

Peterson, W. 1970. A Program for Early Identification of Learning Disabilities. Special Child Publications, Inc., Seattle.

Peterson, D. R. 1961. Behavior problems of middle childhood. J. Consult. Psychol. 25:205–209.

Petre-Quadens, O., and C. DeLee. 1970. Eye-movements during sleep— A common criterion of learning capacities and endocrine activity. Dev. Med. Child Neurol. 12:730–740.

Petric, A., R. McCullough, and P. Kazdin. 1962. The perceptual characteristics of the juvenile delinquent. J. Nerv. Ment. Dis. 134:415.

Piaget, J. 1932. Langauge and Thought of the Child. Harcourt, Brace and Co., Inc., New York.

Piaget, J. 1960. The Psychology of Intelligence. Littlefield, Adams & Co., Paterson, N. J.

Piaget, J. 1962. Play, Dreams and Imitation in Childhood. W. W. Norton & Co., Inc., New York.

Piaget, J. 1963. The Origins of Intelligence in Children. W. W. Norton & Co., Inc., New York.

Piaget, J., and B. Inhelder. 1958. The Growth of Logical Thinking. Basic Books, New York.

Pierson, D. E. 1974. The Second Year of the Brookline Early Education Project: Progress Report and Plans for the Future. Brookline Early Education Project, Brookline, Mass.

Pines, M. 1965. What the talking typewriter says. The New York Times Magazine, May 9, 1965.

Pines, M. 1971. New facts on infant learning. Life Magazine, December.

Pitman, I. J. 1961. Learning to Read: An Experiment. J. Roy. Soc. Arts 109:149–80.

Pope, L. 1970. Motor activity in brain-injured children. Am. J. Orthopsychiat. 40:783–794.

Powell, L. F. 1974. The effect of extra stimulation and maternal involvement on the development of low birth-weight infants and on maternal behavior. Child Dev. 45:106–113.

Pratt, M., L. Giesecke, H. Hagan, M. Konon, and A. Edelin. 1972. Special study: Analysis of U. S. infant mortality by cause of death, color, sex, age at death and degree of urbanization of place of residence, 1962–1967. MCH Exchange 2(3):15–48.

Premack, D. 1959. Toward empirical behavior laws: I. Positive reinforcement. Psychol. Rev. 66:219 33.

President's Committee on Mental Retardation. 1969. The Six-Hour Retarded Child. U. S. Government Printing Office, Washington, D.C.

President's Committee on Mental Retardation. 1972a. Background Papers of Boston Conference: Early Screening and Assessment. U. S. Government Printing Office, Washington, D. C.

President's Committee on Mental Retardation. 1972b. Report of Work Group on Research and Prevention. (Unpublished.)

Preston, M. S. 1974. Visual evoked responses in normal and disabled readers. Psychophysiol. 11:452.

Pribram, K. H. 1971. Languages of the Brain: Experimental Paradoxes and Principles in Neuropsychology. Prentice-Hall, Inc., Englewood Cliffs, N. J.

Provence, S., and R. C. Lipton. 1962. Infants in Institutions. International Universities Press, New York.

Psychiatric Opinion. 1975. Vol. 12, No. 2, February, Framingham, Mass.

Purpura, D. P. 1976. Discussants' Comments on First Plenary Session. In T. J. Tjossem (ed.), Intervention Strategies for the High Risk Infant. University Park Press.

Quay, H. C. 1964. Personality dimensions in delinquent males as inferred from the factor analysis of behavior ratings. J. Res. Crime Delinquency 1:33–37.

Quay, H. C., and D. R. Peterson. 1967. Manual for the Behavior Problems Checklist. Children's Research Center, University of Illinois, Champaign, Ill.

Rabinovich, R. 1959. Reading and learning disabilities. In S. Arieti (ed.), American Handbook of Psychiatry. Basic Books, New York.

Rafael, B. 1973. Early education for multihandicapped children. Children Today 2(1):22–26.

Ramey, C. T., P. Mills, F. A. Campbell, and C. O'Brien. 1975. Infants home environments: A comparison of high risk families and families from the general population. Am. J. Ment. Defic. 80:40–42.

Rappaport, J., W. S. Davidson, M. N. Wilson, and A. Mitchell. 1975. Alternatives to blaming the victim or the environment. Am. Psychol. 30:525–528.

Rawson, M. 1968. Developmental Language Disability: Adult Accomplishments in Dyslexic Boys. Johns Hopkins Press, Baltimore.

Rayder, N. F., B. Bödy, and A. I. Abrams. 1975. Effects of the Responsive Education Program: New data. Far West Laboratory for Educational Research and Development, San Francisco.

Rayder, N. F., and B. Bödy. 1975. The Educational Forces Inventory: A New Technique for Measuring Influences on the Classroom. (Unpublished manuscript.) Far West Laboratory for Educational Research and Development, San Francisco.

Rebelsky, F., and C. Hanks. 1971. Father's verbal interaction with infants in the first three months of life. Child Dev. 42:63–68.

Reger, R., W. Schroeder, and K. Uschold. 1968. Special Education: Children with Learning Problems. Oxford University Press, New York.

Reppucci, N. D., and J. T. Saunders. 1974. Social psychology of behavior modification: Problems of implementation in natural settings. Am. Psychol. 649–660.

Restaino, L. C., P. A. Socher, C. Milligan, and S. Rubenstein. 1971. Curriculum for Young Deaf Children. New York State Education Department, Albany, New York.

Revised Stanford-Binet Test of Intelligence. 1965. Consulting Psychologists Press, Inc., Palo Alto, Calif.

Reyes, E. V., H. Garber, and R. Heber. 1972. Developmental differences in language as measured by a sentence repetition test during the fourth year of life. (Unpublished manuscript, University of Wisconsin), Madison, Wisc.

Rheingold, H. L. 1961. The effect of environmental stimulation upon social and exploratory behavior in the human infant. In B. Foss (ed.), Determinants of Infant Behavior. John Wiley & Sons, Inc., New York.

Richards, I. D., and C. J. Roberts. 1967. The "at risk" infant. Lancet 2:711.

Richardson, S. A., H. G. Birch, and M. E. Hertzig. 1973. School performance of children who were severely malnourished in infancy. Am. J. Ment. Defic. 77(5):623–632.

Riessman, F. 1962. The Culturally Deprived Child. Harper & Row, New York.

Roach, E., and N. Kephart. 1966. The Purdue Perceptual-Motor Survey, Charles E. Merrill Publishing Co., Columbus, Ohio.

Robbins, M. P. 1967. Study of validity of Delacato's theory of neurological organization. J.A.M.A. 202:389–393.

Robinson, H. B., and N. M. Robinson. 1971. Longitudinal development of very young children in a comprehensive day care program: The first two years. Child Dev. 42:1673–1683.

Robinson, M. 1975. Five-year research and development plan regarding mother-infant interaction using Parent Child Development Center models. Office of Child Development, Washington, D. C. (Unpublished.)

Robinson, H. F., and K. D. Wann. 1967. Status report: Study of intellectual stimulation of disadvantaged pre-kindergarten children. Sponsored by Center for Urban Education, Teachers College, Columbia University, New York.

Rogers, C. 1951. Client-Centered Therapy. Houghton-Mifflin, Boston.

Rogers, M. C. 1968. Risk registers and early detection of handicaps. Dev. Med. Child Neurol. 10:651.

Rolcik, J. W. 1965. Scholastic achievement of teenagers and parental attitudes toward and interest in schoolwork. Family Life Coordinator 14:158–160.

Rosenstein, S. N. 1974. "Premature" infants: The relation of dental abnormalities to neurological and psychometric status at age two years. Dev. Med. Child Neurol. 16:158–162.

Rosenthal, R. 1966. Experimenter Effects in Behavioral Research. Appleton-Century-Crofts, Inc., New York.

Rosenzweig, M. R. 1966. Environmental complexity, cerebral change, and behavior. Am. Psychol. 21:321–322.

Rotter, J. B. 1967. Generalized expectancies for internal vs. external control of reinforcement. Psychol. Monogr. 80, No. 1, Washington, D.C.

Rousy, C., and W. Cozad. 1966. Hearing and Speech Disorders among Delinquent Children. Menninger Clinic, Topeka, Kansas.

Rubenstein, J. 1967. Maternal attentiveness and subsequent exploratory behavior in the infant. Child Dev. 38:1089–1100.

Rubin, R. A., C. Rosenblatt, and B. Balow. 1973. Psychological and educational sequelae of prematurity. Pediatrics 52(3):352–363.

Rudnick, M., G. M. Sterritt, and M. Flax. 1967. Auditory and visual rhythm perception and reading ability. Child Dev. 38:581–587.

Rugel, R. P. 1974. WISC subtest scores of disabled readers: A review with respect to Bannatyne's recategorization. J. Learn. Disab. 7(1):48–55.

Rutter, M. 1970. Psychological development: Predictions for infancy. J. Child Psychol. Psychiat. 11:49–62.

Rychener, R. O. 1948. Reading disability and the ophthalmologist. Trans. Am. Acad. Ophthal-Otolaryng. 18:107.

Saltz, R. 1973. Effects of part-time "mothering" on I.Q. and S.Q. of young institutionalized children. Child Dev. 44:166–170.

Sameroff, A. J., and M. J. Chandler. 1975. Reproductive risk and the continuum of caretaking casualty. In F. D. Horowitz, M. Hetherington, S. Scarr-Salapatek, and C. Siegel (eds.), Review of Child Development Research. (In press.)

Samuda, R. J. 1973. Racial discrimination through mental testing: A social critic's point of view. IRCD Bull. No. 42, May.

Sanday, M. 1974. The IQ Debate. Time, February 4.

Sandler, L. 1972. Effectiveness of Screening Instrument in Detection of Developmental Handicaps among Preschool Children. Franklin Institute Research Laboratories, Philadelphia.

Sandler, L., D. Jamison, O. Deliser, L. Cohen, K. Emkey, and H. Keith. 1972. Developmental test performance on disadvantaged children. Except. Child. 15:201–208.

Sandler, L., J. Van Campen, G. Ratner, C. Stafford, and R. Weismar. 1970. Responses of urban preschool children to a developmental screening test. J. Pediat. 77(5):775–781.

Satz, P., and J. Friel. 1974. Some predictive antecedents of special reading disability: A preliminary two-year follow-up. J. Learn. Disab. 7:437–444.

Savitz, R. A., R. B. Reed, and I. Valadian. 1964. Vision Screening of the Preschool Child. Children's Bureau, U. S. Department of Health, Education, and Welfare, U. S. Government Printing Office, Washington, D. C.

Scarr-Salapetek, S., and M. L. Williams. 1973. The effects of early stimulation of low birth-weight infants. Child Dev. 44:94–101.

Schaefer, E. S., and M. Aaronson. 1972. Infant education research project: Implementation and implications of a home tutoring program. In R. K. Parker (ed.), The Preschool in Action—Exploring Early Childhood Programs, pp. 410–434. Allyn and Bacon, Boston.

Schaefer, E. S., and N. Bayley. 1963. Maternal behavior, child behavior, and their intercorrelations from infancy through adolescence. Monogr. Soc. Child Dev., 28(3):1–178.

Schaefer, E. S., and R. Q. Bell. 1958. Development of a parental attitude research instrument. Child Dev. 29:339–361.

Schiefelbusch, R. L., and L. L. Lloyd. 1974. Language Perspectives—Acquisition, Retardation, and Intervention. University Park Press, Baltimore.

Schmitt, B., H. P. Martin, G. Nellhaus, J. Cravens, B. W. Camp, and K. Jordan. 1973. The hyperactive child. Clin. Pediat. 12:154–169.

Science. 1974. International participation and language structure, Vol. 183, p. 4120.

Scott, J. P. 1958. Critical periods in the development of social behavior in puppies. Psychosom. Med. 20:42–53.

Scott, J. P., E. Fredrickson, and J. L. Fuller. 1951. Experimental exploration of the critical period of hypothesis. Personality 1:268–270.

Scott, R., E. R. Kell, and D. L. Salisbury. 1970. Cognitive profiles of "retarded" children: A survey of inter- and intra-child differences. Psychol. Schools 7:288–292.

Scurletis, T. D., and M. S. Headrick. 1972. A System of Comprehensive Health Care Screening and Service for Children. Material presented at AAMD Meeting, May, Minneapolis.

Searls, E. F. 1971. WISC & WIPPSI I.Q.'s and Subtest Patterns Related to First Grade Reading Achievement. Doctoral dissertation, University of Miami, Miami, Fla.

Sears, R. R., E. Maccoby, and H. Levin. 1957. Patterns of Child Rearing. Row-Peterson, Evanston, Ill.

Segner, L., and C. Patterson. 1970. Ways to Help Babies Grow and

Learn: Activities for Infant Education. University of Colorado Medical Center, Denver.

Selye, H. 1974. Stress without Distress. J. B. Lippincott Co., Philadelphia.

Severson, R. A. 1972. Early detection of children with potential learning disabilities: A seven year effort. Proceedings of the 80th Annual Convention of the American Psychological Association, pp. 561—562.

Shaeffer, E. S. 1971. Towards revolution in education: A perspective from child development research. The National Elementary Principal, Vol. LI, No. 1, September.

Shaw, M. C., and D. L. White. 1965. The relationship between child-parent identification and academic underachievement. J. Clin. Psychol. 21:10—13.

Shearer, A. E., and M. J. Shearer. 1972. The Portage project: A model for early childhood education. Except. Child. 15:210—217.

Shearer, M., and A. E. Shearer. 1974. The Portage project. Presented at Conference on Early Intervention for High Risk Infants and Young Children, University of North Carolina, May 5—8. Chapel Hill, N. C.

Shotwell, A. 1964. Suitability of the Kuhlmann-Binet Infant Scale for assessing intelligence of mental retardates. Am. J. Ment. Defic. 68:757.

Simeonsson, R. J., and R. Wiegerink. 1975. Accountability: A dilemma in infant intervention. Except. Child. 18:474—481.

Simons, K., and D. Reinecke. 1974. A reconsideration of amblyopia screening and stereopsis. Am. J. Ophthal. 78:707—721.

Sines, J. O., J. D. Pauker, L. K. Sines, and D. R. Owen. 1969. Identification of clinically relevant dimensions of children's behavior. J. Consult. Clin. Psychol. 33(6):728—734.

Siqueland, E. R. 1973. Biological and experimental determinants of exploration in infancy. In L. J. Stone, H. T. Smith, and L. B. Murphy (eds.), The Competent Infant. Research Commentary. Basic Books, New York.

Skeels, H. M., and H. B. Dye. 1939. A study of the effects of differential stimulation on mentally retarded children. Proc. Addresses Am. Assoc. Ment. Defic. 44(1):114—136.

Skinner, B. F. 1948. Walden Two. The Macmillan Company, New York.

Skinner, B. F. 1971. Beyond Freedom and Dignity. Knopf, New York.

Sklar, B., J. Hanley, and W. W. Simons. 1972. An EEG experiment aimed toward identifying dyslexic children. Nature 241:414.

Sladen, B. 1970. Inheritance of dyslexia. Bull. Orton Soc. 20:30.

Slingerland, B. H. 1962. Screening Tests for Identifying Children with Specific Language Disability. Educators Publishing Service, Cambridge, Mass.

Slosson Intelligence Test for Children and Adults. 1963. Slosson Educational Publishers, Inc., East Aurora, New York.

Small, J. G., M. K. DeMeyer, and V. Milstein. 1971. CNV responses to autistic and normal children. J. Autism Child. Schizo. 1(2):215−231.

Smith, A. C., G. L. Flick, G. S. Ferris, and A. H. Sellman. 1972. Prediction of developmental outcome at seven years from prenatal, perinatal, and postnatal events. Child Dev. 43:495−507.

Smith, F., and G. A. Miller. 1966. The Genesis of Language. Massachusetts Institute of Technology Press, Cambridge, Mass.

Smith, S. M., R. Hanson, and S. Noble. 1973. Correlation of birth weight with intelligence. Brit. Med. J. 4:388.

Sokolov, Y. N. 1963. Perception and the Conditioned Reflex. (Translated by S. W. Wayenfeld.) The Macmillan Co., New York.

Solkoff, N., S. Yaffe, D. Weinstraub, and B. Blase. 1969. Effects of handling on the subsequent development of premature infants. Dev. Psychol. 1:765−768.

Solomon, H. C. (ed.). 1975. The pregnant teenager. Psychiat. Opin. 12:1−42.

Spearman, C. 1927. The Abilities of Man: Their Nature and Measurement. The Macmillan Co., New York.

Speer, D. C. 1971. Behavior problem checklist (Peterson-Quay)— Baseline data from parents of child guidance and nonclinic children. J. Consult. Clin. Psychol. 36:221−228.

Sperry, R. W. 1958. Physiological plasticity and brain circuit theory. In H. F. Harlow and C. N. Woolsey, Biological and Biochemical Bases of Behavior, University of Wisconsin Press, Madison, Wisc.

Spiro, M. 1958. Children of the Kibbutz. Harvard University Press, Cambridge, Mass.

Spitz, R. A. 1945. Hospitalism: An inquiry into the genesis of psychiatric conditions in early childhood. Psychoanal. Stud. Child 1:53−74.

Spitz, R. A. 1946a. Anaclitic depression. Psychoanal. Stud. Child 2:313−342.

Spitz, R. A. 1946b. Hospitalism: A follow-up report. Psychoanal. Stud. Child 2:113−117.

Spivack, G., and M. Levine. 1964. The Devereux Child Behavior Rating Scales: A study of symptom and behavior in latency age atypical children. Am. J. Ment. Defic. 68:700−717.

Spivack, G., and J. Spotts, 1966. The Devereux Child Behavior Rating Scale. Devereux Foundation, Devon, Pa.

Sprague, R. S., J. S. Wherry, and D. E. Christensen. 1972. Experimental psychology and stimulant drugs. Presented at the symposium on the Clinical Use of Stimulant Drugs in Children. March 5−8. Key Biscayne, Fla.

Stallings, J. 1974. What Teachers Do Does Make a Difference—A Study of Seven Follow Through Educational Models. Presented to the Early Childhood Conference on Evaluation, August 6, 1974. Anaheim, Calif.

Starr, R. H., Jr. 1971. Cognitive development in infancy: Assessment, acceleration, and actualization. Merrill-Palmer Quart. 17(2): 153−185.

Starr, R. H., Jr. 1973. Cognitive development in infancy. *In* J. H. Meier (ed.), Screening and Assessment of Young Children at Developmental Risk, p. 84. U. S. Government Printing Office, Washington, D. C.

Stern, E., A. H. Parmalee, Y. Akiyama, M. A. Schulte, and W. H. Wenner. 1969. Sleep cycle characteristics in infants. Pediatrics 43: 65–70.

Stewart, M. A., and S. W. Olds. 1973. Raising a Hyperactive Child. Harper & Row, New York.

Stoltz, S. B., L. A. Wienchkowski, and B. S. Brown. 1975. Behavior modification: A perspective on critical issues. Am. Psychol. 30(11): 1027–1048.

Stott, L., and R. Ball. 1965. Infant and preschool mental tests: Review and evaluation. Monogr. Soc. Res. Child Develop. 30 (101):1–98.

Stowitschek, J., and A. Hofmeister. 1975. Parent training packages. Children Today 4(2):23–25.

Strauss, A., and N. Kephart. 1955. Psychopathology and education of the brain-injured child. *In* Progress in Theory and Clinic, Vol. 2. Grune & Stratton, Inc., New York.

Summer, G. K. 1973–1974. Screening for inborn errors. Developments 1(2):1.

Swartz, J. D. 1974. Motor development and body image: A replay to Ball. Am. J. Ment. Defic. 79(2):227–228.

Tarnopol, L. 1970. Delinquency in minimal brain dysfunctions. J. Learn. Disab. 3:200–207.

Templeton, A. B. (ed.). 1969. Reading Disorders in the U.S.: Report of the Secretary's (HEW) National Advisory Committee on Dyslexia and Related Reading Disorders. Developmental Learning Materials, Chicago, Ill.

Terdal, L. 1970. Behavioral Analysis in Field and Clinic Settings as a Base for Treatment: A Case Study. University of Oregon, Eugene, Oregon.

Terman, L. M. 1916. The Measurement of Intelligence. Houghton-Mifflin Company, Boston.

Terman, L. M. 1925. Genetic Studies of Genius, Vol. 1: The Mental and Physical Traits of a Thousand Gifted Children. Stanford University Press, Palo Alto, Calif.

Terman, E., and M. Merrill. 1961. Stanford-Binet Intelligence Scale Manual. Third Revision. Houghton-Mifflin Co., Boston.

Tharp, R., and R. Wetzel. 1969. Behavior Modification in the Natural Environment. Academic Press, Inc., New York.

Thomas, A., S. Chess, and H. G. Birch. 1968. Temperament and Behavior Disorders in Children. New York University Press, New York.

Thomas, E. D., C. J. Letchworth, G. A. Rogers, M. Jones, M. Akin, and J. Levy. 1973. The diagnosis of learning disabilities: A neurologic screening test to identify children at high risk. Southern Med. J. 66(11):1286–93.

Thomas, H. 1970. Psychological assessment instruments for use with human infants. Merrill-Palmer Quart. 16:179–224.

Thompson, D. L. 1972. Headstart at home: A model for rural areas. Appalachia 5(3):17–20.

Thoresen, C. E. 1973. Behavior Modification in Education. University of Chicago Press, Chicago, Ill.

Thorpe, H. S., and E. E. Warner. 1974. Developmental screening of preschool children: A critical review of inventories used in health and educational programs. Pediatrics 53(3):362–370.

Tjossem, T. (ed.). 1976. Intervention Strategies for High Risk Infants and Young Children. University Park Press, Baltimore.

Toffler, A. 1970. Future Shock. Random House, New York.

Torrance, E. P. 1965. Rewarding Creative Behavior. Prentice-Hall, Inc., Englewood Cliffs, N. J.

Touwen, B. C., and H. F. R. Prechtl. 1970. The Neurological Examination of the Child with Minor Nervous Dysfunction. J. B. Lippincott Co., Philadelphia.

Travis, L. E. 1971. Handbook of Speech Pathology and Audiology. Appleton-Century-Crofts, Inc., New York.

Tronick, E., and P. M. Greenfield. 1973. Infant Curriculum: The Bromley Health Guide to the Care of Infants in Groups. Media Projects Inc., New York.

Trotter, S. 1975. Labeling: It hurts more than it helps. J. Learn. Disab. 8(3):69–70.

Ullmann, L. P., and L. Krasner. 1965. Case Studies in Behavior Modification. Holt, Rinehart and Winston, Inc., New York.

Uzgiris, I. C., and J. McV. Hunt. 1966. An Instrument for Assessing Infant Psychological Development. (Mimeographed paper.) University of Illinois, Urbana, Ill.

Uzgiris, I. C., and J. McV. Hunt. 1975. Assessment in Infancy: Ordinal Scales of Psychological Development. University of Illinois Press, Urbana, Ill.

Valett, R. 1968. Psychoeducational Inventory of Basic Learning Abilities. Fearon Publishers, Palo Alto, Calif.

Valverde, F., and A. Ruiz-Marcos. 1968. The effects of sensory deprivation on dendritic spines in the visual cortex of the mouse. Proceedings of Dyslexia Conference, Lake Mohonk, New York, National Research Council Committee on Brain Sciences.

Van den Berg, B. J. 1968. Morbidity of low birth weight and/or preterm children compared to that of the mature. Pediatrics 42:590.

Van der Veer, B., and E. Schweid. 1974. Infant assessment: Stability of mental functioning in young retarded children. Am. J. Ment. Defic. 79(1):1–4.

Vane, J. R. 1968. Vane Kindergarten Test. J. Clin. Psychol. 24:121–54.

Vuckovich, M. 1967. Pediatric neurology and learning disabilities. In H. R. Myklebust (ed.), Progress in Learning Disabilities. Grune & Stratton, Inc., New York.

Wachs, T. D., I. C. Uzgiris, and J. McV. Hunt. 1971. Cognitive development in infants of different age levels and from different environmental backgrounds: An exploratory investigation. Merrill-Palmer Quart. 17:283–317.

Walker, D. K. 1973. Socio-emotional Measures for Preschool and Kindergarten Children. Jossey-Bass, Inc., San Francisco.

Walker, S., III. 1974. We're too cavalier about hyperactivity. Drugging the American child. Psychol. Today, December, pp. 43–44, 46, 48.

Wallace, P. 1974. Brain–Environment and physiology. Science 185(4156):1035–1037.

Walworth, J., and J. R. Metz. 1971. A Scale for Screening Children at Risk for Abuse: Preliminary Findings. (Unpublished paper.) Permanente Medical Group, San Francisco.

Walzer, S., and P. H. Wolff (eds.). 1973. Minimal Cerebral Dysfunction in Children. Grune & Stratton, Inc., New York.

Warren, S. A. 1973. Pros and cons of normalization. Presented at the New York Medical College Post-graduate Symposium on Mental Retardation/The Sixth Annual International Symposium, March. (Unpublished.) Vienna, Austria.

Weber, L. 1971. The English Infant School and Informal Education. Prentice-Hall, Inc., Englewood Cliffs, N. J.

Wechsler, D. 1949. Wechsler Intelligence Scale for Children. Psychological Corp., New York.

Wechsler, D. 1955. Wechsler Intelligence Scale for Children: Manual. Psychological Corp., New York.

Wechsler, D. 1966. The I.Q. as an intelligence test. New York Times Magazine 26:66, June 26.

Wechsler, D. 1967. Wechsler Preschool and Primary Scale of Intelligence: Manual. Psychological Corp., New York.

Weeds, L. L. 1974. The POMR Patient Book: Problem-Oriented Record, A Key to Better Health Care. Greene, Chicago, Ill.

Weigle, J. W. 1974. Teaching child development to teenage mothers. Children Today 3(5):23–25.

Weikart, D. P. 1966. Preschool programs: Preliminary findings. J. Spec. Educ. 1(2):163–181.

Weikart, D. P. 1971. Early Childhood Special Education for Intellectually Sub-normal and/or Culturally Different Children. High/Scope Educational Research Foundation, Ypsilanti, Mich.

Weikart, D., and D. Lambie. 1968. Preschool intervention through a home teaching program. In J. Hellmuth (ed.), Disadvantaged Child, Vol. II, pp. 435–501. Brunner/Mazel, Inc., New York.

Weikart, D., and D. Lambie. 1969. Early enrichment in infants. Presented at the Meeting of the American Association for the Advancement of Science, December, 1969. Boston.

Wellman, B. L. 1940. Iowa's studies on the effects of schooling. Nat. Soc. Stud. Educ. 39:377–399.

Wender, P. H. 1971. Minimal Brain Dysfunction in Children. John Wiley & Sons, Inc., New York.

Wepman, J. 1958. Auditory Discrimination Test. Language Research Associates, Chicago, Ill.

Werner, E. E. (In press.)

Werner, E. E., J. M. Bierman, and F. E. French. 1971. The Children of Kauai. University of Hawaii Press, Honolulu.

Werner, E. E., M. Honzik, and R. Smith. 1968. Prediction of intelligence and achievement at 10 years from 20 months pediatric and psychological examinations. Child Dev. 39:1063.

Westinghouse Report and Ohio University. 1970. The impact of Head Start: An evaluation of the effects of Head Start on children's cognitive and affective development. From the Executive Summary of the June 1969 Report, reprinted in J. L. Frost and G. R. Hawkes (eds.), The Disadvantaged Child. Houghton-Mifflin Co., Boston.

White, B. L. 1967. An experimental approach to the effects of experience on early human behavior. In J. P. Hill (ed.), Minnesota Symposia on Child Psychol., University of Minnesota Press, Minneapolis.

White, B. L., P. Castle, and R. Held. 1964. Observations on the development of visually directed teaching. Child Dev. 35:349–364.

White, B. L., and B. Kaban. 1971. Manual for Quantitative Analysis of Tasks of One-to-Six-Year-Old Children. Preschool Project. Harvard University, Cambridge, Mass.

White, B. L., B. Kaban, J. Marmor, and B. Shapiro. 1972. Child Rearing Practices and the Development of Competence. U. S. Department of Health, Education, and Welfare, U. S. Government Printing Office, Washington, D. C.

White, B. L., and J. C. Watts. 1973. Experience and Environment: Major Influences on the Development of the Young Child, Vol. 1. Prentice-Hall, Inc., Englewood Cliffs, N. J.

White, R. W. 1959. Motivation reconsidered: The concept of competence. Psychol. Rev. 66:297–323.

White, S. H., M. C. Day, P. K. Freeman, S. A. Hantman, and K. P. Messenger. 1973. Federal Programs for Young Children: Review and Recommendations, Vol. II. Review of Evaluation Data. U. S. Government Printing Office, Washington, D. C.

Whitney, D. C., and R. K. Parker. 1972. A comprehensive approach to early education: The discovery program. In R. K. Parker (ed.), The Preschool in Action: Exploring Early Childhood Programs, pp. 270–297. Allyn and Bacon, Boston.

Willerman, L., S. H. Broman, and M. Fiedler. 1970. Infant development, preschool IQ, and social class. Child Dev. 41:69–77.

Willerman, L., and M. F. Fiedler. 1974. Infant performance and intellectual precocity. Child Dev. 45:483–486.

Williams, B. S. 1971. Your Child Has a Learning Disability . . . What Is It? National Easter Seal Society for Crippled Children and Adults, Chicago, Ill.

Williams, G. Z. 1970. Critique of the subcommittee report. In M. F. Collen, R. Feldman, J. Barbaccia, J. Dunn, R. Greenblatt, and A. Mather. (eds.), Provisional Guidelines for AMHTS. U. S. Government Printing Office, Washington, D. C.

Williams, T. M. 1972. Infant Care: Abstracts of the Literature. Consortium on Early Childbearing and Childrearing, Washington, D. C.

Williams, T. M. 1974. Childbearing practices of young mothers: What we know, how it matters, why it's so little. Am. J. Orthopsychiat. 44(1):70–75.

Windle, W. 1969. Brain damage by asphyxia at birth. Sci. Amer. 221: 76–87.

Wolfensberger, W. 1972. The Principle of Normalization in Human Services. National Institute on Mental Retardation, York University Campus, Toronto, Canada.

World Health Organization. 1968. International Classification of Diseases (ICD-8), Eighth Revision. Geneva, Switzerland.

Wright, C., J. R. Lally, and M. Dibble. 1970. Prenatal-postnatal intervention: A description and discussion of preliminary findings of a home visit program supplying cognitive, nutritional and health information to disadvantaged homes. Presented at the Meeting of the American Psychological Association, September 1970, Miami, Florida.

Wulkan, P. D. (No date.) First Identification of Neonatal Disabilities (F.I.N.D.). (Unpublished.) Southern Arizona Training Programs, Tucson.

Wunderlich, R. 1970. Kids, Brains, and Learning: What Goes Wrong—Prevention and Treatment. Johnny Reads, Inc., St. Petersburg, Fla.

Wunderlich, R. 1973. Allergy, Brains and Children Coping: Allergy and Child Behavior, The Neuro-Allergic Syndrome. Johnny Reads, St. Petersburg, Fla.

Wyatt, G. L. 1971. Early Identification of Children with Potential Learning Disabilities. Wellesley Public Schools, Wellesley, Mass.

Wynne Associates. 1975. Mainstreaming and Early Childhood Education for Handicapped Children: Review and Implications for Research. U. S. Bureau of Education for Handicapped, Washington, D. C.

Yarrow. L. J. 1963. Research in dimensions of early maternal care. Merrill-Palmer Quart. 12:101–114.

Yarrow, L. J. 1968. The crucial nature of early experience. In D. G. Glass (ed.), Environmental Influences, pp. 101–113. The Rockefeller University Press and Russell Sage Foundation, New York.

Zajonc, R. B. 1975. Dumber by the dozen. Psychol. Today, January, 37–40, 43.

Zigler, E. 1971. A new child care profession: The child development associate. Young Child. 27:71–74.

Zigler, E. 1973. Project Head Start: Success or failure? Children, December.

Zigler, E., and V. Seitz. 1975. On "an experimental evaluation of sensorimotor patterning": A critique. Am. J. Ment. Defic. 79(5): 483–492.

Zingg, R. M. 1940. Feral man and extreme cases of isolation. Am. J. Psychol. 53:487–517.

RESOURCES

Bibliography

Adams, M. 1971. Mental Retardation and Its Social Dimensions. Columbus University Press, New York.

Adler, S. 1964. The Non-Verbal Child. Charles C Thomas, Springfield, Ill.

Alford, H. J. 1975. Bibliography of Research Reports: Demonstration Projects, and Other Materials Relating to Early Childhood Education of the Handicapped (1964–1974). Educational Testing Service, Princeton, N. J.

American Alliance for Health, Physical Education, and Recreation. 1975. Annotated Research Bibliography in Physical Education, Recreation, and Psychomotor Function of Mentally Retarded Persons. Washington, D. C.

Apgar, V., and J. Beck. 1972. Is My Baby All Right? Trident Press, New York.

Appalachian Regional Commission. 1970. Federal Programs for Young Children. Washington, D. C.

Arena, J. I. (ed.). 1971. The Child with Learning Disabilities: His Right to Learn. Selected papers on learning disabilities. Association for Children with Learning Disabilities, Pittsburgh.

Arieti, S. (ed.). 1959. American Handbook of Psychiatry, Vol. I and II. Basic Books, New York.

Association for Childhood Education International. 1969. Nursery School Portfolio. Washington, D. C.

Baldwin, A. L. 1967. Theories of Child Development. John Wiley & Sons, Inc., New York.

Bannatyne, A. 1971. Language, Reading and Learning Disabilities. Charles C Thomas, Springfield, Ill.

Barksdale, L. S. 1972. Building Self-Esteem. The Barksdale Foundation for Furtherance of Human Understanding, Los Angeles.

Battle, C. U., and N. C. Ackerman. 1973. Early Identification and Intervention Programs for Infants with Developmental Delay and Their Families—A Summary and Directory. National Easter Seal Society for Crippled Children and Adults, Chicago.

Baumeister, A. A. 1967. Mental Retardation—Appraisal, Education, Rehabilitation. Aldine Publishing Co., Chicago.

Beckwith, L. 1972. Relationships between infants' social behavior and their mothers' behavior. Child Dev. 43(2):397–412.

Begab, M. J. 1963. The Mentally Retarded Child—A Guide to Services of Social Agencies. Children's Bureau, U. S. Department of Health, Education, and Welfare, Washington, D. C.

Bierbauer, E. 1974. If Your Child Has a Learning Disability. The Interstate Press, Danville, Ill.

Bijou, S. W., L. Elliot, V. Armbruster, and T. Ryan. 1971. The Exceptional Child: Conditioned Learning and Teaching Ideas. MSS Information Corporation, New York.

Birch, H. G. (ed.). 1964. Brain Damage in Children. The Williams & Wilkins Co., Baltimore.

Birch, H. G., and J. D. Gussow. 1970. Disadvantaged Children—Health, Nutrition, and School Failure. Grune & Stratton, Inc., New York.

Birth Defects-Genetic Services. 1974. International Directory, 4th Ed. The National Foundation, March of Dimes, White Plains, New York.

Blatt, B. 1970. Exodus from Pandemonium. Allyn and Bacon, Boston.

Blatt, B., and F. Garfunkel. 1969. The Educability of Intelligence: Preschool Intervention with Disadvantaged Children. Council for Exceptional Children, Washington, D. C.

Blatt, B., and F. Kaplan. 1966. Christmas in Purgatory. Allyn and Bacon, Boston.

Blom, G. E. 1971. Motivational and attitudinal content of first grade reading textbooks: Their influence on reading behavior and socialization. J. Amer. Acad. Child Psychiat. 10(2):191–203.

Blom, G., and J. Wiberg. 1973. Attitude content in reading primers. In J. Downing (ed.), Comparative Reading, pp. 85–104. The Macmillan Co., New York.

Bloom, B. S., J. T. Hastings, and G. F. Madaus. 1971. Handbook on Formative and Summative Evaluation of Student Learning. McGraw-Hill Book Co., New York.

Bortner, M. 1968. Evaluation and Education of Children with Brain Damage. Charles C Thomas, Springfield, Ill.

Brewer, W. 1963. Specific Language Disability: Review of the Literature and Family Study. Honors thesis, Harvard University, Cambridge, Mass.

Briggs, L. J. 1968. Learner Variables and Educational Media. Review of Educational Research, Vol. 38, No. 2, pp. 160–176, April.

Brody, S., and S. Axelrod. 1970. Anxiety and Ego Formation in Infancy. International Universities Press, New York.

Broman, S. H., P. L. Nichols, and W. A. Kennedy. 1975. Preschool I.Q.: Prenatal and Early Development Correlates. Lawrence Erlbaum Associates, Hillsdale, N. J.

Bronfenbrenner, U. 1970. Two Worlds of Childhood—U.S. and U.S.S.R. Russell Sage Foundation, New York.

Buckley, W. 1968. Modern Systems Research for the Behavioral Scientist. Aldine Publishing Co., Chicago.

Buktenica, N. A. 1968. Visual Learning. Dimensions Publishing Co., San Rafael, Calif.

Buttaro, P. J. 1973. Legal Manual for Nursing Homes. Western Printing Co., Aberdeen, S. D.

Cancro, R. (ed.). 1971. Intelligence—Genetic and Environmental Influence. Grune & Stratton, Inc., New York.

Chapple, C. C. 1972. Birth Defects—Original Articles Series, Developmental Defects. The National Foundation, March of Dimes, White Plains, New York.

Child Welfare League of America. 1959. Standards for Homemaker Service for Children, New York.

Child Welfare League of America. 1969. Standards for Day Care Service. New York.

Child with Central Nervous System Deficit: Report of Two Symposiums. U. S. Government Printing Office, Washington, D. C.

Child with Epilepsy. 1961. U. S. Government Printing Office, Washington, D. C.

Chomsky, C. 1969. The Acquisition of Syntax in Children from 5 to 10. M.I.T. Press, Cambridge, Mass.

Clarke, A. M., and A. D. (eds.). 1966. Mental Deficiency: The Changing Outlook, 2nd Ed. Free Press, New York.

Clements, S. D. 1966. Minimal Brain Dysfunction in Children. National Institute of Neurological Diseases and Blindness, Monogr. No. 3, U. S. Department of Health, Education, and Welfare, Washington, D. C.

Cratty, B. J. 1970. Perceptual and Motor Development in Infants and Children. The Macmillan Co., New York.

Davis, H. (ed.). 1965. The Young Deaf Child: Identification and Management. Acta Otolaryg. (Stockholm) (Suppl. 206).

deHirsch, K., J. J. Jansky, and W. S. Langford. 1968. Predicting Reading Failure. Harper & Row, New York.

Denhoff, E. 1967. Cerebral Palsy—The Preschool Years—Diagnosis, Treatment, and Planning. Charles C Thomas, Springfield, Ill.

Directory of State and Local Resources for the Mentally Retarded. U. S. Government Printing Office, Washington, D. C.

Dittman, L. 1973. The Infants We Care For. National Association for the Education of Young Children, Washington, D. C.

Dybwad, R. F. (ed.). 1971. International Directory of Mental Retardation Resource. President's Committee on Mental Retardation, U. S. Government Printing Office, Washington, D. C.

Edgerton, R. B. 1971. The Cloak of Competence. University of California Press, Berkeley.

Ekstein, R., and R. L. Motto. 1969. From Learning for Love to Love of Learning. Brunner/Mazel, New York.

ERIC/ECE Publications List. 1975. ERIC Clearinghouse on Early Childhood Education, University of Illinois, Urbana, Ill.

Erikson, E. H. 1963. Childhood and Society. W. W. Norton & Co., Inc., New York.

Eyman, R. K., C. E. Meyers, and G. Tarjan. 1973. Sociobehavioral Studies in Mental Retardation. Papers in honor of Harvey F. Dingman. American Association on Mental Deficiency, Washington, D. C.

Faber, N. W. 1969. The Retarded Child. The Crown Publishing Co., New York.

Falkner, F. 1966. Human Development. W. B. Saunders Co., Philadelphia.

Fantini, M., and G. Weinstein. 1968. The Disadvantaged: Challenge to Education. Harper & Row, New York.

Fellows, B. J. 1968. The Discrimination Process and Development. Pergamon Press, New York.

Fontana, V. J. 1971. The Maltreated Child. Charles C Thomas, Springfield, Ill.

Foss, B. M. (ed.). 1961 and 1965. Determinants of Infant Behavior, Vols. II–IV. Barnes and Noble, New York.

Fraiberg, S. 1968. The Magic Years. Charles Scribner's Sons, New York.

Francis-Williams, J. 1970. Children with Specific Learning Difficulties. Pergamon Press, New York.

Frank, L. K. 1969. On the Importance of Infancy. Peter Smith, Gloucester, Mass.

Frankenburg, W., and B. Camp. 1975. Pediatric Screening Tests. Charles C Thomas, Springfield, Ill.

Full, H. 1967. Controversy in American Education. The Macmillan Co., New York.

Furth, H. G. 1969. Piaget and Knowledge. Prentice-Hall, Inc., Englewood Cliffs, N. J.

Gardner, R. A. 1973. Understanding Children. Jason Aronson, Inc., New York.

Gersch, M. J., and I. F. Litt. 1971. The Handbook of Adolescence. Dell Publishing Co., New York.

Gibson, E. J. 1969. Principles of Perceptual Learning and Development. Meredith Corp., New York.

Gitter, L. L. 1970. The Montessori Way. Special Child Publishing, Seattle, Wash.

Gooch, S., and M. L. Kellmer Pringle. 1967. Four Years On. Humanistic Press, New York.

Goodglass, H., and S. Blumstein. 1973. Psycholinguistics and Aphasia. Johns Hopkins Press, Baltimore.

Gordon, I. J. (ed.). 1972. Early Childhood Education: 71st Yearbook of the National Society for the Study of Education, Part II. University of Chicago Press, Chicago.

Gottsegen, M. G., and G. B. 1960, 1963, 1969. Professional School Psychology, Vols. I–III. Grune & Stratton, Inc., New York.

Gottwald, H. 1970. Public Awareness about Mental Retardation. Council for Exceptional Children, Arlington, Va.

Greene, M. F., and O. Ryan. 1968. The School Children Growing Up in the Slums. Pantheon Books, Random House, New York.

1975 Handbook of Private Schools. Porter Sargent Publications, Boston, Mass.

Haring, N. G. 1968. Attending and Responding. Dimensions Publishing Co., San Rafael, Calif.

Harris, T. A. 1969. I'm O.K.—You're O.K.—A Practical Guide to Transactional Analysis. Harper & Row, New York.

Hartley, R. E., F. Lawrence, and R. Goldenson. 1952. Understanding Children's Play. Columbia University Press, New York.

Hartup, W. W., and N. L. Smothergill (eds.). 1973. The Young Child: Reviews of Research, Vol. I. National Association for the Education of Young Children, Washington, D. C.

Haskell, L. A. 1971. British Primary Education: An Annotated Bibliography. College of Education Curriculum Laboratory, University of Illinois, Urbana, Ill.

Havighurst, R. J. 1952. Developmental Tasks and Education, 2nd Ed. Longmans, Green & Co., Inc., New York.

Hellmuth, J. (ed.). 1965–1966, 1968, 1971. Learning Disorders, Vols. 1–4. Special Child Publishing, Seattle, Wash.

Hellmuth, J. (ed.). 1966 and 1969. Educational Therapy, Vols. I and II. Special Child Publishing, Seattle, Wash.

Hellmuth, J. (ed.). 1970–1971. Cognitive Studies, Vols. 1 and 2. Brunner/Mazel, New York.

Hellmuth, J. (ed.). 1967, 1969–1970. The Disadvantaged Child, Vols. 1–3. Special Child Publishing, Seattle, Wash.

Hellmuth, J. (ed.). 1967 and 1971. Exceptional Infant, Vols. 1 and 2. Brunner/Mazel, New York.

Henshel, A. 1972. The Forgotten Ones–A Sociological Study of Anglo and Chicano Retardates. University of Texas Press, Austin, Tex.

Hess, R. D., and R. M. Baer (eds.). 1968. Early Education: Current Theory, Research, and Practice. Aldine Publishing Co., Chicago.

Hess, R. D., and D. J. Croft. 1972. Teachers of Young Children. Houghton Mifflin Co., Boston, Mass.

Hill, W. F. 1963. Learning–A Survey of Psychological Interpretations. Chandler Publishing Co., Scranton, Pa.

Howard, N. K. 1972. Mother-Child Home Learning Programs: An Abstract Bibliography. College of Education Curriculum Laboratory, University of Illinois, Urbana, Ill.

Howard, N. K. 1973. Open Education: An Abstract Bibliography. College of Education Curriculum Laboratory, University of Illinois, Urbana, Ill.

Hunt, J. McV. 1969. The Challenge of Incompetence and Poverty. University of Illinois Press, Urbana, Ill.

Hunt, J. McV. 1973. Psychological assessment, developmental plasticity, and heredity, with implications for early education. In R. M. Allen, A. D. Cortazzo, and R. P. Toister (eds.), Theories of Cognitive Development: Implications for the Mentally Retarded, pp. 100–160. University of Miami Press, Coral Gables, Fla.

Hymes, J. L., Jr. 1969. The Child Under Six. Prentice-Hall, Inc., Englewood Cliffs, N. J.

Illingworth, R. S. 1970. The Development of the Infant and Young Child: Normal and Abnormal. The Williams & Wilkins Co., Baltimore.

Information Center for Hearing, Speech and Disorders of Human Communications. 1973. Bibliography: Abnormal Language and Speech Development in Children: An Overview. The Johns Hopkins Medical Institutes, Baltimore.

Jarrard, L. E. 1971. Cognitive Processes of Nonhuman Primates. Academic Press, Inc., New York.

Jervis, G. A. 1968. Expanding Concepts in Mental Retardation. Charles C Thomas, Springfield, Ill.

John F. Kennedy Child Development Center. 1974–1975. JFK Instructional Technology Library (video tape/film/audio cassette). University of Colorado Medical Center, Denver, Colo.

Jordan, B. 1973. OCD urges special education's support for new Head Start services to handicapped children. Except. Child 40:45–48.

Kagan, J. 1971. Change and Continuity in Infancy. John Wiley & Sons, Inc., New York.

Kanfer, F. H., and J. S. Phillips. 1970. Learning Foundations of Behavior Therapy. John Wiley & Sons, Inc., New York.

Kanner, L. 1964. A History of the Case and Study of the Mentally Retarded. Charles C Thomas, Springfield, Ill.

Katz, L. G. 1972. Research on Open Education: Problems and Issues. College of Education Curriculum Laboratory, University of Illinois, Urbana, Ill.

Kavanagh, J. F., and I. G. Mattingly. 1972. Language by Ear and by Eye. Massachusetts Institute of Technology, Cambridge, Mass.

Keister, M. E. 1970. "The Good Life" for Infants and Toddlers. National Association for Education of Young Children, Washington, D. C.

Kellogg, E. T., and D. M. Hill. 1969. Following through with Young Children. National Association for the Education of Young Children, Washington, D. C.

Kephart, N. C. 1971. The Slow Learner in the Classroom. Charles E. Merrill, Columbus, O.

Kessen, W., M. M. Haith, and P. H. Salapatek. 1970. Human infancy: A bibliography and guide. In P. H. Mussen (ed.), Manual of Child Psychology, Vol. 1, pp. 287–445. John Wiley & Sons, Inc., New York.

Khanna, J. L. 1968. Brain Damage and Mental Retardation. Charles C Thomas, Springfield, Ill.

Kopp, C. (ed.). 1971. Readings in Early Development for Occupational and Physical Therapists. Charles C Thomas, Springfield, Ill.

Koppitz, E. M. 1971. Children with Learning Disabilities: A Five Year Follow-Up Study. Grune & Stratton, Inc., New York.

Kozol, J. 1967. Death at an Early Age. Houghton-Mifflin, Boston.

Larsen, O. N. 1968. Violence and the Mass Media. Harper & Row, New York.

Leavitt, J. E. 1974. The Battered Child. Selected Readings. General Learning Corp., Morristown, N. J.

Leeper, S. H., R. J. Dales, D. S. Skipper, and R. L. Witherspoon. 1974. Good Schools for Young Children, 3rd Ed. The Macmillan Co., New York.

Leonard, G. 1968. Education and Ecstacy. Delacorte Press, New York.

LeShan, I. J. 1968. The Conspiracy Against Childhood. Atheneum, New York.

Lohr, I. D. 1965. Selected Films on Child Life. Children's Bureau, U. S. Government Printing Office, Washington, D. C.

Luria, A. R. 1966. Human Brain and Psychological Processes. Harper & Row, New York.

Luria, A. R., and F. LaYudovich. 1971. Speech and the Development of Mental Processes in the Child. Penguin Books, Baltimore.

Maier, H. W. 1969. Three Theories of Child Development. Harper & Row, New York.

Manocha, S. L. 1972. Malnutrition and Retarded Human Development. Charles C Thomas, Springfield, Ill.

March, J. G. 1965. Handbook of Organizations. Rand McNally & Co., Chicago, Ill.

Masland, R. L. 1969. Children with minimal brain dysfunction—A national problem. In I. L. Tarnopol (ed.), Learning Disabilities: Introduction to Educational and Medical Management. Charles C Thomas, Springfield, Ill.

Mayer, C. A. 1974. Understanding Young Children: Emotional and Behavioral Development and Disabilities. ERIC Clearinghouse on Early Childhood Education, University of Illinois, Urbana, Ill.

Mayer, J. 1972. Human Nutrition—Its Physiological, Medical, and Social Aspects. Charles C Thomas, Springfield, Ill.

McDaniel, J. W. 1969. Physical Disability and Human Behavior. Pergamon Press, New York.

Miller, A. B. 1974. Physicians' Desk Reference. Medical Economics, Oradell, N. J.

Millon, T. 1969. Modern Psychopathology: A Biosocial Approach to Maladaptive Learning and Functioning. W. B. Saunders Co., Philadelphia.

Moskovitz, S. 1975. Cross Cultural Early Education and Day Care: A Bibliography. ERIC Clearinghouse on Early Childhood Education, University of Illinois, Urbana, Ill.

Mussen, P. H. 1970. Manual of Child Psychology, Vols. I and II. John Wiley & Sons, Inc., New York.

Mussen, P., J. Conger, and J. Kagan. 1974. Child Development and Personality. Harper & Row, New York.

Nash, J. 1970. Developmental Psychology: A Psychological Approach. Prentice-Hall, Inc., Englewood Cliffs, N. J.

Nash, P. 1966. Authority and Freedom in Education. John Wiley & Sons, Inc., New York.

National Information Center for the Handicapped. 1974. Practical Advice to Parents. Washington, D. C.

Nelson, W. E. 1969. Textbook of Pediatrics. W. B. Saunders Co., Philadelphia.

Nimnicht, G. P., and J. A. Johnson. 1973. Beyond "Compensatory Education"—A New Approach to Educating Children. U. S. Government Printing Office, Washington, D. C.

Nimnicht, G., O. McAfee, and J. Meier. 1969. The New Nursery School. General Learning Corp., New York.

Orem, R. C. 1970. Montessori and the Special Child. Capricorn Books, New York.

Parker, R. K. (ed.). 1972. The Preschool in Action—Exploring Early Childhood Programs. Allyn and Bacon, Boston.

Parker, R. K., and S. Ambron (eds.). 1972. Child Development and Education Handbook: Preschool, Vol. II. Office of Child Development, U. S. Government Printing Office, Washington, D. C.

Passow, A. H., and R. R. Leeper. 1964. Intellectual Development: Another Look. Association for Supervision and Curriculum Development, Washington, D. C.

Perkins, B. B. 1974. Adolescent Birth Planning and Sexuality: Abstracts of the Literature. Consortium on Early Childbearing and Childrearing, Washington, D. C.

Perspectives on Human Deprivation: Biological, Psychological, and Sociological. 1968. NIMH, U. S. Department of Health, Education, and Welfare, Washington, D. C.

Pines, M. 1967. Revolution in Learning—The Years From Birth to Six. Harper & Row, New York.

Pribram, K. H. (ed.). 1969. On the Biology of Learning. Harcourt, Brace and Co., Inc., New York.

Pringle, M. L. K., N. R. Butler, and R. Davie. 1967. 11,000 Seven-Year-Olds. Humanities Press, New York.

Public Health Service Publications. 1969. Minimal Brain Dysfunction. National Project on Learning Disabilities in Children, U. S. Government Printing Office, Washington, D. C.

Read, K. H. 1966. The Nursery School. W. B. Saunders Co., Philadelphia.

Reading Disorders in the United States. U. S. Government Printing Office, Washington, D. C.

Redl, F. 1966. When We Deal with Children. The Free Press, New York.

Rembolt, R., and B. Roth. (No date.) Cerebral Palsy and Related Developmental Disabilities: An Annotated Bibliography. United Cerebral Palsy Association, New York.

Robinson, H., and N. M. 1965. The Mentally Retarded Child: A Psychological Approach. McGraw-Hill Book Co. New York.

Rocky Mountain Educational Laboratory. 1968. Individual Learning Disabilities—Bibliography. Greeley, Colorado.

Ross, A. O. 1959. The Practice of Clinical Child Psychology. Grune & Stratton, Inc., New York.

Rourke, B. P. 1975. Brain-behavior relationships in children with learning disabilities. Am. Pschol. 30:911–920.

Sarason, S. 1972. The Creation of Settings and the Future Societies. Jossey-Bass, Inc., San Francisco.

Satz, P., and J. Ross (eds.). 1973. The Disabled Learner: Early Detection and Intervention. Rotterdam University Press, Netherlands.

Schain, R. J. 1972. Neurology of Childhood Learning Disorders. The Williams & Wilkins Co., Baltimore.

Schloss, I. E. (ed.). 1971. The Educator's Enigma: The Adolescent with Learning Disabilities. Academic Therapy Publications, San Rafael, Calif.

Schreiber, M. 1970. Social Work and Mental Retardation. The John Day Co., New York.

Schwebel, M. (No date.) Resistance to Learning. Early Childhood Education Council of New York, New York.

SEIMC/RMC Network Informations Systems. 1974. Instructional Materials Thesaurus for Special Education, 2nd Ed., GEC Information Center on Exceptional Children, Reston, Va.

Siegel, E. 1969. The real problem of minimal brain dysfunction. *In* D. Kronick (ed.), Learning Disabilities: Its Implications to a Responsible Society, pp. 53—67. Developmental Learning Materials, Chicago.

Silberman, C. E. 1970. Crisis in the Classroom. Random House, New York.

Sluckin, W. (ed.). 1971. Early Learning and Early Experience. Penguin Books, Baltimore.

Smith, D. W., and A. A. Wilson. 1973. The Child with Down's Syndrome (Mongolism). W. B. Saunders Co., Philadelphia.

Smith, F., and G. A. Miller, 1966. The Genesis of Language. M.I.T. Press, Cambridge, Mass.

Society for Research in Child Development. (No date.) Child Development Abstracts and Bibliography. University of Chicago Press, Chicago.

Spencer, M. B. 1960. Blind Children in Family and Community. University of Minnesota Press, Minneapolis.

Spotlight on Day Care. Proceedings of the National Conference on Day Care Services, May 13—15, 1965. U. S. Government Printing Office, Washington, D. C.

Stanbury, J. B., J. B. Wyngaarden, and D. S. Fredrickson. 1960 and 1966. The Metabolic Basis of Inherited Disease. McGraw-Hill Book Co., New York.

Stanley, J. C. 1972. Preschool Programs for the Disadvantaged. Johns Hopkins Press, Baltimore.

Stevenson, H. W. 1972. Children's Learning. Appleton-Century-Crofts, Inc., New York.

Stevenson, H. W., J. Kagan, and C. Spiker (eds.). 1963. Child Psychology. University of Chicago Press, Chicago.

Stolurow, L. M. 1963. Readings in Learnings. Prentice-Hall, Inc., New York.

Stone, L. J., and J. Church. 1957. Childhood and Adolescence—A psychology of the growing person. Random House, New York.

Stone, L. J., H. T. Smith, and L. B. Murphy (eds.). 1973. The Competent Infant. Basic Books, New York.

Strother, C. 1971. The Educator's Enigma—The Adolescent with Learning Disabilities. Academic Therapy Publications, San Rafael, Calif.

Szurek, S. A., and I. N. Berlin. 1968. Psychosomatic Disorders and Mental Retardation in Children. Science and Behavior Books, Palo Alto, Calif.

Talbot, N. B., J. Kagan, and L. Eisenberg. 1971. Behavioral Science in Pediatric Medicine. W. B. Saunders Co., Philadelphia.

Teaching the Disadvantaged Young Child. 1966. Compilation of Selected Articles from Young Children. National Association for the Education of Young Children, Washington, D. C.

Torrance, E. P. 1969. Creativity. Dimensions Publishing Co., San Rafael, Calif.

Tredgold, R. F., and K. Soddy. 1970. Tredgold's Mental Retardation. The Williams & Wilkins Co., Baltimore.

Tulkin, S. R., and J. Kagan. 1972. Mother-child interaction in the first year of life. Child Dev. 43(1):31—41.

United Cerebral Palsy Association. 1970. The Second Milestone. New York.

University of North Carolina at Greensboro. 1973. Infant Care Project: Some Aids for Those Who Work with Infants and Toddlers, A Catalog of Materials Available from the Infant Care Project. Institute for Child and Family Development, University of North Carolina, Greensboro, N. C.

Vygotsky, L. S. 1962. Thought and Language. M.I.T. Press, Cambridge, Mass.

Wacker, J. A. 1975. The Dyslogic Syndrome. Texas Association for Children with Learning Disabilities. Dallas, Texas.

Wagner, M. 1975. Sweden's Health-Screening Program for Four-Year-Old Children. U. S. National Institute of Mental Health, Washington, D. C.

Wagner, N. N., and M. J. Haug. 1971. Chicanos—Social and Psychological Perspectives. C. V. Mosby Co., St. Louis.

Warner, J. M. 1974. Learning Disabilities: Activities for Remediation. The Interstate Press, Danville, Ill.

Weber, E. 1970. Early Childhood Education: Perspectives on Change. Wadsworth Publishing Co., Belmont, Calif.

Weber, L. 1971. The English Infant School and Informal Education. Prentice-Hall, Inc., Englewood Cliffs, N. J.

Weber, R. E. (ed.). 1974. Handbook on Learning Disabilities: A Prognosis for the Child, the Adolescent, and the Adult. Prentice-Hall, Inc., Englewood Cliffs, N. J.

Weinberg, M. 1968. Desegregation Research: An Appraisal. Phi Delta Kappa, Bloomington, Ind.

Wender, P. H. 1971. Minimal Brain Dysfunction in Children. John Wiley & Sons, Inc., New York.

Werner, E. E., J. M. Bierman, and F. E. French. 1971. The Children of Kauai. University of Hawaii Press, Honolulu.

Werner, E., K. Simonian, J. M. Bierman, and F. E. French. 1967. Cumulative effect of perinatal complications and deprived environment on physical, intellectual, and social development of preschool children. Pediatrics 39(4):202—208.

White, B. 1971. Human Infants: Experience and Psychological Development. Prentice-Hall, Inc., Englewood Cliffs, N. J.

White, B. (ed.). 1973. Experience and Environment: Major Influences on the Development of the Young Child, Vol. 1. Prentice-Hall, Inc., Englewood Cliffs, N. J.

Williams, B. S. (No date.) Your Child has a Learning Disability ... What is it? The National Easter Seal Society for Crippled Children and Adults, Chicago.

Williams, G., and S. Gordon. 1974. Clinical Child Psychology—Current Practices and Future Perspectives. Behavioral Publications, New York.

Winick, M. 1972. Nutrition and Development. John Wiley & Sons, Inc., New York.

Wolf, J. M., and R. M. Anderson (eds.). 1969. The Multiply Handicapped Child. Charles C Thomas, Springfield, Ill.

Wolman, B. B. 1972. Manual of Child Psychopathology. McGraw-Hill Book Co., New York.

Wortis, J. 1970–1974. Mental Retardation, Vols. I–VI. Grune & Stratton, Inc., New York.

Wright, H. F. 1967. Recording and Analyzing Child Behavior. Harper & Row, New York.

Wunderlich, R. C. 1970. Kids, Brains, and Learning. Johnny Reads, Inc., St. Petersburg, Fla.

Wyatt, G. 1969. Language, Learning and Communication Disorders in Children. Free Press, New York.

Young, L. 1964. Wednesday's Children. A study of child neglect and abuse. McGraw-Hill Book Co., New York.

Young, W. M., Jr. 1969. Beyond Racism. McGraw-Hill Book Co., New York.

Zigmond, N. K., and R. Cicci. 1968. Auditory Learning. Dimensions Publishing Co., San Rafael, Calif.

Zipf, G. K. 1965. The Psycho-Biology of Language: An Introduction to Dynamic Philology. M.I.T. Press, Cambridge, Mass.

Commentaries on Evaluation Instruments, Tests, and Scales for DLDs

Aliotti, N., and A. Bannatyne. 1975. Bannatyne Visuo-Spatial Memory Test. Learning Systems Press, Lafayette, La.

American Medical Association. 1965. Mental Retardation—A Handbook for the Primary Physician. Chicago.

American Psychiatric Association. 1968. Diagnostic and Statistical Manual of Mental Disorders. 3rd Ed. (DSM-II.) Washington, D.C.

Attwell, A. A. 1970. A Handbook for School Psychologists. California State College, Los Angeles.

Benton, A. 1959. Right-Left Discrimination and Finger Localization: Development and Pathology. Hoeber Medical Division, Harper & Row, New York.

Bergsma, D. (ed.). 1973. Birth Defects—Atlas and Compendium. The Williams and Wilkins Co., Baltimore.

Bernstein, L., and R. H. Dana. 1970. Interviewing and the Health Professions. Meredith Corporation, New York.

Berry, M. F. 1969. Language Disorders of Children—The Bases and Diagnoses. Meredith Corporation, New York.

Blom, G. E., and A. W. Jones. 1970. Bases of classification and reading disorders. J. Learn. Disab. 3:606–617.

Bower, H. 1970. Early Identification of Emotionally Handicapped Children in School. Charles C Thomas, Springfield, Ill.

Brazelton, T. B. 1973. Neonatal Behavioral Assessment Scale. J. B. Lippincott Co., Philadelphia.

Bruner, J. S. 1961. The cognitive consequences of early sensory deprivation. In P. Solomon (ed.), Sensory Deprivation: A Symposium

Held at Harvard Medical School. Harvard University Press, Cambridge, Mass.

Bulik, V. E. (No date). A Methodological Approach to Identifying and Defining Objectives for Evaluative Research. Division of Instructional Experimentation, Arsenal Family and Children's Center, University of Pittsburgh, Pittsburgh.

Burns, G., and B. Watson. 1973. Factory analysis of the Revised ITPA with underachieving children. J. Learn. Disab. 6(6):230–234.

Buros, O. K. (ed.). 1965 and 1972. The Seventh Mental Measurements Yearbook, Vols. I–VII. The Gryphon Press, Highland Park, N. J.

Buros, O. K. (ed.). 1968. Reading–Tests and Reviews. The Gryphon Press, Highland Park, N. J.

Caffrey, B., J. D. Jones, and B. R. Hinkle. 1971. Variability in reaction times of normal and educable mentally retarded children. Percept. Motor Skills 32:255–258.

Carter, C. 1966. Mental Retardation Syndromes. Charles C Thomas, Springfield, Ill.

Chess, S., S. J. Korn, and P. B. Fernandez. 1971. Psychiatric Disorders of Children with Congenital Rubella. Brunner/Mazel, New York.

Childs, B. 1972. Genetic analysis of human behavior. Annu. Rev. Med. 23:373.

Collar, A. R. 1971. The Assessment of "Self-Concept" in Early Childhood Education. ERIC Clearinghouse on Early Childhood Education, University of Illinois, Urbana, Ill.

Connors, C. K. 1971. Cortical visual evoked response in children with learning disabilities. Psychophysiology 7:418.

Crome, L., and J. Stern. 1972. Pathology of Mental Retardation. 2nd Ed. The Williams & Wilkins Co., Baltimore.

Cronbach, L. J. 1970. Essentials of Psychological Testing. Harper & Row, New York.

Cusworth, D. C. 1971. Biochemical Screening in Relation to Mental Retardation. Pergamon Press, Elmsford, N. Y.

Drew, A. L. 1956. A neurological appraisal of familial congenital word-blindness. Brain 79:440.

Dubowitz, V. 1969. The Floppy Infant. Clinics of Developmental Medicine. No. 31. The Lavenham Press, Ltd., Lavenham, Suffolk, England.

Educational Testing Service. 1973. Assessment of a Pluralistic Society. Proceedings of the 1972 Invitational Conference on Testing Problems. Princeton, N. J.

Escalona, S. 1954. Understanding Hostility in Children. Science Research Associates, Chicago.

Fredericks, H. D. 1969. A Comparison of the Doman-Delacato Method and Behavior Modification Method upon the Coordination of Mongoloids. Teaching Research, A Division of the Oregon State System of Higher Education, Monmouth, Ore.

Freedman, A. M., and H. I. Kaplan. 1971. The Child: His Psychological and Cultural Development, Vol 1: Normal Development and Psychological Assessment. The Williams & Wilkins Co., Baltimore.

References, Resources, and Glossary   405

Garrett, A. 1972. Interviewing—Its Principles and Methods. 2nd Ed.
Family Service Association of America, New York.
Gilbert, J. 1969. Clinical Psychological Tests in Psychiatric and Medical Practice. Charles C Thomas, Springfield, Ill.
Goodman, J. D., and J. A. Sours. 1967. The Child Mental Status Examination. Basic Books, New York.
Gordon, S. 1969. Psychological problems of adolescents with minimal brain dysfunction. *In* D. Kronick (ed.), Learning Disabilities: Its Implications to a Responsible Society, pp. 78—89. Developmental Learning Materials, Chicago.
Grossman, H. J. 1973. Manual on Terminology and Classification in Mental Retardation. American Association of Mental Deficiency, Washington, D. C.
Hagin, R. A. 1971. How do we find him? *In* I. E. Schloss (ed.), The Educator's Enigma: The Adolescent with Learning Disabilities. Academic Therapy Publications, San Rafael, Calif.
Hainsworth, P. K., and M. L. Siqueland. 1969. Early Identification of Children with Learning Disabilities: The Meeting Street School Screening Test. Meeting Street School, Providence, R. I.
Haslam, R. H., and P. J. Valletutti. 1975. Medical Problems in the Classroom: The Teacher's Role in Diagnosis and Management. University Park Press, Baltimore.
Haynes, U. 1967. A Developmental Approach to Casefinding with Special Reference to Cerebral Palsy, Mental Retardation, and Related Disorders. U. S. Government Printing Office, Washington, D. C.
Holt, K. S. 1973. Early Diagnosis of Neuro-Developmental Problems. First Annual Lecture in Developmental Pediatrics presented by Meyer Children's Rehabilitation Institute, Omaha, Neb.
Illingworth, R. S. 1971. The predictive value of developmental assessment in infancy. Dev. Med. Child Neurol. 13(6):721—725.
International Universities Press, Inc. 1965. The Writings of Anna Freud, Vol. VI: Normality and Pathology in Childhood: Assessments of Development. New York.
Jandron, E. 1972. Psychotic Disorders. The Lansford Publishing Co., San Jose, Calif.
Jedrysek, E. 1972. Psychoeducational Evaluation of the Preschool Child. Grune & Stratton, Inc., New York.
Johnson, O. G., and J. W. Bommarito. 1971. Tests and Measurements in Child Development: A Handbook. Jossey-Bass, Inc., San Francisco.
Kadushin, A. 1972. The Social Work Interview. Columbia University Press, New York.
Karlin, I. S., D. B. Karlin, and L. Gurren. 1965. Development and Disorders of Speech in Childhood. Charles C Thomas, Springfield, Ill.
Karnes, M. B. 1968. An evaluation of two preschool programs for disadvantaged children: A traditional and a highly structured experimental preschool. Except. Child. 34(9):667—676.
Keogh, B. (ed.). 1969. Early Identification of Children with Learning

Disabilities. JSE Monograph No. 1. University of California, Los Angeles.

Kirk, S. A., and W. D. Kirk. 1971. Psycholinguistic Learning Disabilities: Diagnosis and Remediation. University of Illinois, Urbana, Ill.

Kirk, S. A., J. J. McCarthy, and W. D. Kirk. 1968. Illinois Test of Psycholinguistic Abilities, Examiner's Manual. University of Illinois, Urbana, Ill.

Klasen, E. 1972. The Syndrome of Specific Dyslexia. University Park Press, Baltimore.

Koppitz, E. M. 1968. Psychological Evaluation of Children's Human Figure Drawings. Grune & Stratton, Inc., New York.

Lambert, N. M., M. R. Wilcox, and W. P. Gleason. 1974. The Educationally Retarded Child. Comprehensive Assessment and Planning for Slow Learners and the Educable Mentally Retarded. Grune & Stratton, Inc., New York.

Lillywhite, H. S. 1970. Pediatrician's Handbook of Communication Disorders. Lea & Febiger, Philadelphia.

McCandless, G. A., and G. K. Thomas. 1974. Impedence audiometry as a screening procedure for middle ear disease. Trans. Am. Acad. Ophthalmol. Otolaryngol. 78:98–102.

McCarthy, D. 1972. Manual for the McCarthy Scales of Children's Abilities. The Psychological Corporation, New York.

McDonald, E. T. 1964. Articulation Testing and Treatment–Sensory-Motor Approach. Stanwix House, Inc., Pittsburgh.

McLeod, J. 1965. A comparison of WISC sub-test scores of pre-adolescent successful and unsuccessful readers. Aust. J. Psychol. 17(3): 220–228.

Meier, J. H. 1973. Monograph: Screening and Assessment of Young Children at Developmental Risk. U. S. Government Printing Office, Washington, D. C.

Michal-Smith, H., and S. Kastein. 1962. The Special Child–Diagnosis, Treatment, Habilitation. Special Child Publications, Inc., Seattle, Wash.

Moore, D. F. 1971. An Investigation of the Psycholinguistic Functioning of Deaf Adolescents. University of Minnesota, Research and Development Center, Minneapolis.

Morley, M. E. 1972. The Development & Disorders of Speech in Childhood. 3rd Ed. The Williams & Wilkins Co., Baltimore.

Myklebust, H. R. 1965. Development and Disorders of Written Language. Vol I: Picture Story Language Test. Grune & Stratton, Inc., New York.

Myklebust, H. R. 1973. Development and Disorders of Written Language. Vol. II: Studies of Normal and Exceptional Children. Grune & Stratton, Inc., New York.

Norfleet, M. 1973. The Bender Gestalt as a group screening instrument for first grade reading potential. J. Learn. Disab. 6(6).

Novakovich, H., and S. Zoslow. 1973. Target on Language. Christ Church Child Center, Bethesda, Md.

Oakland, T., and F. C. Williams. 1971. Auditory Perception–Diagnosis and Development for Language and Reading Ability. Special Child Publications, Seattle, Wash.

O'Brien, D., and F. A. Ibbott. 1962. Laboratory Manual of Pediatric Micro- and Ultramicro-Biochemical Techniques. 3rd Ed. Harper & Row, New York.

Oliphant, G. 1970. A study of factors involved in early identification of specific language disability. Bull. Orton Soc. 20:81–94.

Palmer, J. O. 1970. The Psychological Assessment of Children. John Wiley & Sons, Inc., New York.

Poser, C. M. 1969. Mental Retardation: Diagnosis and Treatment. Harper & Row, New York.

Rossi, P. H., and W. Williams. 1972. Evaluating Social Programs— Theory, Practice, and Politics. Seminar Press, Inc., New York.

Rubin, E. Z., J. S. Braun, G. R. Beck, and L. A. Illorens. 1972. Cognitive Perceptual Motor Dysfunction. Wayne State University Press, Detroit.

Rugel, R. 1974. The factor structure of the WISC in two populations of disabled readers. J. Learn. Disab. 7(9):329–335.

Russell, E. W., C. Neuringer, and G. Goldstein. 1970. Assessment of Brain Damage. John Wiley & Sons, Inc., New York.

Schulberg, H. C., A. Sheldon, and F. Baker. 1969. Program Evaluation in the Health Fields. Behavioral Publications, Inc., New York.

Simons, K., and R. D. Reinecke. 1974. A reconsideration of amblyopia screening and stereopsis. Am. J. Ophthalmol. 78:707–722.

Small, L. 1973. Neuropsychodiagnosis in Psychotherapy. Brunner/ Mazel, New York.

Smith, D. W. 1970. Recognizable Patterns of Human Malformation— Genetic, Embryologic, and Clinical Aspects. W. B. Saunders Co., Philadelphia.

Smith, W. L., and M. J. Philippus. 1969. Neuropsychological Testing in Organic Brain Dysfunction. Charles C Thomas, Springfield, Ill.

Tait, C. A. (ed.). 1973. Proceedings of a Conference on Audiological Considerations with Acoustically and Visually Impaired Children. ISMRRD, University of Michigan, Ann Arbor, Mich.

Walker, L., and E. Cole. 1965. Familiar patterns of expression of specific reading disability in a population sample. Part 1: Prevalence distribution and persistence. Bull. Orton Soc. 15:12–24.

Wholey, J. S., J. W. Scanlon, and H. G. Duffy. 1973. Federal Evaluation Program, Analyzing the Effects of Public Programs. The Urban Institute, Washington, D.C.

Wold, R. M. 1970. Screening Tests: To Be Used by the Classroom Teacher. Academic Therapy Publishers, San Rafael, Calif.

Wolf, C. W. 1967. An experimental investigation of specific language disability (dyslexia). Bull. Orton Soc. 17:92–97.

Commonly Used Evaluation Instruments, Tests, and Procedures for Assessing DLDs

Assessment of Perceptual Development. 1969. H. P. Martin, E. M. Gilfoyle, H. L. Fischer, and B. B. Grueter, Am. J. Occup. Ther. 23:1–10.

Ayres Space Test. 1962. Western Psychological Services, Los Angeles.

Balthazar Scales of Adaptive Behavior for the Profoundly and Severely Mentally Retarded. 1971. Earl E. Balthazar, Research Press Co., Champaign, Ill.

Bayley Scales of Infant Development Infant Behavior Record. 1969. The Psychological Corporation, New York.

Beery-Buktenica Visual-Motor Integration Test. 1967. Follett Publishing Co., Chicago.

Behavior Characteristics Progression. 1973. Santa Cruz County Office of Education, Santa Cruz, Calif.

Bender Visual Motor Gestalt Test for Children. 1962. Western Psychological Corporation, Los Angeles.

Bender Visual Motor Gestalt Test for Young Children—Koppitz. 1964. Grune & Stratton, Inc., New York.

Benton Visual Retention Test. 1955. Psychological Corporation, New York.

Bristol Social-Adjustment Guides. 1969. D. H. Stott and E. G. Sykes, Educational and Industrial Testing Service, San Diego, Calif.

Buswell-John Diagnostic Test for Fundamental Processes in Arithmetic. (No date.) Bobbs-Merrill, Indianapolis.

Cain-Levine Social Competency Scale. 1963. L. F. Cain, S. Levine, and F. F. Elzey, Consulting Psychologist Press, Palo Alto, Calif.

California Preschool Social Competency Scale. 1969. S. Levine, F. F. Elzey, and M. Lewis, Consulting Psychologists Press, Palo Alto, Calif.

Cambridge Assessment Developmental Rating and Evaluation. 1974. R. J. Welch, J. O'Brien, and F. Ayers, Cambridge Public Schools, Cambridge, Mass.

Camelot Behavior Systems Behavior Checklist. 1974. R. W. Foster, Parsons, Kan.

Child Behavior Rating Scale. 1962. R. N. Cassel, Western Psychological Service, Los Angeles.

Children's Behavior Inventory. 1967. E. I. Burdock, A. S. Hardesty, Springer Verlag, Inc., New York.

Client Assessment Instrument. 1974. Division of Retardation, Department of Health and Rehabilitation Services, State of Florida, Tallahassee, Fla.

Colorado State Plan for the Developmentally Disabled. 1974. Master Planning Guide for Instructional Objectives, Master Planning Committee of the Division of Developmental Disabilities, May.

Columbia Mental Maturity Scale. 1959. Harcourt, Brace and Co. Inc., New York.

Comprehensive Behavior Checklist Experimental Form. (No date.) J. M. Gardner, Columbus State Institute Behavior Modification Projects, Columbus, O.

Consolidated Behavioral Assessment Scale. 1975. Department of Public Welfare, Commonwealth of Pennsylvania, Office of Mental Retardation, Bureau of Research and Training, Pittsburgh.

Critical Behavior Record. 1958. F. W. Schmid, Pittsburgh.

Denver Developmental Screening Test. 1967. W. K. Frankenburg and J. B. Dodds, University of Colorado Medical Center, Denver.

Detroit Tests of Learning Aptitude. 1967. H. J. Baker and B. Leland, Bobbs-Merrill Company, Inc., Indianapolis.

Developmental Profile. (No date.) G. D. Alpert and T. J. Bell, Psychological Development Publishers, Indianapolis.

Developmental Progress Scale Revised Experimental Form. (No date.) R. D. Boyd, University of Oregon, Eugene, Ore.

Devereux Child Behavior Rating Scale. 1966. G. Spivack and J. Spotts, Devereux Foundation, Devon, Pa.

Diagnostic Reading Scales—Examiner's Manual—Examiner's Record Booklet. 1963. G. D. Spache, McGraw-Hill Book Co., Monterey, Calif.

Durrell Analysis of Reading Difficulty. 1955. Harcourt, Brace and Co., New York.

Evanston Early Identification Scale. 1967. Follett Publishing Co., Chicago.

Fairview Developmental Scale. 1971. R. T. Ross and A. Boroskin, Fairview State Hospital, Fairview, Calif.

Fairview Problem Behavior Record. (No date.) R. T. Ross, Fairview State Hospital, Fairview, Calif.

Fairview Self-Help Scale. 1969. R. T. Ross, Fairview State Hospital, Fairview, Calif.

Fairview Social Skills Scale for Mildly and Moderately Retarded. 1971. R. T. Ross, Fairview State Hospital, Fairview, Calif.

First Grade Screening Test. 1966. American Guidance Services, Minneapolis.

Frostig Developmental Tests of Visual Perception. 1961. Consulting Psychologists Press, Palo Alto, Calif.

Gates-MacGinitie Reading Test. 1965. Teachers College Press, Columbia University, New York.

Gates-McKillop Reading Diagnostic Tests—Pupil Record Booklet II—Manual of Directions. 1962. A. I. Gates and A. S. McKillop, Teachers College Press, Columbia University, New York.

Gesell Developmental Schedules, Form IJ. 1949. A. Gesell and associates, The Psychological Corporation, New York.

Gilmore Oral Reading Test. 1968. Harcourt, Brace and Co., New York.

Goals for Trainable Pupils. (No date.) Department of Public Instruction, State of Iowa, Des Moines, Iowa.

Goodenough-Harris Drawing Test. 1963. Harcourt, Brace and Co., New York.

Goodenough-Harris Drawing Test and Manual. 1965. D. B. Harris, Harcourt, Brace and Co., New York.

Harris Test of Laterial Dominance. 1955. Psychological Corporation, New York.

Head Preschool Self-Concept Picture Test. 1969. Woolner, R. *In* R. Boger and S. Knight (eds.), Head Start Evaluation and Research Center, Washington, D.C.

Illinois Test of Psycholinguistic Abilities. 1961. J. J. McCarthy and S. A. Kirk, Institute for Research on Exceptional Children, Urbana, Ill.

Illinois Test of Psycholinguistic Abilities. 1968. University of Illinois Press, Urbana, Ill.

Introduction to Developmental Assessment in the First Year. 1962. R. S. Illingworth, Heinmann, London, England.

Koontz Child Developmental Program Training Activities for the First 48 Months. 1974. C. W. Koontz, Western Psychological Services, Los Angeles.

Kuhlmann Revision of the Binet-Simon Tests. 1922. Wardwick and Co., Baltimore.

Learning Disabilities/Early Childhood Research Project. 1972. Northwestern University, Office of Superintendent of Public Instruction, Evanston, Illinois.

Learning Methods Test. 1966. The Mills Center, Fort Lauderdale, Fla.

Lincoln Primary Spelling Test. 1962. Educational Records Bureau, New York.

Minnesota Developmental Programming System. 1975. W. Bock, C. Hawkings, P. Jeyachandran, H. Tapper, and R. Weatherman, University of Minnesota, St. Paul.

Minnesota Percepto-Diagnostic Test. 1963. Western Psychological Services, Los Angeles.

Money Road-Map Test of Direction Sense. 1965. Western Psychological Services, Los Angeles.

Neurological Organization Evaluation Form. 1966. M. Ozer, Systems for Education, Inc., Chicago.

Palmer Scale. 1931. Rachel and Merrill Stutsman, Stoelting Co., Chicago.

Peabody Individual Achievement Test. 1970. American Guidance Service, Inc., Circle Pines, Minn.

Peabody Picture Vocabulary Test. 1970. L. Dunn, American Guidance Service, Inc., Minneapolis.

Preschool Attainment Record. 1966. E. Doll, American Guidance Service, Circle Pines, Minn.

Preschool Language Manual. 1969. I. Zimmerman, Charles E. Merrill, Columbus, O.

Program Placement Survey. 1974. L. Payne, Tucson, Ariz.

Progress Assessment Chart of Social Development. 1965. H. C. Gunzburg, SEFA Publishers, Burmingham, England.

Psychoeducational Inventory of Basic Learning Disability. 1966. Fearon Publishing Co., Palo Alto, Calif.

Purdue Perceptual Motor Survey. 1966. E. G. Roach and N. C. Kephart, Charles E. Merrill, Columbus, O.

Remedial Inventory One. (No date.) Ellwyn Institute, Ellwyn, Pa.

Rutgers Drawing Test: An Initial Report. 1961. A. S. Starr, New Brunswick, N. J.

Scale of Real-Life Ability. 1950. D. H. Stott and L. H. Duncan, University of Guelph, Scotland.

Screening Test for Identifying Children with Specific Language Disabilities. 1962. B. Slingerland, Educators Publishing Service, Cambridge, Mass.

Slosson Intelligence Test. 1964. Slosson Educational Publishers, East Aurora, N. Y.

Spache Diagnostic Reading Scales. 1963. California Test Bureau, New Cumberland, Pa.

Stanford-Binet Intelligence Scale: Form L-M. 1960. Houghton-Mifflin, Boston.

Stanford Diagnostic Arithmetic Test—Specimen Set, Level I. 1966. L. S. Beatty, R. Madden, and E. F. Gardner, Harcourt, Brace and Co., New York.

Student Progress Record and Curriculum Guide. 1971. Mental Health Division, Community Mental Retardation Section, State of Oregon, Portland, Ore.

The Templin-Darley Tests of Articulation. 1960. M. C. Templin and F. L. Darley, University of Iowa Press, Iowa City, Iowa.

TMR Performance Profile for the Severely and Moderately Retarded. 1963. A. J. D. Nola, B. P. Kaminsky, and A. E. Sternfeld, Educational Performance Associates, Ridgefield, N. J.

Verbal Language Development Scale. 1959. M. Mecham, American Guidance Service, Circle Pines, Minn.

Vineland Social Maturity Scale. 1965. E. Doll, American Guidance Service, Circle Pines, Minn.

Washington Assessment and Training Scales (WATS). 1969. Interinstitutional Assessment and Training Scales Committee, Office of Handicapped Children, Department of Social and Health Services, State of Washington.

Wechsler Intelligence Scale for Children. 1949. Psychological Corporation, New York.

Wechsler Preschool and Primary Scale of Intelligence. 1967. Psychological Corporation, New York.

Wepman Test of Auditory Discrimination. 1958. Language Research Associates, Chicago.

Wide Range Achievement Test. 1965. J. E. Jastak and S. R. Jastak, Guidance Associates, Wilmington, Del.

Intervention Guides

Adams, A. H. (No date.) Learning Abilities: Diagnostic and Instructional Procedures for Specific Early Learning Disabilities. The Macmillan Co., New York.

Ambrose, A. (ed.). 1969. Stimulation in Early Infancy: Proceedings of the Centre for Advanced Study in the Developmental Sciences. Academic Press, Inc., New York.

Ames, L. B. 1970. Child Care and Development. J. B. Lippincott Co., Philadelphia.

Anderson, L. 1970. Helping the Adolescent with the Hidden Handicap. Academic Therapy Publishers, San Rafael, Calif.

Appalachian Regional Commission. 1970. Programs for Infants and

Young Children. Part I: Education and Day Care; Part II: Nutrition; Part III: Health; and Part IV: Equipment and Facilities. Washington, D. C.

Arena, J. I. 1967. Teaching Educationally Handicapped Children. Academic Therapy Publishers, San Rafael, Calif.

Arena, J. I. 1969. Teaching through Sensory-Motor Experiences. Academic Therapy Publishers, San Rafael, Calif.

Artuso, A. A., F. D. Taylor, and F. M. Hewett. 1970. Individualized Reading Skills Improvement. Love Publishing Co., Denver.

Association for Children with Learning Disabilities. 1968. Successful Programming (Selected Papers on Learning Disabilities). Washington. D. C.

Association for Supervision and Curriculum Development, NEA. (No date.) 1) Early Childhood Education Today; 2) Curriculum Decisions—Social Realities; 3) Curriculum Materials; 4) Educating the Children of the Poor; 5) Freeing Capacity to Learn; 6) Humanizing Education: The Person in the Process; 7) Individualizing Instruction; 8) Learning More About Learning; 9) New Curriculum Developments; 10) Theories of Instruction; and 11) What are the Sources of the Curriculum? A Symposium. Washington, D. C.

Axline, V. M. 1947. Play Therapy. Ballantine Books, New York.

Bangs, T. (ed.). 1968. Language and Learning Disorders of the Pre-Academic Child: With Curriculum Guide. Appleton-Century-Crofts, Inc., New York.

Bannatyne, A., and M. Bannatyne. 1975. Bannatyne System: Reading, Writing, Spelling, and Language Program. Learning Systems Press, Lafayette, La.

Barlin, A., and P. Barlin. 1971. The Art of Learning through Movement. Ward Ritchie Press, Los Angeles.

Bassinger, J. F. 1972. Behavior Modification: A Programmed Text for Institutional Staff. Behavior Modification Technology, Inc., Libertyville, Ill.

Bateman, B. D. 1971. The Essentials of Teaching. Dimensions Publishing Co., San Rafael, Calif.

Beery, K. 1972. Models for Mainstreaming. Dimensions Publishing Co., San Rafael, Calif.

Bensberg, G. J. 1971. Habilitative Recreation for the Mentally Retarded. Center for Developmental and Learning Disorders, University of Alabama, Birmingham, Ala.

Bereiter, C. 1968. Arithmetic and Mathematics. Dimensions Publishing Co., San Rafael, Calif.

Bergstrom, J. L., and J. R. Gold. 1974. Sweden's Day Nurseries: Focus on Programs for Infants and Toddlers. Day Care and Child Development Council of America, Washington, D. C.

Biber, B. (ed.). 1971. Promoting Cognitive Growth: A Developmental Interaction Point of View. National Association for the Education of Young Children, Washington, D. C.

Blough, G. O., and M. H. Campbell. 1954. Making and Using Classroom

Science Materials in the Elementary School. Dryden Press, New York.

Bobath, B. 1967. The very early treatment of cerebral palsy. Dev. Med. Child Neurol. 9(4):373–390.

Bogoch, S., and J. Dreyfus. 1970. The Broad Range of Use of Diphenylhydantoin. Bibliography and Review. The Dreyfus Medical Foundation, New York.

Braun, S. J., J. Costello, and B. R. Dahle. (No date.) Curriculum is What Happens. National Association for the Education of Young Children, Washington, D. C.

Bricker, D., and W. Bricker. 1971–1972. Toddler Research and Intervention Project Report, Year I and Year II. IMRID Behavioral Science Monographs 20 and 21. Institute on Mental Retardation and Intellectual Development, George Peabody College of Teachers, Nashville, Tenn.

Briggs, L. J. 1970. Handbook of Procedures for the Design of Instruction. American Institutes for Research, Pittsburgh.

Buist, C. A., and J. L. Schulman. 1969. Toys and Games for Educationally Handicapped Children. Charles C Thomas, Springfield, Ill.

Bush, W. J., and M. T. Giles. 1969. Aids to Psycholinguistic Teaching. Charles E. Merrill Publishing Co., Columbus, O.

Caldwell, B. M. 1967. What is the optimal environment for the young child? Amer. J. Orthopsychiat. 37(1):8–21.

Caplan, F., and T. Caplan. 1973. The Power of Play. Anchor Press/ Doubleday and Co., Inc., Garden City, N. Y.

Chalfant, J. C., and R. G. Silikovitz. 1972. Systematic Instruction for Retarded Children. Part I: Teacher-Parent Guide. The Interstate Printers and Publishers, Inc., Danville, Ill.

Chaney, C., and N. C. Kephart. 1968. Motoric Aids to Perceptual Training. Charles E. Merrill, Columbus, O.

Cholden, L. S. 1958. A Psychiatrist Works with Blindness. American Foundation for the Blind, New York.

Clements, S. D. (ed.). 1969. Minimal Brain Dysfunction National Project on Learning Disabilities in Children. Phase II. Educational Medical and Health-Related Services. U. S. Government Printing Office, Washington, D. C.

Cooke, R. E., and G. Levin (eds.). 1968. Biological Basis of Pediatric Practice. McGraw-Hill Book Co., New York.

Cratty, B. J. 1969. Perceptual-Motor Behavior and Educational Process. Charles C Thomas, Springfield, Ill.

Cratty, B. J. 1971. Movement and Spatial Awareness in Blind Children and Youth. Charles C Thomas, Springfield, Ill.

Curry, N. E. 1972. Current Issues in Play: Theoretical and Practical Considerations for Its Use as a Curricular Tool in the Preschool. University of Pittsburgh, Division of Instructional Experimentation, Pittsburgh.

Dittman, L. L. (ed.). 1968. Early Child Care: The New Perspectives. Aldine-Atherton, Chicago.

Dorward, B. 1960. Teaching Aids and Toys for Handicapped Children. Council for Exceptional Children, Washington, D. C.

Edison Laboratory. 1972. The Edison Responsive Environment Learning System, or the Talking Typewriter. American Institutes for Research, Palo Alto, Calif.

Engelmann, S. 1972. Distar Instructional System. American Institutes for Research, Palo Alto, Calif.

Forrester, B. J. (ed.). 1971. Materials for Infant Development. Demonstration and Research Center for Early Education, George Peabody College for Teachers, Nashville, Tenn.

Foxx, R. M., and N. H. Azrin. 1973. Toilet Training the Retarded—A Rapid Program for Day and Nighttime Independent Toileting. Research Press, Champaign, Ill.

Frankel, M. G., F. W. Happ, and M. P. Smith. 1966. Functional Teaching of the Mentally Retarded. Charles C Thomas, Springfield, Ill.

Frazier, A. 1968. The New Elementary School. Association for Supervision and Curriculum Development, NEA, Washington, D. C.

Frazier, A. 1969. A Curriculum for Children. Association for Supervision and Curriculum Development, NEA, Washington, D. C.

Freedman, A. M., and H. I. Kaplan. 1971. The Child: His Psychological and Cultural Development. Vol. 2: The Major Psychological Disorders and Their Treatment. The Williams & Wilkins Co., Baltimore.

Frostig, M. 1966. The Developmental Program in Visual Perception Beginning Pictures and Patterns. Follett Publishing Co., Chicago.

Frostig, M. 1971. The Frostig Program for Perceptual Motor Development. American Institutes for Research, Palo Alto, Calif.

Frostig, M., and P. Maslow. 1973. Learning Problems in the Classroom—Prevention and Remediation. Grune & Stratton, Inc., New York.

Full, C. (ed.). 1974. Dental Management of the Handicapped Child. Symposium, University of Iowa, Iowa City, Iowa.

Furman, R., and A. Katan (eds.). 1969. The Therapeutic Nursery School. International Universities Press, New York.

Gallagher, J. (ed.). 1973. Program Planning and Evaluation. First Chance for Children. Vol. 2. Technical Assistance Development System, Chapel Hill, N. C.

Gans, R., C. B. Stendler, and M. Almy. 1952. Teaching Young Children. World Book Co., New York.

Gardner, W. I. 1974. Children with Learning and Behavior Problems: A Behavior Management Approach. Allyn and Bacon, Boston.

Gearheart, B. R. 1973. Learning Disabilities—Educational Strategies. C. V. Mosby Co., St. Louis.

Gearheart, B. R., and E. P. Willenberg. 1970. Application of Pupil Assessment Information: For the Special Education Teacher. Love Publishing Co., Denver.

Gibson, E. 1969. Principles of Perceptual Learning and Development. Appleton-Century-Crofts, Inc., New York.

Gordon, I. J. 1970. Baby Learning through Baby Play. St. Martin's Press, New York.

Hall, R. V. 1971. Managing Behavior: Behavior Modification: 1) The Measurement of Behavior; 2) Basic Principles. H & H Enterprises, Inc., Lawrence, Kan.

Haring, N. G. (ed.). 1971. Programs and Projects: Intervention in Early Childhood Education. Educational Technology, Englewood Cliffs, N. J.

Harper, P. A. 1962. Preventive Pediatrics. Appleton-Century-Crofts, Inc., New York.

Haslam, R. (ed.). 1973. Habilitation of the handicapped child. Pediat. Clin. N. Amer. 20(1):272.

Hensley, G., and V. W. Patterson. 1970. Interdisciplinary Programming for Infants—with Known or Suspected Cerebral Dysfunction. The report of an interdisciplinary conference held March 16–18 at Santa Monica, Calif.

Hewett, F. M. 1968. The Emotionally Disturbed Child in the Classroom. Allyn and Bacon, Boston.

Humble, J. W. 1973. How to Manage by Objectives. Amacom, New York.

Humphrey, J. H., and D. D. Sullivan. 1970. Teaching Slow Learners through Active Games. Charles C Thomas, Springfield, Ill.

Hutt, M. L., and R. G. Gibby. 1965. The Mentally Retarded Child: Development, Education, and Treatment. Allyn and Bacon, Boston.

Hymes, J. L., Jr. 1968. Teaching the Child under Six. Charles E. Merrill, Columbus, O.

Instructional Objectives Exchange. 1968. Early Childhood Education. Los Angeles.

Johnson, D., and H. R. Myklebust. 1967. Learning Disabilities: Educational Principles and Practices. Grune & Stratton, Inc., New York.

Karnes, M. B. 1968. Helping Young Children Develop Language Skills. The Council for Exceptional Children, Arlington, Va.

Knott, M., and D. E. Voss. 1968. Proprioceptive Neuromuscular Facilitation—Patterns and Techniques. Harper & Row, New York.

Korner, A. F. 1971. Individual differences at birth: Implications for early experience and later development. Am. J. Orthopsychiat. 41(4): 608–619.

Kritchevsky, S., E. Prescott, and L. Walling. 1969. Physical Space—Planning Environments for Young Children. National Association for the Education of Young Children, Washington, D. C.

Kugel, R. B. 1970. Combatting retardation in infants with Down's syndrome. Children 17:188–192.

Lavatelli, C. S. 1970. Piaget's Theory Applied to an Early Childhood Curriculum. Center for Media Development, American Science and Engineering, Inc., Boston.

Leeper, R. R. 1966. Curriculum Change: Direction and Process. Association for Supervision and Curriculum Development, NEA, Washington, D. C.

Lehtinen, R. L. 1971. How do we teach him? In I. E. Schloss (ed.), The Educator's Enigma: The Adolescent with Learning Disabilities. Academic Therapy Publishers, San Rafael, Calif.

Lewis, H. P. 1972. Art for the Preprimary Child. National Art Education Association, Washington, D. C.

Linford, M. D., L. W. Hipsher, and R. G. Silikovitz. 1972. Systematic Instruction for Retarded Children, The Illinois Program. Part III: Self-Help Instruction. The Interstate Printers and Publishers, Danville, Ill.

Long, N. J., W. C. Morse, and R. G. Newman. 1971. Conflict in the Classroom. Wadsworth Publishing Co., Belmont, Calif.

Lowenfeld, V. 1952. Creative and Mental Growth. The Macmillan Co., New York.

Lowman, E., and J. L. Klinger. 1969. Aids to Independent Living: Self-Help for the Handicapped. McGraw-Hill Book Co., New York.

Lubar, J. F. 1975. Behavioral Management of Epilepsy Through Sensori-motor Rhythm EEG Biofeedback Conditioning. National Spokesman. Vol. VIII, No. 6, pp. 6—7.

Luper, H. L., and R. L. Mulder. 1964. Stuttering: Therapy for Children. Prentice-Hall, Inc., New York.

Mallison, R. 1968. Education as Therapy—Suggestions for Work with Neurologically Impaired Children. Special Child Publishers, Seattle, Wash.

Marzollo, J., and J. Lloyd. 1972. Learning through Play. Harper & Row, New York.

McLean, J. E., D. E. Yoder, and R. L. Schiefelbusch. 1972. Language Intervention with the Retarded—Developing Strategies. University Park Press, Baltimore.

McWilliams, M. 1967. Nutrition for the Growing Years. John Wiley & Sons, Inc., New York.

Meyers, E. S., H. H. Ball, and M. Critchfield. 1973. The Kindergarten Teacher's Handbook. Gramercy Press, Los Angeles. Calif.

Miel, A. 1958. Practical Suggestions for Teaching—Observing and Recording the Behavior of Young Children. Teacher's College Press, Columbia University, New York.

Moustakas, C. E. 1971. Psychotherapy with Children: The Living Relationship. Ballantine Books, New York.

Murphy, P. 1971. A Special Way for the Special Child in the Regular Classroom. Academic Therapy Publishers, San Rafael, Calif.

Mycue, E. 1973. Young Children with Handicaps: Part I: Emotional Disturbance and Specific Learning Disabilities; Part III: Educable and Trainable Mentally Handicapped. College of Education Curriculum Laboratory, University of Illinois, Urbana, Ill.

Myers, P. I., and D. D. Hammill. 1969. Methods for Learning Disorders. John Wiley & Sons, Inc., New York.

Myklebust, H. R., and D. Johnson. 1971. Learning Disabilities: Educational Principles and Practices. Vol. II. Grune & Stratton, Inc., New York.

Newcomb, M. A. (No date.) Infant Stimulation Kit. San Francisco Mental Health Association, San Francisco.

Nizel, A. E. 1972. Nutrition in Preventive Dentistry: Science and Practice. W. B. Saunders Co., Philadelphia.

Noland, R. L. 1972. Counseling Parents of the Emotionally Disturbed Child. Charles C Thomas, Springfield, Ill.

Northcott, W. H. 1973. Implementing programs for young hearing-impaired children. Except. Child. 39(6):455–463.

O'Donnell, P. A. 1969. Motor and Haptic Learning. Dimensions Publishing Co., San Rafael, Calif.

Oren, R. C. 1966. A Montessori Handbook. Capricorn Books, New York.

Painter, G. 1968. Infant Education. Dimensions Publishing Co., San Rafael, Calif.

Painter, G. 1971. Teach Your Baby. Simon and Schuster, New York.

Parad, H. J. (ed.). 1965. Crisis Intervention: Selected Readings. Family Service Association of America, New York.

Pearson, P. H., and C. E. Williams. 1972. Physical Therapy Services in the Developmental Disabilities. Charles C Thomas, Springfield, Ill.

Peter, L. J. 1965. Prescriptive Teaching. McGraw-Hill Book Co., New York.

Pitcher, E. G., and L. B. Ames. 1964. The Guidance Nursery School. Dell Publishing Co., New York.

Poser, C. M. 1969. Mental Retardation: Diagnosis and Treatment. Harper & Row, New York.

Provence, S. A. 1967. Guide for the Care of Infants in Groups. Child Welfare League of America, New York.

Rafael, B. 1973. Early Education for Multihandicapped Children. Child. Today 2(1):22–26.

Reynolds, G. S. 1968. A Primer of Operant Conditioning. Scott, Foresman and Co., Glenview, Ill.

Ribble, M. A. 1965. The Rights of Infants: Early Psychological Needs and Their Satisfaction. 2nd Ed. Columbia University Press, New York.

Robinault, I. (ed.). 1973. Functional Aids for the Multiply Handicapped. Medical Department, Harper & Row, Hagerstown, Md.

Robinson, H. B., and N. M. 1965. The Mentally Retarded Child—A Psychological Approach. McGraw-Hill Book Co., New York.

Rogers, V. R. 1970. Teaching in the British Primary School. The Macmillan Co., New York.

Rosenberg, M. B. 1968. Diagnostic Teaching. Special Child Publishers, Seattle, Wash.

Rosenberg, M. B. 1972. Mutual Education. Bernie Straub Publishing Co., Seattle, Wash.

Rosenberg, M. B. 1973. Educational Therapy. Vol. 3. Bernie Straub Publishing Co., Seattle, Wash.

Sager, C. J., and H. S. Kaplan. 1972. Progress in Group and Family Therapy. Brunner/Mazel, New York.

Schiffman, G. B. 1970. Special programs for underachieving children. In D. Carter (ed.). Interdisciplinary Approaches to Learning Disorders. Chilton Book Co., Philadelphia.

Seeger, R. C. 1948. American Folk Songs for Children. Doubleday and Co., Garden City, N. Y.

Segner, L., and C. Patterson. 1970. Ways to Help Babies Grow and Learn:

Activities for Infant Education. John F. Kennedy Child Development Center, University of Colorado Medical Center, Denver.

Shaver, J., and D. Nuhn. 1971. The effectiveness of tutoring under-achievers in reading and writing. J. Educ. Res. 65(3):107–112.

Siegel, E. 1969. Special Education in the Regular Classroom. John Day Co., New York.

Sloane, H. N., Jr., and B. D. MacAulay. 1968. Operant Procedures in Remedial Speech and Language Training. Houghton-Mifflin Co., Boston.

Smith, J. M., and D. E. P. Smith. 1966. Child Management: A Program for Parents and Teachers. Ann Arbor Publishers, Ann Arbor, Mich.

Stark, E. S. 1969. Special Education—A curriculum guide. Charles C Thomas, Springfield, Ill.

Stendler, C. B., and W. E. Martin. 1953. Intergroup Education in Kinder-garten—Primary Grades. The Macmillan Co., New York.

Streng, A. H. 1972. Syntax, Speech and Hearing—Applied Linguistics for Teachers of Children with Language and Hearing Disabilities. Grune & Stratton, Inc., New York.

Tarney, E. D. 1965. What Docs thc Nursery School Teacher Teach? National Association for the Education of Young Children, Washington, D. C.

Tawney, J. W., and L. W. Hipsher. 1972. Systematic Instruction for Retarded Children, the Illinois Program. Part II: Systematic Language Instruction. Interstate Printers and Publishers, Danville, Ill.

Taylor, F. D., A. A. Artuso, and F. M. Hewett. 1970. Individualized Arithmetic Instruction. Love Publishing Co., Denver.

Thompson, T., and J. Grabowski. 1972. Behavior Modification of the Mentally Retarded. Oxford University Press, New York.

Valett, R. E. 1969. Modifying Children's Behavior—A Guide for Parents and Professionals. Fearon Publishers, Belmont, Calif.

Valett, R. E. 1969. Programming Learning Disabilities. Fearon Publishers, Palo Alto, Calif.

Van Riper, C. 1972. Speech Correction: Principles and Methods. 5th Ed. Prentice-Hall, Inc., Englewood Cliffs, N. J.

Van Witsen, B. 1967. Perceptual Training Activities Handbook. Teacher's College, Columbia University, New York.

Virginia State Department of Health. 1971. A Helpful Guide in the Training of a Mentally Retarded Child. National Association for Re-tarded Citizens, Arlington, Tex.

Waite, K. B. The Educable Mentally Retarded Child. Charles C Thomas, Springfield, Ill.

Watson, L. S., Jr. 1973. Child Behavior Modification: A Manual for Teachers, Nurses, and Parents. Pergamon Press, Ltd., Elmsford, N. Y.

Wedemeyer, A., and J. Cejka. 1970. Creative Ideas for Teaching Excep-tional Children. Love Publishing Co., Denver.

Weikart, D. P., L. Rogers, and C. Adcock. 1971. The Cognitively Oriented Curriculum. National Association for the Education of Young Children, Washington, D. C.

Weiner, F. 1973. Help for the Handicapped Child. McGraw-Hill Book Co., New York.

Welch, I. D., and W. Schutte. 1973. Discipline: A Shared Experience. Shields Publishing Co., Fort Collins, Colo.

Westerman, G. S. 1971. Spelling and Writing. Dimensions Publishing Co., San Rafael, Calif.

Wing, L. 1972. Autistic Children—A Guide for Parents and Professionals. Brunner/Mazel, New York.

Wolfensberger, W. 1972. Normalization—The Principle of Normalization in Human Services. National Institute on Mental Retardation, York University Campus, Downsview, Toronto, Canada.

Wood, M. M. 1975. Developmental Therapy: A Textbook for Teachers as Therapists for Emotionally Disturbed Young Children. University Park Press, Baltimore.

Intervention Materials

Arithmetic for Today Skilltext, Grade Level 1—8. Charles E. Merrill, Columbus, O.

Basic Goals in Spelling (Large Type), Grade Level 2—8. McGraw-Hill Book Co., Hightstown, N. J.

Beginning Arithmetic, Grade Level 1—2. Whitman Publishing Co., Racine, Wisc.

Better Handwriting for You, Grade Level 1—8. Noble and Noble, New York.

Building Language Power, Grade Level 3—8. Charles E. Merrill, Columbus, O.

Checkered Flag Series, Grade Interest Level 6—12. Field Educational Publications, San Francisco.

Continental Press Arithmetic Workbooks, Grade Level 1—9. Continental Press Co., Elizabethtown, Pa.

Continental Press English Workbooks, Grade Level 1—9. Continental Press Co., Elizabethtown, Pa.

Continental Press Visual Motor Tasks, Grade Level Readiness to 1. Continental Press Co., Elizabethtown, Pa.

Count, Color and Play, Grade Level 1—2. Whitman Publishing Co., Racine, Wisc.

Cuisinaire Aids in Mathematics, Grade Level Preschool-7. Cuisinaire Company of America, New Rochelle, N. Y.

Deep Sea Adventure Series, Grade Interest Level 3—10. Field Educational Publications, San Francisco.

Developmental Learning Materials, Ungraded. Developmental Learning Materials, Chicago.

Developmental Reading Text Workbook, Grade Level RR-6. Bobbs-Merrill Co., Indianapolis.

Diagnostic Reading Workbooks, Ungraded. Charles E. Merrill, Columbus, O.

Diagnostic Tests and Remedial Exercises in Reading, Grade Level 1—3. Holt, Rinehart and Winston, Inc., New York.

Dr. Spello. 2nd Ed., Grade Level 4–9. McGraw-Hill Book Co., Highstown, N. J.

English We Need, Grade Level Ungraded. Frank E. Richards Co., Liverpool, N. Y.

Experiences in Wood and Related Materials, Grade Level 4–6. Follett Publishing Co., Chicago.

Exploring English, Grade Level 4–6. Field Educational Publications, San Francisco.

Fitzhugh Plus Program, Ungraded. Allied Education Council, Galien, Mich.

Flash-X, Grade Level K–2. Educational Developmental Laboratories, Huntington, N. Y.

Follett Spelling Program, Grade Level 1–6. Follett Publishing Co., Chicago.

Frostig Program for Visual Perception, Grade Level K–2. Follett Publishing Co., Chicago.

Growth in Arithmetic Series, Ungraded. World Book Co., New York.

Handwriting with Write and See, Grade Level 1–6. Lyons and Carnahan Co., Chicago.

I Want to Learn, Grade Level Readiness. Follett Publishing Co., Chicago.

Learning Readiness System, Grade Level Preschool to Primary. Harper & Row, Evanston, Ill.

Learning Skills Series Arithmetic, Ungraded. McGraw-Hill Book Co., Hightstown, N. J.

Linguistic Block Series, Grade Level Pre-Primer-2. Scott, Foresman, Oakland, N. J.

Mathematics In Action, Ungraded. American Book Co., Cincinnati, O.

Merrill Linguistic Readers, Grade Level K–6. Charles E. Merrill, Columbus, O.

Michigan Tracking Program, Ungraded. Ann Arbor Publications, Ann Arbor, Mich.

Mott Reading Program, Grade Level RR–9. Allied Education Council, Galien, Mich.

New Phonics Skilltext-The Sound and Structure of Words, Ungraded. Charles E. Merrill, Columbus, O.

New Reading Skilltext, Grade Level RR–6. Charles E. Merrill, Columbus, O.

Parkinson, Program for Special Children, Grade Level RR–Ungraded. Follett Publishing Co., Chicago.

Peabody Rebus Reading Program, Grade Level RR. American Guidance Service, Circle Pines, Minn.

Perceptual-Motor Developmental (Fairbanks-Robinson), Grade Level Preschool to Primary. Teaching Resources, Boston.

Perceptual-Motor Teaching Materials (Erie Program I), Grade Level to Preschool to Primary. Teaching Resources, Boston.

Peterson Handwriting, Grade Level 1–6. Peterson Handwriting, Greensburg, Pa.

Phonics and Word Power, Grade Level RR–3. American Education Publishers, Columbus, O.

Phonics We Use Learning Games Kit, Grade Level 1–3. Lyons and Carnahan, Meredith Corporation, Chicago.

Programmed Math Sullivan Series, Grade Level 1–2. McGraw-Hill Book Co., Hightstown, N. J.

Programmed Reading Sullivan Series, Grade Level 1–3. McGraw-Hill Book Co., Highstown, N. J.

Read-Color-Play, Ungraded. Whitman Publishing Co., Racine, Wisc.

Reader's Skills Practice Pads, Grade Level 1–3. McGraw-Hill Book Co., Hightstown, N. J.

Reading Skills Builders, Grade Level 1–8. Reader's Digest Series, Inc., Pleasantville, N. Y.

Read-Study-Think, Grade Level 1–6. American Education Publications, Columbus, O.

Remedial Reading Drills, Ungraded. George Wahr Publishing Co., Ann Arbor, Mich.

Remediation of Learning Disabilities, Ungraded. Fearon Publishing Co., Palo Alto, Calif.

Sensory Enrichment Materials, Grade Level K–9. Flick Reedy Education Enterprises, Bensenville, Ill.

Sounds I Say–Growth In Speech and Phonic Readiness Through Pictures, Grade Level Primary. Chronicle Guidance Publications, Moravia, N. Y.

Stern's Arithmetic Discovering Arithmetic, Ungraded. Houghton-Mifflin Co., New York. .

Symbol Tracking, Ungraded. Michigan Tracking Program, Ann Arbor Publishers, Ann Arbor, Mich.

Teaching Aids in Special Education, Ungraded. Educational Teaching Aids, New York.

Time Machine Series, Grade Interest Level K–3. Field Educational Publications, San Francisco.

Visual Tracing (Groffman), Grade Level Primary. Keystone View Co., Meadville, Pa.

Webster Classroom Reading Clinic, Grade Level 4–9. McGraw-Hill Book Co., Hightstown, N. J.

World of Language, Grade Level 1–6. Follett Publishing Co., Chicago.

References for Parents

Anthony, E. J., and T. Benedek (eds.). 1970. Parenthood: Its Psychology and Psychopathology. Little, Brown & Co., Boston.

Barnard, K. E., and M. L. Powell. 1972. Teaching the Mentally Retarded Child–A Family Care Approach. C. V. Mosby Co., St. Louis.

Barten, H. H., and S. S. 1973. Children and Their Parents in Brief Therapy. Behavioral Publications, New York.

Becker, W. 1971. Parents are Teachers: A Child Management Program. Research Press, Champaign, Ill.

Braga, J. D., and L. L. Braga. 1973. Child Development and Early Childhood Education: A Guide for Parents and Teachers. Model Cities–Chicago Committee on Urban Opportunity, Chicago.

Brazelton, T. B. 1969. Infants and Mothers: Individual Differences in Development. Delacorte, Dell Publishing Co., New York.

Brody, S. 1970. Patterns of Mothering. International Universities Press, New York.

Brown, D. 1969. Learning Begins at Home. Borden Publishing Co., Alhambra, Calif.

Carmichael, B. E. 1972. Home-Oriented Preschool Education: Home Visitor's Handbook. Appalachia Educational Laboratory, Charleston, W. Va.

Children's Bureau. 1967. Selected Reading Suggestions for Parents of M. R. Children. U. S. Department of Health, Education, and Welfare, SRS, Washington, D. C.

Developmental Language and Speech Center, Grand Rapids, Michigan. 1975. Teach Your Child to Talk—A Parent Handbook. Standard Publishing Co., New York.

D'Evelyn, K. E. 1945. Individual Parent-Teacher Conferences. Bureau of Publications, Teacher's College, Columbia University, New York.

Dittman, L. L. 1959. The Mentally Retarded Child At Home. U. S. Government Printing Office, Washington, D. C.

Dodson, F. 1970. How to Parent. Nash Publ. Corp., Los Angeles, Calif.

Ellingson, C. 1967. The Shadow Children. Topaz Books, Chicago.

Emmerich, W. 1969. The Parental Role: A Functional-Cognitive Approach. Mongr. Soc. Res. Child Develop. 34(8):Serial no. 132.

Farson, R., P. M. Hauser, H. Stroup, and A. J. Wiener. 1969. The Future of the Family. Family Service Association of America, New York.

Finnie, N. R. 1968. Handling the Young Cerebral Palsied Child at Home. E. P. Dutton & Co., New York.

Gardner, R. A. 1973. The Family Book About Minimal Brain Dysfunction. Jason Aronson, Inc., New York.

Gersh, M. J. 1966. How to Raise Children at Home in Your Spare Time. Stein and Day, New York.

Gilmore, A. S., and T. A. Rich. 1967. Mental Retardation—A Programmed Manual for Volunteer Workers. Charles C Thomas, Springfield, Ill.

Ginott, H. G. 1965. Between Parent and Child. Avon Books, Hearst Corp., New York.

Golick, M. 1968. A parent's guide to learning problems. J. Learn. Disab. 1(6):366–377.

Gordon, T. 1970. Parent Effectiveness Training: The No-Lose Program for Raising Responsible Children. Wyden, New York.

Gorham, K. A. 1970. Selected Reading Suggestions for Parents of Mentally Retarded Children. U. S. Government Printing Office, Washington, D.C.

Hainstock, E. G. 1968. Teaching Montessori in the Home: The Preschool Years. Random House, New York.

Hall, R. V. 1971. Managing Behavior: Vol. 3: Behavior Modification: Applications in School and Home. H & H Enterprises, Inc., Lawrence, Kan.

Hart, J., and B. Jones. 1968. Where's Hannah? A Handbook for Parents and Teachers of Children with Learning Disorders. Hart Publishing Co., New York.

Heisler, V. 1972. A Handicapped Child in the Family: A Guide for Parents. Grune & Stratton, Inc., New York.

Hewett, S. 1970. The Family and the Handicapped Child—A Study of Cerebral Palsied Children in Their Homes. Aldine Publishing Co., Chicago.

Hunter, M. H. (ed.). 1972. The Retarded Child from Birth to Five: A Multidisciplinary Approach for Parent and Child. John Day Co., New York.

Illinois Office of the Superintendent of Public Instruction. (No date.) Preschool Learning Activities for the Visually Impaired Child—A Guide for Parents. Springfield, Ill.

Koch, R., and J. C. Dobson. 1971. The Mentally Retarded Child and His Family. Brunner/Mazel, New York.

Kramm, E. R. 1963. Families of Mongoloid Children. U. S. Government Printing Office, Washington, D. C.

Kronick, D. 1969. They, Too, Can Succeed: A Practical Guide for Parents of Learning Disabled Children. Academic Therapy Publishing, San Rafael, Calif.

Lillie, D. L. (ed.). 1972. Parent programs in child development centers. First Chance for Children, Vol. I. Technical Assistance Development System, Chapel Hill, N. C.

Love, H. D. 1970. Parents Diagnose and Correct Reading Problems. Charles C Thomas, Springfield, Ill.

Madsen, C. K., and C. H. Madsen. 1972. Parents, Children, Discipline—A Positive Approach. Allyn and Bacon, Boston.

Marx, O. H. 1972. Physical Activities for Handicapped Children in the Home. University of Iowa, Iowa City, Iowa.

Myklebust, H. R. 1970. Your Deaf Child: A Guide for Parents. Charles C Thomas, Springfield, Ill.

Painter, G. 1971. Teach Your Baby. Simon and Schuster, New York.

Patterson, G. R. 1971. Families—Applications of Social Learning to Family Life. Research Press Co., Champaign, Ill.

Patterson, G. R., and M. E. Guillion. 1971. Living with Children: New Methods for Parents and Teachers. Research Press Co., Champaign, Ill.

Perske, R. 1973. New Directions for Parents of Persons Who are Retarded. Abingdon Press, Nashville, Tenn.

Piers, M. W. 1966. Growing Up with Children. Quadrangle Books, New York.

Polansky, N. A., C. DeSaix, and S. A. Sharlin. 1972. Child Neglect: Understanding and Reaching the Parent. Child Welfare League of America, New York.

Robertson, J. 1962. Hospitals and Children: A Parent's-Eye View. International Universities Press, New York.

Rood, L. A. 1970. Parents and Teachers Together. Humanics, Inc., Washington, D. C.

Rotter, P. 1969. A Parent's Program in a School for the Deaf. Alexander Graham Bell Association for the Deaf, Washington, D. C.

Ruben, M. 1973. Parent Guidance in the Nursery School. International Universities Press, New York.

Slavson, S. R. (No date.) Child-Centered Group Guidance for Parents. International Universities Press, New York.

Smith, J. M., and D. E. P. 1966. Child Management: A Program for Parents and Teachers. Ann Arbor Publications, Ann Arbor, Mich.

State of New Jersey, Department of Education, Carl L. Marburger. (No date.) Planning Parent-Implemented Programs. A Guide for Parents, Schools, and Communities. Department of Education, State of New Jersey.

Taichert, L. C. 1973. Childhood Learning, Behavior, and the Family. Behavioral Publications, New York.

Taylor, K. W. 1954. Parent Cooperative Nursery Schools. Bureau of Publications, Teacher's College, Columbia University, New York.

von Hilsheimer, G. 1970. How to Live with Your Special Child. Acropolis Books, Washington, D. C.

Watson, L. S., Jr. 1973. Child Behavior Modification: A Manual for Teachers, Nurses, and Parents. Pergamon Press, Ltd., Elmsford, N. Y.

Wing, L. 1972. Autistic Children—A Guide for Parents and Professionals. Brunner/Mazel, New York.

GLOSSARY

Acalculia—an inability to do simple arithmetic work, to appreciate numerical relationships, to appropriately arrange numerical symbols, or to order on the basis of numerical value.

Adaptive Behavior—ability of an individual to perform usual daily living tasks such as dressing, eating, eliminating, etc., as well as to cope with other ordinary demands his/her particular culture makes on all members of the same age.

Agnosia—malfunctioning of input sensory channels although the sensory organ is not impaired; an inability to interpret or recognize sensory impressions caused by impairment of the central nervous system, as in auditory agnosia, auditory-verbal agnosia, geometric form agnosia, picture agnosia, tactile agnosia, finger agnosia, tactile-verbal agnosia, and visual agnosia.

Agraphia—type of aphasia associated with a lesion of the central nervous system, characterized by inability to recall the kinesthetic patterns that go into writing, to express thought in written form, or to appropriately arrange written symbols.

Alexia—inability to interpret written symbols; severe reading disability often the result of brain dysfunction.

Amblyopia—dimness of sight without any apparent organic defect caused by lack of fusion between both eyes resulting in the suppression of one eye's vision at the CNS level and not correctable by lenses.

Amentia—mental deficiency; severe lack of mental development such as that of profoundly retarded individuals.

Anarthria—inability to form words accurately caused by brain lesion or injury to peripheral nerves which transmit impulses to the articulatory muscles.

Anomia—an inability to name objects or recall and recognize names.

Anoxia—deficiency or lack of oxygen. It may occur in the newborn in the transition from maternal supply of oxygenated cord blood to independent breathing. The brain cells are particularly vulnerable to continued anoxia.

Aphasia—defect or loss of the power of expression by speech, writing, or signs, or of comprehending spoken or written language, caused by injury or disease of the brain centers.

Aphasia, auditory—loss of ability to hear and understand speech; loss of auditory acuity.

Aphasia, semantic—lack of ability to understand meaning of words.

Apraxia—loss of ability to perform purposeful movements, in the absence of paralysis or sensory disturbance; caused by lesions in the cerebral cortex. An inability to perform a motor act. Inability to arrange the sequences in the act.

Astereognosis—form of agnosia in which one cannot recognize objects or their forms by touching them.

Astigmatism—faulty vision caused by irregularity in the curvature of refractive surfaces of the eye.

Ataxia—lack of coordination in the movement of the voluntary musculature and disturbed equilibrium, related to cerebellar damage.

Athetosis—uncontrolled muscular movement marked by slow weaving movement of arms and legs and facial grimaces mainly the result of basal ganglia damage.

Auditory Reception—auditory decoding; understanding words spoken by another person.

Auditory Sequencing—ability to recall details previously heard in their correct order, such as in correctly repeating digits or other spoken sounds.

Auditory-Vocal Association—ability to intelligently respond verbally to a stimulus which has been heard.

Autism, infantile—severe psychiatric disorder in infants and children with severe inability to communicate in social interaction, living in their private and self-centered world.

Autistic—thought-being controlled by the individual's wishes and fantasies rather than by reality: daydreaming, introversion.

Autotelic—that which serves as an end within itself; describes an activity which is pursued for its own regard (intrinsically motivating).

Body Image or Body Schema—the picture or mental representation one has of one's own body at rest or in motion at any moment. Body image is also a synonym of body concept, meaning one's evaluation of one's own body, with special attention to how one thinks or fantasies that it looks to others.

Brain Damage—a structural injury to the brain from accident, disease, or surgery.

Brain Dysfunction—description for a child of average intelligence who exhibits some learning disabilities as a result of a presumed minimal dysfunction of the central nervous system; differentiated from such major brain or cerebral disorders as cerebral palsy and epilepsy by "soft" or minimal symptoms such as poor concentration, hyperactivity or mild perceptual and motor impairments.

Brain-injured Child—one who has suffered brain damage before, during or after birth which damage may interfere with normal learning and/or development.

Cerebral Cortex—external gray layer of the brain containing nearly 14 billion neuronal cells and mediating the most complex human functions such as language, abstract problem-solving, creating and synthesizing ideas, etc.

Cerebral Palsy—paralysis caused by a lesion in the brain which can be found at birth, resulting in a weakening of the limbs; may include ataxia, involuntary movements and possibly some degree of mental deficiency.

Cerebrum—the brain.

Cholinesterase—enzyme reputed to remove acetycholine from cell walls at synapse; appears to act as a circuit breaker in transmission of nerve impulses.

Chorea—motor disorder characterized by jerky, spasmodic movements.

Choreiform Syndrome—term used to describe the symptoms characteristic of children who have reading disabilities, including hyperkinesis, faulty dominance, dyskinesia, visual perceptual difficulties, and poor concentration.

Chromosomes—threadlike structures found in nucleus of cells along which are arranged the genes; in the male there are 22 pairs of autosomes and 1 pair of XY sex chromosomes; in the female, there are 22 pairs of autosomes and 1 pair of XX sex chromosomes.

Cluttering—bursting, nervous speech marked by frequent omissions and substitutions of sound.

CNS—central nervous system; the brain or cerebrum, spinal cord, and peripheral nerves.

Cochlea—shell-like cavity of inner ear containing the endings of the auditory nerve.

Cognitive—the faculty of knowing, of becoming aware of objects of thought or perception, including understanding and reasoning.

Cognitive Process—mental activity in which the individual begins with the concrete level of knowledge and may proceed through the abstract levels of analysis and synthesis.

Communication—interchange of information or thought by speech, print, signs or signals; the message which is communicated.

Concept—a general idea of a class of objects.

Conceptual Disorders—disturbance of the cognitive process in thinking activities dealing with abstract concepts.

Conditioning—repeated response to a stimulus other than the original or normal stimulus through association with the new stimulus: Pavlov's classical conditioned reflex where the dogs salivated at the sound of a bell instead of the presence of food.

Congenital—present at birth, but not necessarily hereditary.

Convergent Thinking—analysis of given data, which, because of its structured nature, produces a single correct answer to the problem; opposite of divergent thinking.

Cross-Dominance—sensorimotor functioning characterized by right-handed and left-eyed, or left-handed and right-eyed performance; occasionally refers to dominance of ear or foot as well.

Cyanosis—blueness of the skin, caused by insufficient oxygen in the blood, as a result of poor circulation or, especially in the newborn, delayed or insufficient breathing.

Deafness, nerve—deafness resulting from lesions associated with sensory receptors of the cochlea or acoustic nerve fibers.

Decode—ability to identify sound value (phonemes) of the printed symbol (grapheme); being able to look at the printed symbol *cart* and to pronounce the word *"cart."*

Defect—incomplete or imperfect as in mental defect or deficit.

Deficiency, mental—term encompassing all the levels below normal intelligence, i.e., more than 1 S.D. below the mean intelligence of approximately 100.

Delta Wave—electroencephalographic record of neural firing in the cerebral cortex characterized by a frequency between 0.5 and 3.5 per second; such a record is found during normal sleep, but, if found in an adult who is awake, it is suggestive of pathology.

Dendrite—part of neuron's structure which carries nerve impulses to adjacent cells.

Denial—unconscious defense mechanism used in temporarily allaying anxiety and resolving conflicts by refusing to admit existence of anxiety-causing objects.

Development—changes in an individual from conception to death.

Developmental Disability—a disability attributable to mental retardation, cerebral palsy, epilepsy, or another neurological condition of an individual found by the Secretary of the U. S. Department of Health, Education, and Welfare to be closely related to mental retardation or to require treatment similar to that required for mentally retarded individuals, which disability originates before such individual attains age 18, which has continued or can be expected to continue indefinitely, and which constitutes a substantial handicap to such individual.

Diagnosis—analysis of available information, subjective and objective, to determine the nature, etiology, and pattern of a disability; such activity has as its goal the development of a prescriptive program for correction.

Diagnosis, clinical—intensive analysis of person's disability made by a specialist or team of specialists representing various disciplines; in current practice, a prescriptive treatment plan is generated from such an evaluation.

Dilantin (diphenylhydantoin)—anticonvulsant drug used for hyperactive children and epilepsy.

Diplopia—condition in which one subject is seen as two; double vision.

Directional Confusion—characteristic of making reversals and substitutions resulting from a left-right or laterality orientation disorder.

Discrimination, auditory—ability to detect likenesses and differences in

428   Meier: Developmental and Learning Disabilities

sound stimuli—also gustatory, kinesthetic, olfactory, tactile, and visual sensory modalities.

Distractibility—inability to hold one's attention; the tendency to be easily drawn to extraneous stimuli or to focus on unimportant details to the abnormal extent of becoming confused by the task.

Divergent Thinking—analysis of a problem resulting in multiple solutions or conclusions which an individual may rank in order of various values; opposite of convergent thinking.

DLD—abbreviation for developmental and/or learning disability, both of which are defined elsewhere in this glossary and are discussed in detail in Chapter 1. These disabilities may have intraindividual or extraindividual origins (see Chapter 3) and may exist singly or in multiple combinations.

Down's Syndrome—a variety of congenital cognitive/intellectual DLD with abnormal physical development characterized by a flat skull, a fold of skin over the inner angles of the eyes giving a "mongoloid" appearance, stubby fingers, and fissured tongue; these characteristics were described in 1866 by J. Landen Down and result from the presence of an extra chromosome on the twenty-first pair (trisomy 21).

Dysacusis—impairment in hearing not involving sensitivity loss but rather distortion of loudness and/or pitch.

Dysarthria—inability to articulate speech sounds intelligibly, usually reflecting a CNS dysfunction in speech/motor musculature.

Dysbulia—confusion in the ability to think and to attend.

Dyscalculia—a partial disturbance of the ability to manipulate arithmetic symbols and to do mathematical calculations.

Dysdiadochokinesis—lack of the ability to perform repetitive movements such as finger tapping.

Dysgraphia—inability to perform the required motor tasks for handwriting and, thus, the inability to express ideas by writing; often a result of a brain lesion or dysfunction.

Dyskinesia—impairment of the power of voluntary movement, resulting in fragmentary and poorly coordinated movement.

Dyslalia—speech impairment of functional origin; sometimes caused by defective speech organs.

Dyslexia—impaired ability to read or to understand what one reads silently or orally; condition generally associated with brain dysfunction.

Dysnomia—condition characterized by the inability to recall words at will even when the individual knows the word he wishes to recall and can recognize it when said.

Dysphasia—difficulty in writing or speaking usually as a result of CNS impairment.

Dysrhythmia—abnormal speech fluency characterized by defective stress, intonation, and breath control.

Echolalia—dysfunction characterized by the repetition of words or phrases spoken by another; such repetition does not convey meaning and is frequently associated with some psychiatric schizophrenic disorders.

Educable Mentally Retarded (EMR)—individual within an IQ in the range of 50–75 as measured by an individualized test of mental ability; now popularly referred to as significantly limited intellectual capacity (SLIC) in many public school systems.

Electrocardiogram (EKG)—a graph of the electrical activity of the heart.

Electroencephalogram (EEG)—a graph of the electrical activity of various parts of the cerebral cortex of the brain.

Electromyogram (EMG)—a graph of the electrical activity of muscles caused by contraction and relaxation.

Electrooculogram—an electrographic tracing of eye movements using the reading eye camera.

Encephalitis—acute inflammation of the brain substance or its membraneous coverings.

Encoding—analysis and conversion of oral language into representative written symbols.

Enuresis—lack of control over urination; bedwetting.

Epilepsy—brain disorder characterized by excessive neuronal discharge, accompanied by temporary episodes of motor, sensory, or psychic dysfunction with or without convulsive movements or loss of consciousness; during an episode that is a marked change in recorded electrical brain activity (EEG); grand mal, gross convulsive seizures with loss of consciousness; petit mal, minor nonconvulsive seizures with momentary lapses of consciousness; psychomotor, recurrent periodic disturbances of behavior often done in repetitive, organized, but semi-automatic fashion.

Etiology—study of the causes of a dysfunction.

Evaluation—process of determining the effectiveness of instruction for an individual, a group, or a whole program; examining subjective judgment, qualitative and quantitative changes in relation of stated objectives; making value judgments about the seriousness and prognosis of diagnostic findings.

Exceptional Child—child with a physical, mental, or learning abnormality who requires an adjusted instructional program to meet his specific needs: as the slow learner, blind, deaf, DLD, and gifted.

Exogenous—originating outside the body; in disability analysis a condition whose etiology is other than hereditary or genetic.

Expressive Language Skills—those required to communicate ideas through language, such as writing, gesturing, and speaking.

Exteroceptors—skin receptors which sense warmth, cold, touch pressure, or other changes in the immediate external environment.

Extraindividual—originating outside of the individual and beyond his control; not organic but ecological in origin (see Table 4, Chapter 7).

Extrinsic Motivation—desire to engage in an activity in order to obtain some other unrelated or external reward; for example, mastering a learning task for money or praise rather than the rewarding experience of the learning itself.

Figure Ground Perception—ability to select a specific pattern or center of attention from the total field of incoming stimuli; the figure is the center of attention; the ground is the balance of the mass of stimuli.

Fine Motor Activities—motor output through which the fine and delicate muscle system is employed in precision movements.

Functional Literacy—level of reading ability which is necessary to function in our society; somewhere between fourth and seventh grade reading level.

Gene—submicroscopic structure or organization of the chromatin in chromosomes; physical unit of heredity.

Genotype—genetic composition of an individual determined by genes and chromosomes; when reflected through interaction with one's environment, the observable product is the phenotype.

Gestalt—a form, a configuration, or a totality that has, as a unified whole, properties which cannot be derived by summation from the parts of their relationships; the whole is greater or more meaningful than the sum of the parts.

Gifted—those with IQ of 120+ who demonstrate a high level of learning ability; talented.

Gnosia—the faculty of perceiving and knowing.

Grapheme—written or printed counterpart of a phoneme; a written language symbol that represents oral language.

Gross Motor Activity—movement in which groups of large muscles are employed and total body rhythm and balance are of major importance.

Halo Effect—tendency to rate an individual consistently high or low on the basis of subjective general impression.

Haptic Perception—process of getting information through the kinesthetic and tactile sensory modalities.

Hawthorne Effect—condition arising in an experimental study which alters group performance because of members' awareness and interest as participants in the research.

Hearing Loss, conductive—loss of acuity as a result of a reduction or total elimination of sound stimulus transmission through external and middle ear processes to the inner ear.

Hearing Loss, sensorineural—loss of acuity as a result of a defect or disease of the cochlea or acoustic nerve.

Hemispheres—left and right halves into which the brain is divided.

Heterogeneous—composed of parts which represent a wide range of difference or variability; in instructional grouping, refers to placing students together with regard for ability, achievement, age, or other characteristics; antonym to homogeneous.

Homogeneous—composed of similar parts which represent a narrow range of variability; antonym to heterogeneous (above).

Hydrocephalus—condition characterized by extreme pressure caused by excessive amount of cerebrospinal fluid within the skull which produces enlargement of the head and atrophy of the brain.

Hyperactivity—excessive activity or energy; overactivity or excessive motor movement sometimes called *hyperkinesis;* describes an individual who seems to always be in motion and, therefore, disturbing to classroom teachers and other students in school or in other structured settings; often associated with reading disability, perceptual difficulties, mixed dominance, concentration problems, moodiness, temper tantrums, antisocial behavior, low frustration tolerance, poor impulse control, imbalance and unpredictability; on tests, this child has difficulties with tasks that involve motor, visual, and auditory areas and scores higher in verbal than performance areas.

Hyperopia—visual condition in which light rays focus behind the retina instead of on it; farsightedness.

Hypoactivity—pronounced lack of physical activity; antonym to hyper-activity.

Iatrogenic—an iatrogenic condition is one which is caused by treatment of related condition; for example, an emotional illness inadvertently induced by a therapist's attitude or comments or setting.

Information Theory—interdisciplinary study, of which communications or theory is the technology, dealing with the transmission of signals or the communication of information; it draws upon cybernetics, engineering, linguistics, physics, psychology, and sociology.

Initial Teaching Alphabet—alphabet, augmented Roman, 44-letter alphabet evolved in England by Sir James Pitman; employs all letters of English alphabet except x and g plus 20 new symbols; each of the 44 letters in the new alphabet stands for only one sound; incorporated in a beginning reading program known as the ITA.

Intelligence—individual's ability to perceive relationships such as logical, spatial, numerical, and verbal; to learn, to recall, and to integrate constructively previous learning and experience to solve new problems; sometimes referred to as mental age or scholastic aptitude; measured by verbal and nonverbal tests of cognitive/intellectual functioning.

Intelligence Quotient (IQ)—ratio of mental age in months (MA), as determined by a test of mental abilities, to chronological age in months (CA) for an individual. IQ = (MA/CA) × 100.

Interindividual—originating as result of interaction between two or more persons.

Intraindividual—originating within an individual's organism and may or may not be subject to his conscious control.

Intrinsic Motivation—desire within oneself to engage in a given activity simply for the satisfaction or reward derived therefrom; autotelic.

Kinesthesis—sensory awareness and impression of movement or strain in muscles, tendons, or joints.

Kinesthetic Imagery—muscle imagery from recalled sense of movement or muscles, not actual.

Laterality—the internal sensorimotor awareness of the two sides of one's body and the ability to identify them as left or right correctly; frequently refers to establishing one dominant side such as right-eyed, right-eared, right-handed, and right-footed.

Learning—change in behavior and/or perception.

Learning Disabilities Specialist—one involved in the diagnosis and classification of severely handicapped children. This includes an estimate of the child's sensory abilities as well as an estimate of his strengths and weaknesses in academic learning. The learning disabilities specialist is aware of and responsive to the individual development of each child, whose individual differences are considered when the educational prescription is made. The learning disabilities specialist is a "child-oriented" learning facilitator.

Learning Disability—a disorder in one or more of the basic psychological processes involved in understanding or in using language, spoken or written, which disorder may manifest itself in imperfect ability to listen, think, speak, read, write, spell, or do mathematical calculations. Such disorders include such conditions as perceptual handicaps, brain injury, minimal brain dysfunction, dyslexia, and developmental aphasia, but such a term does not include children who have learning problems which are primarily the result of visual, hearing, or motor handicaps, or mental retardation, of emotional disturbance, or of environmental disadvantage.

Lesions—any alteration such as a wound, or a scar, caused by injury or disease.

Logorrhea—excessive, uncontrollable talking; diarrhea of the mouth and constipation of the brain.

Maturation—physiological, mental, and neurological development consistent with chronological age.

Maturational Lag—delay in physiological, mental, or neurological development without apparent structural defect.

Mental Retardation—significantly subaverage general cognitive/intellectual functioning existing concurrently with impaired adaptive behavior.

Minimal Brain Dysfunction—a mild neurological abnormality causing various intraindividual DLDs in a child with normal or near normal intelligence; characterized by "soft" neurological signs; also called mild or minimal cerebral dysfunction.

Mixed Dominance—basis for theory that speech or language disorders may be caused wholly or partly by the fact that one cerebral hemisphere does not consistently lead the other in control of sensorimotor perception or bodily movement.

Mixed Laterality—tendency to perform some acts with a right side preference and others with a left side preference; may involve the confused shifting from right to left in differing situations.

Modality—group of common sensory qualities which form pathways for receiving information and learning, as the visual modality, auditory modality, etc.; some individuals seem to prefer one modality for learning others.

Morpheme—smallest meaning-bearing unit in the structure of words, a root, prefix, suffix, or an inflectional ending as singing has two morphemes—*sing* and *ing*.

Myopia—visual condition in which light rays focus in front of the retina instead of on it; nearsightedness.

Neurological Examination—examination of sensory and motor functioning, especially concerned with the reflexes, to determine whether there are localized impairments of the nervous system.

Neurologically Impaired—an individual who manifests hard neurological signs; that is, there is evidence of specific and definable central nervous system disorder.

Neuropsychology—mental aspects of the central nervous system's higher operations; concerned primarily with studying and evaluating brain/behavior relationships.

Nongrading—school organizational plan without grade designations to which children are assigned on the basis of achievement; individualized instruction and learning occur through a planned sequence over a period of years.

Normal Distribution Curve—bell-shaped curve representing the theoretical distribution of an infinitely large number of scores or with deviation from the mean only by change.

Nosological Definition—provides a description of the disorder as to its etiology; usually of an intraindividual origin.

Nystagmus—an involuntary rapid movement of the eyeball; lateral, vertical, rotary, or mixed.

Ontogeny—life cycle or biological development of an individual; distinct from phylogeny.

Operant Behavior—behavior whose rate or form is affected by its consequences.

Ophthalmologist—medical doctor who treats medical and surgical problems of the eye.

Optometrist—vision specialist licensed to evaluate visual functioning, to prescribe refractions (glasses) and to treat the functional aspects of vision; cannot use drugs or treat eye diseases as a doctor of medicine (ophthalmologist).

Organicity—DLD condition which has its source or origin within the individual (intraindividual), usually in the central nervous system.

Otitis Media—inflammation or fluid in the middle ear, acute or chronic, which impairs hearing more or less and can underlie some language DLDs.

Otologist—a physician specializing in hearing defects and diseases of the ear and general hearing apparatus.

Perception—means by which the individual recognizes, and integrates meaningfully, sensory information; the process of reacting to sense presentations and modifying them further by attention, interests, previous experience; the process giving particular meaning and significance to a given sensation; the means by which an individual organizes and comes to understand the phenomena which constantly impinge upon him.

Perceptual Disorder—disturbance in the ability to accurately interpret sensory stimulation of intraindividual or extraindividual origin (see perception, above).

Perinatal—connected with or occurring during the birth process; *prenatal* is before birth, *postnatal* is immediately after birth, and *neonatal* is roughly the first month of life after birth.

Perseveration—tendency to continue the response to a stimulus after the stimulus has been removed or is no longer appropriate; lack of impulse control of a motor or verbal act; for example, an individual may repeat the same words over and over again.

Personality—person's mental, emotional, and temperamental make-up as they affect his personal and social relationships.

Petit Mal Seizures—see Epilepsy.

Phenotype—total interaction of genotype and environment; the individual's observable traits.

Phobia—an excessive, obsessive, persistent, unrealistic fear of an external object or situation.

Phoneme—smallest unit of speech sound or its variants.

Phonics—simplified phonetics used to teach the recognition and pronunciation of words in reading through sound-symbol relationships.

Phonics, analytic (whole word approach)—analytic method in which the specific phoneme is identified within the whole word rather than the sounding of isolated phonemes which are blended into whole words; first a series of sight words is learned, phonemes are then identified, a whole-to-part, gestalt, cognitive-field approach to reading.

Phylogeny—evolution of the race or history of a species.

Play Therapy—child is placed in a free play situation, usually limited only by the four walls, so that he may play (act) out his frustrations, disturbance, or undesirable traits; observations by the therapist lead to evaluation of problems and treatment of them.

Pneumoencephalogram—x-ray taken of the ventricular spaces of the brain immediately following the injection of air or gas.

Prenatal—pertaining to the time during pregnancy before birth.

Psychiatry—medical science that deals with the origin, prevention, diagnosis, and treatment of disorders of the mind and their affect on the body (psychosomatic illnesses); the psychiatrist is a medical doctor with additional training in psychology.

Psychoeducational Specialist—one who evaluates an individual who is having difficulty in learning, using a variety of psychological and educational testing instruments, then recommends and/or applies a variety of psychoeducational techniques to remedy the DLD condition (see Learning disabilities specialist); school psychologists perform these tasks among others.

Psychology—behavioral science dealing with the study of mental processes and behavior in man and animals.

Psychoneurology—area of study that deals with the behavioral disorders associated with brain dysfunctions in human beings; same as neuropsychology.

Psychoneurosis—emotional maladaptation caused by unresolved unconscious conflicts with minimal loss of contact with reality and some impairment of thinking, learning, and judgment.

Psychosis—severe mental disorder in which there is loss of, or disorder in, mental processes, contact with reality, control of elementary processes, and general personality integration.

Psychosomatic—refers to real physical illness which has at least a partial origin in emotional malfunction.

Psychotherapy—use of psychological techniques in the treatment of psychological abnormalities and disorders.

Psychotropic—refers to drugs which have an effect on psychic (mental) function, behavior, and experience.

Reading Disability—situation in which an individual's reading level is significantly, a year or more, below his measured intellectual capacity and estimated reading level.

Reading Readiness—general stage of developmental maturity at which the child can learn to read easily and efficiently; the term may be used to signify ability to begin each succeeding stage of reading development as well as for beginning reading.

Reading Retardation, primary—primary reading disability; dysfunction in which the neurophysiological mechanism for learning is not fully developed or is defective, thus producing a DLD or perceptual limitation; the individual is generally of at least normal intelligence but is unable to learn to read efficiently; the problem is organic and may be sensory, neural, or motoric in character; severe cases involving lack of understanding of words are called alexia and dyslexia.

Reading Retardation, secondary—dysfunction in which an individual with the capacity to learn, who possesses no physiological or mental limitations, does not acquire skill mastery; the origin of such a DLD is typically extraindividual or psychological.

Receptive Language—language that is spoken or written by others and received by the individual; includes listening, reading, understanding sign language, etc.

Reinforcement—technical term in learning theory indicating that learning is strengthened positively by success or reward; negative reinforcement may involve punishment or a penalty for error, sometimes resulting in reduction or extinction of an undesired behavior.

Reliability—extent to which a test will yield the same score or nearly the same score on successive trials; expressed as a reliability coefficient.

Reversal—perceptual inaccuracy caused by a right to left reading of English letters and words; thus, "pan" is "nap."

Ritalin (methylphenidate)—one of numerous somewhat controversial psychotropic drugs given to children to promote cerebral control over their lack of attention/concentration and hyperactivity; improves muscular coordination; may cause occasional insomnia, reduced appetite, and constipation; dosage for children usually varies from 2.5–20 mg two or three times per day.

Saccadic Movements—jerky eye movements from left to right and back again during reading.

Schizophrenia—cluster of psychotic reactions representing basic disturbances in reality relationships and resulting in unusual affective, intellectual and overt behavior such as delusions, hallucinations, regressions, and similar bizarre behaviors.

School Phobia—unfounded fear of or aversion to attending school; generally the causative factor is emotional.

Sensorimotor Skills—auditory, motor, and visual abilities necessary for the development of efficient adaptive behavior, language, and reading competence.

Slow Learner—child with a measured IQ of about 75–90.

Social Worker—person trained to help the individual improve his human relationships with self, family, and community.

Soft Signs—neurological abnormalities that are mild and difficult to detect, as contrasted with the obvious hard neurological abnormalities.

Span, auditory memory—number of items that can be recalled immediately following their spoken presentation.

Specific Language Disability—specific developmental dyslexia; refers to children with adequate intelligence who have not learned to read, write, spell, or communicate, despite environmental opportunities and conventional-type instruction, although they generally succeed in science and math.

Speech Delayed—speech development slowed by emotional blockage, mental deficiency, hearing loss, or other factor.

Splinter Skills—highly specific skills having limited relationship to the activities of the total organism, a motor pattern or skill, usually achieved by rote drill, which exists in isolation from the remainder of the individual's motor activity or ability.

Stereognosis—an ability to somatically perceive objects, forms, materials according to shape, size, quality of materials.

Stimulus-Response Learning—repetitive type of exercises whereby the individual learns to associate the correct response to the selected stimulus by a given schedule of reinforcements.

Strabismus—an eye condition in which there is a lack of coordination of the eye muscles, characterized by a squint or cross-eyes.

Strauss Syndrome—collection of behaviors descriptive of a brain-injured child whose impairment is caused by something other than genetic causes; specific characteristics are hyperactivity, emotionally labile, perceptually disordered, impulsive, distractible, and perseverative.

Strephosymbolia—twisted symbols; a persistent and pervasive reversing of symbols found in children's reading and writing in spite of their normal or above intelligence; mirror reading and or writing as in "was" for "saw," "felt" for "left."

Stuttering—speech impediment characterized by hesitations, rapid repetition of elements, and breathing or vocal muscle spasm; in speech correction practice there are three necessary qualifications: (1) no discerned physical or mental abnormalities, (2) stutterer is aware of speech abnormality, and (3) stutterer tries to force correct speech.

Synapse—communication between neurons; the point at which an impulse passes from an axon of one neuron to a dendrite of another; a synapse is polarized so nerve impulses are transmitted only in one direction; it is characterized by fatigability.

Tactile-Kinesthetic—combining sensory impressions of touch and muscle movement.

Test—a sample of behavior.

Test, achievement—evaluation instrument that measures the extent to which a person has acquired information or mastered skills.

Test, intelligence—group or individual standardized test that measures an individual's ability to perform cognitive/intellectual tasks; IQ test; test of mental ability, as Wechsler Intelligence Scale for Children (WISC) or California Test of Mental Maturity (CTMM).

Test, performance—ambiguous term meaning a test, usually involving special apparatus or materials, minimizing verbal skills, as opposed to a paper-and-pencil or verbal test, as the Arthur-Point Scale, Leiter International Test, or WISC Block Design Subtest.

Test, personality—test, questionnaire, or other device designed to assess an individual's internal and external patterns of adjustment to life.

Test, readiness—test measuring the extent of maturity or the level of prerequisite skill acquisition of an individual for beginning a particular task, as beginning reading.

Test, standardized—test composed of empirically chosen content; has specific directions for administration, scoring, and interpretation; reports data on reliability and validity; and has adequately developed norms.

Test, verbal—test in which results depend on the use and comprehension of words, presented orally or visually, as in most paper-and-pencil tests.

Therapy—treatment for curing or alleviating a disorder.

Trainable Child—one whose IQ, determined by an individual intelligence test, is 50 or less, but who may learn to perform tasks and adaptive behaviors that let him become a functioning member of society.

VAKT—highly structured systems of teaching reading in which kinesthetic and tactile stimulation is employed in conjunction with the auditory and visual modalities which utilize tracing by the child of a word or letter that has been written; the most widely used Visual-Auditory-Kinesthetic-Tactile (VAKT) systems are the Fernald and the Gillingham Systems.

Validity—the degree to which a test measures what it has been designed to measure, expressed as a correlation coefficient.

Visual Coordination and Pursuit—the capacity to effectively synchronize eye movements in following and tracking objects with the eyes.

Visual Figure-Ground Differentiation—the ability to differentiate the essential (figure) from the ground (nonessential) elements of a visual stimulus (see Figure-ground, above).

Visual-Motor Coordination—ability to relate vision with the movements of the body or its parts.

Word-Attack Skills—a pedogogical term that refers to a child's ability to analyze unfamiliar words by syllables and phonic elements and so arrive at their pronunciation and possibly recognize their meaning.

Word Blindness—lack of ability to interpret words, which may be congenital or acquired; alexia.

Word Recognition—process of identifying and understanding words.

Writing—ability to express oneself through written language; an expressive language act; individual's capacity to express himself on paper; the act of constructing graphemes.

Writing, cursive—longhand or script writing with letters joined.

Index